PRAISE FOR MARGARET MILLAR

Mystery Writers of America Grand Master
Winner of the Edgar® Award for Best Novel
***Los Angeles Times* Woman of the Year**

"One of the most original and vital voices in all of American crime fiction."
—Laura Lippman

"No woman in twentieth-century American mystery writing is more important than Margaret Millar."
—H.R.F. Keating

"I long ago changed my writing name to Ross Macdonald for obvious reasons."
—Kenneth Millar (Ross Macdonald), in a letter to the *Toronto Saturday Night* newspaper

"Very Original."
—Agatha Christie

"Stunningly original."
—Val McDermid

"She has few peers, and no superior in the art of bamboozlement."
—Julian Symons

"Written with such complete realization of every character that the most bitter antagonist of mystery fiction may be forced to acknowledge it as a work of art."
—Anthony Boucher reviewing *Beast in View* for the *New York Times*

"Margaret Millar can build up the sensation of fear so strongly that at the end it literally hits you like a battering ram."
—BBC

"Wonderfully ingenious."
—The New Yorker

"Brilliantly superlative . . . One of the most impressive additions to mystery literature—and the word "literature" is used in its fullest sense."
—San Francisco Chronicle

"In the whole of crime fiction's distinguished sisterhood, there is no one quite like Margaret Millar."
—The Guardian

"She writes minor classics."
—Washington Post

"Mrs. Millar doesn't attract fans she creates addicts."
—Dilys Winn, namesake of the Dilys Award

COLLECTED MILLAR

THE MASTER AT HER ZENITH

COLLECTED MILLAR

THE FIRST DETECTIVES

The Paul Prye Mysteries

The Invisible Worm (1941)
The Weak-Eyed Bat (1942)
The Devil Loves Me (1942)

Inspector Sands Mysteries

Wall of Eyes (1943)
The Iron Gates [*Taste of Fears*] (1945)

DAWN OF DOMESTIC SUSPENSE

Fire Will Freeze (1944)
Experiment in Springtime (1947)
The Cannibal Heart (1949)
Do Evil in Return (1950)
Rose's Last Summer (1952)

THE MASTER AT HER ZENITH

Vanish in an Instant (1952)
Wives and Lovers (1954)
Beast in View (1955)
An Air That Kills (1957)
The Listening Walls (1959)

LEGENDARY NOVELS OF SUSPENSE

A Stranger in My Grave (1960)
How Like an Angel (1962)
The Fiend (1964)
Beyond This Point Are Monsters (1970)

THE TOM ARAGON NOVELS

Ask for Me Tomorrow (1976)
The Murder of Miranda (1979)
Mermaid (1982)

FIRST THINGS, LAST THINGS

Banshee (1983)
Spider Webs (1986)
Collected Short Fiction (2016)
It's All in the Family (1948) (semi-autobiographical children's novel book)

MEMOIR

The Birds and the Beasts Were There (1968)

COLLECTED MILLAR

THE MASTER AT HER ZENITH

INCLUDING

VANISH IN AN INSTANT
WIVES AND LOVERS
BEAST IN VIEW
AN AIR THAT KILLS
THE LISTENING WALLS

MARGARET
MILLAR

SYNDICATE BOOKS
NEW YORK

This volume published in 2016 by Syndicate Books

www.syndicatebooks.com

Distributed by
Soho Press, Inc.
853 Broadway
New York, NY 10003

Library of Congress Cataloging-in-Publication Data is available

ISBN: 978-1-68199-027-9
Vanish in an Instant eISBN: 978-1-68199-011-8
Wives and Lovers eISBN: 978-1-68199-025-5
Beast in View eISBN: 978-1-68199-012-5
An Air That Kills eISBN: 978-1-68199-013-2
The Listening Walls eISBN: 978-1-68199-014-9

Cover and interior design by Jeff Wong

Printed in the United States of America

10 9 8 7 6 5 4 3 2 1

COLLECTED MILLAR

THE MASTER AT HER ZENITH

TABLE OF CONTENTS

INTRODUCTION BY TOM NOLAN

"The real fear of the average adult," Margaret Millar supposed in 1983, after four decades as an author of novels filled with menace, anxiety, violence and terror, "must be what lies in the deepest shadows of his own mind."

The author knew whereof she wrote.

A lifelong amateur student of psychology, she had a sharp awareness of her own and others' phobic dreads and neurotic potentials. She drew on such real and imagined experience in creating her most alarming stories. Like a method actor, Maggie (as she insisted on being called) sometimes took on the personalities of her disturbed characters to the point of near-breakdown. While writing the final chapters of a novel about one fatally fearful woman, she recalled, "I shared [her] nightmare . . . Every sound was a threat, its volume exaggerated. The telephone no longer rang, it shrilled. People didn't talk, they screamed . . . Creator and creation had become one."

That book was *Beast in View*, which won the Mystery Writers of America's Edgar® Award as the best novel of 1955. Some sixty years after first publication, it retains its unsettling power to chill.

Millar's earliest few books, though, were light in tone (despite having a psychiatrist as detective-hero). The breakthrough into her mature themes and style came with her fourth work, *Wall of Eyes* (1943). She was well-established with readers and reviewers as a master of psychological suspense by the publication of *Vanish in an Instant* (1952), her twelfth book and the first work collected in this volume.

Set in "Arbana," a fictionalized Michigan town based on Ann Arbor (where Millar, her husband and daughter spent the better, or worst, part of their 1949), *Vanish* presents the disaffected young woman Virginia Barkeley, a highly sensitive child of privilege now accused of murder. "She seems to be . . . rather an unhappy person," ventures Virginia's mother's paid companion. "You have to be pretty unhappy," snaps Virginia's lawyer, "to stab a guy half a dozen times in the neck."

But did she? "How can you tell, with Virginia," muses her own husband, "what's real and what isn't?"

Then an even more confused and confusing figure appears: a man named Loftus, who confesses in convincing detail to the crime of which Virginia is accused—despite never before having met the victim. Deformed in body and perhaps in mind, Loftus admits to looking forward to his death from the fatal illness he carries: "I'm waiting for an end of fear."

Millar took a break from crime fiction with her 1954 mainstream novel, *Wives and Lovers*. But this book's Southern California characters were scarcely less burdened with troublesome secrets and distressing symptoms than her usual cast of suspects.

The seemingly placid life of a married dentist in the Santa Barbara-like town of "Channel City" is thrown into turmoil by the appearance of a young woman he met in San Francisco a few months earlier. The dentist is yanked from his role of long-suffering husband and transformed into a paranoid plotter. His wife is forced to see that her "marriage had been colored by [her] bile-green feeling that she had been cheated"—though, "as a churchwoman and the mother of three children, [she] believed in divorce even less than she believed in marriage and [her husband] . . ." Meanwhile the lovesick young woman, her mind working with "disastrous simplicity," discovers harsh emotions raging beneath her thwarted passion: "I hate him. I'll get back at him. I'll get even. I'll go and see his wife. He'll be sorry."

The book's scope widens to reveal a devastating panorama of early 1950s male-female relationships: a suburban vista of pettiness, bitterness, self-delusion and despair. "I'd like to kill you," an ex-husband tells the former wife he thinks is trying to rob him of his last chance at happiness. "Perhaps in the end," another character muses of society, " . . . everyone in the world was affected by the actions of every other person . . . an interminable string tying them all together in an inextricably knotted mass. There was no escape . . ."

Wives and Lovers is in many ways like Millar's crime novels, except no one goes too far and commits a felony—though several people come close. The book feels as if it's heading towards catastrophe, that at any moment someone may attempt assault and battery, homicide, or suicide. Instead the book settles for the dismantling of several characters' cruel or pathetic protective strategies.

Then came *Beast in View*: a return to genre-form for Millar: a no-holds-barred experiment in terror.

The book starts with a rich young woman in Los Angeles named Helen Clarvoe receiving a strange and threatening telephone call from a person who claims to know her. "I feel very strongly—that this woman means to destroy me," Clarvoe tells the family retainer she asks to investigate the harasser. "I *know* it. If you like, call it intuition." "Call it fear," the counselor says.

This man sees Helen as the neurotic and alienated person she is: cut off from other people (including her own family) and old before her time. "She was a middle-aged woman because she had had nothing to keep her young. She was the chosen victim, not only of [her telephone nemesis], but of life itself."

The roots of her isolation run deep, the lawyer finds when he speaks to Helen's surviving parent. "I don't feel like her mother," this woman admits. "I never did, even when she was a baby. The ugliest baby you ever saw. I couldn't believe it belonged to me. I felt cheated."

The psychic cost has been high. "A plate breaks and you throw it away," another mother says. "A person breaks and all you can do is pick up the pieces and try to put them together the best way you can."

Before all the pieces of this book's victims and victimizers can be reassembled, terrible secrets have been uncovered, and horrible deaths have occurred.

The award-winning *Beast in View* remains perhaps Margaret Millar's best-known book; but some critics felt she wrote even better ones—for instance, *Beast*'s immediate successor, *An Air That Kills*.

Titled from a Houseman poem, and set in Ontario, Canada, *An Air That Kills* is blown into motion by the disappearance of a man en route to meet friends at a hunting lodge. What's become of Ron Galloway? It seems he was leading a double life: married to one woman (with whom he's fathered two children) while carrying on with another man's wife.

Millar's novelist-husband Kenneth (whose pen name was Ross Macdonald) described this book in its jacket notes (which, as was the Millars' practice with her books, he wrote anonymously) as "a unique blend of mystery, tragicomedy, and satire, handled with all the arts of the modern novel." Unique it was, even for Mrs. Millar, who exhibited here an even greater control of her materials and cool mastery of her methods and techniques. In exploring the double lives of not only Ron Galloway but of others, she demonstrates the dual consciousness which allows given characters to alternate between emotional poles of irritation and affection, optimism and pessimism; and she wields that alternating current to build suspense throughout an engrossing puzzle filled with surprises. Her artist's objectivity also succeeds in inducing what critic Luther Nichols found at the time to be a "sympathetic understanding of human frailty . . . When we finally know the guilty and their motives in her books, our wrath is usually turned to compassion."

Maggie Millar had more triumphs in store. Her next title, *The Listening Walls*, was the first of three novels which reviewer and master short-story writer Ed Hoch thought were her finest works: a "special trio" that exemplified "the peak of the mystery writer's art in that each of them withholds the key element of its solution until the very end of the book."

At the book's very beginning, two American women, Amy and Wilma, are on a pleasure trip together in Mexico City. The pleasure dissipates when the women quarrel over an expensive present Wilma buys for Amy's husband. The vacation becomes a disaster when a drunken Wilma falls to her death from their hotel-room balcony, an apparent suicide. Amy's husband flies from San Francisco to rescue his physically and emotionally battered spouse from her hospital bed. But once the couple are back in their Bay Area home, Amy once more leaves—"explaining" by letter that she needs time alone.

Her possessive brother suspects foul play and hires a private detective to find Amy. Needless to say, the detective discovers many other things *en route*—some shocking, some poignant, some fatal.

Kenneth Millar was typically, justifiably proud of his wife's achievement with *The Listening Walls*, praising, in his unsigned jacket copy, the author's "dazzling talent" and "deeply human touch." Then he concluded with this accurate but perhaps unfairly tempting boast about Maggie's latest *chef-d'oeuvre*: "aficionados may notice that its last page ends with the most expertly withheld solution in the long history of mystery fiction."

Don't peek.

Tom Nolan has been a freelance writer since age eighteen and has contributed to dozens of magazines and newspapers, including *Rolling Stone*, *Ploughshares*, and *Oxford American*. For fifteen years he has reviewed crime fiction for the *Wall Street Journal*. Nolan's book *Ross Macdonald: A Biography* (Scribner, 1999) was nominated for the Edgar® Award, the Anthony Award, and the Macavity Award (which it won). His most recent work is *Meanwhile There Are Letters: The Correspondence of Eudora Welty and Ross Macdonald* (Arcade, 2015), which he co-edited with Suzanne Marrs. He lives in Glendale, California.

VANISH IN AN INSTANT

For My Loved Ones
MILL AND LINDA

1

SNOW AND SOOT sprinkled the concrete runways like salt and pepper. Twenty miles to the east, Detroit was a city of smoke and lights. Twenty miles to the west the town of Arbana was not visible at all, but it was to the west that Mrs. Hamilton looked first as if she hoped to catch a miraculous glimpse of it.

On the observation ramp above the airfield she could see the faces of people waiting to board a plane or to meet someone or simply waiting and watching, because if they couldn't go anywhere themselves, the next best thing was to watch someone else going. Under the glaring lights their faces appeared as similar as the rows of wax vegetables in the windows of the markets back home. She scanned the faces briefly, wondering if one of them belonged to her son-in-law, Paul. She wasn't sure she would recognize him—in her mind he had never entirely taken shape as a person, he was just Virginia's husband—or that he would recognize her.

"*I* certainly haven't changed," she said aloud, quite sharply.

Her companion turned with an air of surprise. She was a slim girl in her early twenties, rather pretty, though her fair hair and extremely light eyebrows gave her a frail and colorless appearance. Her eyes were deep blue and round, so that she always looked a little inquisitive, like a child to whom everything is new. "Did you say something, Mrs. Hamilton?"

"People don't change very much in a year, unless it's a bad year. And I haven't really had a bad year until this—until now."

The girl made a sympathetic sound, to which Mrs. Hamilton reacted stiffly. Mrs. Hamilton actively disliked and resented sympathy. In contrast to her plump small-boned body, her nature was brisk and vigorous. Holding her large black purse firmly under her arm she crossed the swept concrete apron toward the entrance to the terminal. As she passed the ramp she glanced up at the vegetable-faces once more.

"I don't see Paul. Do you, Alice?"

"He might be waiting inside," the girl said. "It's cold."

"I told you to be sure and buy a warm enough coat."

"The coat's warm enough. But the wind isn't."

"Californians get spoiled. For winter this is quite balmy." But her own lips were blue-tinged, and her fingers inside the white doeskin gloves felt stiff as though they were in splints. "I didn't ask him to meet me in my telegram. Well, we'll take a taxi to Arbana. What time is it?"

"About nine."

"Too late. They probably won't let me see Virginia tonight."

"Probably not."

"I guess the—I guess *they* have visiting hours like a hospital." She spoke the word *they* as if it had an explosive content and must be handled carefully.

There was a line-up at the luggage counter, and they took their places at the end of it. To Mrs. Hamilton, who was quick to sense atmosphere, the big room had an air of excitement gone stale, anticipation soured by reality.

Journey's end, she thought. She felt stale and sour herself, and the feeling reminded her of Virginia; Virginia at Christmas time, the year she was eight. For weeks and weeks the child had dreamed of Christmas, and then on Christmas morning she had awakened and found that Christmas was only another day. There were presents, of course, but they weren't, they never could be, as big and exciting and mysterious as the packages they came in. In the afternoon Virginia had wept, rocking herself back and forth in misery.

"I want my Christmas back again. I want *my* Christmas!" Mrs. Hamilton knew now that what Virginia had wanted back were the wild and wonderful hopes, the boxes unopened, the ribbons still in bows.

Soon, in two weeks, there would be a new Christmas. She wondered, grimly, if Virginia would weep for its return when it was gone.

"You must be tired," Alice said. "Why don't you sit down and let me wait in line?"

The response was crisp and immediate. "No, thanks. I refuse to be treated like an old lady, at my age."

"Willett told me I was to be sure and look after you properly."

"My son Willett was born to be an old maid. I have no illusions about my children. Never had any. I know that Virginia is temperamental. But that's *all*. There's no harm in her." She rubbed her moist pallid forehead with a handkerchief. The room seemed unbearably hot, suddenly, and she was unbearably tired, but she felt impelled to go on talking. "The charge is false, preposterous. In a small town like Arbana the police are inefficient and probably corrupt. They've made an absurd mistake."

She had spoken the same words a dozen times in the past dozen hours. They had, with repetition, gained force and speed like a runaway car going downhill, heading for a crash.

"Wait until you meet her, Alice. You'll find out for yourself."

"I'm sure I will." Yet the more Mrs. Hamilton talked about Virginia, the more obscure Virginia became, hidden in a thicket of words like an unknown animal.

"I have no illusions," the older woman repeated. "She is temperamental, even bad-tempered at times, but she's incapable of injuring anyone deliberately."

Alice murmured an indistinct but reassuring answer. She had become conscious, suddenly, of being a focus of attention. She turned and looked over Mrs. Hamilton's shoulder toward the exit door. A man was standing near the door watching her. He was in his middle thirties, tall, a little slouched as if he worked too long at a desk, and a little hard-faced, as if he didn't enjoy it. He wore a tweed topcoat that looked new, and a gray fedora and heavy brown English brogues.

"I think your son-in-law just came in."

Mrs. Hamilton turned too, and glanced brightly at the man. "That's not Paul. Too well-dressed. Paul always looks like someone in a soup line."

"He seems to know you, by the way he stares."

"Nonsense. Don't be so modest. He's staring at you. You're a pretty girl."

"I don't feel pretty."

"No woman *feels* pretty without a man. I used to feel pretty, though I never was, of course."

It was true. She had never been pretty even as a girl. Her head was too large for her body and emphasized by thick brown hair that was now burning itself out like a grass-fire and showing streaks of ashes. "You must learn to *pretend*, Alice. After all, you're not a schoolteacher any more. You're a young woman of the world, you're traveling, all sorts of exciting things can happen to you. Don't you feel that?"

"No," Alice said simply.

"Well, try."

The man at the door had come to a decision. He crossed the room briskly, removing his hat as he walked.

"Mrs. Hamilton?"

Mrs. Hamilton faced him, a slight frown creasing the skin between her eyebrows. The encounter, whatever it meant, wasn't in her plans. She had no time to waste or energy to squander on a stranger. She gripped her purse a little tighter as if the stranger had come to steal something from her.

"Yes, I'm Mrs. Hamilton."

"My name is Eric Meecham. Dr. Barkeley sent me to meet you."

"Oh. Well, how do you do?"

"How do you do?" He had a low-pitched voice with a faint rumble of impatience in it.

"You're a friend of Paul's?"

"No."

"Then?"

"I'm a lawyer. I've been retained to represent your daughter."

"Who hired you?"

"Dr. Barkeley."

"In my wire I instructed him to wait until I arrived."

Meecham returned her frown. "Well, he didn't. He wanted me to try and get her out of jail right away."

"And did you?"

"No."

"Why not? If it's money, I have . . ."

"It's not money. They can hold her for forty-eight hours without charge. It looks as if that's what they're going to do."

"But how can they hold an innocent girl?"

Meecham picked up the question carefully as if it was loaded. "The fact is, she hasn't claimed to be innocent."

"What—what does she claim?"

"Nothing. She won't deny anything, won't admit anything, won't, period. She's . . ." He groped for a word and out of the number that occurred to him he chose the least offensive: "She's a little difficult."

"She's frightened, the poor child. When she's frightened she's always difficult."

"I can see that." The line-up had dwindled down to just the three of them. Meecham looked questioningly at Alice, then turned back to Mrs. Hamilton. "You came alone?"

"No. No, I'm sorry, I forgot to introduce you. Alice, this is Mr. Meecham. Miss Dwyer."

Meecham nodded. "How do you do?"

"Alice is a friend of mine," Mrs. Hamilton explained.

"I'm a hired companion, really," Alice said.

"Really? If you'll give me the luggage checks, I'll get your things and take them out to my car."

Mrs. Hamilton handed him the checks. "It was kind of you to go to all this trouble."

"No trouble at all." The words were polite but without conviction.

He carried the four suitcases out to the car and piled them in the luggage compartment. The car was new but splattered with mud and there was a dent in the left rear fender.

The two women sat in the back and Meecham alone in the front. No one spoke for the first few miles. Traffic on the highway was heavy and the pavement slippery with slush.

Alice looked out at the countryside visible in the glare of headlights. It was bleak and flat, covered with patches of gray snow. A wave of homesickness swept over her, and mingled with it was a feeling much stronger and more violent than homesickness. She hated this place, and she hated the lawyer because he belonged to it. He was as crude and stark as the landscape and as ungracious as the weather.

Mrs. Hamilton seemed to share her feeling. She reached over suddenly and patted Alice's hand. Then she straightened up and addressed Meecham in her clear, deliberate voice: "Just what are your qualifications for this work, Mr. Meecham?"

"I took my law degree here at the University and played office boy to the firm of Post and Cranston until they found me indispensable and put my name on a door. Is that what you want to know?"

"I want to know what experience you've had with criminal cases."

"I've never handled a murder case, if that's what you mean," he said frankly. "They're not common around town. You know Arbana?"

"I've been there. Once."

"Then you know it's a university town and it hasn't a crime rate like Detroit's. The biggest policing problem is the traffic after football games. Naturally there's a certain percentage of auto thefts, robberies, morals offenses and things like that. But there hasn't been a murder for two years, until now."

"And they've arrested my daughter."

"Yes."

"I can't, I just can't believe it. All they had to do is take one look at Virginia to realize that she's a—a *nice* girl, well brought up."

"Nice girls have been in trouble before."

There was a brief silence. "You sound as if you think she's guilty."

"I've formed no opinion."

"You have. I can tell." Mrs. Hamilton leaned forward, one hand on the back of Meecham's seat. "Excuse me if I sound rude," she said softly, "but I'm not sure you're qualified to handle this business."

"I'm not sure either, but I'm going to try."

"Naturally you'll try. If murders are as rare in this town as you claim, it would be quite a feather in your cap to conduct a defense, wouldn't it?"

"It could be."

"I don't believe I'd like to see you wearing that feather, at my daughter's expense."

"What do you suggest that I do, Mrs. Hamilton?"

"Retire gracefully."

"I'm not graceful," Meecham said.

"I see. Well, I'll talk it over with Paul tonight."

They were approaching the town. There was a red neon glow in the sky and service stations and hamburger stands appeared at shorter intervals along the highway.

Mrs. Hamilton spoke again. "It's not that I have anything against you personally, Mr. Meecham."

"No."

"It's just that my daughter is the most important thing in my life. I can't take any chances."

Meecham thought of a dozen retorts, but he didn't make any of them. He felt genuinely sorry for the woman, or for anyone to whom Virginia Barkeley was the most important thing in life.

2

ONE WING OF the house was dark, but in the other wing lights streamed from every window like golden ribbons.

The place was larger than Meecham had expected, and its flat roof and enormous windows looked incongruous in a winter setting. It was a Southern California house, of redwood and fieldstone. Meecham wondered whether Virginia had planned it that way herself, deliberately, because it reminded her of home, or unconsciously, as a symbol of her own refusal to conform to a new environment.

The driveway entrance to the house was through a patio that separated the two wings. Here, too, the lights were on, revealing hanging baskets of dead plants and flowerpots heaped with snow, and a barbecue pit fringed with tiny icicles.

Mrs. Hamilton's eyes were squinted up as if she was going to cry at the sight of Virginia's patio, built for sun and summer and now desolate in the winter night. Silently she got out of the car and moved toward the house.

Meecham pushed back his hat in a gesture of relief. "Quite a character, eh?"

"I like her. She's very pleasant to me."

"Oh?" He stood aside while Alice stepped out of the car. "You're a little young to be a hired companion. How long have you worked for her?"

"About a month."

"Why?"

"Why? Well . . ." She flushed again. "Well, that's a silly question. I have to earn a living."

"I meant, it's a funny kind of job for a young girl."

"I used to be a schoolteacher. Only I wasn't meeting . . ." *any eligible men* were the words that occurred to her, but she said instead, "I was getting into a rut, so I decided to change jobs for a year or so."

He gave her a queer look and went around to the back of the car to unlock the luggage compartment. Mrs. Hamilton had gone into the house, leaving the front door open.

Meecham put the four suitcases on the shoveled drive and relocked the compartment. "I suppose you know what you're getting into."

"I—of course. *Naturally*."

"Naturally." He looked slightly amused. "I gather you haven't met Virginia."

"No. I've heard a lot about her, though, from her brother, Willett, and from Mrs. Hamilton. She seems to be—well, rather an unhappy person."

"You have to be pretty unhappy," Meecham said, "to stab a guy half a dozen times in the neck. Or didn't you know about that?"

"I knew it." She meant to sound very positive, like Mrs. Hamilton, but her voice was squeezed into a tight little whisper. "Of course I knew it."

"Naturally."

"You're quite objectionable."

"I am when people object to me," Meecham said. "I've forgotten your name, by the way, what is it?"

Instead of answering she picked up two of the suitcases and went ahead into the house.

Mrs. Hamilton heard her coming and called out, "Alice? I'm here, in the living room. Bring Mr. Meecham in with you. Perhaps he'd like some coffee."

Alice looked coldly at Meecham who had followed her in. "Would you like some coffee?"

"No, thanks, *Alice*."

"I don't permit total strangers to call me Alice."

"Okay, kid." He looked as if he was going to laugh, but he didn't. Instead, he said, "We seem to have started off on the wrong foot."

"Since we're not going anywhere together, what does it matter?"

"Have it your way." He put on his hat. "Tell Mrs. Hamilton I'll meet her tomorrow morning at 9:30 at the county jail. She can see Virginia then."

"Couldn't she phone her tonight or something?"

"The girl's in jail. She's not staying at the Waldorf." He said over his shoulder as he went out the door, "Good night, kid."

"Alice?" Mrs. Hamilton repeated. "Oh, there you are. Where's Mr. Meecham?"

"He left."

"Perhaps I was a little harsh with him, challenging his abilities." She was standing in front of the fireplace, still in her hat and coat, and rubbing her hands together as if to get warm, though the fire wasn't lit. "I'm afraid I antagonized him. I couldn't help it. I felt he had the wrong attitude toward Virginia."

The room was very large and colorful, furnished in rattan and bamboo and glass like a tropical lanai. There were growing plants everywhere, philodendron and ivy hanging from copper planters on the walls, azaleas in tubs, and cyclamen and coleus and saintpaulia in bright coralstone pots on the mantel and on every shelf and table. The air was humid and smelled of moist earth like a field after a spring rain.

The whole effect of the room was one of impossible beauty and excess, as if the person who lived there lived in a dream.

"She loves flowers," Mrs. Hamilton said. "She isn't like Willett, my son. He's never cared for anything except money. But Virginia is quite different. Even when she was a child she was always very gentle with flowers as she was with birds and animals. Very gentle and understanding . . ."

"Mrs. Hamilton."

". . . as if they were people and could feel."

"Mrs. Hamilton," Alice repeated, and the woman blinked as if just waking up. "Why is Virginia in jail? What did she do?"

She was fully awake now, the questions had struck her vulnerable body as hailstones strike a field of sun-warmed wheat. "Virginia didn't do anything. She was arrested by mistake."

"But why?"

"I've told you, Paul's wire to me was very brief. I know none of the details."

"You could have asked Mr. Meecham."

"I prefer to get the details from someone closer to me and to Virginia."

She doesn't want the facts at all, Alice thought. All she wants is to have Virginia back again, the gentle child who loved animals and flowers.

A middle-aged woman in horn-rimmed glasses and a white uniform came into the room carrying a cup of coffee, half of which had spilled into the saucer. She had a limp but she moved very quickly as if she thought speed would cover it. She had a spot of color on each cheekbone, round as coins.

"Here you are. This'll warm you up." She spoke a little too loudly, covering her embarrassment with volume as she covered her limp with speed.

Mrs. Hamilton nodded her thanks. "Carney, this is Alice Dwyer. Alice, Mrs. Carnova."

The woman shook Alice's hand vigorously. "Call me Carney. Everyone does."

"Carney," Mrs. Hamilton explained, "is Paul's office nurse, and an old friend of mine."

"He phoned from the hospital a few minutes ago. He's on his way."

"We are old friends, aren't we, Carney?"

The coins on the woman's cheekbones expanded. "Sure. You bet we are."

"Then what are you acting so nervous about?"

"Nervous? Well, everybody gets nervous once in a while, don't they? I've had a busy day and I stayed after hours to welcome you, see that you got settled, and so forth. I'm tired, is all."

"Is it?"

The two women had forgotten Alice. Carney was looking down at the floor, and the color had radiated all over her face to the tops of her large pale ears. "Why did you come? You can't do anything."

"I can. I'm going to."

"You don't know how things are."

"Then tell me."

"This is bad, the worst yet. I knew she was seeing Margolis. I warned her. I said I'd write and tell you and you'd come and make it hot for her."

"You didn't tell me."

Carney spread her hands. "How could I? She's twenty- six; that's too old to be kept in line by threats of telling mama."

"Did Paul know about this—this man?"

"I'm not sure. Maybe he did. He never said anything." She plucked a dried leaf from the yam plant that was growing down from the mantel. "Virginia won't listen to me anymore. She doesn't like me."

"That's silly. She's always been devoted to you."

"Not anymore. Last week she called me a snooping old beerhound. She said that when I applied for this job it wasn't because Carnova had left me stranded in Detroit, it was because you sent me here to spy on her."

"That's ridiculous," Mrs. Hamilton said crisply. "I'll talk to Virginia tomorrow and see that she apologizes."

"*Apologizes*. What do you think this is, some little *game* or something? Oh, God." Carney exploded. She covered her face with her hands, half-laughing, half-crying and then she began to hiccup, loud and fast. "Oh—damn—oh—damn."

Mrs. Hamilton turned to Alice. "We all need some rest. Come and I'll show you your room."

"I'll—show—her."

"All right. You go with Carney, Alice. I'll wait up to say hello to Paul."

Alice looked embarrassed. "I hated to stand there listening like that. About Virginia, I mean."

"That's all right, you couldn't help it." A car came up the driveway and stopped with a shriek of brakes. "Here's Paul now. I'll talk to him alone, Carney, if you don't mind."

"Why—should—I—mind?"

"And for heaven's sake breathe into a paper bag or something. Good night."

When they had gone, Mrs. Hamilton stood in the center of the room for a moment, her fingertips pressing her temples, her eyes closed. She felt exhausted, not from the sleepless night she had spent, or from the plane trip, but from the strain of uncertainty, and the more terrible strain of pretending that everything would be all right, that a mistake had been made which could be rather easily corrected.

She went to open the door for Paul.

He came in, stamping the snow from his boots, a stocky, powerfully built man in a wrinkled trench coat and a damp shapeless grey hat. He looked like a red-cheeked farmer coming in from his evening's chores, carrying a medical bag instead of a lantern.

He had a folded newspaper under his arm. Mrs. Hamilton glanced at the newspaper and away again.

"Well, Paul." They shook hands briefly.

"I'm glad you got here all right." He had a very deep warm voice and he talked rather slowly, weighing out each word with care like a prescription. "Sorry I couldn't meet you—Mother."

"You don't have to call me Mother, you know, if it makes you uncomfortable."

"Then I won't." He laid his hat and trench coat across a chair and put his medical bag on top of them. But he kept the newspaper in his hand, rolling it up very tight as if he intended to use it as a weapon, to swat a fly or discipline an unruly pup.

Mrs. Hamilton sat down suddenly and heavily, as though the newspaper had been used against her. The light from the rattan lamp struck her face with the sharpness of a slap. "That paper you have, what is it?"

"One of the Detroit tabloids."

"Is it . . .?"

"It's all in here, yes. Not on the front page."

"Are there any pictures?"

"Yes."

"Of Virginia?"

"One."

"Let me see."

"It's not very pretty," he said. "Perhaps you'd better not."

"I must see it."

"All right."

The pictures occupied the entire second page. There were three of them. One, captioned DEATH SHACK, showed a small cottage, its roof heavy with fresh snow and its windows opaque with frost. The second was of a sleek dark-haired man smiling into the camera. He was identified as Claude Ross Margolis, forty-two, prominent contractor, victim of fatal stabbing.

The third picture was of Virginia, though no one would have recognized her. She was sitting on some kind of bench, hunched over, with her hands covering her face and a tangled mass of black hair falling over her wrists. She wore evening slippers, one of them minus a heel, and a long fluffy dress and light-colored coat. The coat and dress and one of the shoes showed dark stains that looked like mud. Above the picture were the words, *held for questioning*, and underneath it Virginia was identified as Mrs. Paul Barkeley, twenty-six, wife of Arbana physician, allegedly implicated in the death of Claude Margolis.

Mrs. Hamilton spoke finally in a thin, ragged whisper: "I've seen a thousand such dreary pictures in my life, but I never thought that some day one of them would be terribly different to me from all the others."

She looked up at Barkeley. His face hadn't changed expression, it showed no sign of awareness that the girl in the picture was his wife. A little pulse of resentment began to beat in the back of Mrs. Hamilton's mind: *He doesn't care—he should have taken better care of Virginia—this would never have happened. Why wasn't he with her? Or why didn't he keep her at home*?

She said, not trying to hide her resentment, "Where were you when it happened, Paul?"

"Right here at home. In bed."

"You knew she was out."

"She'd been going out a great deal lately."

"Didn't you care?"

"Of course I cared. Unfortunately, I have to make a living. I can't afford to follow Virginia around picking up the pieces." He went over to the built-in bar in the south corner of the room. "Have a nightcap with me."

"No, thanks. I—those stains on her clothes, they're blood?"

"Yes."

"Whose blood?"

"His. Margolis'."

"How can they tell?"

"There are lab tests to determine whether blood is human and what type it is."

"Well. Well, anyway, I'm glad it's not hers." She hesitated, glancing at the paper and away again, as if she would have liked to read the report for herself but was afraid to. "She wasn't hurt?"

"No. She was drunk."

"*Drunk*?"

"Yes." He poured some bourbon into a glass and added water. Then he held the glass up to the light as if he was searching for microbes in a test tube. "A police patrol car picked her up. They found her wandering around about a quarter of a mile from Margolis' cottage. It was snowing very hard; she must have lost her way."

"Wandering around in the snow with only that light coat and those thin shoes—oh God, I can't bear it."

"You'll have to," he said quietly. "Virginia's depending on you."

"I know, I know she is. Tell me—the rest."

"There isn't much. Margolis' body had been discovered by that time because something had gone wrong with the fireplace in the cottage. There was a lot of smoke, someone reported it, and the highway patrol found Margolis inside dead, stabbed with his own knife. He'd been living in the cottage which is just outside the city limits because his own house was closed. His wife is in Peru on a holiday."

"His wife. He was married."

"Yes."

"There were—children?"

"Two."

"Drunk," Mrs. Hamilton whispered. "And out with a married man. There must be some mistake, surely, surely there is."

"No. I saw her myself. The Sheriff called me about three o'clock this morning and told me she was being held and why. I wired you immediately, and then I went down to the county jail where they'd taken her. She was still drunk, didn't even recognize me. Or pretended not to. How can you tell, with Virginia, what's real and what isn't?"

"*I* can tell."

"Can you?" He sipped at his drink. "The sheriff and a couple of deputies were there trying to get a statement from her. They didn't get one, of course. I told them it was silly to go on questioning anyone in her condition, so they let her go back to bed."

"In a cell? With thieves and prostitutes and . . ."

"She was alone. The cell—*room*, rather, was clean. I saw it. And the matron, or deputy, I think they called her, seemed a decent young woman. The surroundings aren't quite what Virginia is used to, but she's not suffering. Don't worry about that part of it."

"You don't appear to be worrying at all."

"I've done nothing but worry, for a long time." He hesitated, looking at her across the room as if wondering how much of the truth she wanted to hear. "You may as well know now—Virginia will tell you, if I don't—that this first year of our marriage has been bad. The worst year of my life, and maybe the worst in Virginia's too."

Mrs. Hamilton's face looked crushed, like paper in a fist. "Why didn't someone *tell* me? Virginia wrote to me, Carney wrote. No one said anything. I thought things were going well, that Virginia had settled down with you and was happy, that she was finally happy. Now I find out I've been deceived. She didn't settle down. She's been running around with married men, getting drunk, behaving like a cheap tart. And now this, this final disgrace. I just don't know what to *do*, what to *think*."

He saw the question in her eyes, and turned away, holding his glass up to the light again. "I did what I could, hired a lawyer."

"Yes, but what kind? A man with no experience."

"He was recommended to me."

"He's not good enough. Virginia should have the best."

"She should indeed," he said dryly. "Unfortunately, I can't afford the best."

"I can. Money is no object."

"That money-is-no-object idea is a little old-fashioned, I'm afraid." He put down his empty glass. "There's another point. If Virginia is innocent, she won't need the best. Now if you'll excuse me, I think I'll go to bed. I have to keep early hours. Carney showed you your room, I suppose?"

yourself at home as much as possible. The house is yours," he added with a wry smile. "Mortgage and all. Good night, Mrs. Hamilton."

"Good night." She hesitated for a split second before adding, "my boy."

He went out of the room. She followed him with her eyes; they were perfectly dry now, and hard and gray as granite.

Red-faced farmer, she thought viciously.

3

IN THE SUMMER the red bricks of the courthouse were covered with dirty ivy and in the winter with dirty snow. The building had been constructed on a large square in what was originally the center of town. But the town had moved westward, abandoned the courthouse like an ugly stepchild, leaving it in the east end to fend for itself among the furniture warehouses and service stations and beer-and-sandwich cafés.

Across the road from the main entrance was a supermarket. Meecham parked his car in front of it. Its doors were still closed, though there was activity inside. Along the aisles clerks moved apathetically, slowed by sleep and the depression of a winter morning that was no different from night. Street lamps were still burning, the sky was dark, the air heavy and damp.

Meecham crossed the road. He felt sluggish, and wished he could have stayed in bed until it was light.

In front of the courthouse a thirty-foot Christmas tree had been put up and four county prisoners were stringing it with colored lights under the direction of a deputy. The deputy wore fuzzy orange ear-muffs, and he kept stamping his feet rhythmically, either to keep warm or because there was nothing else to do.

When Meecham approached, all four of the prisoners stopped work to look at him, as they stopped to look at nearly everyone who passed, realizing that they had plenty of time and nothing to lose by a delay.

"Speed it up a little, eh, fellows?" The deputy whacked his hands together. "What's the matter, you paralyzed or something, Joe?"

Joe looked down from the top of the ladder and laughed, showing his upper teeth filled at the gum-line with gold. "How'd you like to be inside with a nice rum toddy, Huggins? Mmm?"

"I never touch the stuff," Huggins said. "Morning, Meecham."

Meecham nodded. "Morning."

"Up early catching worms?"

"That's right."

Huggins jerked his thumb at the ladder. "Me, I'm trying to inject the spirit of Christmas into these bums."

Three of the men laughed. The fourth spat into the snow.

Meecham went inside. The steam had been turned on full force and the old-fashioned radiators were clanking like ghosts rattling their chains. Meecham was sweating before he reached the middle of the corridor, and the passages from his nose to his throat felt hot and dry as if he'd been breathing fire.

The main corridor smelled of wood and fresh wax, but when he descended the stairs on the left a new smell rose to overpower the others, the smell of disinfectant.

The door lettered County Sheriff was open. Meecham walked into the anteroom and sat down in one of the straight chairs that were lined up against the wall like mute and motionless prisoners. The anteroom was empty, though a man's coat and hat were hanging on a rack in the corner, and the final inch of a cigarette was smoldering in an ash tray on the scarred wooden counter. Meecham looked at the cigarette but made no move to put it out.

The door of the Sheriff's private office banged open suddenly and Cordwink himself came out. He was a tall man, match-thin, with gray hair that was clipped short to disguise its curl. His eyelashes curled too, giving his cold eyes a false appearance of naivete. He had fifty years of hard living behind him, but they didn't show except when he was tired or when he'd had a quarrel with his wife over money or one of the kids.

"What are you doing around so early?" Cordwink said.

"I wanted to be the first to wish you a Merry Christmas."

"You bright young lawyers, you keep me all the time in stitches. Yah." He scowled at the cigarette smoldering in the ash tray. "What the hell you trying to do, burn the place down?"

"It's not my . . ."

"That's about the only way you'll get your client out of here."

"Oh?" Meecham lit a cigarette and used the burnt match to crush out the burning remnants of tobacco in the ash tray. "Have you dug up any new information?"

"I should tell you?" Cordwink laughed. "You bloody lawyers can do your own sleuthing."

"Kind of sour this morning, aren't you, Sheriff?"

"I'm in a sour business, I meet sour people, so I'm sour. So?"

"So you didn't get a statement from Mrs. Barkeley."

"Sure I got a statement."

"Such as?"

"Such as that I'm an illiterate buffoon of canine parentage."

Meecham grinned.

"That strikes you as humorous, eh, Meecham?"

"Moderately."

"Well, it so happens that I graduated from the University of Wisconsin, class of '22."

"Funny, I thought you were a Harvard man. You act and talk like a . . ."

"You bright young lawyers kill me." He grunted. "Yah. Well, I don't care if she makes a statement or not. We have her."

"Maybe."

"Even you ought to be smart enough to see that. You'd better start combing the books for some fancy self-defense items. Make sure you get a nice stupid jury, then razz the cops, turn on the tears, quote the Bible—yah! Makes me sick. What a way to make a living, obstructing justice."

"I've heard the theme song before, Sheriff. Let's skip the second chorus."

"You think I'm off-key, eh?"

"Sure you are."

Cordwink pressed a buzzer on the counter. "You won't get away with a self-defense plea. There isn't a mark on the girl, no cut, no bruise, not a scratch."

"I don't have to prove that the danger to her person was objectively real and imminent, only that she thought, and had reason to think, that it was real and imminent."

"You're not in court yet, so can the jargon. Makes me sick."

The Sheriff pressed the buzzer again and a moment later a young woman in a green dress came into the room blithely swinging a ring of keys.

She greeted Meecham with a show of fine white teeth. "You again, Mr. Meecham."

"Right."

"You ought to just move in." She switched the smile on Cordwink. "Isn't that right, Sheriff?"

"Righter than you think," Cordwink said. "If justice was done, the place would be crawling with lawyers." He started toward his office. "Show the gentleman into Mrs. Barkeley's boudoir, Miss Jennings."

"Okeydoke." Cordwink slammed his door and Miss Jennings added, in a stage whisper, "My, aren't we short-tempered this morning."

"Must be the weather."

"You know, I think it is, Mr. Meecham. Personally, the weather never bothers me. I rise above it. When winter comes can spring be far behind?"

"You have something there."

"Shakespeare. I adore poetry."

"Good, good." He followed her down the corridor. "How is Mrs. Barkeley?"

"She had a good sleep and a big breakfast. I think she's finally over her hangover. My, it was a beaut." She unlocked the door at the end of the corridor and held it open for Meecham to go through first. "She borrowed my lipstick. That's a good sign."

"Maybe. But I don't know of what."

"Oh, you're just cynical. So many people are cynical. My mother often says to me, Mollie dear, you were born smiling and you'll probably go out smiling."

Meecham shuddered. "Lucky girl."

"Yes, I am lucky. I simply can't *help* looking at the cheerful side."

"Good for you."

The women's section of the cell-block was empty except for Virginia. Miss Jennings unlocked the door. "Here's that man again, Mrs. Barkeley."

Virginia was sitting on her narrow cot reading, or pretending to read, a magazine. She was wearing the yellow wool dress and brown sandals that Meecham had brought to her the previous afternoon, and her black hair was brushed carefully back from her high forehead. She had used Miss Jennings' lipstick to advantage, painting her mouth fuller and wider than it actually was. In the light of the single overhead bulb her flesh looked smooth and cold as marble. Meecham found it impossible to imagine what emotions she was feeling, or what was going on behind her remote and beautiful eyes.

She raised her head and gave him a long unfriendly stare that reminded him of Mrs. Hamilton, though there was no physical resemblance between the mother and daughter.

"Good morning, Mrs. Barkeley."

"Why don't you get me out of here?" she said flatly.

"I'm trying."

He stepped inside and Miss Jennings closed the door behind him but didn't lock it. She retired to the end of the room and sat down on a bench near the exit door. She hummed a few bars of music, very casually, to indicate to Meecham and Virginia that she had no intention of eavesdropping. *I'll take the high road . . .*

"She sings," Virginia said. "She whistles. She quoted poetry. She's so cheerful it drives me crazy. You've got to get me *out* of here."

"I'm trying."

"You said that before."

"Now I'm repeating it. Mind if I sit down?"

"I don't care."

He sat down at the foot of the cot. "How's your hangover?"

"It's all right. But they've got fleas or something in here. I have more of those red welts all over my ankles. Did you remember to bring the DDT?"

"Sure." He took the small bottle of DDT out of his overcoat pocket and gave it to her.

She read the label, frowning. "It's only two percent."

"I couldn't get it any stronger."

"You could."

"All right, but I didn't."

"What were you afraid of, that I'd drink it in remorse or something?"

"It occurred to me," Meecham said. "Now don't get excited. Your mother will be here soon."

"When?"

"Nine-thirty."

"Do I—do I look all right?"

"You look fine. Very pretty, in fact."

"Don't say that. I know I'm not pretty."

Meecham smiled. "We disagree about so many things, let's not disagree about that. Where did you get the cockeyed idea that you're not pretty?"

"I know I'm not. We won't discuss it."

"All right." He offered her a cigarette and she shook her head in refusal. "Let's discuss Cordwink. Give him a statement today and you'll be out . . ."

"I wouldn't give him the time of day."

"Why not?"

Her lips tightened. "I know what I'm doing. If I refuse to tell Cordwink anything, he won't have anything to trip me up with later on."

"That argument is sound but rather limited."

"Besides, now that my mother's here, she'll handle everything."

"Oh?"

"Wait and see."

"Your mother," Meecham said dryly, "is undoubtedly a strong and persevering woman, but she can't handle an entire sheriff's department."

She looked at him stubbornly. "She *believes* in me."

"I don't care if she thinks you're Queen of the May, a mother's faith isn't enough to go to court on."

"I won't be going to court."

"No?"

"I'm not guilty. I didn't kill him." She raised her voice. "Hear that, Miss Big Ears? I didn't kill Margolis."

Miss Jennings began to hum again: *And you'll take the low road.*

"Well, that's something anyway," Meecham said. "A denial. Can you back it up?"

"That's all I'm saying right now."

"Why?"

"Because it *is*."

"Because you don't remember," Meecham said. "According to the lab report your blood alcohol was 2.23."

"What does that mean?"

"You were loaded."

Virginia's cheeks turned slightly pink. "Does my mother know that?"

"She must, by this time."

"She'll be furious. She's a teetotaler." She said it very seriously, as if the crime of which she was accused was not murder but drinking.

"So you won't give Cordwink a statement."

"I can't. Don't you understand? I can't tell him I don't remember anything, he'll throw the book at me."

"He may anyway."

She bit her lower lip. "I admit I was a little high Saturday night."

"You were quite stupendously drunk, Mrs. Barkeley. You weren't a little high."

"Well, stop repeating it!" she cried. "Why did you come here anyway? I don't need you to tell me what to do."

"Don't you?"

There was a pause. Miss Jennings was wide-eyed with curiosity, but she hummed valiantly on, keeping time with her left foot.

"You weren't drunk all Saturday night. What happened earlier, before Margolis was killed?"

"We danced and had something to eat."

"You also had a fight around eleven o'clock."

"Claude and I were the best of friends," she said stiffly.

"It's on the record, Mrs. Barkeley. A waitress at the Top Hat remembers you both and has already identified your pictures. In the middle of the argument you got up and walked out and a few minutes later Margolis followed you. Where did you go? Or don't you want me to tell you?"

"You like talking so much, tell me." The words were arrogant, but they weren't spoken arrogantly. Her voice trembled, and Meecham wondered if she was frightened at the thought of meeting her mother. She had shown no previous signs of fear.

He said, "You went to a beer-and-pretzel place a couple of doors down the street. It was jammed with the Saturday-night college crowd. Margolis caught up with you there. You were at the bar talking to a man when Margolis arrived. You got up and left with Margolis, and the other man got up and left too, according to one of the bartenders. But he doesn't know whether the man left with you, or whether he was just going home because it was nearly closing time. Which was it?"

"Stop." Virginia pounded the edge of the cot with her fist. "Do we have to go into it like this?"

"Somebody has to. We can't all sit around nursing our amnesia."

"You're pretty insolent, for hired help."

"And you're pretty uncooperative for a girl who might spend her next twenty years sorting out dirty clothes in a prison laundry."

"That was an ugly remark." The girl's face was paper-white, and her skin seemed to be stretched tight and transparent across her cheekbones. "I won't forget it."

"I hope not," Meecham said. "There's one very interesting point about the finding of Margolis' body. His wallet was missing."

"What difference does that make?"

"His friends claim he always carried a fair amount of cash."

"He did."

"It makes me wonder about your anonymous stranger at the bar. I gather you didn't take Margolis' wallet?"

"Why should I?"

"Because you're broke."

"So you've been checking up. Afraid you're not going to get paid?"

"I've been checking. Your car isn't paid for, your house is mortgaged, your husband is . . ."

"Leave Paul out of this," she said sharply. "And get one thing straight—if I want money, I don't have to go around lifting wallets."

"You can ask your mother."

"That's right, I can."

"Well, here's your chance." Meecham glanced at his watch. "She should be arriving right now."

The overhead lights went off suddenly and the feeble rays of the morning sun filtered in through the barred windows like dim hopes.

Virginia got up and looked out the window at her little square of sky. "I can't see her in here. There must be some other place."

"I'll see what I can do." He opened the cell door and stepped out. "Miss Jennings?"

Miss Jennings came up, swinging her keys. "All through for now?"

"Mrs. Barkeley's mother is coming to visit her. They haven't seen each other for a year. I thought we might be able to borrow some other room for a while, Miss Jennings."

"Well, I guess so. I'll see. After all, one's own *mother*." She glanced rather uncertainly at Virginia. "I'll have to stay with you all the time. Mr. Meecham can talk to you in private because he's your lawyer. But anyone else . . . There are rules, even about mothers."

"What do you think she's going to do," Virginia said, "slip me a loaf of bread with a chisel inside?"

Miss Jennings laughed hollowly. "She's a great one for joking, isn't she, Mr. Meecham?"

"Just great." He gave Virginia a warning glance and she went and sat down on the cot again with her back to them both.

Miss Jennings locked the cell door. "I'll go and ask the Sheriff if you can use his private office. But I don't guarantee a thing. He's not at his best this morning."

"Thanks for trying, anyway." When Miss Jennings had gone, he spoke through the bars to Virginia: "It's time you started to win friends and influence people."

"Really?"

"Put on an act. You're an innocent flower, dirt has been done by you, and now your dear old mother has come to visit you from the faraway hills."

"What ham. It's too thick to slice."

"Ham or not, try some," Meecham said. "By the way, do you know Margolis' wife?"

"I've met her. She has a bad complexion."

"How did you meet her?"

"That's none of your business."

"Everything about you is my business until you get out of here for good. How did you meet Margolis?"

"He built the house for me. For me and Paul, that is."

Miss Jennings returned and opened the cell door again. "Your mother's waiting in the Sheriff's office, Mrs. Barkeley. My, she doesn't resemble you a bit, except maybe just around the eyes. Family resemblances fascinate me. Here, you can borrow my compact mirror to see how you look."

"I know how I look," Virginia said.

"Now, is that nice?" Smiling cheerfully, Miss Jennings replaced the compact in her pocket. "You look sulky, if you want the truth."

Virginia opened her mouth to reply, caught another warning glance from Meecham and changed her mind. She followed Miss Jennings silently down the hall. Her face was calm, almost stony, but she walked as if she had trouble keeping her balance.

"Do you want me to stay?" Meecham asked.

Virginia half-turned and said, over her shoulder, "What for?"

"Well, there's my answer."

"Right."

He dropped behind the two women. When they reached the Sheriff's office Virginia went in ahead, taking little running steps. "Momma! *Momma*!"

Meecham wondered grimly whether this was the real thing or whether it was ham too thick to slice.

He walked slowly past the open door. Mrs. Hamilton was holding Virginia in her arms, rocking back and forth in grief and gladness. She was crying, and Virginia was crying, and Miss Jennings' face was all squeezed up as if she too was going to cry. All three of them looked so funny that for an instant Meecham almost laughed.

The instant passed.

"Ginny darling. Darling girl."

Christ, Meecham thought, and walked away as fast as possible to get out of earshot.

At the bottom of the stairs leading up to the main floor a man was sitting on a bench, his back resting against the wall.

Meecham stared at him curiously as he passed, and the man returned the stare, unselfconsciously, like someone accustomed to attracting attention. In spite of the winter weather he wore no coat or hat, and his skin was mushroom-pale as if he had lived underground for a long time, out of reach of the sun. He was still young. His face looked younger than Meecham's, but the shape of his body was like that of a dissolute old man—scrawny shoulders and pipestem wrists and a huge pendulous belly which he tried to hide by keeping his arms folded in front of him.

He looked at Meecham, his eyes enormous in the thin sensitive face, and then he rose heavily and awkwardly like a woman far gone with child and moved on down the corridor.

Meecham went up the stairs. Outside, the Christmas tree lights were in place and turned on, but they didn't show up very well because the sun was shining.

4

WHEN MEECHAM ARRIVED at the house it was almost dark and snow was falling again, a fine light snow, iridescent, like crushed diamonds.

Alice met him at the door. Though he'd only seen her once before, on the previous night, she looked very familiar to him, like a kid sister. He glanced down at her with a critical brotherly eye. She was wearing a cherry-colored dress that didn't suit her; the lines were too straight, the color too vivid.

"Do I come in?" Meecham said.

"Well, I guess so."

"What's the matter? Anything wrong?"

"No. Except that there's no one here but me. Dr. Barkeley and Mrs. Hamilton are out."

"That's all right. Maybe I'm early."

"Early?"

"I was invited for tea." He consulted his watch. "At five. It's now five."

"No one told me anything about it. Mrs. Hamilton's been gone all day."

He took off his coat and laid it across a chair while Alice watched him, still looking puzzled and rather unfriendly.

She said, "Why did she invite you for tea?"

"Maybe she wants to read my tea leaves. That should be interesting," he added with a dry smile. "I might be about to get some money or meet a short suspicious blonde."

"That's not very funny."

"Then stop acting suspicious."

"I'm not."

"Have it your way."

He crossed the room and stood with his back to the mantel, his left arm supporting some of his weight. His body was never quite erect. When he walked he slouched, and when he stood he always leaned against something like a man who had spent too much time in a car and at a desk.

"Where is she?" he asked.

"At the movies. She phoned at noon and told me she intended to stay downtown for lunch and do some shopping and take in a double feature. She sounded quite gay and girlish, as if she was going on a spree."

"Maybe she was."

"Oh, no. She doesn't drink."

"I wasn't thinking of that kind of a spree."

"Then why don't you say what you think?"

"Maybe I will, sometime."

"I can hardly wait."

"Now what are you miffed about?"

"You're so condescending."

"I don't feel that way," he said gravely. "In fact, right now I'm confused. I can go down to lower Fifth Street and look in the window of a house, any house, and tell you quite a lot about the people who live there. But I'm not used to houses like this or girls like Virginia or women like Mrs. Hamilton."

"Or like me?" The question slipped out unintentionally, like a line from a fishing reel left unguarded for a moment.

"I think I know quite a bit about you, Alice."

"Oh? You've met dozens like me, I suppose."

"A few."

She turned away so that he couldn't see the angry flush that stained her face.

He didn't see it, though he guessed it was there. "Why does that make you mad?"

"I'm not mad."

"You wouldn't want to be absolutely unique, would you, like a three-headed calf or something?"

"Of course not." I would, she thought violently. I want to be absolutely unique.

"I'm sorry if I offended you," he said with a trace of a smile. "It's just that I knew a three-headed calf once, and all it ever wanted to be was ordinary."

"This is a ridiculous conversation," Alice said. "I think you'd better stick to looking in windows on lower Fifth Street, Mr. Meecham."

"I *don't* look in. . ."

"You said you did."

"I said I *could*."

"Anybody can. You hardly need any special equipment for window peeping."

"I am *not* a window peeper."

"Well, you said you were."

"I did not say I . . ."

"I heard you distinctly."

Meecham shook his head in exasperation. "All right. All right, I'm a window peeper."

"I can believe it."

"I think I've changed my mind about you, Alice. You *are* unique. Absolutely unique and impossible."

Alice gazed at him blandly. "I'd rather be impossible than ordinary. Mrs. Hamilton says I can be anything if I try."

"Mrs. Hamilton's an authority?"

"On most things."

"I wouldn't be too sure," he said. "Don't get stuck on the old girl. She might let you down."

From outside there came the sound of footsteps hurrying across the patio. A moment later the front door burst open and Mrs. Hamilton came rushing into the room. Her coat was flying open and her hat had slid to the back of her head. She looked blowsy and old and scared.

As she turned to close the door behind her the parcels she was carrying slid out of her arms and dropped to the floor. There was a muffled shatter of glass, and almost instantly the smell of lilacs crept poignantly into the room like a remembered spring.

"Turn off the lights, Alice," she said. "Don't ask questions. Turn them off."

Alice did as she was told. Without lights the smell of lilacs seemed stronger, and Mrs. Hamilton's harsh breathing rose and fell in the darkness.

"Someone is out there. A man. He's been following me."

Meecham coughed, faintly. She took it as a sign of disbelief.

"No, I'm not imagining things, Mr. Meecham," she said sharply. "He followed me from the bus stop. I couldn't get a cab downtown so I took the bus. This man got off at the same corner as I did. He followed me. I think he meant to rob me."

"He may live in one of the houses around here," Meecham said.

"No. He came after me quite deliberately and openly. When I walked fast he walked fast, and when I paused he paused. There was something almost sadistic about it."

"He's probably a neighborhood nut who gets his kicks out of scaring women," Meecham said. Or a policeman, he thought, maybe one of Cordwink's men. "Where is he now?"

"The last I saw of him he had gone behind the cedar hedge." She crossed to the window and pointed. "Right there, at the entrance to the driveway. He might be there yet."

"I'll go out and take a look."

"What if he's dangerous? Maybe we should call the police immediately."

"First, let's see if he's still there," Meecham said.

Outside, the snow was still falling. It felt good, after the heat of the house. Through the patio and down the driveway Meecham walked, a little self-consciously, aware that the two women were watching him from the window and not sure how far they could see, since it wasn't totally dark yet.

By the time he reached the end of the curving driveway the snow didn't feel quite so pleasant. With quiet persistence it had seeped in over the tops of his shoes, and up his coat sleeves and down under his collar. He felt cold and wet and foolish.

He said, in a voice that wasn't as loud or as firm as he intended: "Hey. You behind the hedge. What are you doing?"

There was no answer. He had expected none. The old girl had probably dreamed up the whole thing. Darkness, weariness, a deserted street, footsteps behind—together they were rich food for the imagination.

Pulling up his coat collar against the snow, he was on the point of turning to go back to the house when a man shuffled out from the shadow of the hedge. He moved like an old man, and his hair and eyebrows were white, but the whiteness was snow. He stood with his back to the street lamp so that his face was just a blur in the deepening twilight. The light-colored baggy coat he wore hung on him like a tent.

"What am I doing here?" he said. "I'm waiting for the doctor."

"Behind a hedge?"

"No, sir." He had a rather high, earnest voice, like a schoolboy's. "I intend to go to his office, but I thought I'd stand here a bit and enjoy the night. I like a winter night."

"Kind of cold, isn't it?"

"Not for me. I like the smell of cedar too. It reminds me of Christmas. I won't be having a Christmas this year." He brushed the snow from his eyebrows with the back of his bare hand. "Of course I'm not really waiting for the doctor."

Meecham's eyes were alert, suspicious. "No?"

"Oh, I'll see him, of course. But what I'm really waiting for—and so are you, if you only knew it—is a destination, a finality, an end of something. My own case is rather special; I'm waiting for an end of fear."

I was right, Meecham thought. *He's a neighborhood nut*. Aloud he said, "You'd better pick a more comfortable place to wait. Move on, now. We don't want any trouble."

The man didn't even hear him. "I've died a thousand times from fear. A thousand deaths, and one would have been enough. A great irony."

"You'd better move on, go home and get some sleep. Have you got a family?"

"A family?" The young man laughed. "I have a great family."

"They may be waiting for you."

"I won't be going home tonight."

"You can't stay here." Meecham glanced briefly at the man's shoes. Like the overcoat, they looked new. He said anyway, "I can let you have a couple of bucks."

"What do you think, that I'm a bum wanting a handout? I'm not a bum."

A car came around the corner, its headlights searched the man's face for a moment like big blind eyes. Meecham recognized him instantly. He had seen him that morning in the county jail, the old-young man with the sensitive face and the swollen dissolute body. The body was hidden now under the tent of his overcoat. His face was bland and unlined, and the falling snow had feathered his eyelashes and made his eyes look dewy and innocent. He was, Meecham thought, about twenty-eight.

He said aloud, "We've met before."

"Yes, I know. I know who you are."

"Oh?"

"You're Mr. Meecham, the girl's lawyer."

Meecham had an abrupt and inexplicable feeling of uneasiness. It was, he thought, like turning around suddenly on a dark night and finding at your heels a silent and vicious dog; nothing is said, nothing is done; the walk continues, the dog behind you, and behind the dog, fear, following you both.

"What's your name?" Meecham said.

"Loftus. Earl Duane Loftus." The young man blinked, and the snow tumbled from his eyelashes down his cheeks in a miniature avalanche. "You'd better go and call the police. You wouldn't mind if I waited inside the house until they arrive? I'm not cold—I never mind the cold—but I'd like to sit down. I tire easily."

"Why should I call the police?"

"I'd like to give them a statement."

"What about?"

"I committed a murder."

"Oh."

"You don't believe me," Loftus said.

"Oh sure, sure I do."

"No. I can tell. First you thought I was a bum, now you think I'm a psycho."

"No, I don't," Meecham lied, without conviction.

"Well, I can't blame you, actually. I guess every murder case attracts a lot of tips and confessions from psychos, people who want punishment or publicity or expiation. I don't fit into any of those classes, Mr. Meecham."

"Of course not," Meecham lied again, wishing that a patrol car would come along, or that the young man would go away quietly, and without a fuss.

"I can see you're still skeptical. You haven't even asked whom I killed."

Meecham felt cold and weary, and a little impatient. "What gave you the idea you killed anyone?"

"The body. The dead body." Loftus' long skinny fingers worked nervously at the lapels of his coat. "I didn't come here following the old lady home. We had a common destination, that's all. I wanted to see the doctor and tell him first. His wife didn't kill Margolis. I did."

Meecham's impatience had grown with his discomfort. "How'd you kill him, with a shotgun as he was going into the post-office to mail a letter?"

Loftus shook his head, very seriously. "No, sir, I didn't. I stabbed him in the neck. Four or five times, I believe."

"Why?"

"I had a good many reasons." He leaned toward Meecham in an almost confidential manner. "I look funny to you, don't I? You think like a lot of people that a man who looks so funny must also be funny in the head. Looks are very important. Very deceiving too. I'm quite sane, quite intelligent even. There's only one thing the matter with me; I am going to die."

"Why are you telling me?"

"You asked why I killed Margolis. Well, that's one of my reasons. Ever since I found out, a year ago, what my chances were, I've been pondering the situation. Since I was going to die anyway, I thought I would take someone with me—rid the world of someone it would be better off without, some incorrigible criminal, perhaps, or a dangerous politician. But when the time and opportunity came, it was Margolis. I wish it could have been someone more important. Margolis was very third-rate."

"He had a wife and two kids."

Loftus' calm was unshaken. "He won't be missed. I've done them a favor."

"Well," Meecham said quietly. "Come inside and sit down."

"Thank you, sir."

They walked, side by side, toward the house. It seemed to Meecham that it was the longest and strangest walk he'd ever taken.

5

LOFTUS LOOKED AT the clock on the mantel. 6:10. So the clock was going, all right, time was passing, but slow and soundless. He missed the noise of ticking. The clock he had in his own room ticked so loud that it often kept him awake. Sometimes in the middle of the night he got up and covered it with a glass bowl that he'd bought in the dime store. The glass smothered the noise a little but didn't obscure the face of the clock.

The room was quiet. Mrs. Hamilton and the blonde girl had gone to another part of the house, and the doctor had come, and, after a long whispered conference in the hall, had gone away again. There were only the four of them left, the two policemen, and Meecham, and Loftus himself.

"Loftus."

Loftus turned. "Yes, sir." He wasn't sure if this was the way to address a sheriff. He had never talked to one before.

"When did you write this?" Cordwink said.

"This afternoon."

"Why?"

"I thought it would be better to write it down myself, to get things very clear. They are, aren't they? Clear?"

Cordwink made a noise in the back of his throat. "Clear as a bell. You thought of everything, Loftus."

"I tried to."

"It makes me wonder whether you might have had a little help with it."

"Who would help me?"

"Well, now. Meecham over here is always willing to lend a hand, especially if . . ."

"You're off your rocker, Cordwink," Meecham said flatly. "I never saw the man before in my life."

"No?"

"No. And just what do you mean 'help' him with it? You talk as if we're a couple of school kids and I did his homework for him, or something."

Cordwink rustled the papers he held in his hand. There were eight of them, closely written. By moving his head slightly Loftus could see the top sheet. It had been the most difficult to write. He had made so many copies that he knew it by heart: *My name is Earl Duane Loftus. I am writing this without coercion or advice on the part of anyone, and with the full knowledge that it can be used as evidence in a court of law. . . .*

Cordwink was speaking. "This comes at a convenient time for you, Meecham. Your client's in jail, a lot of evidence against her . . ."

"Circumstantial."

". . . and then out of the blue comes a nice pat answer to all your problems."

"But it didn't come out of the blue," Loftus said, blinking his eyes nervously. "Not at all, sir. I intended to admit everything right from the beginning, but I needed some time. I had to do a few things first, personal things. I'm afraid I didn't give much thought to Mrs. Barkeley being held in jail. But then it didn't do her any harm, did it? She's a little spoiled."

"Is she?"

"I think so."

Cordwink's mouth tightened. "There's nothing in what you've written here to indicate that you knew her before last Saturday night."

"I didn't know her, not actually. I saw her once, a little over a year ago. I had come to consult Dr. Barkeley, I was feeling so tired and heavy, and I minded the heat so much. I . . ." He paused, folding his arms to hide his belly. It was my belly that worried me, he thought. It had begun to swell, bigger and bigger. I had nightmares about being a hideous freak, the only man in the world who ever had a baby. It wasn't a baby, but I was a freak, all right. I didn't know it then. I said, it's my nerves, doctor, maybe I need a rest, a change of climate. You need hospital treatment, he said. I went to him three times, and the third time he told me what I had. It was only a word to me then, a pretty word like a girl's name, Leukemia, Leukemia Smith, Leukemia Ann Johnston. Chronic myeloid leukemia, he said. He didn't tell me I was dying. But I knew, I knew. He never sent me a bill.

"Loftus," Cordwink said.

Loftus jerked his head up. "Yes, sir."

"Go on. You were saying?"

"I—oh, yes. Yes. I saw Mrs. Barkeley once when I went to the doctor's office. She was in the yard raking up leaves."

"Did you talk to her?"

"No, oh no. I just passed by."

"Did she notice you?"

"I don't think so."

"Have you ever talked to her?"

"Just on Saturday night, that's the only time."

Cordwink turned to the deputy he had brought with him, a young intense-looking man in a tweed suit. "Dun- lop, you're getting all this down?"

"Yes, sir," Dunlop said. "'Just on Saturday night, that's the only time.'"

"When Mrs. Barkeley came into the bar, Loftus, did you recognize her?"

"Of course. She's a very pretty woman."

"What was the name of the bar?"

"It's in there, in my confession."

"Tell me anyway."

"Sam's Café."

"Are you sure? I thought it was Joe's."

Loftus shook his head. "It was Sam's. If you're trying to confuse me, you can't. I remember everything very clearly. I only had one drink, a beer. I was just finishing it when Mrs. Barkeley came up to the bar and sat down beside me. This is all written down, but I suppose you want me to repeat it, just to test me, is that it?"

"Go on."

"She smiled at me and said hello. I was flattered, thinking she might have remembered me. Then I saw how drunk she was, eyes glassy and out of focus, and her smile not real at all, just sort of painted on like a doll's smile."

"What else did she say?"

"You mean her exact words?"

"Yes."

Loftus thought a moment. "She said, 'God, this place stinks.'"

Meecham made a sound like a laugh and covered it with a cough. Cordwink turned and stared at him. "Is something amusing you, Meecham?"

"No." Meecham coughed again. "I have a slight cold."

"Is that a fact? Dunlop."

"Yes, sir," Dunlop said.

"Read that back. Mr. Meecham wants a good laugh."

Dunlop bent over his notes. "'God, this place stinks.'"

"There. Is it as funny as you thought it was, Meecham?"

Meecham looked as if he intended to make a sharp reply but he held it back. "No."

"All right then. What else did Mrs. Barkeley say to you, Loftus?"

"She said she wanted a drink but she'd left her purse in the car. I bought her a beer. She had just started to drink it when Margolis came in. He was an impressive-looking man. I'd seen him before at the county hospital where I go for my X-ray treatments and shots. His firm was building the new T.B. wing and he used to hang around a lot, talking to the nurses. Margolis remembered me too. I'm quite a—freak." He looked down at the floor. "Margolis asked Mrs. Barkeley to leave. She said she didn't want to go home, and why didn't all three of us go to another place for a drink. Margolis humored her. When she started for the door he said I was to come along and he'd give me a lift home. I accepted. I wanted a lift home, but there was more to it than that. I was excited, thrilled as a high-school kid at suddenly becoming a part of all that—glamor, I guess you'd call it. I didn't realize until we got out to the car that offering me a lift home wasn't exactly a noble gesture on Margolis' part. He needed me to help him handle Mrs. Barkeley. She passed out in the back seat. Margolis shook her and swore at her, but she was limp as a rag."

He stopped to wipe the sweat from his face with his handkerchief.

". . . and swore at her," Dunlop said in his quick uninterested monotone, "but she was limp as a rag."

Loftus appealed to Cordwink: "I've admitted everything. Why does he have to take all this down?"

"It's routine, for one thing. For another, the statement you're making now will have to be checked with your written confession for discrepancies."

"But I'm guilty, I've . . ."

"No matter if you write five hundred confessions, you still have to be tried in a court of law to determine the degree of your guilt."

"Yes. Yes, I see now. I didn't realize." I sound so meek, Loftus thought. I don't sound like a murderer at all. Maybe I would be more convincing if I acted belligerent, but I hardly know how.

"Are you ready to continue, Loftus?"

"I—yes, of course. Margolis said he couldn't take Mrs. Barkeley home in that condition, and he asked me if I'd mind helping him get her out to his cottage. It wasn't the first time I'd heard of his cottage. There were rumors around the hospital . . . I was there so much that I got to know quite a few of the nurses, and that's how I first heard of Margolis and his affairs."

"The cottage was just outside the city limits, on the river. It didn't look like much on the outside, but it was fixed up nice inside—leather furniture and a stone fireplace and some good reproductions hanging on the walls, a Van Gogh, I remember, was one of them."

"Tell me more about the fireplace," Cordwink said.

"Well, there were a pair of fishing rods, crossed, on the wall above it, and on the mantel itself there were several of those big German steins and two hunting knives in leather sheaths."

"Dunlop . . ." Cordwink made a half-turn. "Was the inside of Margolis' cottage described in any of the papers?"

Dunlop put down his pencil. "A couple of Detroit papers carried a shot of the outside, and the *Tribune*, I think it was, had a shot of the floor where Margolis was found—bloodstains, et cetera."

"No fireplace in the picture?"

"No fireplace."

Loftus smiled anxiously. "I don't read the *Tribune* anyway, sir."

"All right, go on."

"I helped Margolis carry her inside the cottage and put her on the davenport. She was still out cold. Margolis was very angry by this time. I think the two of them must have been quarreling earlier in the evening, and that this was a final straw for Margolis. He began calling her names and shaking her again. It was an ugly scene. I thought of all the things I'd heard about Margolis around the hospital. I thought of—well, it doesn't matter what I thought. I went over to the fireplace. The fire was lit and the room was beginning to get very warm. I picked up one of the hunting knives and took it out of its sheath. Margolis wasn't paying any attention to me. He'd forgotten I was there. I was just a bum, a nobody, a—well, then I did it. I stabbed him in the neck. I'm not very strong and I thought his neck would be the easiest place. It wasn't easy. I had to stab him four or five times. He fell after the first stab, but he didn't die right away. He kept sort of *flopping* around on the floor. The blood was terrible. It got all over me, my gloves and my coat and pants. And the smell—I began to retch. I ran for the door, and I kept on running. I lost my head, forgot about the girl, forgot about everything. All I wanted to do was get away from that blood, that smell. I went home by side streets. I don't know how far I walked, two miles, three miles. No one noticed me particularly. It was late, and it was snowing, big feathery flakes of snow that clung to my clothes and hid the stains. The house was dark when I got home. I let myself into my room and took off the clothes that had blood on them and put them in the back of the wardrobe. That's where they are now."

"In the wardrobe," Cordwink said.

"Yes, 611 Division Street, the left front room. It has its own entrance, that's why the landlady calls it an apartment."

"What did you do on Sunday?"

"I was very weak, I had to stay in bed."

"Didn't see any papers?"

"Not until early Monday morning, that is, this morning. As soon as I read that Mrs. Barkeley was being held, I went down to the jail to see you. You were busy, and I waited in the corridor. Mr. Meecham saw me there."

Meecham nodded. "Yes, I saw him."

"Well, *I* didn't," Cordwink said. "What happened, Loftus? Lose your nerve?"

"No. I suddenly realized, as I was sitting there, that there were a lot of things I hadn't attended to, and that I'd never get a chance, once I'd confessed. So I walked out again."

"A lot of things you hadn't attended to, such as what?"

"Personal things. I closed my bank account, and sold my car, things like that."

"Listen to this, Loftus." Cordwink turned over the pages until he found what he was looking for. "'I stabbed Margolis deliberately and with intent to kill, and not to protect Mrs. Barkley or myself.' You still claim that?"

"Better think before you answer," Meecham said. "That deliberation and intent business will . . ."

"Keep out of this, Meecham," Cordwink said, scowling. "You're not his lawyer."

"He needs one."

"He'll get one." Cordwink faced Loftus again. "Have you any money?"

"A little, yes. The past few months I've been able to work. I'm an accountant. That's what my treatments have been for, not so I could live longer, but so I could carry on with my job, live more efficiently."

"How much money? Two thousand? One?"

"Oh, not that much."

"Lawyers come high. The more crooked they are, the bigger their price. That's how they stay out of the booby hatch, by rubbing the lesions on their conscience with greenbacks."

Loftus looked a little puzzled. "Well, if I have to have a lawyer, Mr. Meecham will suit me fine. He's been very kind."

"Kind?" Cordwink raised his eyebrows, exaggeratedly. "This I must hear."

"When he thought I was just a bum, he offered me two dollars."

"Well, well. Where'd you get the two dollars, Meecham, selling phony oil shares to war widows?"

Meecham's smile was a little strained. "I object to the question on the grounds that it is intimidating and forms a conclusion."

Dunlop put down his pencil, and said, with a faint whine, "When everybody keeps talking like this, I don't know what to write down. Everybody shouldn't keep talking like this."

"Don't write anything," Cordwink said. "Call a patrol car and take Loftus down and book him."

I'm going to jail, Loftus thought. But he still couldn't quite believe it. Jail was for criminals, for thieves and thugs, for brutal angry lawless men. He said, with the surprise and disbelief evident in his voice: "I'm going to—to jail?"

"For the present, yes."

"Why do you say, for the present?"

"We have no facilities at the jail for looking after a dy——a sick man. There's a prison ward at the County Hospital. You'll be transferred there eventually."

"The County Hospital." Loftus laughed, holding his hands over his belly. It hurt him to laugh, but he couldn't help it. "That's funny, isn't it? The final irony. After all that's happened, I'll end up where I started—in a ward at the County Hospital."

The sound of his laughter faded, though his mouth kept grinning. He saw Cordwink and Meecham exchange uneasy glances. "You're uncomfortable, aren't you?—disturbed?—you wish you'd never seen me? Yes, it's the same everywhere I go, I make people uncomfortable. I don't have any friends. No one wants to be near me, people are afraid to be near a man who's walking a step ahead of death. I make them too conscious of their own fate, and they hate me for it. I'm not blaming them, no, I understand how they feel. I loathe myself more than anyone could loathe me. I loathe this decaying body that I'm trapped inside, hopelessly trapped inside. This isn't me, this grotesque body, it is my prison. What prison have you to offer that could be half so terrible?"

He didn't realize that he was crying until he felt the sting of salt on his lips. He sometimes cried when he was alone at night and the hours seemed so ironically endless; but never in front of anyone, not even his wife on the day she left him. He wiped his eyes with his coat sleeve, ashamed that he had broken down in front of these three men.

Cordwink stared out of the window, motionless, his face like granite. Inside, he felt something begin to move, like a steel claw, reaching out and clutching his stomach, squeezing. *It could be me. Or Alma and the kids. Don't let it happen. Me or Alma and the kids.*

A pair of headlights swerved up the driveway. He glanced across the room at Loftus. Loftus had slumped forward in his chair, his hands covering his eyes. The back of his neck looked very young, a boy's neck, thin and vulnerable and white as wax.

"Loftus."

There was no reply, no stirring in response to his name.

"Loftus," Cordwink said again. "The car is here."

Loftus raised his head slowly. He seemed dazed, as if he'd flown his prison, had gone miles and years away, and was now returning, like a soul to hell.

"I'm ready," Loftus said.

6

611 DIVISION STREET was a three-story red-brick house on the outskirts of the college district. Light and noise poured from nearly every window. On the second floor two young men were bending over a microscope. In the adjoining room a boy sat at a table by the window, absorbed in the blare of the radio beside him, his head resting on an open book. Meecham couldn't see into any of the rooms on the top floor, but it sounded as if a party was going on up there. There was a continuous babble of voices punctuated by sudden peals of laughter.

The left part of the lower floor was dark and the shades were drawn.

Following Cordwink up the sidewalk Meecham thought, it's a funny place for Loftus to live—a dying man in the midst of all this noise and youth.

The sidewalk forked to the left. A little path no more than a foot wide had been shoveled through the snow and sprinkled with cinders. This was Loftus' private entrance.

Cordwink took out the ring of keys that Loftus had given him. "Still want to tag along, Meecham?"

"Certainly."

"What do you expect me to find?"

"The bloodstained clothes he was wearing Saturday night."

"You seem to have a lot of confidence in that confession. Wishful thinking, Meecham?"

"Could be."

"You and Loftus are kind of palsy for a couple of guys who never met before."

"I'm palsy with everyone."

"Yeah. You got a heart of gold, haven't you? Cold and yellow."

"You're getting to be a sour old character if I ever saw one."

Cordwink inserted one of the keys into the lock. It didn't fit, but the second one did. The flimsy door, curtained at the top, swung inward. "By the way, it wouldn't be quite ethical to take on a second client while your first client is still in jail."

"She won't be in jail long. Your forty-eight hours are nearly up, Cordwink. By tomorrow morning you have to charge her or release her."

"And if she's released, you'd take on a lost cause like Loftus?"

"One minute you're implying that his confession is a phony and the next minute he's a lost cause. Make up your mind."

"He's a lost cause to you, anyway. He hasn't much money."

"Well?"

"Or at least that's what he claims." Cordwink turned on the light switch inside the door, but he didn't look at the room. He was watching Meecham. "Suppose you were in Loftus' shoes and wanted some money."

"Money isn't much good, where's he's going."

"Suppose he didn't want it for himself. For a relative, maybe, or a close friend. It seems to me that Loftus had something very valuable to sell—his absolutely certain knowledge that he's going to die anyway. No matter what he does, he has nothing to lose."

"So?"

"So he committed a murder. For money."

"Whose money?"

"Virginia Barkeley's."

"That sounds reasonable enough," Meecham said calmly, "except for a few little things. First, Mrs. Barkeley only met Loftus once, in a bar, for about five minutes. That's not quite long enough to arrange a big deal like murder."

"She could have known him before. They'd both deny that, naturally, if there's a deal on."

"In the second place, if she paid him to kill Margolis, she wouldn't have arranged the matter so that she'd be caught as she was."

"Maybe she's very, very subtle."

"In the third place she hasn't any money and neither has her husband. I've checked. They live up to their income, the house is mortgaged and the furniture isn't paid for."

"There are ways of raising money."

"And in the fourth place you don't even know that Loftus has any money."

"I'll find out."

"Your trouble is stubbornness, Cordwink. You were sure Mrs. Barkeley was guilty and you can't admit you were wrong even with Loftus' confession staring you in the face."

"What's staring me in the face is a lot of funny coincidences and right in the middle of them is a lawyer called Meecham."

"Is that a fact?"

"That's one. Another one has just occurred to me. Suppose Loftus was paid for services rendered, what did he do with the money?"

Meecham said wearily, "He dug a hole in the back yard and buried it."

"I figure he gave it to someone, either the party he wanted it for in the first place, or a go-between."

"Me?"

"You."

"Whom am I going between, or between whom am I going? Oh, hell. You know I never saw Loftus until today."

"That's your story."

"His, too."

"It would be, of course, if the two of you are working in collusion."

Meecham lit a cigarette. There was no ashtray in the room that he could see, so he put the burnt match in his pocket. "So now you've dreamed up a place for the money you've dreamed up. Want to see my wallet? Check books? Or maybe I'm wearing a money belt. Why don't you check?"

"Don't worry, I will. When the time comes."

"You can waste a lot of time chasing little bright butterflies, Cordwink."

"I like the exercise."

Meecham raised his head. He saw that the Sheriff was looking rather pleased with himself, and he wondered whether Cordwink really believed in his own theory or whether he was merely needling him. Cordwink hated all lawyers, but his hatred wasn't a personal one. It was a matter of principle: he hated lawyers because he believed their sole objective was to circumvent the law.

Cordwink began to circle the room, his eyes moving from object to object with alert precision.

The room was fairly large, and fitted out for light housekeeping. In one corner, half-hidden by a painted cardboard screen, was a small sink and a two-burner gas plate and a table. The bed was a studio couch neatly covered with a blue and yellow chenille spread, and above it, high on the wall, a trio of college pennants was nailed:

Illinois. Arbana. Yale.

The pennants were very old and very dusty. They probably didn't belong to Loftus, Meecham thought. They had been on the wall when he moved in and he left them there because they were too high to reach. Anyway, there there they were, emphasizing the transient feeling of the room, symbols of college boys who were no longer boys, football teams that were forgotten, textbooks left to mildew, with silverfish camping, sleek and comfortable, between the pages.

A room for transients, with Loftus the last, the most transient of them all. It was as if Loftus had known this and had taken pains to obliterate his traces. The whole room, except for the pennants, was scrupulously clean. There were no clothes or shoes lying around, the top of the bureau held only an alarm clock with a glass bowl inverted over it, and the wastebasket beside the desk was empty. Whatever had been in the wastebasket—letters, bills, check stubs, pages from a diary?—they were all gone now. There was no clue to Loftus' mind and personality in the room except for the books that filled the high narrow bookcase.

The books were oddly assorted: a few novels, two anthologies of poetry, *How to Win at Canasta*, a biography of Pasteur and a Bible—but most of them concerned psychology and medicine. Cecil's *Textbook of Medicine, Cancer and Its Causes, The Neurotic Personality of Our Time, Peace of Mind, Release from Fear, Alcoholism and Its Causes, The Alcoholic and Allergy, A New View of Alcoholism, How to Treat the Alcoholic, Drinking Problems, Glandular Deficiency in Alcoholism.*

Cordwink, too, was staring at the books. "He doesn't look like a lush," he said finally.

"No."

"You can't always tell, though. One of the worst lushes I ever knew used to take up collection in the Methodist church. No one even knew he took a drink until one night he started hopping around the house trying to get out of the way of the fish. He thought there were little fish flopping all over the floor. Bats and snakes and beetles I'd heard of, but never little fish. It was creepy—made the bottom of my feet kind of ticklish. Funny, eh?"

"What happened to him?"

"He hit the real skids after that. Landed in jail four or five times that year for non-support, disturbing, petty theft. He always had a whale of an excuse. Drunks are the wildest liars in the world."

"Loftus isn't a drunk."

"Maybe not."

There was no closet in the room, but between the studio couch and the screen that hid the gas plate, a seven-foot walnut wardrobe stood against the wall. It was a massive piece of furniture, with a big old-fashioned plain lock. There was no key to fit it on the key-ring Loftus had given him, so Cordwink forced the lock with the small blade of his jacknife. When the door opened, the pungent smell of moth crystals filled the room. Cordwink sneezed, and sneezed again.

There was hardly enough clothing inside the wardrobe to justify the lavish use of moth crystals: two suits, well-worn but cleaned and pressed, a sweater, shoes, a pair of galoshes, a khaki baseball cap, some pajamas; and on the floor, three suitcases. Two of them were empty. The third Cordwink took out and placed on the studio couch.

Pasted across the top of the suitcase was a faded Railway Express consignment slip: From Mrs. Charles E. Loftus, 231 Oak Street, Kincaid, Michigan, to Mr. Earl Duane Loftus, 611 Division Street, Arbana, Michigan. Value of contents: $50.00.

"His mother," Cordwink said. "Or maybe his sister-in- law. Or maybe it doesn't even matter."

The value of the original contents might have been fifty dollars. The present contents had little monetary value: an old trench coat, a blue serge suit, and a pair of brown oxfords, all of them stained with blood.

Cordwink pressed down the lid of the suitcase. "I'd like to talk to the woman who runs this place. Loftus said she's a Mrs. Hearst. Go and get her, will you?"

"Why don't you? You have the authority."

"This stuff is evidence. I wouldn't trust you alone with it."

Meecham colored. "What the hell do you think I'd do, grab it and take off for South America?"

"I don't know and I'm not going to find out. Be a good boy now, Meecham, and co-operate, and some day you may be District Attorney, then you can kick me in the teeth if I've got any teeth left by that time."

"Who are you kidding? You haven't got any left now."

Cordwink's eyes narrowed, but he didn't make any reply. He crossed the room to the door that led into the hallway of the house, unlocked it, and motioned Meecham out with a curt nod.

Meecham went out, quite meekly. He felt a little ashamed of himself for making the crack about Cordwink's teeth. Nearly everyone in town knew that Cordwink had had his front teeth knocked out in a fight with two berserk sailors who were equipped with brass knuckles. The sailors went to a military prison, Cordwink went to the dentist, and the brass knuckles went into his pile of impounded weapons that included everything from sawed-off shotguns to paring knives.

Meecham followed the hall past an immense high-ceilinged dining room into the kitchen. It was a big old-fashioned kitchen, designed not merely for cooking and eating, but for all kinds of family living. There was a card table with a plastic canasta set, a rocking chair, a record player, a bookcase and a couch with a blanket neatly folded at the foot. A woman stood at the sink, wiping dishes and humming to herself.

Her voice and figure were youthful, and her light hair was cut girlishly short and curled close to her head. But when she turned, hearing Meecham approach, he saw that she was about forty. Her hair was gray, not blonde as it appeared at first, and the skin around her sharp blue eyes was creased and dry, like crepe paper.

She smiled at Meecham as she rolled down the sleeves of her dress and buttoned them at the wrists. Her smile was not artificial exactly, but facile, as if she was accustomed to smiling in all kinds of situations and at all kinds of people. "Were you looking for someone?"

"Yes, the owner of the house."

"The bank owns it," she said crisply. "Arbana Trust and Savings. I rent it."

"You're Mrs. Hearst?"

"Yes."

"I'm Eric Meecham. I'm a friend of Mr. Loftus."

"A friend of Earl's? Isn't that *nice*, it really *is*." Out of habit, she spoke with a little too much emphasis. It made her enthusiasm, which was real, sound forced. "For a minute there I thought you were going to try and sell me something. *Not* that I wouldn't like to buy something, but nobody ever got rich on college boys. They're nice boys, all of them, boys from *good* homes. But what with taxes the way . . ." She paused, suddenly frowning. "You're from out of town?"

"No, I live here."

"I just wondered. Earl's never mentioned you. He hasn't many friends and he usually tells me things. I—is anything the matter? Where is Earl? Where *is* he?"

"I can't say, definitely."

"I knew something was up. He always has supper with me Monday nights. Tonight he didn't come, didn't phone. I waited an hour. Everything was ruined. Where is he?"

"In jail."

"In *jail*? Why, that's crazy. Why, Earl is one of the quietest, most *refined*. . ."

"The Sheriff is in his room now. He wants to talk to you."

"To me? A sheriff? Why I—I don't know what to say. This isn't some kind of trick one of my boys put you up to? They play tricks on me sometimes, not meaning to be cruel."

"There's no trick," Meecham said. "I'm a long way from college."

"A sheriff," she repeated, in a strained voice. "I'll talk to him, if I must. But I've nothing to say. Nothing. Earl is a perfect gentleman. And more than that, too. You only see him now, when he's sick." She hesitated, as if she would have liked to say more about Loftus, but decided this was not the time or place. "All right, I'll talk to him. Some mistake has been made somewhere, of that I'm sure."

She preceded Meecham down the hall, wiping her hands nervously on her apron and casting uneasy glances up the staircase to her left, obviously afraid that one of the "boys from good homes" would come down and see her talking to a policeman.

Meecham followed her into Loftus' room and closed the door. "Mrs. Hearst, this is the Sheriff, Mr. Cordwink."

Cordwink acknowledged the introduction with a brief nod. "Sit down, Mrs. Hearst. I just want to check up on a few things about Earl Loftus."

The woman didn't sit down. She didn't even advance into the room, but stood rigidly with her back against the wall, her hands clenched in the pockets of her apron. "I don't understand why you're here. Earl hasn't—*done* anything?"

"That's what I'm trying to find out," Cordwink said. "How long has he been with you?"

"Lived here? A year, almost a year."

"You know him pretty well, then?"

"I—yes. We are friends."

"He confides in you?"

"Yes, you understand, I'm not like a *mother* to him, the way I am to some of my boys. No indeed, Earl's different, more mature. Our conversations are very stimulating. Why, he talks as mature as any man my—my own age."

"I notice that he has his own telephone and mailbox."

"Yes, this little apartment is completely separate from the rest of the house."

"Then you wouldn't, naturally, be able to keep as close track of him as you would of your regular roomers."

Mrs. Hearst's mouth looked pinched. "I don't have to keep *track* of anyone."

"What I meant was . . ."

"I know what you meant. You meant, do I snoop in on other people's telephone conversations and examine their mail. No, I don't. And in Earl's case it wouldn't even be necessary. He tells me everything."

There was a brief silence before Cordwink spoke again, in a quiet, amiable voice: "He seems, on the surface, to be quite an exceptional young man."

"Not just on the surface. He's exceptional all through. Very intelligent, Earl is, and very polite and considerate, doesn't drink or smoke or run around with women."

"He's married, isn't he?"

"Married? Why, of course not. He would certainly have told me, and he's never mentioned a wife. Just his mother. He's devoted to his mother. She lives out of town, but she came to see him last summer. A very refined type of woman. She's ill most of the time, that's why she doesn't come to see him oftener. Earl himself isn't very—very well."

"Yes, I know that." Cordwink went over to the studio couch and lifted the lid of the suitcase. "I suppose you're familiar with Loftus' clothes?"

"His clothes? That's a funny question. I don't understand."

Cordwink picked up the wrinkled bloodstained trench coat, quite naturally and casually, as if it was an ordinary piece of clothing. There was no indication, in his movements or expression, of his extreme distaste for the sight of blood, the feelings it gave him, of loss, futility, vulnerability. The blood on this worn and dirty coat had been the end of a man and might be the end of another.

He said calmly, "Do you, for instance, recognize this coat, Mrs. Hearst?"

"I—don't know. It's so wrinkled. I can't . . . What are those marks?"

"Blood."

She drew in her breath suddenly, gaspingly, like an exhausted swimmer. "I don't like this. I don't like it, I say. Where's Earl? Where *is* he? You've got no right prying into his things like this! How do I know you're policemen? How do I know you're not a pair . . .?"

"Here's my identification." Cordwink took his badge out of his pocket and showed it to her. "Mr. Meecham isn't a policeman, he's a lawyer. As for prying into Loftus' things, I'm doing it with his consent. Here are his own keys. He gave them to me."

The woman sat down, suddenly and heavily. "What—what did Earl do?"

"He says he killed a man."

She stared, round-eyed, glassy-eyed, into the corner of the room. "Here? *Here* in this house?"

"No."

"Earl didn't—couldn't—it's impossible."

"He says he did."

"But you can't believe him. I've often thought, time and time again I've thought, that someday that terrible disease would affect his mind, would . . ."

"His mind seems clear enough," Cordwink said.

"But you don't *know* Earl. He could never harm anyone. He hated to kill anything. Why—why, once there was a mouse in his room—last fall—I wanted to set a trap but he wouldn't let me. He said the mouse was so tiny and harmless . . ."

"Mrs. Hearst."

"I'm *telling* you, Earl *wouldn't*."

"This is his coat, isn't it?"

She turned her head away and stared at the wall. "Yes."

"And this suit? The shoes? Please look at them, Mrs. Hearst. You can't identify something without looking at it."

She glanced briefly at the suit and shoes and then away again. "They're Earl's."

"No question about it?"

"I said they're Earl's. Now can I go? I've had a great shock, a terrible shock."

"In a minute," Cordwink said. "The trench coat, and the serge suit—were these the clothes Loftus usually wore when he was going out in the evening, say?"

"Why?" she said bitterly. "Don't you think they were good enough to go out in? Well, maybe they weren't! But they were the only ones he had. He couldn't afford any more."

"When I saw him an hour ago he was wearing a new topcoat, new suit, new shoes. All of them looked expensive."

"I don't care! I don't know what you're implying, and I don't *care*!"

"Did you ever lend him money, Mrs. Hearst?"

"I—no! Never! He'd never have taken it, never have borrowed money from a woman, never!"

"All right," Cordwink said. Privately he wondered how much, and when. "Then you didn't lend him any money, say, this morning?"

"No!"

"Did you see him this morning?"

"Yes."

"When?"

"When I was shoveling off the walk, about seven-thirty."

"What exactly did you say to him?"

"I said—I said, 'Earl you can't go like that, in just a sweater and slacks, it's winter, you'll catch cold.'"

"And he said?"

"That he'd sent his coat to the cleaner's and that anyway he wasn't cold. I asked him where he was off to, so early. And he said he was going downtown to see about selling his car. He said it wasn't working so well, it was just a nuisance in the winter, so he thought he'd sell it, and then, in the spring, maybe he'd—he'd be feeling better and could work more and buy a—a new car. I said, just joking, how about a Cadillac, then you can take me for a ride. And he said there—wasn't anyone he'd rather take for a ride in a Cadillac than—than me."

She looked toward the window as if she was trying to see, not the dark of a winter night, but a morning in spring, with Earl well again and at the wheel of his new car.

"As you know now," Cordwink said, "he didn't send his coat to the cleaner's. It was here all the time, locked inside the wardrobe. He had approximately forty hours to dispose of it, but he apparently made no attempt to. That's curious, don't you think, Mrs. Hearst?"

"Curious," she repeated dully. "Yes. It's curious. Everything's curious."

"Do you clean Loftus' roo——apartment?"

"Go on, *call* it a room. It's not an apartment, it's just a room. I know it's just a room, and Earl knows it and everyone . . ." She stopped, holding the back of her hand to her mouth. "I clean it twice a week, Tuesday and Saturday. I don't have to do it, it's not included in his rent. I do it for—because I like to," she added defiantly. "I *like* to clean."

"Take another look around now, Mrs. Hearst. Is this the way his room usually looked?"

"No."

"What's different about it?"

"A lot of his things are gone."

"Clothes?"

"Not clothes. Personal little things, like his desk set, for instance. He had a very nice desk set, onyx, quite expensive. His mother gave it to him. His mother's picture is gone too, it was in a silver frame. And his radio—he used to keep his radio on the table over there."

"Have you any idea what happened to the missing objects?"

"They could have been—s-stolen." But she stumbled over the answer. It was fairly obvious, both to Meecham and to Cordwink, that she didn't believe the articles had been stolen.

"Or pawned, maybe," Cordwink said. "Was he in the habit of pawning things?"

"He—when he *had* to, when he was desperate. He had such terrible expenses. And then there's his mother, he sends her money. Last fall he scrimped and saved to send her some and when he did she blew it all in—went out and bought the desk set I told you about, and mailed it to him. It was a nice gesture, of course, only it was such a *foolish* thing to do. But then, she's very refined, she doesn't realize that people have to scrounge around for money these days."

"You think, then, that Loftus pawned this stuff of his that's missing?"

"Yes."

"Any idea where?"

"There's a little place in the east end, right next to the bowling alley. Devine's, it's called."

"Did Loftus tell you that's where he usually went?"

"I—no. No, he didn't." Her skin looked flushed. "I found a pawn ticket once when I was dusting his bureau. It was for his wrist watch. He never got the watch back. He told me he'd lost it. It wasn't a real lie, Earl never lies. It was just a fib to save his pride. Being poor," she said, "having to pawn things, that's nothing to be ashamed of. But Earl isn't used to it the way some people are. His father was well-to-do—he was a broker in Detroit before he died—and of course when Earl was working steadily he got a very good salary. Being poor is new to Earl. It's his disease that's dragged him down, his disease and his mom——No. No, I won't say that. His mother can't help herself, she's very refined."

Cordwink lit a cigarette. He rarely smoked, and the package from which he had taken the cigarette looked as though it had been in his pocket for months. He said, "When did you last see Loftus wearing this trench coat?"

"Saturday night. I was on my way to the hockey game, one of my boys is on the team. I met Earl on the sidewalk out in front of the house. I stopped to chat, I always do, and Earl said he'd just finished dinner downtown and that he was going to bed early because he was tired."

"After the game you got home around . . .?"

"Eleven, it was just about eleven. Earl had gone to bed by that time."

"Are you sure of that?"

"Well, I *thought* he'd gone to bed. It never occurred to me that he hadn't, and his lights were off."

"Did you see him on Sunday at all?"

"No, Sunday's my day off. I always go over to Chelsea to visit my sister and her kids. My sister and I had a little disagreement, nothing serious, but I left earlier than usual. I got home around 8:30. Earl's light was on, I saw it shining under the door when I went into the hall. I thought of dropping in on him a minute; I was upset and Earl always cheers me up. But when I stopped outside his door he was talking on the telephone so I went on up to my room."

"How long did you pause there, in the hall?"

"Oh, half a minute, no longer."

"And you heard him talking?"

"Yes."

"But not necessarily on the phone."

"I—no, not necessarily, but . . ."

"In fact, there may have been someone in here with him."

"Well, I can't swear to it, of course, but I'm sure there wasn't anyone here. Earl never has company."

"No girlfriends?"

Mrs. Hearst frowned. "No, *none*. Of that I *am* sure. He doesn't bother with girls, young girls."

"Was it a question of money?"

"No. Earl considers himself—well, deformed. He told me once that he couldn't expect any woman to go out with a freak like he was." She rubbed her eyes with the corner of her apron. "He isn't a freak. It hurt me, his saying that. He *isn't* a freak. A lot of women would be glad to—to look after him, see that he got the proper rest and food and didn't go traipsing around in the cold without his galoshes and overcoat. A lot of women would be—would be . . ."

She hid her face in her apron, in silent grief. Watching her, Meecham wondered if the grief was for Loftus, or for all the women like herself who wanted a man to look after.

His eyes shifted to Cordwink. Cordwink's face was grim and the cigarette he was smoking was chewed at one end like a cigar. He opened his mouth, and Meecham thought he was going to say something to the woman. But the Sheriff didn't speak. Instead, he went over and helped Mrs. Hearst out of the chair and guided her out into the hallway as if she were blind.

When he came back he slammed the door shut behind him and looked bitterly across the room at Meecham. "Okay, you got any smart cracks to make, Meecham?"

"No."

"That's good, because I'm not in the mood to listen to any." He closed the suitcase with a bang, picked it up and turned off the lights. "I'll drop you off at Barkeley's so you can pick up your car."

"Thanks."

Cordwink didn't speak again until he got into his car and pulled away from the curb. "The fact is," he said, "I'm a very emotional man where women are concerned."

7

THE LIGHT OF morning coming in through the barred window was dingy, and along the corridor a cool damp wind blew, erratically, first one way and then the other.

Miss Jennings wore a heavy cardigan over her brown dress, and instead of piling her hair high on top of her head as usual, this morning she had let it hang to keep the draft off her neck. As Miss Jennings was in the habit of pointing out, to anyone who was interested and a great many who weren't, weather never bothered her, she rose above it. The clicking of her heels against the floor was overpoweringly cheerful, and she was humming, off-beat and off-key, but with a good deal of spirit.

Virginia pretended not to hear either the footsteps or the humming. She ignored Miss Jennings right up to the last moment; and then it was no longer possible to ignore her because Miss Jennings took her key-ring and slid it playfully and noisily across the bars of the cell like a child running a stick along an iron fence.

"Hi!" Miss Jennings always addressed her charges in a good loud voice, as if out of a conviction that imprisonment, like age, impaired the hearing. "Well, you're all prettied up already. That's good, because someone wants to see you right away."

"If it's that greasy little psychiatrist again tell him to go peddle his dreams."

"Now, really. Now, is that any way to talk about nice Dr. Maguire? Besides it's not him—he. It's Mr. Meecham. He has a big surprise for you."

"I wonder."

"He has, too. Guess what it is."

"I don't like guessing games."

"Oh, don't be a little old spoilsport. Go on, guess."

"I'm going home," Virginia said.

"Yes! How about that now, aren't you happy? Aren't you surprised?"

"My mother sent me a message last night. So did Meecham."

"Oh. Well, they couldn't have known for *sure*, though. The lab reports weren't in, the blood, and so forth."

"What blood?"

"Why, he had blood all over his clothes, same as you had. They say he's a nice young man, no record or anything. What amazes me is the amount of blood in a person, it's simply amazing."

"I'd rather not talk about it."

"Well, all right," Miss Jennings smiled, rising above the blood as she rose above the weather.

She unlocked the cell door and Virginia stepped out into the corridor. She was pale, and the skin around her eyes looked blue, as if bruised by pressing thumbs.

"My, my," Miss Jennings said. "You don't look one bit happy. 'Fess up now, you're sorry to be leaving us."

"Oh, sure."

"You've been treated well, haven't you?"

"Great. Just great. I'll recommend the place to all my friends."

Miss Jennings was still wearing her smile but it sagged in places like a worn-out dress. "You're a sarcastic little snip, aren't you?"

"So?"

"You think you're so goddam smart all the time. All the time making smart talk. Oh, I heard your remarks about me to Mr. Meecham yesterday."

"I knew you were too good to be true, Jennings."

There was a thin line of white around the edges of Miss Jennings' mouth. "I know you and your type. Jeering all the time, jeering at decent hardworking respectable people. I hate you. You hear that? I just hate you!"

"Oh, can it," Virginia said. "Who cares?"

"And I'm sorry you're leaving. I hope you'll be back, next time for keeps." She unlocked the door into the main corridor and the keys on the big key-ring clanked viciously. "You can go from here by yourself."

"Thanks."

"The girls that come in here and go out again, I always try to give them a nice send-off. But you, I wouldn't even say good-bye to you. I think you're a cold, bad, nasty woman and to hell with you."

She shut the door between them with a decisive bang. All the way down the corridor Virginia could hear the clanking of metal against metal. It sounded as though Miss Jennings was slamming her keys against a wall in time to some rhythm of rage in her heart.

I'm not, Virginia thought, *I'm not a cold nasty woman.*

The door of the Sheriff's office was open, and Meecham was waiting for her inside, with a brief case under his arm. Cordwink was there too, hunched over a desk that was strewn with papers. On a bench along the wall sat a white-faced young man in a gray prison uniform. The young man was staring at Virginia with a curious kind of intensity. She had an uneasy feeling that there was some silent communication in that glance, that he was trying to say something to her, or ask her something.

No introductions were made, no greetings exchanged. Not a word was spoken until Cordwink said, in his low heavy voice, "Do you recognize this man, Mrs. Barkeley?"

"Not by name. I think I've seen him before, though."

"Where?"

"I don't remember. Anywhere—on the street or at Paul's office or in a bar. I get around quite a few places."

"It was in a bar," Loftus said, very quickly. "Sam's—Saturday night, you talked to me . . ."

"Keep out of this, Loftus."

Cordwink slapped the desk to emphasize the order. Loftus blinked nervously, but he went right on talking: "I'm only trying to help, Mr. Cordwink. What difference does it make if she remembers me? I've admitted fifty times that I killed Margolis. All these questions and interviews and tests—they aren't going to change anything." He turned to Virginia. "I asked Mr. Meecham to tell you but now I can tell you myself. I'm sorry about your having to stay in jail for a couple of days like this."

"That's—all right." Under the glaring ceiling lights her face was as white as Loftus', and the half-circles under her eyes made her look old and tired and hard. She whirled suddenly and faced Meecham. "I—couldn't we get out of here? I want to get *out* of here."

"All right," Meecham said. "That suit you, Cordwink?"

"It has to." Cordwink stood up. "The papers are all signed, nothing's stopping you, the door's open, go on."

"What about your suitcase, Virginia?"

"To hell with the suitcase," Virginia said harshly. "I just want to get out of here."

Her departure was as wordless as her entrance. No one said good-bye, see you again, glad to have met you. Virginia walked out of the door and down the corridor so rapidly that Meecham had to hurry to catch up with her. Even when she reached the main door she didn't stop to put on her coat. She just held it around her shoulders as she went out, and the arms of the coat flopped back and forth in the rising wind, making silly boneless little gestures.

The sidewalk was dirty with slush and on the road the cars swished by with splatters of mud. Even the wind was dirty. Somewhere, in the north of Canada, it had started out fresh, but it had picked up dirt on its journey, smoke and dust and particles of soot.

They stood in silence, side by side, at the intersection until the light turned green. Then they crossed the road to the parking lot where Meecham had left his car.

The car was locked. With only a slight hesitation Meecham unlocked his own door first and got in the car. Then he leaned across the seat and unlocked the other door for Virginia. The little amenities of politeness seemed as inappropriate and futile here as they had in the Sheriff's office.

Meecham laid his briefcase on the seat between them and started the car and switched on the heater. A cold blast of air gushed noisily from the heater.

Virginia reached over and turned the heater off again. "It makes too much noise."

"All right."

"Well, I did what you told me to. Didn't I?"

"More or less."

"I said that he looked familiar, that I'd seen him before. Isn't that what you meant in the note you sent me last night?"

Meecham nodded.

"It's not true though. I've never seen him before, not in Sam's or any other bar or any other place."

"You had quite a few memory lapses on Saturday night."

"I remember talking to someone at Sam's but it wasn't this man. I'd have remembered him because he looks like Willett before Willett began to get fat."

"Willett?"

"My older brother. When you meet someone who looks like your own brother, you don't forget him, do you?"

"I haven't got a brother."

"You know what I mean. Don't be so damned annoying, Meecham."

"*Me*, annoying." He turned left at the next intersection. The driver of the car behind him began to sound his horn furiously.

"You didn't make a signal," Virginia said. "If conversation interferes with your driving . . ."

"Your conversation interferes with my thinking," Meecham said acidly. "You forget some things, you remember some things. The things you're supposed to remember you forget, and the things you're supposed to forget you remember."

"I can't help that."

"Look, you just got out of jail ten minutes ago. Do you want to talk yourself right back in?"

"I thought you were my lawyer. Aren't you supposed to be able to tell everything to your lawyer?"

"Theoretically, yes. But let's get one point straight. What you told me just now—and very positively—was that you never saw Loftus before in your life. You may believe that, but I don't. The evidence is against it. The fact that you'd been drinking heavily all evening makes your memory unreliable anyway. Then there's Loftus' own statement, and his report of some of your remarks to him. Loftus claims that you said among other things, God, this place stinks. One of the bartenders at Sam's overheard it, and identified you as the woman who said it. He has a half-interest in the place, and I think you hurt his feelings. Well, are you still sure you never saw Loftus in your life until this morning?"

"I'm positive."

"I know one definition of positive—being wrong at the top of your voice."

"All right, I may be wrong." She sounded depressed, listless. "It doesn't matter much anyway, does it? When is Claude going to be buried?"

"This afternoon." It was the first time he had heard her use Margolis' first name or indicate in any way that she had been interested in him.

"I wouldn't go to his funeral even if I could. I hate dead people." She huddled, shivering, inside the big plaid coat. "I remember once when I was at school, the mother of one of my friends died, and I went home with the girl to cheer her up. Her mother was at the undertaker's, they hadn't quite finished—fixing her up. The girl combed her mother's hair and fixed her glasses. The damned glasses kept slipping down that dead face, the girl kept putting them in place again. It was ghastly; I almost screamed. Do you have a cigarette?"

"Here."

"Thanks. Shall I light one for you, too?"

"All right."

She lit two cigarettes and gave him one. "Tell me, Meecham, are you on the level?"

"Ask a stupid question and you get a stupid answer. Sure, I am."

"I don't think it's so stupid. You must get lots of opportunities and meet lots of funny people."

"I do, indeed," Meecham said dryly.

"Speaking of mothers, how much is my mother paying you?"

"For what?"

"She *is* paying you?"

"She offered to. I haven't sent her a bill."

"How much are you going to bill her for?"

"I haven't thought about it."

"Well, think now. How much?"

"What is this anyway?" Meecham said, turning his head briefly to look at her. "What's up?"

"She owns quite a bit of real estate back home. Two apartment houses in Pasadena and one in Westwood, and so on."

"Why tell me?"

"So that you'd know she could afford to pay—oh, quite a lot."

"I'm supposed to bill her for quite a lot, eh?"

"She can afford it, I tell you."

"Then when Christmas comes around in a couple of weeks I send you a nice little present, is that it?"

"Sort of."

"It sounds nasty," Meecham said. "And you sound nasty."

"It sounds worse than it is. I like my mother. I'm not trying to chisel her on anything. I can get money from her any time, only I hate to ask her. She always has to know why and what for. This way it would be the same money actually, only I wouldn't have to answer any questions."

"It still sounds nasty. What do you want the money for?"

"Questions, questions. Nobody trusts me."

"What do you want the money for?"

"To run away," she said earnestly.

"Where to?"

"It wouldn't be running away if I told you where. Besides, I haven't decided, and it doesn't matter where as long as it's far away and the climate's good."

He glanced at her again. Her listlessness had gone, and she looked very sincere and hopeful about her new project of running away. But it was a childish hopefulness, without a plan behind it or a foundation under it. "Away" would be pleasant simply because it wasn't "here."

"It will be good for me, good for my morale, to get away," Virginia said. "Carney thinks I'm bad, and Paul thinks I'm a fool. They're both very good people, virtuous people. But it's hard to live with anyone who sets up standards you can't ever reach." She paused to draw on her cigarette. "And now this. This business about Claude. I'll never live it down. No one will ever believe that I wasn't one of Claude's *women*. You don't believe it, Meecham. Do you?"

"I could."

"I wasn't, anyway. I went out with him a few times because he was a wonderful dancer."

It wasn't very convincing, in view of the evidence of the quarrel the two of them had had on Saturday night. But Meecham didn't say anything.

They had come to a railroad crossing just as the signal turned red and the crossing barriers were being lowered into place. A freight train began to move very slowly down the track, heading west. Virginia strained forward in her seat and watched it intensely, watched each car roll ponderously past as if she was wishing she was on one of them, heading west to some place where the climate was good.

He felt sorry for her. The feeling disturbed him, so he turned his attention to the printing on the sides of the freight cars. Michigan Central. Rock Island. Burlington. Atchison, Topeka and Santa Fe. Union Pacific. Grand Rapids. C.P.R. Do Not Hump. And, in chalk, on the bulging belly of a tank car, KILROY WAS HERE, followed by a spirited reply, WHO WASN'T, JOE AND HOWIE.

A hundred cars—oil and lumber, automobiles and scrap metal and fertilizer, explosives and people—a vast jumble of everything, and always room for one more, Virginia.

The caboose slid past, the barriers rose and Virginia sat back in the seat, her eyes shining, her breathing accelerated. The train had excited her—its possibilities, its destination, its very movement. Impulsively, she raised her hand and waved at the caboose as it disappeared down the track.

8

MEECHAM STOPPED THE car in the driveway and got out. Pulling his overcoat collar up around his neck, he went around the back of the car and opened the door for Virginia. "Here you are. And good luck."

She glanced up at him in surprise. "Aren't you coming in?"

"No."

"But my mother will want to see you, to thank you."

"She hasn't anything to thank me for. The whole thing has been a pleasure."

"You're sore, aren't you? Just because I suggested that about the bill."

"I'm not sore," Meecham said. "I have to go back to the jail to see Loftus."

"Why?"

"Because he asked me to."

"But why should he . . .?"

"I don't know, and I probably wouldn't tell you anyway."

"Well, thanks for the ride." She got out of the car and went toward the front door of the house. Before she was halfway there the door opened and Mrs. Hamilton came out.

Virginia ran into her mother's arms and her mother held her there, rocking back and forth. It was almost an exact repetition of the scene the previous morning in Cordwink's office.

"Momma!"

"Ginny darling. Darling girl."

"Oh, *momma!*"

Meecham watched them, but this time he felt quite detached, unmoved. He wondered what Mrs. Hamilton would do if she found out how and why Virginia had tried to raise money.

As unobtrusively as possible he slid in behind the wheel of his car and pressed the starter button. Mrs. Hamilton's reaction to the sound was immediate and exaggerated, like an amateur actress' response to a cue that was late in coming.

"Mr. Meecham! Oh, Mr. Meecham, wait a minute."

With an air of resignation Meecham switched off the ignition, set the emergency brake and got out of the car for the second time.

Mrs. Hamilton approached him, her right hand stretched out in greeting. "You weren't leaving?"

"I was. I have some bus—"

"Please come in and have a cup of coffee. Or a drink. Business can wait. This is such a happy occasion for me. I have my girl back safe and sound."

Safe and sound. Meecham almost winced at the phrase, it seemed so incongruous. Her girl would probably never be either safe or sound. He had a suspicion that Mrs. Hamilton knew this and that the phrase had slipped out, in unconscious irony.

"I'd like some coffee," Meecham said. "Nice of you to invite me."

Virginia had gone ahead into the house. Her coat had fallen off one shoulder and the hem dragged in the dirty snow.

"She looks terrible," Mrs. Hamilton said, in a changed voice. "As if she hasn't eaten, hasn't slept."

"Have you?"

"Some. Thank God it's all over now, anyway. It is over. Isn't it?"

"Yes."

"The man is guilty, he's proved it?"

"As far as I know, yes. I'm not the Sheriff's confidant."

The answer seemed to satisfy her. "I think you've brought us luck, Mr. Meecham."

The inside of the house was moist and fragrant, like a florist's shop. Meecham saw that, in anticipation of Virginia's arrival, someone had watered all the plants, watered them too liberally as if to make up for past neglect. The saucers under the flowerpots were brimming and one of the ivy-planted wall brackets dripped with sharp little *pings* onto the waxed concrete floor.

Mrs. Hamilton didn't notice the dripping. She had taken Virginia's coat and was hanging it in the closet. She handled the coat with a kind of nervous tenderness as if it was of great value and she wasn't sure how to treat it. For the first time Meecham took a close look at the coat. Its bold black and white design dazzled the eye, but the material was cheap.

Neither of the women made any move to take Meecham's hat or coat, so he laid them across a chair. He was a little irritated because he was sure that the omission on their part was more than a lapse in manners; it was an unconscious expression of their real feeling toward him. He wondered again why Mrs. Hamilton had invited him in for coffee, and why he had accepted against his will.

"We should do something to celebrate," Mrs. Hamilton said. "Perhaps a little dinner party tonight. Would you like that, Ginny?"

Virginia ignored, or didn't hear, the question. She was gazing at Meecham thoughtfully, part of her lower lip caught between her teeth. "Meecham, I've got an idea."

"Mr. Meecham, dear," Mrs. Hamilton corrected. "Mr. It sounds coarse to . . ."

"Momma, *please*. I'm talking."

"Then talk properly."

"Oh, for heaven's sake, Momma, this is important!" She turned back to Meecham. "I think I'll sue them for false arrest. I suffered grievous humiliation, didn't I, my reputation was damaged, I underwent great privations, et cetera. How about that, Meecham?"

"It's not such a good idea," Meecham said.

"It is, it's a wonderful idea. Why, I could get a fortune if I won."

"You couldn't win because you haven't a case. There was no malicious persecution, and the Sheriff had enough grounds to arr—"

"Stop." Mrs. Hamilton spoke quietly but with such force, such cold anger, that Meecham stopped in the middle of a word, and Virginia turned to look at her mother with an air of surprise. "I'm ashamed of you, Virginia. Ashamed."

"For heaven's sake, Momma, I've got my rights and . . ."

"There'll be no further discussion of this, ever." Mrs. Hamilton's face had changed from white to pink, and now back to white again, as if there was something the matter with her circulatory system and it responded too quickly and too violently to changes in her emotions. "The subject will never be brought up again. Is that clear to you, Virginia? And you, Mr. Meecham?"

"The whole thing was a pipe-dream anyway," Meecham said.

"Of course. Of course it was." She was regaining her composure. "You hear that, Virginia?"

"I heard."

"Now go and say hello to Carney, like a good girl. She can't leave the office."

Virginia turned obediently and walked away, but not before giving Meecham an obvious we'll-talk-about-it-later glance. Mrs. Hamilton must have seen the glance and interpreted it, but she said nothing about it until she and Meecham were settled in front of the fireplace.

Between them, so close to Meecham that he could scarcely move his legs, there was an immense three-tiered glass table that looked as though it weighed a ton. The chair that Meecham occupied was deep and low and soft, one of those chairs it was difficult to get out of even without a table blocking the way.

Meecham felt suddenly and inexplicably afraid. The fear passed over him like a wave, accelerating his heartbeat, and left behind beads of moisture on his forehead and a damp cold sensation across the small of his back. He had to control an impulse to kick away the huge table, spilling the coffee from its silver urn, shattering the china cups and the glass tiers. Violence is the instinctive response to fear. But because the fear was nameless and unimmediate, the violence was vague and unreasoning. He dropped an ashtray. Dropped it, quite unintentionally, and when he saw it break he had no conscious feeling of satisfaction, but he stopped sweating and his heartbeat was normal again.

Mrs. Hamilton dismissed his apologies with a gesture. She looked annoyed, not at the loss of the ashtray, but at the interruption of her thoughts.

She said quietly and firmly, "You understand, don't you, that Virginia gets wild ideas sometimes. You mustn't take them seriously."

"I don't."

"This false arrest business would never do, you understand that."

"Quite." He didn't remind her that he'd said the same thing himself, at least twice.

"Virginia can be very persuasive. I—I *beg* of you not to pay any attention to her. She doesn't realize the consequences of such a thing—more publicity and investigations, policemen prying into things."

"What things?"

"Everything," she said, spreading her small plump hands. "Paul has suffered enough. Crank phone calls and letters, and reporters stopping him on the street."

"It will all blow over."

"Not if Virginia does anything further. Like this suit she wants to start."

"No lawyer would touch it."

It was his third or fourth reassurance. "That's a relief," she said, and Meecham thought the subject was closed until she added, "Why does Virginia want money so badly?"

"You'd better ask her."

"She'd lie."

"Maybe."

"Not that she's a liar, a real liar, but she's secretive sometimes because she doesn't understand how completely sympathetic I am to her." She repeated the word *completely* with emphasis, as if denying an unspoken accusation of lack of sympathy. "I understand her, she's my girl. We've always been very close."

"I see that."

"Tell me frankly, Mr. Meecham. Did you examine any of the reports about Virginia?"

"What reports?"

"While she was in—while she was there, they must have asked her questions, given her tests, things like that. They usually do, don't they?"

"Yes."

"You don't know how they—turned out?"

"No."

"I thought since you were . . . Well, it doesn't really matter. Virginia's normal, of course. A little spoiled, but completely normal."

"I agree," Meecham said. It was futile to say anything else.

Mrs. Hamilton looked at him gratefully. She had received the answer she wanted and now it was time to change the subject before Meecham could reverse or modify his answer. She said, "It's been a sordid business. I'm glad it's over, and I suppose you are too."

"In a way."

"Send me your bill as soon as possible. I don't know how long I'll be staying here. Or I can pay you right now, if you like, in cash."

"That won't be necessary."

Somewhere in the house a telephone rang, twice.

"You'll come to our little celebration dinner tonight, Mr. Meecham?"

"Thanks, but I'm afraid I won't be able to make it." He never wanted to set foot in that house again, to be subtly imprisoned by a soft chair and a glass table and a quiet frantic woman. "I have some business to attend to."

"Of course. You must have other clients, hundreds."

"A few, anyway."

"This man, Loftus. He'll undoubtedly get a good lawyer?"

"Money or no money, he'll get a lawyer of some kind."

"Why do you say, money or no money?"

"If he can't afford to pay, the court will appoint two lawyers for the defense. There's no Public Defender here as there is in Los Angeles."

"I didn't realize we had such a thing. I've never had occasion to be interested in—matters like that."

Quick light footsteps sounded in the hall, and a moment later Alice appeared in the doorway. She looked as if she had been working. Her hair was drawn back tightly behind her ears and tied with a blue ribbon, and she wore an apron that reached almost to her ankles. Her face was warm and flushed and pretty.

Mrs. Hamilton frowned, faintly but pointedly, in Alice's direction, like a mother silencing a little girl, warning her not to interrupt while the grownups were talking. Or, if she had to interrupt, at least to remove her apron first.

"My dear Alice," she said, "what have you been doing?"

"Cleaning."

"You know perfectly well you're not expected to do any of the household work."

"I don't mind. And it needed doing."

Mrs. Hamilton turned to Meecham with a smile that seemed forced. "Now what would you do with a girl like that?"

"I don't know," Meecham said. He felt, quite irrationally, that Alice's appearance had changed something in the room, broken a tension, snapped an invisible wire. He got up from the chair, pushing the glass table away until its bamboo legs shrieked in protest. The table was lighter than he thought.

Alice was watching him gravely from the doorway. "Your office called, Mr. Meecham. You're to drop in there after you talk to Mr. Loftus."

"Thank you."

In the silence that followed Meecham could hear the ivy-planted wall bracket still dripping, very slowly and softly, like the final blood from a death wound.

Mrs. Hamilton had risen too, to face Meecham. "I think you might be quite a clever and devious creature, Mr. Meecham."

"So is a weasel, so I won't bother thanking you for that, Mrs. Hamilton."

"You've been stringing me along," she said in a cold flat voice. "*You're* going to be Loftus' lawyer, aren't you?"

"No."

"You can lie about it. Go on. Everybody else lies."

"I'm not lying."

"How can I believe you? How can I believe anybody?" She crossed the room, moving with agonizing slowness like a deep-sea diver forcing his leaden feet across the ocean floor, fighting a pressure he can't see or understand. "I . . . Alice, I think I'll go up to my room and rest awhile. Please see that Mr. Meecham is—looked after."

Meecham watched her until she disappeared around a corner of the hall. Then he turned his head and looked at Alice, and in that moment he had two wishes, diverging in means, but with a common purpose: to get Alice away from that house. His first wish was that he had a mother or a father or a family of some kind so that he could invite Alice to stay with them. Since he had no family at all, he wished that Mrs. Hamilton would take Alice and board the earliest plane for home. Some day, some remote day when he had surplus time and money, he might go to see her. She might be married, by that time, married and with a couple of children; a placid contented matron, shopping, going to movies, lying in the sun. This projection into the future was so vivid, his sense of loss so acute, that he felt a tide of rage rise in him, rise and ebb, leaving a taste of salt.

He said, abruptly, "When are you leaving for home?"

"You mean L.A.?"

"Yes."

"I don't know. Mrs. Hamilton hasn't told me."

"You could tell her. Tell her you want to leave."

"But I don't want to," she protested.

"Have you seen Virginia?"

"Yes, a few minutes ago, with Carney."

"Suppose I told you I think Virginia is dangerous?"

"Are you trying to scare me? I don't understand. Everything is all right now, isn't it? Everything's been settled?" She took a step back, away from him. "Or has it? Why are you going to see Loftus if you're not his lawyer?"

"Because he asked me to."

"As an old pal?"

"More or less."

"You never saw him before last night, does that make you an old pal?"

"He thought I had an honest face," Meecham said, "so I became his old pal right away. It happens, now and then, especially to a lonely guy in trouble. I'm a lonely guy myself and I've been in trouble, so I know a little about these things." He put on his coat. "Nobody seems to like the idea of me talking to Loftus. I wonder why."

"I don't care, one way or the other. I was just puzzled." She thrust her hands deep into the pockets of the oversize apron. "I guess I'm getting suspicious of everybody. I don't know why."

"That's the trouble with suspicion, it infects even the nicest people. Good-bye, Alice."

"Good-bye."

He bent down and kissed her lightly on the forehead. She didn't react in any way. She just stood there, looking surprised and a little forlorn.

He was halfway to the center of town before he realized that he hadn't had any coffee after all. He wanted, then, to turn around and go back, not for the coffee he had missed, but because the solution of the problem had suddenly struck him. It was quite simple: the house should be abandoned like a ship about to sink under the weight of excess cargo. Alice and Mrs. Hamilton should go home, Carney get another job, Paul rent an office somewhere downtown. And Virginia—there was only one thing to do about Virginia: give her the money to run away, far away where the climate was good.

He thought of the expression on her face as she had watched the train go past and waved at the red caboose. Motion, change, speed, they were essential to Virginia. She should always be on a passing train, one that went round and round the world and never stopped.

9

MEECHAM DIDN'T GO directly to the jail. The place he wanted to see first was on his way. He found it finally, after driving past twice—a small store with a single window, wedged inconspicuously between a bowling alley and a cigar shop.

A sign above the door was lettered in green and white: Doug Devine, Prop. There was no other identification, and none was needed. The window was piled to the ceiling with the scraps and leavings, the hopes and futilities, the desires and fears and evils, of human beings. Wedding rings and automatics, rosaries and hunting knives, worn shoes and violins; and, at the back of the window, the bland, ageless face of a grandfather clock. The clock was running, and on time: 10:35.

Inside the store a middle-aged man was sitting on a wicker bench examining a shotgun. The gun was old and grimy. About four or five inches of the barrel had been sawed off, and the rest of it was mended with black friction tape. It was a desperate weapon, as likely to explode when the trigger was pulled as to discharge its shot. Meecham wondered what desperate man had bought and sold it, and what desperate man would buy it and add another chapter to its dark allusive history.

Devine looked up from his task. He was a black Irishman with coarse curly hair and eyes bright as beetles. "It works," he said briefly. "I tried it."

"Oh?"

"Sure. But you never know what you're going to hit. Aim it at your wife and you end up shooting the neighbor's pet goldfish."

"That could be good."

"Oh, sure. No argument about that. No law against shooting up goldfish." He got up and put the shotgun carefully on the wicker bench. "Anything I can do for you?"

"Maybe."

"Buying or selling?"

"Buying."

"I figure you for an insurance investigator," Devine said. "Right or wrong?"

"Wrong."

"I bet I was close."

"Pretty close."

"I'm always close. Practically the only thing I know in this whole cockeyed world is people and I can't make a nickel out of it. Give me an idea what you're interested in. You want to start music lessons, we got a nice clarinet."

"No, thanks. What I . . ."

"Fellow that sold it to me said it once belonged to Benny Goodman. Funny thing, how a lot of people dream up the same old stuff and think it's new. There's not a clarinet in any pawnshop east of Frisco that ain't been played by Goodman or Artie Shaw. We got some nice bargains in jewelry."

"I was thinking of a picture frame."

"Just the frame?"

"Yes."

"We got some first-class framed oil paintings, some genuine Manderheim's."

"I never heard of Manderheim."

"I never did either, but you'd be surprised how many I've sold." He pointed to a picture of a vase of roses and ivy that was propped against the legs of an up-ended chair. "See that, over there. If I told my customers that somebody's Aunt Agnes painted it on her kitchen table, I couldn't give it away. But Manderheim—well, he's different, he's strictly class. Romantic, even. You want to know why he doesn't sign his pictures? Well, he's run away with another man's wife, see, and he doesn't want to be recognized because the husband is out gunning for him. Yes, sir, people will believe anything if it's preposterous enough." He added, with a touch of gloom, "Funny thing is, I damn near believe in Manderheim myself."

So did Meecham. "Maybe some other time I'll take a Manderheim," he said. "Right now all I want is a frame. My girlfriend had her picture taken last week. By a curious coincidence her name's Manderheim too."

Devine didn't smile. "You want a *silver* frame?"

"Yes."

"About eight by ten?"

"About that."

Devine was silent a moment, rubbing the side of his chin with his hand. His skin was like sandpaper. "I'm in a peculiar business, mister, and I get peculiar people in here asking for peculiar things. Now there's nothing special about a silver picture frame by itself. I buy one occasionally, sell one occasionally. What's peculiar is that this morning, inside of one little hour, I get three calls for a silver frame. You're the third. The second was a cop, and the first was a lady."

"Who was she?"

"State your business, mister."

Meecham took one of his professional cards from his wallet.

Devine accepted the card, read it with a grunt and dropped it on the floor. "I told the cop, and I'm telling you. I didn't know her from Adam."

"You said people are your specialty. You must have noticed her."

"Sure, sure. I figured her for a nurse, or maybe a schoolteacher. She was ordinary, not bad-looking not good-looking, not well-dressed, not poorly dressed. Forty, or thereabouts, thin, had a sharp nose. Looked like she'd been crying or had a bad cold. She was standing outside when I opened up the store at nine. She said she wanted a few odds and ends for her house, and would I mind if she looked around. She went through the whole place very methodically, like someone who's used to looking for things. It took her about twenty minutes to find what she wanted: the silver frame, a table radio, and an onyx pen and pencil set. $48.50 for the works. A steal."

"Have you seen the papers this morning?"

"I've got four kids," Devine said. "When you got four kids you don't read the paper until night when they're all in bed. Why?"

Meecham ignored the question. "I suppose you remember who sold you the articles that this woman bought."

"Certainly. I both remember and I got it written down on my books. He's a young man I've done business with before. Sometimes he pawns a couple things, sometimes sells them outright like yesterday. His name's Desmond. Duane Desmond." He studied Meecham's face for a moment. "That's a phony, eh? I kind of thought it might be. What's his real tag?"

"Earl Loftus."

"Why all the sudden interest in him? He dead or something?"

"He's in jail."

"Is that a fact?" Devine showed no surprise. "Well, like they say, it couldn't happen to a nicer guy. Who was the lady who bought the stuff he sold me?"

"I thought you might have recognized her," Meecham said with a wry little smile. "It was Manderheim's mistress."

Devine blushed like a girl. "Oh, can it now. What the hell." He followed Meecham to the door. "The stuff I got from Desmond—Loftus, I mean—it wasn't hot?"

"No."

"That's a relief. I wonder why the woman bought it all back again?"

"Maybe to return it to him." Maybe to remember him by, he added silently. He thought of the way she had sat in Loftus' room, her head buried in her hands, in silent grief. He said, "There was no picture in the frame?"

"Sure there was. A nice-looking woman, sixty or thereabouts, white hair. I figured at first it must be Loftus' mother. I asked him didn't he want to take the picture out and keep it, and he said no. So I guess it wasn't his mother."

"I think it was."

"Well, now that's strange, eh? You'd think a guy would keep a picture of his own mother."

It was strange. Particularly strange in the case of Loftus, the devoted son. "What did you do with it?"

"Threw it away. It was no pin-up, what else would I do?"

"Maybe you could remember where you threw it."

"Sure I could remember, for all the good it will do. I put it in the furnace and burned it along with the other rubbish. It was just an ordinary picture, ordinary woman. How was I to know anybody'd want it? What do you want it for, anyway?"

"I don't. I'm just curious. I'd like to know why Loftus didn't keep it."

"Maybe he was sore at her. I get sore at my old lady."

"You may be right." Meecham opened the door. After the mustiness of the shop the winter wind felt fresh and clean. "Thanks for the information."

"Welcome. Come in again."

"I will." Meecham stepped out into the street and stood for a moment in front of the cluttered window, buttoning his topcoat. When he looked back into the store, he saw that Devine had returned to the wicker bench and was sitting with the ancient shotgun across his knees.

10

HE FOUND LOFTUS in a small room across the hall from the Sheriff's office. Loftus was alone, and not under restraint of any kind, though there was a policeman outside in the corridor.

Meecham knew the policeman. His name was Samuels; he was nearing retirement age, his legs and feet bothered him, and he suffered from attacks of hiccups that sometimes lasted for hours. Whenever Samuels got the hiccups his colleagues planned intricate, and occasionally hilarious, ways of scaring them away. None of them worked.

"Hello, Samuels," Meecham said. "How are things?"

"Bad. You got here just in time. They're taking your boy in there away."

"Where to?"

"The doc says he should be in a hospital. So as soon as I get the transfer papers, that's where I'm taking him, out to County."

"I'll talk to him first. Mind if I close this door?"

Samuels shrugged, a magnificently eloquent shrug which implied that as far as he was concerned every door in the place should be shut and the whole building blown up.

Meecham went inside and closed the door. The room was very small, furnished with a card table and three folding chairs, all different, a bridge lamp, a davenport with two broken springs, and a swivel chair with a cracked and worn leather seat. Everything in the room seemed to be discards from other rooms and offices, including the pictures that lined the windowless walls: photographs of the Detroit Red Wings, Abraham Lincoln, a sailboat, Dizzy Dean, and a score of unnamed and unremembered magistrates and judges and policemen.

Loftus was sitting in one of the folding chairs, staring up at the ceiling ventilator, his eyes strained and supplicating, as if they saw, beyond the ventilator, the sky; and beyond the sky the great hole of eternity already open for him.

Meecham said, "Loftus?"

Loftus moaned, faintly, the protesting sound of a man returning from a dream.

"Sorry I'm late, Loftus. Are you feeling all right?"

"I've been trying to pray. My mind won't let me, it keeps flying, flying through space." He lowered his head, and his eyes met Meecham's. "They're taking me away. I think I'm dying."

The ventilator whirred like wings.

"No. No, you're not, Loftus. Cordwink thinks you'll be more comfortable in the hospital, have more care, better food." He spoke too heartily, in an attempt to cover his conviction that the care and comfort were too late, the food useless to a man who couldn't eat.

"I don't want to go to the hospital. Please. I don't want to go, Mr. Meecham."

"I can't prevent them doing what's best for you."

"It's not best. I hate that air, smelling of sickness. I—well, I'll go, of course. I'll go. There's no choice." He glanced down at the suitcase beside his feet. It was the first time Meecham noticed it. "Emmy came to see me this morning."

"Mrs. Hearst?"

"Yes. They wouldn't let her in, but they let me have the stuff she brought me, some of my clothes and my radio. I don't know how she got the radio. I sold it yesterday."

"She bought it back from Devine this morning."

"She? God! She must have found out about the name I—I used."

"Maybe not," Meecham said. "I did, though."

"Duane Desmond. How do you like that for a grown man, eh? Funny, isn't it? I don't know what got into me. Duane Desmond. God!" He pounded the flimsy card table with his fist. One of the hinged legs collapsed and the table sagged but didn't fall. Loftus bent down and straightened the hinge, looking a little ashamed of himself. "You won't tell Emmy."

"Why should I?"

"She mustn't find out. She doesn't know I'm a fool." He rested his head on his hands. Meecham saw then the toothmarks on the knuckles of both of Loftus' hands. Even in the dim yellow light of the old bridge lamp they were plainly the marks of teeth, and one of them was bleeding. The blood looked like any other blood to Meecham. But he knew that this blood was venom, and that the long night—when Loftus had sat in silent frenzy biting his knuckles—was only the beginning of a longer night.

Meecham was seized by a sensation of incredible helplessness. He wanted to communicate with Loftus, to express sympathy and friendship, but the words he knew were inadequate as all words are inadequate in the imminence of death. For the first time in his life Meecham experienced a sense of religion, a feeling that the only way he and Loftus could communicate with each other was through a third being, a translator of the spirit.

Loftus turned his head suddenly. "You went to Devine's to check up on me, Mr. Meecham?"

"I had to find out what happened to the articles that were missing from your room, whether you'd given them away, pawned them, sold them."

"Is that so important?"

"It's important because Cordwink has—or had—an idea that someone paid you to kill Margolis."

"Is that your idea too?"

"No. I think you sold the stuff to Devine because you were broke. If you were broke, obviously you weren't paid."

"I could have told you that."

"Certainly. You could tell me anything you like but it wouldn't necessarily be the truth."

"You think I'm a liar, Mr. Meecham?" he said, anxiously.

"You're human."

"All this checking up on me, it's not necessary. I ask no favors. I'm a guilty man and I'm willing to take my punishment. But this prying—this unnecessary. . ."

"What you say isn't evidence unless it's backed by what you've done."

"I guess you're right. But whatever you find out, don't tell Emmy."

"What is there to find out?"

Loftus didn't answer. He was gnawing on his bleeding knuckles again.

"She's very fond of you, Loftus."

"She is, yes, I'm sure she is. I . . . What did . . .? You were talking to her last night, what did she say about me?"

"She was full of praise, of course; how kind and thoughtful you were, and a little bit about your history."

Footsteps passed in the corridor beyond the door. They sounded faint and far away.

"It's hard to admit you're nothing," Loftus said. "I'm admitting it now. My life has been without meaning or purpose or satisfaction. I should never have been born; my father didn't want children and my mother felt trapped by the responsibility. The whole thing has been a mistake from beginning to end. I am afraid of my moment of dying, terribly afraid. But I will be glad to be gone. You don't read poetry, Mr. Meecham?"

"No."

"There's a phrase that Yeats used. I have it written down in my book." He took a little black notebook from his shirt pocket and leafed through it. Each page that Meecham could see was crammed from top to bottom with writing, writing so small that it seemed impossible to read with the naked eye. He wondered whether this was Loftus' natural handwriting, or whether he wrote that way deliberately to save space in the little book.

"Here it is," Loftus said. "I'm not sure exactly what it means, it's out of context. But this one phrase keeps cropping up in my head lately: 'That this pragmatical preposterous pig of a world, its farrow that so solid seem, Must vanish on the instant if the mind but change its theme.'

"'Pragmatical preposterous pig of a world,'" he said, spitting out the words like pits that he'd been chewing too long. "That describes it. I will be glad to leave."

He lapsed into silence again. The only sound in the room was the whirring of the ventilator, though there was a sensation of sound and movement, as if beyond the closed door many things were happening, preposterous things.

Meecham said, "Why did you ask me to come here?"

"I want to hire you. Oh, not to defend me, that won't be necessary. But there are one or two little things that I won't be able to take care of. I'd like you to do them for me."

"What are they?"

"I have some money. I sold my car and a few little articles. It amounted to $716.00. I want my mother to have it."

"Where is it?"

"Emmy will give it to you. It's in an envelope in the middle of a package of letters. Deduct your fee, whatever it is, and give the rest of the money and all the letters to my mother. They're her letters. She wrote them to me when I came here. Tell her. . ." He hesitated, clenching and unclenching his hands. "Tell her to reread them, every one of them, to see. . . No. No, don't tell her that. Let her do what she likes with them. It's too late anyway. Just give her the money and tell her to go away somewhere for a while."

"Why?"

"She can't—can't face things very well. It's better if she goes away. Her address was in one of the morning papers. That's bad. She may be hounded by reporters or—well, Kincaid is a small cruel town."

"I'll deliver your message. I don't guarantee that I can persuade her to leave."

"You can try. Here, I'll write the address down for you."

"Don't bother, I saw the papers," Meecham said. He remembered the address, not from any newspaper, but from the Railway Express consignment slip that had been pasted across Loftus' suitcase: FROM MRS. CHARLES E. LOFTUS, 231 OAK STREET, KINCAID, MICHIGAN, TO MR. EARL DUANE LOFTUS, 611 DIVISION STREET, ARBANA, MICHIGAN. CONTENTS VALUED AT $50.00.

"I know it's asking a lot, Mr. Meecham. But if you could go sometime today, get to her first—it's only a hundred miles. . . ."

"I'll go today."

"Thank you." Loftus rose, clumsily, supporting himself by leaning one hand on the card table and the other on the back of the chair. "Thank you very much."

"Why didn't you keep her picture, Loftus?"

"I wanted to be alone. Entirely alone, without even a picture. Can you understand that?"

"It isn't a good thing to be alone. Relatives have a way of standing by in emergencies. Haven't you got any, except your mother?"

"I had a wife once. She left me, got a divorce. I can't blame her. She was a big, strong, healthy woman. At least she was then, I haven't seen her for a long time."

"Has it occurred to you that your mother might want to come here to see you?"

Loftus shrugged, wearily. "She won't come. Oh, she'll want to come, she may even plan to come, have everything arranged, suitcase neatly packed, everything. She may even get as far as the bus depot. Then she'll take a little drink to calm her nerves. You can guess the rest."

"Yes." He recalled the number of books about alcoholism that Loftus kept in his room.

"She was always death against liquor. She never had a drink until she was nearly fifty. My father had run out on her by that time, and one day she went out and bought a bottle of wine to calm her nerves. It happened right away. One drink, and she was a drunk. She'd been a drunk for maybe thirty years and didn't find it out until then. For her the world vanished in that instant. She has never seen it since. She never will again."

"Perhaps. There are cures."

Loftus only shook his head.

"I'll see to it personally that she comes to visit you, if you want her to."

"No, thank you," Loftus said politely. "I don't want to see anyone."

The door from the corridor opened and the policeman, Samuels, came in. He had taken his handcuffs from the leather case fastened to his belt and he was playing with them, clicking them from wide to narrow and back again, the way Miss Jennings played with her ring of keys and for the same reason, because he was bored and a little embarrassed.

"All through, Mr. Meecham? We got orders to be on the move."

Meecham turned to Loftus. "Are we all through?"

"I think so," Loftus said.

"If something else comes up, let me know. In any case, I'll be around to see you when I've transacted the business we discussed. Perhaps early in the morning."

"Thank you."

"I'll see Emmy right away."

"Tell her not to worry. Everything's going to be fine."

"I will. Good luck."

Meecham stood in the doorway of the small windowless room and watched the two men go down the corridor, handcuffed together, walking slowly and in step. Then he turned, abruptly, and walked as fast as he could in the other direction and out the rear entrance.

It was noon, but there was no sun. The sky hung close over the smoky city like a sagging tent top that would some day blow away, exposing the vast blackness of space.

Meecham waited for the traffic signal to change. A car went through the yellow light and almost sideswiped another car. Both drivers began to curse, ineffectually through closed windows, like little boys hurling threats from the safety of their own doorsteps. A woman came out of the supermarket across the street, jerking the arm of the crying child staggering along behind her. An old man on crutches inched his way across the icy sidewalk to the curb and stood eyeing the speeding cars with hate and fear.

A column of bitterness rose like mercury in Meecham's throat. *Pig of a world*, he thought. *Preposterous pig of a world.*

11

WHEN HE RANG the doorbell Emmy Hearst answered it herself, immediately, as if she'd been there at the door watching from behind the lace curtains of the little window for someone who would never come. Her eyes were so swollen that they didn't look like human eyes at all, but like twin blisters raised by fire. When she spoke she held one hand against her throat as if to ease its aching:

"You saw him?"

Mecham nodded. "Yes."

"I tried to. They wouldn't let me. They said I had no right, no right." She clung to the door for support, a tall strong woman who had come abruptly, in a single day, to the end of her strength.

"They've transferred him to the hospital," Meecham said.

"He'll get good care there. Won't he?"

"Of course."

There was a burst of masculine laughter from one of the rooms on the second floor.

Mrs. Hearst glanced nervously at the staircase. "I can't ask you to come in, I—I'm busy. I have business to attend to."

Mecham said, "I can't stay anyway. Loftus asked me to pick up a package of letters that he wants me to take to his mother."

"His mother," she said quietly. "Always his mother. She's a stone around his neck, drowning him, she's like a . . . Yes, I have the letters. They're in the kitchen. I'll get them for you."

She went down the hall and through the swinging door into the kitchen. Meecham heard her give a little cry of surprise: "Why—why, I thought you were upstairs."

"Well, I'm not upstairs. How do you like that, eh?"

The door stopped swinging and settled into place, entombing the sound waves in its heavy oak. But the woman's little cry of surprise hung in the air for a moment like a question mark of smoke and then disintegrated.

Meecham waited, uneasy and depressed. The front door was still open and he didn't close it; he felt that she had left it open deliberately. The wind blew down the hall and up the stairs, agitating the lace curtains and the coats and sweaters hanging on the old-fashioned hall rack. On the floor beside the rack there was a pile of rubbers and galoshes and a pair of battered tube skates and one gym shoe with the name Kryboski inked on each side.

Meecham looked at his watch and then coughed, a long purposeful cough. A minute later the swinging door opened again and Mrs. Hearst came toward him with a brown package under her arm. She was lurching slightly, as if she was carrying either inside the package or inside herself something heavy that threw her off balance.

She thrust the package at him. It was very light. "Here. Please go. *Please.*"

"Certainly," Meecham said. But he was a little too late. A man had come out of the kitchen, a big ruddy-faced man with fair hair. A hall-length away he looked quite distinguished and physically powerful. But as he came nearer, the shaft of light from the open door exposed the fraud like an efficient camera. His body was running to fat, and his face was disfigured by lines of indecision and self-doubt, ambition gone sour and life gone sour. His pale eyes moved constantly, back and forth, like birds at sea looking for a piece of kelp to rest on. He was one of those men Meecham recognized as a common type; the big boy whose mind and emotions had never been able to keep up with his maturing body. With the years the gap widened and the personality narrowed. He was, perhaps, forty-five.

Mrs. Hearst deliberately turned her head away as he approached. When she spoke she didn't look at either of the men, she seemed to be addressing the grease-darkened lilies that climbed the wall:

"This is my husband, Jim."

"Say, what is all this anyhow?" Hearst said. "Just what is it? Mysterious packages, cops in the house, Emmy bawling all over the joint. A guy has a right to know, don't he?"

He tugged, self-consciously, at his tie. The checked suit he wore was a little too tight around the hips, and the sleeves were too short, so that his wrists stuck out, not the vulnerable pipe-stem wrists of a growing boy, but thick wrists covered with coarse gold hairs. His manner, his clothes, his expression, they all added to his air of chronic failure . . . the air of a man who has tried and quit a hundred jobs in a hundred places, always out of step and off-beat.

"Well? Ain't anybody going to say anything but me? Not that I can't do the talking. I've got plenty to say and plenty to ask too."

"Shut up, Jim," Mrs. Hearst said, without turning.

"Now she tells me, shut up. Mind my own business, she says. Maybe that's my trouble, I have minded my own business. I've winked an eye at things." He looked at his wife. "Some pretty funny things, eh, Emmy?"

"Shut up," she repeated listlessly. "He's not a cop, he's a lawyer. And the package . . . Oh, you tell him, Mr. Meecham. Tell him what's in the package since he won't believe me."

"They're letters," Meecham said. "Written to Loftus by his mother. I'm returning them to her at his request."

Hearst looked disappointed. "Just a bunch of old letters, eh?"

"That's right."

"You mean all the value they've got is just sentimental?"

"Yes." Meecham didn't mention the money in one of the envelopes. He had the notion that if Hearst knew there was money involved he would put up a fight to keep it; a not unreasonable fight, since the package had been left in his own kitchen, and he, Meecham, had no power of attorney for Loftus, and, in fact, no proof that the package even belonged to Loftus.

But Hearst had already lost interest in the package. He was watching his wife, his eyes moving constantly in their sockets but keeping her within range. "He's quite a sentimental guy, Loftus is. Too bad I don't have that sentimental stuff, the ladies are crazy for it. And manners he's got too, real fancy manners that makes an ordinary guy feel like a bum. I'm not a bum. I'm a rough diamond, sure, but I don't go around carving people up either. Eh, Emmy?"

"I don't know what you do when you're out of town," she said distinctly. "And I don't care."

"I work. That's what I do. I *work*." The word seemed to stimulate him. He turned to Meecham, suddenly animated: "Right now I'm pushing a new product we got out, a soapless suds. Best thing on the market, Noscrub it's called. I'm in charge of out-of-town advertising."

"You distribute free samples from door to door," his wife said, still speaking in the same clear and distinct way, like a teacher correcting the repeated lies of a small boy.

"That's right, build me up. That's great. Funny how you could get so mealy-mouthed over Loftus because he read books instead of doing a man's work. Books and soft talk . . ."

"A man's work. A two-year-old could be taught to deliver samples from door to door."

His face purpled and he seemed ready to strike her. He looked, for the first time, decisive, sure of his ground and his rights. But the moment passed. His anger, like his other emotions, was not quite fully developed; it turned against himself so that he was his own victim.

"Wait till the product catches on," he said. "Just wait."

"Yes, Jim."

"I'll be advertising manager; I've got Weber's word for it."

"Yes, Jim."

"Yes Jim, yes Jim, yes Jim." He shook his head, in a new anger and an old despair. "God-dam it, build me up, Emmy. Like a real wife, build me up."

"The higher you're built the sooner you'll fall."

"You built *him* up. Earl this, Earl that, Earl you're wonderful."

"I never said he was wonderful."

"You did. I heard you."

"People who spy at doors will hear anything, and what they don't hear they'll make up."

"I didn't have to spy at doors. It was here, all over the place, right under my nose." His eyes shifted to Meecham. "How about that, eh? You take a guy into your home, you treat him right, treat him like your own . . ."

"You never said a civil word to him in your life." She was examining the wallpaper again. "Not a civil word."

"You said enough for both of us, didn't you? What do you think, I should of shook his hand for making me feel like an old bum?"

"I haven't had a friend since I left school, man or woman, not a friend. That's what Earl is to me, a friend."

"I've kicked around in my life, and one thing I know, there's no such thing as a man and woman being friends. It's not in the books. It's against nature."

"Your nature, maybe. Not . . ."

"Anybody's nature!"

"Keep your voice down. The boys might hear you."

"Let them. Maybe they'll learn a thing or two."

"If you don't mind," Meecham said, "I'd better be going."

Neither of them paid the slightest attention. They were absorbed in each other, like boxers in a ring, each of them intent only on the other's weak spots and unguarded moments.

She had crossed her arms on her chest, as if protecting a vulnerable place. "What are you accusing me of? Say it."

"I will."

"Well, go on. Say it in front of Mr. Meecham here. He's a lawyer."

"Sure, I'll say it. I don't care if he's President Truman."

"Well, what's stopping you? Go on, go on."

"He was your lover," Hearst said. "That piddling little shrimp was your lover."

"You fool," she whispered. "You *terrible* fool." She began to cry, very quietly, her forehead pressing against the wall. Tears fell from her swollen eyes and splattered the greasy lilies of the wallpaper. Her head moved, from one side to another, in misery and denial.

"Emmy?"

"Go away."

"It's not true then, eh, Emmy?"

"What do you think? A sick man—a dying man—what—do—you—think?"

"I—well . . ."

He looked with pathetic uncertainty at Meecham, like a small boy who had made his mother cry and sought reassurance that eventually she would stop and everything would be all right again.

"Emmy?" He touched her shoulder tentatively. "I didn't mean nothing, Emmy. You know me, I shoot off at the mouth, sure, but I wouldn't hurt a hair of your head. If you was only honest with me, Emmy. If you was only honest."

Meecham went out the door with the package under his arm. Neither of them noticed or cared.

Outside, the wind was fresh, but he had a sensation of suffocating heaviness in his throat and chest, as if the slices of life he had seen in the course of the morning were too sharp and fibrous to be swallowed.

12

HIGHWAY 12 RAN due west from Arbana to Kincaid, just over fifty miles of straight road through flat countryside. Under better circumstances it might have been an hour drive. But heavy trucks and heavy weather had pocked and dented the road, and beyond Jackson the snow began to fall in huge wet flakes that clung to the windshield like glue. Every few minutes Meecham had to slow down to give the windshield wipers more power and speed.

When he reached Kincaid it was five, and the street lights were on. Here and there a few houses were already decorated for Christmas, with strings of colored lights along the porches, clusters of pine branches and cones attached to the doors. The shops and the streets were crowded, and the crowds looked gay as if freshened by the new snow.

He had no trouble finding Oak Street. It crossed the main highway at a traffic signal in the center of town.

Two Hundred Thirty-one was a two-story, white-brick apartment house in a neighborhood that derived its brash but decaying air from nearby slums. Meecham parked his car and crossed the street with the brown package under his arm. The building itself was well kept, and nailed to the front door there was a Christmas wreath, a red cellophane bell surrounded by artificial spruce boughs and red wax berries. The snow made the spruce and the berries look quite real.

Inside the small lobby there was a row of locked mailboxes and on the wall a black arrow pointing to the basement, and a sign, Manager's Office. The third mailbox belonged to Loftus' mother: Mrs. C. E. Loftus, Apartment Five.

Meecham walked down the hall. The carpeting was worn but clean, and the air smelled pungently of paint. Someone in the building obviously had a flair for lettering. All over the walls there were elaborately executed instructions: APARTMENTS ONE—FIVE, THIS WAY →→. NO SMOKING IN CORRIDORS. KEEP YOUR RADIO LOW AFTER ELEVEN O'CLOCK PLEASE. NO SOLICITING. PLEASE USE NIGHT BELL ONLY WHEN NECESSARY. NIGHT BELL ↓↓.

Number Five had a fire extinguisher fastened to the wall just outside the door. Meecham pressed the buzzer, waited half a minute, and pressed it again, twice. There was no response. He went back to the lobby and down the steps to the basement following the Manager's Office arrow.

A small man past middle age, in a peaked painting cap and splattered overalls, was squatting in a full knee bend outside the door, putting masking tape around the knob. He turned when he heard Meecham's footsteps, turned without rising and without losing his balance even for a moment. His back was straight as a board.

"Yes, sir?"

"Are you the manager?"

"Yes, sir, I am. Victor Garino."

"I'm looking for Mrs. Loftus. I'm Eric Meecham, a friend of Earl's, her son."

Garino's eyes behind his rimless spectacles looked misty.

"Oh, you are? Earl's a fine boy. You tried her apartment?"

"Yes."

"Well, come in, come inside." He opened the door and Meecham preceded him into a small living room. The room was so crowded with furniture and knickknacks that there was hardly any space to move. In a box beside an electric heater a litter of kittens was mewling, while the mother cat stalked around and around the box with a kind of angry dignity, as if ashamed of the way her children were behaving in front of a stranger.

"You like cats, Mr. Meecham? Yes?"

"Very much." He had never particularly liked or disliked them but the sight of the tiny furry bodies stirred something inside him.

"Yes, I like all animals, but cats, ah, they're quiet and quick, and they earn their keep. We never have any complaints about rats," Garino added proudly. "Never. Sit down, will you? Then I can sit down too. Ah, that's better. You came from Earl, eh? How is he?"

"The same as usual."

"Ah, yes. Did you . . .? You knocked on her door very loud, did you? Sometimes she's hard of hearing. Also she's a deep sleeper."

"Also she gets loaded."

"Yes," Garino said in a melancholy voice. "She gets loaded very bad. Often's the time I let myself in her apartment with my passkey just to see she's not burning the place down or something. She's a problem. She's a nice lady but she's a problem."

"I can see that."

"How we found out, Mama and me, was by the incinerator. Rum bottles. Empty rum bottles kept coming down the chute all the time making a fine mess. Mama said it must be Mrs. Loftus. No, I said, no, how could it be, such a nice dignified lady drinking all that rum. Mama was right, though." Garino's eyes were sad as a hound's. "I went up and asked Mrs. Loftus please not to throw rum bottles down the chute. Right away she denied it, acted real shocked. Why, Victor, she said, why, Victor, you know I never touch the stuff. It must be the young couple upstairs, she said."

The mother cat had settled down beside Garino on the davenport and was purring in her sleep.

"After that," Garino said, "there were no more rum bottles in the incinerator. She took them out and threw them somewhere. I often saw her go down the street with a paper bag full of bottles. It looked funny, her such a lady walking down the street to dispose of her *garbage*. Ah, we feel bad, Mama and me. The bottles didn't make such a great mess, we would have just let her keep on using the incinerator."

"Maybe you should."

"It's too late now. If I went and told her it was all right to use the incinerator she couldn't *pretend* anymore, she couldn't have any pride left. That wouldn't be good. Anyway"—Garino spread his hands—"she's not such a terrible bother. Her rent is always paid, Earl sends it to me. And she is quiet. No parties, no company. She keeps to herself. Sometimes when she forgets to eat, Mama takes her up a little plate of something. She's not a common drunkard, you understand. She's a lady who's had one sorrow too many. Some people get strong under sorrows. Other people, they snap like twigs, they break, it's not their fault."

"What sorrows?" Meecham said.

"First, they lost their money and then her husband ran away, just left one afternoon while she was at a movie. After that her son went out and got married, left her alone. For nearly a year she was alone and then Earl and his wife came back and they all lived together up in Number Five. That was worse than being alone because there were fights all the time, just words, but loud nasty words, between Earl and his wife, and Earl and his mother, and his mother and his wife. Fighting, fighting, over everything."

"What was his wife's name?"

"Birdie, they called her. Such a silly name. She wasn't anything like a bird. She was a big woman, older than Earl, and quite pleasant unless you crossed her. She had a terrible temper, just terrible. Maybe everything would have worked out, though, if the three of them didn't have to live together, if there wouldn't've been that jealousy between the two women. As it was, Birdie left town—she'd only been here a month or so—and a little while afterwards Earl got a legal notice that she'd divorced him in some other state, Nevada, I think."

"When was that?"

"About two years ago. Upped and left just as suddenly as Mr. Loftus had left. After that Earl began to change. No one knew he was sick, he just got quieter and never went out. First we thought it was sadness over Birdie. He was crazy over her, and when she was in a good mood she babied him and fussed over him like a mother. Mrs. Loftus never babied him, being such a baby herself in some ways. Yes, we thought Earl's trouble was lovesick. But he didn't get any better. One day he went to Arbana, he wanted to look up some books in the University Library, he was always book crazy. He never came back here. He wrote his mother, he paid her rent, everything was friendly, but he never came back. Maybe it was true what Mrs. Loftus told me—that he had to stay there for hospital treatments. But we have a hospital here. So . . ." He sighed. "Ah well, I'm getting to be an old gossip. More and more, an old gossip." He got up from the davenport and then reached down and patted the cat's head as if apologizing for making too abrupt a move. "I'll go and ask Mama if she saw Mrs. Loftus go out."

When he opened the kitchen door, a rich odor of oil and garlic spilled out, submerging the smell of paint. Meecham went over to the box of kittens and knelt down beside it. They were all asleep now, piled haphazardly on top of one another in a corner. He touched one of them very gently with his forefinger, and immediately the mother cat sauntered over to the box with the casual but alert air of a policeman who doesn't want to start trouble but intends to be around if trouble appears.

Garino returned, followed by a short broad woman in a cotton housedress. She obviously wasn't Italian like her husband. Her hair was light brown, her eyes green, and she had a certain brusqueness of movement and speech that suggested impatience.

Garino started to speak. "Mama said, yes, Mrs. Loftus went out early this morning. To the grocery store, that's what Mama thought, only Mama thought maybe she'd come back again and . . ."

"I can tell it, Victor," his wife said. "After all, I've got a tongue in my head." She flashed a glance at Meecham. "I guess Victor told you about her?"

"Yes."

"Well, there you have it. When she goes out I never know when she'll come home or how she'll come home or if she'll come home. Nobody knows. She doesn't know herself." Mrs. Garino crossed her arms on her chest with slightly exaggerated belligerence. "She's been gone all day. You know what that means, Victor."

"Yes, Mama."

"Remember last time."

"Yes. Yes, Mama."

"You'd better go and start looking for her."

Garino glanced at Meecham with an air of apology. "Usually she stays in her apartment and drinks quietly by herself. But sometimes . . ."

"This is a *sometime*," his wife said sharply. "You get your coat on, Victor. You find her. We've got other tenants to consider too. Remember last time."

"What happened last time?" Meecham addressed the question to Garino.

Garino looked down at his hands. "She got in trouble, arrested. After that she was in the hospital for two weeks. She was sick."

"She had the D. T.'s." Mrs. Garino's face had gone a little hard. "You hurry up now, Victor."

"All right, all right."

"I'll go with you," Meecham said. "I have to find her anyway."

The woman turned and gave him a long level stare. "Why?"

"I have something for her."

"Money?"

"Yes."

Garino had gone into the next room to get his coat. "She'll blow it all in two days," his wife said in a low voice. "Victor, in there, he thinks I'm getting sour. Yes, and maybe I am. I've got myself to consider too. All this extra work and worry and none of it doing one sliver of good, sure I'm sour. But Victor . . . Ha, Victor thinks she's a *lady*, and *ladies* don't get to be common ordinary drunks. Ha. Victor's been in this country for twenty years and he still thinks like a Wop, still talks about *ladies*. People are people. Everyone's people."

Garino stood in the doorway with his hat and coat on and a woolen muffler crossed at his neck. "You talk too much, Mama." He added, to Meecham, "Scotch women are jealous."

Mrs. Garino's face was white. "Jealous! Me, jealous!"

"Yes, you are." Garino went over and kissed her affectionately on the forehead. "I'll be back as soon as I can."

"As if I cared."

"You could make some fresh coffee and have it ready."

"I wouldn't make you any coffee for all the money in the world."

"I'm not offering you money."

"Me, jealous. That's funny. That's a scream."

"Get me a clean handkerchief, will you, Mama?"

She went into the next room, muttering under her breath. When she returned with the handkerchief she didn't hand it to him; she threw it at him from the doorway. He caught it, one-handed, and then he went out the door, smiling. Meecham followed him up the steps and through the lobby and into the street.

Garino was still smiling. "Ah, now, you mustn't be embarrassed, Mr. Meecham. That wasn't a quarrel. Mama and I have been married for twenty-one years. When I get home there will be fresh coffee on the stove and I will tell Mama I love her and she will admit she's a little jealous."

"That's all there is to it, eh?"

"Not at first, no. But after twenty-one years we have worked out some short cuts. We have a system."

"My car's across the road," Meecham said.

"We could walk. I know some of the places where she goes, only two or three blocks away. But then, maybe you don't like walking?"

"It's all right for women and children."

They crossed the street and got into Meecham's car.

13

AT HALF-PAST eight they were still searching, and Garino was getting hungry and beginning to worry about what his wife would say when he got home.

"Always before, I've found her," Garino said. "She doesn't go from place to place, a drink here, a drink there, like some people. She's shy of strangers. There are only two or three little bars that she ever goes to."

The two or three little bars had expanded into twenty, of all sizes. No one had seen, or admitted having seen, Mrs. Loftus.

Making a sudden decision, Meecham swung the car around in a U-turn at the next corner. "I'll take you home, Garino."

"No, no. Mama said, find her. I've got to . . ."

"There's no point in both of us wasting time and this is my job, not yours," Meecham said. The fact was, that although he enjoyed Garino's company, Garino slowed him down; he seemed to know everyone in town and he stopped to chat, shake hands, inquire after wives and children, like a politician touring the city, not forgetting the details in spite of more important issues in his mind. Meecham's impatience had spread from the weather and the ugly little city to the Garinos and to Mrs. Loftus herself. She was a pathetic figure, but her very pathos was a burden and a nuisance. He wished he had never heard of her.

"This is my job," he repeated. "You've done what you could, Garino."

"Little enough," Garino said gloomily. "I don't know where else. She has no friends anymore."

"I'll take you home."

"To tell the truth, I have a stomach-ache. Yes, and the cats. . . I have to look after the cats. And the furnace too, suppose it needs shaking down and Mama can't shake it down right, and the complaints start coming in, no heat, no hot water . . ."

His voice trailed away. Meecham turned left, in the direction of Oak Street, while Garino sat, stiff and uncomfortable, his back barely touching the back of the seat, as if he was unaccustomed to driving in cars and wasn't sure what disaster the next corner would bring.

"Do you think you'll find her?" Garino said.

"Yes."

"Then what? Then you bring her home, she goes to sleep, and in the morning it starts all over again. One day is like another. Sometimes," he said soberly, "sometimes I think, ah, the hell with everything."

Meecham stopped the car in front of the white-brick apartment building. He could see Mrs. Garino peering out of the window of the basement apartment. She had her face right up against the glass with both hands cupped around her eyes to shut out the kitchen light behind her. When she saw the car, and Garino getting out, she ducked her head in guilty haste.

"I hope you find her soon," Garino said nervously.

"I hope so."

"I will wait up, to see things are all right. Where will you go?"

"I'm not sure," Meecham said. He was almost sure, though. Pulling away from the curb he tried to recall Loftus' words about his mother: *"She may want to come, she may have everything arranged, even get as far as the bus depot . . ."*

The depot was on a little side street toward the west side of town. Half of the small waiting room was taken up by rows of benches and the other half by a newsstand and a lunch counter. A bus had just left, or was loaded and ready to leave, because the benches were empty except for a man with a little girl about ten. Both the man and the little girl were completely absorbed in comic books.

Meecham sat down at the lunch counter and ordered coffee. There was only one other customer, an intense-looking, pimply young man in a bus driver's uniform.

"I've got a few minutes yet," the driver said. "Give me another cherry coke, Charley."

"The way you guzzle that stuff, it's coating the insides of your stomach." Charley put the drink on the counter and wiped his hands on his apron. He was a big burly man with a round face and a worried little smile. "I heard on the radio, more snow coming."

"Snow don't bother me. It's the people asking questions and craning their necks all over the place trying to drive the bus."

"Say, did the old lady get on all right?"

"I didn't see any old lady."

"She bought a ticket. Maybe she's in the rest room and didn't hear the announcement. You better go and check, Roy."

"Listen, Charley, I drive a bus, I don't run no old-ladies' home. You want to check, check."

"Jesus, no one moves a muscle around this place excepting me."

Charley took off his apron and chef's hat and went toward the restroom. Meecham got up and followed him.

"I heard you talking," Meecham said. "About an old lady."

Charley paused at the door of the restroom, his hand on the knob. "So?"

"I'm looking for the mother of a friend of mine, woman in her late sixties, white hair, nice-looking, refined."

"Could be her. Myself, I don't pay much attention to old ladies."

Charley glanced around carefully to see that no one else had come in, and that the man and the little girl weren't watching, before he opened the door of the restroom.

It was a small square box of a room equipped with a chair and a moth-eaten couch, and smelling heavily of wet paper towels and disinfectant.

She was lying on her back on the couch with her eyes closed, a tiny woman, thin to the point of atrophy. Her face had the same look of fragility and innocence as her son's: high cheekbones with shadowed hollows underneath, wide serene forehead, and brown lashes thick and straight as bristles. She was dressed for a winter day in a black cloth coat with a lamb collar and high velvet carriage boots trimmed with black-dyed rabbit fur. Where the boots touched the calves of her withered legs, the fur was entirely rubbed away. At the foot of the couch, on the floor, was a paper bag and a stained and battered calfskin purse with a chain handle.

"I never been in here before," Charley said with interest. "I guess women don't write on walls."

"Mrs. Loftus," Meecham said.

Her breathing paused at the mention of her name, just for a fraction of a second, and then it went on as before, heavy and uneven. Her hands were at her sides, palms up, in a supplicating way, as if she was asking for something, money, help, mercy, love, or just another drink. She wore short kid gloves, and protruding from the wrist of the right glove was her bus ticket. She had put it, not in her purse as a grown woman would, but in her glove for safekeeping. It reminded Meecham of the Sunday School collection nickels he had carried when he was a boy, in the thumb of his mitten or the toe of his shoe; the uncomfortable but wonderfully virtuous feeling of that nickel-for-the-Lord in his shoe. The old lady and the old memory pierced him like unexpected arrows from a long bow.

"Hey, lady," Charley said. "Wake up. Your bus is leaving."

She moved her head to one side and her hat slipped to the floor, exposing her white silky hair, a little yellowed in places from neglect and curling tongs. Charley bent down to pick up the hat, but he didn't reach it. He straightened up with a grunt of surprise. "Hell, she's drunk. Catch that breath, will you? She's kayoed."

The bus driver, too, had come into the room. He stared down at the woman with his pale lips pressed together in disapproval. "It's a fine thing, isn't it, having people like that hanging around our depot."

"Come on, lady. Wake up now."

"You can just save your breath, Charley. I wouldn't *dream* of taking her on *my* bus, not if she's got thirty tickets."

"Oh, shut up. Give the old girl a break. She's somebody's mother."

"Just so long as she ain't mine," the driver said. "Personally, I've got a good mind to call the police. They know how to deal with people like that."

Charley's face hardened. "Call the police and I'll clobber you. Now get out of here."

"You can't order . . ."

"Turn blue. Just turn blue."

The driver backed out of the room, still talking, but inaudibly, under his breath.

"That stinking lily," Charley said. "I ought to poke him, but I don't want to bust my knuckles."

Meecham was bending over Mrs. Loftus. He had taken off her gloves and was rubbing her small bony hands. The skin felt very dry and cold like a leaf in autumn.

"Mrs. Loftus. Can you hear me?"

She stirred a little, and spoke a name without opening her eyes. "Victor?"

"I'm taking you home, Mrs. Loftus."

She didn't answer.

"Maybe if I opened the window," Charley said, "she'd snap out of it sooner."

"Good idea."

Charley went over and pushed up the window over the washbasin. Fresh snow from the sill sifted into the room like a flight of furry white-winged insects coming to rest. "I never figured she was drunk, see. She's been in a couple of times today and I thought first she was waiting for someone and didn't know what bus to meet. Then, about an hour ago, she comes in the third time, buys a ticket for Arbana and sits down to wait. I kept an eye on her because she looked sick and she acted sick; kept coming in here to the restroom and coming out again. I never for a minute figured she was getting herself hootched."

Meecham picked up the paper bag from the floor and looked inside. It contained a half-empty fifth of cheap rum. He twisted the bag shut again and dropped it into the metal trash container.

"I don't want to hurry you, mister," Charley said. "Nothing like that. Only if she's the mother of a friend of yours like you said, maybe you ought to phone your friend."

"He's out of town. I'll take her home myself."

"I don't want to hurry you, I know you're in a spot. Only there's a little kid out there with her father. You know kids, they're always running to the can. Suppose she comes in here and sees the old lady, it might scare her."

Meecham recalled the gruesome cover of the comic book the little girl had been reading, but he said agreeably, "Yes, it might. I'll do my best."

He looked down again at Mrs. Loftus, helpless in her coma of rum and ruin. He wondered if this was how Virginia was on the night Margolis was killed, and if Loftus, watching her, had unconsciously identified her with his mother, had attacked Margolis as the father-rival-invader. It seemed to Meecham that this idea made the murder of Margolis more plausible, that it synthesized the rather vague and philosophical motives Loftus had given into something stronger and closer to the heart. Loftus was a passive man, a man of ideas. For him to become the aggressor, to commit so positive and final an act as murder, must have required a positive motive: not money, as Cordwink believed, and not the childishly rationalized notion of ridding the world of a nuisance; but hate, the obverse of fear, and rage, the obverse of impotence.

"Victor?" Mrs. Loftus said again. She had opened her eyes and was staring up at the ceiling, at one particular spot, as if she realized that she was in a strange place and was afraid to look around and find out where.

"Victor isn't here," Meecham said. "He's waiting for you at home. I'll take you there."

"I'm in the hospital?"

"No, in the bus depot."

"Bus? *Bus*." She struggled to get up, lost her balance and sat down heavily on the couch again. "My bus ticket. Where's my bus ticket? Got to see Earl. Got to see my boy."

Meecham put his hand on her arm to steady her; it felt as fleshless as a broom handle. "The bus has gone, Mrs. Loftus. Besides, you're not well enough to go on a trip by yourself."

"I'm not well." Her pale round eyes took on a crafty expression. "I'm ill, aren't I?"

"Yes."

"I had a fainting spell. I remember now. I felt quite faint, so I just lay down and had a little rest until the feeling passed. That's reasonable, isn't it?"

"Of course."

"You be sure and tell Victor that. Victor's beginning to get some very odd ideas." She picked up her purse from the floor, hanging on to Meecham's coat sleeve to balance herself when she leaned over. "Where is my luggage?"

"I haven't seen it," Meecham said. "Perhaps you checked . . ."

"I had my luggage with me. In a paper bag. I couldn't find my suitcase so I packed a few little things in a paper bag." She had begun to tremble violently, all over her body. Her knees shook, and her mouth and hands and shoulders, and her head kept moving back and forth as if her neck was too feeble to hold it up and it was just balancing there precariously like a ball on the nose of a seal. "It wasn't much, my toothbrush and towel and a few little things like that. But it's a matter of principle. I want my luggage. I want my luggage." She looked up at Charley. "You. Are you the attendant?"

"Me?" Charley said. "Oh, sure."

"Please go and tell the manager I'd like a few words with him."

"He's not in."

"Then I'll wait. I don't like to be insistent but I can't let a thing like this pass. I want my luggage. It's a matter of principle. I want . . ."

"Oh, for crying in the sink," Charley said, "give her the bottle."

There was an instant of dead silence. Then Mrs. Loftus sat down again, covering her eyes with her trembling hands. "Please. I want my luggage."

"I'll take a look around and see if I can find it," Meecham said. He pretended to look under the couch and on top of the towel rack. Then he reached into the trash bin and pulled out the paper bag. "Is this it, Mrs. Loftus?"

She raised her head and stared at the bag with excitement and loathing. "Yes. Yes, that's it. Give it to me."

But she didn't wait for him to give it to her. She rose and staggered toward him, her arms outstretched. She took the bag in her hands, and felt its contours with anxiety and then relief, like a mother feeling the bones of a child who had fallen and might have been injured.

"Yes, this is it. Everything's here—toothbrush, towel—thank you, sir." Her violent shaking had stopped. The very sight of the bottle had steadied her: the sight of land to the seasick sailor. "Thank you very much."

"Don't mention it," Meecham said.

"Now if you'll excuse me, I'll freshen up a bit. After all, this is the ladies' room, you know. I don't understand how you two got in here in the first place. The management must be very lax."

The two men went out into the waiting room, Charley to the lunch counter, and Meecham to one of the hard wooden benches. He sat down and lit a cigarette and kept his eye on the door marked Ladies.

Five minutes later Mrs. Loftus emerged. She'd put on her hat and gloves and rouged her cheeks. Whatever she had drunk from the bottle during the five minutes had worked its dark magic. She seemed quite confident and poised, and when she approached Meecham her step had a spring to it, like a young girl's. It looked grotesque, that semblance of youth in a starved and wasted body.

"There you are, young man." She spoke slowly, letting out each consonant with great care like a fisherman letting out a taut line foot by foot, not sure what is on the other end. "I'm quite ready now, if you are."

"My car's across the street."

"Isn't that nice. Then we won't have to pay taxi fare. Whenever I have one of my little spells Victor calls for me and we take a taxi home. I don't care for taxis. The drivers can be extremely discourteous."

They went out together. When they crossed the street she hung on to Meecham's arm. She was light as a bird but he felt that he was dragging a stone that had been dragged for a long time by many people, had become larger and heavier as it collected debris, until now it weighed a ton.

14

Garino was waiting at the front door of the apartment house. All the lights were turned on, in the lobby, and on the porch, and the walk had been shoveled and sprinkled with cinders. As soon as he saw the car stop he came down the steps and opened the door for Mrs. Loftus.

"Why, there you are, Victor," she said, as if she'd been looking for him all over town.

"Here I am," Garino said, a little grimly. "Have you eaten? It's nine o'clock."

"Nine already? Dear me. Where do the days go, I wonder. They simply . . ."

"Have you eaten?"

"I'm not hungry."

"I'll bring you up something."

"I *said* I'm not hungry, Victor."

"All right. Come on, we'll go inside."

Meecham followed them into the lobby with the package of letters under his arm.

"This very kind gentleman drove me home. A perfect stranger to me, too. But then I sometimes think strangers are often nicer than other people."

"Where were you?"

"My dear Victor, where would I be? I was in the bus depot, of course. When one is going to take a bus one goes to the bus depot."

"What bus?"

"To Arbana, to see Earl. I had this odd letter from him this morning and I decided that Earl needs me. A son needs his mother in time of trouble."

"What trouble?"

"He didn't say anything definite but I can read between the lines. It was as plain as day. Earl needs me, I said to myself, I can't fail my son, I must go and help him. But then . . ." Her voice faltered, and her face wrinkled up in bewilderment and surprise. "But then I didn't go. I didn't *go*, did I?"

"That's a good thing. You're better to stay right here."

"But my son . . ."

"Earl's a good boy. He'll never get into trouble."

Garino unlocked the door of her apartment, pushed it open with his right elbow and clicked on the wall switch with his left hand, all in one easy practiced motion as if he had done the same thing a hundred times. "Please come in, Mr. Meecham."

Meecham went in but he didn't close the door after him. The smell in the small living room was unbearable. It was obvious that someone—probably Garino himself—had tried to straighten the place up in a hurry and hadn't had time to clean out the fireplace. It was a litter of rubbish; cigarette butts, newspapers, apple cores, a whole moldy orange, a shriveled head of lettuce, an empty bottle of ketchup blackened by fire, and a wedge of cheese beaded with oil. Every piece of furniture in the room bore the scars of Mrs. Loftus' daily battles with herself: burns and stains, dents and holes and broken springs.

"Dear me," said the old lady. "It's nice to be home. I think I'll go and make some coffee."

She started for the kitchen, holding the paper bag against her chest with both arms as if she was dancing with it.

Garino intercepted her at the door. "I'll make the coffee. You sit down."

"I'll make it myself. I'm quite . . ."

"Give me the bottle," Garino said.

"What bottle?"

"Give it to me."

"If you're referring to this cough medicine I purchased this afternoon . . . I've had this cough. I'm not well, Victor, you know that. I'm not well. I had a bad spell in the bus depot. Ask the young man. He'll verify it."

Garino looked questioningly over the old lady's head at Meecham. Meecham shrugged and turned away.

"Yes," Garino said. "Yes. I guess you had a bad spell."

"I certainly *did*, Victor. I felt it coming on at noon. I started to cough. You know that nasty cough I have and how you're always telling me to buy some medicine for it?"

"Yes," he said. "Yes."

"Well, I finally did. There, you see? I took your advice. I'm improving, aren't I?"

"Yes, of course."

There was a sound from the hall. Meecham looked up and saw Mrs. Garino standing in the doorway, with an old woolen sweater flung over her shoulders. She didn't speak, or give any indication that she was there. She just stood watching her husband and Mrs. Loftus, her eyes flat and hard and metallic like coins.

"But the medicine didn't agree with me in some way. I began to feel faint. And then I *did* faint, Victor."

"You faint a lot," Mrs. Garino said quietly.

Mrs. Loftus whirled around with a cry of surprise. "Why, *there* you are, Ella. I was just telling Victor that . . ."

"I heard you."

"You must meet this nice young man, Ella. I don't know your name, young man, but I'd like you to meet one of my dearest friends."

Mrs. Garino didn't look at Meecham. She started across the room, holding the old sweater close across her breasts. "So you fainted again."

"Why, yes. Yes, I did, Ella. I swear to you I . . ."

"Mama," Garino said. "Please go home."

"Not yet."

"Please, you mustn't . . ."

"I mustn't *what?*"

"It's better not to say anything."

"That's been your system all along. It's sure worked out swell, hasn't it?"

Garino looked down at the floor, in silence.

"When's it all going to stop, Victor? All this pretending, this silly stupid game we've been playing. Do you think it's doing *her* any good? Take a look at this rotten mess of a room. Smell it."

"Be quiet, I beg of you," Garino said. "You'll only hate yourself afterwards, you'll . . ."

"Who are we all kidding anyway? Headaches, coughs, neuritis, fainting spells, anything. Anything but the truth. It can't go on forever like this. Somebody's got to tell the truth sometime."

"Perhaps the truth can wait for tonight," Meecham said.

"It's been waiting for years," Mrs. Garino said, still addressing her husband. "Go on, tell her, Victor."

"No! No, be quiet!"

"Tell her she's a drunk. Tell her you know it and I know it, we've known it for years and so has everybody else in town."

The steam radiator began to clank, like cymbals heralding the truth.

"Ask her a few things, too. Ask her why Earl left, why Birdie left, why everyone's left except us. You blamed Birdie for fighting with her, didn't you, just like you're blaming me now. Well, there's only one thing to blame. This." She reached out and grabbed the paper bag from Mrs. Loftus' hands. "*This.*"

"No, no." Mrs. Loftus was swaying back and forth like a tower of toy blocks about to fall. "Give it to me. My medicine."

"Medicine. Who do you think you're fooling except yourself? Sometimes I think I could stand anything except this pretending all the time. Can't you admit anything, just once, one word of truth? What's in here? Gin? Whisky? Rubbing alcohol?"

The old lady moved slowly sideways toward a chair and held onto the back of it with both hands, clung to it like an ageing ballerina to the bar, for reassurance and new strength.

"You're not behaving like a lady, Ella," she said in a whisper. "You're making defamatory remarks."

Mrs. Garino threw back her head and began to laugh; her whole body vibrated with harsh tinny laughter. Garino didn't say anything. He went over to her, took the paper bag out of her hand and placed it on the table. Then he put his arms around her waist and the two of them walked out into the hall together, Garino matching his step to hers.

The instant the door closed Mrs. Loftus took the bottle out of the paper bag, uncorked it and put it to her lips, very daintily, a fine lady sipping fine tea from the best of china. An immediate change came over her, the same change Meecham had observed in the bus depot: a revitalizing, a flow of color to her skin, as if the stuff she drank was blood and went directly into her veins.

She put the bottle down and looked across the room at Meecham, her eyes narrowed to slits in an attempt to focus accurately.

"Are you still here?"

"Yes."

"Want a drink?"

"Not now, thanks."

"It's rum," she said. "Ella was wrong. I don't fool myself, and I don't mind admitting to the right people that I take the odd nip now and then, if there's a chill in the air."

Or if it's hot, Meecham added silently, or dry or windy; in a spring rain or on a sunny afternoon, a smoky morning in fall, Indian summer or Easter moon. All weather had a chill to it, every day was winter.

Meecham went over and sat down in the old cherrywood rocker opposite Mrs. Loftus. "I know it's late, but I wanted to talk to you. Earl asked me to."

"Earl?" She put a hand to her throat as if the name had jabbed her there like a needle. "My bus. I missed my bus. I must . . ."

"There are other buses," Meecham said. There could be a thousand buses but she'd never be on any of them. He realized now how hopeless his mission was: he couldn't persuade her to leave town as Loftus wanted her to do, and he couldn't give her the money because she was obviously unfit to handle it.

"Yes, of course there are other buses, aren't there? I'll go tomorrow, early in the morning. But first I must tidy things up a bit. I will not have anyone like Ella casting aspersions on my home. Did you hear what she said?"

"Yes."

"She lied about Birdie leaving, too. Birdie didn't leave, I kicked her out. You're not good enough for my son Earl, I told her. Pack your bags and start moving, we don't need your help to get along, I said."

"What kind of help?"

"Money. Earl was temporarily unemployed—the firm he was working for went out of business—and Birdie took a job as a waitress. That's when they came to live with me. Birdie managed all the money, wouldn't let me do any of the shopping, treated me like a child. She even gave me an allowance. Yes, and you want to know how much? A dollar. A dollar a week. Every Saturday she'd give it to me and say, very sarcastic, don't spend it all in one place. A *dollar*. What can you buy with that?"

Two bottles of dago red, Meecham thought.

"And then she started to accuse me of pilfering, taking money from her purse. She told Earl and Earl came to me, and I said, Earl, I'm only your mother but I have some rights, and what am I going to do when the poor paper boy comes for his money and I don't have a cent? It isn't fair to ask that poor paper boy to come back again and again when Birdie's purse is lying there right out in the open, I said. Earl understood perfectly. You know what happened?" She let out a crow of laughter. "They raised my allowance to five dollars. I beat Birdie at her own game, didn't I?"

"I guess you did," Meecham said.

The little story, with its interlocking links of deceit and truth, humor and sordidness, was oppressive. The old lady had spoken with such a complete sense of right and justification. Petty theft?—never. Saving the poor paper boy a second trip?—of course. Meecham felt a flash of sympathy for the vanished Birdie.

Mrs. Loftus uncorked the bottle again. This time she didn't sip quite so daintily, and her reaction wasn't so immediate and distinct. It came gradually, into her speech and mannerisms—an occasional slurring of s's and omission of final consonants, grand but vague gestures, and a constant widening and narrowing of her eyes in an attempt to blink away a film that wasn't there. Meecham wanted to take the bottle from her and hide it some place, at least temporarily, so that she wouldn't get too drunk to talk. He had a curious and irrational desire to hear more about Loftus and Birdie, as if Loftus' relationship with his wife and mother might explain more about the murder of Margolis. Yet he was sure that there was no link except the psychological one—the effect of A and B on C had determined C's conduct toward D.

"You bet I beat her at her own game. Yes, sir," the old lady went on. "Birdie never fooled me. First time I saw her I had her spotted. She wasn't any twenty-eight, as she told Earl, and she wasn't any innocent virgin. Any woman could have sheen srough her but not Earl. Earl was always a pure boy, a good boy, took after my side of the family. Never smoked or drank like other boys, or went out carousing to parties. He stayed home nights and read, or we played carj together. It was a good innocent life he led until the day he met Birdie. Didden tell me he met her, didden say a word about her till the day he brought her home and said, this is my wife. Like that. This is my wife. And there she stood, with that hennaed hair and that hard look, forty if she was a day, forty, and him just a boy."

She wiped her eyes with the back of her hand, but it was a meaningless gesture. The tears that had been wept had long since dried and formed a crust of salt over an emotion long since dead.

"If you knew Earl—how good he is, this deep feeling of love inside of him. But he gave it all to her. Never saw her as she was, a hard exshperienced woman. The day he got the divorce papers she sent him from Nevada he sat in his room. All day, just sat, looking out the window. You'd think he expected her to walk past. Well, she didden walk past. She coulden. She was in Nevada. Issen at right? Eh?"

"I suppose so."

"You bet it's right. And good ridushe to bad rubbish. Go, I told her. Go." She pointed toward the door with majestic dignity. "Go! And she went. She . . ." Her hand fell to her side. "You go too. I'm tired. You go home."

"I will in a minute. Have you heard from Birdie since she left?"

"No."

"Has Earl?"

"Has Earl? What has Earl?"

Meecham said patiently, "Did she write to Earl?"

"She coulden write her own name. Ignorant, understand? Ignorant. Whyn't you go home?"

"I'm going." He picked up his coat and the package of letters. He stripped the brown paper from the package. Inside, there were about fifty or sixty letters, arranged, as far as Meecham could tell, in order of date. They were addressed to Earl Loftus in writing that was large and hesitant, like a school child's. "*Tell her to reread them*" Loftus had said, and then he'd changed his mind: "*No, don't tell her anything.*"

One of the envelopes was blank and new, and heavier than the others. Meecham put it in his pocket. He felt a kind of helpless anger against Loftus for giving him the responsibility of delivering the money, and against Mrs. Loftus, fumbling around in her twilit world where money could buy only one thing, darkness.

The old lady had closed her eyes, and her head had sunk like a tortoise's into the worn fur collar of her coat.

"Mrs. Loftus, listen to me for a minute."

"Whyn't you go home?"

"These are your letters. I'm leaving them here on the table. I have some money for you too. I'll give it to the Garinos to take care of. The fact is that you were right about Earl. He is in trouble. You'll be hearing about it very soon anyway. If it will make it easier for you I'll tell you myself right now. . . . Mrs. Loftus? Hey, Mrs. Loftus!"

The old lady let out a delicate snore. Darkness had been bought.

Cursing under his breath, Meecham put on his coat, turned out the ceiling light and went into the hall. Mrs. Garino was just coming up the steps from her apartment in the basement. She looked pale and calm, like the sea after a storm. She was carrying a metal tray with a pot of coffee on it and a sandwich cut daintily into diamonds and garnished with a radish rose.

"She's asleep," Meecham said.

"I can wake her. She has to eat."

"She should be in a hospital."

"You know what that means, getting commitment papers for her as a habitual drunk. The booby hatch, that's what it means," she said bitterly. "Did you give her the money you brought?"

"No."

"How much is it?"

"Over seven hundred dollars."

"Where would Earl get that kind of money?"

"He sold his car," Meecham said. "And a few other things."

"But Earl knows his mother. It's not reasonable for him to sell his things and send her a lot of money in a lump sum like that. He knows what she'd do with it."

"He wanted her to take the money and leave town for a while, go on a little holiday."

"A holiday, where?"

"Hasn't she any relatives she can visit?"

"Oh, for heaven's sake, Mr. Meecham. I mean, if she was your relative would you invite her for a visit? Earl must be crazy. A *holiday*. He must be . . ."

"About this money," Meecham said. "I don't want to keep it. I hardly know Loftus, he isn't my client and I'm not taking any fee for this trip."

She was watching him suspiciously. "You must have had some reason for coming."

"Put it down to curiosity. Anyway I came, I accomplished nothing. . . ."

"You found her and brought her home. That's a lot and I'm grateful. *But* I know what you're going to say about the money and the answer is no. I won't keep it for her."

"It was just a passing thought," Meecham said dryly.

"Why should I keep it—and dole it out to her in dimes and quarters, have her come wheedling . . .? No. I won't. Take it back to Earl. Or send it to her a little at a time so at least she won't starve."

"Is her rent paid?"

"Up to the new year."

"I'll pay you for January then, and give you some extra to keep her in food."

"Earl pays her rent."

"He won't be paying it from now on."

"Why? What's happened?"

Meecham told her, while she stood resting the tray on the railing of the banister. She didn't express shock and incredulity as he expected her to and as the other people had who knew Loftus.

When he had finished she said, quietly, "Did you tell *her*?"

"I tried to. She went to sleep."

"It's just as well."

"She has to know sometime. It's probably written up in your own newspaper tonight."

"Maybe. I haven't looked at it yet." She sighed and turned away. "I'll tell her myself, tomorrow."

"She may take it hard."

"You think so, do you? Well, you're wrong. She's not human anymore. She's like one of those things you see at a carnival, pickled in a bottle. I don't know why I try to keep her alive." She looked down at the tray grimly. "I don't know why."

Meecham took a hundred dollars out of the envelope, and put it on the tray.

"I'll give you a receipt," Mrs. Garino said. "If you'll wait a minute."

"That won't be necessary."

"It's a funny way to do business."

"This isn't exactly business." It's not business, he thought, it's life; and it's not money that's involved, but human beings. The dainty sandwich with its radish rose couldn't have been bought for a thousand dollars.

15

THE FOLLOWING MORNING Meecham reached his office a little after ten o'clock. The secretary whose services he shared with the two senior partners in the firm was behind her typewriter, a thin, stringy-haired, vivacious girl with glasses.

She looked at him with highly exaggerated surprise. "My goodness, it's Mr. Meecham. I hardly recognized you, it's been so long."

"I'm a little too tired for banter this morning, Mrs. Christy."

"Wild night?"

"Pretty wild."

"At your age. Well. Here's the scoreboard. Mr. Cranston is howling mad because his wife bought an antique highboy, and Mr. Post just went home with a migraine because the Doretto case has been dismissed. And there's a girl waiting in your office, a blonde."

"Who's the girl?"

"A Miss Dwyer. She's been waiting nearly an hour. I gave her a copy of *Fortune* to read. She looked like the intellectual type."

"She's not."

He opened the opaque glass door of his office. It had his name on it, Eric J. Meecham, in firm black letters, and whenever he saw it he felt a little firmer himself, sharp and clear around the edges.

His office was small and overfurnished, but it had a wide window with a leather-covered seat as long as a couch, where you could sit and watch the street, five stories below, or the sky, a stone's throw away.

Alice was watching the street, her chin cupped in her hand. The morning sun had turned her hair to tinsel, and Meecham wondered whether she bleached it a little. The thought of the small deception pleased him. It seemed to him charming and feminine for a woman to improve on nature.

"Hello."

She jumped in surprise at the sound of his voice and made a motion to get up.

"No, don't move," Meecham said. "You look pretty."

"Do I?"

"I should hire you to come and sit there by the hour."

She gazed at him, unsmiling. "I wish you wouldn't say smooth things to me."

"Why not?"

"It puts me off, makes me feel that you're ordinary. Anyone can be smooth, it's just words."

"You're cross because I kept you waiting."

"I guess," she said. "A little."

He sat down beside her on the window seat. "You shouldn't be."

"I kept *listening* for you so hard, I—well, that's a bad sign, isn't it?"

"Very bad."

He took both her hands and held them against his chest. They looked down at the street together, remote and serene, like angels on a cloud.

Alice stirred finally. "Naturally it isn't going to work out."

"Naturally. What isn't?"

"You know. Even if you feel the same way as I do. Everything's against it. I don't like the town and the climate's terrible and I'm so far from home. And then you're not very young anymore and they say the older a man gets the less adjustable he is to marriage. Naturally it won't work out."

"Naturally."

"You don't have to keep repeating that word."

"I'm agreeing with you. You're such a sensible young woman, I have to. Of course, there are a few other points you didn't mention. You can't cook, for one thing. And you bleach your hair."

"How did you know? Anyway, just a little bit."

"Also my great-uncle James was a crackpot. I don't own a house. I haven't much money, and . . ."

"Oh, *Meecham*."

"Have I forgotten anything?"

"Oh, Meecham, I *love* you."

"At this point I think I might kiss you, if I didn't have one foot in the grave."

"I didn't say you had one foot in the grave. I said you weren't very young and adjustable and . . ."

"I accept the apology."

He took her in his arms and kissed her for a long time, feeling that he had never kissed a girl before, it was so strange and perfect.

She looked very solemn. "I will love you forever, Meecham."

"You'd better. . . . Are you happy?"

She shook her head.

"Well, for Christ's sake," he said helplessly. "Why not?"

"I'm just not, that's all. I feel awful."

"Well, for . . ."

"I can't help it. All that sweet stuff that's been written about love, and this is how *I* feel, just plain awful. I ache, and my insides are hollow as if I could eat forever, only nothing fills me up and the sight of food makes me sick. I'll probably starve to death. I'm too thin anyway."

"No, you're not. You're perfect."

"No. I don't have enough of a *figure*, you know?"

"I have a rough idea."

"I look terrible in a strapless evening gown. I tried one on in a store once. My collarbones project."

"I happen to be very fond of projecting collarbones," he said. "It's a regular complex."

"You know what I mean. I'd like to be perfect for you. I'd like myself to be perfect and things to be perfect."

"If you and things were perfect, you wouldn't look twice at me."

"Oh, I *would*," she said passionately. "I couldn't help it."

"The town isn't so bad. There are worse climates, and you could always go home for visits."

"I know."

"We can work things out. Things don't work themselves out."

She looked up at him, still pale and still solemn. "On top of everything else, you're nice, aren't you?"

"Sometimes I think so. Not often."

"The climate—people get used to it, don't they? And I bet it's pretty in the spring, isn't it?"

"Very pretty."

"With little green sprouts and buds coming out all over. I think I'll like that part of it very much."

"I think you will."

"Anyway, I don't feel quite so hollow anymore."

"That's good." He lifted her tinseled hair and kissed the soft nape of her neck. Standing there, with his mouth against her skin, he felt that he loved all women because he loved Alice.

"We've never even had a date together," she said. "Isn't that funny, Meecham?"

"Yes."

"We haven't had a chance to fall in love. How did it happen? How *could* it have happened?"

"If I knew I'd go out and tell the world."

The buzzer on his desk sounded, harsh and sudden, like an alarm clock disturbing a dreamer.

He reached over and turned on the switch. "Yes?"

"There's a Mrs. Hamilton on the phone," Mrs. Christy said. "Do you want to talk to her?"

"No, but I will."

"Okay, go ahead."

He turned off the switch and reached for the telephone. Alice put her hand on his arm to stop him. "Did she say—Mrs. *Hamilton*?"

"Yes."

"Tell her I'm not here. Tell her you haven't seen me or heard from me."

"All right, if that's what you want me to say." He picked up the phone. "Hello."

"Mr. Meecham, this is Mrs. Hamilton. How are you?"

"Fine. And you?"

"I'm fine too. Everything is." She sounded so falsely cheerful that he wondered if anything at all was fine. "We seem to have a bad connection, Mr. Meecham. Will you talk louder?"

"All right."

"The fact is, I'm a little concerned about something. I suppose it's absurd to worry about a sensible girl like Alice. But then it's sometimes the sensible ones who do and say silly things, isn't it?"

"Sometimes."

"Have you seen her this morning?"

"No, I haven't." He looked across the desk at Alice. She was sitting on the window seat again not watching the street, but watching him, her eyes wide and anxious. He smiled at her reassuringly but she didn't smile back. "What reason have you to worry, Mrs. Hamilton?"

"Perhaps I haven't any reason. I'm not sure. She's acting peculiarly."

"In what way?"

"It's hard to . . . well, I think she's avoiding me. This morning, for instance, she left the house, without breakfast, without saying a word to anyone. She disappeared, in fact."

"She's probably downtown shopping."

"Then why didn't she tell me where she was going? Surely that would have been the natural thing to do? I was right there, having breakfast with Virginia and Paul in the dining room, and Alice went past the door and that's the last I saw of her. It seems odd, doesn't it?"

"Everything seems odd until it's explained."

"Outside of the family, you're the only person she knows in town. I had the notion that she would come to you, if something was—if she had anything on her mind."

"What would be on her mind?"

"I haven't the slightest idea." It was a positive yet somehow unconvincing statement.

"She might come here. If she does, I'll let you know."

"Thank you. You realize that I'm very fond of Alice, she's a very dear girl." She paused. It was a significant pause, Meecham thought, and he waited for the *but*. It came. "But I didn't hire her to go running off like this."

She emphasized the word *hire* quite carefully, as if to put Alice in her place, through Meecham. Meecham resented her tone, but stronger than his resentment was his feeling that Mrs. Hamilton was a desperate woman fighting with her back to the wall against shadows that Meecham couldn't see and shapes he didn't recognize. He thought of Mrs. Loftus in her twilit world where everything was shadow, and shapes were molten and confused. The two women had nothing in common but despair. Yet it seemed that somewhere, at some point, their separate worlds had collided like wandering planets, and one had lost part of itself and the other had cracked through the middle.

"Mr. Meecham, are you still there?"

"Yes."

"You'll let me know for sure then, if Alice turns up?"

"I'll let you know. Good-bye."

"Good-bye, Mr. Meecham."

Meecham replaced the telephone on his desk, and looked at it thoughtfully, then moved it half an inch to the right. "You could have told her you were going shopping."

"I didn't want to face her."

"Why not?"

"I don't trust her anymore. She's changed."

"That's why you came here, to tell me she's changed?"

"No." Alice turned and looked down at the busy street. "A man came to see her last night. I saw him, and I think she knows I saw him."

"Who was it?"

"I don't know. But I'm sure she didn't want me to see him, that the meeting was to be a secret."

"How did you get in on it?"

"I heard a knock on the front door, not the chime, just a short knock, like a signal. I'd been in my room lying in bed, sort of thinking things over. When I heard the knock I got up to answer it because I—well, I thought it might be you. That's another bad sign, isn't it? Every time the phone rings or there's a knock on the door or footsteps on the sidewalk, every time a car stops I think it might be you."

"That's the worst yet," he said, smiling. "Go on."

"I put on my robe and slippers and went down the hall. I got as far as the corner where the hall bends and then I heard voices. I looked around the corner and saw Mrs. Hamilton standing at the door talking to a man, a stranger. I don't know why but I suddenly felt furtive. I wasn't spying or eavesdropping, I couldn't even hear what they were saying. But I had the feeling that the meeting was wrong somehow and the man shouldn't have been there at that time of night."

"What time?"

"Nearly eleven."

"Where was the rest of the household?"

"Carney sleeps out, and the cook was in her room. . . . She has a television set and hardly ever leaves it. And Virginia went with Paul to a movie. The celebration dinner had been kind of a flop. Virginia was terribly nervous so someone suggested a movie."

"Which someone?"

"I think Mrs. Hamilton mentioned it first. Virginia agreed that it was a good idea, and she invited me to go along. It was very—thoughtful of her, wasn't it?"

"Very. But I wonder what the thought was."

"You mean they were trying to get rid of me for the night, Virginia and Mrs. Hamilton?"

"I don't know. It's possible. It's also possible that Virginia invited you because she took a liking to you. She's unpredictable."

"She didn't take anything to me, like or dislike. She ignored me until the movie business came up, and then she tried to sound very cordial and friendly. I don't know, maybe she *was* being cordial and friendly. I can't tell. My judgments of people have gone haywire, so I can't trust my . . ."

"Don't get excited." He put his hand reassuringly on her shoulder. "You refused the invitation?"

"Yes. I said I was going to bed early, and I did. But I couldn't sleep. I kept thinking about you, and what you said about me going back home as soon as possible. I wasn't worried about them trying to get rid of me for the evening. I was worried about you trying to get rid of me forever."

"It seems I failed."

"Miserably."

"It's my nicest failure, to date," he said. "You may regret it, though."

"Meecham, I'm trying to tell you something, only everything seems to come around to *us*, just us." She frowned. "I should try to be impersonal, don't you think?"

"By all means. Be impersonal."

"I—don't look at me then."

"All right." He looked at the wall. "Go on."

"Well, they stood there in the hall talking. The man could have been anybody, a friend, or someone selling insurance or Christmas cards or something. If he had come in the daytime, I'd never have noticed him or thought twice about him. It was the secrecy that disturbed me—the lateness, the soft knock on the door instead of the chime, their low hurried voices. But I didn't try to hear what they were saying. I went back to bed. Then a few minutes later Mrs. Hamilton came down the hall very quietly. If I hadn't been listening for her, I don't think I'd have heard her. She didn't go to her own room directly. She stopped at my door. I could actually hear her breathing, very heavy labored breathing like someone whose air had been cut off, someone who'd been choked. Not that I—not that I really think she was *choked*. . . ."

"What do you think?"

"That she'd had a shock, a bad shock, and that she was checking up on me to make sure I hadn't seen or heard anything."

"You didn't hear anything, though."

"No."

"And all you saw was a stranger at the door. Was the hall light on?"

"One of them was."

"You must have had a fairly good view of him then."

"For a minute I did. He was a tall man, rather handsome, with light hair and a reddish face. He was about forty, I think, and he was wearing a bright green plaid topcoat. I never thought of it before, but he might have been a policeman."

"He might have been," Meecham said. But he knew he wasn't a policeman. He remembered the man and he remembered the green plaid coat hanging with the other coats on the hall rack, swinging in the wind from the open door. *This is my husband, Jim.*

Jim Hearst and Mrs. Hamilton. Another equation to be solved, he thought, and each new equation led to still another, and on and on into the infinity of the human mind. He felt stunted and inadequate, an engineer without a slide rule, a chemist without a formula.

"Of course he was a policeman," Alice said, sounding irrationally pleased, as if she too had discovered an equation and had solved it quite simply, by counting on her fingers. "I guess I was just depressed and dreamed up a lot of nonsense, didn't I?"

For a minute he couldn't answer. He was not sure how much to tell her, or even how much he himself knew.

"Didn't I, Meecham?"

"I suppose you did."

"Things seem so much worse at night, in the dark."

"They do when you're alone."

"I'll *never* be frightened with you, Meecham."

"No." He took her in his arms again. She was warm and soft in her innocence, eager in her new love that would endure forever, burn through the dark of night and the chill of winter. He wondered, with a detachment that was cruder to himself than it was to her, how long it would last.

He said, "You'd better have a story ready for Mrs. Hamilton."

"All right. What?"

"You went to get your hair done."

"But it isn't done."

"Get it done."

"All right," she said meekly. "Meecham, how did you know? About the bleach, I mean."

"I have little birds spying for me all over town."

"No. I mean it. How *did* you?"

"A blind guess, darling."

"I wouldn't like to think you knew too much about women," she said, frowning. "Other women, I mean. I don't care what you know about me. Naturally I'll try to act mysterious sometimes."

"When you do I promise to act mystified."

"Oh, Meecham. I feel—I feel just overcome with love. Do you think I'm making a mistake telling you that? Should I keep you guessing?"

"It's a little late for that," Meecham said. "Besides, I'm tired of guessing. I ought to buy a new slide rule or go back to counting on my fingers like you."

"What does that mean?"

"Nothing." He kissed her lightly on the temple. "Run along now and get your hair done."

"When will I see you? Couldn't we have lunch together, perhaps?"

"Not today. I have to go out to the hospital to see Loftus."

"Loftus again," she said, flatly.

"Loftus again."

"Why?"

"I have some money that belongs to him. I want to know what to do with it."

"Why should he give you money? Why should you still be *involved* with him like this?"

"There's no involvement." He knew there was, though. First a moral and mental involvement, and then gradually a physical one which had him trapped in a net of human ropes. Every way he turned he found new knots in the net. He couldn't fight or talk or buy his way out of it; each knot, tighter and more intricate than the preceding, must be loosened and picked apart—the old lady, the Garinos, Virginia and her mother, the dead Margolis, Emmy Hearst and the husband she despised, and Loftus himself, the first and the final knot, and the most difficult of all.

16

THE COUNTY HOSPITAL was a heterogeneous group of old and new buildings about three miles to the south of town. The so-called prison ward was not a ward but a two-story yellow brick house separated from the other buildings by some fifty yards and a steel fence. Originally the house had been the superintendent's quarters, but as additional hospital facilities became necessary, the superintendent moved out and the house was used as an isolation ward for victims of the more highly contagious diseases like diphtheria and typhoid. Immunization gradually decreased the number of these diseases to almost nothing, but no immunization had been found against crime, and the number of county prisoners had increased considerably. Some of them were physically sick and needed attention, and some were mentally sick and needed even more. This latter fact was recognized after a series of spirited board meetings, newspaper editorials and a petulant statement from the local congressman who was running for re-election.

The conversion from protecting society from diphtheria to protecting it from its own bastard, the criminal, was accomplished with simple economy. The curtains were removed from the windows and bars were substituted; the fence was constructed; nurses were replaced by orderlies, and what had been first the superintendent's parlor, and then the children's ward, was now furnished as a combination chart room, office and lounge for the orderlies.

A sign on the door said, RING AND WALK IN. Meecham rang and walked in.

The orderly on duty was sitting at a small desk in the corner reading a chart.

"Good morning, Gill," Meecham said.

Gill looked up from the chart, frowning. "How did you get past the gate?"

"The trusty's an old friend of mine."

"We have rules, Meecham, you know that."

"I'm not breaking anything."

Meecham had known Gill for a year or more. The orderly was a stocky young man whose principal interest was disease. He was the only employee of the hospital who could listen, with intense concern, to the complaints and symptoms of every patient under his care. He was, accordingly, very popular and much more useful than he himself realized. Migraines and stomach cramps, asthmatic attacks and cardiospasms, had been talked away into Gill's receptive ear, and many a fear had been drowned in his liquid brown eyes.

At his own request he had been transferred to the prison ward because he wanted to study the relationship between crime and disease. He was very conscientious about it; he kept a notebook in which he jotted down all kinds of medical lore and symptoms, and observations and remarks made by his charges. But so far he had reached no conclusion beyond the fact that the prisoners were on the whole quieter and made less fuss over their pains than the men in other wards.

"I just want to talk to him for a minute," Meecham said.

Gill fingered the stethoscope he wore around his neck. It was his own stethoscope, he'd bought it a week ago, and one of the interns was teaching him how to use it and interpret the meaning of its sounds correctly. He wore it with great pride and self-consciousness, like a diamond necklace.

"I told you over the phone, Meecham, no visitors. He's a very sick boy." To Gill all his patients, of any age, were boys, as if by becoming sick they had retrogressed into childhood. Meecham wondered if Gill knew how close to the truth this was.

"I'm not a visitor."

"He had to have a blood transfusion last night. They took a test when they brought him in yesterday morning and they found out his percentage of myleo—myeloblasts was very high."

"What's a myeloblast?"

Gill colored. "It's a bad sign, anyway, very bad. The transfusion perked him up, though. In fact, he got restless and couldn't settle down and go to sleep. He wanted to talk so I stayed with him."

"All night?"

"Sure. I didn't have anything else to do except sleep, and I never had a leukemia case before. The fact is, I think it's a coming disease, so I want to find out as much about it as I can. Then by the time I can afford to go to medical school I'll know a lot of stuff the other guys won't know, the real inside stuff."

"Like myeloblasts," Meecham said. "What did he want to talk about last night?"

"What most of the boys talk about. Himself and women."

"What women?"

"His mother, for one. It seems his mother is an alcoholic. I've often noticed that there's a history of alcoholism in most . . ."

"What other woman?"

"He called her Birdie. She was his wife, but he gave her a raw deal and she left him. Say, what do you want to know stuff like this for?"

"I'm interested. You're interested in Loftus' myeloblasts and I'm interested in his wife."

"Are you trying to find her or something?"

"Just out of curiosity, yes."

"You must be awfully curious, to want to go where she's gone."

"Where is she?"

"She's dead," Gill said. "She was killed in a car accident in Las Vegas about a year and a half ago."

"Killed?"

"Not outright. She died several days later in the hospital."

Meecham felt a little dizzy and off-balance, as if one of the knots in the net of ropes had been cut away under his hand and left him swinging in air.

Birdie was dead, had been dead for a long time. She hadn't just vanished for an instant around a corner, she had walked away into the shadows of some strange street.

"That's—too bad," he said finally.

"It sure is."

"He didn't tell me about it."

"People tell me a lot of things, I don't know why. But I never heard anyone talk as much as Loftus did last night. He must have been crazy about that woman. Birdie this, Birdie that, I damn near went to sleep a couple of times except the chair was so hard. The funny part of it is that he never mentioned what he was in here for until I asked him. And then I got the impression that the murder seemed to him a very trivial thing, like parking beside a red curb. I've had a couple of psychopaths in here and that was their attitude. But Loftus shows no signs of being a psychopath. Except for that one blank spot, the murder itself, he's a very moral and responsible man. Do you know his mother?"

"I've met her."

"From what I heard, she's quite a case, eh? You know, I've been sort of thinking things out this morning and I was wondering when I get enough money to go to medical school if I shouldn't concentrate on psychiatry. I haven't got any education, just what I picked up here and there, but you're an educated man, don't you think psychiatry's the coming thing?"

"We could all use a little."

"That's what I mean. When they get most of the physical diseases licked in a test tube, then I'll have my psychiatry, I won't be left flat on my rear."

"I'll be your first patient," Meecham said, "if you'll let me in to see Loftus."

"I can't, Meecham. The boy's sick. Honest-to-God sick, not like some of the fakers I get."

"I know that."

"Besides, he's sleeping. He had a sedative three hours ago."

"I'll wait." Meecham sat down on the edge of the desk and lit a cigarette. "If he's too sick to talk, all right, I promise not to ask him any questions. That's reasonable, isn't it? After all, the sight of me isn't going to scare him to death. I'll walk quietly in, and if he's asleep, I'll walk quietly out. Where is he?"

"In the bridal suite," Gill said. The phrase had lost any connotations of humor long ago; it was the standard term used to describe the building's only private room where the very ill or the post-operative patients were kept. "You go to a lot of trouble just for curiosity's sake, don't you?"

"Occasionally."

"Who are you working for?"

"Myself only."

"Well, come on. I'll see if he's awake."

"Thanks, Gill. Show up at my office around the middle of February and I'll help you with your income tax."

"Who are you kidding?" Gill reached into a drawer and took out a ring of keys. It wasn't as large as the ring Miss Jennings had at the county jail but there were more keys on it, of every size and shape. "You know, I get kind of sick of locking things up all the time. Lock the doors, lock the windows, lock the lavatory, lock up the thermometers, the rubbing alcohol, the dishes, even the spoons."

Meecham followed him to the door. "Why the spoons?"

"A couple of years ago a guy was in here who'd been beaten up in a family brawl. He tried to choke himself by swallowing some orange peelings and pushing them down his throat with a spoon. So, no spoons and no oranges."

He unlocked a door that led into a long narrow hall. In spite of the sun and air, paint and disinfectant, the odor of rotting wood clung to the old house. It trailed up and down the hall and up and down the hollowed steps like the restive ghost of the superintendent looking for a trace of himself.

There were four rooms on the lower floor. From three of them the doors had been removed and full-length gates had been substituted, made of the same material as the fencing around the grounds.

From inside one of the gates a man began to groan with sudden fervor.

Gill paused. "Oh, stop it, Billings," he said pleasantly. "Be a good boy."

The boy was an elderly Negro with a tobacco-stained beard and white hair that reached his shoulders. "Them prunes I had for breakfast, they's setting hard on my belly like billiard balls."

"Can that phony dialect. Last time you were here you were talking like a Yale man."

"I'se rumblin inside."

"I'll give you something in a little while."

"Listen. Come here and listen, white boy."

"I can't now, Billings. I'm busy."

"Listen. I'se full of sin. It's rumblin round my belly. Oh, sweet Jesus stop that rumblin, stop clackin them billiard balls in my insides."

"There aren't any billiard balls in your insides," Gill said. "It's gas."

"I'm only an old nigger full of sin, sweet Jesus, no one to turn to ceptin you. Now they's gonna cut off my hair, cut off my beard, they's gonna take away what's rightfully mine, saying I got lice. I never had a lice, Lord, all I got's the rumblin."

"Haven't you heard, Billings? Everybody's wearing their hair short these days, even the women."

"You'll be crawlin through the fires of hell, white boy, and I'll be ridin into heaven." The old Negro rolled over on his cot and, face to the wall, he resumed his low melodious groaning.

Gill turned away with a shrug and went on down the hall.

The fourth room had its original oak door, but a small rectangular peephole had been cut out at eye level. Gill looked in through the peephole before he unlocked the door.

The shades were drawn and the room was almost in darkness, so that only light-colored objects were visible at first, the bed, basin, a covered trash container, a white chair lying overturned in the corner, and above the chair Loftus' face. He had grown enormously during the night. His face reached nearly to the ceiling.

The old Negro was groaning to sweet Jesus and Gill was breathing like a tired horse, and there was a rattle of branches against the windowpane.

Gill crossed the room and pulled up the shade. Then he went to the corner and touched one of Loftus' dangling hands. Loftus began to swing very slowly back and forth as if a wind was rocking him.

"It's not my fault," Gill said. "If they want to die bad enough you can't stop them. It's not my fault. I gave him the sedatives and he promised he'd take them and go to sleep."

He'd kept one part of his promise, Meecham thought, but the two yellow capsules were still lying on the metal table beside the bed.

"White boy, you there, white boy? I'se been talkin to the Lord, white boy, and he says you're full of sin, says you oughtn't give a poor old nigger prunes for breakfast. You listenin, boy?"

"How could I have stopped him?" Gill said. "How *could* I? Maybe all night while he was talking, he was making plans, looking around trying to see what he could use."

The room had nothing in it that was sharp or pointed, nothing that could be broken to form a cutting edge; even the light bulbs were inaccessible. But Loftus, like other desperate men, found a way. He pried the wire handle off the trash container and attached it to a ventilation hole in the wall near the ceiling. To the handle he fastened a twisted strip torn off the gray hospital blanket from his bed. Standing on the chair he tied the other end of the strip around his neck. He stood there like that, perhaps a minute, perhaps an hour, before he shoved the chair away with his foot.

He had died quietly, without a fight. On the white wall behind him there were no marks of feet kicking in anguish or struggling to get a hold on the wall to ease the pressure around his neck. There were no scratches or fingernail marks on his throat. It was as if he had died by willing, before the twisted strip of blanket had time to cut off his air.

His face was not discolored, and though his mouth was slightly open, his tongue didn't protrude. He looked quite tranquil, as if the long night that he'd been dreading had turned out well and the dreams it held were pleasant. Its shadows were without terror, and its streets were the same strange streets that Birdie had walked along.

"I hears you, white boy, I hears you talkin and whisperin. You get down on your knees and ask the sweet Jesus to loose the devil in you standin in there whisperin and laughin bout a poor old nigger's insides."

Gill wheeled around suddenly and screamed toward the open door: "Shut up! Shut up, I tell you!"

"Whisperin and laughin . . ."

"Shut up, goddam it!"

"Cursin and yellin and whisperin . . ."

"I'll come in and brain you, goddam it!"

"Threatenin, threatenin a poor old man that's full of sins and lice and gonna have his hair cut off. Get down on your knees, white boy, and ask for the devil to loose you."

Gill stood with his fists pressed against his ribs, the color draining out of his knuckles. "All right, Billings," he said at last. "I got down and the devil loosed me."

"Sing Hallelujah."

"Hallelujah," Gill said, with the tears streaming down his face. "Hallelujah."

17

THE STREET WAS still five stories down, but the sky seemed closer than it had during the morning. Now at twilight it pressed against the window of Meecham's office, a shapeless changing mass, the color of bruised flesh.

Mrs. Christy was gone for the day, and the telephone was ringing. There was a typewritten note propped against the lamp on Meecham's desk and he read it before he reached for the phone.

"E.J.M: Following calls came in. 11:35 Cordwink. 12:10 Mrs. Hamilton, no message. 1:15 Mr. Geo. Loesser, will call back. 1:40 Checker Cab, motion for new trial denied. 3:10 Miss McDaniels can't find her copy of will. 3:15 Sweeney Dry Cleaners, rug shrinkage unavoidable and refuse to settle. 3:45 Mrs. Alistair re: trust deed. 4:05 Mr. Loesser, call him at 5-5988 before six. 4:33 Mr. Post won't be in tomorrow. L. E. Christy."

He picked up the phone. "Hello, Meecham speaking."

"This is George Loesser, Mr. Meecham. I may be wrong, but I think we met a year or so ago at a convention in Chicago." Loesser spoke in a thin nervous voice with a slight New England accent. "Does that ring a bell?"

"It could," Meecham said. He hadn't been to a convention for ten years. "Bring me up to date a little."

"Absolutely. Well, right now I'm with a Detroit firm, Lewenstein, Adler and Birch. The reason I'm in town is that I had to meet a client at the airport this morning and then I drove her over here. My client happens to be very interested in seeing you."

"As a lawyer?"

"Not at all," Loesser said sharply. "My firm handles all her affairs. This is quite a different matter, a personal one. She would like to talk to you because the Sheriff mentioned your name in connection with Virginia Barkeley. You were looking after Mrs. Barkeley's interests, weren't you?"

"For a time."

"My client is Lily Margolis."

"Oh."

"As you may know, she was in Lima visiting her sister at the time of Mr. Margolis' death."

"I knew that, yes."

"She returned as soon as she could. She's been with the Sheriff this morning and part of the afternoon. She hadn't anything much to tell him, of course. It was just a formality."

"If she's seen Cordwink, why does she want to see me?"

"Frankly, I don't know." Loesser sounded sincerely puzzled. "Curiosity, probably. Cordwink didn't tell her a great deal, and you know women, they like details, never get sick of details. That's understandable, of course, in Lily's case. She's never come up against anything like this before. She's led a very sheltered life, you might say, and this business has been a great shock to her emotionally, mainly because of the children. Naturally I've done my best to keep her and the children out of the papers."

"I knew someone had." Loesser had been successful too. No photograph or snapshot of either Lily Margolis or her children had appeared in any newspaper, and very few facts about her personal life had been mentioned. It was possible, though, that there were very few facts to mention, that Lily Margolis was one of those dull and virtuous women who had no interests outside of her children and the mechanical operations of her home. Meecham had met a great many such women, and sometimes their dullness, and often their virtue, was a surface covering, a thin sheet of ice over a running river, dangerous to cross.

"My own feeling about the matter," Loesser said, "is that it would be better to forget it. In fact, I'm phoning you now under protest. I didn't want to, and I don't think anything will be gained by mulling over the sordid details. But Lily wants it that way. If you come and talk to her you'll be reimbursed for your time, of course."

"You realize that the case is settled."

"Of course. Since the young man killed himself this morning . . ."

"How did you find that out?"

"Strangely enough, Lily was in the Sheriff's office when the message was phoned in. She couldn't help overhearing." Loesser coughed, but it was more of a nervous mannerism than a real cough. "I understand you were a friend of the young man?"

"I knew him."

"It's a sad affair all around, but especially for Lily and the two children. Fortunately, they're well provided for. One of the few sensible things Margolis did in his lifetime was to take out enough insurance."

"Double indemnity has healed a lot of broken hearts."

"It helps, and why not?" Loesser said defensively.

"Why not, indeed." Meecham looked at the clock on his desk: 5:10. "I'll be glad to see Mrs. Margolis. When?"

"How about tonight after dinner? Or right away, if you'd prefer."

"That would be better."

"I'm at Lily's house now. Do you know where Lancaster Drive is, near the golf course?"

"Yes."

"It's 1206, a white-and-green colonial house. You can't miss it. The kids have spent all afternoon building a couple of snowmen at the driveway entrance."

"I'll be there in twenty minutes."

The floodlight was on at the entrance gate, and the snow figures stood like sepulchers, one on each side. Loesser had made a mistake about them, though. They weren't snowmen. One of them was a lady, with a pink ruffled apron tied around her lumpy waist and a bandana covering her head to hide its baldness. One of her charcoal eyes had fallen out of its melting socket. She had a witch's nose made out of a carrot and a moist beet-mouth, and stuck in her chest was a long dripping icicle that gleamed in the light like a stiletto with a jeweled handle. The snow lady seemed to be aware of the wound: her blurred beet-mouth was anguished, and her single eye stared helplessly into the night.

Meecham pressed hard on the accelerator and the wheels of the car spun for a moment in the slush and then took hold. The driveway was on a steep grade and it hadn't been shoveled. Neither had the steps of the house, or the wide pillared veranda. There were sounds of dripping everywhere, as in a greenhouse.

Nearly every window was lighted and wide open, as if the rooms were being aired after a period of disease.

Loesser answered the door himself. In contrast to his thin nervous voice over the phone, he was a heavy-set moon-faced man in his forties, with a smile that flashed off and on with the precision of a traffic signal. He had courtroom manners and a way of talking to a person without looking at him, as if he was really aiming his words at an unseen and very critical jury.

"Good of you to come, Meecham." The two men shook hands. "Let me take your coat. The maid's upstairs with the kids."

He took Meecham's coat and hung it in a small closet that opened off the foyer. Meecham noticed that the closet was empty except for a pair of child's rubber boots.

"Lily hasn't had time to unpack or get organized," Loesser said. "I'm her cousin, by the way, in case you were wondering how I come in on all this."

"I wasn't wondering very hard."

"No? Well, I thought you might. The fact is"—he tugged at his tie—"the fact of the matter is that I've stood by Lily all during this unfortunate marriage of hers."

It was the sort of remark that demanded an answer of some kind: *Oh? How interesting. Is that a fact? Good for you, old boy. Stout fellow.* Meecham merely made an indeterminate noise.

"Well, Lily's waiting in the den," Loesser said. "It's the only room in the house that doesn't smell of moth crystals. The place has been closed up, you know."

The den wasn't what Meecham expected from its name, a book-and-pipe sanctuary for a man. It turned out to be a small room on the southeast corner of the house, equipped for activity, not rest. There was a sewing machine, a drawing board, a small hand-loom, a dressmaker's dummy, and a long unpainted wooden table filled with children's toys. The pine walls were covered with children's art, sketches and watercolors and fingerpaintings, some of them hanging from the molding in frames, and some of them fastened loosely to the wall with thumbtacks. The pictures were all signed, most of them right across the middle, Ann M. or Georgie.

Activity had given the room an air of pleasant untidiness. But there was nothing untidy about Lily Margolis. She was a slim muscular young woman in a tweed suit with flecks of blue in it that exactly matched the color of her eyes. Her brown hair was clipped short in rows of curls, and the curls were so uniform that it seemed as though she had weighed and measured each of them before letting herself be seen in public. Her face was deeply sunburned, so that her eyes looked very bright and clear in contrast, and her teeth very white. Her features were plain, but the carefully chosen tweed suit, and the carefully acquired sunburn, gave her quite a striking appearance.

She repeated the words Loesser had used, but her New England accent was stronger than his, as if she had retained it deliberately to show her contempt for the Middle West.

"It was very good of you to come, Mr. Meecham. Please sit down, won't you? And George, would you mind awfully bringing us a drink?"

Loesser got up obediently, but he looked slightly pained and he turned at the doorway to give Mrs. Margolis a don't-say-anything-interesting-while-I'm-gone glance.

Lily Margolis returned to the wooden bench by the drawing board where she'd been sitting before she rose to greet Meecham. She sat, stiff and erect, her feet planted squarely on the floor, her large competent-looking hands crossed on her knees. "You see, Mr. Meecham, I don't know quite what happened, or why. Everything is fuzzy and confused. It's like trying to understand someone else's nightmare."

Someone else's, Meecham noted, not her own. The statement fitted in with his previous conception of her; she seemed to have the occupational schizophrenia of the perfect secretary, a self-effacing manner combined with a positive knowledge of her own superiority. *Yes, boss* on the one hand, and *silly boy* on the other. Perhaps not exactly the perfect wife.

She leaned forward slightly toward Meecham, but without bending her back. "I had taken the children down to Lima to spend Christmas with my sister—her husband is a mining engineer. I was only there two weeks when the message came that Claude had had an accident. Rather delicate wording, don't you think, for what really happened."

"You're weathering the shock very well," Meecham said.

"When you've had as many shocks as I've had in eight years, one more hardly matters. I'm a little punchy by this time, like an old fighter." She smiled, without bitterness, without feeling of any kind. "I've had so much uncertainty. Now at least things are settled. I don't have to wonder where Claude is or what he's doing. I don't have to try and decide whether to divorce him for the sake of the children, or not to divorce him for the sake of the children. Fate stepped in and like a referee stopped the fight. I'm not sorry and I won't pretend that I'm sorry. Claude was a terrible fool. Only a terrible fool would . . ."

She stopped but the idea was clear: only a terrible fool would get murdered. And, in a sense, Meecham agreed; the victim, like the murderer, had a certain choice of fate, a selection of circumstances.

Loesser returned with a pitcher of martinis. He poured a drink for Meecham and one for himself.

"You'll excuse me, Mr. Meecham," Lily Margolis said. "I don't drink."

"It makes her sick," Loesser explained. "Well, here's how."

"It doesn't make me sick in the least, George. I wish you wouldn't keep telling that to everyone."

"Well, it does make you sick. I've . . ."

"George *dear*, what will Mr. Meecham think of us, indulging in a silly family squabble like this?"

Loesser gazed with a stony little smile at the wall behind her head: *Ladies and gentlemen of the jury, I submit to you that the witness is lying, that the effect of alcohol on her system is highly deleterious, and, in fact, it makes her sick.*

Meecham shifted restlessly in his chair. There was a bowl of russet apples on the table in front of him and the sight and smell of them started a hungry gnawing in his stomach. He felt like a man who had come to a banquet as guest speaker and then found himself lost in the shuffle of preliminaries and introductions while the food got cold. So far Mrs. Margolis hadn't asked a single question about her husband's death, and Meecham was almost certain now that she didn't intend to, that he had been invited to the house not to talk but to listen.

"George, there's no point in your staying here," Mrs. Margolis said suddenly. "You have a long drive ahead of you and you know how Marion hates anyone to be late for dinner."

Loesser cleared his throat. "It's my duty to stay. This is a family matter."

"Are you afraid I'll say the wrong thing?"

"Well, no. Not really."

Mrs. Margolis laughed and said to Meecham, "He is. He's afraid I'll make a slanderous remark about Virginia. I will, too."

"Now, Lily," Loesser protested. "Now I suggest that you let bygones be bygones."

She ignored him. "Virginia is your client, I understand, Mr. Meecham?"

"She was."

"Did she mention me?"

"She said she had met you."

"*Met* me? That's a laugh. Yes, indeed, she met me. We had quite a charming brawl before I left for Lima."

Loesser looked extremely uncomfortable. "I wouldn't say it was a brawl exactly."

"It was a brawl. She called me a liar and tried to slap me and pull my hair, and I held her wrists so she couldn't. I'm quite strong."

"Tennis," Loesser explained. "Plenty of . . ."

"George. I wish you'd go home."

"I know you do," he said grimly. "But I'm not going. You're tired and emotional and you may stick your neck out without meaning to."

"It's my neck."

"It was Claude's too."

Her face looked a little sick under its healthy sunburn. "What a—a terrible thing to say."

"Well, I'm sorry. I'm sorry, but damn it, Lily, you won't pay any attention unless I . . . Anyway, I'd forgotten that's where he was . . ."

Meecham interrupted. "We're not getting anywhere."

"We would, if George would go home."

"I'm not going home," Loesser stated.

"Well, then keep quiet." A pulse in Mrs. Margolis' temple had begun to beat hard, moving rhythmically under her skin. "I didn't intend to quarrel with Virginia. I went to her house out of a sense of duty. I knew she was going out with Claude because my maid Rose saw them together at one of those juke-box places outside of town. Rose goes to Dr. Barkeley for allergy shots and she recognized Virginia right away. So I—went to see her." She fidgeted with her plain gold wedding ring, slipping it over the joint of her finger and back again. "I told her the truth, that she was wasting her time on Claude because he was keeping another woman, had been keeping her for years, perhaps before we were ever married. Years and years," she repeated. "The silly girls like Virginia were just cover-ups. He took them dancing or out to dinner. But he was never seen with *her.* She was his—his real love."

Her control was slipping down like a zipper under too much pressure.

"His real love. Isn't that funny? That a man like Claude could actually love one woman all those years? I used to lie awake and wonder, what did she look like, what did she have that I didn't have, what did they talk about . . ."

"Now, now, Lily," Loesser said. "You have no proof at all that Claude knew this woman for a long time or even that he was keeping her. You've always had a wild imagination where Claude is concerned. It's possible that the two of them were merely good friends."

Mrs. Margolis' mouth curved in an ugly little smile. "Old school chums. That's a brilliant idea, George."

"Well, damn it, my own impression of Miss Falconer is that she's a highly respectable woman."

"You've met her?" Meecham said.

"Yes, in a way. It happened accidentally about two months ago. I went into Hudson's at lunch time to pick up a book for my wife. I saw Claude standing at the glove counter and went over to say hello, thinking that perhaps we might have lunch together and I'd have a chance to talk to him about Lily. He didn't come into town often and when he did he avoided me. He knew what I thought of his behavior, especially this latest business involving Virginia Barkeley."

Mrs. Margolis was leaning toward him with a rapt expression on her face like a small girl who had never tired of hearing the same story and wanted it repeated, word for word.

"I didn't realize, of course, that Claude had anyone with him until it was too late for me to retire gracefully. He introduced the woman to me as Miss Falconer. She was a tall, rather common-looking woman about Claude's own age. I knew Lily had been thinking for some time that Claude had a steady mistress, but I couldn't believe it was this Miss Falconer. She wasn't the type and, besides, Claude didn't act embarrassed or anything."

Mrs. Margolis made a sound of contempt. "Claude wouldn't have been embarrassed if he'd been caught making love to her on the steps of the city hall. You can't embarrass a moral imbecile."

"At least give him credit for some sensibility. As I said before, I had the impression that he and the woman were old friends. They were very much at ease with each other and . . ."

"So are lovers."

"Yes, but Miss Falconer doesn't suit the role very well. She's not young or attractive. She's a good ten years older than you are, Lily, and not nearly so pretty."

"Thank you," she said heavily. "Thank you very much, George."

"Well, I mean it. She's just an ordinary woman."

"Ordinary. That's all you ever say about her. How can you tell whether she's ordinary or not? And it isn't what she *is* that's important—it's how she made Claude feel. That's what falling in love must be, meeting someone who makes you feel good, who fills a need for you." She looked down at her own shadow on the floor. "I never found out what Claude's need was."

Loesser went over and patted her shoulder. "It wasn't your fault. He may have had some sort of glandular imbalance."

"Glandular imbalance." She began to laugh. "That's marvelous. Glandular imbalance."

"I must say I don't see anything particularly funny about it." He turned his back on her and addressed Meecham: "Well, that's the story. I told Lily about meeting Miss Falconer and Lily immediately drew her own conclusions as women always do, and decided to leave town for a while. Before she left she went to see Virginia Barkeley. You know the result of that."

Meecham nodded. "Yes."

"I'm not sure you do," Mrs. Margolis said.

"There was a brawl, you claimed."

"That was one result. The other result was that Claude was killed."

"Meaning?"

"Meaning I haven't been taken in by the confession of an unbalanced man with a guilt complex. I know who killed my husband, and George knows it and . . ."

"Leave me out of this," Loesser said.

"They had Virginia in jail, right where she belongs. Why didn't they keep her there?"

"They couldn't," Loesser explained with weary patience. "She was held for questioning as long as they could hold her, for forty-eight hours. After that they had to charge her or let her go. Naturally they let her go because Loftus proved that he committed the murder."

"Proved, George? Proved?" She chewed the word as if it was a stick of sharply flavored gum. "A lot of things can be proved that aren't true, and a lot of things that are true can't be proved. I can't prove that my husband kept a woman called Miss Falconer for years, but I know he did, the same as I know that Loftus was lying. Why did he lie? Because he was insane? Or for money? Or both? You knew him, Mr. Meecham, George told me you knew him. Why did he lie?"

Meecham looked at the bowl of apples on the table. "There's no evidence that he was paid, or insane or lying."

"No evidence but common sense. Tell me, Mr. Meecham, weren't you surprised when Loftus came forward with his story?"

"I wasn't expecting it," Meecham said. He remained uncertain of the degree of his surprise, though he remembered the scene vividly, Loftus half-hidden behind the hedge, his hair whitened by the falling snow. "*I've died a thousand times from fear*," he had said. "*A thousand deaths and one would have been enough. A great irony.*" The words turned over in Meecham's mind like stones in a river.

"Someone was expecting it, someone wasn't surprised," Mrs. Margolis said. "Why should she be? She paid him for it. She bought that confession the way you go into a butcher shop and buy a pound of baloney. And that's what she got, baloney! She bought that con—"

"For God's sake, be quiet, Lily." Loesser was beginning to sweat. "You don't realize the seriousness of what you're . . ."

"I will not be quiet. I have a right to my opinion."

"Keep it an *opinion*, then."

"Very well. In my *opinion*, Virginia Barkeley killed my husband in a jealous rage. It's a common motive, and for a woman like her, I suppose, a strong one. She has an uncontrollable temper, everyone knows that."

"Allegedly," Loesser said.

"All right, *allegedly*!" she shouted. "She was *allegedly* angry and jealous and she reacted against Claude the way she reacted against me the day I told her about Claude and Miss Falconer. She attacked him as she attacked me. According to my *opinion*! Damn you, George. *Damn* you. I *won't* keep modifying everything, qualifying everything."

"You're on safe ground as long as you're damning me," Loesser said. "So go ahead."

But Mrs. Margolis had turned to Meecham again. There was a glassy glare in her eyes, as if she was burning up with a fever of rage and resentment that had been slowly, for years and years, infecting her system. "She was there in the room, wasn't she? Do you think she could have slept through a murder? How quiet is a murder? Do you think Claude wouldn't have fought back if a stranger came at him with a knife?"

"There was no evidence of a struggle," Meecham said.

"That's what I'm talking about. There was no evidence of a struggle because there was no struggle. Claude was taken unawares. Not by a stranger like Loftus. By someone he trusted, someone he thought was just fooling with the knife. Claude was a big man. He could have torn Loftus apart. Can you expect me to believe that he just stood there and let himself be killed?"

"The attack was quick," Meecham said, "and your husband had been drinking quite heavily. So had Virginia. In fact, her blood alcohol concentration was so high it's doubtful that she had sufficient strength and co-ordination to use the knife."

Mrs. Margolis swallowed hard, her hand against her throat. "I have no proof, nothing. But I feel in my heart that she killed him. I don't know how, but she's responsible."

"In your opinion," Loesser said.

"In—in my opinion." She rubbed the throbbing pulse in her temple.

"You're tired out, Lily. Why don't you have a nice hot supper with the children and then go to bed?" He added, to Meecham, "She was up all night on the plane—ran into a storm in the South."

"I understand."

"Naturally, she doesn't see things in their proper perspective. I myself am convinced that Loftus gave a perfectly straightforward account of the affair and then killed himself in remorse. Don't you think so, Meecham?"

"It seems reasonable," Meecham said, though he didn't agree with either Loesser's oversimplified version or Mrs. Margolis' personal and over-imaginative one. The truth lay somewhere between the two extremes like an uncharted island between two shores.

Meecham hoped that someday it would be found, by star and compass, or by blind luck. "Did you tell the Sheriff about your suspicions, Mrs. Margolis?"

"I intended to. George wouldn't let me. He said it would cause trouble."

Loesser flushed. "Confound it, Lily, what I meant was that you'd do yourself and the children a lot more harm than Virginia—more publicity, more scandal. You've got to consider not just your own feelings but the children. They're the real unfortunates in this rotten business."

"I've been a little unfortunate myself," she said dryly. "So was Claude."

And a great many others, Meecham added in silence. Little ones and big ones: Gill who might lose his job, Miss Falconer who had lost a lover, and Loftus who had lost everything. The Garinos, Dr. Barkeley, Mrs. Hearst, cold and bitter in her grief, Loftus' mother buying darkness by the quart, and Virginia herself watching the trains go past.

Then he thought of the snow-lady he'd seen at the entrance gate with the icicle in her heart, and he wondered if Loesser wasn't right, after all—that the children were the real unfortunates. They would carry their scars longer, and with bewilderment, and in inaccessible places.

Loesser accompanied him to the front door. He seemed more at ease now that the interview was over and all statements had been properly qualified as opinions and allegations. "I hope you haven't taken Lily too seriously, Meecham."

"No."

"The tragedy's knocked her off-balance, but she'll right herself. You know how most women are, their emotions are direct and clear like Scotch. There's no hangover. In a few months she'll have forgotten about Virginia and Miss Falconer and all the rest of them."

"I don't suppose you ever looked up this Miss Falconer."

"No, but I tried to find out where she lived just out of curiosity. There was no Miss Falconer—or Faulkner—listed in the 1951 or '50 Arbana directories. The '48 directory listed a Jemima Falconer as a secretary and gave a Catherine Avenue address, I believe. It may or may not have been the same woman, and besides, a lot can happen in four years."

"What about the Detroit vicinity?"

"I found several listings under both spellings, which was as good as a dead end for me. I hadn't the time or inclination to try and track down the woman, especially since the only evidence I had of her connection with Claude was that chance meeting in Hudson's, and Lily's intuition. You've no doubt had some experience with female intuition, in court and out of it. It's almost as fallible as tea leaves or head bumps."

He took Meecham's coat and hat out of the hall closet.

"I repeat, it was nice of you to come out and talk to Lily. I think now that she's gotten a few things off her chest she'll be better."

"Probably."

"Send your bill to me. Please don't be hesitant about it. That was our arrangement over the phone."

"Let's leave it on the cuff," Meecham said. "I might want a favor from you some day."

"Any time. My office is in the First National Building and my house is in Grosse Point."

"I'll remember that."

They parted with a very hearty handshake like a pair of old alumni after a homecoming.

Meecham crossed the wet driveway and got into his car. He drove in low gear down the steep grade to the entrance gate.

During the hour that he'd been in the house the snow-lady had been melting in the soft air like butter in the sun. The icicle was still sticking through her heart, though her nose and her remaining eye had fallen out and the scarf clung moistly to her shrinking head. By morning, if the weather held, she would topple into an indistinguishable mass of gray slush, and no one would remember her existence except two children.

18

GURTON'S CAFÉ WAS on State Street at Main, between a haberdashery and a department store. Gurton had been installed there for thirty years, the chef for nearly twenty, and for five Meecham had been eating his dinners there several times a week. He knew the menus, the waiters, Gurton's children and their children, and every picture on the wall. When the place closed for repainting once a year, Meecham missed it. It was the closest thing to a home, a social continuity, that he had ever had in his solitary life.

Gurton came to the door to meet him, smelling heavily of the cloves he was always chewing. "How've you been, Meech?"

"Fine."

"Somebody's got your table."

"That's all right. I'll sit someplace else."

"I thought you weren't coming. I figured you were out of town. You haven't been around."

"I've been working."

Gurton was an enormous man. He ate too much, and drank too much beer in his off-hours, and the only exercise he ever got was shuffling to the front door to greet his friends and counting his money at night after the place was closed. He enjoyed counting his money and he always took the day's receipts home with him. To protect himself he carried a Colt automatic. He knew, theoretically, how to use it, but he was actually more terrified of the automatic than he was of any robber. Gurton was convinced that someday, in spite of the safety catch, it would go off accidentally and cripple him, or explode in his pocket and blow him to pieces. Like a man putting all his eggs in one basket, Gurton had loaded all his worries and fears into the automatic.

"You got your name in tonight's paper," he said.

"Did I?"

"I rang up all my kids and said, Meech has his name in the paper. You want to see it?"

"No."

"You aren't human." Gurton shook his head and his jowls flapped like a turkey's wattles. "I knew this guy Loftus that you found dead. Not by name, but once I saw his picture I recognized him. He used to come in here about two, three years ago, with his girlfriend, a tall bright-looking redhead. They used to sit and drink coffee, never saw a pair that could drink so much coffee. After a while they stopped coming in and I thought they must have broken up or got married."

"They got married," Meecham said, "and moved to another town."

"Is that a fact? It didn't mention that in the paper."

"They were divorced after a short time and the woman was killed in an auto accident out West."

"That's too bad. I always feel sorry when people get divorced or don't get married at all, which is even worse."

Meecham knew what was coming and tried to avoid it by picking up the menu.

It came anyway. "It's no good for a man, always being alone. You ought to get married, Meech, start having a few kids to put a little zip in your life and to give you something to leave behind you. Take this guy, Loftus, what did he leave behind him, eh?"

"Seven hundred and sixteen dollars."

Gurton looked disappointed. He hadn't expected or wanted an answer. "Now how come you know that?"

"You're getting nosy, Gurton."

"I've always been nosy."

"It's bad for business." Meecham put the menu back in its metal holder. "I'll take the veal cutlets. Mind if I use the phone in your office?"

"Go ahead. The cutlets are no good, it's the wrong time of year for veal."

"It doesn't matter."

"That reminds me, you know what the priest said to the butcher at confession? He said, you're cutting up too much."

"That's a howl."

"*I* consider it funny," Gurton said with dignity. "Thank God I don't work so hard that I have no sense of humor left, like some people."

Gurton's office was a small room on the mezzanine. In contrast to the meticulously neat kitchen downstairs, the office was littered with papers and letters, magazines, canceled checks, watch folders and half-empty packs of cigarettes.

Meecham closed the door and sat down in the swivel chair behind the desk. It took him five minutes to find the telephone directory, which had fallen into the wastebasket. Hearst was listed as Jameson R. Hearst, 611 Division Street. He dialed 2-6306.

Emmy Hearst answered the phone. She sounded as if she'd been crying again and he knew she must have found out about Loftus by this time.

"Hello."

"Hello. Mrs. Hearst?"

"Yes." There was a hum of activity in the background, voices and music and bursts of laughter. It was seven o'clock; Mrs. Hearst's "boys" would all be home. Meecham recalled the first night he'd gone to see Loftus' room; how incongruous it had seemed to him that Loftus should live in a house so full of youth and vitality.

"This is Eric Meecham. Is Mr. Hearst in? I'd like to talk to him."

"What about? Jim doesn't know anything."

"It's a trivial matter," Meecham said, hoping that it was. "I don't want to bother you about it, you've had a bad time."

"I wish I were dead," she said in a low flat voice. "I wish I were dead."

"Words aren't much good, I know, but I'd like to assure you that he didn't suffer. I saw him afterwards."

"He didn't leave any note, any message?"

"No."

"It said in the paper that he talked to the guard all night."

"To the orderly, yes."

"Did he talk about—me?"

"I guess he talked about everything." He couldn't give her the bald truth, that Loftus had talked only about Birdie. Mrs. Hearst didn't even know of Birdie's existence. The first night when she discussed Loftus with Cordwink she'd said, *Earl tells me everything and he's never mentioned a wife.* It would be a cruel blow to her when she found out about Birdie. Meecham knew that eventually she must find out. He said, "I know it's hard to be realistic in a situation like this, Mrs. Hearst. But the fact is, Earl had very little time left anyway. He would have died soon."

"I can't—talk about it anymore. I—I—I'll call Jim."

There was a long pause, then the sudden sharp slamming of two doors and the background noises ceased.

"Yes?" Hearst said. "Who's this?"

"Eric Meecham."

"The lawyer?"

"Yes."

"I don't get it. I expected to hear directly from her."

Meecham made a little sound of surprise, then covered it with a cough. "She couldn't manage it—too many people around."

"She's got no business calling a lawyer in on a thing like this. I don't like it." There was a moment's silence. "Is the agreement ready?"

"She's still thinking it over." He wasn't sure yet who the "she" was—Virginia or Mrs. Hamilton—and he had no idea what agreement she was supposed to have made. He made a blind guess: "Your asking price is a little high."

"I never mentioned money," Hearst said. "I'm an honest man. If she said I mentioned money she's a liar. I wouldn't take a red cent from her. Just try me. Offer me money and I wouldn't take it, see?"

"What exactly do you want?"

"I told her what I want."

"She didn't make it clear to me. She was quite upset."

"I want a chance. A future. There's no future in a town like this for a man like me. I can do things once I get a chance."

"So?"

"Well, supposing she buys a new car and needs somebody to drive it back to California for her."

"You'll drive it back."

"Sure, that's right. And then when we get there, she's got a lot of connections, she could fix me up with a job, maybe around a movie studio, maybe as her regular chauffeur."

"That sounds reasonable."

"Sure, it's reasonable, Mr. Meecham." He sounded almost pathetically eager. "She's got nothing to be upset about. All I'm asking is a favor in return for the favor I'm doing her."

"She didn't tell me what your favor was."

Hearst hesitated, like a small boy playing cards, wanting to win the game on his own but tempted to show everyone what a good hand he had. "It's a personal family matter," he said.

"I see." Meecham was sure now that the "she" was Mrs. Hamilton, and the "family" was Virginia, and the only connecting link between them and Hearst was through Loftus. But he didn't know what this link was. Loftus had not been friendly with Hearst, he wouldn't have confided in him; in fact, he had never even confided in Mrs. Hearst with any degree of truth.

"What I want," Hearst said, "is an agreement."

"What kind of agreement?"

"One that's written down and legal, like a contract."

"You'll have to specify the exact terms. I can't draw up a contract without . . ."

"Sure, sure, I know that."

"We'd better have a talk about it sometime," Meecham said, deliberately evasive.

"*Some* time. Say, what do you think this . . .?"

"How about the day after tomorrow at four, or early next week?"

"Stop trying to stall me. It's now or never, as far as I'm concerned. I want that agreement."

"All right." Hearst had reacted as he expected. "I'll pick you up and we'll go over to my office. Say in about half an hour?"

"I'll be ready."

"Good."

Meecham hung up, replaced the telephone directory exactly where he'd found it, in the wastebasket, and went downstairs to his table. His dinner was waiting for him, not the veal cutlets he had ordered, but a platter of fried chicken over which Gurton was hovering and clucking like a fat old hen.

"Gurton."

"Now listen, Meech, the cutlets were no damn good, understand? Not fit for my mother-in-law. Not fit for a . . ."

"Are you still carrying that Colt automatic?"

"I have to."

"How about lending it to me for a while tonight?"

"What for?"

"I'm going calling on a few friends."

"You with a gun, Meech? That don't make sense. No sir, I wouldn't lend you my gun no more than I'd serve you those cutlets. Suppose it goes off and hits you in the leg and then you have your leg amputated? How about *that*? Anyway, what kind of friends are these, that you've got to carry a gun?"

"That's what I'm going to find out."

"You're mixed in with funny people, eh?"

"Some of them are funny. Some of them are quite serious."

"Bejesus, Meech, I think you're kidding me. You don't want my gun."

"Maybe I don't."

"Guns are for crooks and crazy people and suckers like me who have to carry money around on a dark night. Now here's a funny thing—nobody's my friend in the dark. I see a guy coming up the alley on my way home, and I know him and he knows me, but he's not my friend, understand? I always want to turn around and run. That's what darkness does to people."

"Or money does."

"Well, anyway, I'm glad you were kidding. For a minute there I took you honest-to-God-serious."

"Yes, so did I," Meecham said.

All during dinner he wondered what kind of crazy impulse had made him ask Gurton for the automatic.

I'm nervous, he thought, like Gurton carrying his money in the dark. I have no friends. I know them and they know me, but I want to turn around and run.

19

THE NIGHT WAS turning cold, and an eager new wind raced up and down the streets. Under the lights the sidewalks and the limbs of trees shone icy.

Meecham moved stiffly toward the house with his briefcase in his hand. During the past hour when the weather had changed, some of Mrs. Hearst's boys had made a slide of ice, three or four yards long, from the sidewalk to the porch steps. Meecham would have liked to try the slide, but the briefcase felt heavy and he felt heavy. He thought, if this was another house and if Alice was with me, we might try the slide together.

On the porch, underneath the parlor window, there was a stepladder lying on its side, and a basket of pine branches and a spiral of copper wire, as if someone had started to decorate the house for Christmas and then lost interest. The parlor blinds were up, and the crystal chandelier hanging from the center of the ceiling blazed with light. A group of young men and girls were sitting around a table playing cards.

Meecham went up the steps and pressed the doorbell. The porch light went on instantly above his head like a spotlight. It stayed on for a few seconds and then it went off again, and the door was opened by Emmy Hearst. Her eyes were still puffed, but she'd put on some make-up and a black close-fitting dress that looked new and emphasized her slimness.

"Come in."

"Thanks."

"We'll have to talk in the kitchen. One of the boys is entertaining."

She closed the door behind him and led the way down the hall. Following her, Meecham had the same impression of youth and energy that he'd had the first time he saw her standing at the sink humming to herself. It had been a shock then, as it was now, when she turned around and her face showed the bitter years.

"He isn't here," she said abruptly. "He had to go downtown. He asked me to tell you to wait."

"For how long?"

"He didn't say."

"I had an idea that he wanted to see me as soon as possible."

She crossed her arms as if holding herself together in readiness for a blow. "What about?"

"You'd better ask him."

"I did. He wouldn't tell me. But it's bad, isn't it?"

"I can't very well discuss . . ."

"How bad?"

"I don't know," he said truthfully.

"It's about this murder? Isn't it?"

"I think so."

She sat down on the couch and began to pick bits of wool off the blanket that covered it. The floor was littered with fuzz, as if she had already spent hours sitting there picking at the blanket like an industrious bird gathering material for its nest. She spoke listlessly, without raising her head: "After you phoned him, he phoned someone else."

"Who was it?"

"I heard him dialing but I couldn't hear his words. Afterwards he came and told me he was going downtown for a package of cigarettes."

"And I'm to wait here until he comes back?"

She turned the blanket over and began on the other side. "I don't think he's coming back."

"Why?"

"When he walked out the door I had a feeling that I wasn't going to see him again."

A trickle of sweat ran down the side of Meecham's face leaving a cold moist track like a slug's track. He said carefully, "I think I'd better try to find him."

"Don't. Let him go."

"He has some information. I want it."

"Information," she repeated. "He's taken you in. What information could he have? He was here, right in this house, when Margolis was killed. He was sleeping."

"How can you be sure?"

"I saw him. That was the night I cut my arm. See, it's still bandaged."

She started to push up her left sleeve but Meecham stopped her. "Yes, I remember the bandage."

"Well, that was the night it happened—Saturday. I had gotten up to take a sleeping pill. One of the boys broke the porcelain tap in the basin a week or so ago, and I fell against it in the dark and cut myself. I went into Jim's room to see if he'd help me bandage it. But he was sleeping and I didn't want to wake him up. That was about 12:30." She leaned forward, looking at him anxiously. "You don't understand about Jim. He's like a kid. He's never had much excitement, and when this—this business happened, we weren't mixed up in it at all, but Jim—it went to his head. He'd say anything to be in on things, to be part of the excitement."

"Someone might take him seriously."

"No one who knows him."

"There are a lot of people who don't know him," Meecham said. *Including me*, he thought. *I take him seriously*. "I'll wait for another fifteen minutes. If he doesn't show up I'll start looking for him."

"I don't care." She shook her head. "We're through anyway. I'm going away. The car's mine, I paid for it myself. I'm going to get in it and drive, just drive away somewhere, I don't care where I end up."

They were Virginia's words, but she spoke them with more decision and assurance than Virginia had. Virginia might dream of leaving, pack her vague plans between layers of folded hopes; but Emmy Hearst would leave, get into her car and drive away without a backward glance. She was a forceful woman, and Meecham thought what a comic tragedy it was that such a woman would always choose emotionally stunted men like Hearst, or physically stunted ones like Loftus.

"I'll stay with my sister in Chelsea for a while, and then, after that, I don't know. Everything's so vague and useless. When Earl was alive, no matter how bad things were, I always had a reason for living." She leaned over suddenly, and with nervous fingers gathered up all the fuzz on the floor and squeezed it into a ball. "I loved Earl. He was the only person I've ever loved in my whole life. He was—perfect."

"No," Meecham said. "He wasn't."

"To me he was." She went to the sink and threw the ball of fuzz into the garbage strainer, as if deliberately walking away from the argument. The supper dishes were still on the drainboard, two glasses, two plates, two of everything. Jim's and Emmy's, Meecham thought ironically. His and Hers.

"You're idealizing Loftus," he said. "It will be harder for you if you don't face reality."

"I don't care."

"Not tonight, perhaps, but next week, next year. You'll go on with your life, working, meeting new people. But you'll never meet a living man who'll be as perfect as your image of a dead man. So you'll have to change that image, cut it down to size."

She turned and stared at him. "What are you getting at, Mr. Meecham?"

"Loftus was human. He had bad qualities as well as good qualities."

"You could never shake my faith in him."

"I can," Meecham said. "I think I have to."

"Try. Go ahead and try."

"Did he ever tell you about Birdie?"

"Birdie?" A pulse began to pound in her throat, and she put her hand over it to hide it. "Who was—Birdie?"

"She was his wife."

"No. No, he never had a wife."

"He married her about two years ago. They were divor—"

"Please," she said. "Please. Don't."

"They were divorced—there was trouble over his mother, I believe—and later Birdie was killed in an auto accident out West."

For almost a whole minute she didn't speak or move. Then, with a sudden furious sweep of her hand, she thrust all the dishes off the drainboard into the sink. The crash split the air, and little pieces of glass sprayed out of the sink like water from a fountain.

Some of the glass struck her but she didn't flinch or even notice. She just turned and walked away from the whole mess, looking very composed.

Pausing in the doorway, she said to Meecham in a cold flat voice, "Your fifteen minutes are up. Good night, Mr. Meecham."

20

EIGHT O'CLOCK, AND a church bell was ringing out a Christmas carol, alternately brash and wispy, as the wind carried the tune like a temperamental choir boy.

O Little Town of Bethlehem. As he passed the church Meecham sang with the bells, a nervous obsessive singing that had nothing to do with music but was only an expression of disquiet. People were gathered on the church steps, huddled protectively in groups to withstand the force of the weather and of other groups. O Little Town.

Two blocks beyond the church he saw, in the glare of his headlights, a woman walking alone down the street. She was limping, heading into the wind with her coat and scarf flapping uselessly behind her like sails torn from a mast. Meecham pulled over to the curb. The woman turned abruptly, glanced at the car through her horn-rimmed glasses, and then began walking again with the springy uneven steps of someone accustomed to walking on ice.

Meecham drove ahead a few yards, stopped the car and leaned across the seat to open the window nearest the curb.

"Carney."

She came closer, blinking away the moisture from her wind-whipped eyes. Her cheeks and her chin and the tip of her nose were red and shiny with cold.

She said, "Give me a lift?"

"Hop in." He opened the door and she got into the car. Leaning back in the seat she held her mittened hands against her face to ease the aching of the cold.

"I'm freezing."

"You look it."

"I couldn't get a cab so I decided to walk." Her glasses had steamed up from the heat of the car so that she looked blind. She made no attempt to take off the glasses or wipe them; she seemed content, for the moment, to see nothing, to rest behind the fog like a ship at anchor.

The car moved ahead with a spinning of the rear wheels.

"Where are you going?" Meecham said.

"To the house. Alice phoned and asked me to come. She said it was an emergency."

"What kind of emergency?"

Carney gave a quick nervous laugh. "Any kind. Some people seem to jump from emergency to emergency, and other people like me just wait around to be useful after the fall."

"What's happened, Carney?"

"They've gone, that's what happened. The two of them—Virginia and her mother."

"When?"

"Just a while ago. They sent Alice out on some errand or other, and when she came back to the house they were gone. She phoned me right away and she tried to phone you and Paul too."

"How did they leave?"

"In the new car. I should have known there was something funny about that car. It isn't like Mrs. Hamilton to go out and buy something like that without shopping around. She's not stingy, but she's careful about her purchases—she hates to get stung."

"Where did she buy the car?"

"Right off the showroom floor. You know that Kaiser Frazer branch out near the stadium. She and Virginia went there in a cab this morning, and Virginia drove the car home—a yellow Frazer sedan."

"It's gone now, of course?"

"Yes. Alice checked."

"Why is she so sure they're not coming back?"

"Because they left some money for her in an envelope, her salary and enough to get home on." With a sound of anger she shook her head violently, like a wet spaniel shaking water off its ears. "How could they be so stupid? A middle-aged woman and her married daughter running away like a couple of children. Why? Why did they do it?"

"Figure it out."

"No, I don't want to. It—looks bad, doesn't it?"

"As bad as possible."

"Oh God, I'm tired. I'm tired of emergencies. I'm tired of playing the maiden aunt. When something goes wrong, call Carney. It's been like that ever since I knew them. Well." She took a deep breath. "Well, now something has gone really wrong and I can't help them at all."

Meecham turned left at the next corner. Part of the Barkeley house was visible at the end of the block, but most of it was hidden behind the evergreen hedge where Loftus had stood the first night. It seemed a long time ago.

He said, "Did you have any idea they were planning to leave?"

"No, but I thought something was in the wind. The new car, and then the telegram this morning."

"What telegram?"

"From Willett, her son in Los Angeles. He wired his mother a thousand dollars. She had to go down to the Western Union office to get it. Now why should Willett have wired her that much money?"

"Because she asked him to."

"She must have," Carney said. "But why? She had a lot of money when she came. I remember asking her about Willett the night she arrived, and she said something about Willett being the same old Willett, that he was in a great stew because she was carrying so much cash."

"How much is so much?"

"I can't give you a definite figure, but I know she's always carried very large amounts of cash. She was never afraid of being robbed, as I would be. On the contrary, it gave her a sense of security."

He stopped the car in the driveway but didn't get out. Instead, he said, "What happened to her money?"

Carney hesitated. She had taken off her glasses and was swinging them in a circle, one way and then another. "She gave it away, I guess."

"To whom?"

"Well, to Virginia. She . . ."

"Virginia hasn't a dime," Meecham said. "She was trying to cook up a scheme with me to float enough cash to run away."

"I don't know, I just can't reason things out. Nothing seems—well, sensible. Nothing seems *sensible.*"

"Not yet."

They got out of the car and went toward the house, walking side by side and close together in curious intimacy, like mourners approaching a grave. But the grave was only Virginia's patio, built for sun and summer but now dark and useless, the redwood chairs glazed with ice, the barbecue pit discolored by the soot of winter, and the plants dead in their hanging baskets.

Inside the house it was very warm but Alice and Barkeley still had their heavy coats on, as if in the stress of the moment they had both forgotten their personal comfort.

Alice looked ready to cry, but there was no sign of emotion on Barkeley's face except for a kind of weary contempt.

He addressed Meecham. "Well, what do we do now, call the police?"

"Perhaps that's the best idea."

"I don't want to, but I can't think of any alternative."

"You might try to catch up with them."

"How?"

"We know they're heading west, that's the important point. From here as far as Morrisburg, Highway 12 is the only road west. At Morrisburg they can take 60 southwest. So the problem is to catch them before they reach Morrisburg."

"I'll get the car out," Barkeley said. He was halfway to the door before he finished the sentence. It was the first time Meecham had seen him move quickly.

Carney had sat down and taken off her galoshes. "I won't go along. Alice can, but I won't. Like I said, I'm tired of emergencies."

Meecham looked at Alice. "Do you want to come?"

"I'm not sure."

"It will be safer if you stay here. The roads aren't good and we'll be speeding."

She touched his sleeve, shyly. "It would be worse staying here wondering if anything's happened to you."

"Nothing will happen to me. I want you to stay here with Carney."

"I—all right."

"Well," Carney said with an odd little smile. "So that's the way it is, is it?"

Meecham nodded.

"Well, good luck to you both. Maybe you won't need it as much as Carnova and I did, but you'll need it."

The last Meecham saw of her she was sitting with her right knee crossed over her left, her hand nursing her crippled foot. She looked old and bitter and hard, as if, in the role she'd played as maiden aunt, all the nieces and nephews had turned out bad and she had no faith or charity left.

The two men sat in the front seat. At first they were too tense to talk; they stared in silence at the road ahead while the windshield wipers clicked back and forth like metronomes. There was a light snow, not falling, but sweeping up and across the road in gusts, so that one moment there was nothing to be seen except whirls of white, and the next moment, in the lull of the wind, the air would be clear and everything seemed to be doubly visible—the billboards, the telephone poles, and the heavy piles of snow left at intervals on each side of the road by the snow plough after the last storm.

"They won't get far in weather like this," Barkeley said finally. "Virginia's a terrible driver."

"Virginia isn't driving," Meecham said.

"She must be. Her mother doesn't know how."

"They have a friend with them. A man called Hearst."

Barkeley's only reaction of surprise was to take a tighter grip on the steering wheel. "Who is Hearst?"

"He lives in the house where Loftus lived, he works for a detergent company, and he wants to go to California."

"That's not telling me much."

"It's as much as I definitely know. What I suspect is that he's a very small-time chiseler, and that he knows something your wife and mother-in-law don't want known. So they took Hearst along, not for the ride, but to get him as far away from town as possible."

"What does he know?"

"As far as I can gather from the physical evidence— times, places, actions—there's only one thing he can know. At the time Margolis was killed on Saturday night, Hearst was in his own house. So was Loftus."

"So was . . .? No. No, that's impossible."

"He was watching Loftus because he was jealous of him. Hearst is a traveling man, away from home all week on business. He had time to hatch plenty of suspicions about his wife and Loftus, not without some justification. On Saturday night Mrs. Hearst left the house about 7:30, met Loftus out on the sidewalk on his way home after dinner downtown, and then went on to a hockey game. That's her story, but Hearst didn't believe it. He was pretty sure she intended to meet Loftus somewhere in the course of the evening. He could have followed his wife, of course. But Hearst is a lazy, half-hearted man; it was easier for him to stay right in the house and keep an eye on Loftus. I believe that's what he did. He spied on Loftus and Loftus didn't go out."

"You have no proof of that."

"No, it's merely an opinion," Meecham said. The word reminded him vividly of the scene between Lily Margolis and her cousin, Loesser, a few hours before: "I will not be quiet, George. I have a right to my opinion." "Keep it an *opinion*, then." "Very well. In my *opinion*, Virginia Barkeley killed my husband in a jealous rage!"

He said aloud, "We may never know the truth of what happened. Maybe there isn't any whole truth about anything, just a lot of versions, of different colors and different flavors, like ice cream, and you pick the most palatable. Cigarette?"

"Not while I'm driving."

Meecham lit one for himself, cupping his hands over the lighter so that its sudden glare wouldn't distract Barkeley's eyes from the road. The wind was slackening, and the flakes of snow had become larger, coagulating with moisture into thick fluffy whirls that clung stickily wherever they fell. The windshield wipers had lost their rhythm. They jerked, slowed, stopped, and went on in wild haste, like a hunted man.

Meecham spoke again. "As Carney put it, nothing seems sensible. Loftus was an intelligent young man with a conscience, yet he accepted money to confess to a murder he didn't commit and fabricated enough circumstantial evidence to back it up—his bloodstained clothes, his knowledge of the inside of Margolis' cottage, what kind of knife was used, where it was kept, the temperature of the room, the number of times Margolis was stabbed, and so on. He couldn't have fabricated all that evidence without help."

"Whose help?"

Meecham didn't answer.

"You mean my wife's help," Barkeley said. "Don't you?"

"It seems—logical."

"But the blood on his clothes—how could Loftus have managed that? The Sheriff himself said that it wasn't rubbed on, it was splattered there from a wound, a quart or more of the stuff."

"That's one of two things I hope to find out soon. Where did the blood come from and where did the money go?"

"You think my wife knows."

"It's very possible."

"You might as well make that a definite opinion, Meecham. You seem to have opinions about everything."

"I don't pick them off trees," Meecham said. "They're flung into my lap."

"No opinions about me yet?"

"None."

"That's odd. I had quite a time-honored motive, you know. My wife was Margolis' mistress."

"I don't think she was."

"Very polite of you to say so, anyway."

"It's not politeness. I'm taking Lily Margolis' word for it. Margolis had a real love—that's her phrase—but it wasn't Virginia."

"The degree of Virginia's unfaithfulness hardly matters, does it?"

"I thought you'd be interested."

"Yes, I am," Barkeley said quietly. "I'm disappointed, too, that she didn't get any happiness out of all the grief she's given the rest of us. You'd think somebody would get something out of it. But no, Margolis is dead, and Virginia is running away, and I'm running after her, reluctantly and without hope. If I find her, what then? What then?" he repeated. "I just don't know."

Neither did Meecham. The next hour seemed as imponderable and remote as the next year.

They were passing through a small town identified by a sign over the railroad station door as Algonquin. A layer of fresh snow hid its ugliness like frosting on a soggy cake.

"Morrisburg is only another thirty miles," Barkeley said. "We won't catch them."

"We might."

"I don't think so."

He was wrong. Meecham spotted the bright yellow Frazer about a half-mile beyond Algonquin. Its hood was half- buried in a pile of snow left by a snow plough at the side of the road. A tow truck was parked in front of the Frazer, its red blinker going off and on like a buoy light to warn the approaching traffic.

Barkeley parked his car a few yards beyond the tow truck and Meecham got out and walked back.

A gray-haired angry-looking woman sat behind the wheel of the truck, her arms folded aggressively across her chest. A teen-aged boy in leather cap and windbreaker was busy with a shovel digging away the snow from the Frazer's bumper.

"Need any help?" Meecham said.

The boy looked up and shook his head. "Nope."

"A nasty thing to have happen to a new car like that."

"Not much damage done. Didn't hit nothing except snow."

The woman in the truck cranked down the window and stuck her head out. "What's he want, Billy?"

"Nothing."

"He ain't one of those insurance fellows?"

"How should I know?"

"Just think," the woman said bitterly. "Just think, if your father'd stayed *home* tonight where he *belongs*. But no. Not *him*. He had to go and . . ."

"Oh, for heck's sake, Mom, stop crabbing."

The woman's lips continued moving, but no one heard what she said because she'd closed the window again.

Meecham asked the boy, "Anyone hurt in the accident?"

"One of the women was riding up front and got her head bumped on the windshield. Nothing much."

"Where are the people now?"

"They're waiting for the car at my Dad's place, about five hundred yards up the road. We got a garage and a hamburger stand."

"Good. I'll drop in."

The boy resumed his shoveling and Meecham began walking back to the car.

The woman had opened the window of the truck again. "I bet it was one of those insurance fellows."

"It don't matter anyway."

"It's after eight. I missed Guest Star. Your father knows Wednesday's the best night. And here I sit, in the middle of a snowstorm when I could be . . ."

The snow gradually covered her voice as it covers cat tracks.

21

THE HAMBURGER STAND was one large room built onto the front of an old brick farmhouse. It was equipped with three oilcloth-covered tables, a dozen chairs and a long wooden counter. At one end of the counter, facing the door, there was a small television set on a crude homemade shelf attached to the wall. A boxing match was on the screen showing two boxers, bodies close and heads together in a clinch. They looked as though they were sobbing on each other's shoulders.

A waitress was languidly drying a pile of cups and saucers, her eyes glued to the screen.

Hearst sat at the counter alone. There was a sandwich and a cup of coffee in front of him, but he was too absorbed in the boxers to eat or drink. His face, like that of the waitress, had a curious stupor, as if they were both drugged by the motions on the screen. He didn't turn his head, or even blink when the door opened and Meecham and Barkeley came in.

There was no sign of either Virginia or her mother.

"One of them's getting all bloody," the waitress said, apparently to Hearst though she didn't look at him. "Why can't we get something more cheerful, I'd like to know."

"Leave it on," Hearst said. "It's not real anyway."

Barkeley and Meecham sat down at the counter. The waitress didn't notice, or pretended not to.

"It looks real," she said.

"The whole thing's phony, like wrestling. For blood they use ketchup."

"Is that a fact?"

"Sure it is. I know one of the head guys at the biggest station in Detroit."

"I bet."

"Sure I do."

"Well, I'd just as soon have blood running down my face as ketchup. I hate the smell of ketchup, reminds me of every joint I ever worked in." She wheeled around suddenly and said to Meecham, "We don't have menus, just what's written on the mirror up there."

Hearst turned at the same instant, and recognized Meecham.

"Hello, Hearst," Meecham said.

Hearst's expression of apathy didn't change. He never did anything right and he never expected to do anything right, so his failures were no surprise to him. He cleared his throat. "I didn't know anyone was looking for me. I . . ."

"Where's Mrs. Hamilton?"

"In the washroom. The girl's in there too. Washing up, I guess." He looked at Barkeley as if he thought Barkeley was a policeman. "I didn't hurt the car much. Maybe the headlights are bust, but it wasn't my fault. I went into a skid."

"You were born in a skid," Meecham said, "and never got out of it."

Ignoring the remark, Hearst continued to address Barkeley with earnest righteousness in the manner of a petty crook caught in a misdemeanor on his way to commit a felony. "I didn't steal the car. She hired me to drive out to the Coast. I got the contract right here in my pocket. It's all written down. What's written down is legal, isn't that right, Mr. Meecham?"

"Let's see it."

The "contract" was a piece of paper torn from a scratch pad. The signature was Mrs. Hamilton's, but the rest of it had obviously been written by Hearst himself in an awkward hand, so heavy in places that the ink was blotched and the paper torn by the pen. "I, the undersigned, on this December thirteen, 1950, agree to hire Jameson Ralph Hearst as chauffer for my new Frazer and to retain his services for a period of two years at a salary of $150.00 per monthly plus full maintenance (room and board). Signed, Rachel Mills Hamilton."

Hearst watched Meecham as he read it. "That's legal, isn't it? I made up the words myself but it's legal."

"You did a great job." Meecham folded the paper and put it in his own pocket.

"Hey, give it back. That's my contract. I need it. When I get to California . . ."

"You're never getting to California."

Hearst looked a little sick. "I am. Some day I am. Some day I'll . . ."

"All right, some day," Meecham said. All Hearst's days were *some days*, he thought. There was no definite tomorrow or week after next, just a shady avenue of *some days*.

Virginia came out of the washroom followed by her mother. There was a bluish lump on the right side of Virginia's forehead and the skin around her right eye was slightly darkened. Her hair was smooth, her face powdered and her lips freshly rouged. She looked as tidy and lifeless as a corpse primped for the funeral service. When she saw Barkeley she turned immediately, and brushing past her mother she went back into the washroom and closed the door.

Mrs. Hamilton continued walking toward the three men at the counter, unsteadily, and listing slightly, as if she'd just gotten off a boat and couldn't adjust to the stability of land.

She wore a dark beaver coat that looked like one of Virginia's coats; it reached to her ears at the top, and to her snowboots at the hemline. She was clasping the ill-fitting coat around her with both hands, as if its thick heavy fur was a new skin that held her body together.

She was smiling, but the smile, like the coat, seemed to belong to someone else.

"Well, Paul. I—didn't expect to see you here."

"I guess not," Barkeley said.

"I hardly know what to—to say. I mean . . ."

"Are you all right?"

"C-certainly I'm all right. I'm just fine."

"You don't look it," Barkeley said sharply. "I'm driving you home right away, all three of you."

"Not me, you aren't," Hearst said.

"You, too."

"No, sir. I got this far, I'm not going back. I told Emmy she'd never see me again. You think I'm going to walk in that door and let her think I'm a sap? No, sir. I'm staying here. I got a *legal contract.*"

Mrs. Hamilton turned to him. "Mr. Hearst, please. You must realize that we can't go on with our trip right now. Perhaps—perhaps later. Some other day."

"I got this far. I don't want to go back." He wiped the sweat off his forehead with his coat sleeve. It left a damp dingy stain on the glossy blue serge. "I don't want to walk in that front door and face her like I was a sap that couldn't get along without her."

"We all have to go back," Mrs. Hamilton said gently, as if she was addressing an animal that couldn't understand words, only the tone in which the words were spoken. "I'll go and get Virginia."

"No, I will," Barkeley said. "You sit down and take it easy. Meecham, see that she drinks a glass of milk."

Barkeley went toward the washroom. There was no lock on the door, only a hole where the lock had once been.

"Virginia."

He pushed the door open slowly. Virginia was standing motionless at the washbasin looking at herself in the cheap dust-smeared mirror above it, both fists clenched against her abdomen as if to ease a cramp. The mirror, and the lump over her eye distorted her features.

"I'm ugly," she said. "Look at me. You never knew that before, how ugly I am."

"It's a bad mirror."

"Is it? Is it really?"

"Yes."

She shook her head back and forth in a slow melancholy way. "No, that's not right. I can't blame the mirror. It's too easy."

"You never do anything easy," he said. "You run too fast and stumble. Then other people have to pick you up off the ground."

"Is that why you came—to pick me up off the ground?" She smiled, and the ugly girl in the mirror smiled too, her face doubly distorted. "Well, don't bother. I *like* it here on the ground. Me and Hearst, a couple of flops. Maybe the two of us should just keep on going west together."

"You wouldn't get very far."

"Would you send the police after me?"

"I'm afraid I'd have to."

"Because of Claude."

"Yes."

She reached out her hand and with her forefinger traced an x in the dust on the mirror, then a whole row of x's. "Do you think I killed him?"

"I don't know."

"Why don't you ask my mother? She'll tell you. She knows everything. You and my mother would make almost as good a pair as Hearst and I. She knows everything, and you never do anything wrong. Wonderful combination, isn't it? Unbeatable. I can't beat it anyway and I've quit trying. I can't keep up with all you nice virtuous people who never do anything wrong, who never even *feel* like doing anything wrong!"

He caught her by the shoulders and turned her around so that she had to look at him instead of the ugly girl in the mirror. "Where did you get the idea that there are only white saints and black sinners in this world?"

She stared at him, mute and suffering.

"It's an impossible standard to live by, Virginia. It doesn't leave any room for ordinary human mistakes."

"Like Claude?"

"Like Claude."

Her mouth began to tremble uncontrollably, as if the muscles around it had been stretched too tight and suddenly snapped like elastic bands. "I never—I wasn't anything to him. My mother won't believe that. She says she does, she always says she trusts me and has faith in me, but I know it isn't true. The way she *looks* at me, always expecting that I've done something, that I'm bad. And the awful part is I can't help feeling that she's right, that I *am* bad. It's been like that ever since I can remember."

"You're not bad," he said. "And I believe you. Whatever you say about Margolis, I believe you."

"Do you, honestly?"

"Yes." He was conscious of the passage of time, of the three people waiting for him in the next room, but he didn't want to leave. In the whole year of his marriage he had never understood Virginia's nature so completely, or felt closer to her than he did now in the sordid little washroom.

"If Claude was alive," she said, "I could prove we were just friends, just putting in time together. I didn't have anything else to do, and Claude was waiting for someone to come back, so we both had lots of time to waste." She rubbed the lump on her forehead vigorously with her fingertips. It seemed to Barkeley that the gesture, like so many of Virginia's gestures and actions and words, was a self-punishment.

"Does your head hurt?" he said.

"Yes."

"Then don't rub it like that."

"Was I rubbing it? I didn't mean to."

He took both her hands and held them tightly in his. "Who was Claude waiting for?"

"A woman. Lily Margolis told me about her first. Lily came to the house one day and said she wanted to do me a favor by telling me that Claude was in love with another woman. She started out calmly enough but then she got carried away by her own words and began calling me names. I was afraid Carney or someone in your office would hear her, so I put my hand over her mouth to stop her. I guess her version of it is different, but that's what really happened—I was scared and embarrassed, and I had to shut her up. Carney heard everything, of course," she added with a trace of bitterness. "She always does. She said if I didn't behave myself she was going to write and tell my mother. Carney doesn't like me. She pretends to. She's like my mother, she pretends all the time. That cheerful act of hers—that kindly tolerance—it's all a front."

He didn't agree or disagree, and after a time she began talking again:

"Later on I asked Claude if it was true that he'd been in love with someone for a long time and he said yes, it was true but the woman had left him and he was afraid that this time she wasn't coming back. We didn't quarrel about it or anything like that. I even felt sorry for him. I know how it is to wait for someone who doesn't come."

"Have you waited very often for me, Virginia?"

"You know I have."

"I always came, though. The next time you wait, remember that."

"I'll remember. I promise."

"Come on, Virginia. We're going home now."

"Please. I can't face it."

"You'll have to."

"I don't know what will happen. What will they do to me? What will they do to my mother?"

"I can't answer that."

He held the door open for her and she walked slowly past him, one hand pressed against the lump on her forehead as if it was an excrescence of evil that would shrink under the pain of atonement.

22

THE ROOM WAS one Meecham had never been in before, in the rear of the Barkeley house. It was small and square and almost empty. There were no books, no pictures, and the only furniture was a fluorescent lamp and a davenport with a matching chair that needed reupholstering. The window was a wall of glass that in the daytime looked out on the hills behind the town, but now at night reflected only the room itself, and the mother and daughter sitting at opposite ends of the davenport, like strangers. They were both staring at Meecham as if they expected him to introduce them to each other. He wondered if he could, if he knew the right combination of words that would mean, *this is Virginia* and *this is Rachel Hamilton.*

"I wanted to talk to you both privately," Meecham said. "It's your right and privilege to consult a lawyer before making any official statement." Neither of the women seemed to be listening, but he continued anyway. "Mr. Hearst has already told me what he knows: that Loftus didn't leave his apartment on Saturday night, that he, Hearst, came to you with this information yesterday evening, and you, Mrs. Hamilton, agreed to hire him as your chauffeur provided that he kept the information to himself. Is that right?"

Mrs. Hamilton spoke through stiff dry lips. "You know it is."

"Why did you agree?"

"I didn't want the case reopened."

"Why were you certain that Hearst was telling you the truth?"

"I—well, I just believed him, that's all."

"You had good reason to believe him," Meecham said. "You've known almost from the beginning that Loftus was innocent."

She didn't reply.

"Whose idea was it to leave for California?"

"Mine."

"You thought you'd get away and stay away and that would be the end of the whole business?"

"I thought it was—possible."

"Do you know who killed Margolis?"

She didn't look at Virginia, but her right hand half-rose in an unconscious gesture of defense. "I know nothing about it."

"Go on," Virginia said. "Tell him that I did."

"Keep out of this, Virginia."

"You've handled everything so far, now I have a right to . . ."

"Be quiet, you stupid girl." She added in a softer tone, as if she regretted her words: "Don't you see, I'm trying to help you."

"Paul said I was to tell the truth, to be honest."

"*Honest.* Don't you think everybody would like to be honest? Most people—can't afford the price. They can just afford to be a little honest here and a little honest there, and in front of certain people."

"I'm one of them," Meecham said.

"I hardly think so, Mr. Meecham."

"You can't lie about your age to someone who's holding a photostat of your birth certificate, Mrs. Hamilton."

"You have a photostat?"

"Several. The equivalent of several, anyway."

"I see." In the fluorescent light of the lamp her face looked translucent yet solid, as if the skin had been turned into quartz and the eyes into agate. Even her voice had crystallized, sharp and hard. "I want you to understand one thing, Mr. Meecham. Throughout this whole affair I've acted in my daughter's best interests. From the very first minute that I heard she was in trouble I began to plan, as I've planned so many times before, in spite of her increasing hostility."

She spoke without looking at Virginia or giving any indication that she knew Virginia was still in the room.

"All my life I've done everything possible for her. She's been hard to raise, terribly hard. It's been one crisis after another ever since the day she was born, and I've met each one with all the strength I had. Now I don't have enough left to go on with. I'm a weary old woman. Virginia's on her own now. When she makes a mistake she must correct it herself. I won't be here to help her."

She lapsed into a restless silence. The only sounds in the room were muted and remote, the sounds of breathing, of wind pressing on the pane, and the faint humming of the lamp.

"I was in bed asleep when the telegram came from Paul that night. It seems so long ago now, but it was only Saturday, or rather early Sunday morning, about one o'clock by our time on the Coast. I sent two telegrams back immediately, one to Virginia and one to Paul, advising them to say and do nothing until my arrival. I had no definite plan of action in the back of my mind, not even a definite opinion about Virginia's innocence or guilt. I only knew she was in trouble and it was up to me to help. I didn't go back to bed that night. I made plane reservations, I packed, I checked my bank account, and then I called my son Willett. The next morning Willett drove me to the bank, and I took out $10,000, a thousand of it in cash and the rest in traveler's checks. Willett thought I was crazy, but I realized my expenses were going to be heavy no matter what happened. So I came prepared. I arrived Sunday evening, and early the following morning I went to see Virginia. I was appalled."

For the first time she looked directly at Virginia, and then she repeated the words. "I was appalled. I had expected—well, at least an end to my uncertainty. But there was no end. She couldn't remember what had happened because she'd been drunk. She couldn't affirm or deny anything. I tried not to show my alarm but I felt desperate. The evidence against her seemed so overwhelming, and she was acting as she always does when she's scared to death, brassy and disdainful, deliberately making enemies of people who could be useful—the Sheriff and the matron, and you, Mr. Meecham. Yes, and even me. No wonder I felt despair when I left her that first morning.

"I went out into the corridor. There was a young man sitting on a bench just outside the door of the Sheriff's office. I had never seen him before and he had never seen me. I realize now that he must have been sitting there for some time, listening."

"He was," Meecham said. "I saw him there when I left."

"You know, then, who he was."

"Yes."

"He spoke to me—something about the weather—and then he asked me if I was Virginia Barkeley's mother. When I said I was he told me he wanted to discuss a very important matter with me about Virginia."

Meecham said, "It was Loftus who originated the plan?"

"Yes. Even if I'd had the idea myself, it would have been impossible for me to carry it out, to go around town looking for a man able and willing to do what Loftus did."

"Did his plan seem reasonable to you?"

"At the time, yes."

"You weren't frightened or suspicious? You didn't think he was crazy?"

"You knew him, Mr. Meecham. He wasn't crazy. He had nothing to lose excepting his life which was already lost, and I had nothing to lose except money which I could afford. Those were his very words. To me, the way I felt then, they seemed very logical. They don't anymore." She pressed the back of her hand against her forehead as if to ease the pain of a memory. "We reached an agreement. I—I *bought* him, the way you'd go out and buy a dog. That he wanted it like that is no excuse for me."

"Why did he need the money?"

"For someone else."

"He didn't say who it was?"

"No. Just that the money would help someone else have a decent life. I wonder now, as I've wondered so often in the last two days, if it will." Her hands were working nervously, clenching and unclenching. "Loftus said he would arrange all the details and I was to meet him, with the money, at 4:30 at the bus stop at Arbor and Pontiac."

"That's just a block from here."

"Yes."

"Did he ask you for any information about the murder that he could use—about the hunting knives Margolis had, and the furnishings of the cottage and so on?"

"No. I couldn't have told him anyway because I didn't know."

Meecham turned his gaze on Virginia. "You knew."

"I'd been in the cottage before, yes," she said. "If that's what you mean. But I didn't tell Loftus anything. How could I? The only time I ever saw him was yesterday morning in that room with you and the Sheriff. Remember? The Sheriff asked me if I knew Loftus and I said I'd seen him somewhere before."

"And Loftus said it was on Saturday night in a bar. Sam's bar."

"Yes."

"That wasn't the truth, was it?"

"I don't think so."

"Yet Loftus knew that you were in that bar, and that you did talk casually to a man there. He even knew exactly what you said: *God, this place stinks*. How could he hear you say that and still be at home in his apartment with Hearst watching him?"

"I don't know."

"Someone must have told him. Someone who was there in the bar, who saw you and heard you, who might even have been following you. Who would be interested in following you? Who would be interested in following you and Margolis, Virginia?"

"No one."

"Can't you think of anyone?"

"No!"

"I can. Lily Margolis, for one; only she happened to be several thousand miles away. For another, Margolis' friend, Miss Falconer. Or Carney; Carney was very interested in your welfare. But there's still another possibility. Paul Barkeley."

"If Paul had been there I'd have seen him," Virginia said quietly. "You mustn't try to drag him into this mess. I've been the cause of everything and I'm willing to do the suffering—Momma and I. Aren't we, Momma?"

The two women looked at each other as if through the periscopes of enemy submarines across a fathomless and crawling sea. Then Mrs. Hamilton turned away with a sighing sound. "Yes. Yes, Virginia."

"Paul didn't know anything about the murder or about the arrangement with Loftus. Did he, Momma?"

"No, dear. Nothing at all." She held her hands together on her lap, as she would hold two small restless animals to force quiet upon them. "I met Loftus at 4:30 at the bus stop. I had the money with me. I'd cashed six travelers' checks, at three different banks to avoid unnecessary questions or suspicions. I phoned Alice and told her I was going to a double feature and asked her to invite you for tea, Mr. Meecham. It was Loftus' idea to have you there when he—when he put on his act. I think he wanted to try it on you first before he talked to the Sheriff."

"Like an out-of-town tryout," Meecham said. "Well, it worked."

"Yes, everything worked out very well. Until last night, when I heard from Hearst. He came here to the house and we talked. And I knew then that I had to get Virginia away from this town. Whether she was innocent or guilty, perhaps I would never know. Her memory might be sealed forever, or she might wake up from a dream some night and it would all be sharp and clear in her mind. Look at her, Mr. Meecham. Look at my pretty girl. Somewhere behind those soft eyes there's a record of everything she has ever seen or touched or heard or felt or done. It's all there, but out of context, out of time, out of range."

Virginia stared at her mother with eyes that were not soft at all. "You talk about me as if I was a child or a psychopath."

"You are *my* child."

"Am I?"

Though the two women sat within touching distance of each other, Meecham felt that there was a great space between them, an expanse of sea too violent to sail, of land too mountainous to cross, and of years too long to remember.

Mrs. Hamilton reached out, across the expanse. "Virginia . . ."

"If I have a dream some night, I will never tell you about it," Virginia said. "I promise."

"My dear . . ."

"I'll never tell anyone."

"I—yes. Yes, perhaps that's the best way." She looked at Meecham. "What will happen now, Mr. Meecham?"

"You'll have to call the Sheriff."

"I see. What then?"

"He'll decide what action to take. You've withheld evidence concerning a murder. That's a felony."

"Is it? Fancy that, I've committed a felony. Willett will be very surprised," she said, almost gaily. "Well then, I suppose the next step is to hire a lawyer."

"Yes."

"But not you, Mr. Meecham."

"That's right," Meecham said with a slight smile. "Not me."

"I feel you're very tired of us all. You think we create difficulties where none exist, that our troubles aren't as real as broken legs or measles, or something you can see." She rose and went to the door. "You'll take care of Alice?"

"I'll try."

"Alice is a good girl," she said, thoughtfully. "I wish I knew how . . . Well, I'll go and phone the Sheriff. You needn't wait, Mr. Meecham. Good night."

"Good night."

He walked out the door and down the hall. He didn't look back but he knew she was watching him. He could feel her eyes on the back of his neck, cold and painful as the touch of ice.

23

ALICE WAS waiting for him in his car, a black scarf covering her bright hair, so that he didn't see her until he opened the door.

"Hello," Meecham said.

"Hello."

"Going anywhere?"

"Anywhere at all," she said. "Wherever you go."

"All right." He let the car coast down the driveway to the street. He felt an intense activity inside his body, like hundreds of wheels turning in all directions. He was almost afraid to speak because of what the wheels might do to his voice. But when he finally spoke he sounded quite calm and detached. "I'm going home."

"Then that's where I'll go too."

"Maybe you'd better not."

"I'm twenty-three," she said with naive pride, as if twenty-three was a very special age that conferred great wisdom and rightness on its wearer.

"I was twenty-three once too," Meecham said, "along with a lot of other people. I often made mistakes."

"I won't."

The traffic in the center of town was congested with cars that slid ghostlike along the streets, and students bundled like mummies against the cold. The bell tower was striking 9:15 when Meecham stopped the car in front of a small white duplex.

Hand in hand, they walked across the unshoveled sidewalk and up the porch steps of the right side of the duplex. A card above the doorbell said Eric Meecham. Two bottles of milk stood in a drift of snow outside the door. The milk had frozen and grown out of the tops of the bottles like strange white fungus that springs up overnight after a summer rain.

"I guess I forgot to bring in the milk," Meecham said.

"Does it always do that in the winter?"

"When it's very cold."

"It looks funny. I'll have to get used to a lot of different things, won't I, Meecham?"

"Yes." He tried to unlock the door but the key stuck and wouldn't move. He made three attempts before the door finally opened and a warm draft of air swept out to meet them like a friendly hostess.

Meecham turned on the hall light. "It's not very clean, I guess. It looks clean enough to me, but to a woman . . ."

"It's *very* clean."

"Is it?"

"I don't see how it could be any cleaner, really. I . . . Oh, *Meecham.* Frozen milk and the place being clean—what does anything *matter*?"

He untied the scarf that was knotted under her chin and it fell soft and unnoticed to the floor like a leaf.

"You're beautiful, Alice."

"Oh, I *hope* so. I couldn't live if you didn't like the way I looked."

She was clinging to him with all her strength, like a vine that had been growing alone and whose seeking tendrils had at last touched a tree. He held her tightly in his arms and kissed her, and the wheels inside him began to move with such furious speed that their noise whirred and pounded in his ears. When the telephone rang he hardly recognized it at first as a new and separate sound, but its sharp insistence gradually penetrated his mind like a pain.

Alice stirred in his arms and shook her head as if to shake off the intrusion. "I guess—that's the phone."

"Let it ring," he said.

"Do other women call you very often?"

"Sometimes."

The telephone continued to ring, five, six, seven times.

"You could answer," she said, "and then if it's another woman tell her you're very busy and you'll be busy for a long time."

"How long?"

"Years. Forever."

"All right." He picked up the phone from the hall table. His hands were shaking and his knees felt weak. "Hello."

"Is that you, Mr. Meecham?"

"Yes."

"This is me, Victor Garino. You remember?"

"Of course. Where are you?"

"Here at home, in Kincaid. I've been trying to reach you ever since before supper. Mama and me, we're having a bad time with Mrs. Loftus. It's about the money."

"What money?"

"The rest of Earl's seven hundred dollars. You shouldn't have sent it to her, Mr. Meecham."

Meecham felt the inside breast pocket of his coat. The envelope containing the rest of Loftus' money was still there.

"She's going wild," Garino said. "Buying not just liquor but everything, everything she sees. Records, dozens of records, and nothing to play them on. And a dress for Mama, a great big dress so big Mama could get into it twice. And for me, a new hat and a lamp and a case of wine, a whole case . . ."

"What do you think I can do about it?" Meecham said.

"You must come and take the money back again, what's left of it. I asked her to let me keep it for her and she said no, if I kept it she'd never see more than a dollar at a time like in the old days when Birdie gave her an allowance. I have no right to take the money from her. But you have, Mr. Meecham. You sent it to her and you can take it back again. That would be lawful, wouldn't it?"

"No, it wouldn't, because I didn't send her any money."

There was a silence at the other end of the line. Then Garino's voice again, talking not into the telephone but to someone beside him. "He says he didn't send it, Mama."

"He must have. Where else would she . . .?"

"She borrowed it, maybe."

"Who from? Who'd lend her money?"

"She wouldn't steal."

Then there was another silence, and Mrs. Garino said in a barely audible voice, "I never leave my purse around anymore."

Meecham spoke sharply into the phone: "Garino?"

"I'm here, Mr. Meecham. I was talking to Mama. She says to tell you we're very sorry we bothered you, and—and what else, Mama?"

"Merry Christmas," Mrs. Garino said.

"Oh yes, and a merry Christmas," Garino said gravely.

"Wait a minute, Garino."

"I am embarrassed, making such a big mistake, thinking you sent the . . ."

"Forget it. Is Mrs. Loftus home now?"

"Yes."

"Keep her there."

"By this time she is too drunk to go out anyway."

"I want to talk to her," Meecham said. "It's very important. I can leave right away and I should be there in a little over an hour."

He put the phone down and turned to Alice. She was smiling at him, but not very convincingly.

"You left me behind once tonight," she said. "I don't want to be left behind again."

"Do you like long winter drives in the country?"

"Very much."

"Sure?"

"I adore them." She reached down slowly, bending at the knees, and picked up her scarf from the floor. She said, without rising, "I could sit right down here and bawl."

"Please don't." He pulled her gently to her feet. "Remember, you're twenty-three."

"You're laughing at me."

"No. Here, I'll put on your scarf for you. Will you let me?"

"I guess." She watched him as he tied the scarf awkwardly under her chin. "Meecham, do we *have* to go?"

"We have to." He switched off the hall light and for a moment they stood in the dark facing each other but not touching. "You're not angry?"

"No." She shook her head, rather sadly. "But I don't think I'm twenty-three anymore. I think I'm older."

24

THE LIGHTS IN the Garinos' basement apartment were on. From the sidewalk Meecham and Alice could see right into the kitchen. Mrs. Garino was sitting alone at a big linoleum-covered table, motionless, as if she was listening for a sound or waiting for something to happen.

Garino answered the door. He had a sleeping kitten nestled in the crook of his arm.

"You arrived fast, Mr. Meecham."

"Yes. Miss Dwyer, Mr. Garino. Miss Dwyer is my fiancée. She came along for the ride."

"Come in, come in." Garino stepped back to let them in, and at the movement the kitten awoke and began sheathing and unsheathing its claws against the rough wool of Garino's sweater coat. In and out, the claws moved like iridescent needles being thrust in and out of tiny pink plush cushions. "I will get my keys."

"I could hold the kitten for you," Alice said shyly.

"Ah, you like kittens, eh?"

"I love them."

"This one, he is the littlest. He is always the last to eat, and when he sleeps he is always at the bottom of the pile, so I spoil him a little to make up for this." Alice sat down in an old wicker rocking chair and Garino put the indignant kitten on her lap. "I will go and tell Mama to fix some coffee."

"I already put it on," Mrs. Garino said from the kitchen, sounding rather angry that anyone should have to remind her to make coffee.

"Come out here for a minute, Mama."

"I'm not dressed for company." But she came to the door anyway, smoothing her skirt down over her hips. "We're upset around here today. I didn't have time to fuss with clothes."

Meecham introduced the two women and they eyed each other carefully from an ambush of smiles before they stepped out into the open.

"She can stay down here with me," Mrs. Garino said to her husband. "She wouldn't want to go up there to that . . ."

"Mama."

"How many times a day do you have to say *Mama* to me like that? You might as well be honest and say *shut up*."

"That wouldn't be so polite," Garino answered blandly. The two men went out into the hall and Garino closed the door.

"Is she still in her apartment?" Meecham said.

"Yes, I went up to check fifteen minutes ago. She is drunk, naturally, but not as bad as I expected. I heard her through the door walking around talking to herself."

"Does she know that Earl's dead?"

"I couldn't tell her. She was so happy today, spending that money, how could I spoil it? It's a long time since she had money to spend and it went to her head. When you never have more than a dollar, a hundred dollars seems like it would last forever."

"If my guess is right, there's a lot more than a hundred dollars involved."

"Then you know how she got the money?"

"I don't know how she got it," Meecham said. "But I know where it came from originally."

"She didn't steal it, though?"

"No."

"I didn't think so." But he sounded relieved.

The door of Mrs. Loftus' apartment was locked. Though Garino had the key to it in his hand, he knocked once, and then again, before using it.

The old lady was sitting sideways on the battered davenport, her feet up and ankles crossed, her back to the door. She was smoking a cigarette through a long silver holder, her fingers elegantly extended.

She spoke without moving her head. "Don't I ever get any privacy anymore?"

Garino turned a little white. "I asked you please not to smoke when you're drinking."

"You're a butterinski, Victor. That's what we used to call people like you in my day. What do you want now?"

"I brought someone to see you."

"I've already seen someone." She flicked the ashes off her cigarette in the general direction of an ashtray. Some of the ashes spilled on the floor and the rest on her dress. Meecham noticed that the dress already had two or three scorch marks on it though it looked brand new. Everything she wore looked brand new—the magenta-colored dress with a purple velvet flower at the waist, sheer black stockings, ankle-strap suede pumps and a hat made of sleek black feathers. Nothing fitted her. The hat perched on her head like a reluctant raven, the stockings hung in pleats on her legs, and the full skirt of the dress stuck out from her fleshless hips like a ballerina's tutu.

The room smelled of whisky and of smoke, more acrid than cigarette smoke. Meecham saw then that the old lady had been burning something in the grate. The center of the fire had burned down to a crust of gray and black ash, but around the perimeter some material was still smoldering.

"I didn't know you were going out," Garino said.

She bent her head toward him, slowly, as if to avoid frightening the raven on her head. "I am not going out, Victor."

"I wish you wouldn't."

"I said . . ."

"It's very cold and late, and besides, the bars will be closed pretty soon."

The old lady's eyes flickered. "Why, I wouldn't *dream* of going out on a night like this."

"Promise."

"It never even occurred to me to go out on a night like this. As a matter of fact, I was about to retire when I decided to try on my new clothes."

"It's a pretty dress."

"You really like it? It doesn't fit, but then I didn't buy it for *fit*. I bought it," she added in a very reasonable tone of voice, "for the color. It's such a cheerful color it makes me feel alive."

"Ella can maybe take it in at the seams for you."

She stared at him coldly. "Then you don't really like it, after all."

"Yes, I do. I was only . . ."

"You have no right to force your way into my home and inflict your opinions about clothes on me, Mr. Garino."

"You'd better go to bed before . . ." Garino hesitated, looking down at his hands.

"Before *what*, Mr. Garino?"

"Before Ella has to put you to bed."

She thought this over quietly for a moment. Then she said with an air of triumph, "I can't go to bed. I've got company." She pointed the cigarette holder at Meecham. The cigarette had burned down to the end and gone out. "Who are you, company?"

Meecham repeated his name.

"Well, sit down, sit down some place and we'll all have a cozy drink together. You too, Victor."

"No, I don't want one, thank you," Garino said.

"You needn't pretend, in front of me, that you don't drink. I happen to know that you drink in secret all the time. A lot of people do. Billions. Pour some of us billions a drink, Victor."

Garino's dark skin showed an angry streak of purple across his cheekbones and the bridge of his nose. "You can wait for a while."

"I can't wait. I need the energy. Whisky is a body fuel. I read that in the newspaper. There's no reason why I can't have some body fuel."

"You intend to go out, don't you?" Garino said. "You weren't trying on clothes."

"Why, of all the *absurb* ideas!"

"Where were you going?"

"Give me a drink."

"Where were you going?"

"You dirty foreigner."

Garino's eyes glittered like an oil sludge over moving water. "Watch what you say. I am your only friend."

"Oh no, you're not. I have lots of friends."

Meecham sat down facing her. The scarred and rickety coffee table seemed like a precarious bridge between them that must be crossed carefully, one step at a time.

"Who are they?" he said.

"Who are they is none of your business. I don't go around to other people saying *who are they, who are they* all the time."

"Did your friends give you any money?"

She raised her head high and tried to look haughty. "I wouldn't dream of accepting charity. I'm a woman of independent means."

"I realize that, of course," Meecham said. "But you wouldn't have any objection to accepting money that came from Earl. It did come from Earl?"

"Don't bother me. I'm tired. I need some body fuel."

"All right." Meecham nodded at Garino, and Garino went, silent and tight-lipped, into the kitchen. When he returned he was carrying a plastic tumbler filled to the brim with whisky.

Mrs. Loftus drank it in three gulps. "That newspaper was right. It is a fuel. Why, I feel warmer already."

Meecham said, "Earl is dead, Mrs. Loftus."

The old lady began to tremble, and Meecham thought for a moment that she was going to react violently to the news. But too many nerves of communication had been cut between her and the outside world. Pain was dulled and pleasure remote.

"Did you hear me, Mrs. Loftus?"

"I don't want to hear anything. You leave me alone."

"Before he died he had over six thousand dollars," Meecham said. "How much of that did you get?"

"I've forgotten his face. He was nice-looking, but I've *forgotten*. . . . I can't picture it."

"Who sent money to you? Or brought it to you?"

Though her mouth worked, she didn't speak for a moment, and when she did it wasn't an answer to Meecham's questions but to questions that rose within her like smoke from a forgotten fire. "Such a hard life, a terrible life. Earl is lucky. I wasn't a good mother to him. Something happened to me. What was it? I don't remember. Something happened. I think I was ill and too tired to care."

Meecham recalled the piercing words Loftus had used about her: *One drink and she was a drunk. She'd been a drunk for thirty years and didn't find it out until then. For her the world vanished in that instant. She has never seen it since. She never will again.*

"Earl didn't understand," she said in a whisper. "He wrote cruel things to me sometimes, said I broke my promises, said I didn't *try* hard enough. I burned all his letters. Birdie told me to."

"Who told you?"

"Birdie did. Tonight. I was sitting here and suddenly in comes Birdie through that door like a ghost." She glanced at the locked door expectantly as if she wanted to conjure up the ghost again, a friendly ghost more real than the shadows she lived among.

"Please, Mrs. Loftus," Meecham said sharply. "Take it easy now. Tell me . . ."

"Forget the past, Birdie said, burn it all up. And she's right. From now on things are going to be different. I'm going away, I'm going to start a new life. Birdie says it's bad for me living here like this from hand to mouth in a town full of gossip." *Birdie said and Birdie says* . . . The words seemed to hypnotize her like a new religion with a special chant. "Birdie says I ought to live in the country, in a big house with lots of trees and flowers around and dogs in the yard."

Meecham leaned toward her across the table trying to focus her attention. "Birdie was here tonight?"

"I don't think I'm supposed to tell you that. She doesn't want Victor to know, doesn't like people who snoop."

"I'm not snooping. But you must be making a mistake, Mrs. Loftus. It couldn't have been Birdie."

"I know Birdie. I recognized her right off, she didn't have to open her mouth."

"Earl claimed she was killed in an accident out West."

She didn't seem surprised. "Sometimes Earl told little fibs."

"This was more than a little fib. If he lied about her death, it means that he was deliberately trying to prevent anyone from finding her."

"Well, I found her without even looking. She's alive, all right. Showing her age, I must say," Mrs. Loftus added slyly. "Oh, yes, she's gotten older. And she's had a few knocks in the process, so now she understands better about other people with troubles, like me. She's different, Birdie is. She says I'm different too." She tilted her head at Garino. "You think I am, Victor?"

"Ah—yes." Garino looked sick. "Very different."

"You don't mean that *nice*, do you?" she said slowly.

"I mean it nice."

"At least I haven't gotten stout. So many older women get stout."

Not without food, Meecham thought. "Birdie gave you money?"

"She sent it to me. It came this morning in the mail, a check with a little note. Two hundred dollars."

"And then?"

"Then *what*? I spent it, of course."

"All of it?"

"Not all of it," she said disdainfully. "I'm not a fool. I have twelve dollars left."

"How far do you think twelve dollars will go toward that big house in the country?"

"Birdie says I'm not to worry. She's taking care of everything; Earl asked her to. She knows where the house is. She's going to drive me there tonight. It might be quite a long drive. If I could have another drink, Victor?"

"It would be better not to," Garino said.

"Just one. Then I'll throw the bottle away. I'm going to quit drinking—did you know? I am. I promised Birdie and I promise you, too."

Garino brought the bottle out of the kitchen and poured her a drink. While she drank it he stood over her with melancholy patience like a hen brooding over an egg that has gone rotten in its shell.

"Now I'll throw the bottle away, see, as I promised. Give it to me."

Garino recorked the half-empty bottle and put it in her lap. Then he held out his arm and she pulled herself to her feet by hanging on the sleeve of his old sweater coat. She tottered toward the fireplace, balancing precariously on her new spike-heeled pumps like a child on stilts.

"Didden think I'd keep a promise, eh? Well, you were mistaken, Victor." With loving care she placed the bottle upright in the center of the grate where the fire had died. Then she returned to the davenport breathing hard and noisily, as if she had walked, not the width of a room, but a great distance across a span of years.

She sat down carefully, her eyes avoiding Garino's. Garino didn't say anything. He went over to the fireplace, removed the bottle and took it out to the kitchen again. The silence in the room was unbearable, the silence of terrible words not yet spoken.

"You shouldn't have done that, Victor," she said at last.

Garino's face was like wood. "You could blow the place up. It's a fuel. Remember?"

"You have turned against me."

"I don't want the place blown up."

"You and Ella both. I've only got one friend left."

"Birdie was never your friend," Garino said. "I remember the fighting, fighting all the time the two of you."

"Things have changed."

"Where is this big house she's taking you to, with trees and flowers and dogs in the yard?"

"I don't know exactly."

"Is it a private house?"

"What do you mean, is it private. Of course it's . . . What do you *mean*?"

"I thought it might be some place where they take care of—older people and so on."

"An asylum."

"No, I didn't mean . . ."

"You meant an asylum," she said shrilly. "Earl wouldn't allow it. Do you hear me? He'd never allow it!"

"Earl is dead."

"But he gave her money to look after me and she promised him she would, she *promised*."

"Promises breed like fleas in your family."

"You go away!" she wailed. "I won't listen to you!"

"What if she doesn't show up? What then? You'll be glad enough then to stay here, won't you, even if it's not good enough for you. And me, I'm not good enough either, I'm a dirty foreigner."

"Please, both of you," Meecham said. "This arguing isn't accomplishing anything. Mrs. Loftus, are you listening to me?"

The old lady raised her head slowly like a sick animal. "Birdie will come for me, won't she?"

"She'll be here, sure," Meecham said with conviction. "Are you all packed and ready to leave?"

"Yes."

"Tell me first, where did you cash that check she sent you?"

"At a—little place down the street."

"Store? Bar?"

"A—a tavern. I just happened to be passing by and . . ."

"Yes, I know. What is the name of the place?"

"Peterson's. It's not a bad check, is it? I've spent the money. I couldn't pay it back. I don't want to cheat Mr. Peterson. He's helped me out when I—when I've been ill."

"The check's probably good."

"It's got to be. He didn't want to cash it at first because I told him it was from my daughter-in-law, and he said, how could it be, it wasn't signed Mrs. Loftus. I had to explain to him that Earl and Birdie were divorced and Birdie took back her maiden name of Falconer."

"Of *what*?"

He spoke the words so explosively that the old lady shrank back in fear. "Maybe Birdie wouldn't like me to be telling so much."

"How did she sign that check?"

"J—Jemima Falconer."

"Jemima Falconer," Meecham repeated. The name sounded very familiar yet remote, like the echo of a friend's voice.

"She never let anyone call her Jemima. She thought it sounded as if she was colored. We called her Birdie—that was her nickname at school."

Meecham remembered the descriptions of Birdie that he'd heard from various people. From Garino: "Birdie they called her. Such a silly name. She wasn't anything like a bird. She was a big woman, older than Earl and quite pleasant unless you crossed her—she had a terrible temper." From Mrs. Loftus, the night he had found her at the bus depot: "Didn't say a word about her till the day he brought her home and said, this is my wife. And there she stood, with that hennaed hair and that hard look, forty if she was a day, forty, and him just a boy." From Loesser, at Lily Margolis' house: "My impression is that she's a highly respectable woman. I knew Lily had been thinking for some time that Claude had a steady mistress, but I couldn't believe it was this Falconer woman." From Gurton at the restaurant: "Loftus used to come in here two or three years ago with his girlfriend, a tall bright-looking redhead." And from Gill, the orderly who had spent the last night with Loftus, listening to him talk: "Birdie this, Birdie that. He must have been crazy about that woman."

On that last night, with his own death molded and cast and waiting for him like an iron maiden, Loftus had tried to protect Birdie with the only weapons that were left to him, lies. He had invented her death in the auto accident in the West so that no one would look for her or discover where and who she really was. He had covered her with lies as the snow covers walkers on a winter night and obscures their footprints behind them.

Now, from out of this white ambush Birdie had stepped clear and sharp and real, with blood in her veins and money in her hand and promises on her lips. A big house with trees, and a new life with hope; Birdie said and Birdie says. Why? Why did she come back to say anything? Meecham looked at the old lady. . . . She was intent on fitting a new cigarette into the silver holder, her whole mind and body intent on this small task which would be so easy for anyone else, and he realized the futility of asking her questions.

"I'll do that for you," he said.

"Leave me alone. I can do it. Whyn't you go away?"

"That might be a good idea."

"It's an exshellent idea. Ex—cell—ent."

Meecham rose and went to the door. "I hope you'll send your new address to Mr. Garino."

"Maybe I will and maybe I won't."

"Come on, Garino."

Garino stood where he was. "We can't leave now. I'm going to stay and see that things are all right. I don't trust. . ."

"Things will be all right. Let's go."

"But . . ."

"I can look after myself, Victor," the old lady said firmly. "I'm a woman of ex—pe—rience."

"Good night, then."

She didn't answer. She was peering at the little clock on the mantel, her eyes narrowed to slits to make them focus. It was eleven o'clock. Or perhaps it was twelve. Or ten? The hands of the clock wavered, this way, that way. Ten, twelve, eleven, ten.

"Make up your mind," she said to the clock.

25

ELEVEN-THIRTY BY Meecham's watch. For nearly half an hour he had been waiting in the dark on the bottom step of the basement stairs, his shoulder pressed against the old wooden banister. He couldn't see the front door from this position because there was a turn in the stairs, but he could hear what went on in the hall above. He could even hear, very faintly, Mrs. Loftus walking around in her apartment, making last-minute preparations for the trip. Meecham's shoulder and the back of his neck felt stiff and sore where the draft struck him. He looked at his watch again. Another minute had crawled by, as slow and laborious as a sloth. She's not coming, he thought. Perhaps Birdie had been scared away, or perhaps the whole thing was what he had believed at first, the wish-fantasy of a drunken mind.

Then he heard the front door open, and quiet but firm footsteps moved along the thin carpeting. A pause, the click of a doorknob, and then the old lady's voice, with a sob in it:

"I thought you weren't coming, Birdie."

"Of course I was coming."

"It's so late."

"I had some trouble with the car." The woman's voice was as quiet and firm as her footsteps. "Is this your suitcase?"

"Yes."

"I'll take it. Button up your coat, it's a raw night." A moment of silence. "You've been drinking."

"Just a nip. You said yourself it's a raw night."

"You didn't tell anyone that you were leaving, or about me?"

"Of course not," the old lady lied solemnly.

"You burned everything?"

"Yes."

"Come on, then."

Footsteps down the hall.

Meecham rose quietly and began to ascend the stairs. At the bend in the staircase he paused. The two women were at the front door, Birdie bent under the weight of the suitcase, and the old lady wrapped like a mummy and clinging to Birdie's free arm.

"Where are you going?" Meecham said.

They both swerved toward him, and Meecham felt a column of emotion rise thick in his throat, disbelief and then anger and then sadness. In that one brief moment when Birdie turned, three women merged in her and became one, merged inevitably and naturally like atoms forming a molecule.

Her face was as familiar to him as Alice's: the square forcible jaw, the gentle mouth, and the eyes still blistered from the burning of her tears. He thought back to the last time he'd seen her when she had thrust all the dishes into the sink with a furious sweep of her hand, and the shattered glass had sprayed like water from a fountain.

She was looking down at the old lady with something like pity in her eyes. "You told. You poor fool."

"I didden, Birdie. I didden tell!"

"It's all right."

"You're mad at me. You won't take me along."

"I'm not mad, Clara. I never really expected anything to work out."

Meecham came up the rest of the steps and Mrs. Loftus watched him, peering at him from her heavy wraps like a mole from a thicket, half-dazed and half-blind.

"You go away! Go on! You're spoiling our trip. Birdie, tell him to go away. What about our trip, Birdie?"

"I guess we'll have to postpone it for a while," Mrs. Hearst said quietly. "Mr. Meecham wants to talk to me."

"He's a butterinski."

"Yes. Yes, I guess he is. Come on, we'd better go back to the apartment."

With a decisive movement she picked up the suitcase and went back down the hall, the old lady staggering behind her, whimpering.

"I want to live in the country. I want to have dogs in the yard. I want . . ."

"Sh . . . Sh, now."

"You promised."

"I'll keep my promise," Mrs. Hearst said. "But not tonight, Clara."

She opened the door of the apartment and paused for a moment on the threshold, swaying slightly, as if solid waves of time were beating at her legs.

"I used to live here," she said to Meecham. "Earl and me. Did you know that?"

"I knew it."

"I didn't realize how much you were finding out about me until after supper tonight when you came to see Jim. Then I knew I had to drive over here and cover my tracks somehow." She crossed the room to the old cherry-wood rocker near the window and touched the headrest with her hand. "This was Earl's chair. He was just like a baby; rocking soothed him."

Meecham remembered the rocking chair in the Hearst kitchen and he wondered if Mrs. Hearst had kept it there for Earl to sit in when he came to talk in the evenings.

"We used to fight when we lived here. We were having bad luck. Earl was out of a job and I was trying to support all three of us, working as a waitress. In a small town like this there aren't many jobs, you take what you can get. Nothing worked out for us. Earl felt like a failure and Clara was drinking all the time, and I couldn't see anything ahead but hell. I was younger in those days; I thought I knew what hell was like." She glanced at the old lady who was sitting bolt upright on the davenport with a fixed smile on her face, like a deaf-mute trying to appear interested in a conversation. "Clara knows."

"What's that you say, Birdie?"

"Nothing much. Would you like a drink?"

"I'll get it. We'll celebrate old times, eh, Birdie? Shelebrate old times." She started toward the kitchen, arms outstretched like an amateur tightrope walker. "Don't let me disturb the talking. I love to hear good talk."

Looking at the two women now it was impossible for Meecham to imagine the "old times" when the two strong personalities had clashed. There was no clash any longer; one of them was too weak to make a sound, like a broken drum.

"Well, I divorced Earl. I borrowed the money from my sister and took a bus to Las Vegas. When I came back to Arbana I was single again. I started a rooming house, and that's how I met Jim. I was feeling so empty and old and . . . Anyway, we got married. I guess I'm the kind of woman that don't know how to live without having a man to please and cook for and look after."

For the second time that night Meecham thought what a pity it was that such a forceful woman would always choose emotionally or physically weak men like Hearst and Loftus.

The old lady was still moving around the kitchen, rattling dishes and opening and closing cupboard doors.

"Jim and I got along all right. Nothing special, but all right. Then, about a year ago, I met Earl on the street. I hardly recognized him, he'd changed so much. We stood there in front of Kresge's. . . . It was snowing, and Earl didn't have a hat on and his hair was soaking wet, and he told me that he was sick. He had just found out what was the matter with him and he'd been walking the streets trying to figure things out. Those were the words he used, figure things out.

"I took him home and we sat in the kitchen and he asked me if I had a room for him to stay in. He moved in the next week. I didn't tell Jim or anyone who he was. My sister found out and we often fought about it. But to me it was the right thing to do. We didn't live together as husband and wife, we lived as friends that needed each other. He talked to me when I got upset or lonely, and I looked after him when he was sick, and kept his apartment clean and saw that he got enough to eat. We had a lot of quiet happiness together, Earl and me. There was always in the back of my mind the hope that someday someone would find a miracle cure for his disease. The worse he got, the more I hoped, until it was all I could think about, making him live."

She was looking out of the window, down at the dark and empty street. "If I hadn't hoped so hard he would be still alive."

"I don't believe I understand," Meecham said.

"I went to Claude for money."

"Money for Loftus?"

"Yes, to take him away. I'd read in the paper about a cancer clinic in New York where they were doing research on Earl's disease, and I thought if I could just get him there, there might be a chance for him. I didn't have a cent and nothing to sell except an old car, and no one to borrow from. Except Claude. The more I thought about going to Claude, the more reasonable it seemed. We had known each other a long time, long before Lily ever met him, and when we parted there was no final blowup or anything, we just drifted apart. That's how I thought of it.

"I went to his office a week ago today and waited for him outside. We went and sat in his car and I told him everything. What a terrible mistake I made!" she said bitterly. "If I'd asked him to lend me money for a new house or a trip I'd have gotten it. But Claude was a vain man. He couldn't believe that I loved another man, and that it was the kind of love he and I never had together. He kept saying how he knew I'd come to him, and I kept trying to tell him how I felt about Earl and how serious his condition was. Claude wouldn't listen. I got out of the car and walked home. I was burning up inside, and my head was splitting so I felt like it was going to blow up. You can feel more anger for somebody else than you ever can for yourself."

Meecham knew that she was right. Listening to her, he experienced inside his own head a corresponding pressure of anger and resentment, against Margolis, and against all the tyrannies and tyrants that harass the weak.

"For the next two days I went around as usual. I guess I did all the ordinary things, but I couldn't stop thinking of the money and how easily Claude could have lent it to me if he wanted to, and how much it might mean to Earl. On Saturday night Jim came home after a bad week on the road. He started an argument about me paying too much attention to Earl. I had to get out of the house so I went to the hockey game by myself. That much of what I told you before is true. After the game I was driving through town on my way home when I saw Claude. He was just getting out of his car in front of the Top Hat. There was a girl with him that I didn't know, all dressed up like a Christmas tree. I stopped my car. I had no plan or anything in mind. I think I stopped mostly because I didn't want to go home anyway and because I was curious. At first that was all, I was curious.

"They went into the Top Hat together, and I waited. A long time I waited, picturing the two of them inside, drinking and laughing and dancing like only people can that have their health and some money. I tried to picture Earl and me in there having a good time and I almost laughed, it was so funny.

"I thought of all kinds of crazy things when I was sitting there. I thought of going in and facing up to Claude, demanding money right in front of his new girlfriend. Claude's car was parked across the road, and I even thought of getting behind the wheel and driving it away and selling it some place. Imagine thinking of stealing! Never did I think of stealing before, even when I was a kid, but I thought of it then. Everything began to get very sharp and separated in my mind, so I felt anything I could do for Earl was good and what anyone did against him was bad.

"Maybe I would have stolen the car, I don't know. But I didn't, because the girl came out of the Top Hat. She was alone and I could see when she passed me that she was drunk. She was staggering around and talking to herself. She went on up the street into another bar and I followed her. She was standing at the counter when I got there, talking to the man beside her. I heard her say that she wanted a beer and that she'd left her purse behind, and what a terrible place the bar was."

"That it stank, in fact," Meecham added.

"Yes, those were her words."

"And that's how Loftus knew exactly what happened in that bar, not because he was there but because you told him."

"I told him," she said, painfully. "He made me. He planned everything as soon as he found out what I'd done."

"Margolis came into the bar?"

"Yes. He didn't stay, but took the girl by the arm and steered her outside. It was nearly closing time. A lot of people were leaving and I left too. When I got outside, I saw Claude trying to lift the girl into his car. She had folded up completely and she was hard to handle because she wasn't little, like Clara. I wondered who the girl was. I thought, she must have someone, parents or relatives or maybe a husband, who wouldn't want to see her like that with a man like Claude. And then the idea occurred to me that I should follow them, that maybe the situation might have money in it somewhere, money for Earl."

She went on talking, quietly and earnestly, as if it was very important to her to explain everything and clarify her motives. It seemed to Meecham that the explanation was not for him or for herself but for Earl.

"They went to Claude's cottage on the river. I walked right in. The girl was on the couch asleep and Claude was starting a fire in the grate. Claude said, how the hell did you get here? I didn't answer that. I just told him again I wanted some money and if he didn't give it to me I would phone Lily and the police and the girl's parents, everyone I could think of. He laughed at me. He said the police wouldn't be interested and the girl had no parents and Lily was in South America. When I heard that, I felt that I had nothing left, no hope, no chance, nothing. The whole world was against me and Earl, the whole world, laughing at us, like Claude. I went over to the fireplace. Claude had turned away from me and was poking at the fire again. *You're showing your age, Emmy*, he said. *You'd better start dyeing your hair.* Those were the last words he ever spoke. When I stabbed him he sort of twisted around and nearly fell on top of the girl. Blood spurted all over her dress and coat but she didn't wake up. I stabbed him again, three or four times more, and I stood there and watched him die. I wasn't sorry for him or scared for myself. I just felt kind of relieved, like some awful pressure was gone from inside me."

It was her second mention of the pressure of anger. But Meecham was aware that behind the anger, like a chorus lost in the shadows of a stage while the spotlight followed the principal, there were other pressures; a whole chorus of pressures chosen haphazardly from every period of her life, unrehearsed, dancing out of step and time, screaming off-key.

"I didn't plan anything," she said. "It all just *happened*, and so quick, quicker than telling about it."

"His wallet was missing."

"I took it. I stole it. Sometimes I think I feel worse about that than I do about killing him. I was brought up strict, I never stole or told lies when I was a kid. I—well, there was forty dollars altogether. I kept the money and threw the wallet in the snow on my way home. It was snowing heavy by that time. That was lucky for me because I never thought of tire tracks or footprints or anything. I never even thought of the girl being left there with Claude's body. That seemed like luck too, at first, having her get arrested. I never dreamed it would turn out like this, me with the money I wanted for Earl, and no Earl to make it worthwhile. Six thousand dollars, and no Earl."

From the kitchen came the crash of glass and the old lady's voice, thick with the sleep she wooed and fought with like a lover: "A mesh, an awful mesh, mush clean it up fore Victor sheath it."

"I wasn't scared until I got home and then I realized what I'd done. It hit me the way I'd struck Claude hard and fast, so I could hardly crawl into the house. Everyone was asleep and the lights were off. I rapped on Earl's door and he let me in. I told him what had happened. He didn't get excited, he just kept saying everything would be all right. He fixed me some coffee and when I'd drunk it he made me tell him everything I saw and heard and did, every detail. He wrote down what I said in a notebook. I didn't know then what his idea was, not until he said, *Where will we get the blood*? Where will we get the blood," she repeated dully.

"Where did you get it?"

"From me, from my arm. I told you that I'd cut my arm on the broken tap. . . . I had to tell you something, I knew you'd seen the bandage. But I didn't cut it, Earl did. It took such a long time to get enough blood and Earl was sick from hurting me. But we had to have it to stain the clothes and it had to be mine because it was the same kind as Claude's."

"How did you know that?"

"Once years ago he was hurt on the job and had to have a transfusion. They used my blood, so I guessed it was the same kind. We had to take the chance anyway. Earl bandaged my arm. I guess I broke down then and started to scream because Earl put his hand over my mouth and he kept saying, *I killed Margolis, you were home in bed, you know nothing about it, I killed him.*

"I was crazy with fear but Earl wasn't. He said no jury would convict him because he was going to claim that he killed Claude to protect the girl, and the police would never be able to prove any other motive because there wasn't any. With me it was different, Earl said. They could trace back and find out about my relationship with Claude; they could pin fifty motives on me.

"I don't know how I got through that night. The next morning I drove over to my sister's in Chelsea, like Earl told me to do. It was Sunday, and Earl had to wait until Monday to go to the police because he wanted to sell whatever he could before they locked him up. I didn't find out that the girl had been arrested until Sunday night. I drove back home right away to talk to Earl. Earl said her arrest wouldn't affect his plan. He was wrong. Neither of us imagined how wrong he was, how it was going to affect not just us but everybody.

"On Monday morning Earl left the house early to sell his old Chevy and pawn whatever he could, and went over to the Sheriff's office with the confession in his pocket written out and memorized. You know what happened there. . . . He met the girl's mother, Mrs. Hamilton, in the corridor. Earl was never a schemer, never wanted anything for nothing. But he had a scheme then when he realized Mrs. Hamilton thought her daughter was guilty.

"He came home just before lunch time, terribly excited. He told me all about it, how the girl being a suspect would give me double protection and how the money would take care of Clara and me. He made me promise to look after Clara no matter what happened.

"He brought the money to me late in the afternoon, six thousand dollars. A fortune. Next morning the first thing I did was go down to Devine's and buy back the things Earl had pawned. They were Earl's keepsakes and I thought I'd have them waiting for him as a little surprise when he got out. I did what Earl said to do with the rest of the money. I deposited a little of it in the old account I had under my maiden name and hid what was left. I thought I was safe. Everything seemed so foolproof. Even if Earl's confession was torn apart, suspicion wouldn't fall on me but on the girl. Yes, I felt safe, I even felt hopeful. Earl would get off, we'd go away together, he'd be cured. I was full of crazy dreams like when I was young. I guess Earl didn't have any dreams. This morning he hanged himself."

The old lady's voice drifted from the other room: "Birdie? You there?"

"I'm here."

"Going to bed, very tired."

"I'll help you." She met the old lady at the kitchen door and took her by the arm. Slowly, the two of them moved across the room. "I can't stay with you tonight, Clara. You'll be hearing from me, though. I have to go away for a while but I'll be back, don't worry. I'll be back, won't I, Mr. Meecham?"

He was sure she would.

The snow had stopped. The air was clear and sharp, and the midnight moon traveled with them along the highway.

YOU ARE LEAVING KINCAID. ELEVATION 900, POPULATION 10,550. COME BACK SOON!

"She'll be back," Meecham said. "In a year, two years. Maybe sooner."

Alice pressed closer to his side, as if the mere mention of departures and returns was a threat of separation. "What will happen to her then? What will she be like?"

"She'll be the same. The pattern is the same—for Birdie, Miss Falconer, Emmy Hearst—and she'll follow it."

Alice shook her head in protest. "No, that's too cynical. People can change; they *do*."

"Do they?" The lights of Kincaid were no longer visible, though their reflection shone in the sky. "She'll come back," he repeated. "If Jim is still around she'll take up with him again. If he isn't, she'll find someone else, some man who will depend on her, a prodigal son she can mother."

"You must believe in fate, Meecham," she said gravely.

"Maybe."

"Then I guess you must be my fate. I didn't *choose* you. You just suddenly loomed up like a—well, like an iceberg."

"That's a beautiful thought."

"I mean it to be."

He took his eyes off the road for a second and looked down at her. Her face was a vague white blur in the darkness, anonymous, not Alice's face, but any woman's. He wondered, with a curious feeling of tightness in his throat, how many icebergs were ahead for Birdie and with what reckless skill she'd steer toward them.

Whatever happened, Birdie would survive. Thinking of her and of the girl beside him, Meecham was conscious of a great surge of energy and power, as if he could go on driving forever without food or sleep.

WIVES AND LOVERS

For Lydia and Don Freeman

1

IN HOT WEATHER Hazel liked to sit in the dental chair. Its leather arms and back were cool and there was a fan in the ceiling above it. She loosened the belt of her uniform and leaned back, listening to the hum of the fan and thinking what a fine place it was to sit and realize that except for one bicuspid she didn't have a filling in her head.

From the adjoining room she could hear sharp metallic sounds and the gurgling of water in a basin. Presently the gurgling stopped and Gordon Foster called, "Hazel?"

"Coming."

She climbed out of the chair and, tightening her belt, followed Gordon's voice into the lab. It was a shoebox of a room, with the ceiling pressed down on it like a lid, and Gordon and herself, two mis-mated shoes, tossed together into the box by a careless clerk.

"Did you want something?"

"No."

"You called."

"I thought you might have gone home."

"It's too hot to move. This is the hottest August I've ever experienced." She said this each August, and many times each August, but it always seemed true. "Besides, I brought my lunch."

Gordon looked up from the bridge he was repairing, his eyebrows raised. He didn't talk much when he was working but he often asked silent questions with his brows: Why don't you eat it, then?

"Thin people like you," Hazel said, dabbing at the sweat that trickled down behind her ears, "don't mind the heat so much."

"You could eat your lunch out on the grass where it's cooler."

"I prefer to stay inside."

"Oh."

"The ants. It's a bad year for ants."

Hazel sat on a stool sipping a Coke and looking without appetite at the sandwich she had brought for lunch. Some of the starch that had gone out of her uniform and out of Hazel herself seemed to have found its way into the sandwich. The bread had curled at the edges and the peanut butter filling had dried and stiffened like buckram.

She held the cold bottle of Coke against her forehead for a moment. "Air conditioning would be nice."

"I suppose it would."

"Maybe next summer."

He glanced at her questioningly—next summer? When is that?—then turned away with a sigh. Hazel was not sure whether the sigh meant that she was to be quiet or that next summer seemed a long sad year away.

"Dr. Foster—"

He shook his head. "Elaine says we can't afford an air conditioner." Elaine was his wife, and the final authority on office as well as personal expenditures.

"I know. I wasn't going to talk any more about that."

"Good."

"I just wanted to say, well, the last few weeks you haven't been yourself."

He smiled. He had extraordinarily good teeth for a dentist. "Who have I been?"

"I mean it." Hazel looked stubborn and unamused. "You've lost weight and your color's not good. Those are bad signs in a man your age."

He was thirty-eight, three years younger than Hazel, and sometimes Hazel felt like his mother and sometimes she felt like a mere sprite of a girl beside him. They were never contemporaries.

"Bad signs," she repeated. "You ought to go through one of the clinics and get checked up."

"And you ought to get married again, to some nice fellow who enjoys being fussed over."

"You think I'm fussing?"

"Like an old hen."

"I don't usually."

"No."

"So I must have a good reason for doing it now."

"The reason is, you're a nice normal woman and you don't feel alive unless you're fussing over someone."

"I've never heard you talk like this before. It just goes to show, things aren't *right*."

"No," he said. "No, things aren't right."

She opened her mouth to speak again, but he had turned his back, and his white starched coat was like a blank whitewashed wall.

The buzzer sounded from the front door and Hazel went to answer it, moving heavily on her heat-swollen feet.

She said over her shoulder, "I could make an appointment for you at the clinic."

"No, thanks."

"But if things aren't right—"

"I need a rest, that's all."

"I'm glad you're admitting it. You haven't had any time off since I came here."

"Yes, I have. I went up to San Francisco for the convention in June."

"Just three days. That's no holiday."

He didn't answer. But his shoulders were shaking, as if he was laughing silently to himself. He did that quite frequently lately, laughed to himself, and it annoyed Hazel not to know what the joke was. She never asked him, though, because she was a little afraid that he might tell her and that it wouldn't be quite so funny spoken out loud.

The buzzer sounded again and she went out through the hall to the waiting room. Since it was the doctor's afternoon off, the Venetian blinds were closed tight and the front door was locked.

Hazel opened it, squinting against the sudden sun.

"The doctor is not— Oh, it's you."

The girl said, very brightly and gaily, "Yes, it's me," as if she had enjoyed every moment standing on the roofless stucco porch in the blazing noon. Her face looked stiff; the sun seemed to have squeezed all the moisture out of it. In her right hand she carried a suitcase with "Ruby MacCormick" printed on the side in black crayon, and across her left forearm was a red fox fur.

"Me again," she said blithely. "Is the doctor—?"

"He's working in the lab."

"I won't disturb him then. I only—all I want is some place to sit down for a minute and think. I can't seem to *think* in this weather."

"It's cooler inside."

"I won't bother you." The girl stepped inside and put the suitcase on the floor and laid the red fox across it. "It's just, I want to sit for a minute. I've been walking. The suitcase is very heavy. I ought to have taken a taxi, except I wasn't sure where I was going."

Hazel closed the door. "You're leaving town?"

"No. No, I'm moving. The establishment where I've been staying, well, it's awfully low class. Not what I'm used to. If Mummy and Daddy ever found out, well, they'd kill me. I'm used to nice things."

"I'll get you some water."

"No. No, I don't want to bother you, Miss Philip. I was just passing and I remembered how kind you were last week and I thought I'd drop in and thank you and then be on my way."

"What way, if you don't know where you're going?"

"There must be places for a girl of my background."

Hazel didn't know what her background was. She'd met her only once before, the previous Friday. She had come to the office early in the morning and Gordon had introduced her to Hazel as Ruby MacCormick, a friend of one of his nieces from up north. As it turned out, Gordon himself had arranged the meeting because Ruby was out of a job and he thought Hazel might be able to suggest some type of employment. Ruby was very young and untrained, and the only possibility Hazel could think of was the Beachcomber, a restaurant out on the wharf which was operated, and partly owned, by her ex-husband, George. Because of his temper, and the influx of summer tourists, George was constantly plagued by a shortage of waitresses and he was willing to try anyone who could walk and count up to ten. Ruby could do both.

Hazel poured some water from the cooler and the girl drank it thirstily. She was so thin that her Adam's apple was prominent as a boy's, and moved up and down when she swallowed.

Ruby smiled, her mouth still wet from the water. "That was good. It's funny, I didn't even know I was thirsty. Daddy says I was always like that—I never let physical things bother me, I never squalled for food the way some babies do."

"Have you had any lunch?"

"Not yet. I'm waiting till I go to work. Lunch and dinner are free."

"You got the job, then?"

Ruby widened her eyes. "Didn't I tell you? I guess I forgot. Mr. Anderson hired me right off the bat."

"Good."

"Of course I'm only a waitress, there was no opening as a hostess, but Mr. Anderson says I have a chance to work up . . . I did just what you told me. I went over to the bartender and I said someone had told me he needed a waitress and practically the next minute I was hired. I didn't even have to mention your name, it was that quick."

Hazel didn't bother informing her that this was the way George did all his hiring, and firing, too.

"Are you and Mr. Anderson friends?"

"We were at one time," Hazel said dryly. "We haven't seen much of each other lately." She was usually very quick to tell anyone, even a total stranger, about her personal affairs, including the complete history of her marriage to George, but she had no wish to confide in this girl. Ruby's strange talk disturbed her. It was like listening to a bird talk; the words sounded real, they could be understood well enough, but they had no connection with the bird's thoughts.

"Well, I won't keep you." Ruby rose and picked up the red fox and slung it across her arm with a show of elegant indifference as if she had a hundred such furs stashed away in her drawers at home. But every now and then, as she talked, Hazel had caught her glancing at the fox with anxiety and affection the way a mother glances at a loved but wayward child.

One thing Hazel was sure of—the fox had seen better days; Ruby hadn't.

She said, "What kind of place are you looking for?"

"Oh, just a room. I can't afford anything fancy like I was used to at home. I'm standing on my own two feet now, that's what I wrote and told Daddy."

"My cousin Ruth has a friend who runs a rooming house. She calls it a tourist home. It's on El Camino del Mar."

"That sounds like a very high class location."

"It's the highway. 101."

"Oh." Ruby's jaw tightened but when she spoke again her voice was as gay and blithe as ever: "Well, none of my friends up north will know the difference. They'll think it's high class just like I thought." She paused. "Is it far from here?"

"Ten blocks or so."

"Oh God." Ruby sat down again, holding the fox's head close against her face.

Hazel looked away. Dead things made her nervous.

"I can call you a cab," she said.

"No. No thanks."

"It's a long way, in this heat."

"I don't—I don't mind the heat like most people. I'm just a little tired, but I'll manage. I always do. I'm stronger than I look."

To prove her point she got back onto her feet. She wore winter shoes, black suede pumps scuffed at the toes and heels. Her stockingless legs were very white, as if they'd been frozen.

"I'd better be on my way."

"Hold it a minute while I phone and see if Mrs. Freeman has a vacancy. It might save you a trip."

"You're kind, Miss Philip, you're a kind person," Ruby said, in a surprised voice.

It was too hot to argue so Hazel merely shook her head.

She used the extension phone in the operating room, partly because she didn't want Ruby to overhear her conversation, and partly because she liked to sit in the dental chair while she was telephoning.

Ruth answered the telephone: "Hello? Hazel? I was just doing the lunch dishes." Ruth always made a point of telling people what she was doing, had just done or was about to do. In this way she gave the impression that she did as much work as any six people and so could never be accused of being lazy or not earning her keep. "What do you want? I was just about to start on the Venetian blinds."

"There's a young girl here looking for a room. I thought I'd send her over to Mrs. Freeman's."

"Is the girl respectable?"

"She's a friend of one of Dr. Foster's relatives from up north."

"Then she should certainly be respectable." Ruth was the official babysitter for the Fosters' three children, and while she hadn't much interest in, or use for, Gordon, she admired Elaine Foster tremendously.

Hazel said, "I don't want to send the girl all the way over there unless Mrs. Freeman has a vacancy. Could you give me her phone number?"

"She doesn't have a phone. What with the girls using it all the time, she had it taken out. But I know she has a vacancy. I saw her last night at the organ recital at church."

"What's the house number?"

"1906."

"Thanks."

"Hazel? Are you still there? . . . When I finish the blinds, I have to go over to the Fosters' to babysit, but when I come home I thought I'd wax all the window sills."

"You don't have to."

"Wax is a preservative."

"All right, then. All right." There was no use in arguing with Ruth. Hazel knew that by evening the window sills would all be waxed and Ruth would be lying on the bed with a wet cloth across her eyes.

Gordon came in from the lab and began washing his hands at the basin.

Hazel climbed awkwardly out of the dental chair. "Have you finished?"

"With the bridge, yes. I still have that inlay to cast."

"I can help you."

"It's your afternoon off as well as mine."

"In this weather there's nothing I want to do anyway." There was something, but she would never have admitted it to anyone: she wanted to go down to the beach in a brand-new bathing suit and look the way she had twenty years ago when she and George were married. She had changed in those twenty years, and so had George, but it was characteristic of Hazel that she noticed more changes in herself than in him.

Gordon dried his hands on a linen towel. "Who was at the door?"

"That girl, the one who was here last week."

"Girl?"

"Ruby MacCormick."

"Well," he said, carefully. "What did she want?"

"She's still here."

"Oh."

"She wants a room. She's moving. I was just trying to find a place for her to go."

"And did you?"

"I think so. It's on the highway, 1906."

"Not a very good location."

"The best she can afford, that's my opinion. She talks big, but I can tell. Any woman could."

He threw away the towel and stood for a moment with his clenched fist pressed against the left side of his chest. It was a way he had of standing lately, as if all his problems had gathered together in a tight little bunch around his heart, and the pressure of his fist was meant to dispel them.

Hazel leaned over and picked up the towel and put it in the laundry container. She spoke quietly: "Maybe you'd better go out and say hello to her, just for politeness's sake."

"I'd prefer not to."

"All right then, I'll say it for you."

"Do that." He hesitated a moment. "Did you bring your car this morning?"

"Yes."

"Perhaps it wouldn't be too much out of your way to drive the girl as far as the highway. I feel a certain obligation to her because she's a stranger in town."

"Well, so do I, only I wanted to stay and help you cast the inlay. I'll pour it up for you."

"I can do it alone. Or you can come back later, if you insist."

"I'll come back."

"Thank you, Hazel."

He sounded so deeply grateful that she wasn't sure what he was thanking her for; it couldn't be for anything so trivial as offering to help him with the inlay, or driving Ruby over to the highway.

On the way to Mrs. Freeman's, the girl sat quiet and motionless except when Hazel's old Chevy hit a bump or turned a fast corner, or when Hazel asked a direct question: "What made you decide to come to Channel City?"

"I wanted to get away from home."

"This is a tough place to make a living."

"I have a job."

"You'd do better down south. Some of the big airplane factories—"

"I like it here."

"There's not much chance of promotion being a waitress at the Beachcomber."

"Mr. Anderson says I can work up to cashier or hostess if I try."

"And after that?"

Ruby frowned and then rubbed away the frown lines with the tip of her forefinger. "After that I might get married."

"Have you a boyfriend back home?"

"Loads of them, but they're all silly and immature."

"How old are you, Ruby?"

"Old enough."

Hazel wanted to laugh—the things the girl said were funny, but the way she said them was not. There was an air of stubborn earnestness about her, as if she had in the back of her mind a single and solemn purpose that obliterated all others.

Hazel stopped the car in front of 1906, a two-storied frame house with a sign nailed to one of the porch pillars: "Mrs. Freeman's Tourist Home, Ladies Only, Reasonable Rates, Ocean View." The house, like the scrawny shrubs planted around it and the parched lawn in front of it, bore the marks of the drought years.

"It's not much to look at from the outside, but it's clean inside. Mrs. Freeman is a very clean woman," Hazel added quite severely, as if Ruby had accused Mrs. Freeman of being a very dirty one.

Ruby opened the car door. "Thank you for the ride."

"That's all right."

"I didn't want to admit it but I was awful tired. You just about saved my life."

"It was Dr. Foster's idea."

"It was? Heavens, I didn't think he'd even remember me, honestly."

But the word, honestly, was contradicted by the coy and artificial tone of her voice. She's lying, Hazel thought. She expected to be remembered, and wanted to be. I wonder what her game is.

Ruby put her suitcase on the ground and started to close the car door.

"Leave it open," Hazel said. "It's cooler."

"But you can't drive with it open."

"I thought if you wouldn't be too long I'd wait here for you and drop you off at work on my way back to the office."

The girl looked wary. "I couldn't ask you to do that."

"You didn't ask me. I offered."

"But why? Did Dr. Foster—?"

"No. This is my own idea."

"Thank you." She stood in the blazing sun, stroking the red fox. "You've changed my day, Miss Philip."

"Have I?"

"It started out very bad, worse than I would ever tell anyone. But now it's changed. You've brought me luck. I feel, I honestly feel *lucky*."

"I'm glad you do," Hazel said. She wasn't certain what luck meant to Ruby or how the girl would use it now that it had come her way.

The front door opened and Mrs. Freeman came out on the porch, a tall, stout, middle-aged woman in a printed silk dress that blew around her like a tent. She peered down at the car with the look of chronic suspicion that landladies acquire after years of people. Then, very abruptly, she turned and went back into the house as if she had lost all interest in the car because she'd been expecting someone else.

Inside the house again, Mrs. Freeman leaned against the banister and wiped the sweat off her forehead with the back of her hand. *I thought it was him, I thought for sure. He said, any day now, any day. One of these days . . .*

Ruby picked up her suitcase. "I'm kind of scared. Would you come in with me?"

"I don't know her. She's a friend of my cousin's, not mine. Besides, you're lucky now, remember?"

"Yes, I'm lucky. This is my lucky day. People will like me and I will like them."

So that's her idea of luck, Hazel thought. It had nothing to do with money or jobs. Luck was being liked and liking; and the day which for Ruby had started out very bad, worse than she would ever tell anyone, must have started with hate. Someone had hated Ruby and she had hated in return, and Hazel had changed the day by being kind to her. Hazel wondered who would go to the trouble of hating a girl like Ruby.

Ruby went into the house, and the door closed on her like the page of a book.

Hazel lit a cigarette but the smoke was so hot and acrid that it parched her mouth and stung her eyes. She threw the cigarette out of the window, thinking of George, because it was one of the things she did which annoyed him, throwing lighted cigarettes out of the car. Whenever he read in the newspaper about a forest fire, he practically accused Hazel of being responsible for it even though she'd been several hundred miles away at the time it started and hadn't been smoking anyway. Many of the things for which George held Hazel responsible were justified, but starting forest fires was not one of them.

George was a most unreasonable man. Still, Hazel got out of the car and crushed out the cigarette under the rubber heel of her white nurse's oxfords, wishing that George would pass right that moment and see her. She frequently got a certain sly satisfaction out of correcting the minor faults he'd found in her. The major ones she retained; they were as much a part of her as her skin, but, like her skin, they had sagged a little with the years and no longer fitted so tight.

In five minutes Ruby came out again, without the suitcase and the fox fur. She was smiling and the smile softened the angularity of her jaw and made her look quite pretty.

She got into the car, almost out of breath, as if she'd been running. "She *is* nice, really *nice*, I mean."

"Good."

"She liked me right away, too. I told you I felt lucky, didn't I?" She began to hum softly to herself, "I'm Looking Over a Four Leaf Clover."

Hazel made a quick, illegal U-turn and headed south toward the harbor. Heat rose from the highway in waves, so that the white road markers looked uneven and the outlines of the passing cars were blurred. In the distance a strip of sea was visible, an ice-blue promise of relief from the heat.

"If I brought you luck," Hazel said, "maybe you'll take my advice."

"What advice?"

"Don't stick around this town."

"I have to."

"It's no place for a kid like you with no occupational training. It'd be different if you were going maybe to nurse's school or beauty college, something like that."

"I hate sickness and I hate other people's dirty hair." The girl paused. "Why are you so anxious for me to leave town?"

"I'm not anxious. There's nothing personal in it. I just think it'd be a good idea."

"Well, it isn't." Ruby turned and looked stubbornly out of the window. "I'm staying. I have a job, I'm self-supporting, and I can live where and how I want to."

Hazel was silent, watching the strip of sea expand on the horizon. She said, finally, "That business about all the boyfriends back home—malarkey, wasn't it?"

The girl didn't answer.

"There's only one boyfriend and he's here, in this town. Is that your story, Ruby?"

"You're very nosy," Ruby said.

2

AT TWELVE-THIRTY George Anderson walked along the wharf towards the Beachcomber, a tall, heavy-set man wearing slacks and a sport shirt and a navy blue yachting cap trimmed with gold braid.

Someone had told George once that he moved like an athlete, and ever since then he'd been extremely careful to move like an athlete at all times, eyes straight ahead, shoulders back, stomach in, chin up. This posture was no longer easy to maintain, partly because he was forty now and putting on weight, and partly because in such a position it was difficult to avoid stepping into the holes in the wharf or stumbling against the two-by-fours where it had been patched up.

The wharf was eighty years old. It had been built to last forever but even the proudest citizens of Channel City were forced to admit that it wasn't going to make it. Some of the holes in the planks were as large as fists and when cars drove along it or when a seiner accidentally struck it while docking, the whole structure swayed and tottered and the pilings squawked like gulls.

George took a personal interest in the wharf. He liked boats and he liked money, and the wharf meant both to him since the Beachcomber was built on the end of it. Sometimes, when a particular hole got so big that there was danger of one of the Beachcomber's customers breaking a leg, George himself would come out and repair it, equipped with a bag of nails and a hammer and any piece of wood he could lay his hands on. One of the holes George had rather impulsively mended with the favorite chopping block of the Beachcomber's head chef, Romanelli. After an exchange of bitter words with George over the incident, Romanelli went home and sulked for two days, drinking red wine and planning hot revenge. Unable to think of anything drastic enough and rather pleasantly tired from trying, Romanelli returned to work on the third day, docile and resigned, and George bought him a new chopping block and personally burned Romanelli's initials on the side of it with a soldering iron.

On each side of the wharf "No Fishing" signs were posted but these signs were traditionally ignored and by noon the railings were lined with fishermen of all races and ages and sizes. George nodded pleasantly to each of them because they gave the wharf local color and provided interesting characters for the patrons of the Beachcomber to watch as they dined.

He stopped behind an old woman wearing oil-stained jeans and a wide straw hat pushed back on her head. Her face was brown and lively and covered with wrinkles, like coffee being stirred.

"Hiya, Millie."

Millie jumped, clutching at her hat. "Jees, you scared me!"

"I see you've changed places again. How's the luck over on this side?"

"The same," Millie said. "The same, no matter where I go. I got a jinx, George."

"Go on. You just have to keep trying."

"I tell you, I got a jinx. It don't matter whether I use mussels or squid or sardines, or what I use. Listen, George, I got a proposition."

"Nuts," George said pleasantly.

Millie's propositions were always the same. They were a natural result of her jinx. Other fishermen might occasionally catch a stingray, but Millie hardly ever caught anything else. She usually pulled up at least one a day, and her problem was to get rid of it. If she threw it back into the sea it might be washed up on the beach and some curious child might pick it up and cut himself on the ray's barbed poisonous tail.

After considerable thought on the subject Millie had figured out a way to make a profit on her jinx.

"Listen, George, you cut off the tail, see, and the head, and clean out the guts and what you got left? Filet of stingray. Only you don't have to call it stingray on the menu. Maybe just filet of ray. Don't that sound good to eat?"

"No."

"Hell, George, you're getting old, your mind's narrowing. You think maybe just because a stingray's a mean-looking bastard he won't taste so good. You serve swordfish steaks and swordfish are the meanest-looking bastards ever lived."

Laughing, George put his hands in his pockets and jingled the loose change. He had every intention of some day buying one of Millie's stingrays and taking it over for Hazel to cook.

"I never see you eating any of the things," he said.

"I had one last night for supper," Millie lied solemnly. "No kidding, George, it was a real taste thrill. Maybe like tuna, maybe like abalone. High class stuff."

"I bet."

"Or chowder. How about making it into chowder, George? Chopped up like that, who'd know the difference from clams, I ask you. Be a sport and take a chance, George."

"Ixnay."

Millie sighed. "Oh well, no hard feelings anyway, eh? How's Hazel?"

"The last I heard, fine."

"I saw her drive by a few minutes ago. She went into the Beachcomber. How about that?"

"What do you mean, how about it?"

"I figure you and Hazel—"

"You figure wrong."

"Well, you don't have to bite my head off."

With haughty dignity Millie returned to her fishing. She crossed herself and gave her pole three quick jerks to discourage her jinx.

Hazel's old blue Chevy was standing in the middle of the parking lot next to the Beachcomber. Hazel had never learned to park properly and whenever she came down to the wharf she just left her car with the key in the ignition so that anyone who wanted it moved could move it without bothering her.

George unlocked the front door of the Beachcomber and walked through the foyer into the bar. Hazel was standing at one of the open windows looking out at the sea and breathing very deeply like an underwater swimmer storing up oxygen for the next dive.

He stared at her across the room, wondering why she had come, whether she had heard anything about him and the girl.

"How did you get in?"

"Through the kitchen. Romanelli told me you'd be along in a few minutes so I thought I'd stay and say hello. So, hello."

"Hello." He took off his yachting cap and began rolling up his sleeves. "Nice to see you, Hazel."

"You act overjoyed."

"It's too hot to turn cartwheels."

"Think you still could?"

"Sure, I think so." He put on his bartender's apron, tying it very tight to minimize his paunch. "I've been swimming from here to the breakwater and back every day for a week now."

"Why?"

"Keeping in shape, that's all. How about a beer to cool off?"

"Sounds fine." She crossed the room and perched on one of the red leather bar stools with her legs crossed. "I heard you were on another of your health binges."

"Who told you?"

"Word gets around."

"It seems to me a hell of a lot of words get around to you." He drew two beers from the tap. "Here's to crime. Someday it may pay."

"Right." She sipped her beer. "Gee, this is like old times, eh, George?"

He looked at her uneasily over the rim of his glass. "I guess it is."

"Maybe we ought to drink to old times."

"That's for New Year's Eve."

"What did you do last New Year's Eve, George?"

"I don't remember." He remembered too well: he'd tended bar until two o'clock in the morning and then, in one of the vilest moods he'd ever experienced, he went home and began drinking. He woke up the next morning in a house on East Wilson Street with a plump black-haired girl lying beside him making little snorting noises in her sleep. His wallet was gone but he never reported it to the police.

"I kind of like New Year's Eve," Hazel said. "Don't you?"

"Yeah. Sure."

"Well, what else is new besides the health binge?"

"I wish you'd stop calling it that. I'm just trying to keep fit."

"Romanelli says you've been eating seaweed."

"I don't *eat* it. I sprinkle a little of it on my food."

"Well, I'll be damned," Hazel said earnestly. "How does it taste?"

"Pretty good."

"What's this seaweed supposed to do for you?"

"A lot of things. It's full of vitamins and minerals and stuff like that. Matter of fact, a fellow I know has a kelp-cutting barge and I'm thinking of going into business with him."

"The *seaweed* business?"

"That's right."

"Well, I shall be very damned," Hazel said.

"I might have known better than to mention it to you. It so happens that scientists have discovered many new uses for seaweed."

"Name one."

"There are hundreds. This fellow I know that owns the barge—"

"If I were you I'd stick to the restaurant business. The day may come when we'll all be sitting around munching seaweed but I don't think it's close. Remember the time you sank two thousand dollars in that vacuum cap for growing hair?"

"You've never let me forget it."

"How could I? We nearly starved for a year."

"Look, Hazel, let's not argue. If you're worried about whether I'm going to go broke and you won't get your alimony every month, forget it."

"Maybe I'm a little worried," she said dryly. "I can't keep the house running without it."

"Ruth has no job yet?"

"No."

"I thought by this time she'd be well enough to go back to teaching."

"They'll never take her back, you know that. Maybe she knows it too. I can't tell."

"Poor old Ruth." George disliked Ruth intensely, having suffered too often from her acid disapproval, but now that he no longer had to see her, he could afford to express a little sympathy for her. "How are the others?"

"Fine."

"Another beer?"

"No thanks. I have to get back to work pretty soon." She added, casually, without looking at him, "Harold says he saw you downtown the other night."

"I didn't see him."

"You weren't doing much looking around, Harold said."

"What did he mean by that?"

"You were too busy with the new girlfriend."

George put the two empty glasses into the rinsing trough and wiped his hands carefully on his apron. "So that's why you came—"

"No, it's not. I gave someone a lift and—"

"—to check up on me again."

"Apparently you need some checking up. Harold says the girl was young enough to be your daughter."

"So?"

Hazel gazed at him in a kindly way. About some things, especially women, George was a babe in arms and Hazel sometimes had to be a little rough with him, for his own good. "Just remember what I told you, George, time and again. When some young chick pretends she's interested in you, you go and take a good look in the mirror."

"Oh, for Pete's sake, I—"

"Then you ask yourself: is it *me* or is it the Beachcomber she's batting her eyelashes at? See what I mean, George? I don't want you to make a sap of yourself. It'd be kind of a reflection on me if you made a sap of yourself. Just don't get carried away."

"Well, who's carried away?" George said irritably. "I hardly know the girl."

"Personally, there's nothing I'd like better than to see you married again, to some nice sensible woman, a widow, maybe, with a little something in the bank."

"All right, all right. You find her, I'll marry her."

"I'll look around. Meanwhile, don't you forget what I told you about the mirror."

"No time like the present," George said bleakly, and turned and stared into the mirror behind the bar. There, between a bottle of apple brandy and a bottle of vodka, was his face, and it seemed to him exactly the same face he'd always had, no better, no worse.

"See what I mean, George? You're no spring chicken. You're still a nice-looking man, for my money, but you're not going to set fire to any young girl . . . What's her name?"

"You wouldn't know her. She's one of the new girls I took on last week, a stranger in town."

"I thought you made it a rule not to mess around with the hired help."

"For Christ's sake, who's messing around? I drove her home a couple of times, is all. Now can we drop the subject?"

"What's your hurry? I'm just getting interested."

George leaned across the counter. His face was very red and the pulse in his temple throbbed with the rush of blood. "You won't be satisfied until you know all about her, will you? You can't leave me alone, can you?"

"I just—well, I'd like to see you happy, is all."

"Don't kid me. If you thought I showed the least sign of being happy you'd march down here and plug me full of holes."

"You don't—"

"Well, I'm happy now. Hear that?—I'm happy right now! So what are you going to do about it?"

"Nothing," Hazel said through stiff lips. "I'm glad to hear it. Very glad."

George turned away, exhaling a long noisy sigh like an engine standing in a station letting off excess steam because it was not yet time to move. When he spoke again his voice was quiet and resigned. "Forget what I said. It's not true, that business about plugging me full of holes. It's just that I'm tired, I want to forget about things, including Ruby."

"Ruby." She had known of course that it had to be Ruby but until the actual mention of her name she had kept hoping that it wasn't. The girl, for all her youth, had a shifty way about her, and George, for all his experience, was as artless and as easy to deceive as a baby. "All right," Hazel said, "we'll drop the subject. Forget about her."

"The point is, I can't. She keeps cropping up in my head. I'll be thinking of something else and then suddenly, wham, Ruby will pop up in the middle of it."

"And do you pop up in the middle of what she's thinking?"

"Maybe, but I doubt it." George smiled thinly. "As you pointed out, I'm not the type to set fire to any young girl."

"I didn't mean that as a nasty crack. It was for—"

"For my own good, yes, I know. Well, I haven't set fire to her, and she hasn't to me either. She's just gotten under my skin, is all."

"Oh."

"I feel sorry for her, see. She's a lousy waitress, moves around like I was running an old people's home, and whenever she makes a mistake she stands around for ten minutes apologizing for it. She doesn't realize that a customer would rather have a steak than an apology . . . And sloppy, God, is she sloppy. Half the coffee's in the saucer and the other half's on the floor, and she still manages to have enough left over to splash on the customer. She's just not cut out for this kind of work."

"I guess not."

"But here she is, see?—and she's not doing her job but she keeps trying so hard and the harder she tries the worse she gets. I ought to fire her before she wrecks the joint, but I can't. She needs looking after. If I fired her, she'd be on my conscience."

"You've got a nice roomy conscience, George, there ought to be a place for one more."

Hazel climbed off the bar stool and smoothed her uniform down over her hips. Her arms and legs felt a little heavy, partly from the beer and partly from the depression that had come over her while George was talking. Though she was no longer married to George, or in love with him, she had a deep sense of responsibility for him as she had for all her friends and relatives, and it was a little disturbing to hear George talking about looking after somebody when he was the one who always had to be looked after. George was an impulsive man, and like most impulsive people he had friends who would have been willing to cut off a right arm for him, or at least a finger, and enemies who would have liked to shoot him on sight. It had been Hazel's duty to protect him from both. Even now, when the marriage was ended and Hazel had been relieved of her duties, she still clung to some of them, like a retired general playing with tin soldiers and toy tanks long after the war was won or lost.

She said, "Well, I'd better be getting on my horse."

"Hazel, if you were me, what would you do?"

"About what?"

"You know—Ruby."

"Pension her off. Put her in a good orphanage. Feed her to the sharks. How the heck should I know what to do? It's your life."

"That's the point, I don't feel it *is* my life anymore. I feel like I'm in a box and somebody's sitting on the lid. Or—" George stroked his chin and scowled out the window. "Or like those lobsters way out there caught in the traps. At first they don't realize they're in a trap; they keep going through the same motions they always did, until *zip*, somebody pulls them up and there they are, lobsters Thermidor."

"George Anderson Thermidor," Hazel said.

Blinking, George drew his eyes away from the sea, and the invisible lobster traps. "I don't know why I'm talking like this. It will give you the wrong idea of Ruby. Actually she's a very shy, sweet kid."

"No traps?"

"No."

"Then what are you worrying about? No traps, no George Anderson Thermidor." Hazel reached over the bar and patted him kindly on the shoulder. "You've got another one of your crushes, is all. Cheer up. You'll get over it, same as always."

George stared at her gloomily. "You're a pretty swell woman, Hazel."

"Baloney."

"No, I mean it. You know what we should do, Hazel? We should go out right now and tie one on, for old time's sake."

"We should, eh?"

"We'll go the rounds, how about it? I'll forget all about this joint, and Ruby."

"We'll go the rounds, eh?"

"Why not?"

"You figure out why not."

She began walking toward the door, very slowly, as if she expected to be called back.

George watched her, looking a little bewildered. "Where are you going?"

"Home."

"But I thought you and I—"

"My idea of how not to have a good time is to go the rounds with you and watch you get stinking drunk so you can forget another woman."

"Well, for Christ's sake."

"You give me a pain, George. You give me a big fat pain."

She went out and slammed the door, and a minute later he could hear her racing the engine of the old Chevy. The smell of its exhaust fumes floated in through the open windows along with the smell of kelp and dead fish and hot rolls baking in the kitchen and tar from the underwater oil wells.

George watched the Chevy bounce along the wharf and then he turned and looked at himself in the mirror. His face was the same as it always was, except that it looked terribly surprised: *What did I do or say? I just asked her to go out, to go the rounds.*

It seemed to George that people deliberately or maliciously misunderstood his intentions. He always had the best intentions in the world, but lately every time he opened his mouth he got into trouble, the same as he did when he was a boy. When George was eight he had swollen adenoids and he kept his mouth open a great deal of the time to breathe through. One day when he was playing in the barranca behind his house, a bee flew into his mouth, and before he could spit it out the bee stung the roof of his mouth. For a long time after his adenoids had been removed, George kept his lips pressed together very tightly and he looked like a little old man with no teeth.

George had told this story to nearly everyone he knew, to point a moral, but he never told the sequel: that he was still deathly afraid of bees and that whenever he was worried he kept his jaws clamped together and his lips compressed, and looked like a big middle-aged man with no teeth.

Breathing through his nose George crossed the foyer and the dining room decorated with yacht pennants and abalone shells, and passed through the swinging doors into the kitchen.

While the bar and the dining room were deserted, the kitchen was alive with a kind of hysterical activity. A boy in a brown apron was oiling the dish-washing machine and whistling through his teeth. This boy had a gap between his two front teeth which was bad for talking but fine for whistling so he expressed himself not in words but with a variety of whistles, like a bird. All through the day and night his whistling served as an obbligato to the other kitchen sounds: the hissing of steam, the shrill squawking of the griddle, the banging of oven doors; bursts of Victor Herbert from the pastry chef and Romanelli's eloquent cursing; the buzz of an electric timer measuring the minutes backwards, and the spasmodic peal of Mr. Romanelli's own special alarm clock which he set to remind himself to do all kinds of things, to phone his wife, order turkeys, bawl out the linen-supply service and have the spark plugs checked in his car. At intervals throughout the day Romanelli's alarm went off and the boy with the gap between his two front teeth whistled his allusive obbligatos.

Romanelli put down the chicken he was singeing and came over to George. He was stripped to the waist, but he wore his white chef's hat.

"Lousy hot," Romanelli said.

George nodded, without unfolding his lips.

"Some lady was here. Nice lady. She brought a present to you." Romanelli's eyes danced and his stomach heaved in silent laughter. "On the carving table I put it. Oh my, oh my." Though Romanelli was inclined to be irritable, he dearly loved a joke, and when he laughed he laughed all over. His head bobbed, his chest shook, his feet stamped and his eyes laughed tears. "Oh my. Such a present. Such a nice lady."

On the carving table was a freshly caught stingray. It was not quite dead. Its barbed tail moved now and then, and on each side of its head its dull, vicious eyes stared at George.

George's mouth opened.

"Take that goddamn thing out of here," he shouted. "Do you hear me? Take it out, get rid of the goddamn thing!"

He turned and saw Ruby standing in the doorway, looking pale and surprised. When she met his gaze she moved her arms convulsively and two cups rolled off the table beside her. They didn't break, and Ruby bent over hurriedly to pick them up. Her handbag fell on the floor.

"And you," George yelled. "You over there, you're fired, see? Collect a week's pay and get out! Hear me? You're fired!"

Ruby grabbed her handbag and ran.

Romanelli impaled the stingray on a carving knife and carried it out to the garbage can.

Even after the stingray was gone George could still smell it, its sharp fishy odor mingling with the odor of soap and baking pies and chicken livers and Ruby's Cashmere Bouquet talcum powder.

3

GORDON FOSTER'S OFFICE was one of ten pink stucco bungalows built around a court on the upper end of Main Street. Nine of the bungalows were occupied by physicians specializing in various fields; Gordon was the only dentist.

Whenever Elaine Foster came to call for her husband she took particular care with her grooming and her costume. As she walked through the court, past the goldfish pond and the lantana hedges, she held her head high, not exactly pretending that she was one of the physicians' wives, but half-consciously hoping that passers-by would mistake her for one. It was always a disappointment to her when she had to turn in at Number Seven, which was plainly marked, "Gordon W. Foster, D.D.S."

Elaine believed that Gordon could have been a real doctor if he had had more initiative, or if he'd met her earlier in life, so that she could have supplied the initiative. As it was, when they met, Gordon was already a dentist, and even Elaine's considerable powers couldn't make him into anything else. Their marriage had been colored by Elaine's bile-green feeling that she had been cheated, that Gordon should have become a real doctor because she herself had all the attributes of a perfect doctor's wife. She was energetic, competent, smartly groomed, and she had a low, cultured voice, excellent diction and a smattering of grammar: *I'm very sorry the doctor is not in . . . You may reach him at his office . . . Yes, I shall see that he receives the message . . .*

Elaine was at her best on the telephone. She used it as an actress uses a role, to project her personality and at the same time to hide behind the projection. As a real doctor's wife she could have spent a great deal of time on the telephone, leaving the details of the house and the three children to a maid. As a dentist's wife, she couldn't afford a maid. She couldn't even afford a second car, so that when she needed the Oldsmobile for shopping or errands, she had to drive Gordon to work in the morning and call for him when he had finished for the day.

She went around to the back door of Number Seven and let herself in. She could hear Gordon moving around in the lab, whistling. Elaine was, by nature, extremely suspicious of music or happy sounds in general, and she wondered what Gordon had to whistle about on such a hot day, with the house payment overdue and the tuition fee of Judith's school raised again.

The medicinal smell in the office made her cough. Gordon heard the cough and came out of the lab into the hall, carrying a full set of dentures in his hand.

Elaine turned her eyes away. "*Honestly*, Gordon."

"What's the matter?"

"You know I can't stand the sight of—those things."

"Oh. Sorry." He put the dentures in his pocket. "I'm not quite ready to leave yet."

"I was hoping you would be. The children have been looking forward to this all day. You know how they adore the beach."

"Beach?"

"Don't tell me you've forgotten."

"No. I—"

"But you have. I knew as soon as I walked in that you'd forgotten."

"I have other things on my mind, Elaine. I can't remember everything."

"We talked about it only this morning. You said at breakfast that it was going to be a hot day, and I said, let's get Ruth to look after the baby and you and I and Judith and Paul will go down to the beach . . . You couldn't possibly have forgotten."

"No." He couldn't possibly, but he had. He remembered Elaine mentioning Ruth, but after that his mind had wandered because the name Ruth had reminded him of the name Ruby.

Elaine was watching him, not reproachfully as she had at first, but with careful intensity like a cat about to pounce.

"I hate to mention this, Gordon, but everyone has noticed how absent-minded you've become lately."

"I've been working pretty hard."

"Hard work or not, you still have *ears*. You *heard* me talking about going to the beach this afternoon."

"Yes, I suppose I did."

"But you didn't care."

He put his hand in his pocket. The dentures felt cold and smooth to the touch, not like real teeth, which were warm and often a little rough. The owner of the dentures needed them by tomorrow morning. Elaine needed to go to the beach. It was up to Gordon to decide whose need was the more urgent.

He said, "I didn't really promise that I'd have the afternoon free, Elaine."

"You *implied* a promise."

"I'd like to go to the beach as much as you, perhaps more."

"I'm not concerned with myself. It's the children. You know how much they enjoy the water."

"I know how much they don't."

"I beg your pardon?"

"Nothing."

He was sorry he'd spoken, even though it was the truth. Like Elaine, both of the children were afraid of the water, and yet the beach seemed to hold an intense fascination for all three of them. Elaine would sit staring uneasily at the waves and wonder aloud about the tides and complain about the sand fleas. Paul would wander off by himself to pick up a group of strangers who would be very amused at first by his antics, then bored by his demands for attention, and finally exhausted and unkind. Judith, the seven-year-old, had a subtler approach to self-satisfaction. She would dig vast holes in the sand, large as graves, some of them, and here she would sit and eat her way through the contents of the picnic basket. A day at the beach, which always seemed so much fun for other families, was often a nightmare for the Fosters. Neither Gordon nor Elaine knew why this was so, but in self-defense each blamed the other.

"I don't care about myself," Elaine said. "I'm used to disappointments, all kinds, all sizes."

"I guess you are."

"It's the children I'm thinking of . . . Other families go places together, even the Harrisons, and he's a real doctor. I saw them at the horse show, the night you worked late."

Gordon rubbed his eyes, knowing what was coming, yet feeling utterly powerless to stop it.

"You work late so often recently."

"I have to."

"If your practice is really that good, perhaps it's time to hire an assistant."

"I couldn't make ends meet if I did."

"They're not meeting too well right now."

"Well, I'm doing my best."

"Yes. Yes, I really believe you are, Gordon."

She sounded so sincere and kindly that he turned to look at her in surprise. She was a tall woman, nearly as tall as he. Her self-assured manner, her air of owning the world, had been one of the first things about her that he had noticed and admired. As the years passed Gordon had come to realize that it was not an air or a manner; Elaine really did own her world, and she allowed him to live in a little corner of it at a rent that he found nearly impossible to pay.

"The trouble with some people's best," Elaine said, "is that it isn't good enough."

"Nothing will ever be good enough for you, Elaine."

"Other women are more easily satisfied, are they?"

"I don't know . . . I don't even know what we're talking about, money or sex."

"You know I never discuss sex," she said stiffly.

"Then it must be money. Is that what you want, Elaine? Money?"

"All I want is for our family to be together, to have a decent home life, with warmth and affection."

"I'd like that, too." But he knew that what Elaine meant by warmth and affection was not what he meant. To Elaine, warmth was gay conversation in front of the fireplace after dinner, and affection was a quick hug or a peck on the cheek, and, "*Not now, Gordon, the children might still be awake—*" or it was getting late, or she was tired, or she thought she heard the baby stirring upstairs or a prowler out in the yard.

She stood twisting her wedding ring, pulling it up over the second joint of her finger and pushing it back again. Up and over, over and down, with the diamonds glittering like tears. "What a lovely scene this has been, eh, Gordon? And what a charming couple we make.

Somebody called us that once—remember?—a complete stranger said it when we were walking down Main Street on a Saturday night."

"I think that's what you really want out of life—to be one half of a charming couple walking down Main Street on a Saturday night."

"I don't know what you mean. All I know is that this whole argument started because I made a simple little request. I wanted you to take the children to the beach like any normal father."

"Sorry," he said with a wry smile. "I'm feeling a little abnormal today."

"Is that meant to be a joke?"

"I guess so."

"Well, it's not funny. You *have* been acting abnormal recently—losing all that money on a horse race last week, going for those long walks alone every night, drinking down in that awful café and staying so late I have to phone you to come home."

"I like to walk. And I drink coffee, almost exclusively."

"There's coffee at home."

"Yes."

"But you prefer to go down there."

"Yes."

"Why?"

He had a sudden impulse to tell her the real reason but the impulse went lame before it could move. He knew he would never have the nerve to tell her even half of the truth. "Gomez is an old patient of mine. I feel obliged to patronize him."

"Very considerate of you."

"Besides, when I go for a walk I like to have some kind of destination. Gomez's place is just the right distance."

"Does anyone ever see you in there?"

"If they look around, I imagine they see me. Why?"

"The place seems awfully low class. I wouldn't want any of our friends to see you there."

"Any real doctors, you mean?"

"I didn't say that."

"Well, I'll make you a promise, Elaine. If I ever see any real doctor coming in the front door I'll sneak out through the kitchen."

He expected her to get angry or at least to accuse him of sarcasm. She did neither. "Thank you, Gordon," she said calmly. "That will be very kind of you."

"Elaine, before you go, I'd like to ask you one question."

"Ask it."

"How did you first find out I went down to Gomez's place?"

"You can't keep a secret in this town. Only a fool would try."

"You're sure I have secrets?"

"Your face is crawling with them."

Hazel had come in the back door but they were too engrossed in the quarrel to notice her. They stood in the hot, dark little hall, eyeing each other like fighters planning the next, the most devastating blow.

"Pardon me," Hazel said.

They both turned and looked at her as if she had dropped from another planet to invade their private world. Neither of them spoke.

"I didn't mean to interrupt," Hazel said, addressing Elaine. "I just came back to help Dr. Foster pour up an inlay . . . My, it's certainly hot, isn't it?"

Elaine blinked. "Yes. Yes, it is."

"A perfect day for the beach."

"Yes, I thought so too. Apparently I was wrong." She buttoned the little bolero she wore over her yellow linen sundress, and slung the rope straps of her beach purse over her left shoulder. "Well, I'll be going now, Gordon. I don't want to interfere with anything you and Hazel had planned."

"I'll take you out to the car."

"Don't bother. I'm quite accustomed to finding my way around alone." She walked down the hall to the back door, passing Hazel without a glance. "When you're ready to come home, Gordon, give me a call."

"All right."

"Unless you'd prefer a nice long walk."

Gordon colored. "I'll walk."

"Good. And I'll have a pot of coffee waiting for you. You like coffee so much."

She closed the door behind her very softly to indicate to Gordon that she was not in the least angry.

She went out into the court, past the goldfish pond and the lantana hedges, holding her head high, looking like a real doctor's wife. But when she reached the sidewalk she began to tremble so violently that she could hardly walk. She stood for a moment and pressed the palms of her hands over her eyes. Behind her closed lids there were no pictures, only a moving mass of colors, the reds of rage, the grays of terror.

Gordon turned to Hazel. "Don't say anything."

"I had no inten—"

"In fact, it might be a good idea if you went home."

"But—"

"Now."

"All right."

When both the women were gone, he began to whistle again.

4

FROM A DISTANCE Hazel's house looked like a small white box set right against the foot of the mountains in a grove of live-oak trees. But as Hazel drove up Castillo Street the box enlarged into a house, the live-oak trees stepped back a hundred yards into their proper place, and the mountains were six or seven miles away, the color of violets seen through frosted glass.

Hazel had lived in the town all her life. When she was a child she liked to believe that these mountains were the highest in the world, roadless, inaccessible, to be climbed only by *daring* men with ropes and pickaxes and spiked boots. It was quite a disappointment to her when her brother Harold, at the age of ten, accompanied his Boy Scout troop on a weekend trip to the Lookout Tower and returned unharmed. Harold reported great dangers, some real, like poison oak and rattlesnakes, some imagined, like tigers and man-eating plants; but he had worn ordinary gym shoes and no one in the party had carried a pickaxe.

Hazel stepped out of the car and the roadless, inaccessible mountains were blue dwarfs of hills. She opened the gate of the picket fence and crossed the backyard, stepping carefully around the gopher holes and the clusters of nettles that stung like wasps, ducking to avoid the spider webs spun from the tangle of geraniums to the clothesline, and waiting while a lizard shimmied across her path into the safety of the anise weeds which had grown large as shrubs beside the wall of the garage. Crossing the backyard was as hazardous as Harold's trip up the mountain. When Hazel was feeling a little depressed, and consequently vulnerable to superstition and guilt, she believed that her backyard, with all its sprawling reproduction and confusion of nature, was getting back at her for certain lapses in her own life.

She had tried once to explain it to George: "It's like the minute my back is turned, things *happen*—you know?—they all get together and whoop it up."

Hazel never caught them whooping it up, but the evidence was there: an extra million ants hustling up and down the orange tree, more nests of snails at the roots of the geraniums, new little mounds of earth made by new little gophers, and fresh spider webs strung across the windows and under the eaves. She hosed the ants off the orange tree, she swept away the spider webs and crushed the snails with a spade. She put poisoned grain into the gopher holes. The gophers smelled her scent and avoided the grain, and eventually it sprouted up all over the yard into bright green tufts of wild rice. She set metal traps baited with raw apple and raisins. In order to evade the traps, the gophers dug more and deeper tunnels.

After that she tried an entirely new system, suggested by Josephine's cousin who owned a ranch and presumably knew gophers like the back of his hand. In every open hole, Hazel stuck the top half of a broken beer bottle. Josephine's ranching cousin claimed that gophers were unable to turn around in their holes and that they would commit involuntary suicide on the jagged ends of glass. The beer bottles sticking out all over the yard puzzled everyone, including the gophers. They nibbled a little of the glass, found it too hard to chew, and returned to their normal diet. One of the gophers died of old age and overeating.

Just as the weeds and animals had got out of control in Hazel's backyard, so had the people in her life, her cousin, Ruth, her younger brother, Harold, who drove a truck for a furniture store, Harold's wife, Josephine, and, in a few more months, Josephine's child. There was no longer any minute of the day or any square foot of the house that Hazel could call her own.

Even before she opened the kitchen door, she could hear them talking, Ruth's high, taut, suffering voice, and Harold's quiet worried one.

"—but strawberries and artichokes, that's going too far, Harold."

"The doctor said—"

"The strawberry season is over. You don't seem to realize how much food costs these days."

"Hazel said I was to satisfy Josephine's cravings."

"We all go through life with unsatisfied cravings, Harold. And not just for artichokes and strawberries, either."

"Even so."

"Cabbage is excellent nutrition for expectant mothers. It contains calcium."

"Josephine hates the smell."

"We could use a little Air-Wick."

Hazel came into the kitchen but they didn't interrupt their conversation; it was the kind of household where no fuss was made over arrivals and departures, since there were so many of them. Only the little mongrel, Wendy, paid much attention to these matters. She sprang from her place at Ruth's feet and made a great fuss over Hazel. From somewhere in her obscure ancestry, Wendy had acquired a fine sense of self-preservation, and she seemed to know that Hazel was the head of the house and must be given special notice.

They were seated across from each other at the round, oilcloth-covered table, Harold drinking a cup of coffee, Ruth cutting up a large head of cabbage into a wooden bowl.

Hazel leaned down to pat the dog's firm little rump. "Any more coffee?"

"On the stove," Ruth said. "I was just telling Harold—"

"I heard you from outside."

"Well, don't you agree?"

"If she wants artichokes, let her have artichokes."

"Very well," Ruth said stiffly. "Very well. I shall eat the cabbage myself."

"The calcium will do you good."

"There is no growing child inside of me whose little bones need strengthening."

"Inside of me either, but I'll help you eat the cabbage." She poured herself a cup of coffee and sat down at the table beside Harold. They smiled at each other, very faintly, so that Ruth wouldn't notice.

She noticed anyway. "I don't see what's so humorous about the high cost of food. I realize that I don't contribute any actual *money* to the household, but it's my job to keep expenses as low as possible, even at the risk of incurring unpopularity."

"You're not unpopular," Hazel said. "Now forget it."

Ever since Ruth began having trouble with her nerves, she had to be treated, on occasion, like a child, to be given firm yes and no answers, and sometimes strict orders or very abrupt changes of subject.

It was Hazel who usually provided the change of subject.

"I thought you were going to babysit for the Fosters this afternoon."

"I was, yes."

"What happened?"

"I don't know. Mrs. Foster came home unexpectedly and paid me for a full hour, seventy-five cents, though I was only there half that time. I've saved fourteen dollars now . . . Do you think that's enough?"

"Enough for what?"

"The suit," Harold said and kicked Hazel under the table as a reminder. "The suit she's going to buy to wear in front of the School Board. Herringbone tweed."

"No, not tweed." Ruth paused, looking reflectively up at the plaster ceiling. "I've changed my mind about the tweed. Silk shantung, I think, very simply cut. Don't you think silk shantung would be better, Hazel? It will still be very warm in September . . . And perhaps if I'm lucky enough to get a real bargain on the suit, I'll be able to afford a hat as well. I'd like to cover up my hair."

"There's nothing the matter with your hair."

"I don't want them to see what a change there has been in it. They might think something drastic has happened to me the past year, the way I've suddenly become gray like this . . . A turban would cover it up nicely. Are they wearing turbans anymore, Hazel?"

"Some people are."

"Then I shall aim for a turban."

"Ruth—"

"Then, when I have my outfit all ready, I'll phone the superintendent and ask for an interview. They say the teacher shortage in town is very acute. Of course they say that every year. I mustn't build my hopes too high."

"No, you mustn't."

"By September, I should have at least twenty dollars."

She picked up the wooden bowl of cabbage and carried it over to the sink.

Hazel looked at her brother. "Where's Josephine?"

"Sleeping. I told her to lie down, she looked bad."

"You didn't tell her she looked bad?"

"No."

"I hope to God not."

Harold's responsibilities as a future father weighed heavily on him. He had always been a sweet-natured, dreamy man who could spot a silver lining a mile away, but as soon as Josephine missed her first period, Harold became a worrier. He worried nearly all the time because Josephine looked very frail and had a chronically delicate constitution. Harold had never been ill a day in his life and delicate constitutions fascinated and alarmed him.

"She's so *little*, Hazel."

"You talk like she was a midget or something."

"It's not only her size. It's—well, she's no spring chicken."

"For God's sake, don't tell her that. I got enough trouble on my hands."

"Sure, I know that, Haze."

"For instance, that yard. You'd think a bunch of foreigners lived here the way that yard looks. We might as well go live in a jungle."

Ruth turned sharply. "Are you implying, Hazel, that I should attend to the outside of the house as well as the inside?"

"Speaking of the jungle," Harold said. "You know what a guy down at the plant told me the other day? He said, in the jungle the natives—well, say for instance the natives are going from one village to another, walking, and the native women are pregnant. They just stop walking, have their babies, and catch up with the rest of the tribe again. Can you beat that?"

"I keep this house clean," Ruth said. "There isn't a cleaner house in town. I can't be expected to get out and dig in the yard."

"We ought to plant something," Hazel said. "We ought to have a few flowers around the place, like next-door."

"The people next-door have a gardener once a week. It's easy enough to have flowers if you can afford somebody to look after them. It's a question of money, the same as practically everything else in this world."

Frowning, Hazel picked up her empty cup and began rinsing it under the tap. "I wish I'd meet a millionaire."

Hazel often thought quite seriously about her millionaire. His face and age varied in her mind but always he had in his background a frigid wife. Hazel saw herself opening up vistas for this man and having a few vistas opened up in return.

In a town that was reputedly teeming with millionaires, Hazel had never met one. The closest approximation was her former employer, Arthur W. Cooke, who had a real estate business, a wife, and a black Cadillac big as a hearse. Now and then Mr. Cooke would drop in to inquire after Hazel's health. He never stayed more than half an hour and he never indicated any interest in Hazel other than the state of her health. Though Hazel called these occasions "dates," they were more like visits from the family physician.

"Suppose I did meet a wealthy man," Hazel said, "someone with class like Mr. Cooke, for instance, I'd be ashamed to bring him here with all those weeds around the place and the gopher holes . . . It's a funny thing to me that with all those nice flowers and plants next- door that the gophers don't move over there."

"Maybe they don't appreciate nature." Harold laughed, but no one laughed with him, so he added apologetically, "Listen, Haze, I get Saturday afternoon and Sunday off, and honest to God, I'll get out there and dig those weeds and drown the gophers with a hose."

"You can't drown gophers."

"How do you know?"

"I've tried."

"They can't swim, can they? If they can't swim, they got to drown, don't they?"

"All right, Harold, you win. Next Sunday you go out and catch all the gophers and we'll take them down to the ocean and throw them in."

"Harold isn't concerned with a minor trifle like the water bill," Ruth said contemptuously. "Water costs money. This is desert country, and don't you forget it. Everybody forgets that this is desert country because water has been brought in to irrigate it. But it's still desert country."

"So what," Harold muttered, very softly. He was afraid of Ruth because she sometimes said very intelligent and forceful things. Like that about desert country. Harold admired that. He saw himself down at the plant addressing the manager, or even the president. Gentlemen, said Harold, don't you forget that this is desert country.

Ruth took a sack of potatoes from the vegetable bin and began to peel them very quickly as if supper had to be prepared immediately. The kitchen clock on the wall said ten minutes after three, and supper was at least two hours away. But Ruth had a clock inside herself which never corresponded to the others in the house. Ruth's clock ran fast and Ruth had to run fast to keep up with it. All day she ran, and part of the night; in her sleep her legs and arms twitched and she breathed so hard she woke herself up. There seemed to be no resting place for her, no safety zone where she could pause from the pursuit and catch her breath, no moments of peace except the rare ones when she was alone with the two things she loved best, the Fosters' baby boy and the little mongrel she'd bought at the city pound for two dollars.

The dog lolled against her legs as she stood peeling the potatoes, and the warmth of its body touched cold, loveless places and slowed the clock a little.

Harold said, "I just remembered, a fellow down at the plant told me about some stuff the other day. You spray this junk on, see, and what happens is, it kills all the weeds but not the flowers."

"I don't believe it," Ruth said. "I don't believe that about the jungle and the native women, either."

Harold looked injured. "Well, for crying out loud, I'm not making it up."

"You're gullible, Harold. You've always been gullible."

Harold didn't know what gullible meant, and Ruth knew he didn't know. She stared at him in triumph until Harold dropped his eyes.

"I wonder how much he charges," Hazel said.

Ruth put down the paring knife. "Who?"

"The Mexican gardener that works next-door."

"Have you gone out of your mind? *Hiring* somebody to do a little job like digging? . . . You must be crazy, Hazel. Why, Harold's going to do it. He promised, next Sunday. Aren't you, Harold?"

"Sure, I am. Sure."

"There," Ruth said. "He's promised on his word of honor he'll do it on Sunday. Won't you, Harold?"

"Absolutely."

Hazel walked back to the table and sat down with great deliberation.

"Listen, you two. Who's running this joint? Who pays most of the bills? Who owns the house?"

"Well, I didn't say anything, Haze," Harold said anxiously. "I hardly opened my mouth."

"You better not. It's my house, and if I want it to look respectable, by Jesus it's going to look respectable!"

"Sure, sure it is."

"And if I want flowers around it, by Jesus I'm going to have flowers around it, see?"

"You bet you are, Haze."

"Distinction, that's what I want, a distinguished-looking house with some class to it."

"People in our circumstances *hiring* a *gardener*," Ruth said bitterly.

"I didn't say for sure I was going to. I said I wonder how much he charges."

"A dollar an hour, at least a dollar an hour. And a Mexican, at that. Why, I—I just wouldn't feel safe in the house if he was out there."

"Why not?"

"You can't trust them, any of them . . . Of course I realize I have no voice in the matter. I'm living on your charity for the present."

"Baloney," Hazel said kindly. Her irritation had passed. She was always happiest when she was following her impulses and her current impulse was to hire the Mexican gardener and live in a distinguished-looking house waiting for a distinguished-looking millionaire.

Hazel rarely suffered from second thoughts. Once a decision was made, it seemed good, and Hazel stuck by it the way she stuck by her friends.

A nice yard would (a) increase the value of the house, (b) look pretty, (c) show up the neighbors, and (d) provide a suitable background for gentlemen friends.

Humming to herself Hazel went out into the backyard, gathered up all the broken halves of beer bottles sticking out of the gopher holes, and threw them in the trash can. Then she went over to the house next-door and rang the front doorbell.

Half an hour later she returned with a pleasant glow induced by two glasses of cooking sherry, and a piece of paper bearing the address and phone number of Santana Escobar. She stood looking out of the kitchen window at the backyard. Tomorrow, Hazel thought, everything would be different; the muss and clutter would be gone, and the whole place would be blooming with gardenias and camellias, no more of those lousy geraniums.

Santana. The very name sounded prophetic, a symbol of a brand-new life. She had no clear plans for this new life beyond the fact that it would be different from the old one, and that at some point in it her millionaire would turn up, or at least someone with a little money like Mr. Cooke.

It's the beginning, Hazel thought solemnly. It's the beginning of a new life.

She wanted to communicate this thought to someone, not to Ruth who would blame it on the sherry, or to Harold and Josephine who had their own new life cut out for them, but to someone like George. George was very keen on new beginnings. He would understand perfectly.

She phoned the Beachcomber.

"George?"

"George isn't here. Who's that?"

"It's me, Willie. Hazel."

"Oh, hello, Hazel. This business about George, well, he left about an hour ago. Didn't say where he was going, just walked off. There was some rumpus in the kitchen. He fired one of the girls. He lost his temper. You know George, he gets fussed up. Then, *wham.*"

"You said it, wham. Which girl did he fire, Willie?"

"One of the new ones. I forget her name."

"Ruby?"

"Could well have been Ruby. Anyway, we're short one girl and we're short George. If you run into him anywhere, tell him we've got a crowd here, will you?"

"I'll do that, Willie. So long."

Hazel put down the phone.

In spite of George's defection, it was still the beginning of a new life, and since Harold had gone back to work and Josephine was still asleep there was no one to tell but Ruth. She told Ruth.

"You shouldn't drink in the afternoon," Ruth said.

5

"RUBY? LET ME think a minute." Mrs. Freeman paused, searching for Ruby amid the tissue of fact and fiction that enveloped her mind.

"Ruby MacCormick," George said.

"Oh, that's our new girl, yes. We get so many here. They come and go. I hardly have time to catch their names."

"I'd like to speak to her."

"Now let me think, is she in or out? Wait a minute and I'll go see. Sit down on the porch and make yourself easy."

"Thank you."

George sat down on a redwood bench beside the sign that identified the house: "Mrs. Freeman's Tourist Home, Ladies Only, Reasonable Rates, Ocean View." The bench creaked under his weight and he got up again, brushing off the seat of his trousers. He didn't actually want to sit down anyway. He wanted to do something violent, to run away as fast as he could. But at the same time he wanted to have Ruby running along beside him, just as violent as he. He gazed blindly at Mrs. Freeman's Ocean View—nineteen blocks down the highway a tiny strip of sea was visible—and wondered what he could say to Ruby to make everything all right.

On the highway in front of the house, cars hurried north to San Luis Obispo and San Francisco, and south to Los Angeles and San Diego. George wished that he were in one of them. He felt split in two. Half of him was headed for San Francisco, but the real half stood on Mrs. Freeman's soot-covered porch, nervous and scared like a gangling adolescent.

Mrs. Freeman reappeared. She had taken off her apron, out of deference to George's Buick, silk shirt, and masculinity in general.

"She's in. She'll be right down. What did you say your name was?"

"Anderson."

"Any relation to the Anderson that makes that frozen split-pea soup?"

"No."

"I just wondered." Mrs. Freeman was disappointed. She had made a habit of asking people if they were connected with well-known names ever since she had met, down at the beach, a lady who claimed to be a second cousin of Joan Blondell, the movie actress. Mrs. Freeman had relayed this news to all of her pen pals back East, changing second cousin to first cousin because it was practically the same thing anyway and sounded more interesting.

"All these frozen things they make nowadays, it's a miracle of science," Mrs. Freeman said thoughtfully. "In my opinion, science is making great strides."

George agreed.

"Some people think science is going too far, like this hydrogen bomb for instance. Myself personally, I'm not worried, though the other day something funny certainly happened. I'd bought this fish down at Marchetti's, and when I opened the package it just seemed to fairly *glow.* I thought it might be one of those Bikini fish that got bombed. Do you think that's likely?"

"No."

"I guess not. I ate it and I feel the same. Here's Ruby now."

Mrs. Freeman moved aside with reluctance and Ruby took her place at the screen door. Beside Mrs. Freeman she looked extraordinarily slight and pallid. Her eyes were glowing like Mrs. Freeman's fish, and George had to stifle a wild impulse to laugh.

"Ruby, I just came to—the fact is, you ran off without collecting your pay."

Ruby bent her head and the white skin of her forehead pressed against the screen.

"I thought you might need the money so I looked you up. I had a hard time finding you. You didn't leave an address."

"I'm not so anxious for people to find me that I go around leaving my address," Ruby said with soft scorn. "As for the pay, that's perfectly all right. I broke some dishes anyway."

"That doesn't matter."

"It does to me. You can take the money and buy some new dishes."

"Don't be silly," George said, scowling. "It's your money. You earned it."

"Well, I don't want it. Keep it yourself."

In the background Mrs. Freeman's bosom heaved with pride. This was the kind of tourist home *she* kept, yes-sirree. Her girls might be poor but they had a nice noble attitude towards money. Still, if Ruby had actually earned the money, she would be a fool not to take it.

"If you *earned* the money, my dear," Mrs. Freeman said, "you'll only be accepting your just deserts."

Ruby uttered a sharp little laugh. "Everybody is very concerned about me all of a sudden, I must say. It's certainly funny."

"All right, forget the money," George said. "What I came for was to apologize. I was—I lost my temper and I'm sorry, see? I'm sorry. Damn it"—he turned his scowl on Mrs. Freeman—"isn't there any place we can talk?"

"Talk?" Mrs. Freeman's eyebrows shot up. All her suspicions of men, some born and bred in her and the others picked up along the way of a life with the truant Mr. Freeman, were apparent in the look she gave George. Talk? Talk, indeed. *I know men.*

"You can talk in the parlor," she said, firmly enough to indicate to George that she would be right outside in the hall while the talking was going on.

George opened the screen door and stepped inside. As the door closed his coat sleeve brushed Ruby's bare arm. She shrank away from him, as if the contact had pained her, and ducked into the parlor. She bumped her shin against a leatherette hassock and almost fell, but when George put out his hand to help her regain her balance, she jerked her elbow and its sharp point caught him on a vein in the back of his hand. It stung for a moment like an insect bite.

"Oh." She put her hand up and covered her mouth. "I'm sorry—I didn't mean—"

"Didn't you?"

"No. *No.*"

"All right," George said heavily. "I take your word for it, Ruby."

Mrs. Freeman coughed subtly and closed the parlor door. She was convinced of one thing—that Mr. Anderson was a fool to take Ruby's word for anything. Ruby was a liar. During her fifteen years as a landlady, Mrs. Freeman had become a fairly accurate judge of character and she could invariably spot a liar, all the more readily because she was such a plausible liar herself.

Mrs. Freeman's lies were nearly always written down in letters and were nearly always attempts to conceal her position in life or to justify it. She was a prodigious letter writer. She kept in touch with all her relatives back East, second cousins and nieces by marriage and even the new wives and husbands of divorced or defunct members of the tribe. She also had six pen pals, acquired through a pulp magazine: Middle-aged woman with cultural interests, fond of good music and literature, would appreciate hearing from women of similar interests, eastern background. How about a letter? California Caroline.

Caroline Freeman had become a letter-writer for a number of reasons. She was lonely. She could tolerate her life more easily if she glamorized it on paper, and she could even sometimes force herself into believing some of her own highly idealized versions of the truth: "I honestly felt, Mildred, that it would be a sin and a shame not to open my beautiful home to some of these poor unfortunate girls who have no place to lay their heads."

Occasionally she mentioned Mr. Freeman's spasmodic disappearances: "Poor Robert had not been feeling himself lately and has gone down to Palm Springs for the dry desert air. With the sea practically at our front door we naturally get a good deal of humidity!" When Mr. Freeman returned, in need of funds, badly under the weather, and with his face cherry red from overindulgence, Mrs. Freeman recorded the fact that Robert had come back from Palm Springs with a bad sunburn and the desert air hadn't done him much good after all.

The ink that flowed from Mrs. Freeman's pen was an unguent pouring over reality. It was true that she lived a few yards from the main north-south highway and had to listen all night to the purr and splutter of engines, the squeaking of brakes and the roaring of trucks. But it was also true that this highway had a beautiful and glamorous name, El Camino del Mar, and it was always a great satisfaction to Mrs. Freeman to write her address in the upper right-hand corner of her notepaper: 1906 El Camino del Mar. No one would ever suspect that it was a road lined with wooden shacks, filled eternally with the smoke of diesel engines and the soot from the Southern Pacific Railroad whose tracks lay parallel to the highway.

At times Mrs. Freeman was afraid that some of her correspondents might come to see her and find out about the neighborhood she lived in, and the highway and the tracks. She guarded against this possibility as well as she could by writing to no one further west than Chicago. This allowed a decent mileage between reality and fiction. She was, moreover, fairly certain that none of her correspondents had sufficient money for a long trip west, in spite of the claim of her pen pal, Flossie from Florida, that she owned a huge orange grove. Mrs. Freeman had the same percentage of belief in Flossie's orange grove as she had in Mr. Freeman's sojourns in Palm Springs or the Sierras.

No matter how many letters she wrote, Mrs. Freeman never suffered from lack of material because she had a keen eye, and she was an avid newspaper reader and an enthusiastic walker. She would walk for miles, especially after dinner in the summertime, consciously and deliberately seeing things that most other people would miss. She examined each flower and shrub, every car parked at the curb, the children playing on the sidewalks, the evening strollers like herself. She watched the mountains turn from blue to gray and disappear. She looked into the windows of houses and saw the people inside, eating or reading the paper, listening to the radio, quarreling, washing dishes, and she had a friendly curiosity about all these people.

Afterwards, Mrs. Freeman described her walks in detail, always managing to bring in the exotic street names that she dearly loved. "I strolled up Alameda Padre Serra and over to Plaza Rubio, and finally ended up on Salsipuedes!"

The weather was a constant source of material. Mrs. Freeman, however, did not content herself with mere temperature reports. She injected drama into a cloudy day by describing the fog rolling in from the sea, and into a windy day by stating that "the small craft warnings are up, all up and down the coast!" Calm, sunny days were provided with an element of terror by Mrs. Freeman's favorite phrase, "earthquake weather." The more beautiful the day, the more sinister the growl of the earth beneath it. Thus, Mrs. Freeman's correspondents got the impression that she lived in the crater of a volcano with the earth forever teetering under her house. This impression served two purposes. It made Mrs. Freeman feel that she did indeed live dangerously, and it discouraged her pen pals from planning a visit to this perilous spot. Flossie of Florida had even gone so far as to remark that she wouldn't live in California for all the money in the world—hurricanes Florida might have, yes, but an earthquake practically every day would upset her nervous system. This statement stimulated Mrs. Freeman's imagination, and she replied by return mail, describing how only that morning the whole house had shuddered, the windows rattled, and the chandelier in the parlor swung like a pendulum. She neglected to add that this was a regular occurrence, caused not by an earthquake, but by an S. P. freight train.

Any seed, however small, could grow in Mrs. Freeman's fertile brain. She returned now to her interrupted letter to a third cousin in Michigan. The ink flowed over George and he became a close relative of the Andersons who made that celebrated split-pea soup.

From where she sat, at the round walnut dining-room table, Mrs. Freeman could hear the angry rise and the defensive fall of George's voice. The combination of attack and appeasement in his tone reminded Mrs. Freeman of her husband, Robert. Robert had been gone for nearly three weeks now and she was beginning to worry and to wonder whether she'd better go to the police. This harsh practical thought of going to the police annihilated Mrs. Freeman's writing mood. She put down her pen. She had hoped to finish her letter before making herself a bite to eat, but now she couldn't concentrate on it and for this she blamed George. He had no right to come forcing himself into the house (Mrs. Freeman had no recollection of opening the door for him), using profane language (she couldn't actually distinguish his words but his tone was profane), and browbeating defenseless little women (making them accept money, probably tainted). For the moment, Mrs. Freeman was on Ruby's side. Ruby might be sly, evasive, she might even be a downright liar, but she was a woman, and women should stick together.

In union is strength, thought Mrs. Freeman, who liked an aphorism as well as the next one.

She heard the thud of the evening paper as it struck the porch, and she rose to fetch it. When she passed through the hall she made her step good and loud, a cunning device that didn't escape notice.

"You'd better go," Ruby said. "She's doing that on purpose."

"All right." George got up from Mrs. Freeman's mohair sofa, aware that he had made a fool of himself. He had done what he set out to do, he had apologized for firing Ruby and losing his temper. But the apology had gone wrong. There had been nothing contrite or apologetic about it. He had forced it on her; he had apologized at the top of his lungs.

The apology had a curious effect on Ruby. She lost her air of frightened timidity. She looked composed, even a little ironic.

"She doesn't like men callers to stay too long," Ruby said.

"Do you have other men callers?"

"I can't see that it's any of your business."

"It isn't. I just want to know."

"Well then, sure. Sure I have."

"I don't believe it," George said.

Ruby put her hands on her hips in an exasperated manner. "Well, I like that! I certainly like *that,* Mr. Anderson! You, you just get out of here and don't come back!"

George smiled painfully. "You're not such a bunny after all."

"I certainly don't have to stand here and be insulted."

Thump, thump, thump, Mrs. Freeman's implying feet went down the hall again.

"Why did you leave the other place and move over here all of a sudden?" George said.

"That's my affair."

"Was it the rent? Do you need money?"

"Now I suppose you're thinking that I skipped out without paying my rent! Well, let me tell you one thing, Mr. Anderson. If I were broke I could always go home. You seem to have gotten the wrong idea about me. I'm no orphan. I'm not alone in the world. I can go back to San Francisco any time. My mother and father have a beautiful home there and they're always begging me to come back. But I told my dad, I'm tired of this sheltered life, I want to earn my own way."

"Why?"

"Because. Because I do, that's all. In the modern world a girl has to be able to look out for herself."

"You're not thinking of going home, then?"

"I haven't made up my mind. It all depends."

"I wouldn't like you to leave town."

"That's funny. Someone else told me today that I'd be better off if I did. There are more jobs down south."

"There are jobs here, too. If you don't want to come back to the Beachcomber, maybe I can find something else for you. I've got some connections around town."

Ruby's face lit up. "That would be wonderful. Do you really think you could?"

"I don't see why not."

"A receptionist, maybe. I've always thought I'd like to be a receptionist."

"I don't know about that," George said cautiously. "There's not much call for receptionists in a town this size."

"Still, it's possible, isn't it?—with your connections?"

"Yes."

"Gosh, it'd be nice, sitting instead of standing all the time, and wearing pretty clothes and keeping my nails decent." Her eyes were soft and her cheeks seemed to have already fattened on this dream of pretty clothes and half-inch nails. "I'd have to get a new permanent, though. My hair is a mess."

"It looks fine to me."

"No, it's a mess." She twisted a strand of it between her fingers. "Why should you do me a favor, Mr. Anderson?"

"Because I want to. There's nothing, well, personal in it. I know you need a job, and you're just a kid. In fact—well, to tell you the truth, I'm old enough to be your father."

"You are?" Ruby giggled nervously. "My goodness, you certainly don't look it. You don't look a day over forty."

George, who was forty, thanked her and pulled in his stomach. He knew by her expression that she had meant the remark as a compliment and that she probably thought he was at least fifty.

He felt a little sick, but he smiled and said, "I'll do the best I can for you."

"Oh, I know you will."

"I don't suppose you'd like to come out and have some dinner with me."

"I'd love to, but I can't."

"Oh."

"I really can't. I'm so tired. All this excitement, getting fired first and then having you appear out of the blue with a wonderful new job—"

"I haven't found you one yet."

"But you will, with all your connections and everything."

"I hope so . . . Meanwhile, you'd better come back to the Beachcomber. At least it's a living."

"All right, if you say so, Mr. Anderson."

"Tomorrow, then."

"All right."

They shook hands, in a friendly way, and George opened the parlor door. Out of the corner of his eye he saw Mrs. Freeman descending on him from the dining room. He walked rapidly in the opposite direction to avoid a meeting.

"In a hurry, isn't he?" Mrs. Freeman commented.

"He's a very important businessman," Ruby said. "He's got things to do."

"I knew it the minute I looked at him. A businessman, I said to myself. What business?"

"He owns the Beachcomber."

"All by himself?"

Ruby nodded. Though she knew that George had only a quarter interest in the Beachcomber she didn't think it worthwhile to mention this to Mrs. Freeman. It was a small point, and Ruby believed that it was ridiculous to keep to the strict facts when a few variations served a better purpose. In this respect she was a true spiritual daughter of the house.

"He's got an eye for you," Mrs. Freeman said, with a satisfied nod. "I could tell it the minute I saw him."

"Oh, that's silly, I never heard anything so silly."

"Mark my words, he's a goner."

Ruby colored. "Well, I certainly didn't encourage him."

"Why, I bet you could have him in a minute if you just snapped your fingers. Mark my words, I know men and he's got that look." It occurred to Mrs. Freeman at this point that possibly George was a married man and that she had gone too far in encouraging Ruby. She added, "If he's married, well, that's a horse of another color. I believe in the sanctity of the home and I think that any woman who comes between a man and his wife ought to be horsewhipped."

Mrs. Freeman's eyes hardened, applying the horsewhip to the guilty Ruby. But instead of cringing, Ruby said coldly, "He's divorced, you don't have to worry."

"Not that I was actually worried. I knew as soon as I laid eyes on you that you were a girl that came from a respectable family. There's a lady, I said to myself."

Ruby was unable to resist this blandishment. Over a cup of Mrs. Freeman's hot, bitter coffee she described her parents and their beautiful home atop Nob Hill whence they could see San Francisco Bay and the Golden Gate. Her father, a retired gentleman of the old school, spent all his time now on his collection of rare stamps and coins. Her mother, who had been a beauty in her youth, was now silver-haired but she still rode every day. She was a brilliant horsewoman.

"I know that horsy set," Mrs. Freeman contributed.

"I was terribly spoiled. Then one day I guess I just suddenly grew up. I wanted to live my own life and earn my own way. Daddy nearly had a fit and Mummy cried and cried, but it was no use, they couldn't keep me home. When I make up my mind to do a thing, it's as good as done. Naturally I'll go back someday, but not until I've proved I can stand on my own feet. And now that Mr. Anderson's getting me a job as a receptionist, I feel I'm finally getting some place. I suppose I should really sit down right now and write and tell Mummy and Daddy the good news, but I've got to dress and meet someone."

When Ruby had gone back to her room, Mrs. Freeman poured herself another cup of coffee and sat down at the dining-room table to finish the newspaper.

"What a liar," she said aloud, yet she felt genuinely sorry for Ruby, who was a victim of circumstance like herself. To a lesser degree she felt sorry for George too, because he had what Mrs. Freeman called a "nice open face" and a shrewd eye. From this shrewd eye Mrs. Freeman deduced that George knew quite a lot about women, and it was her opinion that men who understood women could be more easily duped by any individual woman than one who didn't. Take her husband, Robert, for instance. Robert had never understood women, never wanted to, never pretended to, yet he'd had a wife as faithful as the day was long.

As faithful as the day is long, Mrs. Freeman thought, sighing. She turned for comfort to the City News Briefs. Here, in blunt paragraphs, were recorded the mistakes and sorrows, and the petty complaints and transgressions of that large but neglected and anonymous section of the community to which Mrs. Freeman unwittingly belonged. Names were seldom mentioned in the News Briefs. More tactful devices were used for identification: "A woman in the 500 block of W. Los Olivos complained to police of a dog barking in the neighborhood." "An intoxicated middle-aged man was found sleeping in an alley and was given lodging by the police overnight." "A rancher from the Arroyo Burro district reports that two sorrel mares have strayed or been stolen from his premises." "Several juveniles were warned by police when they were found aiming rocks at a boulevard sign near the swimming pool." "Two Mexican nationals were arrested in a local café after becoming involved in an argument with the proprietor."

These items were cunningly spaced between advertisements, so that to make sure of not missing anything Mrs. Freeman read all the advertisements too: slenderizing salons, used cars, potato chips, lost dogs, apartments, lending libraries, Swedish Massage and Hawaiian chocolates.

While she read, Mrs. Freeman talked half-aloud to herself. "Seems a lot of money for a 1939 Ford . . . I wonder what café they were arrested in, seems silly not to mention the name . . . that friend of Mrs. Lambert's lives on Los Olivos, but that's east not west, but it could easily be her anyway, newspapers are always making mistakes like that . . . trying to stop a dog barking. Might as well stop the wind blowing, what are dogs for, I'd like to know . . . sorrel mares, never heard of sorrel, but mark my words they were stolen, human nature can get very low."

She heard one of the girls coming downstairs and she stopped talking abruptly. She didn't want any of them to think she was balmy, talking to herself like that, and she was certain that none of them had enough sense to realize that if you have no one else to talk to, you talk to yourself.

It was Ruby.

"Dressed already?" Mrs. Freeman said cheerfully. "That's a pretty suit. It goes with your eyes."

Ruby blushed with pleasure and averted her eyes, afraid, breathlessly afraid that if she let Mrs. Freeman look at her eyes again Mrs. Freeman might change her mind and say, no, the suit didn't go with her eyes.

She went down the hall, hugging the thin compliment to her heart, letting it nestle there, warm and protected, until it grew fat: she said I have nice eyes. She said, what a pretty suit, it goes with your beautiful eyes. Like stars, she said.

She pictured herself telling Gordon about it tonight, if he could get away from the house to meet her. She would say to him, "Oh, she's a funny old bird, Gordon. You know what she said to me as I was leaving tonight? She said I was beautiful. *Me,* beautiful! Gosh, you could have knocked me over with a feather! She said, with eyes like that, you ought to be in the movies, Ruby."

6

RUBY HAD NEVER lived in a small town before, and she was unaware of the speed and intricacy of its grapevine. She assumed that she had in Channel City the same anonymity she had in San Francisco, and that no one knew about the relationship between Gordon Foster and herself, not even the owner of the café which was their meeting place.

She was not interested in or curious about the other people and she rarely paid any attention to them even when she was sitting waiting for Gordon and had nothing to do but drink coffee. She would have been surprised to learn that at least a dozen habitués of the café knew her and Gordon by sight and guessed the relationship, and several more knew them by name and were sure of the relationship. In the latter group was Al Gomez, who owned the café, and Gordon Foster's wife, Elaine. Neither nature nor experience had equipped Gordon for a life of intrigue, and Elaine had found out about Ruby a week after Ruby arrived in town.

Elaine, as a churchwoman and the mother of three children, believed in divorce even less than she believed in marriage and Gordon, so she didn't discuss the subject of Ruby at all. She merely telephoned the café two or three times in an evening, and asked Mr. Gomez politely to send Gordon home, one of the children had a sore throat, or a wrenched knee, or a headache, or a spot that might be measles. She never asked to speak to Gordon personally; she used Mr. Gomez as the messenger. This proved, at first, to be an effective device, for the messages, delivered in Gomez's harsh, low voice sounded quite alarming. Mr. Gomez would shuffle over to the back booth where Ruby and Gordon were sitting, fix Gordon with his hot little eyes, and croak, "Wife says one of the kids fell out of bed, broke his arm."

These messages, however startling they were in the beginning, had gradually lost their power, and the only people who were affected by them any longer were Gomez, who was tired of answering the phone, Ruby, who was infuriated by Elaine's wily deceptions, and the two older Foster children. They had learned for the first time, listening to their mother on the telephone, that they were frail and mortal, surrounded by their enemy, death. They developed hourly symptoms, and screamed in real terror over a scratch or a bruise. Elaine, who believed she loved her children, was very much concerned because her five-year-old boy suffered from nightmares, and the girl, seven, was disgustingly fat from overeating. The girl found solace in food; even during school hours, or in bed at night, she chewed surreptitiously. As a result she frequently suffered abdominal pains which were relayed to Gordon, via Mr. Gomez: "The wife phoned, says one of the kids got a bust appendix."

"Thank you, Gomez."

"Or maybe polio."

"If she phones again, tell her I've left."

"Check."

"Polio," Ruby said, clenching her fists until the knuckles showed white. "*Polio.*"

"I'd better be leaving, Ruby."

"But you just got here."

"I know."

"I hardly ever *see* you."

"I know that too."

When no one was looking, he kissed her goodbye.

He was often late for their meetings in the back booth, and sometimes he didn't show up at all. Ruby would sit there the entire evening, sipping coffee, which was all she could afford, and watching the front door until her eyes went out of focus and her face looked drunken in its owlish intensity.

Once in a while Mr. Gomez would pause on his way to or from the kitchen.

"Late, eh?"

"Oh, he'll be along. He should be here any minute."

"Maybe the wife says no."

"She's always saying no. That wouldn't make any difference. He'll be here, I'm not worried."

"Married man."

Mr. Gomez's abbreviated speeches, delivered in a cracked monotone, were difficult to understand. Ruby was not certain whether he was telling her that he too was a married man and knew how it was with wives, or whether he was reproving her for having a date with a married man. It worried her. She fancied reproach in his eyes and she wanted to slap his face, the dirty little Mex, but also to explain to him that she loved Gordon, she'd given up everything just to live in the same town he did.

"It's not fair," she screamed mentally at Mr. Gomez, who was frying a hamburger. "It's not fair! She's got everything—Gordon and the house and the kids, and all I've got is the back booth in this lousy little joint!"

The smell of grease rose from the griddle, clung to the walls and seeped into the very pores of Ruby's skin, blending with the cologne she had splashed on her wrists for Gordon. She felt a little nauseated and dizzy from all the coffee she had drunk, but she sat with her eyes fixed glassily on the front door. Whenever the door opened her mouth got set, ready to smile; when it closed again, and Gordon was still missing, her heart shrank and oozed its juices like the hamburger Mr. Gomez was frying on the griddle.

She never gave up hope until Gomez changed the sign on the front door from "Open" to "Closed." Then she rose, picked up her handbag and the fox fur, and said goodnight to Gomez, very gaily, letting him know that she wasn't at all disappointed, and that, Gordon Foster or no Gordon Foster, this was how she liked to spend her evenings, sipping coffee in Mr. Gomez's delightful back booth.

"How the time flies," she said brightly. "I was so interested sitting here watching the people I didn't realize how late it was getting. You certainly have an interesting place here!"

She didn't fool Gomez, who hated the place more than she did, and she didn't fool herself either. As soon as she stepped outside, the cold sea wind slapped the smile off her face. I hate him, she thought, running down the street. I hate him. I'll get back at him. I'll get even. I'll go and see his wife. He'll be sorry.

But Gordon's sorrow had already begun, and it was deeper than Ruby realized. It was the sorrow of failure. He had failed Elaine and the children, he had failed Ruby, and he had failed himself. A more self-assured man might have taken a firm stand one way or the other. The only solution Gordon could think of was to go away for a while and leave the burden of decision up to Elaine and Ruby. A vacation, he called it, when he mentioned it to Elaine. He said he thought he'd take a little trip.

"To San Francisco *again?*" Elaine said with sweet irony.

"What do you mean, *again?*"

"I only meant that you seem to have had such a gay time there a couple of months ago."

"You've got a funny idea of a gay time," Gordon said. "I was at lectures damn near all day, every day." After one lecture he had picked Ruby up in a hotel lobby but he still couldn't understand why Elaine should suspect this. "That was a business trip. A dentist has to keep up with the latest developments and equipment. This time I want a holiday. I thought of Mexico, Ensenada perhaps."

"Mexico?"

"What's the matter with Mexico?"

"Did I say there was anything the matter with Mexico, dear?"

"You said it as if you suddenly smelled a bad smell."

Elaine smiled gently. "There you go imagining things again, dear. You're getting so sensitive. I wonder if it could be glandular."

"Listen, I know how you said 'Mexico.' Don't try and kid me."

"Really, Gordon, you're becoming impossible. I've thought time and again that perhaps you should go and see a doctor. Glandular disturbances are common at your age."

"Jesus Christ," Gordon said, sweating.

"All this fuss simply because I said 'Mexico' in a perfectly ordinary tone of voice. I'm sure I've got nothing against Mexico. Of course I've heard it's terribly dirty. You can't drink the water at all without boiling it, and you have to be awfully careful about the food, cholera and things like that."

Elaine could, with a few well-chosen words, reduce anything to its lowest common multiple. Having deflated Gordon and crushed Mexico, she went to work with undiminished fervor on vacations in general and Gordon's in particular. It was a funny thing, Elaine said, that men took vacations every now and then while women went right on year after year without any kind of rest or holiday at all. Anyway, did Gordon really think it was wise to leave right now?

"After all, dear, you've got your family to think about. It isn't as if you were in some business that could carry on without you. I mean, every day that you're not at the office and don't keep your appointments, you're losing money. You have your overhead, and Hazel's salary, and you know how many new dentists, all of them veterans too, are opening up offices here. After all, you're in a competitive profession. If you're going to be away from the office half the time, your patients are going to feel that they can't depend on you."

In one short speech she had managed to convey to Gordon that he was a shirker who hadn't helped win the war, as well as lazy, impractical, thoughtless, incompetent and irresponsible.

Elaine considered herself a true gentlewoman. She never raised her voice or swore, and even when driven into a corner by fate she used only legitimate womanly weapons like her children, her bed and soft words strung on steel. She had betrayed Gordon on the day she married him by telling her mother that she knew Gordon had a weak character and that she would have to be strong for both of them. Elaine often recalled this speech, which she termed "realistic," and which she considered remarkably shrewd for a girl so "young"—she was twenty-seven on the day she was married. Not six months later, she told Gordon of her speech to her mother. Gordon was shocked, not by her malice, which she had already revealed in many small ways, but by the fact that she despised him. She made it clear that it was only her own iron will and determination which kept Gordon on the straight and narrow and confined him to his office twelve hours a day. Gordon was thirty then, and working very hard to build up a practice so that he could buy Elaine a new house. He was quite surprised to find out that he was a weak character, and inexperienced enough to take the criticism seriously. In the end, after Elaine had given him a gentle heart-to-heart talk, Gordon was convinced that he was indeed weak and that it was Elaine's personal power that turned the drill and kept him confined in the magnetic circle of office-and-home.

With this new self-knowledge inflicted on him by Elaine came a gradual change in personality. He began to doubt himself and his motives. He was grateful to anyone, man or woman, who paid him any attention. He was awed by his three children, who seemed to despise him as much as Elaine did.

"Gordon," Elaine told her friends with a tolerant little smile, "is not the fatherly type." Above the smile her eyes added a personal little message to Gordon alone: *You're a very poor father, admit it, dear.*

Gordon walked through the years in a kind of numb bewilderment.

In the early summer of his thirty-ninth year, in the lobby of the Palace Hotel in San Francisco, a young woman asked him for a match.

She had dark hair and a thin, pointed face. The first thing Gordon noticed about her was her underdeveloped jaw. There wouldn't be room for a normal set of teeth there, Gordon thought, and he wondered whether her teeth were exceptionally small or whether some of them had been removed to prevent overlapping.

"Sorry," he said, patting his coat pockets automatically. "I don't smoke."

"Oh. Well. I'm sorry to have bothered you." She added, with a self-conscious little laugh, "Honestly, I don't smoke either, only about once a year. But I was supposed to meet a certain party here and I've been waiting so long, I just thought a cigarette would help."

They sat side by side under a potted palm tree, Gordon with his newspaper on his lap, and Ruby fingering the clasp of her purse.

"All I'm afraid of is that I missed my party," Ruby said. "The lobby is so crowded, there must be a convention or something."

"Dentists," Gordon said.

"Oh, that's it then. I wondered. Well—" She closed her purse with an air of finality and put on one of her gloves. "Well, I guess my party must be afraid of dentists or something—"

Gordon laughed. "Everybody is."

"Well, I don't blame them! I shiver every time I think of a dentist."

"Are you shivering now?"

Her eyes grew wide. "Why?"

"I'm one."

"No!"

"I am."

"Gosh, and to think I've been sitting beside you all this time without a single shiver! But you don't look a bit like a dentist. You look like, a lawyer or a doctor, maybe."

Gordon was flattered. He had belonged for years to a club for professional men, but he had never got over the feeling that the doctors and lawyers among the members were superior to him, and that dentistry was the poor country cousin of medicine and law. Elaine lent her aid to this feeling. When the club held its monthly Ladies' Night, Elaine was ostentatiously self-effacing, as if to remind everyone that she was, after all, only a dentist's wife and had no right to open her mouth. She sometimes said as much to the other wives. "Of course it's different with you, *I'm* only a poor dentist's wife." This remark caused acute embarrassment among the other women who found themselves forced to belittle their husbands and their husbands' professions to make Elaine comfortable, or else to extol the art of dentistry: *Where would we all be without dentists, I'd like to know. My goodness, dentists are terribly important.*

The fact was that dentists were very important, and after two days of the convention Gordon was beginning to feel proud that he was a man who was doing hard and important work for the welfare of humanity. He was a little afraid for his new pride, though. It was too precious and fragile a thing to survive the journey home, and God knew, he'd never get it past the front door of his house.

He thought of Elaine, not bitterly, but with a kind of helpless pity. Whatever Elaine had wanted and expected from her marriage—great wealth? social position? an idyll of romance?—she hadn't got it and he was unable to give it to her. She was, in the long run, worse off than he was. He had his job, he could become so absorbed in his work that he sometimes didn't think of Elaine for two or three hours. He knew that Elaine had no such respite, that she was always conscious of him as she would have been conscious of a continuous nagging toothache.

He hadn't, come to think of it, remembered Elaine once all day until the girl in the chair beside him asked him for a match. What had the girl said?—that he looked like a doctor or a lawyer. Some answer was expected of him, he must play the game, whatever it was.

"Appearances," he said with ponderous humor, "are deceiving."

"Aren't they just!" She laughed, and he saw that her teeth were very small and even, like canine incisors. "Still, I always say I can tell a nice character by his face, I really can too. Look, isn't that someone waving at you, over there by the cigar counter?"

Gordon turned, and recognizing a colleague of his, he waved back.

"He's from my hometown," Gordon said. He mentioned the name of the town. Ruby said that she'd never been there but she knew lots of people who had, and they all agreed that it was the most beautiful place in the country.

"I certainly intend to go there," she said. "I've just never found the time and my parents are terribly old school. They think girls should stay home all the time."

"Do you work any place?"

"Just for the fun of it I'm working at the perfume counter in Magrim's. Honestly, the people you meet! I never had any idea how the other half lives."

"Didn't you?" Gordon smiled at her innocence.

"Actually I'm not crazy about working, but it's better than sitting at home watching Daddy fuss over his silly stamps and coins. A girl should get out on her own, don't you agree?"

Gordon agreed.

Ruby's "party" failed to appear. Gordon had intended to go to a movie by himself but he couldn't think of any polite way to abandon the girl. She was too young to sit around a hotel lobby alone so Gordon offered to get her a taxi and send her home.

"That's terribly kind of you," Ruby said with a rueful little smile. "But I guess it wouldn't do much good for me to go home this early. Mummy and Daddy are out tonight and I haven't got a key."

Gordon took her along to the movie. She was a trusting little thing. Even though he was a complete stranger she seemed to rely on him already and when they walked down the dark aisle she put her hand on his coat sleeve, tugging at it like a child who doesn't want to be left behind.

Three days later she still didn't want to be left behind.

"Don't go, Gordon, please."

"I have to. You don't understand. I told you about Elaine and the children and my work."

"Take me with you."

"I can't, Ruby."

"Will you be back?"

"You know I will."

"I'm afraid you'll change your mind."

"I would if I could," Gordon said quietly. "It's too late, I love you."

"Say it again."

"I love you."

"What if I never see you again?" she sobbed. "What if you change your mind?"

"I won't." He held her in his arms while she wept. "I'll be back, darling. Don't worry, don't cry."

She sobbed over and over again, "What if I never see you again?"

He drove home alone, buoyant, frightened, intoxicated, ashamed of himself, confused, in love. Once or twice as he drove along the rocky coast he thought of sending himself and the car over the cliff, but he didn't do it, and when he got home, Elaine seemed genuinely glad to see him.

Elaine fussed over him, unpacked his suitcase, and told him he was looking tired.

"Staying up late at all those burlesque shows, I bet!" she said with a gay laugh.

"I didn't go to any burlesque shows."

"My goodness, I thought that's what conventions were *for!*"

He looked at her steadily. "Did you?"

"What's the matter with you, Gordon? Can't you take a joke anymore?"

"It depends on the joke."

"As if I didn't know you have too much self-respect to go to a burlesque show," Elaine said reproachfully. "What did you do with your evenings?"

"I went to the movies," Gordon said. I fell in love with a girl named Ruby. At first I thought she was just an innocent, wide-eyed kid, and then afterwards at the movie I thought she was an ordinary pick-up. When it was too late I found out something else—she was a virgin.

Four days later he had a letter from her. During office hours he kept the letter in his pocket and at night he left it in the office safe.

Dear Gordon:

I guess by this time you've forgotten all about me and I wouldn't blame you, really I wouldn't Gordon; I'm not worthy to shine your shoes. In fact I've got some things on my conscience and I thought I'd tell you, then if you've forgotten me you can just read this and forget it too, but if you haven't and if you still feel about me the way I do about you, you will know anyway that I'm trying to play fair and square with you. Well, here goes, Gordon.

I wasn't waiting for anybody that night in the lobby, I was just sitting there. I was walking home and I got tired so I went and sat there pretending I was waiting for someone because otherwise it wouldn't be good taste. Isn't it funny Gordon that if my feet hadn't been hurting I wouldn't ever have met you. I'm glad I did, no matter what happens to us I'll never be sorry. I swear on my honor I never did that before, talking to a strange man like that and I will never do it again. I haven't even looked at another man since you left—what's the use they look silly beside you.

Point two: I told you I lived with my parents, this isn't true either because my parents are divorced and have married other people and I live with my aunt and cousin; my cousin is older than I and she has a good job. I guess you will think I am a terrible liar. I don't know why I said that about my parents I haven't seen them for years, but I want you to know the truth now anyway because I love you Gordon. I've never been in love before—only crushes.

I guess that's all Gordon. I hope you won't hate me the way I hate myself for telling you those lies, but I wouldn't blame you if you turned against me. I am not good enough for you—maybe I never will be but I'm going to try hard. I think of you all the time, please write to me Gordon. I love you. Ruby.

Every evening, while Hazel was cleaning up the front office, Gordon went into the lab and sat down on the high stool. He read the letter over and over and then he put his head down on the lab table and wept without tears.

Ruby arrived in town three weeks later. She came by bus carrying a suitcase containing two letters from Gordon, a few clothes and her aunt's red fox neckpiece (borrowed for a limited time only). She had nearly two hundred dollars, scraped together from various sources. Seventy dollars was her own, her cousin lent her twenty-five, and a hundred came from her father in Seattle. She had written to him for the first time in two years telling him she was going to be married and needed money for a trousseau. Her father sent her a check and a note wishing her happiness and telling her not to mention the check to her mother under any circumstances.

She took a room in a boarding house a couple of blocks from the bus terminal. Here she unpacked her suitcase, shook out the red fox neckpiece and washed her face. Then she went to the nearest café to phone Gordon and have something to eat.

She sat down in a booth, trembling with weariness and excitement. She was here at last, in the same city as Gordon, perhaps even just a few blocks from him right this minute. From now on all her days would be colored by the possibility of seeing Gordon. He might be walking past the café right now (she looked and could see nothing beyond the closed Venetian blind) and every time she stepped out of the door she might catch a glimpse of his car. She had memorized the license number on that first night, standing on the curb outside Gordon's hotel. She had repeated it aloud over and over, without realizing why. Everything that concerned Gordon had become absorbingly important to her, with the exception of Elaine. She thought of Elaine vaguely as a shadow-figure crossing Gordon's path now and then without touching him or interfering with him. Ruby's one-sided imagination flung a veil over Elaine and her children, her own future, her financial difficulties, Gordon's reputation, and any preconceived notions she had of right and wrong. Right was something you were going to do anyway, and if it didn't justify itself afterwards it became wrong. Ruby's mind worked with disastrous simplicity. It was "wrong" to lie to Gordon about her parents, but it was "right" to follow him here without telling him about it in advance or asking his opinion.

She wanted to surprise Gordon, and she did.

She dialed the number of his office while Mr. Gomez reheated a batch of french-fried potatoes and the juke box moaned a soft, disturbing song. The music brushed her ears and her lips like a kiss.

Watching her from behind the counter Mr. Gomez made one of his quick, wrong analyses of character: kid from a small town, on her way to Hollywood, due for a shock, no jobs around, lousy with pretty girls already, the kid's asking for it.

"I'm not hungry," Gordon told Elaine at dinner. "I think I'll go out for a walk."

Elaine glanced at him across the table. She believed nothing and so she could always spot a lie, an ability which was her pride and joy.

"A walk? I should think after standing on your feet all day a walk would be about the last thing you'd want."

"I don't get enough exercise."

"You have your golf on Sunday afternoons."

"If you've any objections to me going for a walk, say so. Don't beat around the bush. Is there something you want me to do around the house, is that it?"

"You don't have to get irritable, Gordon. I didn't object to your going for a walk, it just seemed peculiar, that's all."

"Well, perhaps I *am* peculiar," Gordon said.

Elaine sighed and thought, how true. Gordon was peculiar, and little did these people who were always telling her how lucky she was to have a good husband, little did they know what she had to put up with. It was quite possible that Gordon's trouble was glandular. If this was the case, Elaine would stand by, she would even nurse him herself, if necessary, until Gordon's glands readjusted and he had completely recovered. Complete recovery, in Elaine's terms, meant that Gordon would be constantly sweet, affectionate, devoted to herself and the children. He would stay home at night and they would all play games together, a gay, happy, united little family. This was Elaine's dream, this picture of Gordon and herself and the children sitting at a table reading aloud or playing Parcheesi and Casino and Snakes and Ladders . . . She and Gordon would touch hands and smile with pride and love at the children's excitement . . . This was what she wanted but she had never told Gordon, and her own attempts in the direction of the dream were hopelessly inadequate. The boys were too young for such games and the girl Judith got overexcited and tried to cheat. Elaine was horrified by this cheating, she could not believe it was natural for a seven-year-old to try to cheat, and in the end she blamed Gordon for passing on his hereditary weakness to his daughter. The gay evenings with the children were nightmares for Gordon and agonizing frustration for Elaine.

Elaine confided in no one. To her friends she appeared invulnerable, and it was only when she said her prayers in the evening that she admitted, even to herself, that she was not.

When Gordon had left she put the children to bed. Then she went into the bedroom she shared with Gordon. Kneeling beside the bed Elaine confided in her doctor-psychoanalyst-father-mother-confessor-God. She talked to Him quite naturally, as to an old friend.

"Dear Father, I need your help, we all do. We turn to you in our unhappiness. I don't ask you to make me happy, only to show me what is wrong and what I should do. Whatever it is I have enough strength and faith to do it. Something terrible is wrong in this house, it is crushing us all, and I know it must be my fault as well as Gordon's. Gordon is out for a walk—it's funny how I keep telling You things You must know—and I miss him the way I did when he was in San Francisco. I think I love him, I don't know. When he's away I love him, but when he comes back everything starts over, all the small irritations and differences. I do my best to lead a virtuous life but sometimes I have wicked thoughts and when I look at Gordon I resent him. Where does this terrible resentment come from? Sometimes I want to hit out at him, and just tonight when he swallowed some soup and it went down the wrong way, I felt glad, really glad! I thought, *that will teach him*—those were the very words that came into my mind. But why? What would it teach him? How could I have been glad? Dear Lord, show me the way, I am lost and wicked—I don't know—what a mess, Oh God, what a mess—"

She remained on her knees for a long time, staring up at the ceiling, a blank relentless heaven.

In terror and exultation Gordon opened the door of Mr. Gomez's café and found Ruby in the back booth.

"Gordon—Gordon, are you glad I'm here?"

"Yes, yes, you know I am—"

"I'm glad too."

He took her hand and held it against his mouth.

"Gordon, I didn't come here to ask you for anything."

"I know. Don't talk."

"I have to say this," she said earnestly. "I mean, I don't want you to give up your family or anything, I wouldn't ask you to. I just came to be near you."

"You shouldn't have come."

"Here I am, though."

"Here you are."

"Are you happy?"

"Very." He smiled at her but his eyes were worried. "I'm very happy."

She noticed his worry and said quickly, "Now don't start *thinking*, Gordon. For one night we won't think or plan or anything, eh?"

"All right."

"If it's me you're worrying about, you can stop right now. I can take care of myself and I know exactly what I'm doing."

"What did you tell your aunt?"

"That I was going to get a job here, and I am, too. She didn't mind. She even let me borrow her red fox fur so I could look more presentable. Naturally I didn't tell her about you—she's death on men anyway."

"Have you any money?"

"Lots. My father sent me some. I had to tell a lie to get it. Does that shock you, Gordon?"

He shook his head. He was beyond the stage of shock, no matter what happened. His life, which for eight years had run like an engine on schedule, had without warning jumped its tracks and roared off into the woods.

It couldn't have happened, Gordon thought in sudden panic, it isn't true. Yet here was Ruby sitting by his side, accepting with mature complacence her new role as mistress to a married man. She seemed to have tossed away her girlhood and walked on without looking back and without looking ahead. She had no goal, no ambition, and no purpose beyond the immediate satisfaction of being near Gordon.

"You'll have to go back home before your aunt finds out the truth," Gordon said wearily.

"I have no home. My aunt's house is no more home to me than the room up the street that I just rented. Why should I go back? Gordon—" She put her hand on his wrist. "Listen, Gordon, after you left, the whole city seemed dead to me. The people were there just the same and they did the same things they always did, walked and laughed and drove cars, but they looked dead to me, like they had motors in them like that dummy that rides the exercycle on Powell Street. Remember when we passed it on the cable car and you said it was wonderful, a typically American invention to get nowhere fast?"

Gordon nodded, marveling at the way she remembered, with absolute accuracy, all the words he had spoken in her presence, as if she had deliberately, right from the first, set out to memorize them. Why? Gordon thought. Why *me?* He saw himself as an ordinary man crowding forty, getting a little bald, a little stooped, a little tired. There was nothing about him to appeal to a young girl, yet for Ruby his departure had murdered a city. She loves me, Gordon thought, and he felt a nameless fear draining the blood out of his head.

Love, I'm not sure what it is, what does it mean? Elaine loves to love things. She loves tweed suits, mushrooms, bleached mahogany furniture, bridge, even me. "I love you, Gordon, naturally I do, for heaven's sake you're my husband, aren't you?" She loves the children too. Eat your custard because Mummy loves you and wants you to be big and strong. Elaine wants to be loved in return; she's always asking me if I love her and I always say I do. "Certainly, of course, absolutely, sure, naturally, why shouldn't I love you, you're my wife, aren't you?" What have we been talking about all these years, Elaine and I? I never killed a city for Elaine.

"I remember," Gordon said.

"I felt dead too, Gordon. I knew I was moving around; sometimes I could feel my legs walking up the streets but they didn't have any connection with *me,* they just walked by themselves automatically."

"I didn't—I didn't mean to make you feel this way about me."

"I know, but I do. It's happened. You don't really want me to go home, do you, Gordon?"

"No."

"Well, that's settled then. And you mustn't worry, promise?"

"I promise, Ruby."

She pressed her head against his shoulder. Her mouth trembled and her eyes were blurred with tears. "I've never loved anyone before and nobody's ever loved me either, not my father or mother or my aunt or another man, no one."

"I'll make it up to you," Gordon said. He felt a new and grave responsibility for her. She had such stubborn naiveté; she was so ignorant of the world and of the difficulties ahead of them both.

In fear and love and desperation he put his arm around her and held her close.

For Gordon, who was by nature a blunt and honest man, life became a series of sly, awkward deceptions.

He lied to Hazel: "You'd better phone Mrs. Hathaway and cancel her five o'clock appointment. I have a bit of a headache." He lied to Elaine: "That walk last night set me up. I think I ought to get more exercise—" and to the children: "Daddy can't read to you tonight, he's going down to the Y to have a swim."

Later, he and Ruby parted at the front door of Ruby's boarding house. The proprietress, who didn't allow visitors of the opposite sex in any of the rooms, had lately become suspicious of one or two of her tenants, and she sat all evening in the parlor with the blinds up, looking alert.

"The old biddy's watching," Ruby said. "Don't kiss me."

"All right."

"Will I see you tomorrow, Gordon?"

"I don't know."

"What did you tell Elaine tonight?"

"That I was going for a swim at the Y."

"You better wet your hair some place."

On his way home he went into the public lavatory and dampened his hair under the tap. He splashed some water in his eyes to make them a little red, and dried his face with his handkerchief. He walked home along the dark quiet streets with the smell of the lavatory in his nostrils and despair and degradation in his heart.

On his arrival Elaine noticed his damp hair and reddish eyes, but she also noticed that he didn't smell of chlorine as he always did after a swim in the pool. She didn't make any comment to Gordon, she merely noted the discrepancy in the little account book she had kept inside her head for years.

The next night Elaine left the children alone, with a bag of chocolates as solace, and followed Gordon down to Mr. Gomez's café. Through the window slot in the front door she saw Gordon enter one of the back booths and greet someone who was already there. After the first vicious thrill of triumph—"I was right! I've been right all along, absolutely right!"—she felt a dazed incredulity. She had followed the wrong man, it was not Gordon (good old comfortable, steady, hard-working Gordon); and the woman who had followed him, dodging behind bushes and trees pretending to be mailing a letter and looking for a certain house number, was not herself, Elaine, the sincere, virtuous, respectable Elaine she knew and loved so well.

Elaine was, during the first few hours, more appalled at herself than at Gordon. How could I, she thought. How could I, following him like that, peering in that window—what would Mama say if she found out?

Neither Mama, nor Gordon, nor anyone else, found out about Elaine's trip in the dark. Elaine managed to forget it herself except when Judith referred to it as "the night Mummy left us alone with the chocolates."

The night of the chocolates, which was for Judith one of her most delightful experiences, was the beginning of what Elaine called her fight for her home and her happiness and the children. She fought indirectly, via the telephone and Mr. Gomez.

The calls infuriated Ruby. "Why can't she leave us alone? She's got everything she wants, what's *she* griping about? I'm the one should be griping."

"What's the matter now, Ruby?"

"I've got to move."

"Why?"

"The old biddy's found out about us. She told me very politely this morning that she didn't keep a house and she wasn't a madam and if I wasn't out by Thursday morning she'd report me to the police and they'd run me out of town. Nice, eh?"

"She must be crazy to talk like that," Gordon said, pale with anger. "My God, Ruby, didn't you defend yourself? Didn't you talk back?"

"Sure I talked back," Ruby said dully. "I said I'd move out Thursday morning and that's *all* I said because it's all I could say."

"But you must have—"

"Well, I didn't. I want to get out of there, anyway. I don't even want to go back there tonight. She scares me, Gordon." She leaned her head on her hands in a picture of weary resignation.

"What's the matter with me tonight? I guess I'm tired. Don't pay any attention to me. Things are getting so much more mixed up than I thought. I just seem to be making a sort of general mess of everything. Even my new job. You know what Mr. Anderson said to me tonight? He said I was the worst waitress he'd ever seen and I guess he's right. In the same breath he asked me to go out with him. I said no. Would you be jealous if I did go out with him, Gordon?"

"I suppose I would," Gordon said soberly. "I don't know. I've never been jealous of anyone before."

"You wouldn't. I mean, that's sort of typical of you. You're just sort of generally nice, aren't you?"

Gordon smiled. "Elaine would like to hear that."

"Don't talk about her tonight. I'm too tired, I'm so tired I could die. What a job, hauling food around all day. You should see some of them eat. God, people are pigs. It makes me so sick watching them that I never want to eat again."

"You've got to quit that job. I'll get some money for you. I'll tell Elaine that—"

He stopped, unable to think of anything to tell Elaine that she would even pretend to believe. Out of the budget Elaine allowed him twenty dollars a week for lunch and incidentals. The budget had always been Elaine's job—an office budget that covered salaries, rent and new equipment, and one for the household. These budgets invariably balanced, and Gordon was grateful to Elaine for taking over the job and making his money stretch further than he would have been able to do. He had never needed more than twenty dollars a week for himself. Now that he did, the only way he could get it was by more lying. If he cashed a check on their joint account Elaine would find out about it and he would still have to lie.

In the end he wrote out a check for fifty dollars and told Elaine he had lost it on a horse race.

"How could you, Gordon," Elaine said, with soft reproach, "when you know how we could have used that money! The children are old enough now to *perceive* things. They see that the Brittons next-door have a slide and swing, but *they* haven't. And poor Paul has had his heart set on a model airplane with a real motor in it. Or a wading pool. I did so hope we'd be able to manage a wading pool this summer. Well—I won't nag, Gordon, I hate nagging wives. But I must ask you for the sake of the children to keep within your allowance."

A little later, while reading the paper, Elaine pointed out to Gordon the picture of an Indian potentate, reputed to be one of the richest men in the world.

"Of course he'd *have* to be rich," Elaine said sharply, "in order to be able to afford a *harem*."

Gordon did not defend himself any more than Ruby had when her landlady asked her to leave.

Monday noon, before she left for work, the landlady knocked on her door and when Ruby failed to answer she let herself in with a passkey.

Ruby was sitting on the edge of the bed in her slip, doubled over as if she had a cramp.

"What's the matter, girl? You sick or something?"

"No."

"You found a place yet?"

"No. I haven't had much chance to look."

"Just so's you're out by Thursday. This is the best room in the house and I want—"

"It's ugly," Ruby said, without raising her head. "It's the ugliest room in the world."

"Mind your tongue or I'll kick you out right now."

"My rent's paid."

"Girls like you, there's a place for them and it's not in any respectable home like this one."

When the landlady had gone, Ruby got up and opened the closet door. The red fox fur was lying on the shelf, its glass eyes bright as jewels. Her aunt wanted the fur back; she'd written two letters about it, stating that she wanted it to wear at the wedding of a relative of hers. Though Ruby didn't actually need the fur, she was reluctant to send it back because it reminded her of Gordon and the first night she had arrived in town—it was a symbol of the happy future she had imagined then. To relinquish the fox fur now would be an admission of failure and an acknowledgment that the happy future had already come and gone. She still loved Gordon but not in the pure distilled sense she had at first. Some of the pollutions of circumstance had seeped in, the squalor of her life, the room she'd lived in, the eternal smell of grease in Mr. Gomez's café, the endless cups of bitter coffee, the endless waiting, the hope that had sickened but refused to die. If she sent the fox fur back she might as well go with it, go home, and never see Gordon again. But at the thought of a world without Gordon her heart contracted in a spasm of fear. She stood for a long time in the dark little clothes closet pressing her face against the red fox and wondering what she could do or say or become to make Gordon love her again.

On Wednesday when she went to work she called Gordon from the pay phone behind the wharf warehouse. He answered the phone himself.

"Dr. Foster's office."

"Hello, Gordon?"

"Hello."

"Is there anybody there? Can you talk?"

"There's no one here."

"Why haven't I seen you? Is there anything the matter, Gordon?"

"I couldn't get away," Gordon said wearily. "Ever since the business about the fifty-dollar check, the assumption is that I'm an insane gambler and not to be trusted even to go for a walk alone."

"You sound so bitter."

"I don't mean to. Are you all right, Ruby?"

"Naturally."

"Did you find a place to move to?"

"Not yet. When will I see you, Gordon?"

"God knows. When I can think up a new lie, I guess."

"I'll be waiting tonight after I get through work."

"No, don't. I can't—I can't stand the thought of you just sitting there in that place waiting for me. You don't understand—I feel as if I've *got* to be there and yet I can't get there. It tears me apart, I can't tell you—I—"

"I won't wait if you don't want me to," Ruby said quickly.

"Do you understand? Just for one night I want to feel that I don't *have* to be two places at once, that no one's expecting anything of me. I know, I guess this sounds childish, but just for this one night I've got to be a free agent. Don't you ever feel like that, Ruby?"

"No. I don't want to be a free agent. I like to wait for you, even if you don't come. What else would I do if I didn't wait for you?"

She hung up, and for a minute she sat staring listlessly into the round black mouth of the telephone. *What else would I do if I didn't wait for Gordon?*

That night after work she walked to the edge of the wharf and stood with her forearms resting on the rail, watching the lights of the town. The lights flickered halfway up the mountain so that the town seemed to be pinned to the side of the mountain with stars. On the wharf the lights were going out one by one. Everyone was leaving, except the customers in the bar. The kitchen was closed, and the waitresses and the kitchen help were departing, in twos and threes. They walked quickly, on the balls of their feet so their heels wouldn't catch in the gaps between the planks. They were all anxious to get back on the dry land since it was common talk that the wharf was heading for disintegration and no one was doing anything to stop it. Occasionally some haphazard repair work was done and a few of the rotting piles were replaced, but this did not mitigate the sense of imminent doom among the people who worked at the Beachcomber. This feeling was nurtured by the cashier, a woman called Virginia, who had escaped certain death for five years now, six nights a week. To newcomers like Ruby, Virginia was careful to point out that the wharf was nearly eighty years old, and aside from the natural deterioration of the years there was also the strong possibility of a bad storm or a tidal wave.

"Mark my words," Virginia said. "One of these days we'll all find ourselves in the ocean hanging onto anything that floats. And you know what I'm going to do then? I'm going to sue them! I'm going to sue the whole damn bunch of them, the owners of the wharf and the city that grants the franchise and Anderson and his outfit, and when I collect I'm going to retire, build a house in the middle of the desert and live the life of Riley. Maybe we could *all* sue them and all of us retire."

The hired help of the Beachcomber were drawn together, by Virginia's enthusiasm, into a common dread and a common dream. The life of Riley appealed to them, and those among them who couldn't swim found themselves eyeing the furnishings of the Beachcomber with the quality of buoyancy in mind.

When Virginia saw Ruby leaning against the railing she paused a moment to proffer advice. She reminded Ruby that the railing was nearly eighty years old, that it was quite a drop into the sea, and the water was cold and deep. Moreover if Ruby drowned she couldn't even sue anybody, being dead.

Having survived one more day, Virginia sped back to land.

Ruby leaned her full weight on the railing. I wouldn't care, she thought. I wouldn't care about drowning except I wouldn't like the water to be very cold. Gordon might be sorry for a while but he'd be glad too. He wouldn't have to think or worry about me anymore; he wouldn't have to feel obliged to me all the time. It would be a relief to him if I died.

She began walking slowly toward shore. She wondered which of the lights of the town belonged to Gordon and what he was doing. Reading? Or perhaps he was already asleep? Poor Gordon. She hadn't meant to cause him so much trouble. Everything had seemed very harmless and right to her in the beginning. All she wanted was to be in the same town as Gordon and to see him now and then. It wasn't a great deal to ask for, but she hadn't foreseen how even this much might affect Gordon's life. Instead of making him happy she had only made him despise himself, and her too. There was no way that she could give back to Gordon his dignity and self-respect. Nothing could dissolve the feeling of degradation that Gordon had had the night he dampened his hair under the tap in the public lavatory. He had told her about it, and Ruby understood his rage and humiliation and guilt. He had said, "I can't stand it," and she believed now that this was true. Gordon was destroying himself and she was the instrument of destruction.

She groped blindly toward the lights of the town, wishing the wharf would rot away under her feet. She seemed to feel it actually moving, not rolling gently with the swell of the water, but throbbing with quick shivers like an old man with palsy. The headlights of a car beamed suddenly behind her. She stepped aside, and as the car passed her, the planks of the wharf rattled and shuddered. She began to run, as fast as she could, toward the shore.

When she reached the boulevard the car was parked along the curb waiting for her. She recognized Mr. Anderson at the wheel but she pretended she didn't see him.

He called after her, "Hop in and I'll give you a lift home."

She stopped, shaking her head. "No, no thanks."

"Might as well."

"It's such a nice night, I don't mind walking."

"You look tired." He opened the front door of the car. "Come on, get in."

She got in, holding the fox fur tight around her throat.

"You don't have to act so scared," George said. "I assure you I'm pretty tired myself." He was smiling, but there was a note of irritation in his voice. "I'm going to have a beer and a steak sandwich. If you want to come with me, fine. If you don't, I'll take you home first."

"I'll—just get out any place and walk home."

"That suits me." He started the car and headed up Main Street. "You're a funny girl. I can't make you out."

She said nothing. She was not interested in Mr. Anderson's opinion of her. She hardly considered him a human being, he was so remote from her thoughts.

"I'm sorry I had to speak a little rough to you about that bar check," George said. "But I'm in business, and if I want to stay in business I have to shoot off my mouth once in a while."

"I didn't mind."

"Good."

"I'll get off at the next corner, if that's all right with you."

"Well, it isn't, but there's not much I can do about it, is there?"

At the next corner he stopped the car. He leaned across her to open the door. She shrank back against the seat to avoid his touch.

George said dryly, "Is there something the matter with me or is there something the matter with you? You're not married or anything, are you?"

"No."

"I'm not, either. I was, but I'm not anymore. Won't you let me take you out sometime?"

"I really don't care much about going out."

"That's that, then."

"Thanks for the ride."

"You're welcome."

As soon as he drove off, she went straight to Mr. Gomez's café. She sat there until closing time, drinking coffee. She kept her eye on the door, out of habit. Gordon didn't even know she'd be waiting, so there wasn't the slightest hope that he would come. But she got a certain bitter satisfaction in watching the door anyway, facing the hopelessness.

She sat there for an hour and a half, seeing quite clearly that there was no future for her and Gordon, and there was no easy way out. The wharf would not rot under her feet, no tidal wave would engulf her, no storm would carry her out to sea.

During the week she sent the fox fur back to her aunt, parcel post, and she let George drive her home two nights in a row. He assumed that she was becoming more friendly toward him and Ruby didn't bother to correct him. She was slipping back into her old habits of evasiveness. It was hardly worthwhile to tell the truth to anyone or explain anything. Let Mr. Anderson assume whatever he wanted to assume, it didn't matter.

On Thursday night she met Gordon at the café for the last time. She arrived full of enthusiasm about the new job Mr. Anderson had promised her. A new job meant a new life, new hope, new chances.

Gordon was waiting for her when she got there. He looked out of place in the regular Thursday-night crowd. He was not watching the door for her arrival. He was watching the people at the bar in sober bewilderment, as if he too was aware of the difference between them and himself, but could not figure out what this difference was. These people were not drunk, yet the possibility of becoming drunk was already coloring their evening. They could cut loose if they liked, and they relaxed into quick friendships, easy laughter, loose wallets. The regulars at the café formed a kind of club for the kind of people for whom ordinary clubs were impossible. They were Mr. Gomez's Rotarian Kiwanis of the Masonic Order of the Elks and Lions. They convened to exchange slaps on the back, stories, political arguments, gossip and news of absentee members, and to mitigate their loneliness.

Gordon, watching them, wished that he could walk over and join the club, or that he could look forward to one night every week when he could relax and forget his responsibilities. One night, not to get drunk, but to sit up at the bar with the regulars and roll thirteenth-ace for the next quarter for the juke box. He felt like a wistful child, on the outside looking in, yet he knew quite well that what he was looking into was nothing that he could accept or enjoy. Gordon could never unlock his chains; they had been forged long before he met Elaine.

"Hello, Gordon." Ruby sat down beside him. She had meant to blurt out her good news right away, but her throat felt clogged and furry and she spoke so softly he had to bend his head to hear her. "I haven't seen you for a long time."

"I know."

"I've missed you terribly. Have you missed me?"

"Yes." He took her hand and held it. There was a desperate strength in his grip as if he knew that something valuable was slipping away from him and he was unable to stop it, unable even to assess its value.

"I missed you," he said, "but I didn't want to see you. I had to reason things out and give you a chance to do the same."

"I didn't want a chance to reason things out. Everything I've done is unreasonable if you look at it that way."

"No, wait, Ruby. I tried—I tried to figure out a way where we'd all come out all right, you and Elaine and I and the kids." He drew in his breath painfully. "And there isn't any way. We all have to suffer for my selfishness."

"We haven't done anything so terrible. Why should you let your conscience bother you like this? Elaine isn't hurt."

"She is, and so are my children, and me, and you most of all, Ruby. What have you gotten out of all this except grief?"

"I don't think of that, Gordon. I love you. I've told you that so often and you never understand it, do you?"

"Understand it? No, I don't. I've tried to figure that out, too. I can't understand why you should love me, I don't know what love is. I only know it needs certain things in order to survive. It can't grow like a mushroom in a pile of dirt in the cellar."

She got up. Her head felt light and empty. "You shouldn't have said that, Gordon. You're right but you shouldn't have said it. It wasn't a very nice thing to say. You hurt me. You *hurt* me, Gordon."

She walked toward the front door. Her eyes were dazed and her mouth still hung open a little in terrible surprise.

7

MR. ESCOBAR ARRIVED for work on Saturday morning. He steered his bicycle with his right hand, and with his left he balanced over his shoulder his own tools, a rake, a spading fork, a hedge clipper and a shovel as polished and sharp as a carving knife. In his bicycle basket he carried an oiled rag, a small wooden box which he used to trap gophers, a bottle of Pepsi-Cola, and three bologna on rye sandwiches moistened with cold beans.

He drove up Mrs. Anderson's lane and parked his bicycle in the garage. A small black and white dog came bouncing across the yard. When Escobar opened the gate the dog danced wildly around his legs and finally flung itself on his heavy boots, stomach up. Escobar leaned down and rubbed its stomach. The friendly dog was a good omen. Only friendly people kept friendly dogs.

"Little fellow," Escobar said. "Hello, pretty little fellow."

Wendy got up and shook herself. Then she started to explore with her nose every inch of his boots. Escobar cleaned his boots almost daily but they never quite lost the smell of fertilizer. Sometimes Lucia, his wife, complained of this. She was a city girl, born and raised in San Diego, and she considered manure (even steer manure swept off cement floors) as rather coarse and unpleasant. When Escobar tried to explain to her that manure was sometimes necessary as food for plants, Lucia wasn't quite convinced. She kept two potted geraniums on the windowsill in the kitchen and they got along nicely without fertilizer, only a little water now and then.

The boots moved across the yard and Wendy followed them, sniffing, and yelping in frustration when they wouldn't stand still.

Ruth came to the screen door. "Be quiet, Wendy."

"He is a pretty little fellow," Escobar said.

"It's a she. A girl. Her name's Wendy."

"She's a pretty little fellow."

"She's only a pup, eight months old. Naturally"—Ruth's laugh came through the door, sharp and defensive—"naturally she's not a thoroughbred."

Escobar nodded cautiously. He was not certain what a thoroughbred dog was, since he had always connected the word with horses. He could not see Ruth clearly through the screen door, but he didn't like her sound, and in spite of the omen of the friendly dog, Escobar was uneasy. He hoped the woman would stay on the other side of the screen door.

"Mrs. Anderson's gone to work," Ruth said. "I'm her cousin. I'll be here all morning if you want to consult me."

"Yes, boss."

"Mrs. Anderson said just to start in. The tools are in the garage. I noticed, I happened to be looking out the window, and I noticed you brought some extra ones."

He nodded again and began to back away from the porch. The dog followed him and Ruth called her back.

"Wendy, come here."

"Go on, little fellow," Escobar said, waving his hand toward the house. "Go on."

The dog paused and Ruth said, "Come and get your goody. Here's your goody. Come on."

She opened the door and the dog streaked into the house. Escobar had a momentary glimpse of her before she closed the door again. She was an old lady with white hair.

Ruth fed Wendy the rest of the scrambled eggs from breakfast, bit by bit, and as she fed her she talked. This was Ruth's hour—two of them had gone to work, and the other one was still in bed—and she intended to spend it as she usually did. But with the Mexican out in the yard, she felt self-conscious, as if he might be eavesdropping. He couldn't hear anything, of course, since she talked in whispers to avoid waking Josephine, but still he was there, and the words she used to the dog were a little different from usual.

"There, my pretty, there's your goody. What a glutton you are. What a fat little glutton. And the manners! Sniffing people like that, my goodness, what bad manners!"

He probably smells, Ruth thought. He looked clean enough but they all smelled under the surface. Their dark skins didn't show the dirt and they were too lazy to wash if it wasn't necessary. Bone-lazy. She would have to supervise him and see that he didn't cheat Hazel out of her hard-earned money by standing around watering things instead of really working, or by taking too much time to eat his lunch. Hazel was too easy on other people and too easy on herself as well.

You had to watch these Mexicans very carefully. They were sly. They put on a great show of innocence and stupidity but Ruth saw through that clearly enough. She had had several of them in her fifth-grade class before she lost her job, and one of them in particular was very sly. He had curly black hair and brown eyes like an angel's, but Ruth knew that the instant she turned her back the Mexican boy *did* something. What this something was or how he did it, she never knew, but she knew it was done. The boy terrified her and she reported him to the principal at least once a week. "He *does* something, Mr. Jamieson, I swear it, I *feel* it!" "I think you need a rest, Miss Kane."

That had been two years ago, but she still thought of the Mexican boy, she thought of his smooth innocent forehead and the dark angel's eyes. In the middle of the night she tried and tried to figure out what he had done, until desperation seized her and she had to cram her fist into her mouth to keep from screaming and waking Hazel. The boy had become a symbol of fascinating, exciting, evil things she dared not name.

You need a rest, Miss Kane.

To: The Superintendent of Schools, Ernest Colfax, A.M.

From: Percy Hoag, M.D.

I advise an immediate medical leave of absence for Miss Ruth Kane, such leave to extend for an indefinite period of time.

She was only thirty-six, but her hair was white and her skin and eyes were pale as if she had been bleeding internally for years.

Josephine called from the bedroom, "Ruth."

"Coming."

She went through the dining room, drying her hands on her apron, and opened the door of Josephine's bedroom.

"Oh dear," Josephine said. "I woke up—what time is it?"

"Nine."

"Oh dear."

"How do you feel?"

"I don't know. I haven't moved yet." She hadn't moved at all during the night. She'd gone to sleep on her back with her head propped on two pillows, and now she was awake in the same position, and not a strand of her long brown hair was out of place. Nearly every night Josephine slept like this, quietly and without dreams, and when she woke up she lay without moving for a long time, remote and self-contained. During the day she brooded or wept, she had placid daydreams or she quarreled, she had headaches and spells of overwhelming fear. But at night she entered another world, and emerging from it in the morning she was rejuvenated. Her face was untroubled, her eyes clear and lustrous, and her skin seemed to glow. It was as if she drew nourishment, during sleep, from a part of her mind or body that she didn't know existed.

"Something woke me," Josephine said. "A noise. There, you hear it?"

They listened and heard just outside the window the spasmodic sounds of Escobar's shovel. The faint shriek as it cut the ground, and the *smack* as Escobar spanked each clod of earth to free the roots of the weeds.

"That's the Mexican," Ruth said.

"So *early.*"

"Do you want a graham cracker before you get out of bed?"

"No, no, I think—" Josephine moved her head experimentally. "No. Is Harold—? Of course. Oh dear. I guess I'll get up. It's Saturday, isn't it?"

"Yes."

"Harold's off this afternoon. It's nice having Harold around. The days—" She helped herself up with her elbows—"awfully long sometimes. The waiting—hand me my corset, will you?—four months yet, oh dear."

She stood up and began lacing up the maternity corset, not too tight, just tight enough to give her some support. She was small-boned and slender, and her condition was becoming much too noticeable.

"I wish I was taller," she said. "If you're tall you can carry things off. Like clothes."

Ruth was making the bed. When Josephine paused between sentences Ruth could hear the gentle *shriek, smack, shriek, smack,* of Escobar's shovel. He's working. Well, he'd better be. I'll keep an eye on him. I'll see Hazel doesn't get cheated.

She went to the window and peered out through layers of mauve net curtains. He was only two feet away from her. He had rolled up the sleeves of his plaid shirt and opened the collar. He wore a yellow undershirt. Sweat glistened on his forehead and in the crooks of his elbows, and his hair was a cap of wet black silk. He was breathing through his mouth. She could see part of his lower front teeth, and they were very white, almost as if he'd cleaned them.

He looked up suddenly and his eyes pierced the mauve net curtains like needles. She stepped back with a shock, feeling the needles in her breasts and her stomach. Her insides curled up and then expanded, disintegrated, dissolved into fluid. I feel quite faint. It's the heat. It's going to be a hot day.

"It's going to be quite a hot day," she said.

"Oh, I hope not," Josephine said. "I feel the heat so. Remember?—I never used to mind the heat— Remember?—I never even sweated. And now—it's the extra weight, don't you think? Harold says I should sweat if I'm hot. Otherwise the poison stays in my system."

Josephine said the same things nearly every morning. Her mind revolved in ever-decreasing circles as her body became larger. I feel, how do I feel? Have I a headache? I wish I was taller. The heat bothers me. Harold says. Harold, Harold.

Always she referred to Harold. No matter how small the circle got, Harold was right there in the middle of it, sometimes sliding along smoothly and sometimes getting bounced and jostled and bruised beyond all recognition.

Harold was Josephine's second husband. Her first had been a silent irascible man, a veterinary doctor named Bener. Though he kept no pets of his own, Bener had a great deal of patience with the animals he boarded and treated. He had none at all with Josephine, and it was rather a relief to both of them when he died quietly one night, of coronary thrombosis, leaving all his money to his mother and his brother Jack. Josephine later received some of it under the Community Property Law. She spent it on clothes and then she married Harold.

She married Harold partly because he was handsome and partly because he was the exact opposite of Bener. In their three years together Harold had never spoken to her sharply, and even lately, when she wept or abused him and all men, including God, Harold remained tender and took the abuse as being well deserved.

Harold was no ball of fire, but he was a good deal sharper than most people thought. He showed up badly in front of Hazel (his older sister) and Ruth (his conscience). In their presence he was always making inconsequential remarks, holding his hand up to his mouth as he spoke, as if in apology. Alone with Josephine he was different and talked quite freely about the government and the Teamsters Union, which had nice new headquarters downtown with a neon sign, and the atom bomb, which something would have to be done about, no matter if the baby turned out to be a boy or a girl.

The others might underestimate Harold, mistaking his good nature for laziness, and his dreaminess for impracticality, but Josephine knew better. Make no mistake, Harold thought great thoughts as he drove his truck.

Josephine took her toothbrush and tube of toothpaste from her bureau drawer and carried them into the bathroom. She squeezed a quarter of an inch of paste onto her brush and thought, *by the time this tube is finished, I'll know. I'll be dead or the baby will be dead or we'll both be alive and all right and Harold will be a father. By the time—*

She had an impulse to press the tube and squeeze out the future inch by inch, an inch for each day, squeeze out the time, a long white fragile ribbon of toothpaste.

She replaced the cap, soberly. It was a brand-new tube, giant size, eighty-nine cents, and it would last a long, long time.

"—for breakfast?" Ruth's voice floated into the turning pool of her thoughts.

"Oh. Anything. I'm not very hungry. Shredded wheat, maybe."

"Hot or cold?"

"Cold. It's going to be a hot day." She was sweating already. The poison was seeping out of her system through her pores, underneath the maternity corset and the wraparound skirt and flowered smock. "No, I think I'll take it hot, don't you think so, Ruth?"

"I don't know, it depends on how you feel."

"Oh, cold then. It doesn't matter. Anything."

She followed Ruth into the kitchen like a sheep, and sat down heavily at the table.

"It's such a nice day," she said. "We should all do something, go down to the beach."

"We can't," Ruth said sharply. "Not with the Mexican here. He'd probably go to sleep if he thought no one was watching him."

Josephine smiled pensively. "Mexican babies are cute."

"The *very* small ones."

"And Chinese babies. I saw a Chinese baby in a buggy outside the Safeway yesterday. The way it looked at me! So *knowing*. It seems a shame—to grow up, I mean. Ruth, I know what we could do this afternoon. We could all go down to the harbor and see George. Maybe he'd lend us his sailboat, Harold's crazy about boats."

"I don't know that it'd be good for you, all that up and down motion."

"I don't think it would hurt."

"Anyway, you know my feelings on the subject of George." Ruth let her feelings about George show on her face. They pulled down the muscles around her mouth and shriveled her eyes. "It's my opinion that when you divorce a man you ought to stay divorced from him and not go phoning him and asking him over all the time the way Hazel does."

"She feels sorry for him. He gets lonesome."

"Even so. It's a matter of taste. I have nothing against George, and I have nothing against Hazel, but if they want to see each other they should never have gotten divorced. It's the principle of the thing."

"Oh well. It doesn't matter." Josephine sighed imperceptibly. It was hard to talk to Ruth without coming eventually on something which was a matter of principle or good taste. Divorce, George, drunkenness, Mexicans, horse racing, leaving dirty dishes overnight, teenaged girls who giggled, motor scooters, two-piece bathing suits, dyed hair, chewing gum, not airing blankets every week and the School Board.

It was becoming increasingly difficult for Josephine to excuse Ruth, but each time she did it anyway.

"I bet the ocean looks nice today," she said.

"The rest of you can go down if you want to. There's nothing to stop you."

"There's nothing to stop you either."

"I want to take the curtains down and wash them. Besides—" She left the word hanging in the air, radiating implications. Besides, there was the Mexican, he couldn't be left alone to be lazy. And besides, she didn't like the sea. Its soft inexorable voice spoke of violence and eternity. When she went out onto the pier where George worked, she felt the water beneath her and the water on each side of her and she always had the wild idea that the sky itself was part of the ocean and ready to drop down on her and slowly and gently drown her. Watching the sea gave her a feeling of expansion and disintegration inside her.

"Besides," she said after a time, "there's too much to be done around the house."

She rose briskly, unable to resist her own bait. Something would have to be done about something, and everything about everything, and right now. Like a professional soldier ready to take up arms against anyone, for any reason, she marched out into the backyard on the offensive.

Escobar was on his knees digging out a root of wild morning glory with a knife. He looked up at her, squinting.

"Those are flowers," Ruth said. "What are you digging them up for?"

"The lady of the house said on the phone to plant gardenias on this side,"

"Gardenias."

"Yes, ma'am."

"Gardenias. You'd think she was made of money. How much—how much do they cost?"

"For the one-gallon size, maybe about five dollars."

"How many did she tell you to plant?"

"Six. She likes the smell, she said, ma'am."

"*Six*, That's thirty dollars. She must be out of her mind."

"Yes, ma'am."

"You mustn't do it, until I get a chance to talk to her . . . Geraniums are plenty good enough. Some people get ideas beyond their pocketbooks. Some people think money grows on trees." She let out a sudden harsh laugh. "For you it does. That's funny. For you money *grows on trees*."

A spot of bright pink appeared in the center of her throat, as if someone had, with malicious accuracy, aimed a spoonful of paint at her. Knowing the spot was there, she covered it with her hand while Escobar wiped off his knife on his brand-new levis. His wife had told him to wear his old ones and he was sorry now that he hadn't; it was a dirty job.

At noon, sitting with his back propped against the wall of the house, he ate his sandwiches and drank the warm Pepsi-Cola. Then he washed his face with the hose and dried it with his bandana.

A pile of weeds burned slowly in the yard. There was no open flame but the pile was diminishing, eaten away at the core, and the smoke rose thin and straight into the windless sky.

When Hazel came home after doing the weekend shopping she noticed with satisfaction that the eugenia hedge had been clipped, the yard raked, and the orange tree pruned, but Escobar was nowhere in sight.

She opened the screen door and went inside.

"Ruth," she called. "Hey, Ruth! Where's the Mexican gone?"

A gentle moan slid through the house. It seemed to come from nowhere and to mean nothing, except that somewhere, in any of the six rooms, something was still half-alive.

"Ruth, where are you?"

A second sound, louder and more definite than the first. Hazel tracked it down to the locked door of the bathroom.

"Anything the matter, Ruth?"

"No."

"Are you crying?"

"No."

"What on earth are you crying about?"

"No, no—"

On the other side of the locked door, Ruth leaned her head against the medicine chest over the wash basin. The tap was turned on, and the tears slid down her cheeks and dripped off her chin to mingle with the tap water.

Ruth opened her eyes. She saw Hazel's toothbrush and her own, blurred and magnified by tears, and the blotches of tooth powder on the mirror, and the smudge of fingers around the catch of the medicine chest. I really must wipe things off, I must wipe—

"Ruth, are you all right?"

"Yes."

"I thought—"

"I'm all right."

And she was. She was not crying. From some inner reservoir filled to capacity the overflow dribbled out. She did not weep passionately and convulsively as Josephine had been doing lately. Ruth's tears were without cause, without meaning.

I am not crying. It's my eyes, they get so dry sometimes. They feel so small and shriveled, they need moisture. This is desert country, Harold, and don't you forget it. The sun pours down, day after day. My eyes get dry and dusty.

"I bought a couple of pounds of ground round," Hazel said. "We can have meatloaf. Then if there's any left over we can make some sandwiches tonight in case Mr. Cooke drops in."

"All right."

Meatloaf. The oven would be on. The hot dry air would seep out of its cracks and the hot dry air would pour in the windows from outside. Her eyeballs would feel crisp and hard, like little dried peas.

"I'll be out in a minute," Ruth said. "I'm bathing my eyes, they felt gritty."

Everything in the house was gritty, though she dusted every day. There was a school playground across the street, and the faintest breeze swept up the dust and wafted it into the neighboring houses. The children didn't seem to mind the dust. Ruth watched them often from the windows of the living room. Some of the younger ones flung themselves boisterously into the dirt as if it were clean white snow. They sat in it, they threw it at each other, they scooped it up in their hands, they ate it mixed with ice cream, bubble gum, lollipops and peanut butter sandwiches.

It was August now and the children were not in classes, but they arrived at the playground early in the morning to play. The school, built to resist earthquakes, was a one-story L-shaped structure with all the classrooms opening on to an outside corridor. This corridor was asphalt, ideal for roller skating, and the long summer days echoed with the steady whirr of roller skates punctuated by sharp rhythmic clacking as the wheels slid over the cracks in the pavement. The playground was to Ruth, at first, an interminable chaos of noise which tore at her ears in a merciless, meaningless way. But she had gradually learned to distinguish the sounds and finally to identify them and speculate about them. The teeter-totter squeaked and banged, and Ruth could tell, from listening to the rhythm of the bang-squeak-bang, whether the children on the teeter-totter were the same size or not. If the rhythm was uneven Ruth wondered whether she should go over to the playground and tell the heavier child to sit further toward the center of the teeter-totter, but she never went.

The teeter banged, the swings creaked, the basketballs plopped, wide of the net, the flying rings gave off a brassy clang, and the children communicated naturally with each other by shouts and screams. A hundred times a day the derisive chant of I'm-the-king-of-the-castle filled the air. The tune was always the same, no matter how the words varied: Can't catch a flea . . . Billy's got a girlfriend . . . Brown Brown went to town, with his britches upside down . . . Red red wet the bed wipe it up with gingerbread . . . Lewis is a stinker . . . Helen is a tattletale . . . Rita is a garlic face . . .

Every time the chant rose, Ruth's heart cringed and she thought, cruel, children are cruel, I must not let it bother me. I must ignore everything.

Miss Kane is a Cross Teacher—written in chalk on the sidewalk.

Miss Kan madam My son Manuel on his raport says poor reeder Home Manuel reeds good or else—

Dear teacher please excuse Annie from being absent as she had to go to the circus. And oblige, Mrs. Mendel.

Dear Miss Kane: I must say I was extremely surprised when Lillian Mae told me she was not chosen for the Christmas Pageant. Lillian Mae has been taking private dancing lessons for a whole year and her teacher says she is as graceful as a bird. I certainly am mystified as to why Lillian Mae was not chosen for the Pageant. Yours truly, Katherine C. Robinson, (Mrs. John H. Robinson, Jr.).

Miss Kane Chews Nails.

Dear Miss Kane: Would you drop into my office tomorrow at four, as there are several matters, pertaining to your grade, which must be discussed.

I think you need a rest, Miss Kane.

Miss Kane splashed water into her eyes and the grit from the playground and the dust raised by the cruel children plunged down the drain.

She emerged from the bathroom, red-eyed and composed.

Hazel was sitting on the edge of her bed. She had her shoes off and she was rubbing her instep where the pump had cut into the skin. The dog, Wendy, had picked up one of the discarded pumps and retired under the bed to chew at the heel. With perseverance and lack of human interference, she could, within an hour, demolish the heel entirely, grinding the lift off with her molars and then peeling the leather away bit by bit with her tiny sharp front teeth.

"She's got your shoe," Ruth said.

"Take it away from her, will you?"

Ruth got down on her knees and pulled up the bedspread. "You bad dog. Bring it here."

"You were so crying," Hazel said.

"Don't be silly. Bring it here, Wendy."

"You never admit anything. Maybe if you did, well, people might be able to help you."

Ruth raised her brows exaggeratedly, repudiating the idea that she was in a position where people could help her. The dog squeezed out from under the bed, wagging her tail to indicate that the whole thing had been an accident. She pressed against Ruth's apron, burrowing her nose in the pocket.

Ruth laughed. "There, she didn't mean it. Look, Hazel, she's apologizing, did you ever see the like? There, there, her mother knows she didn't mean it."

"The hell she didn't," Hazel said.

"Anyway, I don't believe in burdening other people with my troubles, even if I had any."

She rose to her feet, and the dog quietly and with great caution returned to the shoe under the bed.

"I am tired," Ruth said, "and hot. That's all. My goodness, when I see those children over there playing so hard all day and getting so dirty . . . It's a wonder their mothers don't look after them." She went to the front window of the bedroom. Four o'clock, the peak of the day, when the children were dirtiest and noisiest. Their shouts were shriller and their movements had a frenzied quality, as if they knew their hours of play were numbered and they must crowd everything they could into every minute that was left.

"Some people should never have children."

"Tell it to God," Hazel said, rubbing her foot, "not to me."

"I had one little girl in my class . . . It was almost funny how dirty she was, and without realizing it. I often had to wash her ears, they were so dirty you'd wonder how she could hear out of them. She had beautiful hair, that red-gold color, and naturally wavy. I bought her a little comb to keep in her desk, and whenever she washed her own ears and face I gave her a penny."

My goodness, how nice you look this morning, Margaret. Here's your penny.

Thank you, Miss Kane.

Margaret never used the comb or the pennies. She hoarded them in a corner of her desk. On Valentine's Day Miss Kane received a paper penny valentine, "To a Cross Patch Teacher," bearing the picture of an old witch in spectacles riding a yard ruler. When Miss Kane took the valentine out of the valentine box, the other children watched in silence while Margaret sat at her desk, snickering behind her hand.

Thank you for the valentine, Margaret.

I didn't send you no valentine, Miss Kane.

Any valentine.

I didn't send you any valentine.

I was under the impression, Margaret, that you did.

I wouldn't have no money to buy one.

Any money.

I wouldn't have any money to buy one.

"I bought her a little comb," Ruth repeated. "She was an odd child, I could never get close to her."

"You took your job too seriously."

"I hoped, I wanted to give her some pride in herself. It was impossible, I see now. The home factor is so much stronger than the school factor. I couldn't make up for poverty and neglect and brutality. Years and years—"

The years were numbered, like the hours of the children's play, and into the last one she had crammed frenzied activity. The last year brought the angel-eyed Mexican boy, Manuel, who never talked.

Thank you, Lucy. And now it's Manuel's turn to read. Begin at the top of page 79, Manuel.

Manuel sat mute, unmoving.

Manuel, it's your turn. Now see if you know what the first word is. It's a hard one.

Manuel looked weary and innocent while the children giggled, and whispers fluttered in the air like invisible moths.

Is there anybody who can help Manuel with the first word? Janie? That's right—gradually. There now, Manuel, you have the first word, gradually, can you go on from there?

The book lay unopened on Manuel's desk.

Home Manuel reeds good or else—

Manuel didn't play with the other children. As soon as the recess bell rang he dashed across the school yard and swung himself up to the top bars of the jungle gym. There he sat all during recess, with his legs twined around the bars and a faint smile on his face, as if he enjoyed the sensation of being high up, above the other children.

Once he had, without being seen, shinnied up the trunk of the old pepper tree beside the swings, and hidden himself in the feathery leaves. When the time came to return to class Manuel remained in the tree, plucking the pepper berries one by one and letting them slide out of his hand to the ground. He counted them in a whisper—"thirty-six, thirty-seven, thirty-eight"—and as they bounced and rolled in the dirt like tiny marbles, Manuel followed each one with his eyes, dreamily. He was Dick Tracy and the berries were drops of his life's blood. He was Superman and the berries were atom bombs. He was Manuel and Miss Kane was calling him. He heard her calling him and he watched her looking for him, but he made no move to get out of the tree. He would have liked to stay there forever shedding his blood and dropping his bombs, high up above the other children.

Miss Kane knew that Manuel liked to climb, and so she looked first on the roof of the Boy Scout shack, and then on the roof of the kindergarten sandpile. Re-crossing the yard she saw the falling berries, and looking up into the pepper tree she saw Manuel. His eyes were closed, and he seemed to be asleep, entwined gracefully among the boughs. In sleep his right hand dropped the berries, one by one, and the delicate leaves slid over his wrist like lace. He looked so beautiful, so innocent, that she couldn't say the ordinary words: *You know the rules about climbing that tree, Manuel . . . The bell rang some time ago . . . The principal wouldn't like . . . The bell rang . . .*

"It's time to come to class," she said quietly.

Manuel slid down the trunk of the tree and followed her across the yard.

She never again asked him to read, but one afternoon she kept him in and tried to talk to him and to make him talk to her. She tried too hard and Manuel was puzzled and a little contemptuous. When he was gone Miss Kane put her head down on her desk and cried because she had failed. All her failures came back to her and gathered like cysts inside her head and her breasts and her throat. Her tears did not dissolve these cysts, but they altered their substance. The benign *I have failed* became the malignant *They have failed me*, and the Mexican boy, Manuel, became the crux and the symbol of this change.

When the janitor came in to sweep the room and collect the waste baskets he found Miss Kane sitting behind her desk, swollen-eyed, reckless.

"As you can see, I've been crying, Mr. Thursten. No, don't go away. It doesn't matter. We all have our moments." As she talked she scratched one spot on her head, near her left temple, over and over again. "I do my best. Everyone knows that. I've always done my best, without any help from anyone least of all from the ones I'm trying to help. There's this one boy, Mr. Thursten. It was funny, he climbed the pepper tree, and you know he looked so odd up there, as if he belonged. I didn't want to bring him down. Perhaps I ought to have left him. It's difficult, difficult to make decisions all the time. Some of the African tribes live in tree houses to protect themselves from the wild animals."

She saw Manuel in his tree house, surrounded by the yapping snarling faces of the little human animals. Manuel, I will help you. Manuel spat into the dirt.

Mr. Thursten shuffled up and down the aisles, pushing his brush ahead of him, gathering up the litter of the day. He knew Miss Kane was speaking but he didn't hear her words. He was immune to noise and engrossed in his passion for cleaning up. All his aggressive and destructive instincts had been channelized into this one great passion. He loved to collect little piles of rubbish and thrust them savagely into the incinerator. At home he burned his mail as soon as he had read it. He was a bachelor, and did his own housework, and when he cooked his own meals he always washed and dried the dishes from one course before he began eating another course. After the meal he emptied the garbage on a newspaper, squeezing and compressing it into a small neat satisfying bundle. Nearly every day he hung all his blankets and his rugs on the clothesline and beat them into submission. He cleaned the mirrors and windows until they squeaked in protest, and he scrubbed his kitchen with chlorine water until the linoleum peeled and his hands were raw. Mr. Thursten was fortunate. His peculiarities accorded with his job and were misinterpreted as virtues.

"Mr. Thursten—"

The brush paused.

"Mr. Thursten, I wonder if—I feel quite giddy—is there, could you fetch me a glass of water?"

Mr. Thursten brought her some water in a paper cup. When she had finished the water, he took the cup and folded it over and over into a tight, tiny rectangle. Mr. Thursten took particular care of this rectangle. He put it into the incinerator separately, and as it snuffled and expired he had a nice loose feeling inside.

Mr. Thursten, Margaret, Manuel, they had all been a part of the last year. When the year ended Miss Kane ceased to exist. She became Ruth again, and it was Ruth who stood at the bedroom window looking out at the playground of another school, watching the anonymous children whose faces seemed so familiar.

"You took your job too seriously," Hazel repeated.

Ruth turned from the window, wiping the palms of her hands on her apron. "I guess I'll start the meatloaf."

"You never admit anything. If you won't tell people things they can't help you."

"My goodness, as if I—"

"Why were you in there bawling?"

"I tell you I wasn't, Hazel."

"Has it anything to do with the Mexican?"

"What—?" Ruth stopped, on the point of asking, what Mexican? She had been thinking of Manuel, but she realized at once that Hazel didn't know about the boy in the pepper tree and that she must mean Mr. Escobar. "I don't even know what you're talking about."

"I just wondered," Hazel said carefully. "I just thought maybe he'd been rude to you or something. I mean, sometimes you get ideas in your head about certain people, you imagine things."

"Oh?"

"Well, you do. And I just thought—oh well, skip it. Where'd he go?"

"He said he had to go home and get something; a sprayer. He says the eugenia hedge has some disease called scale."

"It doesn't look diseased to me."

"He showed it to me himself. You know that part at the end where you thought the hedge was just dirty? It isn't dirt at all. The sap has been sucked out. He showed me some of the things that do it. They're like little bumps on the wood, hardly noticeable. He scraped some of them away with his thumbnail to show me. I told him, I said, why show *me? I'm* not the lady of the house, I just work here. And do you know what his answer was? He said he thought I'd be interested. Me, *interested*." Ruth laughed, and color splashed across her cheeks. "I said—"

"Little bumps," Hazel said bitterly. "Jesus Murphy, I thought we had everything, gophers, snails, sowbugs, ants, and now we got little bumps besides."

"They can be sprayed."

"I don't know what's the matter with this damn place."

"Neglect is the matter."

"Or maybe it isn't the place, maybe it's just me. I attract things, that's all there is to it. I'm like Millie, I've got a jinx."

Ruth looked blank. She didn't know Millie or the nature of her jinx. "He said if the hedge is sprayed now the other things in the yard won't catch the disease. He says it's very catching."

Like measles, Escobar had said, scraping the little bumps away with this thumbnail while Ruth watched him with fastidious distaste. She did not want to be out in the garden with a Mexican laborer, and she experienced a sense of shock and unreality at finding herself there, and even more strongly, the feeling that a cruel fate had driven her there. I did not come, I was driven.

Persecuted by fate, she stood beside the eugenia hedge and watched Escobar's thumb. It was thick and blunt, the nail heavy with dirt and every crack in the skin outlined as if in charcoal. The thumb moved, bent on destruction, but without hurry, without savagery.

Like measles, Escobar said.

She jerked her eyes away, she laughed nervously, without mirth, she put her hand in the pocket of her apron and shifted her weight to her other foot. She coughed to clear her throat, and when her throat was cleared she had nothing to say. The rays of the sun pelted her face and she thought of the dark house with the blinds drawn and she could not believe that she had left it to come out here. I was driven.

Still she couldn't force herself to return to the house, and in the end it was Escobar who left. He said, "I have a hand spray at home. I will go and get it. It is not far."

She moved with quick jerky steps toward the back door, her head ducked as if to avoid a blow.

Escobar wheeled his bicycle out of the garage. A bicycle was a delicate and expensive vehicle, and Escobar lavished great care on his. It was over four years old now, but there wasn't a single dent in the mudguard or a nick in the red and green paint. Throughout the years he had equipped it with several pounds of gadgets. It had two headlights, one reflector (plain) and a larger one bearing the words "Watch My Speed!" On the handlebars there was a bell, a horn, a speedometer, a basket and a rabbit's foot, and from the end of the carrier at the back dangled a skunk's tail. The original seat was softened with a lamb's wool cover, and between the seat and the cover a St. Christopher's medal was hidden.

Escobar adjusted the pedals and swung his right leg over the bar. He rode away, moving his feet up and down in a proud, ponderous, dignified manner. The reflectors winked behind his back, "Watch My Speed!"

From the kitchen window Ruth had seen him pedaling down the street like a grave and happy child.

"It's a jinx," Hazel said. "We're a pair, Millie and me. Where's my other shoe?"

"I thought you had it."

"I haven't."

"I thought you took it away from her."

The shoe was located under the bed with the lift flapping loose from the heel, but the dog Wendy had disappeared.

"Jesus *Murphy*!"

"She didn't mean it," Ruth said anxiously. "It can be fixed. Look, it's easy as pie to fix." She held the lift in place. "All it needs is a nail or two. I'll pay for it, naturally. I'm going over to the Fosters' tonight to sit with the children, and I'll have the money."

"Oh nuts, forget it."

"Very well."

From outside came a rhythmic hissing sound. A pulse began to beat in Ruth's temple and the spot of color reappeared at the base of her throat.

"The Mexican's back," she said.

She went out into the kitchen and stood at the screen door.

Escobar was spraying the orange tree. She could see his face, among the leaves. It was beautiful and innocent, like Manuel's face looking down at her through the green feathers of the pepper tree.

Some of the African tribes live in tree houses to protect themselves from the wild animals.

I think you need a rest, Miss Kane.

8

MRS. FREEMAN HEARD the click of the front door. She laid aside her pen and waited, with a pleasant feeling of alarm and anticipation. Doors were, in her opinion, one of the most interesting inventions of man. A closed door held a secret, on the other side there could be practically anyone: Robert returning from his travels, one of the girls coming in after an early movie, a stranger looking for another stranger, an old friend or a pen pal arriving unexpectedly. It could be a lunatic, an escaped convict, a man with a gun. Mrs. Freeman had had considerable mental practice handling these eventualities. To the convict, the lunatic, and the man with the gun, she would be very amiable; she would disarm them by kindness (food, conversation, hot coffee, and if worst came to worst, the bottle of rum she'd saved from last Christmas). Having allayed their suspicions, she would then maneuver them into the kitchen, lock the door very fast, run over to Mr. Hitchcock's place next-door and phone the police. Sometimes, when she was alone in the house as she was now, she thought of possible hitches in these plans. The man with the gun might shoot her before she had a chance to be amiable to him, the lunatic might be beyond understanding and the convict, with the police on his trail, might be in too much of a hurry to dally over food and drink. There was also the fact that Mr. Hitchcock's telephone had recently been disconnected.

Mrs. Freeman was, on the whole, rather glad to see Ruby.

"You gave me a start," she said, drawing a deep breath. "I confess, I've never gotten used to staying alone in the house. You never can tell. Look at all those sex murders down in L.A. Even a town like this, I bet you'd be surprised at the things that are going on. My advice to young girls, and I see a lot of them, running a place like this, my advice is to stay out of bars. Bars are the breeding place of crime, also they don't wash the glasses properly, I've heard, just rinse them in cold water. By the way, that Mr. Anderson phoned for you. Wait a minute, he left a number for you to call. Here it is, 23664."

Without answering, Ruby started up the stairs.

"Aren't you going to call him?"

"No—no, I'm too tired."

"Maybe it's about the job he promised you."

"I don't care."

"Well, for heaven's sake," Mrs. Freeman said. "You ought to care. Jobs don't grow on trees. What's the matter with you?"

"I don't know." She paused, leaning against the banister. "I don't want to talk to him. He makes me feel crawly."

"Crawly, for goodness sake. I thought he was such a nice man, clean-cut looking. Crawly. The way you girls talk, I don't understand you."

Ruby merely stared at her woodenly.

Mrs. Freeman said, offended, "It's none of my business, but I can't help taking an interest and when I see a nice-looking man obviously all gone on a girl—and what with the war and so many young men being killed, girls can't afford to be too choosy."

"I'm not looking for a young man."

"Even so, you should be sensible. You can't have too many irons in the fire." Mrs. Freeman shook her head in sincere bewilderment. "Here is this man, putting himself out to get you a job and you won't even call him, no, he makes you feel crawly, you put on an emotional display."

Some of the bitter resentment Ruby felt against Gordon spilled over on Mrs. Freeman and George. "I know it's none of your business, but I don't like him and I don't like the way he looks at me. Also he's too fat and his face is too pink and shaved-looking. And I don't like the way he talks to me as if I was a worm."

"Even so," Mrs. Freeman said helplessly. "Even so."

She had no daughters of her own and so she had developed a proprietary interest in the young unmarried women who came to her house. Her chief concern was to get them married. In spite of her own experience, she still believed that marriage had curative qualities and that a bad husband was better than no husband at all. She was worried by the fact that most of the girls she knew were like Ruby. They had left their homes in search of romance, and overweight pink-faced men didn't belong in their dreams.

Mrs. Freeman read the Vital Statistics in the paper every night and she was shocked by the number of divorces in the town. She blamed it partly on the town itself. People who saw it for the first time believed that they had reached the end of the rainbow, here between the violet mountains and the jeweled sea. And it *was* the end of the rainbow, Mrs. Freeman knew that; but she knew, too, how difficult it was to live there. The romantic postcard perfection of nature contrasted too sharply with the ordinary human existence. The stretches of beach, the parks, the bridle paths, the mountain trails—they were there, free for everybody, except the girls like Ruby who worked all week and washed and ironed their clothes on Sunday. Living beside a subway in Flatbush or in a small flat town in Kansas, they could have held on to their dreams of traveling some day to a tropical Eden. Now that they had reached Eden they were all the more discontented to find themselves leading the same old lives. The end of the rainbow was no longer around the corner; it was six miles north to the mountains and nineteen blocks south to the sea. Yet these blocks were more difficult to travel than three thousand miles across the country.

"I don't know," Mrs. Freeman said, still with her air of helplessness. "Maybe it's true about every place, but here it's very true, people expect too much."

"I expect nothing," Ruby said.

"I remember once when I first came here years ago. It was in the spring and I was standing out in the yard at night. The acacia tree was in bloom and the moon was so bright that the shadows were as sharp as sun shadows and I could see the little yellow acacia blossoms like chenille. I picked a sprig and held it against my face, so soft, like a baby's fingers. The sky was full of stars, and the air wasn't just air, it was rich and thick and cold, I can't describe it. There was a bird at the top of the tree making a funny little noise, a mockingbird perhaps. I had such an odd feeling, standing there, as if anything might happen in the midst of all this beauty, something wonderful. I saw Robert's shadow against the kitchen blind, this very kitchen, and he looked as handsome as a god. Oh, the *feeling* I had."

She paused, twisting the wedding ring round and round her finger.

"Well?" Ruby said.

"Well, then Robert flung open the kitchen window, and told me to come in, he was hungry and wanted a grilled-cheese sandwich." She added, very earnestly, "I'm glad he did. It was a good lesson for me. Acacia doesn't last long after it's picked. I put it in water but the blossoms got smaller and smaller and finally they fell off."

The doorbell pealed. Smoothing down her dress and adjusting her face into an expression of amiability, just in case, Mrs. Freeman answered the door.

She was agreeably surprised to see George, who was not too pink-faced or fat, merely a sturdy, healthy-looking man.

"She just came in," Mrs. Freeman said. "Ruby, here's Mr. Anderson."

Ruby came down the stairs slowly.

"I left my number for you to call," George said.

"I just got home."

"I thought you might like to go for a drive or something."

"It's a nice evening," Mrs. Freeman said. "And too late in the year for acacia."

She returned to her letters.

"What'd she mean by that?" George said.

"I don't know."

"You look tired, Ruby."

"You're always telling me that."

"Am I? I'm sorry. I can't help paying attention to how you look. It's getting to be a habit, I guess. Will you be warm enough in that suit?"

"It's getting late—"

"You can't turn me down all the time. Anyway, it's Saturday night, and everybody celebrates on Saturday night."

"What do they celebrate?" Ruby said dully.

"Anything." He held the screen door open and she went out on the porch. "Are you going to be warm enough? Maybe you'd better get a coat."

"No, I'll be all right."

He put his hand on her elbow, and guided her down the porch steps and across the clay path that substituted for a sidewalk. She didn't shrink away from him as she usually did. She felt too remote to bother about it, as if she had had a great deal to drink and while she was still conscious of what was happening to her she had no interest in it.

George started the car. "Is there any special place you'd like to go?"

"No."

"We'll just drive around then,"

"Where's Garcia Road?"

"What number?"

"Twenty-three hundred."

"That'd be up in the hills. Why?"

"Nothing. I just overheard a—a customer say he lived there, that's all. I wondered what it was like."

"We'll go and find out," George said cheerfully. "Got to check up on our customers, see that they come from the right kind of houses."

"No—no, I'd just as soon not. I'd just as soon drive along the beach."

"All right." He sent her a quick, puzzled glance. Her evasions irritated him. She had no reason to treat him as if he were a district attorney and she was accused of a crime. Yet this was actually how he felt about her. He wanted to put her on a spot and question her about herself, find out a few things about her. Her face rarely revealed anything but a kind of resigned unhappiness, and it was this expression of hers that agitated him. If she had cause for her unhappiness—money troubles? sickness in the family? loneliness?—he wanted her to break down and tell him, to bawl on his shoulder the way Hazel used to do.

They drove along toward the Mesa and George thought about Hazel and the night she had said out of a blue sky, "Jesus, I feel just like bawling the house down." And bawl the house down she did, for a solid hour, until the police drove up to the front of the house, summoned by a neighbor to stop George from beating his wife. Hazel was delighted and she brought out two quarts of beer to celebrate the unexpected company. Neither of the two policemen could drink anything, since they were on duty, but Hazel invited them to come back during their off hours. They came back every now and then, bringing a friend or two, until eventually Hazel knew the whole police department.

"It must be lonely for you," George said, "not knowing anyone in town."

"I get along," Ruby said. "I—read a lot. And write letters home."

"How are your mother and father?"

"Fine."

"Don't you miss the big city?"

"Sometimes."

"And your friends?"

"I'm not much for parties or things like that."

"Maybe you should get out more, have a little fun and excitement."

"I'd just be bored."

"You should try it anyway."

"I used to go to parties at school. I never had a good time. I was scared to death of the boys. I couldn't even open my mouth."

"You still are," George said. "Scared, I mean."

"No, I'm not."

"Of me, anyway."

"No."

"Then I wish you were. I'd like to think I rang some kind of a bell with you somehow." He kept his attention for a minute on the narrow winding road that crept up the Mesa. Then he said, "I need a drink. How about you?"

"If you want one, all right."

"You certainly are an enthusiastic gal tonight. Is there anything worrying you?"

"No."

"And you wouldn't tell me anyway, I get it." He made a right turn at the next crossing. "Here's your Garcia Road."

"I didn't want to— Say, what's the big idea anyway?"

"I didn't believe that about 'one of the customers.'"

"I don't care what you believe, Mr. Anderson."

"Here's your twenty-three hundred." George put the car in low and they went very slowly past a white frame ranch house. "Satisfied?"

She didn't even look at the house. "Yes, thank you."

"Who lives there?"

"I don't know."

"I can easily look it up in the City Directory."

"Why bother?"

"Because it worries me. I think you told me a lie. Who lives there?"

"One of the customers, I don't know his name. And you can let me out of this car right now. I'll walk home. I never wanted to come anyway. You're always accusing me of things."

Instead of stopping the car he raced the engine and they shot ahead, up the hill.

"Why should I lie?" Ruby said. "If it was anyone I knew lived in that house why should I have mentioned it?"

"Maybe you thought I was too dumb to catch on, eh?"

"You can't catch on when there's nothing to catch on to, no matter how smart you are."

"I didn't say I was smart. I only want to be sure. I suppose I'm jealous of you, but if I tell you that you'll only say I have no right to be jealous of you. Which is perfectly true."

"Well, it is."

"I said it first," George said flatly. "Where do you want to go for a drink?"

"Anywhere."

"You know what? I'd like to see you drunk sometime, Ruby. I bet you can be pretty vicious."

"*You'll* never find out," she said with a sharp laugh.

"I wouldn't want to. I like you better the way you are, so full of secrets you're bursting at the seams."

"You certainly have some funny ideas about me, Mr. Anderson. I can't understand why you want to take me out all the time, when all you do is quarrel with me. Maybe you're just a bully."

"I'd hate to think that."

"And whenever we're out together all you want to talk about is me and what's the matter with me and what a funny girl I am. I don't talk about you like that."

"That's because you're not interested."

"Why can't we ever talk about something else for a change? I'm—I'm so *sick* of myself I never even want to hear my own name again." She covered her face with her hands, and with her closed eyes she saw Gordon looking at her with such quiet loathing that she wanted to tear at her own face for inspiring such a look. "I'm so sick of myself I could die. I hate—"

"Be quiet," George said harshly. "That's a hell of a way to talk."

"I hate my own face, I hate it so much I'd like to slash it with a razor, I'd like to slash everything, everything I see!"

He pulled the car over to the curb and turned off the ignition. He said, with pain in his voice, "That's kid stuff, Ruby, stop it."

"A lot you know about it!"

"I do. You're just depressed. You'll snap out of it."

She shook her head over and over again, refusing to be comforted. Powerless, he listened to her flow of words: it was a bad world, with bad people in it, she was as bad as the rest, worse, hateful.

Finally he started the car again. He didn't know what to do about Ruby. He couldn't force himself to try and stop her hysteria with a slap, and he couldn't take her back to Mrs. Freeman's until she calmed down.

He thought suddenly of Hazel. Her house was less than half a mile away; he could stop there and leave Ruby in the car while he got some whisky from Hazel. Hazel wouldn't mind, as long as she didn't know it was for Ruby.

"I'll stop off and get you something to drink," George said. "It will make you feel better."

"A drink—*you* think a drink will cure anything, anything in the world—"

"It helps, sometimes."

"It can't help me, nothing can."

"Let's try it."

"You don't know, you don't *know*—"

"I don't want to know. Just take it easy."

She kept silent until he parked the car in front of Hazel's white stucco house. Then she said, in a low voice, "You're being very kind to me. It's no use, though."

"Why not?"

"I don't know, it's just no use."

"We'll see."

He got out and walked around the lane to the back of the house. Parked beside the fence there was a car he didn't recognize, a black Cadillac with a monogram on the driver's door which was too elaborate to be deciphered at one glance.

George passed the car and went through the gate toward the back door. The moon had come up and it hung like a fruit among the top branches of the oak tree behind the garage. From the garage itself there came the scurrying and bustling noises of the wood rats as they raced along the ceiling and up and down the walls. Sometimes when George used to get his car out of the garage in the mornings he found their tiny paw marks in the dust on the engine hood. Aside from the paw marks and the dust they shook down from the ceiling, the wood rats did no harm. Their noise disturbed Hazel, though, and she used to go out now and then and bang on the garage roof with a broom. The wood rats froze in their tracks while Hazel banged away, breaking one or two of the tiles in her fury; but as soon as she returned to the house they started again, louder than ever, until the garage seemed to be cracking open. George had never been able to trap a wood rat, in fact he had never even seen one. The evidence that they existed at all was purely circumstantial, the noise and the paw marks on the roof tiles or on the engine hood of the car, like the tracks of the invisible man.

The sounds from the garage suddenly ceased, as though the rats had sensed the presence of an intruder. They seemed to be watching from under the tiles, listening, waiting for the stranger to leave the yard. George was struck by a feeling of loss and resentment. He thought, by God, I used to *live* here, this was *my* yard. I planted those two orange trees myself, with my own hands. And the hedge too . . . the hedge has been clipped, it looks too neat, like Willie's mustache . . . I ought to get back to work, what in hell am I doing here anyway?

The hedge had grown, as thick as a wall and as high as Ruby. He looked at it as he crossed the yard, feeling almost betrayed, as if he'd half-expected it to stop growing during his absence.

He went up the steps of the back porch and rapped, hesitantly, on the screen door.

Harold and Josephine were at the kitchen table, making sandwiches. Harold was buttering bread and Josephine was slicing some meatloaf. Whenever a crumb of meat fell on the table Josephine picked it up and popped it in her mouth in a natural, unself-conscious way. They were both sunburned from their afternoon in the sailboat, and a row of freckles had sprung up out of nowhere along the bridge of Josephine's nose.

George rapped again and said, "Hey."

"Well, for crying out loud." Harold put down the butter knife and wiped his hands on the apron of Ruth's that he was wearing. "Come on in. Josephine, look who's here."

"I see him," Josephine said placidly. "Hello, George. What brings you to these parts?"

"I just dropped in to see Hazel for a minute."

"She's got company."

"Yeah, I saw the car."

Harold whistled. "Some car, eh? They say a Caddy like that will do over a hundred miles an—"

"How fast a car goes doesn't matter," Josephine said, giving her husband a glance of disapproval. "If its owner happens to be married. Which he is."

"Sure, honey. Sure—"

"Mr. Cooke's interest in Hazel is purely businesslike, and vice versa. After all, she used to work for Mr. Cooke and there's nothing more to it than that."

Although both Harold and George were inclined to doubt this statement, neither of them cared to argue with Josephine. She had reached the stage where every remark, every incident, had a personal application for her. Harold knew this, and George sensed it.

The two men exchanged glances, then Harold said, hurriedly, "Say George, I didn't get a chance to thank you for the boat this afternoon."

"That's all right."

"We had a wonderful time. Josephine wasn't scared a bit. Were you, Josephine?"

"I was so, at first," Josephine said. "I would have been scared to death without Harold. Harold kept asking me if I was getting seasick, and finally *he* was the one got seasick!"

Harold looked very proud, as if he had deliberately shouldered the burden of seasickness to spare Josephine. "Josie makes a swell sailor. You'd think, with the baby and everything, she'd feel queasy."

"Well, I didn't, not one bit. And don't think those waves weren't high, George. They came at us, whoosh, didn't they, Harold?"

She and Harold exchanged contented smiles. Together they had braved a new element, the sea. They had fought and won, and now after their shared victory they were relaxed, united.

"You're both looking fine," George said.

"I'm certainly not losing any weight, am I?" Josephine laughed. "The doctor thinks maybe I'll have twins."

"Holy cats."

"That's what I told Harold, holy cats. But Harold says it'd be sort of a bargain to get two for the price of one. Considering how much everything costs nowadays, it'd be nice to get a bargain for a change . . . How about a sandwich, George?"

"No thanks."

"Well, the least you can do is sit down and make yourself at home."

"I can't. I'm in kind of a hurry." George shifted his weight from one foot to another, already regretting his decision to bring Ruby here. Everything was so normal—the warm little kitchen, the pungent smell of the meatloaf, Harold with his pride and Josephine with her unborn child—that by contrast Ruby seemed eccentric, even depraved. "I've got someone waiting for me in the car."

"Aha."

"I'd like to speak to Hazel a minute, though."

"Sure thing," Harold said. "I'll get her."

When Harold had gone, Josephine said, casually, "Is it anyone we know?"

"No."

"I just thought if it was, bring her in."

"Thanks just the same."

"If you ask me, George, you're acting sort of jumpy."

"Not as jumpy as I feel."

"What's the trouble?"

"Call it business."

"I didn't mean to be nosy," Josephine said rather stiffly. "It just surprises me when a man of your iron constitution starts acting jumpy."

"I left my iron constitution behind years ago."

"I wish you wouldn't say things like that. It makes me nervous. After all, I'm not terribly much younger than you are, and here I am, going to have twins." She turned to him, her eyes suddenly anxious, seeking reassurance. "Maybe I waited too long and my bones are too set or something?"

"Baloney," George said cheerfully. "Listen, any time you're in doubt about your health take a look in the mirror. Go on, do it now."

"No."

"Go on. Look at yourself."

Awkwardly, Josephine rose from her chair and approached the small oblong mirror hanging between the two windows over the sink. Her eyes were clear and glowing, her dark hair glossy, her cheeks pink from the sun.

"I *do* look healthy, don't I, George?"

"Wonderful."

"There can't be anything wrong if I look so healthy."

Harold came back with Hazel, who was wearing her pearl choker and her black crepe dress, an outfit she reserved for sober and important functions. She looked warm and strained, and when she walked she took mincing little steps because her feet hurt; flesh bulged from her new patent-leather pumps like rising dough.

"I tried to get you on the phone," she said to George. "Willie told me you weren't there. You just up and blew, didn't say a word to anybody, just blew. That's no way to run a business, George."

"I'll make a note of that. Thanks loads."

"Whenever you're in the wrong you always sound like that."

"Like what?"

"You know like what. Whenever you make a mistake you get sore. Isn't that right, Harold?"

"You leave Harold out of it," Josephine said sharply. "Harold and me, we mind our own business. Live and let live."

"All right, all right, skip it." Hazel dabbed at her moist forehead with the back of her hand. "My God, it's hot. Come on out and I'll show you the yard."

"I saw it," George said. "It looks fine."

"Cost me eleven bucks. I need some air." She opened the screen door and went outside on the porch. George followed her, feeling a little hurt that she wasn't in a friendlier mood. "The place looks pretty good, eh?"

"Just great."

"You don't sound very enthusiastic. Maybe you don't realize how a nice yard increases the value of a home."

"Sure, sure I do," George said. "It increases it plenty."

"You can't tell. After all, some day I might want to sell the place, I might get married."

"I guess you might."

She leaned against the porch railing, easing a little of the weight off her feet. "I suppose Harold and Josephine told you I have company?"

"Yes."

"You remember Arthur Cooke that I used to work for."

"Sure."

"He's very refined."

"Hazel—"

"Doesn't drink or smoke and always dresses in the best of taste."

"I'm sorry to bust in on you like this."

"That's all right. He was just leaving anyway. He's a very busy and important man, he—"

"Look, Haze, I don't mean to change the subject or anything, but I'm in kind of a hurry. I've got someone waiting for me in the car."

Hazel raised her eyebrows. "So?"

"She's not feeling very well, and I thought if you had a little brandy or one of those pills you used to take when you got upset, the ones the doctor gave you—"

"I've got a quart of warm beer and some aspirin," Hazel said curtly. "Who is it, the new girlfriend?"

"Yes."

"Why bring her here?"

"Well, we were passing by and I figured I'd drop in and get her a pill or something to calm her down." He scowled at a point in the darkness where a mockingbird sat trying to stir up his sleepy friends, hi there! hi there! "She's so darned unhappy, Hazel."

"I should give one half of one per cent of a good goddamn whether she's unhappy."

"All right, all right. I'll shove off."

"You can have the beer and the aspirin."

"No thanks. Sorry to have bothered you."

He went down the porch steps, stumbling slightly on the last one where the wood had been undermined by termites and sagged in the middle.

"Well, don't go away mad," Hazel said.

"I'm not mad."

"Not much you aren't."

"I am not mad." He scuffed the coco mat at the bottom of the steps with his shoe. "The thing is I want to do what's right, only I don't know how. She's just a kid, she needs help. I get the feeling that she's on the edge of something, something bad." He kicked at the mat again, more violently this time, as if it were an obstacle that had to be kicked away. But the mat didn't budge. It had been there for a long time and was so heavy with the dirt of years that during the rainy winters weeds sprouted in it and grew two or three inches high.

"I know what she's on the edge of," Hazel said. "And it's not so bad."

George looked at her hopefully, and for a moment Hazel wished that she didn't have to say what she had every intention of saying both for George's own good and for her own personal satisfaction.

"It's not so bad," she repeated. "Hooking you and cutting herself in on your share of the Beachcomber."

"You've got the wrong idea, as far as Ruby's concerned anyway. She's not interested in me." In an unconscious gesture, he put his left hand to his head and smoothed back his hair, as if to reassure himself that he still had hair left, that he wasn't quite so old as some people might think. He remembered what Ruby had said when he'd gone to Mrs. Freeman's to give her the back pay she hadn't stopped to collect: "*You don't look a day over forty—*"

"To her I'm a nothing." He cleared his throat. "A big fat nothing."

"I don't believe it," Hazel said, sounding a little angry, as if Ruby, by repudiating George, was casting an aspersion on Hazel herself. "Maybe she's just playing hard to get."

"You think so, Hazel? Honest?"

"I said, maybe."

"Could you tell if you met her?"

"I don't know. How should I know?"

"I mean, suppose I brought her in and you talked to her, sort of sounded her out a little? . . . Then maybe I could find out if I had a chance, and if I haven't, well, that's that, I'll chalk it down to experience. Would you do it, Hazel, just talk to her?"

"Why should I?"

"No reason, I guess. Except—well, suppose you find out she's not interested, then you wouldn't have to worry so much about me getting married again."

"I am *not* worried about your getting married again," Hazel said, in a very calm, reasonable tone. "It's who you marry that concerns me. It beats me why you can't find some nice sensible widow with a little cash or some real estate."

"You already said that, a hundred times."

"Isn't it true a hundred times?"

"Sure, sure. But—"

"There's always a but." She shifted her weight impatiently. The porch railing squawked a protest, and from his new position on the television antenna next-door the tireless mockingbird answered, oh my, oh my, oh my. "The world would be okay if it wasn't for the buts."

"Haze—"

"All right, all right. I'll talk to her. Bring her in the house."

There was a slight edge to her voice, but George was too pleased to notice it. He had great faith in Hazel's ability to handle people, to make them feel at home and get them talking about themselves. It was exactly what Ruby needed, an older woman to confide in. Perhaps—who could tell?—they might even become friends.

George was an incurable optimist. Like an alcoholic who needs only one drink to set him off, George needed only one happy thought, and the happy thought was that Hazel and Ruby should become real pals, lunching together, shopping together, telephoning each other at all hours. Each passing second made the idea more irresistibly logical: Ruby and Hazel, Damon and Pythias.

Oh my, said the mockingbird. *Oh my, oh my.*

"You'll be crazy about her," George said warmly. "She's shy, kind of hard to know at first, but once you get underneath the surface you'll see how sweet she is."

Hazel made an impatient gesture as if she were swatting at an invisible mosquito. "I saw her, the day she came to Dr. Foster's office."

"That's right, you did. What did you think of her? She's not an ordinary girl at all, is she?"

"I only saw her for a few minutes."

"Couldn't you tell she was different?"

"I told you I only saw her for a few minutes. What could have happened in a few minutes, that we should've become bosom pals or something?"

"Not exactly." But it was too close for comfort, and George was unpleasantly surprised at the easy way Hazel could reach into his mind and pick out one of his dreams and pinch it out of shape like a marshmallow.

He said, "I'll get Ruby," and started across the yard, stepping slowly and carefully because he knew Hazel was watching him and he didn't want to appear too eager.

She called after him, "Hey, George."

He stopped.

"George, hold your stomach in."

"Jes—"

"And stick out your chest more. You might as well show up to the best advantage."

"Jesus Christ," he said, but Hazel didn't hear him. She had gone back into the house and the slam of the screen door was loud and final.

Straightening his shoulders George walked back to his car. Ruby was half-sitting, half-lying, with her head pressed against the back of the seat and her eyes closed.

"Ruby?"

She blinked in a surprised way, as if she had been hundreds of miles away and couldn't understand how George had gotten there.

"How are you feeling?"

"All right, I guess."

"You're looking better."

"Am I?" She yawned, making a funny little squeaking noise like a puppy. George wanted to laugh at the noise, which seemed to him charming, but he didn't dare. He was beginning to realize how deadly serious Ruby was about everything. She seldom laughed herself, and the laughter of others always carried a note of menace.

"We've been invited to come in," George said.

"I heard laughing. Is it a party? I don't like parties, I really don't, I wish you'd take me home."

"There's no party. I just want you to come in and meet Hazel, my ex-wife."

Her entire face seemed to tighten, around the eyes and the nostrils and the mouth, as if it had been splashed by a strong astringent. "I guess this is your idea of a big joke, Mr. Anderson."

"It's not a joke. Hazel asked me to bring you in."

"Why?"

"I told her you were waiting in the car. Hazel likes people. She invites everybody to come in."

"She won't like me."

"Sure she will, and I'll bet a nickel you'll like her too." He spoke with confidence. Nearly everyone liked Hazel. She could always make people feel good about themselves, and George had such implicit faith in her generosity that it didn't even occur to him that possibly she wouldn't care to make Ruby feel good.

"It doesn't seem proper," Ruby said. "Besides, I wouldn't want to inflict myself."

"You won't be. Come on."

He opened the car door and Ruby got out. She brushed off her skirt and the shoulders of her suit, and smoothed down her hair. "Do I look all right?"

"You look fine." He wanted to say, beautiful, but he was afraid that the word would only increase her self-consciousness and that she wouldn't believe him anyway. "Let's go around to the back. Hazel's in the kitchen."

"Is it your house?"

"Not anymore. We had a property settlement and Hazel got the house."

"It's funny you're still friends like this."

"Like what?"

"Well, calling on her like this, and bringing me here."

"It doesn't strike me as funny. Why should it?"

"I thought when two people break up, they wouldn't ever want to see each other again."

"It'd be pretty hard not to see Hazel again," George said dryly. "She's all over the place. I don't mean she checks up on me or anything. But it's a small town and we have mutual friends, and so we bump into each other."

"I'd hate that. If I ever got a divorce I'd run away, far away. I'd never want to see him again, never, I'd run away."

"Well, don't get excited. You're not even married yet." He paused. "Not even considering it, I guess."

"No."

"You'll change your mind someday when you meet the right man."

She didn't bother to answer. In silence they went across the yard and up the steps of Hazel's back porch.

Hazel opened the screen door, wearing a fixed smile on her face that looked as if it had been attached with glue. During the time it had taken George to go out to the car and get Ruby, Hazel had freshened her make-up and combed her hair, but already along her upper lip and the hairline of her forehead little pinpoints of sweat were oozing up through the new layer of powder.

When she spoke she used her office-voice which had a professional lilt to it intended to make Dr. Foster's patients feel at ease. "Come on in and make yourself at home—Ruby, is it?"

"Yes."

She looked at Hazel, dully, with no sign of recognition. It was as if the two days since they had met had lengthened into years for Ruby and these years had numbed her memory.

"George tells me you're not feeling very well," Hazel said.

Ruby shook her head. "I feel fine, just fine."

"That's good."

"I get nervous sometimes, that's all. Everybody does. It's nothing. I wouldn't dream of imposing—"

"You're not imposing." Hazel turned to George. "Harold's in the front room. He wants to talk to you about the boat."

"My boat?"

"Yes. He says it's sprung a leak."

"A leak? He must be imagining things. Sure, on a day like this, she ships a little water, naturally."

"All right, so it doesn't leak. Talk to Harold about it. I never said it leaked."

"He didn't either."

"Go and ask him."

"I will. If that suits Ruby."

Ruby glanced at him listlessly, as if the conversation and the moods and tensions beneath it had been too difficult to follow. "What did you say?"

"Is it okay with you if I leave you here with Hazel for a while?"

"I don't care."

"I won't be long."

"I don't care."

He paused in the doorway and looked back, but she was no longer watching him. Letting the door swing shut behind him he was conscious of a feeling of relief, and of gratitude to Hazel for insisting that he go and talk to Harold. Sometimes he wanted to leave Ruby and couldn't; he deluded himself into thinking that if he stayed another minute, or five, or ten, his words, his presence and the very passage of time would change her in his favor.

The door swung into place with a squeak of hinges. The noise seemed to focus Ruby's attention more sharply than any human voice. She looked at the door thoughtfully, as if it had said something to her, without words to distort its meaning.

"It needs oiling," Hazel said. "Everything does around here. Including me. Want some beer?"

"No. No, thanks. You go right ahead, though."

"I don't mind if I do." She took a quart of beer out of the refrigerator and poured out a glassful. The beer was warm and foamed out over the sides of the glass like soapsuds. "Sit down, why don't you, before you drop."

"I won't drop." But she pulled out one of the straight-backed wooden chairs and sat down at the kitchen table. "I feel fine."

"Ruby—"

"Just fine."

"Ruby, snap out of it."

"What?"

"Listen, you haven't been taking drugs or anything, have you?"

"Drugs? No, I never take drugs."

"You don't remember me, Ruby?"

"Remember?"

"We've met before."

Ruby shook her head, slowly, unable for the moment to make any connection between the plump and perspiring woman holding the glass of beer, and the composed efficient nurse in the white uniform who ran Gordon's office and answered the telephone. Even the voices were different.

"What you need," Hazel said, "is some food and rest."

"No, thank you." She stared at the table in front of her, at the half-prepared sandwiches, the buttered bread and the thick slices of meatloaf containing bright blobs of green which might have been peas or green pepper but which looked to Ruby like some phosphorescent decay. She had missed dinner—she hadn't, in fact, had a square meal for a week now—and the sight of the meat and its strong oniony smell nauseated her. She never wanted to see food again. There was no fight, no resolution, left in her, only the numbness of despair that made her want to lie down in a quiet place and go to sleep for a long time until many things were forgotten. She hadn't even the energy to get up and leave. She was bound by sheer inertia to a chair at Hazel's kitchen table, shrouded by the smell of meatloaf and the sweet, fermented memories of the summer with Gordon.

"You're Gordon's Hazel," she said, and a nerve began to twitch in her left cheek, contracting the muscle and pulling up the corner of her mouth. It was as if, minutes before Ruby herself could see any humor in the situation, her face was preparing to smile. But instead of smiling, she threw back her head and laughed, and kept on laughing while Hazel watched her uneasily over the moist, foamy rim of her glass.

"You're George's Hazel and you're Gordon's Hazel and they both begin with a G!" It was so excruciatingly funny that tears oozed out from between her eyelids and fell down her cheeks almost to the point of her chin. She did not weep like Josephine who had a wealth of tears, fat and silver and smooth like ball bearings. Ruby's tears came out pinched and meager, little coins squeezed out of shape between a miser's fingers. Josephine wept from a great reservoir of self-regard and self-pity; Ruby wept from the dry ducts of self-hate.

"You're punchy." Hazel took a piece of Kleenex from the window ledge over the sink. "Here. Use this."

"I don't want anything from you, I don't want anything from anybody."

"All right, but not so loud. George might hear you."

"I don't care." She took the piece of Kleenex and rubbed her face, savagely, as if she had a grudge against her own skin. "He brought me here on purpose. It was a trap. He wants to find out things about me."

"He wants to help you."

"I hate him. I hate him and his help."

"Now listen—"

"He's a fat creepy old man and when he looks at me I feel like screaming, my skin crawls. I know what he's thinking. I know what he wants. And it's not to help me. He wants to *help* me, what a laugh."

"Shut up," Hazel said, but without authority, without even conviction. "He'll hear you."

"Let him. I want him to hear. All this time him putting on the big act, poor Ruby, Ruby needs help, there's something the matter with her. Well, I know who there's something the matter with and it's not me. It's him. Him and his greasy eyes that never let you alone, that you can't ever get away from because even when he's not around I feel them looking at me and I get sick in my stomach!"

"You're imagining things."

"Am I? That's what you think. I've been around. I know men like him."

Hazel finished the beer and put the empty glass on the sink. With one part of her mind she felt pity for George and the need to defend him: *George has nice eyes, they're not greasy, they're luminous—and he always tries to help people, not just you.* But from another and deeper part of her mind, words gushed up like water from an underground river: *Go on, tell me more. Show me how you hate him. Talk louder and he'll hear you. Let him find out. Raise your voice, Ruby.*

"Shut up," she said roughly. "You've got no right shooting off your mouth about one of my best friends."

Ruby didn't answer. She had picked up a crumb of meat from the table and was rolling it between her fingers until it looked like a little brown pill.

"You've got no right," Hazel repeated. "And anyway, what are you doing going out with him if you can't stand the sight of him?"

"I don't know."

"You must have a reason."

"No. He came to the house and wanted to take me for a drive and I was too tired to argue, that's all, too tired." She made another brown pill and placed it carefully beside the first one on the oilcloth table cover. "We drove up Garcia Road."

"You don't have to tell me where you—"

"I've never been in that part of town before. It's very pretty, all the trees and flowers, and the houses with such wide windows like the people in them have got nothing to hide. I'd like to live in a place like that with big wide windows and never pull the blinds. I would keep myself very well groomed so that people walking by on the sidewalk would never catch me looking sloppy or anything. I would always have on a pretty dress or one of those quilted satin housecoats, and I'd keep the house very clean and tidy, nothing lying around.

People walking by would glance in and wonder who I was and think how lucky, that girl, to have such a beautiful clean house with such shiny furniture." She paused for breath, sucking the air in through her mouth greedily as if it was not air at all but an ether to prolong the dream. "Blue is my color but a red robe would be nicer. It's more cheerful, like Christmas. Red always reminds me of Christmas at home."

But she had stretched the dream too far—there had never been a Christmas at home that she could remember without bitterness—and it snapped like an elastic band and stung her skin and brought moisture to her eyes. Through the moisture she could see Hazel looking blurred and fuzzy as if she had just grown a crop of tiny feathers.

"You should have something to eat," Hazel said.

"No. No, please, I'm not hungry."

"A glass of milk, then."

"No." She blinked the moisture out of her eyes. "Gordon lives in a house like that, doesn't he?"

"Like—? Oh. Yes, kind of like that."

"Did you ever go there?"

"Once."

"It's like I said, isn't it, when you walk by you can look right into the windows?"

"I don't remember. Maybe you can."

"I bet she keeps the place very clean. Just judging from what I've heard of her, I bet she's very tidy."

"I guess she is," Hazel said. The girl was making her nervous. She wished George would come back and take her away. "I don't notice those things much."

"Naturally, being a friend of Gordon's, I've had invitations to dinner and things like that, but I've always been too busy to go, so I've never even met his wife. I guess you know her pretty well."

"Well enough."

"What's she look like?"

"She's kind of blonde and pale."

"Pretty?"

"She has nice teeth. She gets them cleaned every three months. That's the only time I ever see her, when she comes to the office, except the once I went out to the house to take her the car keys."

"I thought you might be friendly with her, she might tell you things."

"No. She isn't the kind that confides in the office help."

"You don't like her much, I can tell that."

"I don't think about her."

"I do," Ruby said in a whisper. "I think about her a lot."

Hazel gave her a wary, uneasy glance. "If that's your idea of fun, go ahead."

"I think about her, what is she like, and is she prettier than I am, and what do her and Gordon talk about and what does she give him for breakfast and do they sleep in the same room—all the things that Gordon never tells me, that's what I think about. Gordon and I—Gordon—" She put her head down on the table and cradled it with her arms for comfort. Her voice came out, muffled by the press of flesh: "You wouldn't understand. Nobody would, nobody."

Slowly and stiffly Hazel crossed the room and sat down at the table opposite her. Her hands were shaking and her teeth were clenched together so tight that her jaws ached.

"So you're the girl," she said, sounding helpless and confused, as if the fact had struck her like a fire in the night, exposing her nakedness. "The one he talks to on the phone, that's you."

"We never talked more than a minute. We—"

"Why did you have to tell me? I've got troubles of my own. I didn't want to know. Why did you have to tell me?"

"I—don't know."

"I've kept out of it. I knew something was going on but I managed to keep out of it. It's none of my business what Gordon does, or you." But she was aware as soon as the words were out that they were a lie. What Gordon did was her business because he was her employer, he paid her salary; and what Ruby did was her business because it affected not only Gordon, but George as well. "Why drag me into it, for God's sake?"

"I didn't mean to."

"How many other people have you told?"

"No—no one."

"Does anyone else know?"

"Just her—Elaine."

"Just Elaine," Hazel said with a brief, mirthless laugh. "That's very funny, if you know Elaine. Just." She paused a moment. Through the closed door she could hear George's bass rumble and she thought, *so that's why she hates George so much, not for what he is or does, but because he isn't Gordon.* "How did Elaine find out?"

"I don't know. Suddenly one night she phoned the café where I meet Gordon and asked for him. She told him the children were sick and he was to come right home. I said to Gordon, we'll have to meet some place else, and he said it was no use, no matter where we went she would find out." She raised her head. Her eyes were dry and glassy like marbles, and there was a round red indentation on her left cheek where it had pressed too long and tight against one of the buttons on her sleeve. "He's scared of her. There's no fight in him."

"I've seen him fight."

"Not her. Not against her. He means to, he says he will, and then when the time comes he can't. It's like she paralyzes him and he can't even talk to her. How can anything be settled if he won't talk to her? What will happen to us?"

"You already know. It's already happened."

"You mean bad things."

"What else?"

"They show, here?" She reached up and touched her face, running her fingertips along her forehead and down her cheeks to the point of her jaw. "You can see them?"

"Not exactly. I didn't—"

"I've always looked old for my age," Ruby said stiffly. "It's because I got such fine skin, it wrinkles easier than other people's."

"I didn't mean you had wrinkles."

"You were just trying to scare me, that's what you meant."

"I'm trying to warn you what you're messing around in. The top's been ready to blow off that house for years."

"Let it blow."

"You think you can pick up the pieces?"

"Yes."

"Your own, maybe. Not Gordon's. There'll be nothing to pick up."

Ruby leaned across the table. "You don't want Gordon to go away with me and be happy, do you? You want things to stay like they are. You don't care about Gordon, it's your job you care about."

"There are other jobs," Hazel said grimly. "And probably other Gordons. But if there's a sure thing on God's green earth, there's only one Elaine."

"Trying to scare me—what can she do to me?"

"She can twist you out of shape like you were a pipe cleaner. I've seen what she does to him."

"I can fight back. I'm stronger than I look. I'm tough."

Hazel turned away. "Sure. Sure you are."

"Wait and see. Someday, when everything's settled and Gordon and I are married, I bet you'll look back on tonight and have a big laugh about how you tried to scare me."

"I like a big laugh," Hazel said wearily. "Good luck to you anyway, Ruby."

"Why do you say it like that, like I was going to die or something? I've got a future, me and Gordon. No matter what it is, it'll be better than this. You can see that, can't you?"

"I guess I can."

"I'm strong and I'm tough."

"Sure."

The door from the hall swung open and George came in. His face was flushed and his eyes crinkled at the corners, and he was rubbing his hands together as if he'd just told a good joke and had led the laughing. George knew a million jokes.

"Time to break this up, isn't it?"

Neither of the women answered.

"You girls been having a nice little chat?"

"Swell," Hazel said. "Dandy."

He approached Ruby's chair, almost shyly. "I told you Hazel was a real tonic. You look better already, that's a feat."

She kept her eyes fixed on the table. "I look a mess."

"No, you don't."

"My hair—"

"Your hair looks great." He reached out to touch it, but she shrank away from his hand.

"I left," she said, "I left my purse in the car."

"I'll get it for you."

"No!"

"Is anything the matter?"

"No! I just want to get my purse so I can comb my hair."

"All right," he said. "All right."

He stepped back and she darted toward the door, quick and frightened, like a bird. A moment later, through the open window, they could hear her frantic footsteps.

For a long time George didn't move or speak. Then suddenly he reached down and picked up a whole slice of meatloaf and crammed it into his mouth. He began to chew, his cheeks distended like a squirrel's. A moist blob of food dribbled out of the corner of his mouth and fell on his lapel. He didn't wipe it off. He just stood there, chewing, out of rage and defiance and humiliation, chewing until his jaws ached and his throat contracted in revulsion and a lump formed in his chest like a knot of leather. And then, because he could not swallow, he opened the screen door and spat across the porch railing into the summer night. He came back into the kitchen, wiping his mouth with the back of his hand, breathing noisily like a sprinter at the tape.

"You don't," Hazel said coldly, "have to act like a pig."

"I am treated like a pig. I will be a pig."

"Well, pick somebody else's kitchen to—"

"Shut up." Going to the sink he turned the cold water on full and splashed his face, sucking the water into his mouth. Then he dried himself carefully on a tea towel, folded the towel and replaced it on the rack,

"That's a dish towel," Hazel said.

He looked at her bitterly, his eyes bloodshot from the water. "Well, I'm a dish. That makes it all right. Ask Ruby what a fancy dish I am."

"I didn't have to ask her. She told me."

"Give it to me straight."

"I'd like a cigarette."

"Here."

He lit it for her and she took three quick puffs, as if she intended the smoke to blur George's outlines and take the edge off reality.

She spoke slowly: "Ruby thinks you're a fine man and all that, but she—well, you're more of a father to her, see?"

"She said that?"

"Not exactly."

"What did she say, exactly?"

"She implied that—"

"What did she *say?*"

"Goddamn it, are you threatening me? Get your hands off me!"

"Tell me, tell me the truth."

"Or you'll what?"

"I'll shake it out of you."

"Try."

His hand was still on her shoulder but force and urgency had gone out of it. It lay like a dead thing on Hazel's black crepe shoulder, and when she moved to one side his hand fell away. He looked down at it, a little surprised, and then he put it in his pocket.

"Hazel?"

"Get out of here."

"Tell me the truth, what she said."

"Why should I?"

"Because I've got to know one way or another."

"You already know. You just can't face it. You want me to face it for you, just like in the old days; I got to spell it out for you because it's easier to take that way. Well, I won't. Get out and leave me alone."

"You can't—"

"And the next time you come bursting in here with one of your two-bit heart throbs I'll have you both thrown out on your ear. Now start moving before she comes back. I don't want her in here."

"She's not coming back," George said. "She didn't have any purse."

He began moving toward the door, his head bent, and swinging slightly with each step like a bear's.

"Listen, George—"

"No. I guess you won't have to spell it out for me this time."

"You're lucky she's not coming back. You may not think so right now, but you're really lucky, George."

"Sure. I'm a very lucky guy."

He went out on to the porch and down the creaking steps. From the shadowy denseness of the live-oak tree the relentless mockingbird chortled his derisive little song: Lucky guy, lucky guy, oh my!

George picked up a pebble from the driveway and threw it hard and accurately into the heart of the tree. The mockingbird skittered through the prickly leaves and across the garage roof to a telephone pole where it sat in silence. But the alarm had sounded: the whole tree seemed to come alive with squawks and twitterings and the whirring of wings; the wood rats responded, and began their noisy racing up and down the walls of the garage and across the hood of Hazel's car; and from a clump of bushes came the gentle regret of the mourning dove, lamenting the sad things of this world.

The sound reminded him of Ruby. He quickened his step, stung by a sudden wild hope that he had been wrong about her; she had had her purse with her after all, and she had just gone to the car to get it; she would be there now combing her hair.

"Ruby!" he shouted, and broke into a run.

There was no one in the car, no one on the street. He looked carefully around as if he half-expected to find her hiding somewhere behind a tree or hedge, needing only a little encouragement to come out, like a half-tamed animal.

"Ruby?"

But the only sign of life was the blinking taillight of the East Beach bus and the gray plume of its exhaust as it rolled down toward the sea.

He got into his car. The air was stale because the windows were all shut, and the smell of Ruby's powder mingled with the smell of dead cigars and souring hopes. He cranked down the window on his own side and was leaning across the seat to do the same to the other when he noticed that the door to the glove compartment was open. He knew he hadn't left it that way. He rarely used the compartment except on trips, and then only to store his road maps and sunglasses and the five-dollar bill in the money clip which he kept for an emergency, using the same bill year after year because the emergency hadn't occurred.

The clip was still there but the money was gone.

"Ruby," he said, sounding very surprised. "Ruby."

He thought of her waiting in the car while he went to talk to Hazel, waiting, catlike and curious, exploring the glove compartment to pass the time: *What's this? Money. How nice. I don't have any. It's mine now. Finders keepers.*

Had it been that simple and childish? He knew in his heart that it had not, that she had taken the money not at the first opportunity, when she was left alone in the car, but at the second, when she had run out of the house; and she had taken it not like an amoral child, but like a woman, desperate to get away.

For a full minute he sat there staring into the night and seeing in its deformed shadows a mocking image of the truth. Then he started the car and turned it around and headed back toward the sea. He had no destination but it seemed easier to follow the descent of the road.

Six blocks down he caught up with the bus. As it pulled into a curb the interior lights switched on like stage lights suddenly revealing a new set and cast of characters. The set was almost empty. Two women in nurses' uniforms were at the front of the bus talking to the driver, and behind them, oblivious to their chatter, an old man slept, knees up and chin on chest, in a return to infancy. At the back of the bus a girl sat with her forehead pressed against the window pane, her hands shielding her eyes from the interior lights as if she was trying to see into the darkness outside. She was very young and did not look like a thief.

"Ruby!"

He stopped his car alongside the bus and pressed the horn once and then again.

The old man did not awaken. The young girl turned away from the window and closed her eyes. The bus lights went out.

9

ELAINE CALLED FROM the bedroom, "Is that you, Gordon?"

"Yes."

"Where on earth have you been?"

He heard her sharp footsteps approaching the head of the stairs, and in the background the sounds of the children quarreling: Gimme it, it's mine, gimme it.

Elaine came down the steps with quick, exasperated movements. She wore her old housecoat, but her face was made up and her hair was swirled on top of her head, pinned with a large Spanish comb.

"You know we were going to the party at the club tonight, Gordon. Where have you been?"

"I took a drive."

"All this time? I even phoned Hazel to see if you had an emergency appointment or something. She said no, she left the office at twelve noon and so did you."

"I forgot about the party."

"I kept your dinner hot for a full hour."

"Well, I'm sorry, Elaine."

"You're sorry, well, that's just fine," she said with a bitter little smile. "You go off for eight hours without letting me know and then you say you're sorry."

Gordon said dryly, "I keep getting sorrier and sorrier, if that's any consolation to you."

"And now you've got the nerve to turn around and be sarcastic about it! I suppose you expect me to believe that, about your going for a drive."

"I went for a drive, you don't have to believe it."

"I wonder."

"I can't stop you wondering. I still went for a drive."

At the top of the stairs there was a faint rustle, a flutter of white. Gordon looked up and saw Judith and Paul standing there listening. They were in their pajamas, Paul delicate and nervous, and Judith round as a ball. She had a candy stored in her mouth and one cheek was distended.

"Hello, Judith," Gordon said with forced cheerfulness. "Hello, Paul."

The boy lowered his head and took a step back. Judith said, "Hello."

"Well. And what have you two been doing all day?"

"We went for a drive." She began to giggle. "We went for a drive. Didn't we, Paul? Didn't we went for a drive?"

The boy began to giggle too, and the giggles grew into long shuddering sobs of laughter. "We went for a drive, we went for a drive!"

They started to jump up and down, in time to the words, up and down the hall they went in a frenzy of excitement, repeating the magic, mysterious and somehow forbidden words: "We went for a drive!"

"Stop it!" Elaine shouted. "If you don't go right back to your rooms, I'll tell Miss Kane not to come tonight."

The boy stopped jumping immediately and said, "I want Ruth to come. I want Ruth."

"Then go quietly to your room."

"Is Ruth coming?"

"She's coming if you behave yourself."

"She's not coming, you said she's not coming!"

"I said I'd tell her not to come if you make any more fuss."

"She's not coming, she's not coming!" The boy went, wailing softly, back to his room. He felt betrayed, cheated. She was not coming. His mother was a black witch and his father told lies.

The parents were too ashamed to look at each other. Elaine turned and started up the steps, her shoulders sagging.

"Elaine—"

"I pressed your costume. It's on your bed."

"Thanks." He wanted to apologize, to his children, to his wife, but the children couldn't understand and his wife wouldn't listen.

He did the next best thing to please them all. He gave Paul and Judith a dollar each and he put on his Fiesta costume without argument. The embroidered caballero coat was too tight and the gold braided trousers flapped around his ankles when he walked, like broken wings. Under the dangling pompons of his broad-brimmed hat, Gordon's eyes held a vast bewilderment.

He heard the front doorbell ring and Judith and Paul dashing down the stairs shouting for Ruth.

Elaine came in from the dressing room. She was dressed as a Spanish bride in white lace with a heavy white lace mantilla over her hair. A red velvet rose was caught in the mantilla, and another was pinned to her waist. She had painted her mouth larger than usual, going beyond its own firm outline. The new mouth changed the emphasis of her face and made her look like a stranger to Gordon.

"Ruth's here," Elaine said. "Are you ready?"

"I guess so."

"That coat's a little tight this year. You must be gaining weight."

"Probably."

"Gordon—" She sat down cautiously on the edge of the bed. "I wonder why Paul does that. I mean, he gets ideas in his head, he deliberately misunderstands. You heard me tell him Ruth was coming. He refused to believe me. He was practically hysterical, I don't understand it."

"I don't either," Gordon said. He would have liked to sit down and discuss Paul's difficulties, to try and trace their origin. But he knew that Elaine didn't want a discussion, she merely wanted to be reassured that it wasn't her fault, that she was a good mother. Any serious discussion of the children would lead to a scene, to Elaine weeping, *I did the best I could singlehanded without any help from you, they might as well not have had a father, you've never loved them, you've never even played with them like a normal father.*

No, Gordon thought, I didn't. She never gave me a chance. If I so much as picked one of the children up, she always found reasons why I shouldn't—I was holding them the wrong way, or watch-out-for-his-arm-Gordon!, or it was too soon after a meal for them to be jostled around, or it was time for their nap.

"I feel," Elaine said virtuously, "that it's we parents who are to blame."

Gordon nodded, and the pompons on his hat danced in wild irony.

"I might have known that *something* would happen tonight, it always does when I've been looking forward to something, like this party."

"I'm sorry if—if I've spoiled it for you."

Elaine gave a hard brief laugh. "You haven't, don't worry! I wouldn't *let* anything spoil it. I'm not like some people. I don't *let* circumstances get the best of me."

To Gordon, her eyes added, I'm not like you, Gordon, you poor weak mouse, *letting* people, *letting* circumstances, *letting*—

Letting you too, Elaine.

Well, that just shows how weak you are. And you'll go on letting me, forever and ever!

Gordon took off his hat and wiped the sweat off his forehead.

"It's too bad you couldn't have grown a beard like some of the other men," Elaine said. "You'd look more authentic."

"You look very authentic."

"And what does that mean?"

"Nothing."

"It was the way you said it that I don't like."

"Listen, Elaine. Would you mind if I had a drink before we leave?"

Elaine wrinkled her forehead in exasperation. "What on earth for? There's going to be plenty of liquor there. The liquor was included in the price of the tickets like last year. Anyway," she added as an afterthought, "Ruth is here."

"What's Ruth got to do with it?"

"Well, you know, she's death on liquor. If she saw you taking a drink she'd probably go home and tell Hazel and Hazel would spread it all over the town, exaggerating it, of course. A dentist can't be too careful of his reputation. Anyway, why do you want a drink now, just when we're ready to go?"

"So I'd feel a little less foolish in this outfit, to dull my sensibilities, in brief."

Elaine shook her head in wry satisfaction. "I *knew*, I said to myself, if we get out of this house tonight without Gordon making some kind of a fuss about his costume, it'll be a miracle."

"I wouldn't call this a fuss."

"I can't understand why other people can dress up and go out and have a good time and you can't even seem to make the effort. My goodness, what difference does it make whether you're dressed up like a businessman or a gay caballero?"

"I don't feel like a gay caballero," Gordon said dryly. "That's the difference."

"Well, all right then! We won't go! We'll stay home! We'll spend one of our nice jolly evenings at home for a change!"

"Not so loud, Elaine. Ruth and the kids will hear you."

"Well, it's time somebody heard me. It's time somebody heard my side of the story!"

"Come on, Elaine, let's go."

"I won't." She sat rigidly on the edge of the bed, refusing to budge.

"Look at it sensibly, Elaine. You're getting your own way. I'm wearing the costume, I'm not having a drink. I'm a gay caballero, see, come hell or high water, and lips that touch liquor shall—"

"You've got a nerve getting sarcastic again."

"I wish I had a nerve. Or two nerves."

"What would *you* do?"

"I don't know, I haven't quite figured that out yet."

"That's a very vague threat," Elaine said, but she got up and went to the door. She seemed to have a sixth sense about how far she could go without rousing Gordon's temper, and when she reached that point she stopped. Not that Gordon would actually do anything—he never had, the presumption was that he never would—but he could spoil the party for her by sulking or refusing to dance with some of her bridge-club friends or by drinking too much, as he had on one occasion.

Elaine folded her troubles away in one corner of her mind, neatly and carefully, so that it wouldn't be hard to find them again and unfold them as good as new.

The caballero and his Spanish bride went down the steps together, trailing the faint odor of mothballs and the fainter but more pervasive and sour odor of a quarrel.

Ruth was sitting on the davenport in the front room, with Paul on her lap and Judith pressed against her side. ". . . and this little girl was in the first grade, just like you, Judy, and she had a little brother who was just going to start to school, like you, Paul. And they had a baby brother too, and a dog."

"I want a dog," Paul said. "That's what I want, is a dog as big as a pony to ride and sleep in my bed and I sleep on the floor, or maybe both of us sleep in the bed."

Ruth laughed, and stroked his hair gently. "Ah, I'm afraid Mother wouldn't like that."

"I'm afraid she *wouldn't,*" Elaine said with a smile.

"I want a small dog," Judith said, "to go in my baby buggy."

Elaine put on her sweetly reasonable expression. The children recognized it and knew what was coining. They waited, bored and resentful, for the judge to lay down the law and hurry out of court.

"Now children, I believe we've settled the dog question before. We're going to get a dog when I feel that you're both old enough to appreciate a dog and take the responsibility of looking after it properly."

"Ruth has a dog named Wendy," Judith said. "Ruth says it's a Heinz dog."

"A *what?*" Elaine said.

"A Heinz dog, fifty-seven varieties." Judith howled with laughter, and Paul joined in, laughing even harder than Judith because he didn't understand the joke.

"Hush now," Elaine said. "Be quiet. We'll be later than usual tonight, Ruth, but Dr. Foster will drive you home and you can take a nap if you like."

"Oh, I won't get tired, Mrs. Foster, I never do."

"Don't wake the baby to give him his bottle. He'll wake up about eleven or so. I guess that's all. Well, goodbye, children. Be good now, won't you?"

She hesitated for a moment, half-hoping the children would come over and kiss her goodbye. They made no move, so she waved goodbye to them from the doorway, very gaily, with her arm feeling heavy as lead.

Gordon was waiting in the car with the engine running (indicating, to Elaine, impatience). He looked tired (sulky), and he had taken off the hat which was too hot and heavy on his head (fussing about his costume).

"Did I keep you waiting?" Elaine asked, getting into the car awkwardly so she wouldn't disarrange her mantilla or dirty the white lace skirt.

"No."

"You must have gotten gas if you went for that long drive today. The gas tank's nearly full."

"That would be the first thing you'd notice, wouldn't it?"

Elaine widened her eyes. "Well, my goodness, I wasn't checking up on you. I always look to see how much gas we have."

"Okay."

"And if you're mad because I kept you waiting all of two minutes, well, all I can say is, you might at least have stopped to say hello to Ruth. She's very sensitive about lapses in good manners, you know that."

"I didn't know that. I hardly know her, so I couldn't be expected to know she's sensitive."

"She's got a very sensitive face."

"Good."

"You're certainly in a mood tonight, Gordon. I hope you're not going to sulk all evening the way you did at the Lamberts' party."

"I can't remember sulking at the Lamberts' party. I can't even remember the Lamberts."

"It was right after we were married. They're moved away now."

"Your memory has a long arm, hasn't it, Elaine?"

"I never forget any unpleasant scenes, if that's what you mean. Who does?"

"A lot of people."

"I'm not one of these soft-headed women who forgets a quarrel just because it ends in a kiss. If a quarrel took place, then I'm justified in remembering it, surely. Anyway, people can't help themselves from remembering things."

"I guess not."

All the way to the U-Club Gordon tried to recall the Lamberts and couldn't.

He parked the car in the palm-lined driveway and locked the doors.

The club was an L-shaped structure made of adobe brick. Here, the more successful men of the community—the professional men, lawyers, doctors, real-estate agents, retired army and navy officers—found a sanctuary from their wives and families. They lunched and dined, played poker and billiards and gin rummy, secure in the knowledge that no female trespasser could get past the front door. About once a month a special entertainment was held in the form of mildly dirty movies. No one, not even the head waiter in the dining room who ran the projection machine, knew where these movies came from, or who owned or rented them. This uncertainty gave rise to considerable speculation, especially among the members who were embarrassed and disgusted by the movies and were afraid the members of the Don Cabrillo Club would find out about them and act even more insufferably superior. Suspicion settled on various members, and there was a great deal of dissension and hard feeling in the club. Mr. Westervelt, who sold insurance, was one of the chief suspects because he liked to look at women's legs. He subsequently resigned, refused to pay his outstanding bill, and threatened to sue everybody in the club for slander, including the bus boys. Dr. Lavery, who took Westervelt's place as chief suspect because he'd had three wives, was made of sterner stuff. He wrote a scathing letter to the newspaper, and only the fact that the publisher of the paper was a loyal member of the U-Club prevented the scandal from becoming public.

No one member was entirely free from suspicion except Judge of the Superior Court, old Anton Bowridge. A childless widower, Bowridge led a dull life. Nearly every day he sat on the judge's bench amid the somber beauty of the Superior Court. The high windows were heavily draped against the sun. The chandeliers that hung threateningly from the ceiling gave just enough light to accentuate the gloom, the twilight of guilt. No one in the court ever felt like a free man, least of all Bowridge.

The judge's bench was a masterpiece of design. It looked comfortable, and yet it was just uncomfortable enough to prevent one from going to sleep. Sometimes he sat upright, sometimes he held his head in both hands, or rested his chin in his right hand, then his left hand; he crossed his legs and leaned way over on the right, or the left. But always the chair prodded him sternly in the vertebrae, the eyes of the chandelier accused him of inattention, and conscience lurked in the rigid drapes of the closed windows.

Bowridge had no interest in watching the movies himself. He had spent most of his life in courtrooms and there was nothing that he hadn't seen or heard. His interest lay in watching the people who watched the movies—Johnston kept opening and closing his eyes, repelled, fascinated; poor old Coolidge often had sneezing fits, and the young architect with the buck teeth (McTavish? MacGregor? McSomething) cleared his throat, *ahem!* Afterwards they were all embarrassed, they smiled sheepishly at each other, some of them left in a hurry and others stayed around to discuss the question of where the movies came from. They asked Judge Bowridge if it wasn't illegal to make or possess these movies and Bowridge ruled that it was, but that they were not, however, to accuse any one member of being the guilty party unless they were convinced, beyond a reasonable doubt and to a moral certainty, that such was the case.

Watching the watchers not only amused Bowridge, they restored to him some faith, not in the essential goodness of most people, but in their essential harmlessness. The poor fellows, they felt so guilty at watching the movies it was impossible to imagine them committing a felony. They were really quite simple, harmless fellows who would never crack a safe, take a potshot at their wives, embezzle or commit mayhem. Simple assault, perhaps (no deadly weapon, no intent to kill), or manslaughter involving a motor accident—but none of them, he was convinced, would ever repeat the crime. Their sins were little, their fears great, their lives short, and always in store for them was the Superior-Superior Court with God on the bench (looking a little like Bowridge except that He had a beard), God on the hard bench with an aching back, a little weary and bored, given to inattention, leaning His chin on His right hand, then His left hand, and wondering why someone didn't push aside the drapes and open the windows and turn off the infernal lights of the chandelier.

The Little Sinners was Bowridge's private name for his fellow members of the U-Club. He never missed any of their parties, mainly because they gave him an opportunity to see the wives and so fill in a number of blank spaces about their husbands.

Bowridge entered the club on the heels of Elaine and Gordon. (This young man Foster, now, had a lot of blank spaces. He didn't attend the special movies, he didn't play poker or bridge after dinner. When he came to lunch he left immediately afterwards. A shy duck.)

"Hello, Mrs. Foster," Bowridge said. "Hello, Gordon."

"Why, Judge Bowridge," Elaine said. "You didn't dress up!"

"I prefer to stay on the sidelines watching the beautiful señoritas."

"That's no excuse. Honestly, I think you're mean. Don't you, Gordon? Don't you think he's mean?"

"The fact is," Bowridge explained dryly, "when no one forces me at the point of a gun to dress up, I don't dress up. What caliber weapon did you employ, Mrs. Foster?"

"None at all, so there," Elaine said. "Gordon, wait here a minute while I fix my hair. Excuse me, will you, Judge?"

"Certainly."

They both watched her as she went down the hall toward the powder room.

"We're early," Bowridge said.

"I guess we are."

"The others, I presume, are judiciously getting pie-eyed before they start. The punch they serve at these affairs is highly suspect. Come and try some."

"Thanks, I'll wait for Elaine."

"She'll be able to find you."

"Well—"

"Come along, come along." Bowridge walked ponderously ahead, with his head down and his hands clasped behind his back, as if he were thinking great and solemn thoughts. "As a matter of fact, I have a little surprise for you."

"For me?"

"Well, not strictly for you. You happened to come along at the correct psychological moment and so we will share the surprise. Look."

The judge removed from his hip pocket a pint bottle without a label.

"Gin," Gordon said.

"You're absolutely wrong. Compared to this stuff, gin is mother's milk."

"Alcohol."

"Correct, one hundred percent pure grain alcohol. A medical friend of mine gave it to me for my birthday. Most unusual gift, I consider. His instructions were to mix it with grapefruit juice and the resulting potion is termed a Graveyard Special, I believe. I suggest that we try some—very, very cautiously, mind you—in a glass of punch. Or—" He squinted up his face in such a jovial frown that one of the waiters, who had just received a ticket for overtime parking, scurried back into the kitchen for sanctuary. "Or we might—and I grant that this suggestion has a faint touch of the macabre—we might simply pour the whole bottle into the punch, thus sharing it with the common herd. What do you think, Gordon?"

Gordon smiled helplessly.

"Both are tempting, I must admit," Bowridge said. "But on the whole I think we'd better keep it to ourselves rather than dissipate its energy, as it were. Of course if we had *two* bottles there'd be no question involved. We could keep one and put the other one in the punch, eh? *But* the one we would put in the punch is the one we haven't got, so, come along, come along."

Gordon came along, trailing Bowridge like a spaniel. The ballroom, ex-dining room, was swathed in red and yellow bunting, and a few couples were dancing to the Latin American music of Miguel Escalante. Escalante himself was handling the maracas, tossing them in the air, rolling his eyes, swaying his hips.

"I like bouncy music," Bowridge said, approaching the nearest punch bowl. "Here we are. Now, let me see. What proportions would you suggest, Gordon?"

"I don't know."

"We wouldn't want to become intoxicated. On the other hand we wouldn't want to be niggardly with ourselves. Mean to say you have no experience in these matters, Gordon?"

"None."

"Nor I. It will have to be guesswork, I fear." He poured some alcohol into Gordon's glass of punch.

"Whoa," Gordon said.

"Pleasant flavor."

"Very nice." Now that the drink was in his hands Gordon realized how badly he'd needed it. If he could have three, just three drinks, as a sort of buffer between him and Elaine—

"You're a quiet fellow," Bowridge said. "Something on your mind?"

"No."

"No guilty conscience?"

Gordon shrugged his shoulders.

"By the way," Bowridge said, "how *did* she get you to put on that costume?"

"I put it on voluntarily."

"Ha, to avoid argument."

"It's getting hot in here. I wonder whether Elaine—"

"Have another drink and relax, Gordon. That's what I'm going to do, relax. Relax like a damn little kitten."

Gordon was beginning to understand that Bowridge's relaxation had started several hours ago.

"All right, I'll have another," Gordon said.

"Fine, fine." Bowridge ladled out two more glasses of punch. When he added the alcohol he had to narrow his eyes to the merest slits to make them focus.

"There's your wife," Bowridge said.

Gordon saw Elaine standing in the doorway haughtily glancing over the couples on the dance floor. She's self-conscious, Gordon thought, she always looks like that when she's self-conscious. He turned his back on her and deliberately finished his drink.

"Well. There you are, Gordon," Elaine said pleasantly. "I've been looking all over for you. I thought you were going to wait for me in the hall."

"I was."

"It isn't as if I kept you waiting very long."

"I persuaded him to run away," Bowridge said.

Elaine laughed. "You're a bad influence on my husband, Judge Bowridge!"

"I hope not."

"And just for that, I'm going to persuade him to run away from *you!* Come and dance, Gordon. You'll excuse us, won't you, Judge? We haven't danced together for ages."

Gordon steered her out into the middle of the floor. She felt very light and soft in his arms. She was nearly as tall as he was and their cheeks brushed as they danced. Her skin was scented, some sweet, innocent, nostalgic scent that penetrated to Gordon's heart: *If only we could start over, if we could forget the million sour words and acid looks*—Elaine had closed her eyes, the lids had closed softly over the sharp ironies in her eyes, the unspoken reproaches. *I wish she would never open her eyes again. I wish—*

"Why on earth are you staring at me, Gordon?"

"Was I staring? Sorry."

"Your face looks funny. What have you and that old goat been drinking? And that's the second time you've stumbled."

"Sorry," Gordon said again. "I was thinking about you. I was thinking it would be nice if you kept your eyes closed all the time."

"My eyes closed? What a silly thing. Now you listen to me, Gordon. How many drinks did you have with that old goat?"

"Two."

"Two drinks," Elaine said contemptuously. "You should know by this time you can't hold your liquor. Two drinks, and already your face looks funny and you're starting to talk silly."

"I don't think it was silly. I was pretending, it was a game, you see. As long as you keep your eyes closed I can pretend that you love me and we have some sort of chance of going on together."

"I do love you," Elaine said. "I've always loved you. As for going on together, we haven't much choice, have we? We're not the kind of people who do foolish things on the spur of the moment. We have a sense of responsibility." She turned her face away from his in a gesture of impatience and withdrawal. "Oh, let's sit down. What's the use of dancing, what's the use of coming to a party at all if we've got to talk about things like this."

The dining room was half-filled by this time. Elaine paused to greet two of her bridge-club friends, reminding Gordon by pressing his hand that he wasn't to forget to ask them to dance. Gordon returned to the punch bowl, while Elaine explained to her friends that Gordon was keeping an eye on Judge Bowridge for the evening, he and Gordon were such pals, and you know how Bowridge gets sometimes, stiff, my dear, positively stiff. I know he lost his wife, but *still!*

Bowridge had sat down on a bench behind the punch bowl. He had taken his spectacles out of his pocket and was cleaning them with a handkerchief.

"Ha," he said, breathing air on the lenses. "Ha, ha. Didn't think you'd be back, Gordon."

"Here I am."

"Sit down. Do you feel anything?"

"No."

"Nor I. A little in the eyes, perhaps. My eyes are my weakest part. Those damn lights in the courtroom, not enough of them. Have to peer and peer to distinguish the defendant from the prosecution." He pinched his spectacles on the bridge of his nose and glanced around the room. "In my opinion this straight alcohol is vastly overrated, unless we're diluting it too much. Do you think that could be it?"

"Possibly."

"Then let us mend our ways." The judge rose. He walked steadily and ponderously, without a tremor. Gordon saw Elaine dancing with Dr. Lavery. She was talking very gaily, shaking her head and laughing, but he knew very well that she was watching him out of the corner of her eye. She was watching Bowridge too, as he ladled the punch and spiked it with alcohol from the bottle. Gordon felt like a little boy who is aware that he is doing wrong but keeps on doing it because he knows he won't be openly reprimanded or punished in front of strangers. There'd be only the sweet steely smile, the secret pinch on the arm, the whispered wait-till-I-get-you-home, Junior!

And, like the small boy who knew he was doing wrong, Gordon pretended he was not afraid. His face smiled, while the fear pressed on his chest, stifling his breathing. Wait-till-I-get-you-home, Gordon! He knew now that he had always been afraid of her. This was no new fear that had sprung up because of Ruby, because he had finally given Elaine a weapon. It was an old growth, its multiple roots buried twenty feet under the ground, crossing and re-crossing each other, a maze of roots and at the core, Gordon's personal minotaur.

"Wake up, Gordon," Bowridge said.

"I wasn't asleep."

"Pardon?"

"I—wasn't—asleep."

"I didn't say you were. You were dreaming. Sometimes I dream too, and I can look very alert when I'm dreaming but this takes practice." The judge sat down on the bench and handed Gordon his glass. "In court, sometimes I dream, and sometimes I worry, about fifty-fifty. I worry about people, I try to clarify issues. I boil them down in a crucible, I boil and boil, and when I've finished there isn't a thing left in the crucible, not an ash, not a drop of liquid. I also worry about my cough. Have you ever heard my cough?"

"No."

"It sounds like this—*chmm*—there. Very dry. It could be anything. What do you suppose it is, Gordon?"

"Phlegm."

"That's no answer. Why do you suppose I have phlegm?"

"I don't know."

"Well, there you are," Bowridge said with gloomy satisfaction. "You don't know and I don't know."

Gordon frowned. "I don't get that about boiling the issues."

"Ah, well, you boil off the extraneous matter, you vaporize the irrelevancies, and then what have you got? Nothing. It's very clear, a child could understand. For a child there are no irrelevancies, everything is equally important, a fire, a bowel movement, a caterpillar on a leaf, the pattern of a print, a kiss, a bruise, a passing motor scooter, the smell of a certain cake of soap. I have no children, I am only making this up by the method of contrasts. I'm old. I'm too tired to be interested in fires or caterpillars. I don't notice prints. My sense of smell is feeble, my bowel movements difficult. No one has kissed me for years. I hate the noise of motor scooters. You see?"

"I don't know."

"Ah, even a child can understand, it's very clear." The judge coughed twice, *chmm, chmm,* very dry. Then he put his glass down, took off his spectacles again and cleaned them, blowing on them, ha! ha! ha! and wiping the mist off with his handkerchief. He began to hum with the orchestra. "Catchy tune that. Spirited." Escalante sang "Chuy, chuy," and the Judge sang too, "Chewy, chewy, chewy chewy!"

"I feel," Bowridge said, "that I'm getting into the spirit of things."

Gordon took off his hat and put it on the floor. "It's getting warm in here."

"I like warmth. You and I could sing a duet, Gordon. That fellow up there can't sing. Who ever told him he could sing? Someone should apprise him of the true facts. Come along, come along, you and I will sing a duet."

"I don't know the words."

"They're very simple, just chewy chewy, chewy chewy."

"I don't know the music either."

"No matter. Just follow me."

Gordon looked around for Elaine, but there were too many people on the dance floor and they all looked rather vague and trivial.

Gordon and the judge raised their voices in song.

10

GORDON HUNG ONTO the palm tree with both his hands. The tree was swaying, so he knew there must be a high wind. Against his forehead the bark of the tree felt harsh and dry, like the skin of a very old man. He decided to sit down under this tree and rest.

"Get up," Elaine said.

"I lost my hat."

"Get up. I'm warning you, Gordon."

"A little rest, that's all."

"You disgusting fool, humiliating me in front of all those people. Get up, we're going home. After the exhibition you've made of yourself you'd think you'd want to go home. Do you hear me, Gordon?"

He heard her, of course, but he was listening to other things as well, trying to give them equal importance as the judge said. He heard the engine of a car starting, *za za za za za oom,* and the faint click of heels on the distant sidewalk. He heard Miguel Escalante and his Latin American Rhythms, and the noise of the palm tree. It didn't make the same kind of noise as other trees did. It crackled an incantation, waving its arms in grandiose sweeps like a demented evangelist. What a remarkable woman Elaine was—the wind that swayed the tree left her untouched.

"I lost my hat," Gordon said.

"I have it. Can't you even *see?*"

He peered up at her very earnestly, and of course she had the hat. Elaine never forgot such things. She would, after the Fiesta was over, pack the hat away in mothballs until the next Fiesta. It was a way of measuring time, counting Fiestas instead of birthdays. Next Fiesta he would be one year, three pounds and two moth holes older. *I'm old,* the judge said. *My sense of smell is feeble—I'm too tired—I don't notice—I hate—no one has kissed me—*

"Are you going to sit there all night?" Elaine said.

"A little rest. You could rest too, Elaine. The grass is damp but it's not very damp."

"Thanks. I'll stand up." She took a step nearer to him and leaned over, staring at him. Her face was white and furious. "All my life I've had to apologize for you and make excuses for you, and I'm sick of it, do you hear? I'm sick of it! I've apologized to the children because they've never had a decent father to play games with them or spend some time with them. I've apologized to my friends because every time we go out together you sit in the corner like a lump of lead, and don't open your mouth. I swear, sometimes you act half-witted. Well, the great silent act wasn't enough, oh no! Tonight you have to put on another one. You get drunk as a lord and sing, *sing,* mind you, in front of all those people. Out of tune, too."

"I didn't know the tune, I had to make it up."

"That's lovely! That makes everything all right, I suppose. Yes, and I've had to apologize to my mother, too. Little did she think that I'd be living from hand to mouth, without a maid or a car of my own. She thought you'd have enough gumption to go out and make some money the way other men do." She took a deep breath. "Look, I'm trying to be reasonable, I'm trying to control myself, but there are limits. You just don't seem to have any character, Gordon. You can't resist things, you have no will power."

Answers formed in his mind, rather cleverly, but he remained silent. Whatever he said, she could say more. It could go on all night and all tomorrow, it could go on until one of them died. Gordon, beloved husband of Elaine—

The thing to do was to attach equal importance to all sounds, the car, the heels on the sidewalk, the music, the mad tree. But the car had gone, the heels were silent, the tree drowsed. The music that seeped out of the windows was melancholy and sensuous. It whispered of love and betrayal, Perfidia. The notes ground into his wounds like salt. He thought of Ruby, and the tears welled in his eyes.

Elaine went on talking. She hadn't raised her voice, it was flat, controlled, reasonable: now let us both admit, calmly, that you lack character, will power, earning power, social graces and fatherly instincts; in brief, let us admit that you bear no resemblance to a man.

"There's one more thing," Elaine said. "I swore for the sake of my own pride that I'd never discuss this with you. But I haven't got any pride left anymore. You managed that, all right. You were with your girlfriend this afternoon, weren't you?"

Gordon shook his bowed head, not trusting himself to speak for fear Elaine might hear the tears in his voice.

"So you're still going to lie about it, are you? I suppose you're even going to deny that you have a girlfriend."

Gordon shook his head again.

"They say a wife is always the last to know about it. But I wasn't, I was one of the first. How you could hope to get away with it, in a town like this where everybody knows you—you, a man your age, with three children— Everyone's laughing at you. Not at *me*, because they know I know. If they don't know, I tell them. Everyone was laughing, and it was a case of me joining in the laughs or getting laughed at along with you. So I joined in."

Gordon looked up at her, his mouth open with shock. No matter what happened to him she would always be on the opposite side, joining in the laughs.

"Surprised, aren't you?" Elaine said harshly. "You didn't think I'd do it, did you? I laughed with the rest of them. Yes, and if they didn't know what the joke was, I'd *tell* them! I'd say, 'Gordon? Oh, Gordon's fine. Of course I don't see much of him anymore, he's got a new interest in life.' Then I'd smile, like this. You aren't watching me, Gordon, don't you want to see how I'd smile?"

She was leaning far over now, her face only a foot or so from his, and she was smiling viciously, her mouth drawn back from her teeth, her eyes narrowed to slits.

"You poor slobbering idiot, you thought you could make a fool of me, didn't you? But I got there first, I turned the tables on you! When we were invited some place, you know what I'd say? I'd say, I'm sorry we won't be able to come tonight. Gordon has a date. I haven't the faintest idea whether it's the same girl or not. You know how men get at that age and poor old Gordon needs a little fling. Heaven knows it's better for some girl who gets paid for it to bear the brunt of it rather than me."

He struggled to his feet, clutching at the palm tree. One of the shoulder seams of his coat ripped. He began to run clumsily across the grass to the driveway.

Elaine stood there under the tree, watching him. It was only when she heard the engine of the car start that she realized his intention, and she began to run after him, waving the hat. The car streaked out of the driveway with Elaine stumbling along behind it. Gordon didn't look back.

She returned to the club, limping. She had turned her ankle while she was running, and it was already beginning to swell. Judge Bowridge was at the checking counter putting on his coat and still humming.

"I was wondering where you disappeared to," Bowridge said. "What's happened to Gordon?"

"He's gone," Elaine said curtly.

"Gone?"

"He took the car and left. We had a disagreement."

"I hope I didn't precipitate it."

"No."

"You must let me drive you home."

"No thanks, I'll call a cab. Do you think I should report it to the police?"

"Report what?"

"Gordon. He's drunk, he shouldn't be driving around in his condition, he might wreck the only car we have. And who knows where he's gone? I could report that my car was stolen, couldn't I?"

"Is it registered under your name?"

"Gordon's."

"Then it isn't stolen, obviously. Now, if a divorce was pending and the car was listed as community property, Gordon could be enjoined from removing it from the premises without your consent, until the community property was equably divided."

"There's no divorce pending, I assure you."

"Then if I were you I'd go home. You'll probably find Gordon there ahead of you."

The checkroom attendant called a cab, and Elaine waited for it outside. It was a long time in coming, and her ankle throbbed, but she couldn't go back inside and face the smiles of her friends. She stood haughtily on the stone steps, holding her head high. She had done what she thought was right in bringing up the subject of the girl, but now that it was done she felt a slight anxiety at the back of her mind. Gordon hadn't reacted as she thought he would. He had made no denials, no protestations of shame; he hadn't promised to give the girl up and never see her again. He simply got in the car and drove off.

She half-expected that the judge was right and that she'd find Gordon at home, already asleep, when she got there. But when the cab stopped in front of the house she saw that the garage doors were still open and the garage was empty. Judith had left her scooter out. It was on the front lawn propped up against the pyracantha bush. Elaine picked it up and put it on the veranda beside Paul's little bicycle. Judith's one-legged doll, Nancy, was seated on the bicycle, draped in one of Paul's sweaters. Elaine looked down at the abandoned toys of her sleeping children, and her throat thickened with regret and a growing fear.

In the dim light of the front room she saw Ruth asleep on the davenport. She had her tweed coat flung over her as a blanket, and she had spread a newspaper on the end of the davenport so that her shoes wouldn't soil the slipcovers.

Elaine knew how nervous Ruth was about intruders, so she turned on another lamp in order that Ruth might see her immediately when she woke up.

"Ruth?"

"Who— Oh, dear." She sat up and put her feet hastily on the floor. "My goodness, you're home early. It's not even midnight."

"A quarter to."

"What happened to your leg?"

"I turned my ankle on the dance floor," Elaine said. "I thought I'd better come home. There was no sense in spoiling Gordon's good time. I took a cab. I'll call you one, when you're ready to leave."

"Oh no," Ruth protested. "I can walk, it's not a bit far." It wasn't, actually, very far, but the nights were dark, and all along the way there were high, dense hedges and massive shrubs. In the daytime they were pretty, with their bright green foliage, but at night they darkened to deep slate and black, shadows within shadows. The least sound, an exploring snail, a gopher, a bird threshing about in the leaves, would send her charging down the street seeking the shelter of the next street lamp. "I can walk," she repeated stubbornly.

"No." Elaine's tone was final, and Ruth felt a deep gratitude toward her. No matter what some people might say, Hazel, for instance, Ruth had always found Mrs. Foster a lady, with a lady's sense of obligation. It was hard for her to believe that the Fosters had quarrels, yet she knew it was true. Not only had Hazel told her, but Judith gave her detailed reports every Saturday night. The child had a wonderful memory, and sometimes she mimicked her mother with appalling cruelty. Ruth would try not to be shocked: "Now, Judith, it isn't nice to imitate people." "Well, she said it, she did so, didn't she, Paul?" "She did so," Paul agreed. "Well, you know," Ruth said, "when we hear something we're not supposed to hear, we must close our ears." "Yes, but my ears won't close," Judith said earnestly.

Ruth got up and folded the newspaper and carried it out to the kitchen. When she returned, Elaine was sitting in the wing chair staring straight ahead of her at the lamp beside the davenport. Ruth glanced at the lamp too, to see if anything was wrong. No, the shade was on straight and there wasn't a speck of dust to be seen.

When she had put her coat on, she said hesitantly, "Well, I guess you won't be needing me anymore tonight. Let's see, I've been here three and a half hours, but we needn't count the half, and you don't have to pay me tonight if it's not convenient."

There was a long pause. Ruth kept buttoning and unbuttoning her coat, nervously. She was beginning to fear the worst—that Mrs. Foster had been drinking.

Without taking her eyes off the lamp, Elaine said, "Why don't you stay here overnight?"

"Here?" Ruth said, immediately flustered. "Overnight? Oh, I couldn't. Hazel's expecting me, and what will Dr. Foster say when he gets home?"

"I don't know. I don't even know whether he's coming home."

"A party can't last forever."

"He isn't at the party," Elaine said in a cold, dry voice. "He took the car and ran away."

"Oh dear."

"He was drunk and we had a fight."

"What a shame." *We must close our ears. Yes, but my ears won't close!* "If he drives around, the air will sober him up."

"I said some things I shouldn't. Some of them were lies. I only lied to protect myself. I didn't want him to think that he'd made a fool of me. I didn't—I tell you I never did say anything to other people about Gordon and his—girl. I pretended she never existed. I never mentioned her, I don't even know her name."

She transferred her eyes, very carefully, as if they would break under any swift movement, from the lamp to Ruth. "You're shocked."

"No, no, I'm not." Ruth's face was burning.

"Yes, you are. So am I. I never thought anything like this would happen to me."

"Perhaps it hasn't," Ruth said anxiously. "Perhaps you're imagining. At certain times in the month I often get depressed and start to imagine the awfullest things, mostly about myself, but about other people too."

"He didn't deny it," Elaine said.

"Oh, but if he was drunk—you can't take drunk people seriously. I wouldn't tell this to another living soul, but my father—drank. That's why I'm a little prejudiced against spirits. My goodness, the things he'd say when he was in his cups. But Mother learned not to take them seriously. She knew that as soon as he'd sobered up he'd be his real self again."

"No, no, this isn't like that." She heard a car coming up the hill. She listened, extremely relieved because she knew it was Gordon. The relief passed and gave way to a deep anger. She was already planning how she'd act and what she'd say, when the car passed the house without a pause.

"Hazel must have known," she said wearily. "Hazel must have said something to you."

"Hazel? My goodness, no. Even if she did know she'd never breathe a word to anyone. Hazel's very loyal, and you know what she thinks of Dr. Foster. She's always said he was a wonderful man."

"And she never mentioned a girl? A young girl?"

Ruth shook her head, embarrassed, uneasy, trying to recall anything that Hazel had said about Dr. Foster. But her remarks were all ordinary: Dr. Foster had removed two impacted wisdom teeth in half an hour; Dr. Foster had gone home early with a cold; one of Dr. Foster's patients was an old lady who talked to herself, and even with her mouth crammed with instruments her words were miraculously clear and articulate; Dr. Foster wondered if Hazel could do anything about getting a job for a friend of his, a young girl, pretty inexperienced.

Ruth frowned, annoyed at herself for remembering this at such an awkward time. It couldn't be the same young girl—Dr. Foster must have hundreds of friends and acquaintances whom he helped. Besides, Hazel said later that George had given the girl a job, and if this girl really was Dr. Foster's kept woman she wouldn't have needed a job, she would be kept. In the back of her mind Ruth saw a fleeting image of a heavily draped, heavily scented boudoir, with a large canopied bed; Dr. Foster would never fit such a place.

"No, really," Ruth said earnestly. "Hazel's never said a word."

"She'd be on Gordon's side anyway." Elaine unpinned the velvet rose in her mantilla, and took the high Spanish comb out of her hair. She held them in her lap, moved by the same feeling she had had when she picked up Judith's abandoned scooter and put it on the veranda; as if something was gone, lost, dead, and only its death gave it any value. "Not that it matters, whose side anybody's on. It isn't a tug-of-war. It isn't a case of me winning if I get twenty people on my side and Gordon has only ten. It's a case of what we are going to do. I pray—" She raised her eyes suddenly to the ceiling, as if she were half-afraid that the person she prayed to was listening in, checking up on her. "I pray every night. I was brought up very religious, but now, I don't know, I seem to have lost my faith, I can't really believe that anyone is listening to me. Or if He is, He's not going to help, He's going to judge me, very harshly."

"You're wrong. I'm sure you're wrong."

"I know I have lots of faults, but I try to restrain myself, I try to be just. I try to be humble too, but I can't. Something comes flooding over me like acid, it's terrible, it spreads all over me. When I'm alone and calm, I think to myself, I will do anything for the sake of my children, I will control myself, I will by sheer determination keep my family together. Then I start thinking about Gordon going to meet that girl in the cafe. That's where they meet, at an awful little place down on lower Main Street. Only drunks go there, and people like Gordon, people with secrets."

Ruth turned her face away. "Perhaps you're just imagining—"

"No. I know it."

"Even so," Ruth said helplessly. "Even so. He might be quite innocent."

"He might be," Elaine said with a sharp laugh. "That's the crazy part of it. I don't even know if anything *happens.* I don't know if they sit there and hold hands and stare at each other, or if they go to her place, or take a room in a hotel, or park down by the ocean." She broke off suddenly, her face squeezed up with pain. "I've always done Gordon's planning for him. I suppose if I wanted to save my reputation, I should have planned this affair of his too. As it is, everyone in town is laughing at me. They never laugh at the man, the one who's making a fool of himself. Oh no! They laugh at the wife, the one who gets left, who gets the wool pulled over her eyes." Tears were burning the inside of her eyelids. She turned off the lamp beside her and said in a controlled voice, "Did the baby take all his bottle?"

"Every drop. Honestly, he's the greediest little angel I ever saw. He must have gained two pounds since I saw him last."

"Nearly."

"Paul didn't want to go to bed after our story was finished, but I told him—" Ruth flushed guiltily. "I told him that maybe next Saturday night I'd bring Wendy, my dog, with me. Would that suit you, Mrs. Foster?"

"I guess so."

"Then I gave him his pretend-dog which he promptly named Wendy, and he popped right off to sleep holding the dog in his arms." She saw the look on Mrs. Foster's face (grief? remorse? fright?) and she added, uncertainly, "If you really want me to stay the night, I'd be glad to."

"It's very kind of you, Ruth."

"I'll just phone Hazel, then, so she won't worry."

She phoned Hazel, and then she tiptoed upstairs to the baby's room. She checked to see if his blankets were straight, she listened to his breathing, and she felt his cool, soft forehead. Then she lay down in her slip, on the cot beside the baby's bed.

11

GORDON SWUNG THE car off the highway and switched off the ignition. He had turned the radio on very loud, to keep him awake. As long as this fast, jerky music continued, he didn't feel like sleeping and he didn't feel like thinking. He didn't know the tune the orchestra was playing but he sang anyway, "chewy, chewy, chewy," and honked the horn to emphasize the rhythm.

By squinting up his eyes and concentrating, he could make out the row of houses along the highway, dark, locked for the night. In one of these houses Ruby was sleeping. He couldn't see very well but he was pretty sure which house it was, so he honked the horn insistently. As if in answer, a train came wailing around the bend, and all other sounds were lost in its dismal echo, Yoo hoo, yoo hoo hoo! The road shuddered, the houses trembled, their windows vibrating like chattering teeth. Long after the light on the caboose had disappeared, Gordon could hear the train mourning its farewell, adieu, adieu! He would have liked to follow the train, driving along the tracks, until he caught up with it. But this was impracticable, he realized. The wheels of the car wouldn't fit the tracks, and even if they did it would be hard to keep on them. And suppose another train came along from behind? It would smash the car to pieces, and Elaine would be mad.

He honked the horn again, to drown out the echo of the train whistle.

In one of the houses a light appeared in an upstairs window. A shadow moved behind the blind, and a minute later a light went on in the downstairs hall. A woman in a bathrobe came out on the porch, carrying a flashlight. She shone the flashlight at the car, then directly into Gordon's face. Gordon blinked. The woman came down the porch steps, cautiously, as if she didn't quite trust them. She was middle-aged, heavily built. Her gray hair swung in pigtails against her shoulders. She had some kind of grease plastered on her neck and around her eyes.

"What do you want?" Mrs. Freeman said. "Waking decent people in the middle of the night, you ought to be ashamed. Turn that radio down, my land, do you want to attract the cops?" She sounded very cross, but it was a surface crossness. Mrs. Freeman was, in fact, rather relieved at seeing a total stranger. When she had wakened to the sound of the horn and the blare of the radio, she'd been half-afraid that it was Robert coming home all of a sudden, as he usually did, with one of his noisy friends.

"What do you want?" she repeated, when Gordon had turned down the radio.

"I want Ruby," Gordon said. "Tell Ruby—you tell Ruby—"

"Ruby's asleep like everyone else with a grain of sense to them. The trouble with you is, you're drunk."

"I know. I know I am. I'm very sorry."

"You better be more careful. There are cops going up and down here all night. The highway patrol is just a couple of blocks up."

"It is?" Gordon said, blinking. "I never knew that."

"Well, you know now. You just skiddoo on home and go to bed like everyone else."

Gordon shook his head, apologetic but obstinate. "I prefer to sleep here. I won't disturb anyone. I'll go to sleep in the car and when Ruby wakes up, you tell her I'm here."

"You can't sleep here. They'll pick you up and put you in jail."

"They can't put me in jail just because I'm very tired."

"You and who else," Mrs. Freeman said in disgust.

"It wouldn't be cricket."

"Go on, skiddoo home now." She fluttered her hand at him as if she were shooing away a chicken. "I got enough trouble without a drunk man being picked up in front of my house." She broke off suddenly and exclaimed, "My land, you aren't even dressed proper!"

"It's because I lost my hat," Gordon said. "I put it down some place and lost it. It belongs to the costume. You see, the costume isn't complete without the hat." He knew that the hat wasn't important to him, yet he was filled with an overwhelming sense of loss. I've lost my hat. I've lost something. I'm no longer a man, Elaine said so. I bear no resemblance to a man.

Mrs. Freeman was staring at him in disapproval. "You people that get drunk at Fiesta time, it's you people that give Fiesta a bad name."

"I'm very sorry." He leaned his head against the back of the seat, closing his eyes. He was sorry. He didn't want to give Fiesta a bad name or to cause Mrs. Freeman any trouble. All his desires of the evening—to sing with Judge Bowridge, to hit Elaine, to cry, to follow the train up the tracks, to go back and find his hat—they had all congealed into one great desire, to go to sleep. But Mrs. Freeman turned the flashlight full on his face again and he had to open his eyes.

"All right," she said in a resigned voice. "I'll go and wake her up. Now don't go off to sleep while I'm gone, will you?" She reached in and shook his arm. "Don't go to sleep now, you promise."

"I promise," Gordon said earnestly. "Tell Ruby—tell Ruby—"

"You tell her yourself," Mrs. Freeman said, and went up the porch steps, muttering under her breath.

He had promised not to go to sleep, and he didn't. He merely closed his eyes and floated, until he heard Ruby opening the door of the car. She was breathing hard, as if she was angry or had hurried to get out of the house.

"Ruby?" He moved his hand towards her in a helpless gesture of appeal.

She took his hand and held it, stroking it very gently, as if she was soothing a hurt. He still wasn't sure whether she was angry or not, until she spoke: "Where ever did you get so dirty?"

He opened his eyes. She was smiling at him, amused. She had her beige coat on over her pajamas, and a scarf around her head to hide the pin curls.

"I was sitting on the ground under a tree," Gordon said.
"I've never seen you dirty before."
"Am I dirty?"
"There's mud on your coat, and see, here's a grass stain on your hand. And your fingernails—you are a disgrace. Mrs. Freeman thinks so anyway."
"I'm very, very sorry," Gordon said. "Would you like some music?"
"All right."
He turned the radio up a little. "There. How do you like that?"
"What did you get drunk for?"
"Oh, now. Oh, now, now, now."
"I just wondered. I've never seen you drunk before either."
"I am full of surprises."
"Well, yes," Ruby said slowly. "I guess you are."
"I'm not going home."
"Nobody said you had to."
"That woman said I did. I said, no—I was very polite, though."
Ruby laughed. "I'm sure you were."
"You're a funny girl. You sound so happy. Let me look at you."
"No," she said, quite sharply, turning her face away. "I haven't any make-up on and my hair's done up."
"Well, *I'm* dirty. That makes us a pair. We're a pair, aren't we, Ruby?"
"Don't say it like that."
"Well, but we are. We're a pair. Both victims. Can't fight back. Soft." He felt something closing in his head, like a sliding door. He saw it closing, slowly and inexorably, and he reached out to stop it. "No character, will power."
He put his head on Ruby's shoulder and watched the door close.
"Chewy, chewy, chewy," Gordon said, and went to sleep.
With her free hand Ruby switched off the headlights of the car and turned off the radio. She saw that Mrs. Freeman was still up, moving around the house, and she thought, with detachment, *She will probably ask me to move. I'll have to move again. Well, that's all right.*
She sat listening to the beat of Gordon's heart and the ticking of the dashboard clock, until Mrs. Freeman came outside again. She was carrying a cup of coffee, and the flashlight. The steam rose from the coffee like mist.
"Well," she said. "Well. I guess you know him, eh?"
Ruby nodded.
"I made some coffee. Here."
"Thanks, thanks ever so much."
"It will sober him up." She stared at Ruby. There was hostility in her face, but a certain stoical tolerance too. Facts were facts, and she might disapprove of the fact of a drunken man outside her house, but there he was. "What will the neighbors think?"
"There's no one up, no lights."
"They're probably all peeking out the windows. I have a hard enough time holding my head up."
"I'll move," Ruby said. "I'll move out tomorrow if you want me to."
"It's not your fault," Mrs. Freeman said soberly. "My land, the things that happen. The things that happen that aren't really anybody's fault." She sighed. "What's his name?"
"Gordon."
She went over to the other side of the car and, grasping Gordon's left arm, she pulled him to a sitting position, saying his name over and over in a stern whisper: "Gordon. Wake up, Gordon. Gordon! Now you just sit up, Gordon."

She shook him until his eyes opened. Then she held him upright while Ruby fed him the coffee. Whenever she saw a car approaching Mrs. Freeman switched off the flashlight and the three of them were left in the darkness.

They put him to bed on the studio couch in Mrs. Freeman's dining room. He lay on his side, with his legs drawn up. His shirt stuck out from the ripped seam of his coat, and he slept with his cheek resting on his grass-stained, muddy hands. Ruby covered him with two blankets.

"Look like kids when they're sleeping," Mrs. Freeman said with a kind of bitter melancholy. "I guess he'll be warm enough with two blankets. Anyway, it's all I have."

"He'll be fine. I—it's—it's very nice of you—letting him stay."

"I couldn't do anything else."

"It's very nice of you not to be mad."

"I *am* mad," Mrs. Freeman said decisively. "I *am* mad. But I don't know who at."

She flung a look of disapproval at the sleeping Gordon, but Ruby stepped between her and the couch, as if to shield Gordon. "He wouldn't put anyone out like this intentionally," she said. "He never would. Something must have happened."

"Something always does." Mrs. Freeman pulled the chain hanging from the beaded chandelier. "Always. Well, no matter. There's some coffee left, if you want some."

"Yes, I would. Thanks very much."

"We'll have to drink it in the kitchen. We don't want to wake him up. Who knows, he might come to life and want to dance and make whoopee. You can't tell with drunks."

"He's not a drunk," Ruby said stubbornly. "He hardly ever drinks. Something must have happened."

The kitchen was cold and damp. Mrs. Freeman lit the gas oven and left the oven door open. Then she poured the coffee, and the two of them sat facing each other across the linoleum-covered table. The table had already been set for Mrs. Freeman's solitary breakfast. None of the dishes matched—they were the surviving odds and ends of old sets, the remnants of the years. The salt shaker was shaped like an orange, the pepper shaker was silver plate, with some of the silver still clinging to its surface. Her cup was a shaving mug left behind by one of her tourists. Repeated washings in hot water had peeled away some of the lettering on it but it was still partly legible, Gr in s f El so, Texas. Her knife and fork belonged to her wedding present from her father, a set of silver, but the spoon didn't match. It had been a gift from Robert several years ago. He had arrived home unexpectedly one morning, broke, without a suitcase, without anything: *Carrie, it's me. Now don't be sore, Carrie, don't be like that. Look, I brought you something, it's a present, Carrie.* He had wrapped the spoon up carefully in tissue paper and tied it with a broken shoelace. He watched her eagerly while she unwrapped it. *I hope you like it, Carrie. You're always saying we need some decent silver.* The spoon bore the imprint "Hilton Hotels." *I knew you'd be pleased.*

She picked up the spoon now and stirred some sugar in her coffee. She felt a savage anger welling in her stomach. It spread down her arm into her hand, making her stir the coffee violently.

"I don't know who at," she said, as if to herself. "In the daytime it's all right. I write my letters and make the beds and do my work. I'm not bothered. It's when the night comes on that I begin to worry. It's funny out here—as soon as the sun goes down it gets cold. Not like back home where you could sit on the porch in the twilight and rock a bit. No, out here it gets cold right away, a kind of bleakness sets in. Such a change, all of a sudden, it makes you kind of scared that the sun's not going to come out again the next day. I'm getting like all the other old fogies around here, I depend on the weather too much, like it's a religion. It creeps up on you, gradual, and you get superstitious—like, if the sun shines, well, that's good, there's still plenty of life left in the old girl, that's how you feel. Dying seems awfully far away when I go out into the backyard in the morning and the sun warms my head. I feel quite youthful and confident, like God was smiling at me." She added curtly, "Downright heathenish. A graven image."

She sipped her coffee, a cool and bitter syrup that soured at the base of her throat.

"So something must have happened," she said. "Yes. It always does. Excuses, I know all the excuses there are in this world. He's married, I suppose."

Ruby said, "Yes."

"And what's to happen now?"

"I don't know. It's up to Gordon." She traced the pattern of the linoleum with her forefinger. "He's the one that has to figure things out. He's got ties, other people to think about, and I haven't."

With an air of impatience Mrs. Freeman got up and rinsed out the coffee cups at the sink.

"Not anyone I care about," Ruby said.

"And that nice Mr. Anderson—" She turned off the oven and banged the door shut. "Well, that's the way it goes. You better set your alarm early. Miss Hodgins gets up at seven and I don't want her to find him sleeping on the couch like that. It wouldn't look right, him in costume and everything."

"I'll get up at six."

"Well, good night then."

"Mrs. Freeman—thanks for all your kindness."

"Kindness," Mrs. Freeman said. "You're going to need more than kindness before you're through. Well. I told you I get feeling blue at night like this, don't pay any attention to me. Goodnight."

"Goodnight."

Ruby set her alarm for six. Then she took off her coat and hung it in the closet, moving slowly because she dreaded to go to bed and lie in the darkness, thinking. *I get feeling blue at night like this.* She would have liked to read for a while but there was no reading light in the room. The crudely painted Mexican pottery lamp on the bureau didn't work, and the only other light in the room was the ceiling light with a chain suspended from it. The chain was too short to reach, so someone had tied a strip of pink cloth to the end of it. Ruby pulled the strip of cloth, then lay on the bed with her eyes open, wondering why Gordon had come and what he was going to do.

We're a pair, both victims, can't fight back. In the darkness she shook her head violently as if Gordon was there to witness her denial. In the same motion she denied Mrs. Freeman too: *You're going to need more than kindness.*

No, no, her head rocked back and forth on the pillow. *They don't understand about me, I'm tough. I'm tough.*

When she came downstairs in the morning Gordon was already awake. He was sitting on the couch holding his head in his hands. She came toward him, very shyly, as if she were half-afraid he wouldn't remember who she was.

"Are you all right, Gordon?"

"I'm fine."

She sat down beside him. He was pale and his eyes were bloodshot. The pulse in his temple was beating hard and fast.

"Thanks for letting me sleep here," he said. "What time is it?"

"A little after six."

"The beginning of a new day." He turned to look at her, smiling. "You brushed your hair out. Last night you had a scarf around it, you looked very pretty."

"I didn't think you'd remember."

"I remember everything, I think. I've got to go out and buy some clothes."

"It's Sunday."

"I forgot. Well, I've got an old outfit at the office, I can wear that."

"You have clothes at home."

"I'm not going home. It's too bad it's Sunday. That's going to make things harder, getting some money, etcetera."

"Why do you need money today?"

"I told you, I'm not going home. I'm running away, I suppose you'd call it. I haven't run away since I was seven and I've forgotten how you go about it, but I think money is pretty essential. I hope you'll come with me, will you, Ruby?"

"Gordon—listen Gordon, you're not still sort of half-drunk?"

"I'm sober."

"What about Elaine? Did you talk to her?"

"Yes, we had quite a talk," Gordon said dryly. "Last night."

"Did you tell her you were going away? With me?"

"No, I'm going to let her be surprised."

She looked at him anxiously for a moment. "Gordon, what is this? Are we just going on a little holiday, or are we going to stay together for good? I know, maybe I shouldn't ask that—"

"We're staying together. God knows what she'll do. I'm hoping she'll get a divorce. I'm hoping she'll realize when I'm gone that that's what she's wanted all along." He got to his feet. His head felt heavy and brittle, and for a minute he could see nothing but blackness shot with flashes of light. But his physical discomfort merely accentuated the peace in his mind. Elaine had freed him. She didn't intend to, but she had, and now he was free. He said, "We'll drive over to my office for some clothes and then we'll have breakfast, I'll bring you back here and you can pack your things while I'm trying to gather together some money."

"I haven't much to pack."

"More than I have." He glanced down at her, smiling at her earnestness. He would have liked to bend over and kiss her but he was afraid his head might split in two. He put his hands on her shoulders. "We'll never come back to this town, Ruby."

"We'll have to. This is where your work is."

"I'll sell my practice and start another one, wherever you want to go."

"I'll help you," she said. "I'll work hard."

"We'll start all over. I hate this town, I never want to see it again."

She stared up at him, thinking, he will never love me the way I do him, I am looking forward just to being with him, and he's looking forward to getting away from Elaine—not the town, he doesn't hate the town, it's just that she's in it. But it doesn't matter. I'm lucky and I'm tough.

She turned away and began to fold the blankets on the couch. A desert wind had begun to blow over the mountains in the middle of the night and the blankets felt dry and dusty. Everything in the house was covered with a film of powdered sand, and there was a rawness in Ruby's throat and nasal passages.

When they went outside the wind was still blowing, warm and furious. Gordon's car was gray with dust, and still the dirt came spinning along the road. The houses trembled, as if a procession of freight cars was lunging up the tracks.

The keys were in the car.

"It's a nice day to get out of town," Gordon said.

They drove to his office and Ruby waited in the car while he went inside. It was quite a while before he returned, wearing the gabardine slacks and shirt that he kept for golfing. He looked very stern when he got back into the car.

"Gordon, you're sorry to be leaving?"

"No," he said quietly. "I was just looking around for the last time. Sentimental, isn't it? I'm not sorry I'm leaving. I would just like to take some things with me. It's funny how you can get attached to an electric machine. Habit, ownership."

"You don't have to sell your practice, Gordon. Couldn't we just go away for a while and then we could come back and you could start to work just where you left off?"

"That's the hard way."

"Why? You haven't tried it. People in this day and age don't look down on a man for living with a woman."

"An insurance man, maybe not, or a truck driver. But a schoolteacher, a doctor, a dentist—it's not enough to be able to teach or perform an operation or fill a tooth. We have to set an example. This isn't L.A. or Hollywood, Ruby. They're a hundred miles and fifty million light years away. My ability to fill teeth isn't half as important as my morals." He shook his head. "No, I couldn't swing it, I'm too soft. It would hurt me if they said, 'I certainly will not pay him any five dollars for cleaning my teeth just so he can spend it on that woman he's living with.' Don't look surprised. People are funny, they're pretty hard on people who do some of the things they themselves would like to do. So what I'd get if I stayed here is just that—unpaid bills, patients who want a bargain because they figure I couldn't afford not to cut my prices, and maybe a few new patients who believe that any dentist who lives in sin should be willing to sell drugs on the side. No, I couldn't face it."

He added, after a time, "I don't dare hope she'll divorce me. She doesn't believe in divorce, but there's a chance, maybe, if she can come to believe that it would be better for her, too. It would be, of course. She'll never be happy living only to spite me. It's funny about Elaine. I think that if she'd never married me she'd have been all right. She wouldn't be so filled with vengeance and petty spite. Maybe even yet she will have some kind of decent life with a little softness in it." A gust of wind blew a piece of newspaper against the windshield. It shivered there for a minute and then lurched wildly off down the street. "Where would you like to have breakfast?"

"Any place that's open," Ruby said.

They drove down Main Street. The sun had already risen and in the distance they saw the sheen of the ocean. But the town looked dead, parched by the hot wind. Along the curb were abandoned cars under a pall of dust. Two women were hurrying across the street heading into the wind, shielding their eyes with their hands. An old man sat on a bench at a bus stop, like a victim resigned to the sacrifice, his legs apart, his lunch pail resting on his stomach, his head thrown back with his neck ready for the knife. The old man moved, coughed, spat into the gutter. A cardboard box rolled down the sidewalk and a piece of ripped awning flapped against a store window. A painted sign swung in the wind, squeaking on its hinges. The supple palm trees leaned to the ocean, their fronds streaming out like seaweed, and the air was filled with a continuous rustling noise.

It wasn't a very high wind, like the wind that came in from the ocean and blew the fog off the top of the mountains and cluttered the beaches with kelp and stranded starfish and pieces of tar from the underwater oil wells. Gordon liked the sea winds, they were natural, they suited the town. But the desert wind was an intruder, an alien from the other side of the mountain. Sometimes it hung around for days, like an unwelcome guest in the house who produced tension but must be tolerated. Gordon felt the tension in his hands as they gripped the steering wheel, and in his throat which seemed swollen and grimy.

Yet he was grateful to the wind, too. It was a good day to be leaving, a day when the town looked unnatural, squalid, hidden under scurf. He let his mind dwell, deliberately, on the things he didn't like in the town. Over on Gioconda Street, where the highway bisected the town, lay the nucleus of the slum section. Here lived the Negroes, the Mexicans, and the remnants of what had once been a large Chinese community, in sagging shacks and chicken houses and barns. These slums were worse than anything he had ever seen even in the large cities. If they had existed in Chicago or New York, at least some attention might have been drawn to them, but here they were ignored. The rickety children played in the dirt on Gioconda Street and went to school when they had clothes and shoes to wear, or to the General Hospital if they got sick enough. The town bulged with doctors and elaborate clinics, but many of the residents of the slums felt that it was easier to die than to make the long trek out to the General Hospital and wait all day for a turn, only to be told to eat more eggs and T-bone steaks, take a long rest free from worry, go to Arizona, wear a custom-made truss, buy contraceptives, take vitamin pills. Every Saturday morning they came to Gordon's office for free dental treatment and Gordon had come to dread this day in the week because he, too, had to give them impossible advice: *If you could try to keep Susie off carbohydrates, Mrs. Haley. Sure, sure, Doc. Say, I still got this awful pain in my side and I been told I oughta have an operation on my insides but I got my cleaning jobs to do, I can't take no time off with all those mouths to feed.*

He forced himself to think of Mrs. Haley. When she first came to the office she had the holes in her teeth plugged with candle wax. She had all her children with her, for moral support, and Gordon had given them each a ride in the dental chair, two at a time.

Thinking of Mrs. Haley, he was sure that he hated this pretentious little town. It wore culture on its head like an ageing, kittenish dowager, wearing a picture hat with artificial roses, and needing a good hot bath.

He was glad to be leaving.

The only place they could find open was the lunch room across from the S. P. station. The counter was already half-filled with railroad men. They talked back and forth to each other and to the two waitresses. One of the men took a snapshot out of his wallet and passed it to the stout waitress.

"Gee whiz," she exclaimed. "They're cute! They're as cute as bugs! You musta had a good-looking iceman." She handed the picture to Ruby. "Pass it along, will you? It's Joe's twins."

Joe's twins were standing in a playpen wearing identical expressions of surprise.

"They *are* cute," Ruby said. "Aren't they, Gordon?"

Gordon glanced briefly at the picture and passed it on.

"They don't like to have their pictures took," Joe explained. "Maybe scared of the camera."

"G'wan," said the waitress. "You probably beat them. G'wan, admit it."

"You're a great kidder," Joe said.

The waitress brought Ruby and Gordon some scrambled eggs. She had a good-natured, careless attitude that reminded Gordon of Hazel. He hadn't, until that moment, thought of trying to get some money through Hazel. Hazel wouldn't have any herself, not enough anyway, but if he gave her a check she might be able to cash it through George Anderson.

Without tasting his eggs, he went to the phone booth and dialed Hazel's number.

12

GEORGE DIDN'T GET up till noon on Sundays, and when the phone started ringing before eight he struggled out of bed, cursing.

"George? It's Hazel. Are you all right?"

"Why shouldn't I be?"

"Oh, I don't know. Sometimes you take things like last night kind of hard and I wanted to make sure you were feeling all right because I've got something important to ask you."

"Ask ahead."

"I need some money for a friend of mine. Today. Right now."

"How much?"

"Five hundred dollars."

"You give me a pain," George said.

"Listen to the deal first before you blow a fuse."

"I'm listening."

"Well, this friend of mine is going on a holiday. He intended to leave tomorrow but he's got this chance to leave today and he needs five hundred dollars. He's giving me a check and I'd like you to lend me the money so I can give it to him, and then tomorrow morning I'll cash the check at the bank and pay you back. See?"

"It sounds damned peculiar. I can scare up the money, maybe, but why the complications?"

"Because. Will you do it, George?"

"No."

"For heaven's sake, why not?"

"If your friend wants five hundred dollars bring him over here. Then if he has an honest face and a reasonable balance in his bank book, I'll cash a check for him."

"No. It's better the way I suggested."

"Why?"

"Well, he has a joint account with his wife, see, and his wife doesn't know yet that he's going away. If the check's made out to me I can be at the bank sharp at ten when the doors open, and if I see her there I can just push ahead of her."

"Holy catfish."

"That's what he told me," Hazel said, stubbornly. "If his wife suspects that he's going away she might try and draw out all the money before this check can be cashed. Now do you understand?"

"It sounds like a perfect set-up for you to keep your nose out of."

"Wait a minute, I want to close the dining-room door. I think Josephine and Harold are getting up." There was a pause. "It's all right now. They can't hear."

"What difference would it make if they did?"

"This friend of mine doesn't want everybody to know his business."

"He's running out on his wife, is that it?"

"Yes."

"Why?"

"My gosh, George, do you have to know everything?"

"Five hundred bucks," George said, "is five hundred bucks."

"He's got his reasons."

"I hope you know what you're doing, aiding and abetting whatever you're aiding and abetting."

"I know, all right." She thought how surprised he would be if he knew too. She felt a little sorry for George that he should have to finance Ruby's and Gordon's trip, but it was, actually, for his own good. Eventually he'd be glad and realize that Ruby would never have married him anyway. "It's a matter of principle," she said, her conscience leaping slightly. "Will you get the money, George?"

"I guess I can try."

"You'll do it. You have hundreds of friends."

"I can't think of a better way of losing them."

"Everyone's going to be paid back. This friend of mine is a very respectable man. Just because he's leaving his wife doesn't mean he's a crook."

"All right. I said I'd try."

"Shall I pick it up at your apartment?"

"No." He didn't want Hazel to see the apartment in its present condition. It hadn't been cleaned for a month. "How about meeting me at the Beachcomber?"

"When?"

"In an hour or so."

"I'll be there."

"I still hope you know what you're doing," George said gloomily.

"You're always such a pessimist where money's concerned."

"Five hundred bucks is—"

"Yes, I know, George. Anyway, this is very nice of you. I appreciate it. I'll do something for you someday."

"Cut the violins," George said and hung up.

He got dressed and made his breakfast. This was the part of living alone that he hated most, getting up to an empty apartment and having to make his own breakfast. When they were married Hazel had always cooked very elaborate breakfasts. She told everyone that George had a large frame to fill, and she filled it, in the mornings, with hot cakes and sausages and fried potatoes and blueberry muffins.

The kitchen was a mess and the refrigerator smelled sour, jammed with odds and ends of stale food. He managed to find three eggs, one of them cracked. He fried them while the coffee percolated. Some day he'd have to clean out the refrigerator but he didn't know how to go about it. It seemed kind of drastic to take everything out, and he wondered if women had some special easy system for cleaning out refrigerators, and what they did about the smell.

While he was drinking his coffee he counted the money in his wallet. Forty-seven dollars. That meant shopping around for the difference, four hundred and fifty-three dollars. There was some cash in the safe at the Beachcomber but he had made it a rule not to touch any of it and not to borrow any money from the till even for twenty-four hours. It was the kind of thing that, once started, was hard to stop, and he was afraid his partners wouldn't like it if they found out.

He thought of two men who would be likely to have quite a bit of cash over a Sunday. One was a small-time gambler who played poker every Saturday night in the back of a Chinese herb shop. The gambler lived with his sister who didn't approve of gambling. She took his winnings, when she could find them, and gave them to the church and to relatives. She had become so skillful at finding his hiding places that the gambler was occasionally compelled to leave his money with George over the weekend.

The other man was a fisherman called Mix. He was the co-owner of a small Monterey fishing boat that went out to the islands for two or three days at a time. He'd been bringing in eleven or twelve hundred pounds of lobsters from every trip. George had seen him yesterday morning on the way to Vasco's fish market to settle up his accounts for the past two weeks. He figured that Mix, after deducting expenses, should have around five hundred dollars as his share. Like a lot of other fishermen, Mix hated to put his money in the bank right away. He liked to keep it around and look at it, though sometimes, if he was afraid he was going out to get stewed, he gave George some of his money to keep for him. The rest he went out and spent. As soon as he had two or three drinks, Mix suffered an acute attack of generosity. He bought presents for all his relatives back in Missouri, and shipped them off, live turtles, chocolates, clothes, toys, souvenirs of Channel City. He picked up all kinds of people in bars and bought them drinks and promised them free lobsters. Once he bought up all the papers a newsboy was selling and sent the boy home. The newspapers were heavy to carry, so Mix gave them away to various people. He'd brought a gift to George once, a second-hand set of the Harvard Classics. They were the only books George owned.

When Mix was stone broke he returned to his boat to sleep, and the next morning he would get the rest of his money from George and put it in the bank. George didn't like to throw anything away, so he had a whole drawerful of receipts that Mix had returned to him when George handed back the money. *Received from Mix Jorgen, to be held in trust until Monday, the sum of Two Hundred Dollars, signed, George Anderson. Mix Jorgen gave me $175.50 to keep for him, signed, George Anderson.*

George put the forty-seven dollars back in his wallet. He felt suddenly very annoyed with Hazel, not because she'd asked him to do her a favor, but because she shared his own weakness. She was always getting involved with people. He didn't like the sound of the five hundred dollar deal. He and Hazel could easily be left holding the bag.

He got the car out of the garage and drove down to the wharf to find Mix.

George left his car in the small parking lot beside the Beachcomber. He didn't like to take it beyond this point, because further on some of the holes in the planking had been covered up by thick pieces of board nailed to the planking. When one of the fish trucks hit these boards it bounced in the air, making the whole dock shudder. George preferred to walk.

The wharf was fairly quiet. The amateur fishermen were already lined up at the edge, beside the signs: "No Fishing." "Absolutely No Fishing." "No Fishing Beyond This Point." As George walked on, the fish odors became stronger. A pile of empty abalone shells lay stinking in the sun. The conveyor machines, silvered with scales, smelled of dried fish blood. A young Mexican girl, all dressed up in a tight flowered crepe dress, was tying on some bait which she kept in an abalone shell. The bait was gray and black and it smelled worse than anything George had ever smelled. A small lobster boat was tied up alongside, waiting to unload. The lobsters trailed along behind the boat in crates made of laths.

He found Mix sitting against the wall of the warehouse, smoking a pipe and reading a magazine. He was a man about forty, a Middle Westerner who hadn't seen the ocean until the war. Although he'd been a fisherman now for two years, he was still self-conscious about it. When he was not on his boat he spent hours hanging around the wharf, trying to get over the feeling that he was an impostor. He wore rubber boots, a cowboy hat, a corduroy shirt and dirty army pants.

"Improving your mind?" George said.

Mix threw down the magazine and yawned. "Habit. I started reading in the army and I can't get over it. It's a disease, like."

"How's business?"

"Hell, fishing's no business, it's a bum's game. For the little guys like me, anyhow. Look." He held out his hands. They were covered with scars and scabs and cuts. One of the cuts looked infected. "Fish poisoning. Listen, George, you take a good look at these hands and figger you're lucky to be in a white-collar racket. Sweet Jesus, the way I work! And for what? Thirty-five cents a pound for lobster from Vasco when I could be getting forty-five at San Pedro. People like you, George, you think fishing is just sitting around sailing over the ocean blue. Sweet Jesus, if I was a sensible guy I'd go back in the army so I could do my reading by electric lights again and my pay'd come in regular instead of in fits and starts, and I wouldn't have nothing to do with octopuses. Those things, Jesus, they get me. They get in the pots, see, and I have to gaff them. The other day one of them got me on the arm with one of his suckers. I nearly died," he said solemnly. "I wouldn't tell this to everybody, but when that thing got onto my arm I nearly died."

He tapped the ashes out of his pipe for emphasis. "Eels too, I don't like. Lobsters, now there's something pretty about lobsters. You take a big fifteen-pound bull and watch him flopping around, he looks kinda noble. No sneaking suckers on him, by God."

"What was the take yesterday?" George said.

"Not so good. I figure this way, somebody's been robbing our pots, and it ain't just starfish and eels and octopuses, it's human. So help me Jesus, if I ever catch them I'll use the gaff on them. Last time we only brought in eight hundred pounds."

"Did you settle up with Vasco yesterday?"

"Sure."

"How much?"

"Jesus, I don't ask you how much you—"

"I need some cash until tomorrow."

"We may be going out tomorrow."

"Don't kid me," George said. "You wouldn't go out without putting the money in the bank and by the time the bank's open you'll have your money back, Boy Scout's honor."

"I used to be a Boy Scout," Mix said reminiscently. "Back in St. Louis. The pride of Troop Twenty-Two, and look at me now. I haven't had a bath in a month. I wash, sure, but washing's not like having a hot bath. Maybe some day I'll get me a nice little apartment in town with a bathroom and a kitchen with a refrigerator, cook myself some decent meals for a change. Like this morning, you know what Pete and I had for breakfast? We figured on bacon and eggs, see, with toast. We bring out the bacon and it's moldy. No butter, no lard. The bread don't look so good and the eggs are getting kinda old. So Pete cooks them anyway, scrambles them in Dago red to hide the flavor. Sweet Jesus, it's a wonder my stomach ain't rotting away."

"How do you know it's not?" George said.

"I'm feeling pretty good. I feel pretty good all over except my hand is sore." He pulled up his shirt and unfastened the money belt he wore around his middle. "How much do you want?"

"Four hundred and fifty-three dollars."

"I'll see if I got that much."

He counted his money, while George watched him, amused. Mix knew down to a cent how much money he had in the belt. When he wasn't drinking he was inclined to be careful of money, and George knew that Mix, like a lot of other fishermen around the dock who looked like bums, had a very pretty bank balance.

"Yeah," Mix said. "Yeah, I think I got that much."

"You know damn well you have."

"I have to be sure, don't I? Here. That's four fifty-seven. Now you give me an I. O. U."

George wrote an I. O. U. on the back of an envelope. Mix folded the envelope and put it in his money belt with the air of a man who has made a very bad bargain.

"You'll have it back tomorrow," George said. "On the honor of Troop Twenty-Two."

He showed signs of wanting to leave, but Mix pretended not to notice. Mix was in a conversational mood. Often when he was alone on the boat or at one of the fishing camps over in the islands, he planned conversations. He seldom had a chance to use them because the right situation never turned up and it was hard finding a good listener.

"With me," Mix said, "with me money is a very personal thing. I'm not tight, don't get that idea."

"God forbid."

"No sir. It's like this. When you make money the hard way like I do, you get kinda interested in what happens to it. I mean, you own it, see, you hold it in your hands maybe a couple of days and then off it goes. Maybe you put it in the bank or lend it to somebody or spend it. No matter what, you have a real personal interest in what happens to it because it belongs to you. For example, if I put a hundred dollars in the bank I like to think of all those bills working and accumulating interest, bringing home the bacon to Poppa. It's almost like they were kids I was sending out into the world. See what I mean, George?"

"I think so."

"It don't sound nuts to you?"

"No." George patted the pocket containing his wallet. "These kids of yours are going on a trip."

Mix was pleased.

"Yeah? Where?"

"Missouri."

"Missouri? Well, I'll be goddamned, that's where I come from, St. Louis. Going on an airplane, even?"

"Absolutely."

"Well, I'll be goddamned." Mix shook his head. "How's that for a coincidence, me coming from Missouri and my money going to Missouri. On a plane, too. I never been on a plane."

"I've gotta shove off now, Mix."

"What's your hurry?"

"Well, the plane's leaving pretty soon and the kids here don't want to miss it. They're raising hell in my pocket."

Mix threw back his head and roared. As soon as George left Mix tried to tell a couple of dockhands about the joke, but even though he explained it right from the beginning and told them how funny it was, they didn't laugh.

George walked carefully across the wharf toward the Beachcomber. The money in his pocket felt heavy and he had half a notion to give it back to Mix, but he couldn't think of any logical explanation to offer Hazel: *Listen, Hazel, I've got a funny feeling about this money, we shouldn't mess with it, I've got a hunch . . .*

Although it was not yet nine o'clock the Beachcomber was open and Willie was behind the bar straining a martini for the lone customer, an elderly man wearing rimless spectacles and a wrinkled tuxedo.

Neither Willie nor the man paid any attention to George. They were both intent on the work in progress like alchemists about to test the results of a new formula.

"Here you are," Willie said. "Very dry, like you asked for, Judge."

"I did not say very dry. My exact words were very, *very* dry. Subtle difference there, lad."

"Yes sir, but a martini can only get so dry. When it gets drier, it's straight gin."

"Mere rhetoric. A splitting of the hair of the dog that bit me." Judge Bowridge laughed softly to himself. "You forgot the olives, lad. Three, if you please, on the side."

"Yes sir."

"One should never drink without eating. I learned that at my mother's knee. Anton, she said, Anton, promise me by your dear dead father's mustache, that you will never drink a martini without olives on the side. I have never violated that sacred trust."

He picked up the first olive, slipped it off the toothpick and swallowed it whole like an aspirin. It made a little squeaking noise as it passed down his throat.

"Delicious," he said.

Willie went down to the other end of the counter where George was changing into his white coat. He meant to say something unpleasant and cutting to George for running out on the business the night before but he was afraid to. Instead, he glanced back sourly at Bowridge. "He was sitting on the steps outside when I opened up. I had to let him in."

"How'd he get here?"

"God knows. His car's not around."

"I'll take care of him." George took Willie's place behind the bar. "Good morning, Judge."

"Oh, there you are, Anderson. I was inquiring after your health just a moment ago. Willie informs me you keep well."

"Well enough."

"I am delighted to hear it. There are altogether too many half-dead people running around these days."

"You been up all night, Judge?"

Bowridge took off his spectacles and rubbed them thoughtfully on his coat sleeve. "Now that you mention it, I don't seem to recall going to bed. I was at a party."

"The party still going on?"

"Oh, no, no, no. It wasn't that type of party. It was, frankly, a lugubrious affair. Weak drinks and dull women. Bad combination. I tried to help matters by singing a few songs. Do you happen to know 'Chewy Chewy'?"

"Not offhand."

"A very spirited number. Like this." He snapped his fingers in time to an invisible orchestra. "Gordon Foster and I perfected a duet. You know Foster."

"Not personally. Hazel's mentioned him to me."

"An interesting fellow. Fine tenor voice, but unable to hold his liquor. The trouble with Foster is that he doesn't eat when he drinks." As if to set a good example, Bowridge swallowed the remaining two olives, pits and all, as he had the first. "How is Hazel?"

"Fine. I expect her here any minute."

"Ah. In what capacity?"

"Not what you're thinking," George said dryly.

"I've been acquainted with Hazel for a great many years."

"I know that."

"She's a remarkable woman."

"I know that, too."

"Frankly, Anderson—you don't mind if I speak frankly?"

"No."

"Well then, frankly, I never wanted to sign those divorce papers, Anderson, no, I did not. Oh, I signed them all right, but my heart wasn't in it. I kept putting it off until it was time to go home. My secretary said, you haven't signed these papers yet, and I said, goddamn it, I won't sign them, there's no reason on earth why these two people shouldn't stay married. And she said, you should have thought of that while court was in session, the case is over. And so it was. I signed the papers."

George turned away, looking stubborn and a little resentful. "It was Hazel's idea, not mine."

"So it would seem."

"So it *was*," George said stiffly. "You want to know what happened?—the real thing, I mean, not what Hazel's lawyer said in court."

"I would be very interested."

"Well, I was late getting home one Saturday night and Hazel was waiting up for me in the front room. I was just sitting there having a beer and some potato chips and telling her a few odd things that happened during the day, and suddenly she got up, walked over to me and said, 'I'm getting damn good and tired of your boyish blubberings.' Just like that. Out of a blue sky."

"A most provocative remark. What did you do?"

"Finished my beer and potato chips and went to bed. What else? She was spoiling for a fight."

"She may simply have wanted your attention."

"She wanted a divorce, she got it," George said. "Let's forget it."

"As you wish." Bowridge finished his martini and pushed the empty glass toward George. "One more, very, very dry. And do not look at me askance. *De gustibus non disputandum. De mortuis nil nisi bonum.*"

"Maybe I'd better call you a cab."

"You may call me a whole fleet of cabs if you like," Bowridge said graciously. "It's only fair to warn you, however, that I have no intention of leaving. I must wait for Hazel. Besides, I like it here. The sea air is very bracing. It makes me feel alive and nimble."

He inhaled deeply and extravagantly, opening his mouth wide to receive the bracing air. But his ageing lungs were not accustomed to such largess; he began to cough, pressing both hands against his chest as if to ease its troubles. His face looked pale and withdrawn and he seemed suddenly to have lost interest in George and the martini and the bracing air, in everything but himself. The judge was as ignorant of his body as he was aware of his mind, and this periodic rebellion inside his chest mystified and frightened him. If the day was warm and bright, and his calendar easy, he jeered at the cough, it was nothing. But on a day with a crowded calendar and pellets of rain exploding on the tiled roof of the courtroom so violently he could hardly hear what was going on inside, the cough was death, it had come like the bailiff to take him away, and away he would go, down long corridors to a dark and single cell.

"Devilish thing—don't know what—causes it—maybe —the olives—did the olives—have pits?"

"Yes."

"That's it then—the pits have—lodged somewhere—devilish—damn."

He coughed for a full minute, and when he had finished he took off his spectacles, wiped the moisture out of his eyes with a handkerchief. His chest was a little sore and his throat raw, but, having convinced himself that the cause was nothing more serious than an unfortunate lodging of olive pits, he felt quite cheerful again; the bailiff and the dark cell were years and miles away, the cough was nothing, the pits, wherever they were, would dissolve. A very dry martini would no doubt assist in their dissolution.

The judge repeated his order and when the martini came he sipped it very slowly and gravely as if it were medicine which had been prescribed for him and which he had to take whether he liked it or not.

George went out to the telephone booth in the foyer and called a cab. Through the window in the top of the door he could see Hazel's blue Chevy coming toward the Beachcomber, bouncing over the worn planks of the wharf like a jeep. With a familiar feeling of irritation he watched her as she tried to park. Back and forth she maneuvered, three times, four times, and when she had finished the Chevy was still a good four feet from the wharf railing and straddling two parking spaces.

He opened the door and crossed the parking area. Hazel was just getting out of the Chevy, panting a little from exertion. She hadn't dressed up as she usually did when she came to the Beachcomber. Her hair was tied up in a scarf, and she wore faded blue jeans, a striped T-shirt which had once belonged to Harold and a pair of rhinestone-studded sunglasses which she had borrowed from Josephine since Josephine was too sunburned to go out today anyway.

She gave George a long direct stare as if challenging him to make any remarks about her costume or the way she'd parked the car.

George could never resist a challenge. "You're going to leave it *there?*"

"I don't see why not."

"Look, all you've got to do when you want to park is pull up parallel with the car ahead, back in toward the curb until your engine is just about even with the rear window of the other car, then come to a full stop, reverse your wheel and—"

"That's exactly what I did, and anyway you told me all that before."

"You couldn't have done it like that or we wouldn't be standing out here in the middle of the road."

Hazel colored slightly. "You seem to be pretty burned up about something. Is it the money?"

"No. And I'm not burned up."

"You're acting like it. It's not my fault if I can't park right. I do everything just like you taught me, but it doesn't work out."

"It isn't the parking. It's—" It was everything; it was the judge, the money, Ruby, it was life itself. "Hell, I don't care if you park in the center of 101. It's your funeral."

"Thanks."

He turned away, squinting up at the sun. "I guess I owe you something for last night. I guess you did your best."

"I'd just as soon forget about it."

"So would I."

"Did you—you got the money all right?"

"Yes, sure." He hesitated. "You want it now, or have you got time to come in for a drink?"

"I don't know, it's kind of early. The whole five hundred, did you get?"

"Here it is. Count it."

"No. No, really—"

"Count it, go on."

She counted the money quickly and put it in the back pocket of her jeans as if she was trying to get it out of sight as fast as possible.

"I don't want to pry," George said, "but I'd kind of like to know who the guy is. I deserve that much for my trouble, don't I?"

"You're going to get paid back. What difference does it make who the guy is?"

"Just say I'm nosy."

"Sorry, I can't tell you."

"All right, it's your business."

Hazel turned away, avoiding his eyes. She was tempted to give him back the money right away and make a confession: *I was going to play what you'd think was a dirty trick, George, only I've changed my mind.*

But her mind refused to change. She thought, it isn't actually a dirty trick, it's for his own good. He said himself he wished he'd never met her. It's my fault that he did and now it's my fault that she's going away. Everyone will be better off.

She said, looking a little guilty: "Maybe I could use a drink at that. I'm not dressed, though. I didn't figure on coming in."

"That's all right. There's nobody around except Judge Bowridge."

"Is he—?"

"He is."

"That's too bad."

They went inside. The judge was still sitting at the bar, his arms forming a circle around the half-finished martini. He was talking quietly but distinctly to himself in a language which neither George nor Hazel recognized but which George from past experience assumed was Latin.

"Carpe diem," said the judge, *"quam minimum credula postero.* What happened to you, Anderson?"

"I went out to meet Hazel."

"Hazel. My dear lady, I did not recognize you without your hair. Here, sit down, take off your glasses, let me admire you. *O mater pulchra filia pulchrior.*"

"I bet you say that to all the girls," Hazel said, laughing.

"No, indeed. I speak from the heart. Sit down, sit down, the night is young."

"It's morning."

"I was merely using a figure of speech. I am quite aware that it's morning. Sunday morning, as a matter of fact. I am always perfectly oriented, even when I've been drinking. And I might as well confess that I've had one or two drinks throughout the night."

"Maybe it's time you thought about going home."

"I have thought about it," Bowridge said solemnly. "It seems like an excellent idea."

"Then—"

"But not one which appeals to me. *Carpe diem,* I say. Seize the day. Swing it by the tail. Let it know who's boss."

Hazel's smile was a little forced. For one thing she wasn't sure what he was talking about, and for another she had never before seen Judge Bowridge when he'd been drinking. She had heard about his periodic bats, from George and a dozen other people, but she hadn't witnessed one, and it embarrassed her.

"I sense opprobrium in the air," Bowridge said. "Chide me no chides, Hazel."

"It sounds like you're talking in riddles."

"Like the Sphinx. Yes. But that is not my sole resemblance to the Sphinx. We are both old, desiccated, frangible. I know many fine riddles. For example, what is it that can go up the chimney down, but not down the chimney up?"

Hazel took a careful sip of the beer George had drawn for her, and tried to look thoughtful.

"It's very simple," the judge said. "Go on, guess."

"I can't."

"Give up?"

"Yes."

"It's an umbrella."

"Oh."

"A very fine riddle, that. You don't happen to know any, do you?"

"I don't think so."

"Well, no matter, no matter. We will play Twenty Questions instead. Would you like that?"

"I really don't know," Hazel said earnestly. "I've never played them. Besides, I've got to go, I have an important engagement."

Bowridge frowned. "It's very peculiar, every time I suggest a game of Twenty Questions, people suddenly discover that they have an engagement somewhere. Is there something intrinsically repulsive about the game itself, or am *I* the repelling factor?"

"I really have a date. I've got to deliver some money."

"Money. How very interesting. To whom?"

They were both watching her, the judge owlishly, over the top of his spectacles, and George with obvious eagerness, as if he believed that Hazel, now that she was in the presence of a Judge of the Superior Court, must tell the whole truth and nothing but the truth. To some extent Hazel shared this feeling but it did not alter her decision to lie, it only made it more difficult to carry out.

George said, earnestly, "Listen, Hazel, has it entered your brain that if you give this guy money to run out on his wife, you're kind of responsible for what happens?"

"I am not."

"Just think about it."

"I already have. He could get the money from someone else. The only reason he asked me is because, well, he just thought of me first, is all. He has lots of friends he could have asked." She knew that this was a lie. Gordon had no close friends. "He would go away anyway, even without any money. I'm not responsible one bit. And I don't see why you're acting so petty about it."

"It isn't the money, it's the way you let yourself get dragged into everybody's business. You can't walk up the street without getting involved with somebody."

"You don't have to worry about me."

"I am not worried about you," George said stiffly. "I'm pointing out to you a simple fact."

"I already know some simple facts."

"For instance, just for instance, remember the day you got the bright idea of driving over to Ojai to look up your mother's long-lost cousin Gladys. That was all right, if it would have stopped there. But no. It turns out Gladys has a sister and the sister is living right here in town, teaching school. So naturally you look up the sister too, and by a strange coincidence she happens to be having a nervous breakdown and has to give up her job and has nothing to live on. The rest is history."

"You're getting awfully stuffy in your old age, George. I remember the bums you were always bringing home with you."

"They didn't stay for a couple of years."

"I used to dread getting up in the mornings, never knowing how many bodies I'd have to step over to get to the kitchen."

"That was different. We were married then, you had me to protect you."

"The only thing you ever protected me from was having a good time."

"That's a lie, by Jesus!"

"And it's none of your damned business who lives in my house because it's *my house*."

"I gave it to you."

"The judge gave it to me."

"I signed the prop—"

"Now, now," the judge said, looking sad. "Now, now, now."

"I signed the property settle—"

"Order in the court."

"—ment."

"You're in contempt, Anderson. I fine you one martini."

George looked down at the floor, mute and stubborn.

"You refuse to pay, Anderson?"

"That's right. I called you a cab."

"You realize what this means, of course. If you should ever be forced to appear in my court, I shall take a very dim view of your innocence, a very dim view indeed."

"I'll ask for a jury trial."

"Naturally. But in my instructions to the jury I always have the last word." Bowridge rose unsteadily, hanging on to the ledge of the counter, and addressed the rows of glasses behind George's head. "Ladies and gentlemen, you have heard the evidence. This niggardly fellow, Anderson, is—"

"You'd better sit down before you fall down."

"Very well. I always address the jury in that position anyway." He sat down with cautious dignity, but he looked suddenly very tired, as if the act of rising, or the change of emotional atmosphere in the room, had exhausted him. He tried to revitalize himself by humming, "Chewy Chewy," but he couldn't remember the tune, and the sound that came from his throat was a sad sighing which had no connection with music.

"A fine melody, that," he said, pretending that he could sing it perfectly if he chose to. "Foster sang high and I sang low, but Foster couldn't hold his liquor and finally I had to go it alone. That's life for you—one ends up going it alone. *Lacrimae rerum.* You know what that means, Anderson?"

"I guess it's Latin."

"It means the tears of things, the sorrows of the world."

"Sure, sure. Just don't start on a crying jag in here."

"Preposterous remark," Bowridge said. The truth was, he did want to cry a little and then go to sleep. Simple, human desires; there was no real reason why he shouldn't gratify them. A few tears, a little sleep, and one would wake up, refreshed, forgetting the long night.

Though his eyes felt moist he could not cry and when he folded his arms on the counter and buried his head between them like a scrawny sparrow hiding from the cold and desolate winter, he could not sleep. The spinning of his heart and the ticking of his mind kept him awake. It seemed to him that he was a freak, that the simple and commonplace gratifications were always just beyond his grasp, or around the corner, or in the middle of next week.

"Your cab's here," George said.

13

RUTH CAME HOME at noon, her cheeks pink from the walk and from excitement. Dr. Foster had stayed out all night, and never in all her born days had such a thing happened to someone who was as close to her as Elaine was. It was dreadful, it was scandalous, but the excitement kept flooding through her in waves. She greeted Wendy with almost hysterical fondness and the dog responded, leaping up at her, turning in circles, barking in ferocious delight.

"Quiet," she said. "Be quiet. Down, down, Wendy. Quiet." But the dog was positive she didn't mean it and kept leaping up at her and nibbling affectionately at her clothes with its tiny front teeth. "Ah there, there. Yes, I'm home. Now that's enough. Yes, yes, of course you're glad to see me, oh my, yes, you are!" *Dr. Foster didn't come home!* "She's always glad to see her mother, yes, she is. Now get down, Wendy." *Dr. Foster ran away!* "That's a good girl, you get down. You get down like your mother's good girl." *And I am the king of the castle.*

She was not consciously aware of the children's chant running through her head, but the derisive notes picked their way out of her memory and she thought of Manuel who climbed the pepper tree, and Margaret and the pennies she hoarded in her desk. Where were they now, all the children? Carrying the dog she went to the window and looked out at the playground across the street. The dust was rolling across it like a wall of yellow fog pushed by the wind.

She thought, some day soon I will go back. I feel much better. I feel very strong, actually.

The dog squirmed out of her arms and headed for the kitchen. She turned from the window, laughing, filled with a sense of power because Dr. Foster had run away from his wife. In contrast to Elaine, she had very little, only a dog instead of children and a husband, but the dog was all hers. It would never run off and stay out all night and get drunk.

"There," she said, "did someone forget to give my girl her breakfast? We'll fix that."

Josephine was in the kitchen, sipping a glass of milk and gazing placidly into space. Sometimes she could sit for hours without thinking of anything, only seeing a lot of warm rich color in her mind.

"Nobody had any breakfast," she said in a vaguely surprised voice, "except me and Harold. I was wondering if I should do the dishes but there's hardly enough to bother about."

"I had breakfast at Mrs. Foster's house. She asked me to stay there all night."

With her mind swathed in the warm rich colors, Josephine was incurious. "Harold went out to look at an apartment. The ad was in the paper this morning, three rooms, it said, and no pets and no children allowed. Harold said I'd better stay home on account of someone might suspect my condition."

"Mrs. Foster," Ruth said, rather annoyed at Josephine's obtuseness, "didn't want to stay alone with the children."

"Is she scared of the dark? I am, once in a while. I know very well it's the same room in the dark as it is in the light, but I can't be positively *sure* unless I turn the light on again for a minute."

"Of course she's not afraid of the dark. She was upset because *he* didn't come home. He took the car and ran off last night, and this morning he phoned. She told me every word he said. He's not coming back, he said, he doesn't want to live with her anymore and she's to get a divorce."

"My goodness." Josephine was shocked. "I thought they were a very happy couple."

"So did I. You can't tell from appearances. He said no matter what grounds she gets a divorce on, he promises to give her reasonable alimony and not to ask custody of any of the children. That's not all, either. There's a girl mixed up in it. Mrs. Foster thinks they've been living in sin together. She's not sure, but that's what she thinks. Quite a young girl too. It doesn't put him in a very good light, I must say."

"I don't believe it. No man would leave his kids like that." The warm colors were gone, the scene was gray. She was having her baby and Harold was leaving her. The baby cried pitifully, and she herself held out her arms, pleading, but Harold turned away. A very slim, pretty girl was smiling at him. "Not a decent man like—like Harold."

"Who can tell who's decent nowadays? Look at Dr. Foster. There wasn't a person in town who didn't think he was the soul of honor. He fooled everybody, even Hazel."

"What if he never comes back? Hazel won't have a job."

"I never thought of that."

"It seems a shame," Josephine said. "Just when she was all settled and getting the yard fixed up and everything."

Ruth flung back her head as if she'd been challenged. "Well, at least that's the end of the Mexican anyway. Good riddance to bad rubbish, I say."

She walked decisively to the sink and began to rinse off the dishes under the tap, but she felt such a sudden sharp pain in her chest that she had to stop. She leaned over the sink, pressing her dripping hands against her bosom. It's nothing, she thought. I feel very strong, actually. It's one of those silly meaningless pains that everybody gets now and then. I'm really quite strong.

"Do you feel all right?" Josephine asked.

"Yes—dizzy spell—it's over now."

"It's from that walking. If you walked all the way from Fosters' house at your age—not that you're old, my goodness, but it's the way you walk, so fast no one can keep up with you. You'd think someone was chasing you."

The pain was gone. She wiped her hands and dabbed at the water on the front of her dress, the damp imprint of two hands, one over each breast.

"I like to walk fast," she said.

Josephine giggled. "I can't say the same for myself, right now. I've gotten so I just hate to move, unless Harold's around to help me up out of chairs and things like that."

"I should change my dress."

"It'll dry in a minute on a day like this."

"I'll go and change it. I shouldn't be working around in the kitchen in a good dress like this. It's wasteful."

She went into her bedroom, shutting the door against Josephine. Quite frequently lately, the sound of Josephine's gentle voice talking about Harold, and the sight of her distended abdomen and swollen breasts, set Ruth's nerves on edge. She wasn't sure why she had these violent reactions to Josephine. They came at her suddenly, in the midst of quite ordinary conversations about the baby's name, or the number of diapers that would be necessary, or the house Josephine meant to have someday down by the sea.

"Not a big house. Two bedrooms, that will be enough."

"You'll get the fog down there."

"I don't care, I never get tired looking at the sea."

"If you build above the fog line it would be better for the baby."

"And wistaria vines over the front veranda. I'm crazy about wistaria."

"It's all right when it's in bloom, but think of when it isn't. It looks like old dead twigs."

"And maybe a very small orchard, a couple of orange trees and an avocado. And a jacaranda, just to look at."

"They say you've got to plant two avocados side by side, a single one won't bear fruit."

"I never heard of that."

"You've got to be careful about jacarandas too. Some of them never bloom and some bloom in fits, maybe every few years. They're very temperamental, someone told me."

"My goodness, Ruth, you've said something kind of unpleasant about every single one of my ideas."

"No, I haven't."

"You have so. About the fog line and the wistarias and the jacaranda—"

"I was just urging you to be careful."

"Well, it didn't sound like it. It sounded like—"

Josephine couldn't explain what it sounded like, and Ruth, who might have explained, didn't try. It sounded as if she was jealous of Josephine with her baby who hadn't arrived yet, the two-bedroom house that hadn't been built, and the jacaranda that wasn't planted. But she knew she wasn't jealous of the baby, the tree, the house, only of Josephine's capacity for dreaming of such things.

She took off the crepe dress she always wore to the Fosters' on Saturday nights. Where the water had touched it, the crepe had puckered and the imprint of her hands was now indistinct and no larger than a child's. She hung the dress on her side of the closet she shared with Hazel.

Standing in her white cotton slip, Ruth heard her heart knocking against the bones of her chest, extraordinarily loud and distinct in the stifling closet. It was the heartbeat of fear.

She felt that her life was changing, but she didn't know in which way and she was afraid to have it change at all. The indications of change were there. They were very small things that someone else mightn't notice, little wings beating against the thin brittle walls of her world like moths at a window.

Dr. Foster had left, and though he scarcely knew she was alive, his leaving affected her. There would be no more Saturday nights for her, telling stories to Paul and Judith and giving the baby his bottle, and probably even no more job for Hazel. The four of them, and the fifth to come, would be forced to live on Hazel's alimony and Harold's wages, while the cost of living kept going up and up and up.

The excitement she felt when she entered the house had been only carbonated fear and now that the bubbles had disappeared she recognized it for what it was. She was terrified by the intricate complexities of even one small human act. A man who was almost a stranger to her had decided to leave his wife, and by this decision he had involved not only himself and his family and the girl, but herself and Hazel and Josephine and Harold and the baby, even the dog. Perhaps in the end, she thought desperately, everyone in the world was affected by the actions of every other person, a chain reaction was set up that never ceased. It went on and on, an interminable string tying them all together in an inextricably knotted mass. There was no escape, it was a universal law: one drop of water couldn't be displaced without affecting all the other drops.

She stood in the narrow closet listening to her fearful heart and the pressing of the wind against the windows. She couldn't move, she couldn't take one step forward or backward for fear that step would be heard around the world.

At that moment she came, as close as she'd ever come, to some kind of revelation, but the moment passed and her mind had to withdraw to protect itself. She began to grope for some simple easy explanation that would shift the weight of responsibility. It's this wind, she thought. I always get nervy like this when the wind blows in from the desert. It used to affect my classes too. The children were all cross and I had quite a time controlling them. They used to sag over their desks, their eyes reddened with dust—

She put on a wrap-around cotton dress that Josephine had given to her when Josephine had become too big to wear it any longer. She felt quite ashamed of herself for becoming irritated with Josephine. It was the wind, of course. Now that she realized that fact, she could discipline herself better. For the rest of the day she would force herself to be pleasant and to smile when she didn't feel like it. She had the will power, she could do it. Ignore the desert wind.

She heard the front door slam and she knew it must be Hazel coming home because Harold always closed doors very softly to avoid startling Josephine. Bracing herself (against the wind, the drop of water, the knot of string) she went out to the living room.

She told Hazel the news while Hazel sat on the davenport rubbing her eyes.

"You don't seem very surprised," Ruth said.

"Not so very. My God, it's hot. Is there some cold juice or something in the refrigerator?"

"Grapefruit juice. Don't rub your eyes like that. You're only rubbing the dust in, not getting it out."

"It feels good anyway."

"If you're not surprised it means you must have had your suspicions all along. Mrs. Foster asked me that last night, and I said, of course not. Hazel's never said a word except what a wonderful man Dr. Foster is. I said, I'm sure Hazel would never condone anything like that."

"Like what?"

"His running around with other women."

"He didn't," Hazel said deliberately. "There was just one woman."

"How do you know?"

"Someone told me."

"That's even worse. It—it practically proves that they were—cohabiting."

"If they weren't, they soon will be."

"I'm shocked to the core by your attitude, Hazel. You don't seem to realize—"

"How's Elaine taking it?"

"How would anyone take it? She's beside herself, the poor woman. This morning he had the nerve to phone her and tell her, bold as brass, to go out and get a divorce. Naturally she refused. She said never, no matter what happens, will she disgrace her church and her parents and her children by becoming a divorced woman. And I agree with her. She's convinced that divorce is wrong and I admire her for standing by her convictions."

"Crap."

Ruth's face grew pale with disapproval. "I wish you—you really shouldn't use words like that, Hazel. I know it's your house and all that but—"

"All right, I'll say baloney then, but it's the same thing no matter how you slice it."

"Really, Hazel!"

"I get so damn tired of your admiration for that snippy little bitch. I know why she's not getting a divorce, because she's too damn mean for one thing. It would kill her to see Gordon have a life of his own. And also because she knows she'll never get another husband if she lets Gordon go."

"Such a thought would never occur to her," Ruth said harshly. "And I'm surprised at you, Hazel. You talk as if you actually *approve* of Dr. Foster and what he's done."

"I've always approved of him, why should I change now? A good man doesn't turn into a bad man overnight."

"That's all very well, but we must judge people by their actions. There's no other way to judge them, and you—"

Hazel raised her voice to interrupt. "I don't want to judge them. I want to go on liking the people I like and making excuses for them when I have to, and having a few excuses made for me too."

"Moral softness. I want no excuses made for me, ever."

"You need them, like everyone else."

"I wouldn't take them!" Ruth shouted, making a wild gesture with her fists. "I wouldn't listen!"

"Don't get so worked up. I wasn't trying to—"

"I don't want any excuses from anybody. Discipline, not excuses, that's what we need in this world, more self-denial and discipline. Oh yes, I can see what you're thinking now—poor Ruth, she can't help getting worked up, she had a nervous breakdown and lost her job, and she's an old maid too, of course, and her father was—"

"Stop guessing," Hazel said. "If you want to know what I was thinking I'll tell you. I was thinking that people who are hard on themselves the way you are, are usually pretty hard on other people too."

"Not hard enough."

"Elaine Foster's kind of like that too. I can't explain it so well, but maybe if she liked herself a little better and had a little more self-respect, she'd be better off."

"Well, well! You're getting to be quite a psychologist, Hazel Anderson. You've got Mrs. Foster and me all figured out, and the trouble with us is we have no self-respect!"

"I meant, respect for yourselves as you really are, not expecting to be perfect and accepting the fact that you've got a few human weaknesses that maybe aren't so bad after all."

"No self-respect, eh?" Ruth cried. "And what do you think you've got, the kind of things you do, drinking and carrying on and traipsing after your divorced husband—"

Josephine came to the door with an anxious little smile on her face. "Gee whiz, the way you two sound you'd think you were quarreling. Mrs. Hatcher's outside working in her garden, she's bound to hear every word you say."

"That's all right," Hazel said. "We're finished."

"We *have* finished," Ruth corrected her. "We *are* finished would mean we are dead."

"Close enough to suit me."

"The least I can do in exchange for your analysis of my character is to give you a free lesson in English grammar."

Josephine turned on her and said hotly, "That's no way to speak to Hazel after all she's—"

"You stay out of this," Hazel said. Then she addressed Ruth in a quieter voice, "I'm sorry if I said anything to hurt you. I didn't mean to."

"Hurt me," Ruth sneered. "You can't hurt me. I don't *allow* myself to be hurt."

"There you go again. Don't kid yourself."

"And I repeat, you don't have to make any excuses for me, Hazel Anderson. I don't require them and I don't believe in them, for me or anybody else, let alone a man like Dr. Foster. A man that leaves his wife and children and runs off with another woman is a bad man. He stands condemned by his own action in the eyes of all decent people."

"Maybe I'm not decent."

"If the shoe fits, wear it."

"There's a car stopping out front," Josephine said nervously. "You two just better quit arguing right now."

Hazel got up to look out of the window. Then, without a word of explanation, she picked up her purse from the top of the radio and went outside.

Gordon was alone in the car. Though Hazel had seen him only twenty-four hours ago, he seemed to have changed more than a day's worth. Wearing the old slack suit that she'd seen hanging in his office and needing a shave, he looked like an ordinary workingman relaxing on a Sunday morning. There was none of that do-or-die air about him that he put on along with his white surgeon's coat.

He smiled at her as she came down the walk. "I was just coming in."

"It'd be better if we talked out here. Too many people." She opened her purse and took out the roll of bills bound together with an elastic. It looked like a lot of money and Hazel wondered if Gordon knew how little it actually was in these times. Maybe to him it looked like more because it meant his freedom for a week or two and he was too excited at the prospect to think further ahead than that.

He handed her two checks, one for five hundred dollars made out to Cash, and the other for a hundred made out to Hazel.

"What's this for?"

"Your salary for the next two weeks."

"What am I supposed to do to earn it?"

"Answer the phone. Cancel all appointments for the next month. If there are any emergencies send them over to Dr. Tower. Appointments for routine check-ups and cleanings you can step up till next month if the people are willing to wait. If they aren't ask Dr. MacPherson to take them. Tell everyone I'm on a holiday, naturally."

"Then you're coming back?"

"I hope so. You'll hear from me anyway." He paused for a moment. "Thanks for everything, Hazel. Not just getting the money, but for understanding that this is the only way I could do it. It seems pretty sordid, I guess, for me to be sneaking away like this. But I couldn't go home to say goodbye because I know I wouldn't get away. Elaine would pull out every stop on the organ, and I'm afraid I'd change my mind. I want to do now what has to be done eventually. Ruby isn't the issue, I want you to understand that. It's true that if I didn't know her and if she didn't love me, I probably wouldn't have the guts to leave Elaine now. But Ruby has *caused* nothing, do you see that?"

"Yes."

"She's over at her room packing. She's been at it all morning and she's only got one suitcase. I wonder if she's giving me a chance to change my mind, or if she actually doesn't want to leave under the circumstances."

"Maybe she's just particular," Hazel said.

"That must be it."

"It must be."

Gordon drew in his breath. "Well, I guess that covers everything. Be sure and be at the bank when it opens tomorrow."

"I will."

"It's a hell of a thing to say about your wife, but she might try to close our joint account and I don't want you to be caught with two bad checks."

"You'd better tell me where you're going."

"San Francisco, probably. Then if anything happens Ruby will at least have her aunt's place to go to. Anything could happen you know, an accident or something like that."

"Don't sound so gloomy, Gordon." It was the first time she had ever called him Gordon. She was surprised how the name slipped out so easily, as if she never expected him to come back and change into Dr. Foster again.

The wind veered suddenly, and picking up the dirt from the playground hurled it across the street. They both closed their eyes automatically until the sound of the wind died down.

"Nothing's going to happen," Hazel said.

"I guess not. Well, thanks again, Hazel. I'd better get going, with four hundred miles to drive."

They shook hands, and Hazel said, "Goodbye and good luck."

"Goodbye, Hazel."

She waited on the sidewalk until his car reached the corner, then she waved to him and Gordon waved back, very gaily.

Though she had a premonition that she'd never see him again, she wasn't depressed at the prospect of losing a good job with a pleasant boss. It occurred to her then, for the first time, that she mightn't have been so eager to help Gordon get away if he hadn't been taking Ruby with him.

She stood on the small roofless porch reluctant to go inside and face the questions of Josephine and Ruth. A mockingbird flew up out of the pyracantha bush. Though the berries were barely beginning to show orange, the birds had already been at them. She resolved now, as she did every year, to save the berries for Christmas decoration by screening them with nets, but she knew perfectly well that by Christmas the bush would look as it always did. The red berries would be crushed and half-eaten, showing their yellowish pulp, like ruined immature apples, and every tiny leaf would be partly nibbled to its spine by snails and beetles. Even if she could save the bush from the birds it was hard to wash the beetles off before bringing the berries into the house. The beetles hid and clung, and only after they'd been in the house for a day or two would they abandon the berries and seek the bright yellow patches in the slipcover of the davenport. Motionless and rapt, they would sit absorbing the color. They never returned to the berries, and they never went anywhere else in the house.

The mockingbird came back and began to squawk insults at her from the porch railing.

A teenaged girl was coming up the street on a bicycle, riding very slowly, wobbling from side to side to keep her balance. She had long black hair that danced in a frenzy around her head with every gust of wind. Perched on the carrier behind her was a boy of five or six, hanging on to the girl's waist and holding his legs out in the air to avoid interfering with the girl's pedaling. In the basket at the front sat a fat sunburned baby with a soother in his mouth. Every time the bicycle wobbled the baby lurched to one side, but he didn't make a sound, either because he didn't want to lose the soother, or because he was enjoying the ride. The girl paid no attention to the baby or the boy behind her. Like the captain of a well-run ship, she seemed to assume that they each knew their places and would perform their duties.

The bicycle zigzagged again, and Hazel started down the porch steps and called out, "Aren't you afraid he'll fall?"

The girl stared at Hazel suspiciously for a moment. Then she applied the brakes and put her left foot down on the road. Simultaneously, as if from long habit, the boy put his left foot on the road, and slid off the carrier. "I didn't hear what you said, lady."

"I was just wondering if the baby would fall when you're going so slow and wobbly like that."

"He won't fall," the girl said flatly, blinking her dark eyes at the baby. "I got him tied in. Anyway, I'm only going slow because I'm looking for something. I can ride perfect, without hands even."

"*And* backwards, *and* standing on the seat," the boy added.

"My goodness," Hazel said. "I never even heard of that."

"Connie can do it," the boy said. "Go on, Connie, do it for her."

Connie hesitated, torn between the desire to show off and the desire to appear sophisticated. "Naw," she said. "That's baby stuff, and Pop wouldn't like it anyway." She explained to Hazel, "It's my pop's bicycle."

"He goes to work on it," the boy said. "He's a gardener."

"A *landscape* gardener," the girl corrected him with a frown.

"I wouldn't know the difference," Hazel said.

"There's *lots* of difference. You get more money if you're landscape."

The soother fell out of the baby's mouth and he let out a howl of rage. The girl glanced at Hazel with some contempt. "See? I told you. He's yelling because he thinks the ride's over." She picked the soother up off the road, wiped the dirt off on her blouse and popped it back into the baby's mouth. "He's not afraid of falling, even if he could. Which he can't. Are you, Bingo?"

Bingo rolled his eyes and Hazel laughed. "He's very cute."

"He's called Bingo because my mother was at a Bingo game just before he was born, only his real name's Truman." The girl added, with infinite scorn, "My parents haven't the faintest idea how to name children."

"Is that right."

"I wouldn't *dream* of using my real name at school. It's Consuela, but I just call myself Connie, Consuela sounds so foreignish. If I just call myself Connie, people think my real name is Constance which stinks too, only at least it sounds as if I was *born* in this *country*. Which I was."

"We all was," the boy said. "My mother, too."

"*His* name's Vicente," Connie said, with a worldly shrug. "Only he's not old enough yet to realize how awful it is."

"I do so," the boy protested.

"If you realize now when you're only six, just think how much *more* you're going to realize when you're nearly *sixteen*."

The boy hung his head under the weight of this future, and began to shuffle his feet in the dust. Connie glanced at Hazel as if she wasn't certain whether to continue the conversation or not. Then she said curtly, "Come on, Vin," and she and the boy took their places on the bicycle simultaneously.

It wasn't until they had moved a couple of yards ahead that Hazel recognized the skunk tail hanging from the carriage, and the reflector that spelled out "Watch My Speed." She called out, and the bicycle stopped again, and the boy and girl turned their heads at exactly the same time and with equal suspicion.

"Maybe I can help," Hazel said. "What are you looking for?"

"A hedge clipper," Connie answered. "My pop lost it and it cost five ninety-five."

"Enough for one hundred and nineteen ice cream cones, Pop said," the boy added.

"That's not counting tax," Connie said severely. "If we don't find it on the road, Pop said to go to Mr. Anderson's house, 2124 the number is."

"That's my house."

Connie blinked. "I know."

"You can come in the yard and look around if you like."

"Pop said to look up and down the road first."

"It would probably be picked up by now if he lost it on the road," Hazel said. "He may have left it at my house, I'll go and see. Do you want to come inside and wait?"

"*I'll* come inside," Connie said, flashing a look at the boy. "Vin can ride Bingo up and down the street."

"He can come inside too," Hazel said quickly. "He doesn't look big enough to sit on the seat and reach the pedals."

"You don't have to sit on the *seat* to ride a bicycle. Go on, Vin, show the lady."

Vin obliged.

"See?" Connie said, and Hazel admitted that she saw and the two of them went into the house.

The front room was empty but it had the air of having just been abandoned at the approach of company.

"Sit down, Connie," Hazel said.

"I'd just as soon stand. I *like* to stand, I do it all the time."

She stood along the wall with her hands behind her back. She felt too sophisticated to stare at the furniture with the crude curiosity of a child, the way Vin would have done. She narrowed her eyes and gazed out of their corners in a manner meant to indicate a bored indifference. It was the expression she used at school when one of the teachers asked her a question she couldn't answer. She merely lifted her eyebrows and narrowed her eyes to show that she didn't care but that she certainly would know the answer if she did care.

Every few minutes she heard Vin ride past the house yelling, "Honk, honk!" and "Yippee, bang bang!" She would have liked to open the door and order him to be quiet, but she didn't want to move for fear the lady of the house might think she'd been snooping while she was gone.

When Hazel returned Connie had barely moved a muscle.

"I can't find it," Hazel said. "My sister-in-law and I both hunted for it."

Though Connie continued to look bored, there was an undertone of anxiety in her voice: "Pop said not to bother you too much, but he's pretty sure he couldn't have dropped it on the road. It's heavy, it would have made a noise and he'd have heard it. Pop's awful careful about his tools."

"Yes, I saw that."

"And this was the last place he went to."

"Well, I certainly can't find it," Hazel repeated. She was beginning to feel quite uncomfortable under the girl's oblique gaze. The girl had not accused her of deliberately withholding the hedge clipper; the accusation lay in the facts themselves. Mr. Escobar had brought his hedge clipper to Hazel's yard, and when he arrived home the clipper was missing. It was practically impossible, Hazel thought, for it to have fallen from the bicycle basket without Escobar noticing it.

"Maybe someone stole it," Connie said.

"I don't see how. Your father was working out in the yard all the time, and there wasn't anyone else around, not while I was here anyway. Wait a minute and I'll go and ask my cousin about it."

"Pop said not to bother you too much, maybe I better just go."

"It's no bother," Hazel said quite sharply. "I want to get this thing cleared up."

She went into the bedroom and shut the door behind her. The blinds were drawn, and Ruth was lying on the bed with a cloth over her eyes. She was absolutely motionless, yet Hazel had the same impression that she'd had when she and Connie had come into the house, an impression of activity that stopped a split second before she opened the door. She wondered if Ruth had been listening at the door and if she'd been able to hear anything with the wind blowing so loud outside.

"What's the matter?" Hazel said.

"I have a headache."

"I'm sorry to bother you, but Mr. Escobar's girl is here."

Ruth sat up and the cloth fell off her eyes into her lap.

"What?" she said stupidly. "Who?"

"The Mexican's daughter."

"Daughter?" She let out a sudden sharp laugh. "This is a surprise. He's got a daughter, has he? Who'd have guessed it, from the look of him? What's she like?"

"Quite pretty."

"Pretty, is she? That *is* funny." She laughed again. "She can't take after *him!*"

"Don't laugh like that."

"Like *what?*"

"You know exactly what I mean."

"I don't! I was laughing because it's so funny, him having a daughter, and pretty at that. What's she doing here?"

"She came to get her father's hedge clipper. He says he left it here yesterday."

"He's lying!"

Hazel looked annoyed. "Why should he lie about it?"

"So he can get a new one out of you. His was old, I saw it, it was all rusty."

"The girl told me it was brand new."

"They're all lying," Ruth cried. "They're all the same, sly and scheming behind those innocent eyes of theirs! Yes, those innocent velvet eyes, they can hide a lot."

"Keep your voice down. She's right in the front room."

"I don't care."

"I do."

Ruth picked up the cloth that she'd had over her eyes and began to twist it in her hands. Hazel watched her uneasily. She was afraid that Ruth was going to have another of her nervous spells. They always followed the same pattern—there was the hard mirthless laughter, the talk about self-discipline, and then the moment when the discipline broke open at the seams, exposing a quivering and uncoordinated mass of tissue.

"*I* certainly didn't take his hedge clipper," Ruth said. "What are you looking at *me* for? Why even ask me about it?"

"I thought you might have seen it."

"I didn't."

"You said you did."

"Only for a minute, long enough to see that it was old and rusty." She fell back on the pillow, and when she spoke again her voice was high and suffering: "Anyway, it's all a lie. The whole thing is a lie from beginning to end. Perhaps there never was a hedge clipper, perhaps I only imagined I saw it or I mistook it for something else. That's it, I'm sure—I don't believe there ever was such a thing, so I couldn't have taken something that wasn't there. You mustn't accuse me."

"I wasn't accusing you."

"You were, with your eyes."

"I'm only trying to get to the bottom of the matter," Hazel said. "I feel responsible for a loss that took place on my property."

"That's how he wants you to feel, so you'll buy him another."

"I have no intention of buying him another. I intend to find the one he left here and I'll find it, by Jesus, if I have to take the whole damn house apart."

"You'll never find it," Ruth said softly. "There never was such a thing. It's all a lie, it was all meant to take you in because you're innocent. You talk so rough, Hazel, and you know so many different kinds of people, but you're very innocent."

She put the cloth over her eyes again, as a gesture of dismissal.

"Listen, Ruth," Hazel said quietly, "if you know anything about where that hedge clipper is, you better tell me now. I'll find out anyway."

Ruth lay on the bed, mute and rigid.

"Let's put it this way, suppose you had one of your screwy ideas and decided to take the hedge clipper and put it away some place. Maybe you were going to teach him a lesson, or maybe you even did it for my sake, to save money or something—I don't care what reason you had. Just tell me where you put it and then we'll forget the whole thing."

"I've already forgotten."

"Listen, you've got to tell me where it is."

"I don't know. I never saw it."

"You don't realize, this is one of those small things that can turn out to be very serious. He's a poor man, he might go to the police. We'll all get in trouble."

"See? You *are* accusing me. I felt it when you came in the room."

"I wasn't accusing you when I came in. I only got suspicious when you began to talk about seeing it and not seeing it."

"I'm not a liar. Sometimes I *appear* to lie, but it's only that my imagination is so vivid, pictures form so clear and real in my head. But I'm not a liar."

"I know that," Hazel said patiently.

"So that's where I must have seen it, in my head. It was lying on a shelf, or on the grass, I'm not sure which."

"Ruth, did you take it or didn't you?"

"It wasn't there to take, and besides, I'd have no reason to do such a thing. I can't think of any reason at all." Though there had been no change in her voice and no overt sign of weeping, the cloth over her eyes was wet with tears. "If I could think of a reason, any reason—for your sake, perhaps, for your sake—"

"The reason doesn't matter. Did you take it?"

"No, no, I didn't!"

"All right," Hazel said. "We'll forget it for now."

"What are you going to do?"

"Send the girl home and then find the hedge clipper. Maybe we'd both better hunt for it, you and me."

"I can't, I have this headache."

Hazel stood looking at her indecisively for a moment, then she burst out, "Oh, for God's sake, Ruth, be sensible and tell me where you hid it."

Ruth turned her face to the wall.

When Hazel went back to the front room the girl was gone. Thinking she might have decided to wait outside, Hazel opened the door in time to see the bicycle just turning on to Castillo Street. At the hole in the corner which Hazel was always careful to avoid when she was driving, the baby and the boy and Connie herself all bounced in the air, but Connie kept pedaling furiously and in a moment the bicycle had disappeared behind the stucco wall of the school.

Hazel turned back into the house. Through the closed door of the bedroom she could hear Ruth talking to herself in a thin, reedy monotone that sounded as though Ruth had not intended to talk, she had merely opened her mouth and the desert wind blew through it like a pitch pipe.

She opened the door. Ruth was sitting on the edge of the bed with the little dog cradled in her arms. The dog looked uncomfortable and puzzled, but it did not attempt to escape.

"Ruth."

"I will come out and speak to her personally," Ruth said.

"You can't. She's gone."

"Gone? Why?"

"I don't know. She had her little brothers with her, maybe she wanted to get them home."

"Brothers. Yes, of course. They breed like pigs." The little dog squirmed out of her arms, sensing danger in their sudden contraction, and went to hide under the bed. "Like pigs. It's disgusting. He probably has a new child every year."

"That's his business."

"I'm sure it *is* his business. He seems to do very little else."

"There's no sense in—"

"But then they're all lazy, every one of them."

"I thought he worked very hard yesterday."

"You weren't here. I was. I watched him. I watched him the whole day."

"Yes," Hazel said slowly. "Yes, I guess you did."

"You can rest assured that I did. Josephine wanted me to go along on the boat ride but I stayed home deliberately. They've got to be watched."

"Do they?"

"Every minute of the time."

Hazel had turned quite pale. "You stood outside and watched him?"

"Not outside. In here."

"In where?"

"In—Why are you looking at me like that? Stop it. Stop it immediately."

"Ruth."

"I won't tolerate it."

"Listen to me a minute. I'm only trying to get at the truth."

"Truth. Truth. There's no such thing—it's all a pack of lies."

"What is?"

"All, all of it. Lies. Slander. You can't believe anything you're told."

"Nobody told me anything. I figured it out for myself."

Ruth laughed. "Oh, you did, did you? You're quite a figurer for a woman with no education, who never got past high school."

She was trembling so violently that the bed rattled and the dog hiding under it made a sudden dash for the door.

"I can figure, all right," Hazel said. "You didn't know he was married."

"I didn't know, or care. I wasn't interested enough to think about it."

"You thought about it."

"No!"

"If you watched him all day, you must have."

"How can you imply such a thing?—A Mexican—a dirty Mexican—" She took a long, shuddering breath. "We've always held our heads high, all the Kanes, we're a good family."

"Why did you take the clipper? So he'd have to come back for it?"

"No, no, how can you—how—"

"It's the only reason I can think of."

"No, no! I did it for your sake, Hazel, for you. I knew he was going to try and cheat you. I cheated him first. That's fair, isn't it, isn't it fair?"

"You're talking crazy. Why should he try to cheat me?"

"Because they all do. Everybody knows that. You can't trust them. They're sly, deceitful. He didn't let on he was married, never gave a sign. We talked, I remember every word. Nothing about a wife and family, nothing. It shows, doesn't it, how deceitful they are, how they can't be trusted? I remember every word. We talked about Wendy, him pretending to be interested in her but all the while sizing me up with those innocent eyes of his. Ah, but I was too smart for him. I cheated him before he cheated me. You see that?"

"Yes, I think I see it. I think I do." Hazel walked over to the window, her hands jammed in the pockets of her jeans as if it was necessary to keep them under control. The sun poured through the net curtains, a golden stream of warmth and light. "Where did you hide it?"

"In the garage."

"Whereabouts in the garage?"

"I—can't tell you."

"You've got to."

Ruth stared down at the floor, mute and suffering.

"Now try and be sensible, Ruth. I looked in the garage a few minutes ago and couldn't find it. You're sure you hid it there?"

"Yes."

"What part? Tell me."

"I want to, I want to, but I—" She moved her head from side to side, like an animal with a pain it couldn't understand or communicate.

"Ruth. Listen to me."

"Yes."

"You're over the bad part, you've admitted you took it and hid it some place. That was hard for you, but you did it."

"Yes."

"The rest can't be any harder. Tell me where it is and I'll take it back to him and we can forget the whole thing. Are you listening to me, Ruth?"

"Yes."

"Where is it?"

"The—the buggy."

"Buggy."

"That Harold got for the baby. It's right—right there. I didn't hide it. I just put it down—it seemed—such a good place for it."

"Yes," Hazel said quietly, "I guess it was."

"You won't—tell Josephine?"

"No."

"She'd be mad—germs and everything."

"I won't tell her."

"I don't know—why I took it. It's only a clipper."

"Sometimes things have a special meaning."

"What meaning could it have? Only a clipper." She raised her head, slowly. "To you it must seem—quite humorous."

"No."

"But it is, it *is* humorous, in a way. I often see the funny side of things only I can't laugh easily like some people. Oh, yes, I see the humor in it. You must, too, only you won't admit it—a grown woman spying on a Mexican gardener, yes spying, and then stealing his hedge clipper and hiding it in a baby buggy. That's humorous enough. You're a great laugher, why don't you laugh?"

"I don't feel like it," Hazel said. "I'll go and get the clipper."

"Wait. I'll go with you."

"I wish you wouldn't."

"I must." She grasped the bedpost and pulled herself to her feet. Two spots of color had appeared over her cheekbones like round red poker chips. "I must learn to face things."

The garage smelled of oil and dust and dead leaves. Each time a gust of wind blew past the door the leaves were sucked up into the vacuum it left behind; they jerked and spun for a moment like frenzied dancers and then drifted down to the concrete floor, rustling with self-applause.

Throughout the morning dust had sifted into the garage like snow, and now it covered everything, the oil leavings from Hazel's car, the broken chair from the kitchen, the bicycle Harold had used on his paper route years and years ago, Ruth's trunkful of books, George's collection of shells and driftwood; and, in the far corner near the window, the buggy which Harold had gotten, fourth- or fifth-hand, from the furniture store where he worked. Someone (Josephine? Ruth?) had covered the buggy with an old yellow slicker.

Ruth approached it slowly, holding a handkerchief against her mouth, partly to control its trembling and partly to protect it from the dust.

Her voice came through the handkerchief, muffled and strange. "Everything is so dirty. I must clean." *I must face things, I must expiate, I must clean, I must, I must . . .* She removed the yellow slicker and a faint odor of urine rose from the mattress pad and vanished.

The hedge clipper lay snugly on its side, but it did not breathe or move; it did not look or smell or feel like a real baby, and yet for a brief time in Ruth's mind it had been real. It had breathed against her scrawny chest and warmed her arms and made loving sounds in her ear.

She reached into the buggy and pulled the clipper out roughly by one handle.

"Only a clipper," she said with a sharp little laugh. "You see? It *is* funny."

"Yes."

"I wish you'd laugh. You laugh at other things, why not at this?"

Hazel didn't answer.

"I suppose you think I'm crazy. Well, I'm not. I sometimes wish I were. Life can be so dirty, so cruel, so terrifying." Life is dirty, I must clean; it is cruel, I must be kind; it is terrifying, I must be brave, face things.

"Where does he live?"

"Who?"

"Mr. Escobar." It was the first time she had ever called him by his name.

"On Quincy Street, 509, I think."

"You said the hard part was over, Hazel. You were wrong."

"I don't know what you mean."

"I'm going to take the clipper back myself. That will be the hardest part, explaining to him."

"For God's sake, Ruth, be sensible. You can't explain to him, you—"

"I must."

She turned and walked back through the dead leaves and the dust, with the hedge clipper hanging loosely from her hand, striking her thigh as she moved.

She took a bus across town in the direction of Quincy Street. Since it was Sunday, the bus was nearly empty and the driver had to go very slowly to kill time. On weekdays, in order to keep to his schedule, he was compelled to drive at a wild clip, dodging in and out of traffic, blowing his horn, spurting through the streets like a grounded pilot demoted to the wheel of a dilapidated bus but not admitting it for a minute.

Sunday was different, low gear, five miles an hour. He had time to look around and enjoy himself and study his passengers through the rear-view mirror. The young Negro couple were in love, probably newly in love, from the way they sat and looked at each other in utter silence; the old man behind them was smiling drowsily to himself as if the bus was his own private Cadillac and he was taking a Sunday drive.

Only the gray-haired woman sitting taut and rigid near the rear exit door with a parcel across her knees seemed anxious for a destination. She kept peering out at the street signs.

"Driver?"

"Yes, ma'am."

"You heard me say Quincy Street?"

"Yes."

"You'll be sure and—?"

"Yes, ma'am."

He looked at her curiously. Her features reminded him of a teacher he'd had years ago in Jefferson grade school, a very gentle, pretty, young woman who had trouble keeping the class quiet. When she said goodbye on the last day of school she had cried a little and most of the children had cried too. Miss Kane. He hadn't thought of her for years.

"Quincy Street," he said, and the woman got up, clutching her parcel, and headed for the door.

He swung around in his seat and stared at her, his *eyebrows* raised, as if he expected an answer to some question.

Miss Kane?

She stared back at him for a moment, and then turned away. *Sorry, Miss Kane doesn't live here anymore.*

The door closed behind her and the bus moved away, its ageing insides grumbling and letting off wind.

She stood and watched, remembering the bus driver perfectly, his name, his age, his report card. Melvyn Schlagel, grade three. *Dear Mrs. Schlagel, Melvyn is a bright and lovable boy, and I am sure his indifferent marks are merely the result of high spirits and will improve greatly in time to come. Sincerely, Ruth Kane.*

Miss Kane?

Yes, Melvyn.

She raised her hand and waved, just as the bus reached the corner. She was not sure whether Melvyn waved back or whether he was making a left-turn signal. No, they never make signals, she thought, he must have waved back at me. He knew me after all these years. I can't have changed so much. Perhaps next time, if I see him again, we will have a little chat about old times. What a noisy class I had that year, but I loved them all.

The bus turned the corner and Ruth began to walk in the opposite direction down Quincy Street, a new glow in her eyes and a bounce in her step, as if the unexpected reminder of happy years made them more real in the past and more possible in the future. The gap between the two seemed suddenly smaller, its walls lower, its moats easier to leap across, its doors already half-open.

Quincy Street was packed solid with small square frame shacks, their front windows no more than six feet from the sidewalk. Five hundred and nine was in the middle of the block, indistinguishable from its neighbors except for two potted geraniums precariously balanced on the sagging railing of the tiny porch. On the front door someone had printed in chalk, "*Viva la Fiesta*," and in ink, on a card above the doorbell, "Out of Order."

She banged on the door with the side of her fist to make herself heard above the street noises, the rumble of roller skates, the shrieks of children, the barking of dogs. She was aware that people were watching her as they watched anyone new or different in the neighborhood. Windows were raised, blinds snapped up, lace curtains parted, eyes narrowed.

She knocked again and waited, half-hoping that Escobar would answer right away so that she could get the whole thing over with, and yet dreading the moment when she would come face to face with him and try to explain: *Here is your hedge clipper, Mr. Escobar. You didn't lose it, you didn't leave it anywhere. I took it, yes, quite deliberately. I committed a sinful act. I must pay for it. I must—*

A young Negro in a T-shirt and a straw hat came around the side of the house and looked at her over the porch railing.

He said, in a monotone, "Ain't nobody in."

"Oh."

"They went away couple hours ago. Fishing. They eat a lotta fish." He folded his arms on his chest and teetered back and forth on the balls of his feet. He was wearing very long pointed shoes the color of mustard. "I live next door. Name's Jenkins."

"I'm Miss Kane."

He tipped his hat briefly. "Pleased to meet you."

"I—you have no idea when they'll be back?"

"Depends on the fishing."

"Could I—I wonder if I could leave this parcel here on the porch? It's Mr. Escobar's hedge clipper."

"Oh, that. I heard them talking about it. The walls are thin," he added, as if that explained everything. "It fell off his bicycle."

"No. No, it didn't."

"Just saying what I heard at supper."

"He never had it on his bicycle!"

"Yes, ma'am." Still holding his arms over his chest he took a step back, as if her voice had struck like a spear at his vital organs.

"I know, because I took it. I—"*I stole it, I committed, a sin. I must expiate. Viva la Fiesta. Out of Order.* She inhaled deeply and the hot dusty air rattled in her throat like gourds. "I took it and put it away in the garage—for safekeeping."

"Yes, ma'am."

"Tell him—tell him I found it in the backyard, just where he left it." She propped the clipper up against the front door and turned away, wiping her hands on her skirt. "Tell him he is to be more careful of his tools in the future."

"Yes, ma'am."

"Thank you. Thank you very much, Mr. Jenkins."

She walked back toward the bus stop, feeling extraordinarily light and agile without the weight of the hedge clipper. The noises of Quincy Street, the children, the dogs, the passing freight train, mingled with the remembered noise of the classroom into a pleasant dissonance she had not heard before.

Sitting on the concrete bench at the bus stop with her eyes closed against the wind and the sun, she breathed a quiet prayer. Thank you, Hazel, for being kind. Thank you, Mr. Escobar, for going fishing. Thank you, Mr. Jenkins. Thank you, God.

14

On Sunday night after church Elaine Foster went to her minister for advice. The minister, a worldly man called Kriger, knew perfectly well that Elaine was incapable of taking advice, so he didn't offer any. Instead, he let her talk. She talked for over an hour, being as truthful as she ever had to anybody, and when she had finished she went home and phoned Ruth.

The following morning about eleven o'clock, Ruth arrived carrying a suitcase and leading Wendy by a leash.

Elaine met her at the door. She looked coldly at the dog but didn't say anything.

She spoke in a stage whisper: "The children are playing in the kitchen. I don't want them to know you're here until we've had a chance to discuss matters. They get so excited."

"Have you told them yet?"

"Just that Grandma was sick and I have to go to Chicago to look after her for a week or so. They wouldn't understand the truth."

"Perhaps not." Ruth hesitated, and then reached down and took off the dog's leash. "I hope you don't mind my bringing Wendy. I thought the children might like—it might take their minds off things."

"I don't mind in the least."

"Besides, there's no one at home to look after her. Harold and Josephine are moving today. They found a small house in the canyon."

"I am very fond of dogs," Elaine said, and leaned over and patted the little dog firmly on the head.

Leaving the suitcase on the hall stairs the two women walked on tiptoe into the living room. The drapes were drawn so that the morning sun wouldn't fade the carpet and the slipcovers, and the room was twilight dark. From the kitchen came the sounds of the children playing, muffled by closed doors. Everything seemed muted, as if somewhere in the house, a person was about to die and mustn't be disturbed by noise or light or movement.

"I hate to leave," Elaine said. "But the Reverend Kriger told me it was the best thing to do, go away for a while and gain some perspective, think things out. If I sat around here feeling sorry for myself, I'd go mad."

"You're holding up wonderfully well."

"That's what he said, too. Some women would be simply prostrate, he said, having the bottom drop out of their lives like this. But I can't afford to give in to my emotions." She paused. "I wired Mother last night. Not that she'll be surprised, she's never had much use for Gordon. She was practically heartbroken when I married him. Reverend Kriger didn't actually say so, but he implied that perhaps I am being punished for not taking Mother's advice in the first place."

She began to pace up and down the room, and the little dog, thinking that she might be taking a walk, followed, sniffing, at her heels.

"I told you about the charge accounts at the market and the pharmacy."

Ruth nodded.

"You'll need some cash too, for the laundry and the paperboy and things like that. I've left fifty dollars for you in the top left-hand drawer of the buffet in the dining room. We haven't discussed your salary yet."

"There's no hurry."

"I don't even know how much I'll be able to pay you."

"You mustn't worry about it."

"That's what Reverend Kriger said, I mustn't worry about other people so much, I must think of myself." The Reverend Kriger had done nothing more than nod and make a sympathetic sound, but out of these Elaine had fabricated a whole moral philosophy: *You must be completely selfish, Mrs. Foster.* "He said, what about money, and I said, I don't know, I just don't know how we'll manage. With the house to pay for and three children to feed and clothe we've never been able to put much aside."

"Dr. Foster certainly won't let you starve."

"Won't he?" Elaine's mouth twitched with a grim little smile. "How will he make a living?"

"Hazel says he's a wonderful dentist."

"Really?"

"First-rate, she said."

"It seems to me Hazel might be a little prejudiced."

"Why?"

"That's what I wonder, why." She had stopped pacing and the little dog had stopped too, and was standing at her side looking up into her face, trying to read her expression. "I saw her this morning."

"Hazel? Where?"

"At the bank. She avoided me."

"Oh, I'm sure she didn't mean—"

"It was quite intentional."

"She's nearsighted."

"Not that nearsighted. She was in line at the very next window."

"Well."

"She cashed a check, a large check, judging from the number of bills the teller gave her."

"They could have been ones."

"They could have been, but they weren't. *I* am *not* nearsighted. They were twenties."

"Hazel doesn't keep much money in the bank. I can't understand it."

"I can. It wasn't her money, it was mine. Half mine, anyway."

"I don't see—"

"When my turn came I asked the teller to check the joint account I have with Gordon. There was five hundred dollars missing. It adds up, doesn't it? She wasn't cashing that check for herself but for Gordon. She knows where he's gone. She must, if she's going to send the money to him. It's laughable, isn't it?—she and Gordon may have planned this whole thing weeks ago."

"She never said a word about it, not a word."

"She wouldn't. She and Gordon are hand in glove, always have been."

The sun had passed the front window. Elaine went over and pulled back the drapes. In the morning light she seemed tired, but every curl was in place and her light shantung traveling suit looked very smart and new. When she was a girl, Elaine had shown few signs of youth, and now that she had reached her middle thirties she showed almost no signs of age.

She said, contemptuously, "How typical of Gordon, to drag other people into his childish schemes. He can't even manage his own love affair. Wait until the girl finds him out. Just wait. He'll come slobbering back to me wanting me to wipe his chin for him and change his bib. Just wait until his dear little Ruby catches on to him."

"Hello, Judith," Ruth said in a falsely bright manner.

Elaine turned abruptly. The girl was standing pressed against the door frame with a slice of bread in one hand and a piece of clay in the other.

She looked gravely at Ruth. "I made something. Do you want to see it?"

"I'd love to," Ruth said. "It looks very interesting."

"It isn't interesting, it's just a worm. But it's a good worm. Paul screamed at it blue murder."

"I don't blame him. It's such an excellent worm I feel like screaming myself."

"Why don't you?"

"Perhaps I will, later on when your mother leaves."

"It doesn't count if you don't do it right away like Paul did." For the first time since she entered the room she turned her eyes on her mother. "Who is Ruby?"

"She's just a girl, a woman," Elaine said. "And how many times have I told you not to go around in your bare feet like that prying into grown-ups' conversations? It's cheating."

"Linda's mother has ruby earrings."

"Well, that's nice."

"They cost a million or two dollars."

"Now, Judith, you know perfectly well that a pair of earrings doesn't cost a million dollars."

"Linda's mother's did."

"All right, all *right*."

"She got them from her boyfriend."

"Really now, Judith, you mustn't—" Elaine turned, sighing, to Ruth. "She makes up the weirdest things, honestly."

Ruth smiled at the girl. "I brought Wendy along."

"I know."

"Don't you want to pet her?"

"No."

"Why not?"

"I'll pet her later on when my mother leaves."

She put the clay worm on the table beside Ruth and walked silently out of the room.

"It's always like that," Elaine said. "Always. The least little thing and she turns against me. You'd think I was an ogre or something. Why does she do it?"

"I don't know."

"Well, it's no time to be worrying about it. I ordered the cab for eleven-thirty."

"It's almost that now."

"I—it's hard to believe I'm really leaving. I haven't been anywhere for so long." She hesitated. "Do I look all right?-—I mean, not like a country bumpkin?"

"You look very citified."

"Do I, really? People *dress* in Chicago, you know. Not like out here."

When the cab came, Ruth gathered the children on the front porch to say goodbye to their mother. Since Elaine never went as far as the corner grocery store without last-minute admonitions, a trip to Chicago was worth a record number: promise not to eat too many sweets, to say your prayers, brush your teeth, stay out of the loquat tree, watch for cars, don't spill anything on the new rug, keep out of the gopher poison in the garage, drink your orange juice, don't catch poison oak; be good, obedient, neat, careful, wise, polite, clean and healthy.

The air was thick as jelly with promises. The baby went to sleep in Ruth's arms, Paul played with the dog, Judith ate three bananas.

Elaine departed in the cab, laughing a little because she had wanted this trip for a long time, and crying a little too, because this wasn't how she had planned it. She had meant to go with Gordon and the children, a happy little family off on a visit to Grandma. "What a beautiful *family* you have," people would say. Or, "Such lovely, well-mannered children. It isn't often in this day and age—"

No, it wasn't often.

She leaned out of the back window of the cab and waved her lace handkerchief in farewell. But there was no one left on the porch except the little white mongrel scratching its ear.

Elaine put the lace handkerchief back in her pocketbook and dabbed at her eyes with a piece of Kleenex. She must keep the handkerchief clean for the plane trip. Kleenex looked common.

15

ON MONDAY NIGHT the wind stopped and fog began to move in from the sea across the city like a giant cataract across an eye.

Mrs. Freeman watched it from her dining-room window. It settled down into the trees and between the houses and crept under the cracks of doors; lights grew hazy, people vanished; the foghorn began to bray from the lighthouse on the Mesa.

Mrs. Freeman closed all the windows and pulled down the blinds and went back to the letter she had received in the morning mail. It was written on cheap hotel stationery and the handwriting was like a child's, hesitant and uneven, and punctuated with blobs of ink.

Dear Carrie, I bet you're sore at me not writing before this but you know me "old girl," I'm no good writing letters and stuff. Anyway here goes.

I am in Vegas where all the "big shots" come here to gamble. Every day you see somebody famous like movie stars and gangsters. I've been working steady for a week now a swell job with tips. I "turn on the charm" for them and the tips really roll in. You have to smile a lot that's the secret, the others haven't got wise to it yet.

It's pretty hot here now in the day but the nights are just right. People come here with azsma and go away cured, also T.B. Well that's about all Carrie. Just wait I'll hit the jackpot yet and then I'll be home and we'll live in "the lap of the gods," you can buy a whole new outfit. I miss you a lot and would sure love a home cooked meal for a change. I miss the ocean too, they can have the desert, give me a view of the sea any time. Well I guess that's it.

Love,

Robert.

P.S. Happy birthday on the 3rd of Sept. Ha, ha, I bet you thought I forgot!

Her birthday was on the fifth, but it was the nicest letter she had ever received from him. When the doorbell rang her heart quickened for an instant in the hope that it might be Robert, that the act of writing to her had made him homesick and he had decided to come back right away for a home-cooked meal and a view of the sea.

She opened the door and saw George, his outlines blurred by fog, his voice muffled.

"Is Ruby here?"

She looked at him dully, as if he had spoken a name she'd never heard before.

He coughed and said, "May I come in?"

"Yes. Yes, come in." She closed the door behind him, trembling a little. "It's cold, a cold night. I can smell winter in the air and here it isn't even fall yet. But that's Channel City for you, we get some of our best weather in December or January."

"I suppose so, but—"

"We can talk in the dining room. I have the heater going."

They sat down at the round oak table under the beaded chandelier. In spite of the gas heater hissing in the corner, the room was chilly, as if the old walls had absorbed one too many fogs.

"Ruby," Mrs. Freeman said. "She didn't call you?"

"No."

"I asked her to. I said you must be sure and tell Mr. Anderson before you leave. He'll want to know, I said, he'll be around asking for you."

"She's gone, then?"

"Yes."

"When?"

"Yesterday morning. It was very sudden."

"It must have been."

"Even so she ought to have told you. It's not fair leaving it to me. She could have called you."

"Maybe she tried. Maybe the line was busy."

"I'll bet you that's what happened."

He leaned across the table. "But you wouldn't bet much, would you?"

"No," she said, turning away. "Not much. She was—I tried to talk to her. She was a headstrong girl. Nothing mattered to her except what she wanted at the moment."

"And what did she want?"

"Him," Mrs. Freeman said quietly. "Just him. Nobody else counted. Some women are like that."

Not many, she thought. *But some. The unlucky ones. And the men they love are unlucky too. Like Robert.*

She looked at the bowl of wax fruit in the center of the table. The fruit came from the dime store but Robert had made the bowl himself out of a cracked phonograph record according to directions he'd found in an old magazine, steaming the record over the teakettle and when it was soft shaping it into a scalloped bowl. "Why, Robert, it's beautiful!" "It's not bad, is it?" "It's just beautiful." "Maybe I can get hold of a bunch of old records and start a whole new business." "That's a wonderful idea." "Honest to God, I think we got something here. I think we're going to hit the jackpot, Carrie, old girl." "Of course, of course we are, dear."

Of course. Because she couldn't bear to hurt him, she had encouraged him beyond all reason and reality. The hurt came anyway, and it was shattering and final. He tried to sell one of the bowls to Mrs. Haggerty next door and Mrs. Haggerty said her kids had been making bowls like that for years at the Y.M.C.A. crafts club.

"I'm sorry," Mrs. Freeman said, but it wasn't clear from her tone whom she was sorry for, George or Robert or Ruby or herself.

George lit a cigarette and the smoke curled up into the beaded chandelier and softened its glare.

"Where did she go?"

"I don't know. It wouldn't be any use anyway, trying to find her."

"But you know she went with him—with the man?"

"I saw them leave in his car. A nice-looking car. Green. When she said goodbye to me she put her arms around me, can you beat it?" Mrs. Freeman's mouth tightened. "You'd think we'd been friends or something, the way she said goodbye to me like that, as if she was kind of sorry she had to leave. Well, I can't be responsible for all the girls that cross my path. It's just—I took kind of a personal interest in Ruby. She reminds me of someone I knew years ago. Ruby's a little harder than this other girl I knew. Maybe she'll have better luck. She's not a bad girl."

"Ruby," George said carefully, "is a liar and a thief and a cheat."

She shook her head. "It might seem that way to you, you've been hurt. She lies, yes. People lie when the truth is too hard to bear."

"She didn't tell me she was interested in someone else, never even hinted at it."

"She didn't tell me either. No one ever came here for her or called her except you. It was a shock to me when he turned up on Saturday night looking for her. I thought it was just a common drunk making all that noise outside. When I went out to quiet him down he asked for Ruby. That was the first I knew about it."

"Saturday night," George repeated.

"Early Sunday morning, more like it. He'd been to one of those Fiesta parties and was all dressed up like a caballero or whatever you call them. I couldn't let him wander around in that condition and not even dressed proper, so I went upstairs and woke Ruby and between the two of us, we got him in here on the couch. He fell asleep right away."

"What was he like?"

"Like?" Mrs. Freeman blinked. "Well, sometimes it's kind of hard to tell when a man's drunk, but he seemed nice enough. Nothing special that I could see except he had lovely manners. I guess you'd say he was a gentleman."

"Would I?"

"It takes a gentleman not to forget his manners when he's had a few too many. I asked Ruby, is he a drunk, I asked her. And she said, no, he hardly ever touched the stuff, this was an unusual occasion. I can't tell you much more, Mr. Anderson, I don't know any more. It all happened so fast and unexpected. Maybe I should have phoned you just as soon as—"

"No," George said sharply. "No. I'm glad you didn't."

"I'd like to feel I did my best. I tried to talk to her, reason with her. But girls that age, they know everything, they know the score before they even find out what game they're playing."

She rose, and George rose too, and followed her down the long drafty hall to the front door. They shook hands soberly and formally, like mourners at a funeral.

"Thank you for your trouble," George said and tried to smile but his mouth felt dry and stiff. "You've been very kind."

"I tried, I wanted to help the girl. I wanted her to get interested in someone steady and dependable, well, like you, Mr. Anderson, no flattery intended. A girl like that needs a firm hand, a good strong marriage."

"Maybe she'll have it."

"How can she? He's already married, this man, married and with three kids."

George looked at her in silence for a long time, then he turned and opened the door and stepped out on the porch.

"Mr. Anderson?"

"It's getting late. I'd better—"

"I didn't mean to tell you that. It just popped out."

He didn't answer.

"You're not thinking of doing anything drastic, Mr. Anderson? I mean, it wouldn't be any use trying to find her. She's gone. She made that clear, she's gone for good."

"For good. Yes, I guess you're right."

They stood facing each other on the porch. The fog had shut everything else out, and it was as if they were alone together in a cold gray little world of their own.

Moisture condensed on Mrs. Freeman's home permanent and wiry curls began to spring up all over her head. "I'm sorry, Mr. Anderson. She should have told you herself."

"What's the man's name?"

"I don't—I can't remember."

"You've remembered everything else."

"Even so. Even so, I don't think I ought to—"

"Tell me."

"Gordon," Mrs. Freeman said. "She called him Gordon."

By ten o'clock the fog had covered the city. It hung from the old oak behind Hazel's house like angel hair on a Christmas tree.

There were no lights on in Hazel's house and when George knocked on the front door no one answered. He walked around to the back, found the key where Hazel always left it, under the doormat, and let himself into the kitchen.

He switched on the ceiling light and went over to the sink and poured himself a glass of water. The water left a long cold trail all the way down to his stomach. The rest of his body felt like fire.

Hazel came in from the dining room, heavy-eyed and yawning. "I thought I heard someone."

He stared at her without speaking.

"What do you want at this time of night?"

"I think you know."

"How should I know? What's the matter with you, are you drunk or something?"

"Come here, Hazel."

"What for?"

"Come here. I want to look at you."

"You can see me from there."

"Not well enough."

"Say, what's wrong with you, anyway? Are you losing your mind?"

"Hazel." He went over and took hold of both her wrists. "Tell me about the money, Hazel."

"What money?"

"You bitch. You creeping little bitch. I'd like to kill you."

She was afraid of him but she made no attempt to free herself or to scream for help. Letting her wrists dangle limply from his hands, she thought, it wouldn't really matter so much anyway; Ruth is settled, Harold and Josephine have a place of their own, Gordon is gone.

"Let go of me, George."

"Why? You've got something important to do, maybe? You want to cook up another of your fancy schemes?"

"Oh, stop it. I didn't—it wasn't a scheme. Gordon had to have the money. I got it for him the best way I could."

"There was no scheme, eh?"

"None."

"No idea of getting rid of Ruby because you couldn't stand the thought of me getting married again?"

"No."

"You're a liar."

"Maybe, in a way."

"Maybe, what is that supposed to mean?"

"I mean, the idea might have been in the back of my mind at the time, but I didn't know it was there."

He let go of her wrists and took a step back as if to see her in a new perspective. "You don't want me to get married again, do you?"

"Not to someone like Ruby."

"To someone like who, then?"

"We've talked about it before."

"Oh yes. The nice sensible widow my own age with a little cash and some real estate."

"There must be lots of women like that."

"In my business I don't meet them. Most of the ones I see are already married again, to a bottle."

"Well, I keep looking around."

"Do you?"

"Naturally I do. I'd like to see you settled down. It would be a load off my mind, in fact. I can't seem to—well, to get interested in anyone myself until I see you settled."

He glanced at her dryly. "Is that supposed to be an insult or a compliment?"

"It's how I feel anyway."

"So you're looking around for a nice sensible widow for me?"

"Sure. Sure I am. Just today at lunch in the cafeteria I met a very—"

"What a liar you are, Hazel. You almost make me laugh."

"Laugh yourself sick if you want to. I'm going back to bed. I have to get up early for work."

"Wait a minute."

"Why should I? All you can do is swear at me and call me names."

"I can do more than that."

"I wish you'd—"

"I can do a lot more than that, even without your cooperation."

"You'd better leave. I think you're drunk."

She stepped back, pulling her bathrobe closer around her throat.

"Afraid of me, Hazel?"

"No."

"You are, though. You're shaking like a leaf. What do you think I'm going to do to you?"

She shook her head.

"What would you like me to do?"

"Take—take your hands off me."

"That's what you really want?"

"Yes," she whispered. "Yes."

"When I touch you like this you feel no response?"

"No."

"Sure?"

"No! Yes! I'm sure."

"All right. I just thought I'd ask."

He took his hands away, looked at them for a moment as if they were strange new parts of his body, and put them in his pocket. The color had drained out of his face and his eyes bulged, dark and glassy like marbles.

Walking over to the table he pulled out a chair and sat down and crossed his legs, moving stiffly as if he was in pain.

He said in a low voice, "You'd better start looking a little harder for that widow. I don't like living alone."

"George."

"I guess I owe you an apology. All right. I'm sorry."

"I'm sorry too."

"You? What for?"

"The money."

"The money," he repeated with a grim little smile. "That seems like a long time ago. It hardly matters anymore."

"What does matter?"

"Nothing that I can think of."

"Did you—" Hazel stopped and swallowed hard. "Did you love her very much?"

"Christ. What a question."

"That's no answer."

"I thought about her a lot. When she was away I wanted to see her, but when I saw her she made me nervous, I couldn't stand her sometimes. If that's love, I loved her."

"That isn't how you used to feel about me, is it, George?"

"No."

"We had a lot of laughs together, didn't we? Remember the time you brought home that wrestler from New Jersey and he damn near wrecked the place and finally you had to pin him down?"

"I didn't pin him down," he said flatly. "He practically passed out. He could have broken my neck if he'd have been sober."

"That's not true. You're very strong."

"Oh stop it, Hazel."

"Well, you are."

"Stop it. I'm tired, I'm sick of myself. I'm a big fat nothing, let's face it."

"You're just feeling a little low tonight. Tomorrow morning you'll—"

"Tomorrow morning, next week, next month. It seems to me that all I've had for the past year is a future. The hell with it. I'd sell thirty years of future for ten minutes of present."

"You're pretty hard up then."

"Sure I am. What do you expect? I haven't had a wife for over a year."

The phone began to ring in the dining room and Hazel went to answer it. It was impossible to tell from her expression whether she was relieved or disappointed by the interruption, but when she spoke into the telephone she sounded quite cross.

"Hello? Yes, it's me . . . Now wait a minute, take it easy. Are you sure? . . . Well, lock all the doors and call the police . . . Who cares what she'd think, she's halfway to Chicago by this time . . . You're sure you're not imagining things? . . . Well, wait a minute. George is here. Talk to him."

She turned to call George but he was already there at her elbow.

He said, "Who is it?"

"Ruth. She's staying with the Foster kids while Elaine's away. She says there's a burglar trying to get into the house."

"Oh, for Christ's sake."

"I know, but suppose there really is?"

"I'll talk to her." He took the phone from Hazel's hand. "Ruth, it's George. Now what's this about a burglar?"

Ruth's voice came over the wire, dripping bitterness. "Oh, I heard what you said. I know what you're thinking, that it's all in my imagination. Well, I didn't imagine the dog barking, I didn't imagine someone trying the back door, I didn't im—"

"All right, Ruth, you didn't."

"He's out there now. I saw him with my own eyes, standing in the yard. And there's a car parked out on the street. I can't see if anyone's in it but there might be, there might even be a whole gang of them. A man came around this afternoon trying to sell vacuum cleaners. I told him the Fosters were away, I was only the housekeeper. It could be the same man. I can't tell, it's too foggy."

"Well, sit tight until I get there."

"I hate to put you to this trouble."

"No trouble at all," George said dryly. "I haven't anything else to do. It'll keep me out of mischief."

Hazel followed him to the front door. "I could go with you, George."

"I'm in a hurry and you're not dressed."

"I could slip a coat on. It won't take me a minute. I'd like to go."

"Why?"

"Well, the excitement, I guess."

"Is that all?"

She shook her head, rather shyly.

"What's the real reason, Hazel?"

"I don't know."

"I do," George said. "You don't want to be left alone. You'd rather come with me, not because it's me—I'm nothing special as far as you're concerned—but just to get out of an empty house."

"That's not true, not all of it is, anyway." She opened the door for him and the fog drifted into the room like ectoplasm. "You could come back and tell me all about it."

"I could. Do you want me to?"

"Yes."

"I'll be damned," George said and went out to his car. He walked very quickly as if purposely gathering momentum to carry him along in case his decision to leave should begin to falter.

Ruth put down the phone, and tiptoed through the darkness to the front hall. Here, on the bottom step of the staircase, she sat with the brass poker across her lap and the little dog at her feet, a pair of strange sentinels guarding the sleeping children.

The whole house was quiet. All the noise and confusion, the screams for help, the wail of sirens, the shriek of brakes, she had heard merely in her own mind. The only real noises had been the barking of the little dog and the faint but unmistakable click of the back-door latch.

She was afraid, but pushing its way up through the cold layers of fear was a feeling of triumph. The prowler outside was her enemy, the synthesis of all her enemies; he was real and alive and identifiable, and she was armed against him, guarding the children, with help on the way.

16

EVEN ON A SUNNY day it was a quiet neighborhood. Men went to their offices early in the morning and returned in the evening to eat dinner and read the newspaper and watch television behind closed blinds. Young children were kept off the street in nursery schools or walled patios, and dogs were fenced. It was a neighborhood built by and for retired people and members of the younger professional set who were on the way up.

Gordon didn't belong there; he had never felt any sense of belonging. When he came home from his office after the day's work he usually hesitated a moment outside the front door as if he was not sure whether it was his own door, or what lay behind it, his wife, Elaine, or some hostile stranger.

There was only one light on in the house, the night light in the upstairs bathroom. Elaine always left it on for the children so he knew they must be there, all four of them, sleeping quietly and not caring whether he came back or not. His absence seemed to have made only two differences: Elaine had been more careful about locking the doors, and she had bought a dog. He wondered whether the dog was intended as protection or as compensation for the children. A dog in exchange for a husband. *Well, that's fair enough*, he thought wryly. *Elaine doesn't like either breed.*

He leaned back against the slippery trunk of the loquat tree. Fog condensed on its leathery leaves and dripped on the ground with a monotonous little tune, *plink, plunk,* like a dozen leaking faucets. *Plink, plunk,* the tune was taken up by the bougainvillea over the garage and the hibiscus along the patio wall and the row of red-flowering eucalyptus that bordered the street. The sound reminded him of when he was a boy in Minnesota; in the spring the icicles that had hung stiff as quartz from the eaves throughout the winter started to melt until they fell loose and shattered, and the ice on the pond split open and water began to gurgle up through the cracks. Water sounds, dripping sounds everywhere. The first thaw in spring was almost as noisy as the first storm in autumn.

A cold trickle of moisture slid down the back of his neck. He pulled up his collar and walked silently through the fog to the front of the house. He had meant to arrive earlier, he had started out at dinner time from San Luis Obispo but as soon as the highway curved west to the coast the fog had struck like a crippling plague. Sleek young cars became gray and slow and anemic and moved like a procession of old men.

He went up the porch steps and sat down on the blue canvas glider, and from the inside of the house the dog began to bark again, in a higher pitch of hysteria and frustration. It wants to get out and bite me, chase me away, Gordon thought. I am an intruder. The house already belongs to him.

He was certain that the dog's barking would wake Elaine, and now that the moment was at hand when he must face her he felt uneasy and afraid. He couldn't remember all the compelling arguments he'd thought of during the day. He had planned each one carefully, using words and phrases that Elaine would understand and respond to emotionally. The arguments were still there inside his head but they had lost form, had thawed and dripped out of shape, like the icicles under the eaves, until they were blobs of slush.

He looked at the front door expecting it to open and not knowing what to say when it did. The door was solid mahogany because that's what Elaine wanted. She said it gave people a good impression from the start if they were faced with a solid mahogany door. But, as it turned out, she was mistaken. Hardly anyone came to the house, and of those who did not one had recognized that the door was solid mahogany, and Elaine was forced to tell them: "How do you like our door?" or "I hardly heard, you know, the door is so thick. Solid mahogany, you know."

Solid mahogany, closed and impenetrable. The key to it was on a key ring in his pocket. He could open the door if he wanted to, it was a simple matter, except for the dog. This was no ordinary dog. It sounded larger, stronger, fiercer. Its hoarse barking set up disturbing echoes in his mind, and each echo set up a new echo of its own until his eardrums reverberated with a cacophony of fears.

He sat motionless on the canvas glider with the fog dripping down his face.

A car came over the crest of the hill, languid and yellow-eyed. It crept past the house and paused with a sigh of brakes. The headlights went out, a door slammed, shoes scraped along the wet cement of the driveway.

A man walked out of the fog, like an actor making his entrance from behind a gray plush curtain. He crossed the lawn and came up the porch steps, a heavy-set man with a fedora pulled down low on his forehead. In the dark he could be anyone; but even in the light

Gordon would not have recognized him. He knew George only as the half-hero, half-child of Hazel's conversation.

Gordon leaned forward as if he was about to rise to welcome the stranger. The glider creaked.

The man turned with a little jump of surprise and said harshly, "What the hell."

"I didn't mean to startle—"

"What are you doing here?"

"I was about to ask you the same question."

"Ruth called me, said there was a prowler hanging around the house."

"Ruth? You must have the wrong address. This is my house."

"So?"

"It's not paid for, but I have the deed, so you might say it's my house. Are you a policeman? It's funny somebody should call a policeman because a man wants to get a little fresh air."

"If it's your house why don't you go inside?"

"Well, I would, except for the dog. It isn't any of your business but I don't mind telling you. She bought a dog while I was away. It sounds like a fairly large dog. You heard it a moment ago?"

"I heard it."

"Don't you think it sounds like a fairly large dog?"

"It's a little white mongrel," George said, "about the size of a fox terrier."

Inside the house there was silence, as if the dog was eavesdropping on the conversation.

Gordon rose, wiping the moisture from his forehead with the sleeve of his topcoat. "A little dog," he said quietly. "How could you know that?"

"I know a lot of things about you, Foster."

"You have the advantage of me. I don't even know your name."

"Anderson."

"You're Hazel's—"

"That's right."

"Well." Gordon looked down at the floor. Six inches from his left foot lay the doll he had given Judith the previous week. He had bought it, not for a special reason like a birthday, but in a moment of guilt and compunction, as if he could give to her in the form of this doll the happy babyhood she had missed. He had been able to buy off his conscience to some extent, but he hadn't bought off Judith. Within two days the doll was naked and almost scalped, one arm was gone, its china eyes had been carefully pushed back into its empty head, and into its slightly open mouth between the rows of tiny perfect teeth, Judith had thrust Elaine's ivory-handled nail file.

"Well," he said again. "I suppose it's time we met, even under circumstances like these. I'm not sure," he added wryly, "what circumstances they are."

"Aren't you?"

"No. No, I confess I'm puz—"

"Where's Ruby?"

"Ruby." Gordon repeated the name in a flat voice as if it aroused no interest or memory in him. "She's all right. Nothing happened to her."

"Tell me where she is."

"She's—I left her in San Luis."

"You *left* her."

"She has a cousin there. I—she decided to stay with her until—while I came back and settled things with Elaine. So I came back."

George stepped closer. He was laughing, soft derisive laughter that echoed back against the wall of fog.

"Lover boy," he said, and the laughter bubbled up again, not from his throat but from a source deep inside him. "A real honest-to-God lover boy, eh, Foster?"

Gordon shook his head, mute, resigned.

"That's your technique, is it, Foster?—Get them as far as San Luis, leave them with a cousin, and then come crawling back to your wife? That's it? Eh, lover boy?"

"You can't talk to me like that." But the words were frail and wistful, like the clenched fist of a little boy, the sting of a butterfly, the bite of a glowworm.

He thought of Elaine the last time he'd seen her standing in the wind beneath the wild palm tree, her voice calm and quiet: you fool, you idiot, no character, no will power, not a man, no resemblance to a man . . .

"You can't talk to me like that. I must—" *I must defend my human dignity*, he wanted to say. But there was no time, no place, for words. He drew back his arm and jerked it loosely like a piece of rope. His fist, an inert object at the end of it, incredibly, almost involuntarily, snapped up in front of him and struck George's chin.

George stumbled sideways and stepped on the doll's moist plastic head. The doll slipped out from under his foot with a squeaking noise and slid across the porch.

His arms flailed for a moment as he tried to recover his balance, then he fell heavily, his head striking the iron base of the glider.

From somewhere close by came the first soft muted wails of a police siren. Gordon turned and began to run. As he ran, his trembling muscles gained strength and a feeling of elation rose inside him like bubbles of adrenalin.

He climbed into his car and pressed the starter button. His right knuckles were painful and already swelling so that he couldn't bend his hand around the steering wheel. But the pain was not unpleasant. He drove toward the business section of the city, steering with his left hand, his right hand resting on the seat beside him like a trophy.

He checked in at a hotel on lower State Street and from his room he called Ruby long distance. Although it was very late Ruby answered the phone on the second ring, as if she had been waiting beside it for hours expecting him to call.

"Ruby?"

"Gordon. Where are you?"

"I'm staying at a hotel for the night."

"Did you talk to her? Did you ask her—?"

"I'm not going to ask her anything. I'm going to tell her."

"You sound funny, Gordon. Have you been—do you feel all right?"

"I'm going to tell her," he repeated and looked down at his bruised knuckles. *You can't talk to me like that.* "I'll see her tomorrow morning, first thing tomorrow morning."

"Why didn't you see her tonight?"

"It's hard to explain." Because it was foggy, because there was a dog barking, because Judith left her doll on the porch and a man stumbled over it. "I'll see her tomorrow. I'll make it perfectly clear that I'm not going to be run out of town like a criminal. I'm going to stay put and fight. I'm going to—"

"Yes."

"What did you say?"

"Nothing. Just yes." And she made a little sighing sound that was almost inaudible. But he heard it. He had heard the same sound a thousand times from Elaine and he knew its meaning and its intent; it was a complete negation of everything he was trying to say.

"Ruby?"

"Yes."

"I'll see her first thing tomorrow and then we can make our plans definite."

"Yes."

"You can stay there for a few more days. Then I'll find some place here for you to live, a little apartment, and then I'll drive up and get you. How's that?"

"Yes."

Yes. Not a word of agreement, in fact not a word at all. A sigh. Elaine's sound. A new sound for Ruby. He must destroy it before it grew as Elaine's had grown.

"If you want me to," he said, "I'll drive up and get you tomorrow. We'll face things together."

He heard her gasp of surprise and pleasure. "Gordon, you're not just saying that for my sake, because you know I'm scared?"

"No, I mean it. I'll be there at noon."

"Oh, Gordon."

"Goodnight, darling. There's nothing to be scared of."

His hand had started to throb, heavily and irregularly, like a fluttering heart. He went into the bathroom and held it under the cold water tap.

"There's nothing to be scared of," he said and began to laugh.

The sun rose early and hung like an orange-red spotlight behind a gauze curtain. By seven-thirty most of the fog had burned away, and when Hazel went out into the backyard to empty the trash baskets the roofs of the houses were steaming as if the whole city was on fire. All the dust that the desert wind had laid over everything was washed away and the air was clean and sweet.

To hell with him, he didn't even phone, Hazel thought, and banged the trash baskets upside down into the incinerator. Out came the remnants of the week: the letters and cigarette butts and apple cores, used pieces of Kleenex and empty food cartons and all the odds and ends from the drawers Harold and Josephine had cleaned out before they left, bits of ribbon, old grocery lists written on the corners of envelopes, some snapshot negatives, several newspaper clippings about pregnancy, a pamphlet on skin care, a sachet yellow and soured with age, and a woolen tie riddled with moth holes.

Hazel set a match to the rubbish and walked away because she did not want to see it burn. It seemed too final.

Slowly she crossed the yard. It had been only three days now since Escobar had cleaned it up, but already the grass had grown, more in some places than in others, so that the lawn looked uneven. The desert wind had deposited a fresh pile of dead leaves and acorns and eucalyptus pods beside the picket fence, and in the irrigation ditch Escobar had dug along the eugenia hedge there was a burst of new little weeds, tendrils of devil grass and sprigs of filaree and clusters of toadstools. Under the ground beside the garage an enterprising gopher had built himself some additional runways and storage rooms and his excavations had left little mounds of earth. During the night a dog or cat, bent on food or mischief, had upset the ant pot underneath the orange tree and the syrupy poison had seeped out and crystallized. The ants ignored the poison and marched as usual up and down the orange tree milking the aphids and, when it was necessary, carrying them to the more tender tips of the branches, like good farmers guiding their cattle to greener pastures.

It was as if, during a space of three days, a whole new cycle of life had begun. Under Hazel's feet the ground seemed to move with bursting seeds and hatching eggs, with blind, brainless, soundless cells of things dividing and redividing; earthworms, sow bugs, nematodes, thrips, like rich man, poor man, beggarman, thief.

It's no use, Hazel thought, a dozen Escobars wouldn't change anything.

She heard the click of the gate, and turned and saw George. He looked tired and there was a bandage wrapped around his head so tightly that it crinkled his forehead and gave him a puzzled expression.

"Hello, Hazel."

"Hello."

"I thought you'd be up by this time. I'm on my way home and, well, I decided to drop in and see you first."

"Oh."

He touched the bandage lightly with his fingertips. "No questions?"

"You look like you had quite an evening."

"I did."

"In fact you look like you got into a fight."

"In a way I did."

"You'd think at your age you'd have learned to stay out of fights."

"You're sore, aren't you, because I didn't come back last night? Well, I couldn't make it. Ruth phoned the police and they hauled me off to the hospital and wouldn't let me go until a few minutes ago. The nurse hid my clothes so I couldn't get away. And a couple of detectives kept asking me questions about who was my assailant, that's what they called him, my assailant."

"And who was he?"

"How should I know?" George said flatly. "It was foggy and dark. I didn't get a good look at him. He jumped me, took me by surprise. I slipped on something and hit my head on the glider."

"Is that what you told the police?"

"Yes."

"Is it the truth?"

"Close enough."

"What really happened?"

"What really happened," he repeated thoughtfully, as if he had already spent a great deal of time trying to decide on an answer. "I don't know. Maybe a lot happened, maybe I only got a cut on the head."

"George, was it—is it a bad cut?"

He looked down at her irritably. "Don't go into that Florence Nightingale routine. I'm a big boy, I can take care of myself."

"Then why the hell don't you?"

"Here we are quarreling again. Always quarreling."

"Well, I can't help it." She turned and went up the porch steps. "There's some coffee on the stove, let's have a cup."

He made no move to follow her. "No thanks."

"Aren't you even coming in?"

"No."

"What's the matter with you?"

"Nothing. I like it out here. Besides I can get a cup of coffee downtown. Any downtown. I can go anywhere in the world and get a cup of coffee."

"Whatever that means."

"It means a cup of coffee isn't what I want." He came up the porch steps, his head bent like a charging bull. "Listen to me. I did everything I could to get back here last night. I fought nurses and doctors and even policemen. I would have given my right arm to get back to you. It seemed the most important thing in the whole world to me, not because I'm hard up, as you put it, but because, well, I don't know how to say it. I'm no good at saying things, you might laugh. And if you laughed, I might—I don't trust myself—maybe I'd kill you."

"I don't feel like laughing."

"Don't I seem funny to you?"

"No."

"I am, though. I'm pretty funny. What are you crying about?"

"I'm not crying. And if I am, I can if I want to."

"What did I do to make you cry?"

She shook her head, holding her fists against her eyes. "Nothing."

"I must have. Goddamn it, Hazel, don't cry. I'm sorry. You hear that? I'm sorry. I don't know what for, but I'm sorry. Now will you stop crying?"

"No."

"Well, all right," he said. "All right."

He put his arms around her and she buried her face against his chest, and presently they went together into the house.

BEAST IN VIEW

for Betty and John Mersereau
best friends and unseverest critics

1

THE VOICE WAS quiet, smiling. "Is that Miss Clarvoe?"

"Yes."

"You know who this is?"

"No."

"A friend."

"I have a great many friends," Miss Clarvoe lied.

In the mirror above the telephone stand she saw her mouth repeating the lie, enjoying it, and she saw her head nod in quick affirmation—*this lie is true, yes, this is a very true lie.* Only her eyes refused to be convinced. Embarrassed, they blinked and glanced away.

"We haven't seen each other for a long time," the girl's voice said. "But I've kept track of you, this way and that. I have a crystal ball."

"I—beg your pardon?"

"A crystal ball that you look into the future with. I've got one. All my old friends pop up in it once in a while. Tonight it was you."

"Me." Helen Clarvoe turned back to the mirror. It was round, like a crystal ball, and her face popped up in it, an old friend, familiar but unloved; the mouth thin and tight as if there was nothing but a ridge of bone under the skin, the light brown hair clipped short like a man's, revealing ears that always had a tinge of mauve as if they were forever cold, the lashes and brows so pale that the eyes themselves looked naked and afraid. An old friend in a crystal ball.

She said carefully, "Who is this, please?"

"Evelyn. Remember? Evelyn Merrick."

"Oh, yes."

"You remember now?"

"Yes." It was another lie, easier than the first. The name meant nothing to her. It was only a sound, and she could not separate or identify it any more than she could separate the noise of one car from another in the roar of traffic from the Boulevard three floors down. They all sounded alike, Fords and Austins and Cadillacs and Evelyn Merrick.

"You still there, Miss Clarvoe?"

"Yes."

"I heard your old man died."

"Yes."

"I heard he left you a lot of money."

"That's my business."

"Money is a great responsibility. I might be able to help you."

"Thank you, I don't require any help."

"You may soon."

"Then I shall deal with the problem myself, without the help from any stranger."

"Stranger?" There was a rasp of annoyance in the repetition. "You said you remembered me."

"I was merely trying to be polite."

"Polite. Always the lady, eh, Clarvoe? Or pretending to be. Well, one of these days you'll remember me with a bang. One of these days I'll be famous; my body will be in every art museum in the country. Everyone will get a chance to admire me. Does that make you jealous, Clarvoe?"

"I think you're—mad."

"Mad? Oh no. *I'm* not the one who's mad. It's you, Clarvoe. *You're* the one who can't remember. And I know why you can't remember. Because you're jealous of me, you're so jealous you've blacked me out."

"That's not true," Miss Clarvoe said shrilly. "I don't know you. I've never heard of you. You're making a mistake."

"I don't make mistakes. What you need, Clarvoe, is a crystal ball so you could remember your old friends. Maybe I should send you mine. Then you could see yourself in it, too. Would you like that? Or would you be afraid? You've always been such a coward, my crystal ball might scare you out of your poor little wits. I have it right here with me. Shall I tell you what I see?"

"No—stop this . . ."

"I see you, Clarvoe."

"No . . ."

"Your face is right in front of me, real bright and clear. But there's something wrong with it. Ah, I see now. You've been in an accident. You are mutilated. Your forehead is slashed open, your mouth is bleeding, blood, blood all over, blood all over . . ."

Miss Clarvoe's arm reached out and swept the telephone off the stand. It lay on its side on the floor, unbroken, purring.

Miss Clarvoe sat, stiff with terror. In the crystal ball of the mirror her face was unchanged, unmutilated. The forehead was smooth, the mouth prim and self-contained, the skin paper-white, as if there was no blood left to bleed. Miss Clarvoe's bleeding had been done, over the years, in silence, internally.

When the rigidity of shock began to recede, she leaned down and picked up the telephone and placed it back on the stand.

She could hear the switchboard operator saying, "Number please. This is the operator. Number please. Did you wish to call a number, *pullease?*"

She wanted to say, *Give me the police*, the way people did in plays, very casually, as if they were in the habit of calling the police two or three times a week. Miss Clarvoe had never called the police in her life, had never, in all her thirty years, even talked to a policeman. She was not afraid of them; it was simply a fact that she had nothing in common with them. She did not commit crimes, or have anything to do with people who did, or have any crimes committed against her.

"Your number, please."

"Is that—is that you, June?"

"Why, yes, Miss Clarvoe. Gee, when you didn't answer, I thought maybe you'd fainted or something."

"I never faint." Another lie. It was becoming a habit, a hobby, like stringing beads. A necklace of lies. "What time is it, June?"

"About nine-thirty."

"Are you very busy?"

"Well, I'm practically alone at the switchboard. Dora's got flu. I'm warding off an attack of it myself."

Miss Clarvoe suspected from the note of self-pity in her voice and the slight slurring of her words that June had been warding off the flu in a manner not approved by the management or by Miss Clarvoe herself. She said, "Will you be going off duty soon?"

"In about half an hour."

"Would you—that is, I'd appreciate it very much if you'd come up to my suite before you go home."

"Why, is there anything wrong, Miss Clarvoe?"

"Yes."

"Well, gee whizz, *I* didn't do any . . ."

"I shall expect you here shortly after ten, June."

"Well, all right, but I still don't see what I . . ."

Miss Clarvoe hung up. She knew how to deal with June and others like her. One hung up. One severed connections. What Miss Clarvoe did not realize was that she had severed too many connections in her life, she had hung up too often, too easily, on too many people. Now, at thirty, she was alone. The telephone no longer rang, and when someone knocked on her door, it was the waiter bringing up her dinner, or the woman from the beauty parlour to cut her hair, or the bellboy, with the morning paper. There was no longer anyone to hang up on except a switchboard operator who used to work in her father's office, and a lunatic stranger with a crystal ball.

She had hung up on the stranger, yes, but not quickly enough. It was as if her loneliness had compelled her to listen; even words of evil were better than no words at all.

She crossed the sitting-room and opened the French door that led on to the little balcony. There was room on the balcony for just one chair, and here Miss Clarvoe sat and watched the boulevard three flights down. It was jammed with cars and alive with lights. The sidewalks swarmed with people, the night was full of the noises of living. They struck Miss Clarvoe's ears strangely, like sounds from another planet.

A star appeared in the sky, a first star, to wish on. But Miss Clarvoe made no wish. The three flights of steps that separated her from the people on the boulevard were as infinite as the distance to the star.

June arrived late after a detour through the bar and up the back staircase which led to the door of Miss Clarvoe's kitchenette. Sometimes Miss Clarvoe herself used this back staircase. June had often seen her slipping in or out like a thin, frightened ghost trying to avoid real people.

The door of the kitchenette was locked. Miss Clarvoe locked everything. It was rumored around the hotel that she kept a great deal of money hidden in her suite because she didn't trust banks. But this was a common rumor, usually started by the bellboys, who enjoyed planning various larcenies when they were too broke to play the horses.

June didn't believe the rumor. Miss Clarvoe locked things up because she was the kind of person who always locked things up whether they were valuable or not.

June knocked on the door and waited, swaying a little, partly because the martini had been double, and partly because a radio down the hall was playing a waltz and waltzes always made her sway. Back and forth her scrawny little body moved under the cheap plaid coat.

Miss Clarvoe's voice cut across the music like a knife through butter. "Who's there?"

June put her hand on the door jambs to steady herself. "It's me. June."

The door was unchained and unbolted. "You're late."

"I had an errand to do first."

"Yes, I see." Miss Clarvoe knew what the errand was; the kitchenette already reeked of it. "Come into the other room."

"I can stay only a minute. My aunt will . . ."

"Why did you use the back stairs?"

"Well, I didn't know *exactly* what you wanted me for, and I thought if it was something I'd done wrong I didn't want the others to see me coming up here and getting nosy."

"You haven't done anything wrong, June. I only wanted to ask you a few questions." Miss Clarvoe smiled, in a kindly way. She knew how to deal with June and people like her. One smiled. Even in an agony of fear and uncertainty, one smiled. "Have you ever seen my suite before, June?"

"No."

"Never?"

"How could I? You never asked me up before, and I didn't get my job here until after you moved in."

"Perhaps you'd like to look around a bit?"

"No. No thanks, Miss Clarvoe. I'm in kind of a hurry."

"A drink, then. Perhaps you'd like a drink?" One smiled. One coaxed. One offered drinks. One did anything to avoid being alone, waiting for the telephone to ring again. "I have some nice sherry. I've been keeping it for—well, in case of callers."

"I guess a nip of sherry wouldn't hurt me," June said virtuously. "Especially as I'm coming down with flu."

Miss Clarvoe led the way down the hall into the sitting-room and June followed, looking around curiously now that Miss Clarvoe's back was turned. But there was very little to see. All the doors in the hall were closed, it was impossible to tell what was behind any of them, a closet or a bedroom or a bathroom.

Behind the last door was the sitting-room. Here Miss Clarvoe spent her days and nights, reading in the easy chair by the window, lying on the divan, writing letters at the walnut desk: *Dear Mother: I am well . . . glorious weather . . . Christmas is coming . . . my best to Douglas . . . Dear Mr. Blackshear: Regarding those hundred shares of Atlas . . .*

Her mother lived six miles west, in Beverly Hills, and Mr. Blackshear's office was no more than a dozen blocks down the boulevard, but Miss Clarvoe hadn't seen either of them for a long time.

She poured the sherry from the decanter on the coffee table. "Here you are, June."

"Gee, thanks, Miss Clarvoe."

"Sit down, won't you?"

"All right. Sure."

June sat down in the easy chair by the window and Miss Clarvoe watched her, thinking how much she resembled a bird, with her quick, hopping movements and her bright, greedy eyes and her bony little hands. A sparrow, in spite of the blonde hair and the gaudy plaid coat, a drunken sparrow feeding on sherry instead of crumbs.

And, watching June, Miss Clarvoe wondered for the first time what Evelyn Merrick looked like.

She said carefully, "I had a telephone call an hour ago, June, about nine-thirty. I'd be very—grateful for any information you can give me about the call."

"You mean, where it came from?"

"Yes."

"I wouldn't know that, Miss Clarvoe, unless it was long distance. I took three, four long distance calls tonight, but none of them was for you."

"You recall ringing my room, though, don't you?"

"I don't know."

"Think hard."

"Well, sure, Miss Clarvoe. I *am* thinking hard, real hard." The girl screwed up her face to maintain the illusion. "Only it's like this, see. If someone calls and asks for Miss Clarvoe, then I'd remember it for sure, but if someone just asks for room 425, well, that's different, see."

"Whoever called me, then, knew the number of this suite."

"I guess."

"Why do you guess, June?"

The girl fidgeted on the edge of the chair, and her eyes kept shifting towards the door and then to Miss Clarvoe and back to the door. "I don't know."

"You said you *guessed*, June."

"I only meant I—I can't remember ringing 425 tonight."

"Are you calling me a liar, June?"

"Oh no, Miss Clarvoe, I should say not, Miss Clarvoe. Only . . ."

"Well?"

"I don't remember, is all."

They were the final words of the interview. There were no thank-you's or farewells or see-you-soon's. Miss Clarvoe rose and unlocked the door. June darted out into the corridor. And Miss Clarvoe was alone again.

Laughter from the next room vibrated against the wall and voices floated in through the open french door of the balcony:

"Honestly, George, you're a kick, a real kick."

"Listen to the girl, how cute she talks."

"Hey, for Pete's sake, who took the opener?"

"What do you think the good Lord gave you teeth for?"

"What the Lord gaveth, the Lord tooketh away."

"Dolly, where in hell did you put the opener?"

"I don't remember."

I don't remember, is all.

Miss Clarvoe sat down at the walnut desk and picked up the gold fountain pen her father had given her for her birthday years ago.

She wrote: *Dear Mother: It has been a long time since I've heard from you. I hope that all is hell with you and Douglas.*

She stared at what she had written, subconsciously aware that a mistake had been made but not seeing it at first. It looked so right, somehow: *I hope that all is hell with you and Douglas.*

I meant to say well, Miss Clarvoe thought. It was a slip of the pen. I hold no resentment against her. It's all this noise—I can't concentrate—those awful people next door . . .

"Sometimes you behave like an ape, Harry."

"Send down for some bananas, somebody. Harry's hungry."

"So what's so funny?"

"Take a joke, can't you. Can't you take a joke?"

Miss Clarvoe closed and locked the French doors.

Perhaps that's what the telephone call was, she thought. Just a joke. Just someone, probably someone who worked in the hotel, trying to frighten her a little because she was wealthy and because she was considered somewhat odd. Miss Clarvoe realized that these qualities made her a natural victim for jokers; she had become adjusted to that fact years ago, and behind-the-hand snickers no longer disturbed her the way they had in school.

It was settled then. The girl with the crystal ball was a joke. Evelyn Merrick didn't exist. And yet the very name was beginning to sound so familiar that Miss Clarvoe was no longer absolutely certain she hadn't heard it before.

She pulled the curtains closed across the windows and returned to her letter.

I hope that all is hell with you and Douglas.

She crossed out hell and inserted well.

I hope that all is well with you and Douglas. I don't though. I don't hope anything. I don't care.

She tore the sheet of paper across the middle and placed it carefully in the wastebasket beside her desk. She had nothing really to say to her mother, never had, never would have. The idea of asking her for advice or comfort or help was absurd. Mrs. Clarvoe had none of these things to give, even if Helen had dared to ask.

The party in the next room had reached the stage of song. "Down by the Old Mill Stream." "Harvest Moon." "Daisy, Daisy." Sometimes in close harmony, sometimes far.

A hot gust of anger and resentment swept through Miss Clarvoe's body. They had no right to make so much noise at this time of night. She would have to rap on the wall to warn them, and if that didn't work she would call the manager.

She started to rise but her heel caught in the rung of the chair and she fell forward, her face grazing the sharp edge of the desk. She lay still, tasting the metallic saltiness of blood, listening to the throbbing of the pulse in her temples and the panic beat of her heart.

After a time she pulled herself to her feet and moved slowly and stiffly across the room towards the mirror above the telephone stand. There was a slight scratch on her forehead and one corner of her mouth was bleeding where the underlip had been bit by a tooth.

"*. . . I have a crystal ball. I see you now. Real bright and clear. You've been in an accident. Your forehead is gashed, your mouth is bleeding. . . .*"

A cry for help rose inside Miss Clarvoe's throat. Help me, someone! Help me, Mother—Douglas—Mr. Blackshear . . .

But the cry was never uttered. It stuck in her throat, and presently Miss Clarvoe swallowed it as she had swallowed a great many cries.

I am not really hurt. I must be sensible. Father always boasted to people how sensible I am. Therefore I must not become hysterical. I must think of something very sensible to do.

She went back to her desk and picked up her pen and took out a fresh sheet of notepaper.

> *Dear Mr. Blackshear:*
>
> *You may recall that, at my father's funeral, you offered to give me advice and help if the occasion should ever arise. I do not know whether you said this because it is the kind of thing one says at funerals, or whether you sincerely meant it. I hope it was the latter, because the occasion, you may have already inferred, has arisen. I believe that I have become the victim of a lunatic. . . .*

2

> *. . . It is distressing to me to have to confide these sordid details to anyone. I do not lightly cast my burdens on other people, but since you gave my late father such expert counsel, I would very much appreciate your advice in the situation I have described to you.*
>
> *If you would be so kind as to telephone me when you receive this letter and let me have your opinion in the matter, I would be extremely grateful. I intend, of course, to express my gratitude in more practical terms than words.*
>
> *Yours very truly,*
> *Helen Clarvoe*

The letter was delivered to Mr. Blackshear's office and then sent to his apartment on Los Feliz because he had gone home early. He no longer appeared regularly at his office. At fifty, he was retiring gracefully, by degrees, partly because he could afford to, but mostly because boredom had set in, like a too early winter. Things had begun to repeat themselves: new situations reminded him of past situations, and people he met for the first time were exactly like other people he'd known for years. Nothing was new anymore.

Summer had passed. The winter of boredom had set in and frost had formed in the crevices of Blackshear's mind. His wife was dead, his two sons had married and made lives of their own, and his friends were mostly business acquaintances whom he met for lunch at Scandia or the Brown Derby or the Roosevelt. Dinners and evening parties were rare because Blackshear had to rise long before dawn in order to be at his office by six o'clock when the New York Stock Exchange opened.

By the middle of the afternoon he was tired and irritable, and when Miss Clarvoe's letter was delivered he almost didn't open it. Through her father, who had been one of Blackshear's clients, he had known Helen Clarvoe for years, and her constrained prose and her hobbled mind depressed him. He had never been able to think of her as a woman. She was simply Miss Clarvoe, and he had a dozen or more clients just like her, lonely rich ladies desiring to be richer in order to take the curse off their loneliness.

"Damn the woman," he said aloud. "Damn all dull women."

But he opened the letter because on the envelope, in Miss Clarvoe's neat, private-school backhand, were the words: Confidential, Very Important.

> *. . . Lest you think I am exaggerating the matter, I hasten to assure you that I have given an exact account both of the telephone call and my subsequent conversation with the switchboard operator, June Sullivan. You will understand, I am sure, how deeply shocked and perplexed I am. I have harmed no one in my life, not intentionally at any rate, and I am truly amazed that someone apparently bears me a grudge.*

When he had finished reading the letter he called Miss Clarvoe at her hotel, more from curiosity than any desire to help. Miss Clarvoe was not the kind of woman who would accept help. She existed by, for, and unto herself, shut off from the world by a wall of money and the iron bars of her egotism.

"Miss Clarvoe?"

"Yes."

"This is Paul Blackshear."

"Oh." It was hardly a word, but a deep sigh of relief.

"I received your letter a few minutes ago."

"Yes. I—thank you for calling."

It was more like the end of a conversation than the beginning. Somewhat annoyed by her reticence, Blackshear said, "You asked me for advice, Miss Clarvoe."

"Yes. I know."

"I have had very little experience in such matters, but I strongly urge you to . . ."

"Please," Miss Clarvoe said. "Please don't say anything."

"But you asked me . . ."

"Someone might be listening."

"I have a private line."

"I'm afraid I haven't."

She must mean the girl, June Sullivan, Blackshear thought. Of course the girl would be listening, if she wasn't busy elsewhere; Miss Clarvoe had probably antagonized her, or, at the very least, aroused her curiosity.

"There have been new developments," Miss Clarvoe's voice was guarded. "I can talk about them only in the strictest privacy."

"I see."

"I know how busy you are and I hate to impose on you, but—well, I must, Mr. Blackshear. I *must.*"

"Please go on." Behind her wall of money, behind her iron bars, Miss Clarvoe was the maiden in distress, crying out reluctantly and awkwardly, for help. Blackshear made a wry grimace as he pictured himself in the role of the equally reluctant rescuer, a tired, detached, balding knight in Harris tweeds. "Tell me what you want me to do, Miss Clarvoe."

"If you could come here to my hotel, where we can talk—privately . . ."

"We'd probably have more privacy if you came over here to my apartment."

"I can't. I'm—afraid to go out."

"Very well, then. What time would you like me to come?"

"As soon as you can."

"I'll see you shortly, then, Miss Clarvoe."

"Thank you. Thank you very much. I can't *tell* you how . . ."

"Then please don't. Good-bye."

He hung up quickly. He didn't like the sound of Miss Clarvoe's gratitude spilling out of the telephone, harsh and discordant, like dimes spilling out of a slot machine. The jackpot of Miss Clarvoe's emotions—*thank you very much.*

What a graceless woman she was, Blackshear thought, hoarding herself like a miser, spending only what she had to, to keep alive.

Although they communicated quite frequently by letter, he hadn't seen her since her father's funeral the previous year. Tall, pale, tearless, she had stood apart from the others at the grave; her only display of feeling had been an occasional sour glance at the weeping widow, Verna Clarvoe, leaning on the arm of her son Douglas. The more tears her mother shed, the more rigid Helen Clarvoe's back had become, and the tighter her lips.

When the services were over, Blackshear had approached Miss Clarvoe, aware of her mute suffering.

"I'm sorry, Helen."

She had turned her face away. "Yes. So am I."

"I know how fond you and your father were of each other."

"That's not entirely accurate."

"No?"

"No. I was fond of him, Mr. Blackshear, not he of me."

The last time he saw her she was climbing stiffly into the back of the long black Cadillac that was used to transport the chief mourners, Mrs. Clarvoe, Helen and Douglas. They made a strange trio.

A week later Blackshear received a letter from Miss Clarvoe stating that she had moved, permanently, to the Monica Hotel and wished him to handle her investments.

The Monica was the last place in the world he would have expected Miss Clarvoe to choose. It was a small hotel on a busy boulevard in the heart of Hollywood, and it catered not to the quiet solitary women like Miss Clarvoe, but to transients who stayed a night or two and moved on, minor executives and their wives conducting business with pleasure, salesmen with their sample cases, advertising men seeking new accounts, discreet ladies whose names were on file with the bellhops, and tourists in town to do the studios and see the television shows. All the kinds of people Miss Clarvoe would ordinarily dislike and avoid. Yet she chose to live in their midst, like a visitor from another planet.

Blackshear left his car in a parking lot and crossed the street to the Monica Hotel.

The desk clerk, whose name-plate identified him as G. O. Horner, was a thin, elderly man with protuberant eyes that gave him an expression of intense interest and curiosity. The expression was false. After thirty years in the business, people meant no more to him than individual bees do to a beekeeper. Their differences were lost in a welter of statistics, eradicated by sheer weight of numbers. They came and went; ate, drank, were happy, sad, thin, fat; stole towels and left behind toothbrushes, books, girdles, jewelry; burned holes in the furniture, slipped in bathtubs, jumped out of windows. They were all alike, swarming around the hive, and Mr. Horner wore a protective net of indifference over his head and shoulders.

The only thing that mattered was the prompt payment of bills. Blackshear looked solvent. He was smiled at.

"Is there anything I can do for you, sir?"

"I believe Miss Clarvoe is expecting me."

"Your name, please."

"Paul Blackshear."

"Just a moment, sir, and I'll check."

Horner approached the switchboard, walking softly and carefully, as if one of his old enemies had scattered tacks on the floor. He talked briefly to the girl on duty, hardly moving his mouth. The girl looked over her shoulder at Blackshear with sullen curiosity and Blackshear wondered if this was the June Sullivan Miss Clarvoe had mentioned in her letter.

Blackshear returned her stare. She was an emaciated blonde with trembling hands and a strained, white face, as if the black leech of the earphones had already drawn too much blood.

Horner bent over her, but the girl leaned as far away from him as she could and started to yawn. Three or four times she yawned and her eyes began to water and redden along the upper lids. It was impossible to guess her age. She could have been a malnourished twenty or an underdeveloped forty.

Horner returned, his fingers plucking irritably at the lapels of his black suit. "Miss Clarvoe didn't leave any message down here, sir, and her room doesn't answer."

"I know she's expecting me."

"Oh, certainly, sir, no offence intended, I assure you. Miss Clarvoe frequently doesn't answer her telephone. She wears earplugs. On account of the traffic noises, a great many of our guests wear . . ."

"What is the number of her suite?"

"Four twenty-five."

"I'll go up."

"Certainly, sir. The lifts are to your right."

While he was waiting for a lift, Blackshear glanced back at the desk and saw that Horner was watching him; he had lifted his protective veil of indifference for a moment and was peering out like an old woman from behind a lace curtain.

Blackshear disappeared into the lifts and Mr. Horner lowered his net again, and let the lace curtain fall over his thoughts: *That suit must have cost a hundred and fifty dollars . . . these con men always put up a good appearance . . . I wonder how he's going to take her and for how much . . .*

Miss Clarvoe must have been waiting behind the door. It opened almost simultaneously with Blackshear's knock, and Miss Clarvoe said in a hurried whisper, "Please come in."

She locked the door behind him, and for a few moments they stood looking at each other in silence across a gully of time. Then Miss Clarvoe stretched out her hand and Blackshear took it.

Her skin was cool and dry and stiff like parchment, and there was no pressure of friendliness, or even of interest, in her clasp. She shook hands because she'd been brought up to shake hands as a gesture of politeness. Blackshear felt that she disliked the personal contact. Skin on skin offended her; she was a private person. The private I, Blackshear thought, always looking through a single keyhole.

The day was warm for November, and Blackshear's own hands were moist with sweat. It gave him a kind of petty satisfaction to realize that he must have left some of his moisture on her.

He waited for her to wipe her hand, surreptitiously, even unconsciously, but she didn't. She merely took a step backward and two spots of color appeared on her high cheekbones.

"It was kind of you to go to all this trouble, Mr. Blackshear."

"No trouble at all."

"Please sit down. The wing chair is very comfortable."

He sat down. The wing chair was comfortable enough but he couldn't help noticing that it, like all the other furniture in the room, was cheap and poorly made. He thought of the Clarvoe house in Beverly Hills, the hand-carved chairs and the immense drawing-room where the rug had been especially woven to match a pattern in the Gauguin above the mantel, and he wondered for the dozenth time why Miss Clarvoe had left it so abruptly and isolated herself in a small suite in a second-rate hotel.

"You haven't changed much," Blackshear lied politely.

She gave him a long, direct stare. "Do you mean that as a compliment, Mr. Blackshear?"

"Yes, I did."

"It is no compliment to me to be told that I haven't changed. Because I wish I had."

Damn the woman, Blackshear thought. You couldn't afford to be nice to her. She was unable to accept a compliment, a gift of any kind; they seemed to burn her like flaming arrows and she had to pluck them out and fling them back with vicious accuracy, still aflame.

He said coldly, "How is your mother?"

"Quite well, as far as I know."

"And Douglas?"

"Douglas is like me, Mr. Blackshear. He hasn't changed either. Unfortunately."

She approached the walnut desk. It bore no evidence of the hours Miss Clarvoe had spent at it. There were no letters or papers visible, no ink marks on the blotter. Miss Clarvoe did not leave things lying about. She kept them in drawers, in closets, in neat steel files. All the records of her life were under lock and key: the notes from Douglas asking for money, her bank statements and cancelled checks, gardenia-scented letters from her mother, some newspaper clippings about her father, an engraved wedding invitation half torn down the middle, a bottle of sleeping pills, a leash and harness with a silver tag bearing the name Dapper, a photograph of a thin, awkward girl in a ballet dress, and a sheaf of bills held together by a gold money clip.

Miss Clarvoe picked up the sheaf of bills and handed it to Blackshear.

"Count it, Mr. Blackshear."

"Why?"

"I may have made a mistake. I get—flustered sometimes and can't concentrate properly."

Blackshear counted the money. "A hundred and ninety-six dollars."

"I was right, after all."

"I don't understand."

"Someone has been stealing from me, Mr. Blackshear. Perhaps systematically, for weeks, perhaps just once, I don't know. I do know that there should be nearly a thousand dollars in that clip."

"When did you discover some of it was missing?"

"This morning. I woke up early while it was still dark. There was some argument going on down the hall, a man and a woman. The woman's voice reminded me of the girl on the telephone, Evelyn Merrick, and I—well, it upset me. I couldn't go back to sleep. I began to wonder about Miss Merrick and when—whether I would hear from her again and what she hoped to get out of me. The only thing I have is money."

She paused, as if giving him a chance to contradict her or agree with her. Blackshear remained quiet. He knew she was wrong, but he didn't feel that anything could be gained, at this point, by stating it: Miss Clarvoe had another thing besides money which might interest a woman like Evelyn Merrick, and that was the capacity to be hurt.

Miss Clarvoe continued quietly. “I got up and took a pill and went back to sleep. I dreamed of her—Evelyn Merrick. I dreamed she had a key to my suite and she let herself in, bold as brass. She was blonde, coarse-looking, made up like a woman of the streets—it’s so vivid, even now. She went over to my desk and took my money. All of it.” Miss Clarvoe stopped and gave Blackshear a long, direct stare. “I know such dreams mean nothing, except that I was disturbed and frightened, but as soon as I woke up again I unlocked my desk and counted my money.”

“I see.”

“I told you about the dream because I wanted to make it clear that I had a *reason* for counting the money. I don’t usually do such a thing. I’m not a miser poring over a hoard of gold.”

But she spoke defensively, as if someone in the past had accused her of being miserly.

“Why do you keep such a large amount of cash in your room?” Blackshear said.

“I need it.”

“Why?”

“For—well, tips, shopping for clothes, things like that.”

Blackshear didn’t bother pointing out that a thousand dollars would cover a lot of tips, and the black jersey dress Miss Clarvoe was wearing indicated that her shopping trips were few and meagre.

The silence stretched out like tape from a roller until there seemed no logical place to cut it.

“I like to have my money around,” she said, finally. “It gives me a feeling of security.”

“It should give you the opposite.”

“Why?”

“It makes you a target.”

“You think that’s what Evelyn Merrick wants from me? Only money?”

He realized from her stressing of the word “only” that she too suspected other factors were involved.

“Perhaps,” he said. “It sounds to me like an extortion racket. It may be that the woman means to frighten you, to harass you, until you are willing to pay her to be left alone. It may be, too, that you’ll never hear from her again.”

Miss Clarvoe turned away with a little sighing sound that whispered of despair. “I’m afraid. I’m afraid sometimes even to answer the phone.”

Blackshear looked grave. “Do you know more than you’re telling me, Helen?”

“No. I wrote everything in my letter to you, every word that was spoken. She’s—she’s crazy, isn’t she, Mr. Blackshear?”

“A little off-balance, certainly. I’m no specialist in these matters. My business is stocks and bonds, not psychoses.”

“You have no advice for me, then?”

“I think it would be a good idea if you took a vacation. Leave town for a while. Travel. Go someplace where this woman can’t find you.”

“I have no place to go.”

“You have the whole world,” Blackshear said impatiently.

“No—no.” The world was for couples, for lovers, for husbands and wives, mothers and daughters, fathers and sons. Everywhere in the world, all the way to the horizon, Miss Clarvoe saw couples, like her mother and father, and, now, Douglas and her mother, and the sight of them spread ice around her heart.

“England,” Blackshear was saying. “Or Switzerland. I’m told St. Moritz is very lively in the wintertime.”

“What would I do in such a place?”

“What do other people do?”

"I don't really know," she said seriously. "I've lost touch."

"You must find it again."

"How does one go about finding things that are lost? Have you ever lost anything, Mr. Blackshear?"

"Yes." He thought of his wife, and his endless, silent prayers when she was dying, his bargains with God: take my eyes, my arms, my legs, take anything, but leave me Dorothy.

"I'm sorry," Miss Clarvoe said. "I didn't realize—I'd forgotten . . ."

He lit a cigarette. His hands were shaking with anger and remembered grief and sudden loathing for this awkward woman who did everything wrong, who cared for no one and gave nothing of herself even to a dog.

"You asked me for advice," he said with no trace of emotion. "Very well. About the missing money, you'll have to report that to the police. Whether you like it or not, it's your duty as a citizen."

"Duty." She repeated the word after him, slowly, as if it had a taste that must be analyzed, a flavor pungent with the past: castor oil and algebra and unshed tears and hangnails and ink from leaky pens. Miss Clarvoe was a connoisseur. She could pick out and identify each flavor, no matter how moldy with age.

"As for the woman, Evelyn Merrick, I've already given you my advice. Take a vacation. There are certain disordered persons who get a kick out of making anonymous phone calls to strangers or people they know slightly."

"She gave me her name. It wasn't an anonymous call."

"It was as far as you're concerned. You don't know her. You've never heard of her before. Is that right?"

"I think so. I'm not sure."

"Do you ordinarily remember people well—names, faces, conversations?"

"Oh yes." Miss Clarvoe gave a nod of bitter satisfaction. "I remember them."

Blackshear got up and looked out of the window at the traffic below. After-five traffic, with everyone hurrying to get home in all directions; to Westwood and Tarzana, to Redondo Beach and Glendale, to Escondido and Huntington Park, to Sherman Oaks and Lynwood. It was as if the order had gone out to evacuate Hollywood and the evacuation was taking place with no one in command but a single traffic cop with a tin whistle.

Blackshear said, over his shoulder, "You're not good at taking advice."

"What you suggest is impossible. I can't leave Los Angeles right now, for personal reasons." She added vaguely, "My family."

"I see. Well, I'd like to help you but I'm afraid there isn't anything I can do."

"There is."

"What?"

"Find her."

He turned, frowning. "Why?"

"I want to—I must see her, talk to her. I must rid myself of this—uncertainty."

"Perhaps the uncertainty is in yourself, Helen. Finding a stranger may not help you."

She raised her hand in an autocratic little gesture as if she meant to silence him. But almost immediately her hand dropped to her side again and she said, "Perhaps not. But you could try."

"All I have to go on is a name."

"No. There's more than that. Remember what she said, that one of these days she'd be famous, her—her body would be in every art museum in the country. That must mean that she poses for artists, she's a model."

"Models are a dime a dozen in this town."

"But it at least gives you a place to start. Aren't there such things as model booking agencies?"

"Yes."

"You could try there. I'll pay you, of course. I'll pay . . ."

"You're forgetting something."

"What?"

"I'm not for hire."

She was quiet for a moment. "Have I offended you by mentioning money? I'm sorry. When I offer to pay people, I don't mean it as an insult. It's simply all I have to offer."

"You have a low opinion of yourself, Helen."

"I wasn't born with it."

"Where did you get it?"

"The story," she said, "is too long to tell, and too dull to listen to."

"I see." But he didn't see. He remembered Clarvoe as a tall, thin, quiet-mannered man, obviously fond of and amused by his frilly little wife, Verna. What errant chromosomes or domestic dissensions had produced two such incongruous children as Helen and Douglas, Blackshear could not even guess. He had never been intimate with the family although he'd known them all since Helen was in college and Douglas was attending a military prep school. Once in a while Blackshear was invited out to the house for dinner, and on these occasions the conversation was conducted by Verna Clarvoe, who would chatter endlessly on the I-me-my level. Neither of the children had much to say, or, if they had, they had been instructed not to say it. They were like model prisoners at the warden's table, Douglas, fair-skinned and fragile for his age, and Helen, a caricature of her father, with her cropped black hair and bony arms and legs.

Shortly after Clarvoe's death, Blackshear had been surprised to read in the society page of the morning paper that Douglas had married. He had been less surprised when a notice of annulment followed, on the legal page, a few weeks later.

"I know what you are thinking," Miss Clarvoe said. "That I should hire an experienced investigator."

Nothing had been further from his thoughts but he didn't argue. "It seems like a good idea."

"Do you know of anyone?"

"Not offhand. Look in the yellow pages."

"I couldn't trust a stranger. I don't even tr—" Her mouth closed but her eyes finished the sentence: I don't even trust you. Or mother, or Douglas. Or myself.

"Mr. Blackshear," she said. "I . . ."

Suddenly, her whole body began to move, convulsively, like that of a woman in labor, and her face was tortured as if she already knew that the offspring she was going to bear would be deformed, a monster.

"Mr. Blackshear—I—Oh, God . . ."

And she turned and pressed her forehead against the wall and hid her face with her hands. Blackshear felt a great pity for her not because of her tears but because of all the struggle it had taken to produce them. *The mountain labored and brought forth a mouse.*

"There, there, don't cry. Everything's going to be all right. Just take it easy." He said all the things that he'd learned to say to his wife, Dorothy, whenever she cried, words which didn't mean anything in themselves, but which fulfilled Dorothy's need for attention and sympathy. Miss Clarvoe's needs were deeper and more obscure. She was beyond the reach of words.

Blackshear lit another cigarette and turned to the window and pretended to be interested in the view, a darkening sky, a dribble of clouds. *It might rain tonight—if it does, I won't go to the office in the morning—maybe the doctor was right, I should retire altogether—but what will I do with the days and what will they do to me?*

He was struck by the sudden realization that he was, in his way, as badly off as Miss Clarvoe. They had both reached a plateau of living, surrounded by mountains on the one side and deep gorges on the other. Blackshear had at one time scaled the mountains and explored the gorges, Miss Clarvoe had not done either; but here they were, on the same plateau.

"Helen . . ." He turned and saw that she had left the room.

When she returned a few minutes later, her face was washed and her hair combed.

"Please excuse me, Mr. Blackshear. I don't often make a fool of myself in public." She smiled wrly. "Not such a *damned* fool, anyway."

"I'm sorry I upset you."

"You didn't. It was—the other things. I guess I'm an awful coward."

"What are you afraid of, the thief or the woman?"

"I think they're the same person."

"Perhaps you're interpreting your dream too literally."

"No." Unconsciously, she began to rub her forehead, and Blackshear noticed that it bore a slight scratch that was already healed over. "Do you believe that one person can influence another person to—to have an accident?"

"It's possible, I suppose, if the suggestion is strong enough on the part of the first person, and if it coincides with a desire for self-punishment on the part of the second person."

"There are some things you can't explain by simple psychology."

"I suppose there are."

"Do you believe in extrasensory perception?"

"No."

"It exists, all the same."

"Perhaps."

"I feel—I feel very strongly—that this woman means to destroy me. I *know* it. If you like, call it intuition."

"Call it fear," Blackshear said.

She looked at him with a touch of sadness. "You're like my father. Nothing exists for you unless you can touch or see or smell it. Father was tone-deaf; he never knew, in all his life, that there was such a thing as music. He always thought that when people listened to music they were pretending to hear something that wasn't really there."

"It's not a very good analogy."

"Better than you think, perhaps. Well, I won't keep you any longer, Mr. Blackshear. I appreciate your taking time out to come and see me. I know how busy you are."

"I'm not busy at all. In fact, I've practically retired."

"Oh. I hadn't heard. Well, I hope you enjoy your leisure."

"I'll try." What will you do with the days, he asked himself. Collect stamps, grow roses, sit through double features, doze in the sun on the back porch, and when you get too lonely, go to the park and talk to old men on benches. "I've never had much leisure to enjoy. It will take practice."

"Yes," Miss Clarvoe said gently. "I'm afraid it will."

She crossed the room and unlocked the door. After a moment's hesitation, Blackshear followed her.

They shook hands again and Blackshear said, "You won't forget to report the missing money to the police?"

"I won't forget to do it, Mr. Blackshear. I will simply *not* do it."

"But why?"

"The money itself isn't important. I sit here in my room and get richer without even raising my hand. Every time the clock ticks I'm richer. What does eight hundred dollars matter?"

"All right, then, but Evelyn Merrick matters. The police might be able to find her for you."

"They might, if they bothered to look."

Blackshear knew she was right. The police would be interested in the theft but there wasn't the slightest evidence that Evelyn Merrick was the thief. And as far as the phone call was concerned, the department received dozens of similar complaints every day. Miss Clarvoe's story would be filed and forgotten, because Evelyn Merrick had done no physical harm, had not even voiced any definite threats. No search would be made for the woman unless he, Blackshear, made it himself.

I could do it, he thought. It isn't as if I'd be investigating a major crime where experience is necessary. All I have to do is find a woman. That shouldn't require anything more than ordinary intelligence and perseverance and a bit of luck. Finding a woman is better than collecting stamps or talking to old men on benches in the park.

He felt excitement mounting in him, followed by the sudden and irrational idea that perhaps Miss Clarvoe had contrived the whole thing, that she had somehow tricked or willed him into this reversal of his plans. *"Do you believe in extrasensory perception, Mr. Blackshear?" "No."*

No? He looked at her. She was smiling.

"You've changed your mind," she said, and there was no rising inflection of doubt in her voice.

3

THE FOLLOWING AFTERNOON, after spending the morning at the telephone, Blackshear arrived at the establishment advertised in the yellow pages of the Central Los Angeles phone book as the Lydia Hudson School of Charm and Modelling. It was one of two dozen similar schools listed, differing only in name, location and degree of disregard for the laws of probability: We will make you a New Person . . . Hundreds of Glamorous Jobs awaiting our graduates . . . We Guarantee to Improve your personality, poise, posture, make-up, figure, and mental outlook . . . Walk and Talk in Beauty, our Staff will teach you . . .

Miss Hudson performed her miracles on the second floor of a professional building on Vine Street. The outer office was a stylized mixture of glass brick and wrought iron and self-conscious young women in various stages of charm. Two of them were apparently graduates; they carried their professional equipment in hat-boxes, and they wore identical expressions, half-disillusioned, half-alert, like travelers who had been waiting too long for their train and were eyeing the tracks for a relief car.

They spotted Blackshear, and immediately began an animated conversation.

"You remember Judy Hall. Well, she's *finally* engaged."

"No! How did that happen?"

"I wouldn't *dare* to guess. I mean, her methods are pretty stark, aren't they?"

"They have to be. She's let herself go terribly in the past year. Did you notice her complexion? And her posture?"

"It isn't her posture that's so bad. It's her figure."

"I bet Miss Hudson could do wonders . . ."

Walk and Talk in Beauty, our Staff will teach you.

Blackshear approached the reception desk and the travelers stopped talking. Another train had passed without stopping.

"I have an appointment to see Miss Hudson. The name is Blackshear."

The receptionist's eyelids drooped as if from the weight of her mascara. "Miss Hudson is in Conversation Class at the moment, Mr. Blackshear. Will you wait?"

"Yes."

"Just have a seat over there."

She undulated across the room, walking in beauty, and disappeared behind a frosted glass door marked, PRIVATE. A minute later a short woman with hair the color of persimmons and a mouth to match came out of the same door. She didn't undulate. She walked briskly with her shoulders back and her head thrust forward at a slightly aggressive angle, as if she expected to be challenged by a high wind or a disgruntled client.

"I'm Lydia Hudson." Her voice was incongruously soft and pleasant, with a faint trace of a New England accent. "Sorry to keep you waiting, Mr. Blackshear."

"You didn't."

"I was rather surprised by your phone call. You sounded so mysterious."

"Let's say mystified, not mysterious."

"Very well." She smiled a professional smile, without disturbing her eyes. "You're not a policeman, are you, Mr. Blackshear?"

"No."

"Maybe you're a lawyer, and the Merrick girl is a long-lost heiress. That would be fun."

"It would."

"But that's not it, eh?"

"No."

"It never is." Miss Hudson glanced at the two models who were making a noble pretense of not listening. "Your call hasn't come through yet, girls. Sorry."

One of the models put down her hat-box and started across the room. "But, Miss Hudson, *you* said be here at two and here we . . ."

"Patience, Stella. Patience and poise. One moment of distemper can be as damaging to your skin as two éclairs."

"But . . ."

"Remember, you're a *graduate* now, Stella. You can't afford to behave like a freshman." To Blackshear, she added softly, "Come into my office. We can't talk here in front of these morons."

Miss Hudson's office was artfully devised for the acquisition of new students. On each side of the desk where she sat was a lamp with a pink shade that flattered her complexion and made her hair look almost real. The other side of the room, reserved for prospective clients, was illuminated from the ceiling with fluorescent rods that gave a dead white light, and two of the walls were decorated with full-length mirrors.

"This is our consultation room," Miss Hudson said. "I never give the girls any personal criticism. I simply let them study themselves in the mirrors and *they* tell *me* what's wrong. That way, it makes for a more pleasant relationship and better business. Please sit down, Mr. Blackshear."

"Thanks. Why better business?"

"I often find that the girls are much harder on themselves than I would be. They expect more, you see?"

"Not quite."

"Well, sometimes a very pretty girl comes in and I can't find anything the matter with her at all. But *she* can, because she's probably comparing herself to Ava Gardner. So, she takes my course." Miss Hudson smiled dryly. "Results guaranteed, naturally. Cigarette?"

"No, thanks."

"Well, now you know as much about my business as I do. Or," she added, with a shrewd glance, "as much as you care to, eh?"

"It's very interesting."

"Sometimes the whole thing makes me sick, but it's a living and I've got three kids to support. The youngest is fourteen. When I get her through college or married off to some nice, steady guy, I'm going to retire. I'm going to loll around the house all day in a bathrobe and bedroom slippers and I'm never going to open another jar of face-cream as long as I live, and every morning when I get up I'm going to look in the mirror and chortle myself silly over a new wrinkle and another grey hair." She paused for breath. "Don't mind me. I'm only kidding. I think. Anyway, you didn't come here to listen to my blatting. What do you want to know about this Evelyn Merrick?"

"Everything you can tell me."

"It won't be much. I only saw her once and that was a week ago. She read my ad in the *News* offering a free consultation for a limited time only, and in she came, sat in the same chair you're sitting in now. A scrawny brunette very poorly dressed and made up like a tart. Pretty impossible, from a professional point of view. She had one of those Italian boy haircuts gone to seed. They're supposed to look casual, you know, but actually they require a lot of expert care. And her clothes . . ." Miss Hudson stopped sharply, "I hope she's not a friend of yours?"

"I've never seen her."

"Why do you want to find her, then?"

"Let's stick with the long-lost heiress story," Blackshear said. "I'm beginning to like it."

"I always have."

"You gave her the free consultation?"

"I did the usual thing, tried to put her at ease, called her by her first name and so on. Then asked her to stand up and walk around and watch herself in the mirror and tell me what she thought needed correction. Ordinarily the girls are embarrassed at this point, and sort of giggly. She wasn't. She acted—well, odd."

"In what way?"

"She just stood there looking into the mirror, without making a sound. She seemed fascinated by herself. I was the one who was embarrassed . . ."

"Walk around a bit, Evelyn."

The girl didn't move.

"Are you satisfied with your posture? Your skin? How about your make-up?"

She didn't speak.

"It is our policy to let our prospective students analyze themselves. We cannot correct faults that the student doesn't admit having. Now, then, would you say that you are perfectly happy about your figure? Take a good honest look, fore and aft."

Evelyn blinked and turned away. "The mirror is distorted and the lights are bad."

"They are not bad," Miss Hudson said, stung. "They are—realistic. We must face facts before altering them."

"If you say so, Miss Hudson."

"I say so. I—How old are you, Evelyn?"

"Twenty-one."

She must consider me a fool, Miss Hudson thought. "And you want to be a model?"

"Yes."

"What kind?"

"I want to pose for artists. Painters."

"There's not much demand for that kind of . . ."

"I have good breasts and I don't get cold easily."

"My dear young woman," Miss Hudson said with heavy irony. "And what else can you do besides not get cold easily?"

"You're making fun of me. You simply don't understand."

"Understand what?"

"I want to become immortal."

Miss Hudson lapsed into a stunned silence.

"I couldn't think of any other way to do it," the girl said. "And then I saw your ad., and the idea came to me suddenly, suppose someone paints me, a really great artist, then I will be immortal. So you see, it makes sense, if you think about it."

Miss Hudson didn't care to think about it. She had no time to worry about immortality: tomorrow was bad enough. "Why should a young woman like you be concerned about death?"

"I have an enemy."

"Who hasn't?"

"No, I mean a real enemy," Evelyn said politely. "I've seen her. In my crystal ball."

Miss Hudson looked at the cheap rayon dress stained at the armpits. "Is that how you make your living, telling fortunes?"

"No."

"What do you work at?"

"Just at the moment I'm unemployed. But I can get money if I need it. Enough to take your course."

"You understand we have a waiting list," Miss Hudson lied.

"No. No, I thought . . ."

"I shall be most happy to put your name on file." And leave it there. I want no part of your immortality. Or your crystal ball. "How do you spell your last name?"

"M-E-R-R-I-C-K."

"Evelyn Merrick. Age 21. Address and phone number?"

"Well, I'm not sure. I'm moving out of my present place tomorrow, and I haven't decided just where I'll go."

No address, Miss Hudson wrote on her memo pad. Good. It will give me the perfect excuse for not calling her.

"I'll phone you when I get settled," Evelyn said. "Then you can tell me if you have an opening."

"It might be quite some time."

"I'll keep trying, anyway."

"Yes," Miss Hudson said dryly, "I believe you will."

"I'll call you, say, a week from today?"

"Listen to me a minute, Evelyn. If I were you, I'd reconsider this modelling business, I'd . . ."

"You are not me. I will call you in a week . . ."

"The week was up yesterday," Miss Hudson told Blackshear. "She didn't call. I don't know whether I'm glad or sorry."

"I think," Blackshear said, "that you ought to be glad."

"I guess I am. She's a real mimsy, that one. God knows my girls aren't mental giants, not one of them has an I.Q. that would make a decent basketball score. But they're not really *screwy* like her. You know what I wonder, Mr. Blackshear?"

"No."

"I wonder what she saw in that mirror when she stood there half-hypnotized. What did she see?"

"Herself."

"No." Miss Hudson shook her head. "*I* saw herself. She saw somebody else. Gives you the creeps, doesn't it?"

"Not particularly."

"It does me. I felt sorry for her. I thought, suppose it was one of my kids—suppose something happens to me before they're safe and grown-up, and they're cast out into . . . Well, we won't go into that. Very depressing. Besides, I'm healthy and I drive carefully. Also, I have a sister who's perfectly capable of taking over the kids if anything happened to me . . ." In sudden fury, Miss Hudson reached out and slapped the fragile mauve-and-white desk with the palm of her hand. "*Damn* that girl! You go along for years, doing your best, not worrying about dying, and then something like this happens. Some screwball comes along with a bunch of crazy ideas and you can't get them out of your head. It's not fair. Damn her hide. I'm sorry I tried to help her."

Blackshear raised his brows. "How exactly did you help her, Miss Hudson?"

"Maybe I didn't. But I tried. I could tell she was broke, so I gave her the name of a man. I thought he might give her an odd job to tide her over until she came to her senses if any."

"What kind of job?"

"Posing. He's an artist, a good one too, which means he has to teach to make ends meet. He uses live models in his classes, not just pretty girls, but all kinds and shapes and sizes. I figured it wouldn't do any harm to send Evelyn over there. He might take a fancy to her earlobes or her big toe or something. Moore's a stickler for details."

"Moore?"

"Harley Moore. His studio is on Palm Avenue, just off Sunset near Santa Monica Boulevard."

"Has she actually done any posing, do you know?"

"She said she had. She said she'd done some work for Jack Terola. He's a photographer, ten or twelve blocks south of here. I don't know much about him except that he pays pretty well. He does photo illustrations for one of those confession magazines—you know, where the wife is standing horrified watching her husband kiss his secretary, or the young Sunday school teacher is being assaulted in the choir loft—that sort of thing. My youngest kid reads them all the time. It drives me crazy trying to stop her. Stuff like that gives kids the wrong idea about the world—they get to thinking all secretaries get bussed by the boss and all Sunday school teachers are assaulted in choir lofts. Which isn't true."

"I hope not."

"Well, there you are."

Blackshear wasn't exactly sure where he was. But he knew where he was going.

The means to charm were apparently more profitable than its ends: Miss Hudson could afford glass bricks and mahogany paneling; Terola's place was a long, narrow stucco building between a one-way alley euphemistically named Jacaranda Lane, and a rickety three-story frame-house converted into apartments. Black stenciling on the frosted glass window read:

PHOTOGRAPHIC WORKSHOP
JACK TEROLA, PROPRIETOR
PIN-UP MODELS
LIFE GROUPS FOR AMATEURS AND PROFESSIONALS
RENTAL STUDIOS FOR ART GROUPS
COME IN ANY TIME

Blackshear went in. In spite of the rows of filing cabinets and the samples of Terola's work which lined the walls, the office still looked like what it had been originally, somebody's front parlor. Near one end of the room was a dirty red brick fireplace which had a desolate and futile appearance, as if it had become, from long disuse, a mere hole in the wall which a careless workman had forgotten to plaster over. To the right of the fireplace was a curtained alcove. The curtains were not drawn and Blackshear could see part of the interior: a brown leather chair, the seat wrinkled with age, a daybed partly covered with an old-fashioned afghan, and above it, the stenciled front window. The alcove reminded Blackshear of his childhood in the Middle West—all the best people had had a "sunporch", which was indescribably hot in the summer and equally cold in the winter and no good for anything at all except social prestige.

Terola's sunporch seemed to be not a mark of prestige but a sign of necessity. The daybed was obviously used for sleeping; a dirty sheet dribbled out from under the afghan and the pillow was stained with hair oil.

There was no one in sight, but from behind the closed door at the other end of the room came sounds of activity, the scraping of equipment being moved across a wooden floor, the rise and fall of voices. Blackshear couldn't distinguish the words but the tones were plain enough. Somebody was giving orders and somebody else wasn't taking them.

He was on the point of knocking on the closed door when he noticed the printed sign propped against the typewriter of Terola's desk: FOR ATTENTION, PLEASE RING.

He rang, and waited, and then rang again, and finally the door opened and a young girl came out, wearing a printed silk bathrobe. She wore no make-up and her face glistened with grease and moisture. Water dripped from the ends of her short black hair and slid down her neck, and the damp silk of the bathrobe clung to her skin.

She seemed unconcerned. "You want something?"

"I'd like to speak to Mr. Terola."

"He's busy right now. Sit down."

"Thank you."

"I'm supposed to be drowning but Jack can't get the water right. It's supposed to be Lake Michigan, see."

Blackshear nodded politely to indicate that he saw.

"Jack's a sucker for drowning scenes," the girl added. "Me, I like to stay dry. The way I look at it is, I could just as easy been stabbed. All this fuss trying to make like Lake Michigan. Don't you want to sit down?"

"I'm perfectly comfortable."

"Well, all right. You here on business?"

"In a way. My name is Paul Blackshear."

"Pleased to meet you. I'm Nola Rath. Well, I better get back now. You want a magazine to read?"

"No, thanks."

"You may have quite a wait. If Jack gets this shot right he'll be out here in a jiffy, but if he don't, he won't."

"I'll wait."

"I could just as easy been stabbed," the girl said. "Well, I'll tell Jack you're here."

She left behind a trail of water drops and the smell of wet hair.

Nola Rath. Blackshear repeated the name to himself, wondering how old the girl was. Perhaps twenty-five, only a few years younger than Helen Clarvoe, yet a whole generation seemed to separate the two. Miss Clarvoe's age had very little to do with chronology. She was a middle-aged woman because she had had nothing to keep her young. She was the chosen victim, not only of Evelyn Merrick, but of life itself.

The thought depressed Blackshear. He wished he could forget her but she nagged at his mind like a broken promise.

He looked at his watch. Three-ten. A wind had come up. The curtains of Terola's alcove were blowing in and out and the cobwebs in the fireplace were stirring, and somewhere in the chimney there was a fidgeting of mice.

"You wanted to see me?"

Blackshear turned, surprised that he had not heard the opening of the door or the sound of footsteps.

"Mr. Terola?"

"That's right."

"My name's Blackshear."

They shook hands. Terola was in his early forties, a very thin, tall man with a habitual stoop as if he were trying to scale himself down to size. He had black, bushy brows that quivered with impatience when he talked, as if they were silently denying the words that came out of the soft feminine mouth. Two thin parallel strands of iron grey hair crossed the top of his bald pate like railway ties.

"Just a minute." Terola walked over to the alcove and drew the curtains irritably. "Things are in a mess around here. My secretary's home with the mumps. Mumps, yet, at her age. I thought they were for kids. Well, what can I do for you, Blackshear?"

"I understand you employ, or have employed, a young woman called Evelyn Merrick."

"How come you understand that?"

"Someone told me."

"Such as who?"

"Miss Merrick used your name as a reference when she went to apply for training as a model. She claimed she had done some work for you."

"What kind of work?"

"Whatever kind you had to offer," Blackshear said, attempting to conceal his impatience. "You do quite a bit of, shall we call it art work?"

"We shall and it is."

"Have it your way. Do you remember Miss Merrick?"

"Maybe I do, maybe I don't. I'm not answering a lot of questions unless there's a good reason. You got a good reason, Mr. Blacksheep?"

"Blackshear."

"It's not that I don't want to co-operate, only I kind of like to find out first who I'm co-operating with in what and for why. What's your business, mister?"

"I'm an investment counsellor."

"So?"

"Let's say that there's an estate to settle and Evelyn Merrick may get a piece of it."

Terola spoke tightly, barely moving his mouth, as if he was afraid there might be lip-readers around peering in through the curtains of the alcove or the chinks in the chimney: "The kind of piece that babe gets won't come out of any estate, mister."

"She came here, then?"

"She came. Gave me a hard-luck story about a dying mother, so I let her have a couple of hours' work. I'm a sucker for dying mothers, just so's they don't change their minds and stay alive, like mine did."

"Did the Merrick girl give you any trouble?"

"I don't take trouble from chicks like that. I bounce them out on their ear."

"Did you bounce her?"

"She got nosy. I had to."

"When was this?"

"Couple of weeks ago, maybe less. When they get nosy, they get bounced. Not," he added with a wink, "that I have anything to hide. I just don't like snoopers. They get in my hair, what's left of it."

"What else did she do besides snoop?"

"Oh, she had some screwy idea about me making her immortal. At first I figured she was kidding and trying for a laugh. I have a pretty good sense of humor, so I laughed, see? She got sore as hell. If you want the truth, I don't think she's playing with all her marbles."

"Exactly what kind of work did you give Evelyn Merrick?"

"She posed."

"For you personally? Or for one of your 'art' groups?"

"What difference does it make?"

"It might make a lot of difference to me."

"How so?"

"If she posed for you, for a magazine story layout, you might give me a print of the picture. If she worked with your art group, I don't think you will."

Terola ground out the stub of his cigarette in an ashtray. "I never give away prints."

"What do you do, peddle them?"

"Peddle is a very nasty word. You'd better leave before I push it back down your throat."

"I didn't realize what a sensitive fellow you were, Terola."

"I don't want any trouble with your kind. Blow."

"Thank you for the information."

Terola opened the door. "Go to hell."

Blackshear walked down the alley and got into his car. It was the first time in thirty years that he'd been close to having a fight and the experience aroused old memories and old fears and a certain primeval excitement. His hand on the ignition key was unsteady and anger pressed on his eyeballs like iron thumbs. He wanted to go back and challenge Terola, fight him to the finish, kill him, if he had to.

But as he drove in the direction of Harley Moore's studio, the brisk sea wind cooled his passions and neutralized the acid in his mind. I'm not as civilized as I like to think. There was no need to antagonize him. I handled everything wrong. Maybe I can do better with Moore.

4

BERTHA MOORE HAD waited fifteen years for a child, and when the child, a girl, was born, Bertha could not quite believe in her good fortune. She had constantly to reassure herself. At all hours of the day and night she tiptoed into the nursery to see if the baby was still there, still alive. She could not settle down to read or sew even for a minute; she seemed to be half-suspended in air like a gas-filled balloon held captive only by a length of string. At the other end of this string, fixed and stationary, was her husband, Harley.

She did not make the mistake of ignoring Harley after the birth of the baby. She was, in fact, extremely kind to him, but it was a planned and unemotional kindness; at the back of her mind there was always the thought that she must take deliberate pains to keep Harley contented because the baby would be healthier and better adjusted if it had a happy home and a good father.

What spare time Bertha had was spent in conversations with friends and relatives about the perfections of her child, or in frantic calls to the pediatrician when it vomited its food or to Harley when it cried without apparent reason. During nearly twenty years of marriage Bertha had learned not to disturb Harley at his studio. She unlearned this in a single day, easily, and without the slightest compunction. These calls were "for the baby's sake", and as such were beyond reproach and above criticism. The baby flourished, unaware of its demands on its parents. Bertha called her Angie, which was short for Angel and had no connection with her registered name, Stephanie Caroline Moore.

At four o'clock Angie was in no mood for her bottle. Bertha was waltzing her back and forth across the living room when the telephone rang. She shifted the baby gently from her left arm to her right and picked up the receiver.

"Hello?"

"Hello. Is that Mrs. Moore?"

"Yes."

"You don't know me, but I'm a friend of your husband's."

"Really?" Bertha said, in a lively manner, though she was hardly paying any attention. The baby's hair felt so soft against her neck and its warm skin smelled of flowers and sunshine.

"I'm Evelyn Merrick. Perhaps your husband has mentioned me?"

"He may have." With considerable effort the baby turned her head to listen to the conversation, and she made such a droll face that Bertha laughed out loud.

"Are you alone, Mrs. Moore?"

"I'm *never* alone. We have a new baby, you know."

There was a pause. "Of course I knew."

"She was just four months old yesterday."

"They're so sweet at that age."

"Aren't they, though. But Angie's more like six months than four, even the doctor says so." This was practically true. The doctor, had, after considerable prompting from Bertha, agreed that Angie was "quite advanced" and was "developing nicely".

"That's such a cute name, Angie."

"It's only a nickname, really." What a nice voice the woman had, Bertha thought, and how interested she was in the baby. "Speaking of names, I'm afraid I didn't catch yours."

"Evelyn Merrick. Miss Merrick."

"It does sound familiar. I'm almost sure Harley's mentioned you. Most of the time I'm so busy with the baby I don't hear what people are saying . . . Stop that, Angie. No, no, mustn't touch . . . She's trying to pull out the telephone cord."

"She sounds just adorable."

"Oh, she is." Bertha had admired other women's babies for so many years—telling the truth, if the baby was cute, fibbing if it wasn't—that she felt it only just that other women now had to admire hers. The nice thing was that none of them had to fib about Angie. She was perfect. There was no compliment about her so bulky, no piece of flattery so huge, that Bertha couldn't swallow with the greatest of ease and digest without the faintest rumble.

"Does the baby look like you or like Harley?"

"Oh, like me, I'm afraid," Bertha said with a proud little laugh. "Everyone thinks so."

"I'd love to see her. I'm quite—mad about babies."

"Why don't you come over?"

"When?"

"Well, this afternoon, if you like. Angie's restless, she won't go to sleep for hours." It would be fun to show the baby off to one of Harley's friends, for a change. Harley was very modest about Angie and hardly ever brought anyone to see her. "Harley won't be home until six. We can have some tea and a chat, and I'll show you Angie's baby book. Are you an artist, by any chance, Miss Merrick?"

"In a way."

"I just wondered. Harley says the baby's too young to be painted, but I—well, never mind. You will see for yourself. You know our address?"

"Yes. It will be a pleasure meeting you, Mrs. Moore."

They said good-bye and Bertha hung up, feeling a pleasant glow of anticipation and maternal pride.

She was not, by nature or experience, a suspicious woman—Harley had dozens of friends of both sexes—and it didn't strike her as odd that Evelyn Merrick hadn't explained the purpose of her call.

"A nice lady," she told Angie, "is coming to admire you and I want you to be utterly captivating."

Angie chewed her fingers.

When the baby's diapers and dress had been changed and her half-inch of hair carefully brushed, Bertha went back to the phone to call Harley.

Harley himself answered, sounding sharp and distrustful the way he always did over the telephone, as if he expected to be bored or bamboozled.

"Har? It's just me."

"Oh. Anything wrong with the baby?"

"Not a thing. She's bright as a dollar."

"Look, Bertha, I'm awfully tied up right now. There's a man here who . . ."

"Well, I won't keep you, dear. I just wanted to tell you not to hurry home, I'm having company for tea. A Miss Merrick is coming over to see the baby."

"Who?"

"A friend of yours, Evelyn Merrick."

"She's coming there?"

"Why, yes. What's the matter, Har? You sound so . . ."

"When is she coming?"

"Well, I don't know. It was kind of indefinite."

"Listen to me carefully, Bertha. Lock the doors and stay in the house until I get home."

"I don't under—"

"Do as I say. We'll be there in fifteen minutes."

"What do you mean, we?"

"There's a man in my studio right now looking for that woman. He says she's crazy."

"But she sounded so sweet—and she was so interested in Angie and wanted to see . . ."

But Harley had hung up.

She stood, wide-eyed and pale, hugging the baby to her breasts. Angie, sensing the sudden tension, and resenting the too tight and desperate embrace, began to cry.

"Be a good girl now, Angie," Bertha said, sounding very calm. "There is nothing the matter, nothing to be afraid of."

But the calm voice did not reassure the baby; she heard the quickened heartbeat, she felt her mother's trembling muscles, and she smelled fear.

"We will simply lock the doors and wait for Daddy. There's nothing to cry about. My goodness, what will the neighbors think, such a little girl making so much noise . . ."

Carrying the howling child, Bertha locked the three outside doors and pulled the heavy drapes across the bay window in the living room. Then she sat down in the rocking chair that Harley had bought her because she'd said no one could raise a baby without one. The darkened room and the gentle, rocking motion quieted the child.

"That's a sweet girl. You settle down now and go to sleep. My goodness, we mustn't get excited about a little thing like a crazy . . ."

The door chimes pealed.

Without even glancing towards the door, Bertha carried the sleeping child to the nursery and laid her in the crib and covered her with a blanket. Then she walked slowly back to the front hall as the chimes pealed again.

She stood, waiting and listening, her face like stone. There were no sounds of cars passing or children playing or women hurrying home from the supermarket. It was as if everyone, forewarned of danger, had moved to another part of town.

"Mrs. Moore?" The voice came, soft but persistent, through the crack of the oak door. "Let me in."

Bertha pressed the back of her hand tight against her mouth as if afraid words might come out without her volition.

"I hurried right over. I'm dying to see the baby. Let me in . . . I know you're there, Mrs. Moore. What's the matter? Are you afraid of me? I wouldn't harm anyone. I only want to see Harley's baby . . . Harley and I may have a baby, too."

The words seeped through the crack of the door like drops of poison that could kill on contact.

"Does that shock you, Mrs. Moore? You don't know much of what goes on in that studio of his, do you? What do you think happens after I pose naked?"

Make her stop, Bertha prayed silently. She's lying. She's crazy. Harley would never—he's not like that—he told me they were all like pieces of wood to him . . .

"Oh, don't think I'm the only one. I'm just the latest. After the posing it comes so natural, so inevitable. Have you been fooled all these years? Haven't you wondered, in the back of your mind? Aren't you wondering now? I should lend you my crystal ball. Oh, the things you'd see!"

And she began to describe them, slowly and carefully, as if she were instructing a child, and Bertha listened like a child, not understanding some of the ugly words she used but hypnotized by their implications of evil. She couldn't move, couldn't get out of range of the poison. Drop by drop it burned into her heart and etched nightmares on her mind.

Then, quite suddenly, from the corner, came the quick, tinkling song of a Good Humor man. "My Bonnie lies over the ocean . . . Oh, bring back my Bonnie to me." The song ended and began again, but in the interval between the two, Bertha heard the tap of heels on concrete. Moving lifelessly, like a dummy on hinges, she walked into the living room and parted the heavy drapes on the bay window.

A woman was running down the street, her dark hair lashing furiously in the wind, her coat flapping around her skinny legs. She turned the corner, still running, heading south.

Bertha went back to the nursery. Angie was sleeping on her side with her thumb in her mouth.

Bertha stood by the crib and looked down at the baby, numbly, wondering what kind of man its father was.

"Bertha. Are you all right, dear?"

"Of course."

"We got here as soon as we could. This is Mr. Blackshear. My wife, Bertha."

"How do you do." She shook hands with Blackshear. "Would you like a drink?"

"Thanks. I would," Blackshear said.

"I will, too. I was going to have tea, but—I was going to have company for tea. A nice lady was coming to admire the baby. I dressed Angie up and brushed her hair. I was feeling happy, I remember. That was a long time ago."

"Bertha, you're sure you're feeling all right?"

"Yes," she said politely. How odd Harley looked, with his crew cut and his sunburn and his horn-rimmed glasses. Not like a painter at all. Perhaps that was because he didn't do much painting anymore—other things went on in his studio that were more important—

Harley mixed her a bourbon highball. It tasted weak and sour, and after the first sip she just held the glass to her lips and looked over the rim of it at Blackshear. Quiet, dignified, respectable. But you couldn't tell. If you couldn't tell about Harley, you couldn't tell about anyone in the whole world.

Her hand shook, and some of the highball spilled down the front of her dress. She knew both the men had seen the little accident. They were staring at her in a puzzled way, as if they realized that something was wrong and were too diffident or polite to ask her what.

"She was here," Bertha said. "She asked me to let her in, and when I wouldn't, she talked at me through the crack of the door. I didn't answer, or make any noise, but somehow she knew I was there, listening." She glanced quickly at Harley and away again. "I can't tell you what she said, in front of a stranger."

"Why not?"

"It was about you, your relations with her."

"I had no relations with her except one day last week when she came to the studio for a job and I turned her down."

"She said she was one of your—models."

"Go on," Harley said grimly. "What else?"

"She said you and she—she used terrible words—I couldn't repeat them to anyone . . ."

The blood had drained from Harley's sunburned face, leaving it grey-tan and lifeless, like sandstone. "She implied that I had sexual relations with her?"

"*Implied.*" Bertha began to laugh, *implied.* "That's funny, it really is. If you could have heard her . . ."

"You listened to her, Bertha?"

"Yes."

"Why?"

"I don't know. I didn't want to. I hated it, but I listened."

"Did you believe what she said?"

"No."

He accepted the faint and unconvincing denial without pressing her further. He even tried to give her a reassuring smile, but he looked sick and exhausted as he turned to Blackshear. "Is this the kind of mischief the Merrick woman goes in for?"

"It's a little more than mischief, I'm afraid."

"Well, she may be insane, but she seems to know a lot about human frailties."

"She does." Blackshear thought of the things Evelyn Merrick had said to Miss Clarvoe. She had used Miss Clarvoe's own special set of fears as she had used Mrs. Moore's, and to a lesser extent, Lydia Hudson's, not creating new fears but working on ones that were already there. In each case she had taken a different approach, but the results were the same, uncertainty, anxiety, dread. Miss Hudson had a strong enough personality to settle her own problems; Helen Clarvoe's, perhaps, would never be settled; but Mrs. Moore had a need for, and the ability to accept, help.

Blackshear said, "Evelyn Merrick gets her satisfaction out of other people's pain, Mrs. Moore. Today it was yours. But there have been others."

"I didn't—know that."

"It's true. There is absolutely no limit to what she would say to cause trouble, and perhaps in your case she had an extra motive. Mr. Moore tells me that he was busy at the time she came to the studio and he gave her a quick brush-off."

Bertha smiled, very faintly. "Harley's quite good at that."

"The Merrick woman may have wanted to pay him back. Little episodes like that, which the ordinary person would pass off easily and forget about, often become terribly exaggerated in the mind of an unbalanced woman."

"Of course, I didn't believe her for a minute," Bertha said, in a very firm, reasonable voice. "After all, Harley and I have been happily married for nearly twenty years . . . I suppose Harley's told you about our little girl?"

"He did."

"Would you like to see her?"

"I'd like it very much."

"Let me get her," Harley said, but Bertha had already risen.

"I'll get her," she said, smiling. "I have something to tell her."

Angie was still asleep. She woke up at Bertha's touch, and made a squeak of protest that turned into a yawn.

Bertha spoke softly into her tiny ear. "Your father is a good man. We mustn't either of us forget that. He is a *good man.*"

She carried the child into the living room, walking fast, as if she could get away from the whispers that echoed against the walls of her memory: *You don't know much of what goes on in that studio . . . Have you been fooled all these years? . . . Oh the things you'd see in my crystal ball . . .*

Bertha listened.

5

"HELEN? IS THAT you, Helen, dear?"

"Yes."

"This is Mother."

"Yes."

"I must say you don't seem very happy to hear from me."

"I'm trying." Helen thought, she sounds the same as ever, like a whining child.

"Please speak *up*, dear. If there's one thing I can't bear it's telephone mumblers. Helen? Are you there?"

"I'm here."

"That's better. Well, the reason I wanted to speak to you, I just had a very mysterious phone call from Mr. Blackshear. You remember, that broker friend of your father's whose wife died of cancer?"

"I remember."

"Well, suddenly out of a blue sky he called and asked if he could come and see me tonight. You don't suppose it has anything to do with *money*?"

"In what way?"

"Perhaps he's discovered some misplaced stocks or bonds that belonged to your father."

"I hardly think so."

"But it's possible, isn't it?"

"Yes, I suppose."

"Wouldn't it be a lovely surprise, say just a few shares of AT&T stuck away in a drawer and forgotten. Wouldn't that be *fun*?"

"Yes." She didn't bother pointing out that her father had never bought any shares of AT&T, and if he had, they wouldn't be stuck in a drawer and forgotten. Let Verna find it out for herself; she had a whole closetful of punctured dreams, but there was always room for one more.

The expectation of money, however remote, put a bright and girlish lilt into Verna's voice. "I haven't seen you for ages, Helen."

"I realize that."

"How have you been?"

"Fine, thank you."

"Are you eating properly?"

It was an impossible question to answer, since Verna's ideas of proper eating varied week by week, depending on which new diet attracted her attention. She dieted, variously, to grow slim, to gain weight, to correct low blood sugar, to improve her complexion, to prevent allergies, and to increase the flow of liver bile. The purpose of the diet didn't matter. The practice was what counted. It gave her something to talk about, it made her more interesting and unusual. While her liver bile continued at the same old rate, Verna flitted from one diet to another, making other women who could and did eat anything look like clods.

"*Do* speak *up,* Helen."

"I didn't say anything."

"Oh. Well. The fact is, Dougie and I are having lunch tomorrow at the Vine Street Derby. It's so close to where you are that I thought you might like to join us. Would you?"

"I'm afraid not. Thanks just the same."

"But it's quite a social occasion. In the first place, it's Dougie's birthday, he'll be twenty-six. *Tempus fugit*, doesn't it? And in the second place, someone else will be there whom I'd like you to meet, Dougie's art teacher, a Mr. Terola. I'm told he's a terribly fascinating man."

"I didn't know that Douglas was interested in painting."

"Oh, not painting. Photography. Dougie says there's a big future in photography, and Mr. Terola knows practically everything there is to know about it."

"Indeed."

"I do wish you'd make an effort to come, dear. We'll be at the Derby at one o'clock sharp."

"I'll try to make it." She knew why her mother was anxious for her to be there: she expected her to bring a check for Douglas as a birthday present.

"Are you still there, Helen?"

"Yes."

"These long silences make me nervous, they really do. I never know what you're *thinking*."

Helen smiled grimly into the telephone. "You might ask me some time."

"I'm afraid you'd answer," Verna said with a sharp little laugh. "It's all set, then? We'll see you tomorrow at one?"

"I won't promise."

"My treat, of course. And listen, Helen dear. *Do* wear a little lipstick, won't you? And don't forget it's Dougie's birthday. I'm sure he'd appreciate some little remembrance."

"I'm sure he would."

"Until tomorrow, then."

"Good-bye."

Helen set down the phone. It was the first time in months that she had talked to her mother, but nothing had changed. Animosity still hung between them like a two-edged sword; neither of them could use it without first getting hurt herself.

"A hundred dollars," Verna said aloud. "Or two, if we're lucky. She wouldn't miss it. And if Mr. Blackshear has found those shares of AT&T, we'll be able to keep going for a little while anyway."

Verna was down to a single car, a second mortgage and a part-time servant. She had had the telephone company take out the extra phones in her bedroom and in the patio, and she'd covered the bare spot in the dining-room carpet with a cotton mat, and hung a calendar over the cracking plaster of the kitchen wall. In brief, she had done everything possible to cut expenses and keep the household running. But the household didn't run, it shuffled along like a white elephant, and each week it got further and further behind.

There were occasions, usually at the beginning of the month when the bills poured in, when Verna thought it would be a good thing if Douglas went out and got a job. But most of the time she was content to have him around the house. He was good company, in his quiet way, and he did a great deal of the gardening and the heavier work, when he wasn't studying. In Verna's opinion, Douglas was a born student. He hadn't finished college because of some highly exaggerated incident in the locker room of the gym, but he had continued studying on his own and had already covered ceramics, modern poetry, the French impressionists, the growing of avocados, and the clarinet. The clarinet hurt his lip, the avocado seedlings in the backyard had withered and no one seemed interested in exhibiting his ceramics or listening to him read Dylan Thomas aloud.

Through all this, Douglas remained good-natured. He didn't openly blame the public for its stupidity or the nurseryman for selling him defective avocados, he simply let it be understood that he had done his best and no one could expect more.

No one did, except Verna, and the day he'd sold his clarinet, even though she hated the shriek of it, she went up to her bedroom and wept. The sale of the clarinet wasn't like the gradual loss of interest in ceramics and poetry and all the other things. There was an absolute finality about it that hit her like a fist in the stomach. Her pain was so actual and intense that Douglas sent for the doctor. When the doctor came he seemed just as interested in Douglas as he was in Verna heself. "That boy of yours looks as if he needs a good tonic," the doctor had said.

The "boy" would be twenty-six tomorrow.

"Two hundred at least," Verna said. "After all, it's his birthday and she's his sister."

She covered the canary cage for the night, checked the kitchen to see if the maid had tidied it properly before she left, and went into the den, where Douglas was lying on the couch, reading. He was wearing beaded white moccasins and a terry-cloth bathrobe with the sleeves partly rolled up revealing wrists that were so slim and supple they seemed boneless. His coloring was like Helen's, dark hair and the kind of chameleon grey eyes that changed color with their surroundings. His ears were like a woman's, very close-set, with pierced lobes. In the right lobe he wore a circle of fine gold wire. This tiny earring was one of the things he and Verna frequently quarreled about, but Douglas would not remove it.

When he heard his mother enter the room, Douglas put down his book and got up from the couch. Verna thought, with satisfaction, *at least I've brought him up to show some respect for women.*

She said, "Go and put some clothes on, dear."

"Why?"

"I'm having company."

"Well, *I'm* not."

"Please don't argue with me, dear. I have one of my headaches coming on." Verna had a whole battalion of headaches at her disposal. They came on like a swarm of native troops; when one of them was done to death, another was always ready to rush forward and take its place. "Mr. Blackshear is coming to see us. It may be about money."

She explained about the shares of AT&T that might have got stuck in a drawer, while Douglas listened with amiable skepticism, tugging gently at his golden earring.

The gesture annoyed her. "And for heaven's sake take that thing off."

"Why?"

"I've told you before, it makes you look foolish."

"I don't agree. Different, perhaps, but not foolish."

"Why should you *want* to look different from other men?"

"Because I am, sweetheart, I am."

He reached out and touched her cheek lightly.

She drew away. "Well, it seems to me . . ."

"To you, everything seems. To me, everything is."

"I don't understand you when you talk like that. And I won't have another argument about that earring. Now take it off!"

"All right. You don't have to scream." There was a thin line of white around Douglas's mouth and the veins in his temples bulged with suppressed anger. He unfastened the earring and flung it across the room. It ricocheted off the wall on to the blond plastic top of the spinet piano, then it rolled forward and disappeared between two of the bass keys.

Verna let out a cry of dismay. "Now look what you've done!"

"I'm sick of being ordered around."

"You've wrecked my piano. Another repair bill to pay . . ."

"It isn't wrecked."

"It is so." She ran over to the piano, almost in tears, and played a scale with her left hand. The C and D keys were not stuck, but they made a little plinking sound. "You've ruined my piano."

"Nonsense. I can fix it easily."

"I don't want you to touch it. It's a job for an expert." She rose from the piano bench, her lips tight as if they'd been set in cement.

Watching her, Douglas thought, there are some women who expand with the years, and some who shrink.

Verna had shrunk. Each week she seemed to grow smaller, and when Douglas called her old girl, it wasn't a term of endearment, it was what he really thought of her. Verna was an old girl.

"I'm sorry, old girl."

"Are you?"

"You know I am."

"Will you go up and change your clothes, then?"

"All right." He shrugged as if he'd known from the very beginning that she would get her own way and it no longer mattered because he had his own methods of making her regret her authority.

"And don't forget to put on a tie."

"Why?"

"Other men wear ties."

"Not all of them."

"I don't see why you're in such a difficult mood tonight."

"I think it's the other way around, old girl. Take a pill or something."

As he passed the piano on his way out of the room, he ran his forefinger lightly along the keys, smiling to himself.

"Douglas."

He paused in the doorway, holding his bathrobe tight around his waist. "Well?"

"I met Evie and her mother downtown this afternoon."

"So?"

"Evie asked after you. She was really very pleasant, considering what happened, the annulment and everything."

"I will be equally pleasant to her, if and when."

"She's such a lovely girl. Everyone said you made a very attractive couple."

"Let's not dredge that up."

"I don't suppose there's any chance you might want to see her again? She didn't ask me that, of course, but I could sense she was still interested."

"You need a new crystal ball, old girl."

When he had gone, she began to circle the room, turning on the lamps and straightening the odd-shaped ceramic pieces on the mantel which had been Douglas' passing contribution to the art. Verna didn't understand what these pieces represented any more than she understood Douglas' poetry or his music. It was as if he moved through life in a speeding automobile, now and then tossing out of the windows blobs of clay and notes in music and half-lines of poetry that he had whipped up while stopping for the red lights. Nothing was ever finished before the lights changed, and what was tossed out of the windows was always distorted by the speed of the car and the rush of the wind.

Verna Clarvoe greeted Blackshear with an effusiveness he didn't expect, desire or understand. She had always in the past made it obvious that she considered him a dull man, yet here she was, coming out to the car to meet him, offering him both her hands and telling him how simply marvelous it was to see him again and how well he looked, not a day, not a minute, older.

"You haven't changed a bit. Confess now, you can't say the same about me!"

"I assure you I can."

She blushed with pleasure, misinterpreting his words as a compliment. "What a charming fibber you are, Mr. Blackshear. But then, you always were. Come, let's talk in the den. Since Harrison died, we practically never use the drawing-room. It's so big Dougie and I just rattle around in it. Helen no longer lives at home."

"Yes, I know that. In fact, it's one of the reasons I'm here."

"You've come about *Helen*?"

"Yes."

"Well," she said with a sharp little laugh. "Well, this is a surprise. I thought perhaps you were coming to see me about money."

"I'm sorry if I gave you that impression."

"It wasn't an impression, Mr. Blackshear. It was a *hope.* Very silly of me." She turned her face away. "Well, come along; we'll have a drink."

He followed her down the dimly-lit hall to the den. A fire was spluttering in the raised fieldstone fire pit and the room was like a kiln. In spite of the heat, Verna Clarvoe looked pale and cold, a starved sparrow preserved in ice.

"Please sit down, Mr. Blackshear."

"Thank you."

She mixed two highballs, talking nervously as she worked. "Harrison always did this when he was alive. It's funny what odd times you miss people, isn't it? But you know all about that . . . That's some of Dougie's work on the mantel. It's considered very unusual. Do you know anything about art?"

"Nothing at all," Blackshear said cheerfully.

"That's too bad. I was going to ask your opinion. Oh well, it doesn't matter now. Dougie's taken up something new. Photography. He goes into Hollywood to classes every day. Photography isn't just taking pictures, you know."

This was news to Blackshear but he said, "Tell me more."

"Well, you have to study composition and lighting and filters and a lot of things like that. Dougie's crazy about it. He's a born student."

She crossed the room, carrying the drinks, and sat down beside Blackshear on the cocoa rattan couch.

"What shall we drink to, Mr. Blackshear?"

"It doesn't matter."

"All right. We'll drink to all the millions of things in this world that don't matter. To them!"

Blackshear sipped his drink uneasily, realizing that he had never actually known Verna Clarvoe. In the past he had seen her in character, playing the role she thought was expected of her, the pretty and frivolous wife of a man who could afford her. She was still onstage, but she'd forgotten her lines, and the props and backdrop had been removed and the audience had long since departed.

She said abruptly, "Don't stare at me."

"Was I? Sorry."

"I know I've changed. It's been a terrible year. If Harrison only knew—do you believe that people who have passed on can look down from Heaven and see what's happening on earth?"

"That wouldn't be my idea of Heaven," Blackshear said dryly.

"Nor mine. But in a way I'd like Harrison to *know.* I mean, he's out of it, he's fine, he has no problems. *I'm* the one that's left. I'm—what's that legal term? Relict?—that's what I am. A relict." She gulped the rest of her drink, making little sucking noises like a thirsty child. "This must be very boring for you."

"Not at all."

"Oh, you're always so *polite.* Don't you ever get sick of being polite?"

"I do, indeed."

"Why don't you get *im*polite then? Go on. I dare you. Get *im*polite, why don't you?"

"Very well," Blackshear said calmly. "You can't hold your liquor, Mrs. Clarvoe. Lay off, will you, please?"

"Please. *Please,* yet. You just can't help yourself, you're a gentleman. A born gentleman. Dougie's a born student. He's learning photography. Did I tell you that?"

"Tell me again, if you like."

"Mr. Terola is his teacher. He's a very interesting man. Not a born gentleman, like you, but very interesting. You can't be both. Tragic, isn't it. Why don't you be impolite again? Go on. I can't hold my liquor. What else?"

"I came here to talk about Helen, Mrs. Clarvoe, not about you."

Blotches of color appeared on her cheekbones. "That's impolite enough. All right. Go ahead. Talk about Helen."

"As you may know, for the past year I've been handling her investments."

"I didn't know. Helen doesn't confide in me, least of all about money."

"Yesterday she asked me to serve in another capacity, as an investigator. A woman in town has been making threatening and obscene telephone calls; Helen is one of her victims. From what I've learned about this woman today, I believe she's dangerous."

"What do you expect me to do about it? Helen's old enough to take care of herself. Besides, what are the police for?"

"I've been to the police. The sergeant I talked to told me they get a dozen similar complaints every day in his precinct alone."

The effects of the drink were beginning to wear off. Verna's hands moved nervously in her lap and a little tic tugged at her left eyelid. "Well, I don't see how *I* can help."

"It might be a good idea if you invited her to come and stay here with you for a little while."

"Here? In my house?"

"I'm aware that you're not on very friendly terms, but . . ."

"There are no buts, Mr. Blackshear. None. When Helen left this house I asked her never to come back. She said unforgivable things, about Dougie, about me. Unforgivable. She must be out of her mind to think she can come back here."

"She doesn't know anything about the idea; it was entirely my own."

"I ought to have guessed that. Helen wouldn't ask a favor of me if she were dying."

"It isn't easy for some people to ask favors. Helen is shy and insecure and frightened."

"Frightened? With all that money?" She laughed. "If I had all that money, I wouldn't be scared of the Devil himself."

"Don't bet on that."

With a defiant toss of her head, she crossed the room and began mixing herself another drink. As was the case with the first drink, she began reacting before she'd even uncorked the bottle.

"Mrs. Clarvoe, do you think it's wise to . . ."

"No, it's not wise. I'm a very stupid and ignorant woman. So I'm told."

"Who told you?"

"Oh, a lot of people, Harrison, Dougie, Helen, lots of people. It's a funny thing being told you're stupid and never being told how to get unstupid." She raised her glass. "Here's to all us birdbrains."

"Mrs. Clarvoe, do you do this every night?"

"Do what?"

"Drink like this."

"I haven't had a drink for months. As you said, I can't take the stuff. And I don't usually try. But tonight's different. Tonight's an end of something."

She held the glass in both hands, rotating it as she talked so that the clink of ice cubes punctuated her words.

"You think of an end as being definite, being caused by something important or calamitous. It's not like that at all. For me tonight is final, but nothing special happened, just a lot of things. Some bills came in, the maid was rude about waiting for her salary, I met Evie on the street, the girl Dougie married, Dougie put on his earring and I made him take it off and he threw it and . . . you see? Just little things." She stared into the glass, watching the bubbles rise to the surface and burst. "Evie looked so sweet and pretty. I thought what lovely children they might have had. My grandchildren. I don't mind getting old but I'd like to have something to show for it, like grandchildren. Mr. Blackshear . . ."

"Yes."

"Do you think there's something the matter with Douglas?"

A trickle of sweat oozed down the side of Blackshear's face, leaving a bright moist trail like a slug. "I'm afraid I can't answer that."

"No. No, of course not," she said quietly. "I shouldn't have asked. You don't know him, really. He's a—very sweet boy. He has many fine qualities."

"I'm sure he has."

"And he's extremely talented; everyone says that. Harrison was so strict with him, I tried to make it up to Dougie on the side, I encouraged him to express himself." She put the half- empty glass on the mantel and leaned closer to the fire, her bony little hands stretched out until they were almost touching the flames. "Harrison was a very cruel man sometimes. Does that surprise you?"

"Not much. Most of us are cruel on occasion."

"Not the way Harrison was. He used to—but it doesn't matter now. I can tell I'm depressing you." She turned from the fire, making an obvious effort to control her emotions. "You've listened to my troubles. Now you may tell me yours, if you like."

"They aren't very interesting."

"All troubles are interesting." Perhaps that's why we have them, to keep ourselves from being bored to death. Go on, tell me yours."

"Sorry, there isn't time, Mrs. Clarvoe."

"Don't leave yet. You haven't seen Dougie. He's upstairs getting dressed. Tomorrow's his birthday. We're having a little party at the Brown Derby."

While the maid waits for her salary, Blackshear thought grimly. "Wish Douglas a happy birthday for me."

"I will."

"There's just one more thing, Mrs. Clarvoe. Do you know a young woman named Evelyn Merrick?"

She looked surprised. "Well, of course."

"Of course?"

"She's Dougie's wife. She was, I mean. The marriage was annulled and she took back her maiden name."

"She lives here in town?"

"In Westwood. With her mother."

"I see." It was as simple as that. There'd been no need to ask Miss Hudson or Terola or Harley Moore. Evelyn Merrick wasn't a waif or a stranger. She had been Douglas Clarvoe's wife, Helen Clarvoe's sister-in-law. "Did Helen know the girl?"

"Know her? Why, that's how Douglas first met her. Evie and Helen went to a private school together years ago in Hope Ranch and Helen used to bring Evie home for weekends. After graduation they went to different colleges and lost touch, but Evie used to come over here once in a while, mostly to see Douglas. Douglas had always adored her, she was such a lively, affectionate girl. She used to tease the life out of him, but he loved it. There was never any malice in her teasing."

There is now, Blackshear thought. "Tell me about the wedding."

"Well, it was a very quiet one, being so soon after Harrison's death. Just the family and a few friends."

"Was Helen there?"

"Helen," she said stiffly, "had already moved out. She was invited, of course, and she sent a lovely gift."

"But she didn't come?"

"No. She was ill."

"How ill?"

"Really, Mr. Blackshear, I don't know how ill. Nor did I care. I didn't want her to come anyway. She might have ruined the wedding with that gloomy face of hers."

Blackshear smiled at the irony: Helen might have ruined the wedding, but Verna had ruined the marriage.

"Besides," Verna said, "she and Evie weren't best friends anymore, they hardly ever saw each other. They had nothing much in common, even when they were at school together. Evie was quite a bit younger, and the very opposite in temperament, full of fun and laughter."

"You saw her this afternoon."

"Yes."

"Is she still full of fun and laughter?"

"Not so much anymore. The break-up of the marriage was hard on her. Hard on all of us. I wanted grandchildren."

The second drink had brought color to her face and made her eyes look like blue glass beads in a doll's head.

"I wanted grandchildren. I have nothing to show for my life. Nothing."

"You have Helen. I think perhaps the two of you have reached the stage where you need each other."

"We won't discuss that again."

"Very well."

"I don't want any advice. I hate advice. I don't need it."

"What do you need, then?"

"Money. Just money."

"Money hasn't helped you much in the past. And it's not helping Helen much now. She's in the position of being able to indulge her neurosis instead of trying to do something about it."

"Why tell me?"

"I think you're the logical person to tell, since you're her mother."

"I don't feel like her mother. I never did, even when she was a baby. The ugliest baby you ever saw, I couldn't believe it belonged to me. I felt cheated."

"You'll always be cheated, Mrs. Clarvoe, if you put your value on the wrong things."

She raised her clenched right fist and took a step forward as if she meant to attack him.

Blackshear rose to meet her. "You asked me to be impolite."

"I'm asking you now to get out and leave me alone."

"All right. I'll go. Sorry if I've disturbed you."

Her hands dropped suddenly and she turned away with a sigh. "I'm the one who should apologize. I've had—it's been a bad day."

"Good night, Mrs. Clarvoe."

"Good night. And when you see Helen, tell her—tell her hello for me."

"I'll do that."

"Good night."

As soon as he had gone, she went upstairs to Douglas' room, leaning heavily on the banister for support. I must be firm, she thought. We must reach some decision.

The door of his bedroom was open.

"Dougie, there are some things we should—Dougie?"

He had changed his clothes as she had ordered him to—the terrycloth robe and the beaded moccasins he'd been wearing were on the floor beside the bed—but once again he'd made her regret the order. Instead of coming down to the den to meet Blackshear, he had left the house.

She said, "Dougie" again, but without hope. She knew he was gone, she could even visualize the scene: Douglas coming downstairs, pausing at the den door, listening, hearing his name: *Do you think there's something the matter with Douglas, Mr. Blackshear?*

She turned and moved stiffly towards the staircase. As she walked through the empty house she had a feeling that it would always be empty from now on, that the day had held a finality for Douglas as well as for herself, and he had fled the knowledge of it.

Pressing her fists against her mouth, she thought, I mustn't get silly and hysterical. Of course Dougie will be back. He's gone out to get a pack of cigarettes. Or for a walk. It's a lovely evening. He likes to walk at night and name the stars.

The telephone in the hall began to ring. She was so sure that it was Douglas calling that she spoke his name as soon as she picked up the receiver.

"Douglas. Where are . . ."

"Is that the Clarvoe residence?"

The voice was so muffled and low that Verna thought it was Douglas playing one of his tricks, talking through a handkerchief to disguise his identity. "Where on earth did you disappear to? Mr. Blackshear was . . ."

"This isn't Douglas, Mrs. Clarvoe. It's me, Evie."

"Evie. What a coincidence. I was just talking about you."
"To whom?"
"A friend of mine, Mr. Blackshear."
"Did you say nice things?"
"Of course I did." She hesitated. "I said hello to Douglas for you. He was very pleased."
"Was he?"
"I—I know he'd love to see you."
"Would he?"
"He said, why don't you come over some time; we'll talk about old times."
"I don't want to talk about old times."
"You sound so funny, Evie. Is anything wrong?"
"Nothing. I only called to tell you something."
"What about?"
"Douglas. I know you're worried about him. You don't know what's the matter with him. I'd like to help you. Mrs. Clarvoe. You were always kind to me; now I will repay you."

She began to explain in detail what was the matter with Douglas and some of the things that went on in the rear of Mr. Terola's studio.

Long before she had finished, Verna Clarvoe slumped forward on the floor.

6

It was nine-thirty.

The woman had been in the telephone booth for half an hour and Harry Wallaby was still waiting to call his wife in Encino and tell her the old Buick had broken down and he was going to spend the night with his brother-in-law.

"You'd think the dame's tongue'd drop off," Wallaby said over his third beer.

The bartender, a middle-aged Italian sporting a bow tie in Princeton colors, shook his head knowingly. "Not hers. The more exercise it gets, the stronger it gets. Phoneitis, that's what she has, phoneitis."

"Never heard of it before."

"It's like a disease, see. You gotta phone people. With her it's bad."

"Who is she?"

"Just a dame who comes in once in a while. Every time it's the same routine. A couple of drinks and it hits her, wham. She gets a buck's worth of dimes and parks herself in the phone booth, and there she sits, yackity, yackity, yackity. I've often wondered what in hell she talks about."

"Why don't you find out?"

"You mean go over and listen?"

"Sure."

"It wouldn't look right, me being the owner and proprietor," the bartender said virtuously.

"The same don't go for me. Is there a law says a guy can't stand beside a telephone booth, innocent-like?"

"It's a free country."

"Damn right it's a free country."

With an elaborate pretense of casualness, Wallaby slid off the bar stool, walked towards the front entrance as if he intended to leave, and then crept up on the telephone booth from the left side. He listened a moment, his hand cupping his ear, and returned to the bar, grinning a little sheepishly.

The bartender raised his eyebrows in silent inquiry.

"Douglas' husband," Wallaby said.

"What?"

"That's what she was talking about, a guy called Douglas who has a husband."

"That don't sound right to me. Maybe you heard wrong."

"No, I didn't. She was talking about Douglas' husband."

"Who's Douglas?"

"How the hell should I know who's Douglas? I'm just telling you what she said."

At a quarter to ten Evelyn Merrick stepped out of the telephone booth, stretched her left arm to relieve the cramp and smoothed her skirt down over her hips. Usually, after making a series of telephone calls, she felt a certain relief and relaxation, but tonight she was still excited. The blood drummed double-time in her ears and behind her eyes, and she lurched a little as she made her way back to the bar. Her old-fashioned was untouched on the counter. She didn't pick it up, she just sat down, staring at it suspiciously, as if she thought the bartender had added something to it in her absence.

"Okay, Wallaby," the bartender said loudly and pointedly, "you can phone your wife now."

Evelyn caught his meaning at once and looked up, a flush spreading across her cheekbones. "Did I use the telephone too long?"

"Just nearly an hour, that's all."

"It's a public phone."

"Sure, it's a public phone, meaning it's for the public, for everybody. Someone like you ties it up and the rest don't get a chance. If this was the first time, I wouldn't beef."

"Do you talk to all your customers like this?"

"I own the joint. I talk how I please. People that don't like it don't gotta come back. This includes anybody."

"I see." She stood up. "Is that your liquor license beside the cash register?"

"Sure, it's my license. Paid for and up to date."

"Your name's Florian Vicente?"

"That's right."

"Well good night, Mr. Vicente."

Vicente's jaw dropped in astonishment at her pleasant smile and friendly tone, and he felt a little ashamed of himself for being so brusque with her. After all, she was harmless.

Outside, the first rain of the season had begun, but Evelyn Merrick didn't notice. She had more important things to think about: Mr. Vicente had been rude and must be taught a lesson in manners.

She began walking along Highland towards Hollywood Boulevard, repeating the bartender's name to imprint it on her memory, Florian Vicente. Italian. Catholic. Very likely a married man with several children. They were the easiest victims of all, the married ones with children. She thought of Bertha and Harley Moore and threw back her head and laughed out loud. The rain sprayed into her open mouth. It tasted fresh and good. It tasted better than Mr. Vicente's old-fashioneds. Mr. Vicente should serve drinks like that. *Give me a double rain, Mr. Vicente. In the morning I will phone Mrs. Vicente and tell her that her husband is a pimp for niggers.*

She tripped down the slippery street, her body light and buoyant, bobbing like a cork on the convulsed seas of her emotions.

People huddling in doorways and under awnings looked at her curiously. She knew they were thinking how unusual it was to see such a gay, pretty girl running alone in the rain. They didn't realize that the rain couldn't touch her, she was waterproof; and only a few of the smart ones guessed the real reason why she never got tired or out of breath. Her body ran on a new fuel, rays from the night air. Occasionally one of the smart ones tried to follow her to get her secret, to watch her refuelling, but these spies were quite easy to detect and she was always able to evade them. Only in the strictest privacy did she store up her rays, breathing deeply first through one nostril and then the other, to filter out the irritants.

She turned east on the boulevard, towards Vine Street. She had no destination in mind. Somewhere along the way there would be a small bar with a telephone.

She hurried forward across the street, not seeing the red light until a woman yelled at her from a passing car and a man behind her grabbed her by the coat and pulled her back up on the curb.

"Watch your step, sister."

She turned. The man's face was half-hidden by the collar of his trench coat and the pulled-down brim of a green fedora. The hat splashed water like a fountain.

"Thank you," she said. "Thank you very much."

He tipped his hat. "Welcome."

"You probably saved my life. I don't know how to . . ."

"Forget it."

The light turned green. He brushed past her and crossed the street.

The whole episode had not taken more than half a minute, but already it was expanding in her mind, its cells multiplying cancerously until there was no room for reason. The half-minute became an hour, the red light was Fate, the touch of his hand on her coat was an embrace. She remembered looks that hadn't been exchanged, words that hadn't been spoken: Lover. Dear one. Beloved. Beautiful girl.

Oh, my dear one, wait for me. I'm coming. Wait. Lover. Lover dear.

Soaked to the skin, exhausted, shivering, lost, she began to run again.

People stared at her. Some of them thought she was sick, some thought she was drunk, but no one did anything. No one offered her any help.

She re-fuelled in an alley between a hotel and a cinema building. Hiding behind a row of dustbins, she breathed deeply first through one nostril and then the other, to filter out the irritants. The only witness was a scrawny grey tomcat with incurious amber eyes.

Inhale. Hold. Count four.

Exhale. Hold. Count three.

It must be done slowly and with proper care. The counting was of great importance. Four and three make seven. Everything had to make seven.

Inhale. Hold. Count four.

By the time she had finished re-fuelling, she had completely forgotten about lover. The last thing she remembered was Florian Vicente, who had called her wicked names because she had discovered his secret, that he was a pimp for niggers. What a shock it would be to his wife when she found out. But the poor woman must be enlightened, the truth must be told at all costs, the word must be spread.

Shaking her head in sympathy for poor Mrs. Vicente, Evelyn walked on down the alley and into the back door of the hotel bar. She had been here before.

She ordered a martini, which had seven letters.

A young man sitting on the next stool swung round and looked at her. "It's still raining, eh?"

"Yes," she said politely. "It doesn't matter though."

"It matters to me. I've got to . . ."

"Not to me. I'm waterproof."

The young man began to laugh. Something about the sound of his laughter and the sight of his very white, undersized teeth reminded her of Douglas.

"I'm not joking," she said. "I *am* waterproof."

"Good for you." He winked at the bartender. "I wish I was waterproof, then I could get home. Tell us how you did it, lady."

"You don't do anything. It happens."

"Is that a fact."

"It just happens."

"Is that a fact."

He was still laughing. She turned away. She couldn't be bothered with such an ignorant fool who had teeth like Douglas. If he persisted, of course, if he became really rude like Mr. Vicente, she would have to get his name and teach him a lesson. Meanwhile, there was work to be done.

She paid for the martini, and without even tasting it she approached the phone booth at the rear of the room and opened the folding door.

She didn't have to look up any numbers. She forgot other things sometimes, she had spells when the city seemed foreign as the moon to her and people she knew were strangers and strangers were lovers, but she always remembered the telephone numbers. They formed the only continuous path through the tormented jungle of her mind.

She began to dial, shaking with excitement like a wild evangelist. The word must be spread. Lessons must be taught. Truth must be told.

"The Monica Hotel."

"I'd like to speak to Miss Helen Clarvoe, please."

"I'm sorry. Miss Clarvoe has had a private telephone installed in her suite."

"Could you tell me the number?"

"The number's unlisted. I don't know it myself."

"You filthy liar," Evelyn said and hung up. She couldn't stand liars. They were a bad lot.

She dialed Bertha Moore, but as soon as Bertha recognized her voice, she slammed down the receiver.

She called Verna Clarvoe again. The line was busy.

She called Jack Terola's studio, letting the phone ring for a full minute in case he was busy in the back room, but there was no answer.

She called the police and told them a man had been stabbed with scissors in the lobby of the Monica Hotel and was bleeding to death.

It was better than nothing. But it wasn't good enough. The power and excitement were rotting away inside her like burned flesh, and her mouth was lined with grey fur like the tomcat's in the alley.

The cat. It was the cat that had ruined everything. It had contaminated her because it saw her re-fuelling. She liked animals and was very kind to them, but she had to pay the cat back and teach it a lesson, not with a phone but with scissors. Like the man in the lobby.

The man was no longer part of her imagination but part of her experience. She saw him clearly, lying in the lobby, white face, red blood. He looked a little like Douglas, a little like Terola. He was Douglas-Terola. He was the symbol of their marriage. He was dead.

She returned to the bar. One of the bartenders and the young man who had laughed at her were talking, their heads close together. When she approached they pulled apart and the bartender walked away to the other end of the bar. The young man gave her a hurried, uneasy glance and then got up, and he, too, walked away towards the back exit.

Everyone was deserting her. People did not answer their phones, people walked away from her. Everyone walked away. She hated them all, but her special hate was reserved for the three Clarvoes and, of the three, Helen in particular. Helen had turned her back on an old friend, she had walked away, first and farthest, and for this she must suffer. She couldn't hide forever behind an unlisted telephone number. There were other ways and means.

"I'll get her yet," Evelyn whispered to the walls. "I'll get her yet."

The fur in her mouth grew long and thick with hate.

7

DAWN CAME, A misty, meager lightening of the sky. The storm had intensified during the night. A banshee wind fled screaming up and down the streets, pursued by the rush of rain.

But it was not the wind or the rain that awakened Miss Clarvoe. It was the sudden stab of memory.

"Evie," she said, the name which had meant nothing to her for a long time was as familiar as her own.

Her heart began to pound and tears welled up in her eyes, not because she remembered the girl again, but because she had ever forgotten. There was no reason to forget, no reason at all. Right from the beginning they had been the closest of friends. They exchanged clothes and secrets and food from home, giggled together after the lights were out, met between classes, invented a language of their own to baffle the interceptors of notes, and shared the same crush on the science master who was married and had four children and large romantic brown eyes. Other crushes, too, they shared, but they were all Evie's to begin with. Helen just followed along, content to have Evie take the lead and make the decisions.

We were friends, always. Nothing ever happened that I should forget her. There's no reason, no reason.

They had attended their first dance together one Halloween, dressed alike, at Evie's suggestion, in gypsy costumes. Evie carried a goldfish bowl as a substitute for a crystal ball.

The dance, to which all the upper school girls had been invited, was held in the gymnasium of a private boys' school in the valley. Mr. Clarvoe drove Helen and Evelyn to the school and left them at the gym door. They were nervous and excited and full of the wildest hopes and the most abysmal fears.

"I can't go in, Evie."

"Don't be silly. They're only *boys.*"

"I'm scared. I want to go home."

"We can't walk ten miles dressed like this. Come on in; be a sport."

"Promise you won't leave me?"

"I promise."

"Cross your heart."

"Listen to the music, Helen. They've got a real orchestra!"

They went inside and almost immediately they were separated.

The rest of the evening was a nightmare for Helen. She stood in a corner of the room, rigid, tongue-tied, watching Evie surrounded by boys, laughing, humming snatches of music, floating gracefully from one partner to another. She would have given her soul to be Evie, but no one offered her the chance.

She went into the lavatory and cried, her forehead pressed against the wall.

When the dance was over, her father was waiting in the car outside the gym.

He said, "Where's Evie?"

"A boy asked to take her home. She's going with him."

"She's altogether too young for that sort of thing. If she were my daughter I wouldn't allow it." He pulled away from the curb. "Did you have a good time?"

"Yes."

"Tell me about it."

"There's not much to tell. It was fun, that's all."

"That's not a very good description. Your mother and I went to considerable trouble to get you to this dance. We'd like some report on it at least."

She knew from his tone that he was angry, but she didn't know what caused the anger and why it should be directed against her. "I'm sorry if I kept you waiting, Daddy."

"You didn't." He'd been waiting for three-quarters of an hour, but it was not her fault. He had come early deliberately, because it was her first dance and he was as uneasy about it as she was. He had sat in the car, listening to the chaos of laughter and music coming from the gym, imagining the scene inside, and Helen in the very center of it, bright and gay in her gypsy costume. When at last she came out, alone, with that stiff, sullen look on her face, disappointment rose up and choked him so that he could hardly breathe.

"Did you dance with anyone?"

"Yes."

"Who?"

She didn't want to lie but she knew she had to, and she did it well. Without hesitation she described some of the boys she'd seen dancing with Evie and gave them names and invented conversations and incidents.

She talked all the way home, while her father smiled and nodded and made little comments. "That Jim sounds like a real cut-up." "Too bad the Powers boy was shorter than you." "Now, aren't you glad we made you go to dancing school?"

Later, when she kissed him good night, he gave her an affectionate little pat on the bottom. "I'll have to watch out for you now, young lady. One of these days I'll be driven out of house and home by those little idiots hanging around."

"Good night, Daddy."

"I forgot to ask about Evie. Did she have as good a time as you did?"

"I guess so. I was too busy to pay her any attention."

She went to bed, half-believing in her own lies because her father's belief was so complete.

The following day the dean of Helen's school, who had been one of the chaperones, telephoned Mr. Clarvoe. She wanted, she said, to check up on Helen and see if she was all right, she'd been so unhappy at the dance.

Nothing was said at dinner in front of Verna and Douglas, but later Mr. Clarvoe called Helen into the den and shut the door.

"Why did you lie, Helen?"

"About what?"

"The dance."

She stood, mute, scarlet with humiliation.

"Why did you lie?"

"I don't know."

"If it had been just one lie—but it was a whole string of them. I can't understand it. Why?"

She shook her head.

"Nothing of what you told me was true?"

"No, nothing," she said with a kind of bitter satisfaction, knowing he was hurt almost as much as she was. "Not a word."

"All the boys—they weren't even real?"

"I made them up."

"Helen, look at me. I want the truth. I demand it. What really happened at the dance?"

"I hid in the lavatory."

He stepped back, as if the words had struck him across the chest. "You hid—in the lavatory."

"Yes."

"Why? For God's sake, *why?*"

"I couldn't think of anything else to do."

"My God, why didn't you phone me? I'd have come and taken you home. Why didn't you let me *know*?"

"I was too—proud."

"You call that pride? Skulking in a lavatory? It's almost obscene."

"I couldn't think of anything else to do," she repeated.

"What about Evie? Was she with you?"

"No. She was dancing."

"The entire evening, she was dancing and you were hiding in the lavatory?"

"Yes."

"For heaven's sake, why?"

"She was popular and I wasn't."

"Going off and hiding like that, you didn't give yourself a chance to be popular."

"I wouldn't have been anyway. I mean, I'm not pretty."

"You'll be pretty enough in time. Why, your mother is one of the prettiest women in the state."

"Everyone says I take after you."

"Nonsense, you look more like your mother every day. What on earth put the idea in your head that there's anything the matter with your appearance?"

"The boys don't like me."

"That's probably because you're too standoffish. Why can't you try to be more friendly, like Evie?"

She didn't tell him what he should have known for himself—that she would have given anything in the world to be like Evie, not just at the dance, but any time, any place.

His anger, which in the beginning had boiled out like lava, was now cooling, leaving a hard crust of contempt. "You realize, of course, that I'll have to punish you for lying?"

"Yes."

"Are you sorry you lied?"

"Yes."

"There's only one true test of penitence. If you had a chance to repeat the lies, knowing you wouldn't be found out, would you do it?"

"Yes."

"Why?"

"It would have made both of us happier."

It was true and he knew it as well as she did, but he shook his head and said, "I'm disappointed in you, Helen, extremely disappointed. You may go to your room."

"All right." She lingered wanly at the door. "What about my punishment?"

"Your punishment, Helen, is being you, and having to live with yourself."

Later in the evening she heard her parents talking in their bedroom and she crept down the dark hall to listen.

"Well, heaven knows I've done everything *I* can," Verna said. "You can't make a silk purse out of a sow's ear."

"What about my idea of giving her a big party, inviting a bunch of boys . . ."

"What boys?"

"We must know some people who have boys about her age."

"I can think of exactly two, the Dillards and the Pattersons. I loathe Agnes Patterson, and besides, the whole idea of a party wouldn't work."

"We've got to think of something. If she goes on like this she may not even marry."

"I just don't understand you, Harrison. For years you've been treating Helen as if she were about four, and now suddenly you're thinking about her marriage."

"Are you blaming the situation on me?"

"Someone's to blame."

"But never you."

"I," Verna said righteously, "am bringing up Dougie. The girl is the father's responsibility. Besides, she takes after you. Half the time I don't even understand her. She won't speak out, let anyone know what she's thinking or how she feels about things."

"She's shy, that's all. We must find a way to get her over her shyness."

"How?"

"Well, for one thing, I think we should encourage her relationship with Evie. The girl's a good influence on Helen."

"I agree." There was a silence, and then a sigh. "What a pity we didn't have a girl like Evie."

Barefooted, shivering with cold and fear, she trudged back to her room and got into bed. But the walls and ceiling seemed to contract, to press down on her until they fitted her like a coffin. She knew then that her father had been right. This was her punishment, to be herself, and to have to live with herself forever, a living girl inside a locked coffin.

She lay awake until morning, and the emotion that was strongest in her heart was not resentment against her parents but a new and bitter hatred for Evie.

She did nothing about this hatred. It was buried with her inside the coffin and no one else knew it was there. Things went on as before, with her and Evie, or almost as before. They still shared a crush on the science master with the romantic eyes, they wrote notes in their secret language, and exchanged clothes, and food from home, and confidences. The difference was that Helen's confidences were not real. She made them up just as she'd made up the boys, and the incidents at the dance, for her father.

At the end of the spring semester, when Evie acquired a boyfriend, Helen acquired two. When Evie was promised a horse as a reward for good grades, Helen was promised a car. It became as difficult for Evie to accept these lies as it was for Helen to keep on inventing them, and the two girls began to avoid each other.

There was trouble about it at home, but Helen had anticipated it and she was ready.

"Why didn't you bring Evie with you for the weekend?" her father asked.

"I invited her to come. She didn't want to."

"Why not?"

She hesitated just the right amount of time to rouse his curiosity. "I promised not to tell."

"I'm your father, you can tell me."

"No, I can't."

"Well, is it anything *we've* done?"

"Oh no. It's just—she's busy, she wanted to stay at school and study for the Latin test."

"That doesn't sound like Evie to me, staying at school when she could be here having a good time."

"Oh, she"ll be having a good—I mean, she likes to study."

"You mean she's not going to be studying, isn't that it?"

"I promised not to tell."

"This sounds like the kind of thing I'd better get to the bottom of, right here and now. Where is Evie?"

"At school?"

"Why?"

"I can't tell you. I made a solemn vow."

"I want an immediate and truthful answer to my question. Do you hear me, Helen?"

"Yes. But . . ."

"And no buts, ifs and whens, please."

"She—she has a boyfriend."

"Yes. Go on."

"She doesn't want her parents to find out about him because he's a Mexican."

"A *Mexican.*"

"He works on a lemon ranch near the school. She climbs out of the window after the lights are out and meets him in the woods." She began to cry. "I didn't want to tell. You made me. You made me a liar!"

Miss Clarvoe lay in bed with her right arm across her face as if to shield herself from the onslaught of memories. The ceiling pressed down on her, the walls contracted, until they fitted her like a coffin, tight, airless, sealed forever. And locked in with her were the mementos of her life: *"Your punishment is being you and having to live with yourself." "What a pity we didn't have a girl like Evie!"*

8

THE HOUSE WAS set in the middle of a tiny walled garden on Kasmir Street in Westwood. An engraved card in a slot above the doorbell read, Mrs. Annabel Merrick, Miss Evelyn Merrick.

The house needed paint, the woman who answered Blackshear's ring did not. She looked like a farmer's wife, plump and tanned and apple-cheeked, but her clothes were city clothes, a smart black-and-white striped suit that hinted at severely disciplinary garments underneath.

"Mr. Blackshear?"

"Yes."

"I'm Annabel Merrick." They shook hands. "Come in, won't you? I'm just making breakfast. If you haven't had yours, I can pop another egg in the pan."

"I've eaten, thank you."

"Some coffee then." She closed the front door after him and led the way through the living room into the kitchen. "I must say I was surprised by your early phone call."

"Sorry if I got you out of bed."

"Oh, you didn't. I work, you know. In the flower shop of the Roosevelt Hotel. Sure you wouldn't like an egg?"

"No, thanks."

"I've been divorced for several years, and of course alimony payments don't rise with the cost of living, so I'm glad to have a job. Somehow it's not so much like work when you're surrounded by flowers. Delphiniums are my favorite. Those blues—heavenly, just heavenly."

She brought her plate of eggs and toast to the table and sat down opposite Blackshear. She appeared completely relaxed, as if it was the most normal thing in the world to entertain strange men before eight o'clock in the morning.

"Blackshear, that's an odd name. Do people ever get mixed up and call you Blacksheep?"

"Frequently."

"Here's your coffee. Help yourself to cream and sugar. You didn't tell me what business you were in."

"Stocks and bonds."

"Stocks and bonds? And you want to see Evelyn? Heavens, you're barking up the wrong tree. Neither of us is in a position to invest a nickel. As a matter of fact, Evelyn's out of a job right now."

"It won't hurt to talk to her."

"I guess not. As I told you on the phone, she's not here at the moment. She's spending two or three days with a friend whose husband is out of town. The friend hates to stay alone at night and Evelyn's always anxious to oblige. She's that kind of girl, she'd do anything for a friend."

Her tone was proud and maternal and Blackshear deduced from it that Mrs. Merrick was as blind about her daughter as Verna Clarvoe was about her son. He said, "May I have this other woman's name and address?"

"Certainly. It's Claire Laurence, Mrs. John Laurence, 1375 Nessler Avenue, that's near U.C.L.A. Evelyn won't be there during the day, she's looking for a job, but she'll arrive around dinnertime, I expect."

"What kind of job is she looking for? I might be able to help."

"I'm afraid stocks and bonds aren't in Evelyn's line."

"What is her line, Mrs. Merrick. Is she stage-struck? Does she want to be a model, or something like that?"

"Good heavens, no! Evelyn's a sensible and mature girl. What on earth gave you the idea she might want to be a model?"

"A lot of pretty girls do."

"Evelyn's pretty enough, but she's not vain, and she has far too many brains to enter a profession that's so temporary. Evelyn wants a future. More coffee?"

"No, thank you." But she didn't seem to hear him. She poured more coffee into his cup, and he noticed that her hand was trembling.

He said, "I hope I haven't upset you in any way, Mrs. Merrick."

"Perhaps you have. Then again, perhaps I was upset to begin with."

"Are you worried about Evelyn?"

"What else does a mother worry about, especially when there's only one child? I want Evelyn to be happy, that's all I ask for her, that she be happy and secure."

"And isn't she?"

"I thought she was, for a while. And then she changed. Ever since her marriage she's been different." She looked across the table with a bleak little smile. "I don't know why I should tell you that. You said on the phone you didn't even know Evelyn."

"I don't. I've heard of her, though, through the Clarvoes."

"The Clarvoes are friends of yours?"

"Yes."

"You know about the marriage, then?"

"Yes."

"Is that why you're here? Did Verna send you to make amends?"

"No."

"I thought perhaps—well, it doesn't matter now. It's over. Spilled milk and all that." She took her empty plate to the sink and began rinsing it under the tap. "My own marriage failed. I had high hopes for Evelyn's. What a fool I was not to *see*."

"See what, Mrs. Merrick?"

"You know what." She turned so suddenly that the plate fell out of her hands and crashed in the sink. She didn't even notice. "My daughter married a pansy. And I let her. I let her because I didn't know it, because I was blind, I was taken in, the way Evelyn was, by his gentleness and his pretty manners and his so-called ideals. I thought what a kind and considerate husband he would make. Do you begin to see the picture Evelyn had of him?"

"Yes, clearly."

"I guess it's happened to other girls, getting tied up with a pansy, but it wouldn't have happened to Evelyn if I hadn't been divorced, if her father had been here. He'd have known right away that there was something wrong with Douglas. As it was, we had no hint, no warning at all.

"They went to Las Vegas for their honeymoon. I had a postcard from Evelyn saying she was fine and the weather was beautiful. That was all, until the doorbell rang one night a week later, and when I opened the door there was Evelyn standing on the porch with her suitcases. She didn't cry or make a fuss, she just stood there and said in a matter-of-fact way, 'He's a pervert'.

"It was a terrible shock, terrible. I kept asking her if she was sure, I told her some men were like that at first, timid and embarrassed. But she said she was sure, all right, because he had admitted it. He had apologized. Can you beat it?—he apologized for marrying her!

"Evie left her suitcases out on the porch, wouldn't even let me bring them into the house, and the next day she took them down to the Salvation Army, her whole trousseau, wedding dress and all. When she came back about around lunchtime she looked so pale and exhausted my heart turned over with pity, yes, and guilt, too. I should have known. I've been around. I was responsible."

Mrs. Merrick turned back to the sink, gathered up the bits of broken plate and tossed them into the trashcan. "A plate breaks and you throw it away. A person breaks and all you can do is pick up the pieces and try to put them together the best way you can. Oh, Evelyn didn't break, exactly. She just—well, sort of lost interest in things. She's always been an outgoing and lively girl, very quick to express her opinions or her feelings. On the night she came home she should have made a fuss, I ought to have encouraged her to talk out and cry out a little of the hurt. But she was withdrawn, detached . . ."

"Evelyn, dear, did you have dinner?"

"I think so."

"Let me heat up a little soup for you. I made some chowder."

"No, thank you."

"Evelyn—baby . . ."

"Please don't get emotional, Mother. We have to make plans."

"Plans?"

"I'll get an annulment, I suppose. Isn't that what I'm entitled to when the marriage wasn't consummated, as they say?"

"I think so."

"I'll see a lawyer tomorrow morning."

"There's no need for such haste. Give yourself a chance to rest up."

"Rest up from what?" Evelyn said with a wry smile. "No. The sooner, the better. I've got to shed that name Clarvoe. I hate it."

"Evelyn. Evelyn dear. Listen to me."

"I'm listening."

"He didn't—mistreat you?"

"In what way?"

"He didn't, well, make any indecent advances?"

"I did the advancing."

"Well, thank God for that."

"For what?"

"That he didn't mistreat you."

"You have," Evelyn said distinctly, "quite the wrong picture. I'll give you the right one, if you like."

"Not unless you feel like it, dear."

"I don't feel one way or the other. I just don't want you to get the idea in your head that I was physically abused." As she talked she rubbed the third finger of her left hand, as if massaging away the marks of her wedding ring. "It began on the plane when he became sick. I thought at the time it was airsickness, but I realize now he was sick with fear, fear of being alone with me, of having to do something that was repugnant to him. When we arrived at the hotel, he went into the bar while I unpacked. He stayed in the bar all night. I waited for him, all dressed up in my flossy nightgown and negligée. Around six o'clock in the morning two of the bellboys brought him up and poured him out on the bed. He was snoring. He looked so funny, yet so pathetic, too, like a little boy. As soon as he began to show signs of waking up, I went over and spoke to him and stroked his forehead. He opened his eyes and saw me bending over him. And then he let out a scream, the queerest sound I ever heard, an animal sound. I still didn't know what the trouble was, I thought he merely had a hangover." Her mouth twisted with distaste and contempt. "Well, he had a hangover, all right, but the party had been years and years ago."

"Oh, Evelyn. Baby . . ."

"Please don't fuss."

"But why, why in heaven's name did he marry you?"

"Because," Evelyn said dryly, "he wanted to prove he wasn't a fairy."

Blackshear listened, pitying the woman, pitying them all: Evelyn waiting in her flossy nightgown for the bridegroom, Douglas sick with fear, Verna trying desperately to hide the truth from herself.

"Yesterday," Mrs. Merrick continued, "Evelyn met me downtown at noon to do some shopping. For the first time since the wedding, we saw Verna Clarvoe. I was quite upset. I could think of nothing but bitter things to say. But Evelyn was perfectly controlled. She even asked about Douglas, how he was and what he was doing and so on, in the most natural way in the world.

"Verna went into that spiel of hers—Dougie was fine, he was taking lessons in photography, and doing this and doing that. It seemed to me that she was trying to start the whole business over again, trying to whip up Evelyn's interest. And then it struck me for the first time, she doesn't *know*, Verna still doesn't know, she still has hopes, doesn't she?"

"I think she has."

"Poor Verna," she said quietly. "I feel especially sorry for her today."

"Why especially?"

"It's his birthday. Today is Douglas' birthday."

9

DOUGLAS' DOOR WAS locked; it was the only way she had of knowing that he had come back some time during the night, perhaps because he wanted to, perhaps because he had no place else to go.

She knocked and said, "Douglas," in a harsh heavy voice that was like a stranger's to her. "Are you awake, Douglas?"

From inside the room there came a mumbled reply and the soft thud of feet striking carpet.

"I want to talk to you, Douglas. Get dressed and come downstairs. Right away."

In the kitchen, the part-time maid, a spare, elderly woman named Mabel, was sitting cross-legged at the dresser ledge, drinking a cup of coffee and reading the morning *Times*. She didn't rise when she saw Verna, who owed her back wages in civility as well as cash.

"There's muffins in the oven. Yesterday's. Heated up. You want your orange juice now?"

"I'll get it myself."

"I made a grocery list. We're out of eggs and coffee again. I need a drop of coffee now and then to steady myself and there's barely a cup left in the pot."

"All right, go and buy some. You might as well do the rest of the shopping while you're at it. We need some 100-watt bulbs and paper towels, and you'd better check the potato bin."

"You want I should do it now, before I have a bite to eat?"

"Our understanding was that you were to eat before you come here."

"We had *other* understandings too."

"You'll be paid this week. I expect a check in the mail today."

When the maid had gone, Verna took the muffins out of the oven and tested one. It was rubbery, and the blueberries inside were like squashed purple flies.

She added water to the coffee and reheated it, and then she poured some orange juice out of a pitcher in the refrigerator. It smelled stale. The whole refrigerator smelled stale, as if Mabel had tucked odds and ends of food into forgotten corners.

Hearing the wheeze and rattle of Mabel's ancient Dodge as it moved down the driveway, Verna thought, I'll have to let her go, as soon as I can pay her. How awkward it is to have to keep her on because I can't afford to fire her.

Douglas came in as she was pouring herself a cup of coffee. He hadn't dressed, as she'd asked him to. He was wearing the terrycloth robe and beaded moccasins he'd had on the previous night before Blackshear's visit. He looked haggard. The circles under his eyes were like bruises, and from his left temple to the corner of his mouth there ran three parallel scratches. He tried to hide the scratches with his hand, but the attempt only drew attention to them.

"What happened to your cheek?"

"I was petting a cat."

He sat down beside her, on her left, so that she would only see the uninjured side of his face. Their arms touched and the physical contact jabbed Verna like a needle. She got up, feeling a little faint, and walked over to the stove.

"I'll get you some muffins."

"I'm not hungry." He lit a cigarette.

"You shouldn't smoke before breakfast. Where did you go last night?"

"Out."

"You went out and petted a cat. A real big evening, eh?"

He shook his head wearily.

"What kind of cat was it that you petted?"

"Just an ordinary alley cat."

"Four-legged?"

She paused. "Not the one that scratched you."

"I don't know what you're getting at, I really don't." He turned his eyes on her, dove-colored, full of innocence. "What are you so angry about, Mother? I went for a walk last night, I saw this cat, I picked it up and tried to pet it and it scratched me. God help me, that's the truth."

"God help you, yes," she said. "No one else will."

"What brought on this somber mood?"

"Can't you guess?"

"Certainly I can guess."

"Go ahead then."

"You tried to borrow money from Helen and she turned you down."

"Wrong."

"Mabel asked for her back wages?"

"Wrong again."

"It has something to do with money, that's for sure."

"Not this time."

He got up and started towards the door. "I'm tired of this guessing game. I think I'll go up . . ."

"Sit down."

He stopped at the doorway. "Don't you think I'm too old to be ordered around like . . ."

"Sit down, Douglas."

"All right, all right."

"Where did you go last night?"

"Are we going to start that all over again?"

"We are."

"I went out for a walk. It was a nice night."

"It was raining."

"Not when I left. The rain started about ten o'clock."

"And you just kept on walking."

"Sure."

"Until you got to Mr. Terola's place?"

He stared at her across the room, unblinking, mute.

"That was your destination, wasn't it, one of the back rooms of Terola's studio?"

He still didn't speak.

"Or perhaps it wasn't Terola's, perhaps it was just anybody's back room. I hear your kind isn't particular." She heard herself saying the words, but still she didn't believe them. She waited, her fists clenched against her sides, for the reactions she wanted from him: shock, anger, denial.

He said nothing.

"What goes on in that studio, Douglas? I have a right to know. I'm paying for those so-called 'photography' lessons of yours. Are you really learning anything about photography?"

He walked unsteadily back to the dresser and sat down. "Yes."

"Are you behind the camera or in front of it?"

"I don't know—what you mean."

"You must know, other people do. I heard it myself last night."

"Heard what?"

"About the kind of pictures Terola takes. Not the sort of thing one would want in a family album, are they?"

"I wouldn't know."

"Who would know better than you, Douglas? You pose for them, don't you?"

He shook his head. It was the denial she'd been waiting for, praying for, but it was so fragile she couldn't touch it for fear it would break.

"Who's been talking to you?" he said.

"Someone called me last night after you went out."

"Who was it?"

"I can't tell you."

"If rumors are going around about me I have a right to know who's passing them along."

She clutched at the straw. "Rumors? That's all they are then, Douglas? None of it's true? Not a word?"

"No."

"Oh, thank God, thank God."

She rushed at him across the room, her arms outspread.

His face whitened and his body tensed as he braced himself for her caress. She stroked his hair, she kissed his forehead, she touched the scratches on his cheek with loving tenderness, she murmured his name, "Dougie. Dougie dear. I'm so sorry, darling."

Her arms entwined around him like snakes. He felt sick with revulsion and weak with fear. A scream for help rose in his throat and suffocated there: *God. God help me. God save me.*

"Dougie dear, I'm so sorry. You'll forgive me, won't you?"

"Yes."

"Oh, what a horrible mother I am, believing those lies. That's all there were, lies, lies."

"Please," he whispered. "You're choking me."

But the words were so muffled she didn't hear them. She pressed her cheek against his. "I shouldn't have said those terrible things, Dougie. You're my son. I love you."

"Stop it! Stop!"

He tore himself out of her grasp and ran to the door, and a moment later she heard the wild pounding of his feet on the stairs.

She sat for a long time, stone-faced, marble-eyed, like a deaf person in a room of chatterers. Then she followed him upstairs.

He was lying spread-eagled across the bed, face down. She didn't go near him. She stood just inside the door.

"Douglas."

"Go away. Please. I'm sick."

"I know you are," she said painfully. "We must—cure you, take you to a doctor."

He rolled his head back and forth on the satin spread.

Questions rose on her tongue and died there: When did you first know? Why didn't you come and tell me? Who corrupted you?

"We'll go to a doctor," she said more firmly. "It's curable; it must be curable. They cure everything nowadays with all those wonder drugs they've got, cortisone and A.C.T.H., things like that."

"You don't understand. You just don't *understand.*"

"Try me. What it is? What don't I understand?"

"Please. Leave me alone."

"Is that what you want?"

"Yes."

"Very well," she said coldly. "I'll leave you alone. I have an errand to do anyway."

Something in her voice alerted him, and he rolled over on the bed and sat up. "What kind of errand? You're not going to see a doctor?"

"No; that's your duty."

"And what's yours?"

"Mine," she said, "is to see Terola."

"No. Don't go there."

"I must. It's my duty, as your mother."

"Don't go."

"I must confront this evil man, face to face."

"He's not an evil man," Douglas said wearily. "He's like me."

"Have you no shame, no sense of decency, defending a man like that to me, your own mother?"

"I'm not defen—"

"Where's your self-respect, Douglas, your pride?"

He had so many things to say to her that the words became congested in his throat and he said nothing.

"I'm going to see this Terola and give him a piece of my mind. A man like that being allowed to run around loose; it's a disgrace. He's probably corrupted other young men besides you."

"He didn't corrupt me."

"What are you saying, Douglas? Of course he did. He was responsible. If it weren't for him you'd be perfectly normal. I'll see to it that he pays for the . . ."

"Mother. Stop it."

There was a long silence. Their eyes met across the room and went on again, like strangers passing on a street.

"Terola," she said finally. "He wasn't the first, then."

"No."

"Who was?"

"I've forgotten."

"When did it happen?"

"It was so long ago that I can't remember."

"And all these years—all these *years* . . ."

"All these years," he repeated slowly, using the words like weapons against both her and himself.

He didn't hear her leave, but when he looked up again, she was gone and the door was closed.

He lay back on the bed, listening to the beat of rain on the roof, and the cheep-cheep of a disgruntled house wren complaining about the weather from under the eaves. Every sound was clear and sharp and final: the cracking of the eucalyptus trees as the wind increased, the barking of the collie next door, Mabel's old Dodge wheezing up the driveway, the slam of a car door, the murmur of the electric clock beside his bed.

It seemed that he had never really listened before, and now that he had learned how, each sound was personal and prophetic. He was the wren and the rain, he was the wind and the trees bending under the wind. He was split in two, the mover and the moved, the male and the female.

All these years, the clock murmured, *all these years.*

Verna tapped on the door again and came in. She was dressed to meet the weather, in a red plaid raincoat and a matched peaked cap.

She said, "Mabel's back. Keep your voice down. She has ears like a fox."

"I have nothing to say, anyway."

"Perhaps you'll think of something by the time I get back."

"You're not going to see Terola?"

"I told you I was."

"Please don't."

"I have some questions to ask him."

"Ask me instead. I'll answer. I'll tell you anything you want to know."

"Stop wheedling like that, Douglas. It annoys me." She hesitated. "Don't you see, I'm only doing my duty? I'm only doing what your father would have done if he were still alive. This man Terola, he's obviously corrupt, and yet you're trying to protect him. Why? You said you'd tell me anything. Why?"

He lay motionless on the bed, his eyes closed, his face grey. For a moment she thought he was dead, and she was neither glad nor sorry, only relieved that the problem had been solved by the simple stopping of a heart. Then his lips moved. "You want to know why?"

"Yes."

"Because I'm his wife."

"His—*What did you say?*"

"I'm his wife."

Her mouth opened in shock and slowly closed again. "You filthy little beast," she said quietly. "You filthy little beast."

He turned his head. She was standing by the bed watching him, her face distorted with loathing and contempt.

"Mother. Don't go. Mom!"

"Don't call me that. You're no part of me." She walked decisively to the door and opened it. "By the way, I forgot. Happy birthday."

Alone, he began to listen again to the clock and the wren and the rain and the trees; and then the sound of the Buick's engine racing in response to Verna's anger. She's leaving, he thought. She's going to see Jack. I couldn't stop her.

He got up and went into the bathroom.

For almost a year, ever since his marriage to Evelyn, he'd been saving sleeping pills. He had nearly fifty of them now, hidden in an Epsom salt box in his medicine chest, capsules in various gay colors that belied their purpose. He swallowed five of them without difficulty, but the sixth stuck in his throat for a few moments, and the seventh wouldn't go down at all. The gelatin coating melted in his mouth and released a dry, bitter powder that choked him. He did not try an eighth.

He removed the blade from his safety razor, and standing over the washbasin, he pressed the blade into the flesh that covered the veins of his left wrist. The razor was dull, the wound was hardly more than a scratch, but the sight of his blood oozing out made him dizzy with terror. He felt as if his knees were turning into water and his head was filling with air like a balloon.

He tried to scream, "Help, Mother!" but the words came out like a whimper.

As he fell forward in a faint, his temple struck the projecting corner of the washbasin. The last sound Douglas heard was sharp and clear and final, the crack of bone.

10

AT TEN O'CLOCK, Miss Clarvoe, who had slept late, was just finishing her breakfast. When she heard the knocking on the door she thought it was one of the busboys from the dining room coming to collect her tray and his tip.

She spoke through the crack of the door. "I haven't quite finished. Come back later, please."

"Helen, it's me. Paul Blackshear. Let me in."

She unlocked the door, puzzled by the urgency in his voice. "Is there anything the matter?"

"Your mother's been trying to reach you. The telephone company wouldn't give her your unlisted number, so she called me and asked me to come over."

"To tell me she's cancelled the birthday luncheon, I suppose."

"She's cancelled it, yes."

"Well, she needn't worry about Douglas receiving a present from me. I sent a check out last night; he should get it today."

"He won't get it today."

"Why not?"

"Sit down, Helen."

She went over to the wing chair by the front window but she didn't sit down. She stood behind it, moving her long thin hands nervously along its upholstered back, as if to warm them by friction.

"It's bad news, of course," she said, sounding detached. "You're not an errand boy; even Mother wouldn't use you as an errand boy to tell me about a cancelled luncheon."

"Douglas is dead."

Her hands paused for a moment. "How did it happen?"

"He tried to commit suicide."

"Tried? I thought you said he was dead."

"The doctor believes Douglas swallowed some sleeping capsules and cut one of his wrists, but the cause of death was a blow on the head. He struck his temple against the washbasin as he fell, probably in a faint."

She turned and looked out of the window, not to hide her grief, but to hide the grim little smile that tugged at the corners of her mouth. Poor Douglas, he could never finish anything properly, not even himself.

"I'm sorry, Helen."

"Why should you be? If he wanted to die, that was his affair."

"I meant I was sorry for you."

"Why?"

"Because you don't feel anything, do you?" He crossed the room and stood facing her. "Do you?"

"Not much."

"Do you ever feel anything? For anybody?"

"Yes."

"For whom?"

"I—I wish you would not get personal, Mr. Blackshear."

"My name is Paul."

"I really can't call you that."

"Why not?"

"I just can't, that's all."

"Very well."

"I . . ." She stepped back and stood against the wall with her hands behind her back, like an embarrassed schoolgirl. "How is Mother taking it?"

"I'm not really sure. When she called me on the telephone she seemed more angry than anything else."

"Angry at whom?"

"Evelyn Merrick."

"I don't understand. What had Evelyn to do with Douglas' death?"

"Your mother holds her responsible for it."

"Why?"

"Evelyn called your mother last night and gave her some information about Douglas and Jack Terola, the man who's supposedly been giving Douglas lessons in photography. I won't repeat the information. It wasn't pretty, though; I can tell you that. This morning your mother taxed Douglas with it and he admitted that some of it, at least, was true. Your mother wanted a showdown with Terola and actually started out to see him. Whether she saw him or not, I don't know for sure. She says she didn't, that she turned around and came back to the house. Meanwhile, the maid had found Douglas' body when she went to clean his room, and she called the doctor. The doctor was there when your mother arrived. She tried to get in touch with you immediately, and failing that, she called me and asked me to come over here."

"Why?"

"The telephone company . . ."

"I meant, why was she so anxious to have me informed right away? So she could be sure I'd send a nice fat wreath, as I sent a nice fat check?"

"That's uncharitable, Helen."

"Yes, I guess it is. I'm sorry. Life has taught me to be suspicious. I've learned the lesson too well."

"Perhaps you can unlearn it someday."

"Perhaps. It's harder to unlearn, though."

"I can help you, Helen."

"How?"

"By giving you something that's been too scarce in your life."

"What?"

"You can call it love."

"*Love.*" Violent pink spread up from her neck to her cheekbones. "No. No. You—you're just trying to be nice to me."

"I'm not trying," he said with a smile. "I *am* being nice to you."

"No. I don't want your love, anyone's. I can't accept it. It—embarrasses me."

"All right. Don't get excited. There's no hurry. I can wait."

"Wait? What will you wait for?"

"For you to unlearn some of those lessons you've been taught."

"What if I can't. What if I never . . ."

"You can, Helen. Just tell me you'll try. Will you?"

"Yes, I'll try," she whispered. "But I don't know where to start."

"You've already started."

She looked surprised and pleased. "I have? What did I do?"

"You remembered Evelyn Merrick."

"How do you know that?"

"You referred to her quite casually a few minutes ago as Evelyn. Do you remember her clearly now?"

"Yes."

"In her phone call to you the other night, when she said you'd always envied and been jealous of her, was she right, Helen?"

"She was right."

"That's no longer true, is it?"

"No. I don't envy her anymore. She's to be pitied."

"Pitied, yes," he said, "but watched, too. She's all the more dangerous because she can appear quite rational on the surface."

"You've seen her, then."

"Not yet. I'll see her tonight. But I discussed her with your mother last night before the phone call, and early this morning I talked to Evelyn's own mother. Neither of them had the faintest suspicion that the girl is insane. She appears to have a completely split personality. On the one hand, she's the affectionate, dutiful daughter, as well as your mother's idea of a perfect daughter-in-law—and the latter would take quite a bit of doing, since your mother's not easy to please."

"I'm aware of that."

"On the other hand, the girl is so full of hatred and vengeance that she wants only to destroy people by turning them against one another. She's crafty, she hasn't had to do any of the destroying herself. She just throws in the bone and lets the dogs fight each other over it. And there's usually some meat of truth on the bone."

She thought of her mother and Douglas, and how they had fought throughout the years, not like dogs, or like boxers in the ring face to face, but like guerrillas stalking each other in a dark forest. Into this forest Evelyn had thrown a giant flare which lit up the trees and the underbrush and scorched the enemies out of their cover.

Poor Douglas. He was always a boy, he could never have grown up in a dark forest.

"I sent him a check for his birthday," she said dully. "Perhaps if I'd sent it sooner . . ."

"A check wouldn't have made any difference, Helen. The doctor found nearly fifty sleeping capsules in the medicine chest. Douglas had been planning this for a long time."

"Why does Mother blame Evelyn for it, then?"

"She has to blame someone. And it can't be herself."

"No," she said, thinking: Mother was trapped in the forest just as much as Douglas was. Years ago someone should have led them out, but there was no one except Father and me, and Father was too harsh and I was lost myself.

She covered her face with her hands and tears slid out between her fingers.

"Don't cry, Helen."

"Someone should have helped. Years ago someone should have *helped.*"

"I know."

"Now it's too late, for Douglas, for Mother." She raised her head and looked at him, her eyes softened by tears. "Maybe it's too late for me, too."

"Don't think that."

"Yes. I feel inside me that I've lived my life, I'm only waiting, like Douglas with his hoard of sleeping capsules. Perhaps I'll get another phone call, perhaps it will light up the underbrush and I won't be able to bear what I see."

"Stop it." He put his arms around her, but her body grew stiff as wood at his touch and her hands clenched into tight fists. He knew the time had not yet come, and perhaps never would.

He walked away to the other side of the room and sat down at the desk, watching the change come over her at his retreat, the relaxation of her muscles, the easier breathing, the levelling off of color in her face. He wondered if this was how they must remain for all time, a room's width away from each other.

"You're very—kind," she said. "Thank you, Paul."

"Forget it."

"I suppose now I must go home and stay with Mother. That's what is expected of me, isn't it?"

"By her, yes."

"Then I'll get ready, if you'll excuse me."

"I'll drive you over, Helen."

"No, please don't bother. I'll call a cab. I don't want to interfere with your investigation."

"My investigation, as such, is almost finished. You asked me to find Evelyn Merrick. Well, I've found her."

"You think it's all over, then? Everything's settled?" Her voice was insistent. "You have no further work to do on the case?"

"There's work to be done, but . . ."

"More than ever, in fact."

"Why more?"

"Because there's been a death," she said calmly. "Evelyn's not going to stop now. I think Douglas' death will actually spur her on, give her a sense of power."

It was what Blackshear himself feared, but he hadn't wanted to alarm her by saying so. "It could be."

"Where did she get her information about Douglas?"

"From Terola himself, I guess."

"You mean they could be together in some extortion racket?"

"Perhaps Terola intended it that way, but Evelyn needs deeper satisfactions than money can give."

"But you think they were partners?"

"Yes. When I went to see Terola about her, he was pretty cagey. I got the impression he knew the girl a lot better than he admitted."

"So if there's any evidence against her, this man Terola would have it?"

"Evidence of what?"

"Anything that can be used to put her away some place. So far she's done nothing actionable. In Douglas' case she didn't even tell a lie. She can't be sued or sent to jail just for phoning Mother and telling her the truth. And yet, to a certain extent, she's morally guilty of Douglas' death. You've got to stop her, Paul, before she goes on." She turned so that he couldn't see her face. "I may be next."

"Don't be silly, Helen. She can't call you, she doesn't know your number. And if she comes to the door, don't let her in."

"She'll think of some other way. I feel she's—she's waiting for me."

"Where?"

"I don't know."

"Look, if you're nervous about going over to your mother's house, let me drive you."

She shook her head. "I'd rather you went to see Terola. Tell him about Douglas, force him to talk, to give you information that can be used in court."

"That's a tall order, Helen. Even if he knows Evelyn like a book, he's not going to read it aloud to me. He'd incriminate himself."

"You can try, can't you?"

"That's about it. I can try."

He waited while she went into the bedroom to dress for the street. When she came out she was wearing a dark grey woollen coat and an old-fashioned black felt hat with a broad brim turned down over her forehead. The outfit made her look as if she'd stepped out of the previous decade.

"Helen."

"Yes?"

"Mind if I say something personal?"

"You usually do, whether I mind or not."

"You need some new clothes."

"Do I?" she said indifferently. "I never pay much attention to what I wear."

"It's time you started."

"Why?"

"Because you and I will be going places together. All kinds of places."

She smiled lightly, like a mother at the exaggerated plans of a small boy.

They took the lift downstairs and walked through the lobby together. Mr. Horner, the desk clerk and June Sullivan, the emaciated blonde at the switchboard, watched them with undisguised curiosity and exchanged small, ugly smiles as they paused at the swinging door that led to the street.

"My car's a couple of blocks away. Sure you don't want me to drive you over to your mother's?"

"It isn't necessary."
"I'll come there later to see you, if you like."
"I'm afraid it won't be a very cheerful household. Perhaps you'd better not."
"Shall I call you a cab?"
"The doorman will."
"All right. Good-bye, then."
"Good-bye."
Outside, on the busy street, Evelyn Merrick was waiting for her.

11

THE WIND HAD blown the storm out to sea and the streets, which had been fairly quiet half an hour before, now came alive, as if the end of the rain was an all-clear signal for activities to resume immediately and simultaneously. People marched briskly up and down the sidewalks like ants patrolling after a storm, but on the road traffic came almost to a standstill. Cars moved slowly, if at all, defeated by their own numbers.

It took Blackshear ten minutes to get his car out of the parking lot and another thirty minutes to reach the long, narrow stucco building on Vine Street which served as Terola's studio.

For the second time Blackshear read the black stenciling on the frosted-glass windows, but now the words had more sinister implications:

PHOTOGRAPHIC WORKSHOP
JACK TEROLA, PROPRIETOR
PIN-UP MODELS
LIFE GROUPS FOR AMATEURS AND PROFESSIONALS
RENTAL STUDIOS FOR ART GROUPS
COME IN ANY TIME

The office was exactly as it had been the previous afternoon except that someone had recently used the old brick fireplace. The remains of a fire were still smoking, and whatever had been burned had generated enough heat to make the room uncomfortably hot.

The heat drew out other odors, the smell of boiled-over coffee and of a sharp, musky perfume. The coffee smell came from Terola's alcove, concealed from view by a pair of dirty flowered chintz curtains. The odor of perfume came from the girl seated behind, and almost hidden by, the old-fashioned rolltop desk. She was leaning back in the swivel chair at an awkward angle, and her eyes were closed. She appeared to be asleep.

Blackshear recognized her as Nola Rath, the young girl who'd been posing for one of Terola's magazine layouts the preceding day. At that time her long black hair had been wet and she'd worn no make-up. Now her hair was compressed into a roll on top of her head and she had on a layer of cosmetics so thick it was like a mask. She looked years older.

He approached the desk, diffident and a little embarrassed, feeling that he was intruding on her privacy by watching her in her sleep.

"Miss Rath?"

Slowly, as if the movement hurt her, she opened her eyes. There was no recognition in them, of Blackshear, or of anything else. She seemed dazed.

"I'm sorry if I woke you up."

"I wasn't—asleep." Her voice matched her eyes; it was flat and dull and expressionless. She held her hand to her throat as if the act of speaking, like the act of moving her eyelids, was painful to her.

"Are you feeling all right, Miss Rath?"

"All right."

"Let me get you a glass of water."

"No. No water." She shifted her weight and the chair creaked under it. "You better get out of here."

"I just came."

"That don't matter; you better go."

"I'd like to see Mr. Terola, if I may. Is he in?"

"He's not seeing anybody."

"If he's too busy right now, I'll come back later."

"He's not busy."

"Well, is he ill or something?"

"He's not ill. He's something. He's very something." She began to move her head back and forth. "I been sitting here. I don't know what to do. I been sitting. I ought to get out of here. I can't move."

"Tell me what's happened."

She didn't answer, but her eyes shifted towards the alcove. Blackshear crossed the room, drew back the curtains of the alcove and stepped inside.

Terola was lying on his back on the day bed with a pair of barbers' shears stuck in the base of his throat. A soiled sheet and a blood-spattered pink blanket covered the lower half of his body; the upper half was clothed in an undershirt. On the table near the foot of the daybed the hot plate was still turned on and the coffee pot had boiled dry. It looked as though Terola had got up, turned on the coffee, and then gone back to bed for a few more minutes. During those few minutes he'd had a visitor.

Whoever the visitor was, Terola had not been alarmed. There were, except for the blood, no signs of violence in the room, no evidence of a struggle. Terola's hair was not even mussed; the same thin, parallel strands of grey crossed the top of his pate like railway ties. Either Terola had known the visitor well and been taken completely by surprise, or else he'd been killed in his sleep.

The thrust of the scissors had been deep and vicious and accurate. It was a woman's weapon, a pair of scissors, but the hand that used it had a man's strength.

In life Terola had been unprepossessing enough, in death he was monstrous. The eyes bulged like balls of glass, the fleshy mouth hung slack, the tongue, greyish pink and thick, lolled against the tobacco-stained teeth. Blackshear thought of Douglas and his youth and good looks, and he wondered what dark paths had led him to Terola.

Without touching anything, he returned to the girl in the office.

"Have you called the police?"

She blinked. "Police? No?"

"Did you kill Terola?"

"No. For God's sake, no! He was my friend, he gave me a job when I was down and out, he treated me good, never slapped me around like some."

"You found him the way he is now?"

"Yes, when I came to work."

"When was that?"

"Fifteen, twenty minutes ago, I guess. Be here at noon, he said, only I always come a little early so's I can get ready."

"Was the door locked when you arrived?"

"No. Jack doesn't—didn't keep it locked unless he's—unless he was out."

"Did Terola always sleep at the office?"

"No. He and his mother and his brother have a little ranch out in the valley where they raise avocados, only Jack wasn't stuck on the place, or the company either, I guess, so he often stayed here in town." She pressed a handkerchief to her eyes. "Oh, God, I can't believe he's dead. He was going to do big things for me, he said. He said I had a great future, all I needed was some publicity. He promised he'd get me all the publicity I wanted."

Blackshear was grim. "Well, he kept his promise."

"Kept it? No, he didn't. What do you mean?"

"You'll get all the publicity you want, Miss Rath. Maybe more."

Her reaction was not what he expected. "My God, that's right. Say, there'll be newspaper photographers and everything. The works. How do I look?"

"Great."

"Gee, maybe I could even write an article for the Sunday papers about what a stinker Jack was, except to me. How's that for an angle? Here is this bum Terola, who everybody hates his guts, only he puts himself out to be kind to a down and out orphan girl. How does that sound?"

"Are you an orphan, Miss Rath?"

"I could be," she said with a cold little smile. "Depending on the stakes, I could be anything."

"Including a liar."

"Oh, that. Sure."

"You didn't phone the police, did you?"

She shrugged. "No. I will, though. As soon as you get out."

"Why should I get out?"

"Because you'll wreck everything for me. My future depends on this. It's gotta be done right, see?"

"I don't see."

"Well, put it this way. Suppose I didn't have so many clothes on, and suppose I run screaming into the street that I found a murdered man—get the picture?"

"Vividly."

"Then you see how you'd gum things up by being here." She stood up and leaned across the desk towards him. "I didn't kill Jack and I won't touch anything, I promise. Go away, will you, mister? I need a chance. A real chance."

"And you think this is a real chance for you?"

"It's *got* to be. I'll never get another. Now will you go? Will you *please* go, mister?"

"After you call the police."

She picked up the phone and dialed. While she waited for an answer, she began unbuttoning her dress.

Blackshear went out to his car. He would have liked to stay behind the wheel for a few minutes to witness Nola Rath's performance, but he had a more important matter to attend to. Sometime during the morning Verna Clarvoe had set out to see Terola. Had she, in spite of her story to the contrary, seen him, talked to him? Or had she despaired of words as a weapon and used scissors instead? Perhaps other people had motives for killing Terola, but Verna's was fundamental, for in her, love and hate had merged and exploded like two critical masses of uranium. In the explosion, Douglas had died. Perhaps Terola was the second victim of the chain reaction.

12

A RED-EYED maid answered the door.

Blackshear said, "May I see Mrs. Clarvoe, please?"

"She's not seeing anybody. There's been an accident."

"Yes, I know. I have something urgent to tell Mrs. Clarvoe."

"What's more urgent than being allowed to be alone with your grief, I'd like to know."

"What's your name?"

"Mabel."

"Mabel, I want you to tell Mrs. Clarvoe that Paul Blackshear is here on important business."

"All right, but I warn you, she's been carrying on something awful. When the hearse came to take him away, she screamed, such screaming I never did hear in all my born days. I thought she'd bust a blood vessel. She called someone on the telephone and kept shouting things about a girl named Evelyn. It was fierce."

"Didn't the doctor give her a sedative?"

"Some pills he gave her. *Pills.* Pills is a pretty poor substitute for a son." She opened the door wider and Blackshear stepped into the hall. "I'll go up and tell her. I don't guarantee she'll come down though. What can you expect, at a time like this?"

"Has Miss Clarvoe arrived yet?"

"*Miss* Clarvoe?"

"Douglas' sister."

"I didn't even know he had a sister. Fancy that, no one mentioning a sister."

"She should be arriving any minute now," Blackshear said. "By the way, when she comes, you needn't let on that she isn't mentioned around here."

"As if I'd do a thing like that. Will she be staying—I mean, sleeping and eating and so forth?"

"I'm not sure."

"Well, it's a queer household; make no mistake about that."

"I won't."

"You can wait in the drawing room, if you like."

"I prefer the den."

"I'll show you . . ."

"I know the way, thanks."

The den smelled of last night's fire, and the morning rain. Someone had started to clean the room and been interrupted; a vacuum cleaner was propped against the divan, and a dust cloth and a pile of unwashed ashtrays were sitting on a piano bench. The glass door that led out to the flagstone patio had been slid back and the November wind rustled across the floor and spiraled among the ashes in the fireplace.

Verna Clarvoe came in, her step slow and unsteady as if she was wading upstream in water too deep, against a current too strong. Her eyes were swollen almost shut, and there were scratches around her mouth as if she'd clawed herself in a fury of grief.

She spoke first. "Don't say you're sorry. Everyone says they're sorry and it doesn't matter, it doesn't *matter* whether they're sorry or not." She slumped into a chair. "Don't look at me. My eyes, they always get like this when I cry. I've forgotten where I put my drops. It's so cold in here, so *cold.*"

Blackshear got up and closed the door. "I talked to Helen. She offered to come home."

"Offered?"

"Yes, offered." It was true enough. He hadn't suggested it. "She should have been here half an hour ago."

"She may have changed her mind."

"I don't think so."

"Why didn't she come with you?"

"I had some business to attend to first. It concerns you, Mrs. Clarvoe. If you're feeling well enough, I think I'd better tell you about it now."

"I feel all right."

"Terola is dead."

"Good."

"Did you hear what I said, Mrs. Clarvoe?"

"You said Terola is dead. I'm glad. Very glad. Why should you be surprised that I'm glad? I hope he suffered, I hope he suffered agonies."

"He didn't. It happened pretty quickly."

"How?"

"Someone stabbed him with a pair of scissors."

"Someone murdered him?"

"Yes."

She sat, quiet, composed, smiling. "Ah, that's even better, isn't it?"

"Mrs. Clarvoe . . ."

"He must have been scared before he died, he must have been terrified. You said he didn't suffer. He must have. Being scared is suffering. A pair of scissors. I wish I'd seen it happen. I wish I'd been there."

"And I wish," Blackshear said, "that you could prove you weren't."

"What a silly remark."

"Perhaps; but it had to be made."

"I told you on the phone, I started out to see Terola, but I changed my mind and came back."

"How far did you get? As far as the studio?"

"Yes."

"But you didn't go in?"

"No. The place looked so squalid. I lost my nerve."

"Did you get as far as the door?"

"No. I never left the car. There's a yellow curb in front of the place, I just stopped there for a while."

"For how long?"

"A few minutes."

"Did anyone see you?"

"I was there, people must have seen me."

"What kind of car do you drive?"

"A black Buick sedan, last year's. There are hundreds like it, if that's what you're getting at."

"It is."

"Well, I didn't race up in a flame red Ferrari. There's no reason why anyone should have paid any particular attention to me."

"Let's hope no one did."

"What if they did?"

"If they did," Blackshear said patiently, "you'll probably be questioned by the police. You had a pretty good reason for hating Terola."

"If I killed everyone I hated, people would be dying like flies all over town."

"I don't believe that, Mrs. Clarvoe."

"Oh, stop. Stop that boy-psychiatrist approach. You don't know me. You don't understand. I'm filled with hatred. How can I help it? I've been cheated, duped, tricked—what do you expect? Everyone's let me down, everyone. Harrison, Douglas, they're out of this mess of a life. I'm the one that's left, always the one that's left."

From the driveway came the squeal of a car's moist brakes. They both heard it simultaneously, Verna with dread, Blackshear with relief. He hadn't admitted even to himself that he'd been worried about Helen's delayed arrival.

"That must be Helen now," Verna said. "I don't know what I'll say to her, how I'll act. We've been apart for so long, we're strangers."

"Then act like strangers—they're usually polite to each other, at least."

Blackshear went to the glass door and looked out across the patio towards the driveway. A woman was paying off the cab driver, a plump grey-haired woman in a black and white suit. When the cab backed out towards the street, she stood for a moment staring at the house as if she wasn't sure it was the right one. She saw Blackshear and appeared to recognize him. Instead of going to the front door, she started across the patio towards the den with quick, aggressive strides.

Sensing trouble, Blackshear went out to meet her, closing the glass door behind him.

"Hello, Mrs. Merrick."

Her face was stiff and hostile. "Is she in there?"

"Yes."

She tried to brush past him but he reached out and clasped her arm and held it.

"Wait a minute, Mrs. Merrick."

"The sooner this is done, the better. Let go of my arm."

"I will, after you tell me what you have in mind."

"You mean, am I going to strangle the little bitch? No. Much as I'd like to."

He released her arm but she didn't move away from him. "Much as I'd like to," she repeated. "The things she said about Evelyn—incredible, terrible things. I can't, I won't, let her get away with it. No mother would."

"When did she make these remarks?"

"Less than an hour ago. She called me at the office—at the office, mind you: God knows who heard her, she was shouting so loud. She made the most terrible accusations against Evelyn. I can't even repeat them, they were so vile. She kept shouting something about giving Evelyn a dose of her own medicine. I don't know what she meant. Evelyn's always been so nice to her. Then she said that Evelyn was a murderer, that she murdered Douglas. I hung up, but she called back right away. I had to take the call, there were other people around. When she finally finished, I asked the boss for the rest of the morning off and here I am. I've got to get to the bottom of this."

"Isn't it rather a bad time?"

"It's a bad time, but it's not going to get any better. I have to find out why she said those things about Evelyn. If she's crazy with grief over Douglas, well, all right, I can understand that, I've had a few griefs of my own. But why should she take it out on Evelyn of all people? My daughter has never hurt anyone in her life, it's so *unfair* that she should be attacked like this. She isn't here to defend herself, but I am. I'm here. And don't try and stop me this time, Mr. Blackshear. *I'm going to see Verna Clarvoe.*"

He watched her go into the house.

The two women faced each other in silence for a long time.

"If you've come for an apology," Verna said finally, "you won't get one. A person isn't obliged to apologize for telling the truth."

"I want an explanation, not an apology."

"You have the explanation."

"You've said nothing yet. Nothing."

"I gave Evelyn back some of what she gave me. The truth." Verna turned away, pressing her fingertips against her swollen eyelids. They felt hot, as if they'd been scalded by her tears. "She called me last night. She was quite friendly at first, she said I'd always been kind to her and she wanted to do me a favor in return. Then she told me about Douglas, the kind of life he was leading, the friends he had—sordid, terrible things, in words so vile. I don't see how a girl like Evelyn would know them, let alone speak them. That's your explanation, Mrs. Merrick."

"You can't be talking about Evelyn. Not *my* Evelyn."

"Why not?" Verna said, through clenched teeth. "She was talking about *my son.*"

"I don't believe it. Evelyn would never do such a thing. She felt vindictive, perhaps, for a time after the marriage, but she's all over that. She has no hard feelings now. You saw that for yourself when you met us yesterday. She was pleasant and friendly, wasn't she? Wasn't she nice to you? You said so yourself, she bears no grudge."

"I am not arguing. I am too tired to argue. I told you what happened."

"You must be mistaken." Mrs. Merrick's plump face was like rising dough. "At least admit the possibility that you're mistaken."

"There's no such possibility."

"What time did she—what time was the call?"

"About ten."

"There. You see? You're wrong. Evie stayed with some friends last night. They had tickets for a play at the Biltmore Bowl."

"It was Evelyn who called me. I recognized her voice. And no one else, no woman, anyway, would know such things about Douglas."

"These things—how can you be sure they were true?"

"Because he admitted them, my son admitted them. And then he killed himself." She began to sway back and forth, her arms hugging her scrawny breasts. "Dougie. Dougie is dead. It's his birthday. We'd planned a little party—Oh God, go away, leave me alone."

"Mrs. Clarvoe, listen to me."

"No, no, no."

"I'd like to help you."

"Go away. My son is dead."

She left the way she had come, across the patio. Blackshear was waiting for her on the driveway, his suit collar turned up against the wind, his lips blue with cold.

He said, I'll drive you back to work, Mrs. Merrick."

"No, thanks. You'd better go in to her." She began putting on her suede gloves. "At least Evelyn is alive. No matter what she's done, at least she's *alive.* That's enough to thank God for."

She turned and walked briskly into the wind, her head high.

13

THE WET PATCHES on her dress, where she'd washed off the blood in the lavatory of the public library, were dry now, and it was safe to venture out into the street again. Even if the wind should blow her coat open, people wouldn't notice the faint stains left on her blouse, or if they did, they couldn't identify them.

She closed the book she'd been pretending to read for the past hour and returned it to the reference shelf. She knew no one in the library, and no one knew her. Still, it was dangerous to sit too long in any one place, especially a quiet place, because sometimes her mind clicked noisily like a metronome and spies could tell from its frequency what she was thinking.

One of these spies was an old man sitting at a table near the information desk, half hidden behind a copy of *U.S. News and World Report.* How innocently engrossed he seemed, like a child gazing at a picture book, but something about the angle of his head gave him away. She began to hum, quite loudly, so he couldn't hear her thoughts. He lowered the magazine and gave her a sour look, realizing that he'd been outwitted.

As she passed the table, she bent towards the old man and whispered, "It won't do you any good to follow me." Then she headed for the door, pulling her coat tight around her.

The victory was hers, of course. Still, the clicking of her mind was becoming annoying. It came and went at odd moments, varying with the intensity of her thoughts, and if she was excited by an idea the noise was almost deafening, enough to drive her crazy.

Crazy. Not a word to use lightly. Terola had tried.

She walked quickly down the library steps and turned north, thinking of Terola. She'd been perfectly nice to him, perfectly polite. He had had no reason to act as he did.

When he answered the door he was wearing striped pajama bottoms and an undershirt.

"Hello, Mr. Terola."

"What do *you* want?"

"I just thought I'd pop in and . . ."

"Look, kid, pop out again, will you? I'm hung over."

He started to close the door but she was too quick for him. "I could make you some coffee, Mr. Terola."

"I've been making my own coffee for years."

"Then it's high time you tried mine. Where's the stove?"

Yawning, he led the way to the alcove and sat down on the edge of the daybed while she plugged in the hot plate and filled the coffee pot with water.

"How come the ministering angel act, kid?"

"I like to do a favor for a friend, now and then."

"And then the friend is supposed to do a favor right back at you?"

"That would be nice."

"What's the angle?"

"Those pictures you took of me," she said. "Burn them up."

"Why?"

"They didn't do me justice."

His eyebrows humped like black, bushy caterpillars. "So?"

"So burn them up and take new ones. Good ones, the kind they hang in museums."

"Look, Elaine, Eileen, whatever your name is . . ."

"Evelyn."

"Look, Evelyn, you go home now like a good girl and I'll consider your proposition."

"You don't mean it."

"Sure, sure, I do." He lay down on the bed and pulled the covers up to his waist.

"Do you promise, Mr. Terola?"

"Promise what?"

"To make me immortal."

"You crazy or something?" he said, punching the pillow irritably. "People hear you talking like that, they'll haul you off to the loony bin."

"Mr. Terola . . ."

"Blow, will you? I'm tired. I had a big night."

"Mr. Terola, do you think I'm pretty?"

"Gorgeous," he said, closing his eyes. "Just gorgeous, sweetheart."

"You're making fun of me."

"No, I'm not. Why should I make fun of you? Now blow, like a good girl, Eileen."

"Evelyn," she said. "*Evelyn*."

"All right. Sure."

"Say it. *Say Evelyn*."

He opened his eyes and saw her standing over him. "What's the matter with you, kid? Are you crazy?"

Crazy. Not a word to use lightly.

As she turned the next corner she looked back towards the library. The spy, disguised as an old man, was standing on the steps watching her, with the *U.S. News and World Report* tucked under his arm. She began to run.

The old man went back into the library and stopped at the information desk, where a red-haired girl sat surrounded by telephone directories from all over the country.

The girl smiled and said, "Here I thought you were running off with one of our magazines again, Mr. Hoffman."

"Not this time. Did you happen to notice the young woman who just left. The one with the dark coat?"

"Not particularly. Why?"

"I've been observing her for the past half-hour. Very peculiar, she seemed to me."

"We get a great many peculiar people in here," the girl said cheerfully. "Public institution, you know."

"I thought perhaps—well, the fact is, I couldn't help noticing she had red stains on the front of her dress."

"She probably had spaghetti for lunch. You know how it dribbles."

"All the time I was watching her she kept a book open in front of her, but she wasn't reading. A book on birds, I believe, though my eyes aren't what they used to be. Then, as she was leaving, she leaned down and whispered something to me. I didn't quite catch it. Odd, wouldn't you say?"

"Rather."

"I was wondering if I should, perhaps, report it to the police?"

"Now there you go again, Mr. Hoffman, imagining things!"

Because of the clicking of her mind and the danger of spies, she tried never to go into the same bar twice, but it was difficult to tell one from another, they were so similar. It was as if the decorations, the neon signs, the furniture, the customers, the bartenders, had all come from the same warehouse in a package deal.

The important difference was the location of the phone booth. At the Mecca it was in the rear, near the entrance to the gentlemen's and cut off from the view of the people at the bar by a massive tub of philodendron.

With the folding door of the phone booth shut tight, she felt safe and warm and secluded, beyond the reach of society, like a child in a playhouse or a poet in an ivory tower.

She dialed, smiling to herself, breathing the stale air deeply into her lungs as if it were pure oxygen. Crestview 15115. As she waited for an answer, she totaled the numbers. Thirteen. Add one and divide by two, that made seven. Everything had to make seven. Most people didn't know this, and even when they were told, exhibited skepticism or frank disbelief.

On the fifth ring (plus two) a woman's voice said "Hello".

"Is this the Clarvoe residence?"

"Yes."

"Mrs. Clarvoe?"

"She's not in."

"But I recognize you, Mrs. Clarvoe."

A sharp sound came over the wire, like a metallic object striking the floor. "Who—Is that you, Evelyn?"

"Didn't you expect to hear from me again?"

"Yes. Yes, I expected to."

A pause at the other end of the line, then a flurry as if people were moving about, and a man's voice, low and hurried, but distinct: "Ask her about Helen. Ask her where Helen is."

"Who's that with you?" Evelyn said. As if she didn't know. Poor old bungling Blackshear, looking for her all over town, like a blind man feeling his way through a forest. One of these days I will pop out at him from behind a tree.

"No one's with me, Evelyn. There was, but I—I sent him away. I felt you—you and I could talk better alone. Evelyn? Are you still there?"

Still there. Safe, warm, secluded, the poet in the playhouse, the child in the ivory tower.

A man, barrel-chested, bald, passed the phone booth, and she peered out at him through the dirty, narrow glass door. But he didn't even notice her. His mind was on other things.

"Evelyn? Answer me. *Answer me.*"

"Well, you needn't shout," Evelyn said coldly. "I'm not deaf, you know. I have 20-20 hearing."

"I'm sorry I—shouted."

"That's better."

"Listen to me, please. Have you seen Helen? Have you talked to her?"

"Why?" She smiled to herself because she sounded so sober and earnest when all the time she was bursting with laughter. Had she seen Helen? What a marvelous joke. Prolong it. Draw it out. Make it last a bit. "Why do you want to know about Helen, Mrs. Clarvoe?"

"She was due here hours ago. She said she was coming home."

"Oh, that."

"What do you mean? Have you . . . ?"

"She changed her mind. She didn't really want to come home anyway. She didn't want you to see her in her present condition."

"What is her—condition?"

"I promised not to tell. After all, we were friends once, and I ought to keep a promise to a friend."

"Please. For God's sake . . ."

"You keep shouting. I wish you wouldn't."

"All right," Verna whispered. "I won't shout. Just tell me, where's Helen and what's the matter with her?"

"Well, it's a long story." It wasn't really. It was short and sweet, but Mrs. Clarvoe must be taught a lesson: It was rude to shout.

"Evelyn, please, I beg of you . . ."

"No one has to beg me for the truth. I give it freely, don't I?"

"Yes."

"Whatever else people say about me, I'm not a liar."

"No. Of course not. You're not a liar. About Helen, she's all right, isn't she?"

"I don't know."

"But you said . . ."

"I didn't say she was all right or all wrong. All I said was that she changed her mind, she's not coming home."

"Where is she?"

The barrel-chested man passed again, on his way back to the door. He had glass eyes and wooden lips.

"She's working," Evelyn said, "in a call house."

She began to tremble in excitement and anticipation, waiting for Verna's reaction, shock, disbelief, protest. None came.

"Did you hear me, Mrs. Clarvoe? Helen's working in a call house. It's down on South Flower Street. No place for a lady, I can tell you. But then, Helen never wanted to be a lady. A little excitement, that's what she needs. She'll get it, too. Oh my, yes. She'll get it."

Still no answer, not even the click of the receiver. The excitement began to spill out of her, like blood from a severed artery. She stuffed words into the wound to stem the flow.

"I got her the job. I met her outside her hotel this morning. She said she was sick of the idle life she was leading, she wanted to have something interesting to occupy her time. So I said I knew of something. Come with me, I said. And she came."

"Now I know you're lying," Verna said flatly. "Helen would never have gone anywhere with you. She's been warned."

"Warned? About me?"

"What have you done with her?"

"I told you, I got her a job."

"That's preposterous."

"Is it?" She hung up softly.

It was preposterous, nothing could be more preposterous than poor old Helen in a call house. Yet it was true.

She began to laugh, not ordinary laughter, but sounds with claws that tore at her chest and at the tissues of her throat. Burning with pain, she stumbled out into the street.

14

DURING CLASSES SHE was known as Dr. Laurence, but after five she was Claire and she lived near the U.C.L.A. campus in Westwood with her husband, John, and an overweight spaniel called Louise. She was a tall, well-built young woman with long, beautiful legs and black hair which she wore in a coronet of braids. The style was old-fashioned and not particularly becoming, but it made her look unique, and she was well aware that this was about as much as she could expect with her limited equipment.

Frank, intelligent and unpretentious, she got on well with her students and had a great many friends, most of them university people. Her closest friend, however, had nothing to do with the faculty.

She had met Evelyn Merrick about eight months previously on a double date with one of John's fraternity brothers. On the way home she asked John, "Well, how do you like her?"

"Who?"

"Evelyn Merrick."

"She's okay," John said.

"You certainly are enthusiastic."

"Thank God *one* of us doesn't form snap judgments of people."

"Snap judgments are the only valid ones."

"How so?"

"Otherwise you get to like people, just because they satisfy a need in you and not because of their intrinsic worth."

"Don't look now, but your PhD is showing."

"Let it show," Claire said. "I'll bet she's suffered. And don't say *who* again. You know perfectly well who."

"Most of us suffer here and there."

"I don't think it was here and there with Evelyn. It seems to me that she's had a tremendous shock of some kind."

"Maybe she had shock treatments."

"You meant that to be funny, I suppose."

"Very, very slightly funny."

"As a matter of fact, I've seen people just after they've had shock treatments, and they show the same kind of wary attitude. Even if they hear a question the first time, they like to have it repeated. Things like that."

"So you think your new friend is a parolee from Camarillo."

"I think nothing of the sort," Claire said briskly. "My opinion is that she's suffered a shocking experience. I wonder what it could have been."

"Well, I know you, angel, you'll have the whole story out of her the second time you meet."

He was wrong. During the next few months the two women met frequently, sometimes accidentally, since they lived only eight blocks apart, and sometimes by arrangement, for lunch or dinner or an early movie; but whatever Evelyn's shock had been, she didn't mention it, and any hints that Claire put out or direct questions she asked, were met with silence or a gentle remonstrance. At first, Evelyn's ability to keep a secret tantalized and annoyed Claire, but in time she came to respect it.

When John, who taught in the biology department, had to go away on field trips, Evelyn frequently came over to spend the night because Claire was nervous about being alone.

John liked to tease his wife about these occasions. "Afraid of the dark, at your age and weight."

"I can't help it."

"What did you do before you were married?"

"Before I was married, I lived in an apartment house with people below me, above me, and on both sides of me. The walls were so thin you could hear a pin drop, so there wasn't much chance of being murdered in your bed. It's quite different living in a house, like this. You're cut off from people."

"By a driveway and two flowerbeds."

"No, you know what I mean."

He knew exactly what she meant. She'd been brought up in a large family and lived in dormitories at school. There had always been people around, brothers and sisters, and friends and cousins and cousins of cousins. Being left in a house by herself made Claire feel insecure, and John was grateful to Evelyn for keeping her company in his absence. He had long since lost his original distrust of Evelyn and he believed now that, in her quiet way, she was just about the nicest girl in the world.

On Wednesday morning John took some of his freshmen students on a field trip to Los Padres National Forest and in the late afternoon Evelyn came over to the house to have dinner with Claire and spend the night. The two women had planned on going to see a play at the Biltmore Bowl, but the arrangements were cancelled when Claire arrived home with a severe cold. She went to bed at eight, drugged with anti-histamines and codeine, and slept around the clock.

She woke up the next morning to the sound of dishes rattling and the smell of burning bacon. Slipping on her husband's old Paisley bathrobe, she went out into the kitchen and found Evelyn making breakfast.

Claire said, yawning, "I could eat a horse."

"You may have to. I just ruined the last of the bacon."

"I like it well done."

"It isn't well done; it's charred."

"Well, Johnny says everybody should eat a certain amount of carbon. It acts as a purifying agent."

"You're making that up."

"It sounds rather plausible, though, doesn't it?"

"I can tell you're feeling better this morning."

"Oh, I am. How about you?"

Evelyn turned, her face white and aloof. "Me? There was never anything wrong with me."

"You're looking rocky. If I didn't know you better I'd say you'd been out on a binge."

"Binges aren't much in my line."

"I was just kidding. I didn't mean to offend you."

"I'm afraid I offend easily, these days."

"I know you do. John and I—well, we've noticed, and we couldn't help wondering."

"Wondering what?"

"If you shouldn't get married."

Evelyn was silent.

"I mean," Claire said with awkward earnestness, "marriage is a wonderful thing for a woman."

"Oh?"

"It really is. I don't know why you're looking amused. What's funny?"

"I'm afraid," Evelyn said, smiling, "you wouldn't understand."

On Thursday afternoon Claire arrived home from her classes a little earlier than usual, around four-thirty. It was already getting dark and she didn't notice the car parked at the curb until she let the cocker spaniel out. The dog streaked across the lawn towards the car and began pawing at the door.

A man wearing a grey felt hat leaned out of the window and said, "That's not doing the finish of my car much good."

"So I see." She picked up the squirming spaniel.

"You're Mrs. Laurence?"

"That's right."

"I'm Paul Blackshear. I called you at the University this afternoon."

"Oh yes."

"Is Miss Merrick here?"

"Not yet. She will be though. If you'd like to come inside and wait . . ."

"Thanks, I would."

She led the way across the lawn, feeling apprehensive about letting the stranger into the house and yet unable to think of an adequate reason or a polite way to get rid of him.

In the living room she turned on all four of the lamps and left the drapes open, and when Blackshear had settled himself on the davenport she sat down in a straight-backed chair at the opposite end of the room.

"My husband," she lied firmly, "will be home at any minute."

Blackshear gave her a quizzical look. "Good. I'll need all the help I can get."

"Help with what?"

"I am trying to find a woman. I have reason to believe that Evelyn Merrick knows where this woman is."

"You mean you think Evelyn helped her to disappear?"

"I mean that, yes, but not in exactly the same sense that you do."

"I don't understand."

"The woman's disappearance was involuntary."

Claire stared at him, her face pale and astonished, her clenched fists pressed against her thighs. "What are you—implying?"

"It's obvious, isn't it, Mrs. Laurence?"

"No, it's not obvious. Nothing is obvious. I'm confused. I don't understand."

"I don't understand either, but I'm trying to. That's why I'm here. The woman who disappeared is Helen Clarvoe, a friend of mine. She was also, at one time, a friend of Evelyn Merrick's."

"At one time. Does that mean they quarreled?"

"Let's say they lost touch. Until last Monday night. At that time Miss Merrick telephoned Helen Clarvoe at her hotel. I won't go into detail, but I assure you it wasn't an ordinary call from one old friend to another. As a result of it, Miss Clarvoe asked me to try and find Evelyn Merrick."

"Why?"

"She was disturbed and frightened by Miss Merrick's remarks. During the course of the week I've discovered that unusual telephone calls are Evelyn Merrick's specialty. Some people, when they have a grievance, blow their top, some brood, some write crank letters. Evelyn Merrick telephones."

"Nonsense," Claire said sharply. "I don't believe it. Ev hates to talk on the phone. I should know; I'm her best friend."

"Look, Mrs. Laurence, there may be some things about this woman that even her best friend doesn't know because Miss Merrick herself may not know them."

"That's not possible. Unless she's—are you trying to tell me she's insane?"

"It's a form of insanity."

"What is?"

"Multiple personality."

Claire rose abruptly and began to pace the room. "Ev is my best friend. You're a stranger. You come here and tell me some monstrous things about her and expect me to believe them. Well, I can't. I won't. What right have you got to go around diagnosing people as multiple personalities?"

"The theory isn't mine. It was advanced as a possibility by Miss Merrick's own doctor. I talked to him this afternoon. Miss Merrick has already suffered two emotional disturbances, one after her parents were divorced and her father went east to live, and the other after the break-up of her own marriage last year."

"Marriage," Claire repeated. "Ev's never been married."

"It's a matter of record."

"She's never said a word to me about it. I—why, just this morning we were talking and I said something about marriage being good for a woman and she—well, it doesn't matter now."

"Go on, Mrs. Laurence. She what?"

"Nothing. She just smiled, as if I'd said something unintentionally funny."

"You did."

"It wasn't a happy marriage, then?"

"No."

"Who is the man?"

"Helen Clarvoe's brother, Douglas." Blackshear hesitated, feeling a sudden and acute distaste for the job he had to do. "The young man died this morning."

"Why do you say it in that particular tone?"

"I wasn't aware of my tone."

"I was. You sounded as if you thought Evelyn had something to do with the man's death."

"There's no question in my mind. And two men have died."

She was shaken but obstinate. "There must be some terrible mistake. Ev is the gentlest creature in the world."

"Perhaps the one you know is. The other . . ."

"There is no other!" But the strength had gone out of her. She slumped into a chair, the back of her right hand pressed against her trembling mouth. "How—how did her husband die?"

"He killed himself."

"And the other man?"

"He was stabbed in the throat with a barber's shears sometime this morning."

"My God," she said. "My God." And her hand slid down to her throat as if to try to staunch an invisible flow of blood. "She'll be here at any time. What am I going to do?"

"Nothing. Act as if nothing's happened."

"How can I?"

"You must. Helen Clarvoe's life may be at stake."

"There's no chance you've—made a mistake?"

"There's always that chance, Mrs. Laurence, but it's pretty small. When she called Mrs. Clarvoe about Helen this afternoon she made no secret of her identity; she was even proud of herself."

He told her the content of the telephone call; she listened in stunned silence, rubbing the same place on her neck over and over again.

Outside, the spaniel began to bark. Blackshear turned and looked out of the window. A young woman was coming up the walk, laughing, while the spaniel jumped around her in frenzied delight. As she reached the steps of the porch, she leaned down and put out her arms and the spaniel leaped up into them. Both the girl and the dog looked very pleased with themselves at this remarkable feat.

It was Blackshear's first sight of Evelyn Merrick, and he thought how ironic it was that he should see her like this, laughing, greeting a dog—*the gentlest creature in the world,* Claire Laurence had said.

He turned and looked at Claire. There were tears in her eyes. She brushed them away with the back of her hand as she went to unlock the door.

"Did you see that, Claire? She finally did it, jumped right up into my arms! John said he's been trying to teach her that for years. How's your cold?"

"Much better, thanks," Claire said. "We have company."

"Company? Good."

"Come in and meet Mr. Blackshear."

"Just a sec, I'll shed my coat."

When she came into the room she was smiling slightly, but it was a guarded smile, as if she already suspected that the company wasn't the kind she would enjoy. She had short dark hair and grey eyes that borrowed a little blue from the shirtwaist dress she was wearing. When Blackshear had first seen her greeting the spaniel she had seemed strikingly pretty. Now her animation was gone and she looked quite commonplace. When she shook hands, her clasp was limp and uninterested.

Blackshear said, "I heard Mrs. Laurence call me company. The term isn't quite accurate."

She raised her dark straight brows. "No?"

"I would like to ask you some questions, if I may, Miss Merrick."

"You may. I may even answer them."

"Mr. Blackshear is trying to find a woman who disappeared." Claire said. "I told him you probably don't know a thing about it." She caught Blackshear's warning glance and added, "I'll go and make some coffee."

When she had gone, Evelyn said lightly, "This sounds very intriguing. Tell me more. Is it anyone I know?"

"Helen Clarvoe."

"*Helen*. Good heavens, I think that's the last name in the world I expected to hear. You say she's disappeared?"

"Yes."

"That is odd. Helen just doesn't do that *sort* of thing. She's shall we say, on the conservative side."

"Yes."

"Still, she's old enough to do what she likes and if she wants to disappear, why should anyone try and find her?"

"I'm not sure she wanted to."

"Oh, really?" She seemed amused. "Helen isn't quite as dull as she acts, you know. There may be a man involved."

"I doubt that."

"In any case, I don't see how *I* can help you, Mr. Blackshear. I'll try, though."

"Thank you."

"Fire ahead."

"Are you acquainted with South Flower Street, Miss Merrick?"

"South Flower? That's downtown, isn't it?"

"Yes."

"I suppose I've driven along it. It's not the kind of section I'm familiar with, however."

"How long is it since you've seen Helen Clarvoe?"

"Over a year."

"Have you talked to her on the telephone?"

"Of course not. Why should I? We have nothing to discuss."

"There's no bad feeling between you?"

"There's no feeling at all between us. Not on my side, anyway."

"You were good friends at one time."

"In school, yes. That," she added with a shrug, "was a long time ago."

"You married Helen's brother, Douglas."

"I wouldn't say married. We went through a ceremony. Do you mind if I ask *you* a question now?"

"Not at all."

"Where did you get all your information about me?"

"From your mother."

She looked genuinely amused. "I might have guessed. Mother's a great talker. She bares her soul to the milkman or the boy who delivers the groceries. Unfortunately, she bares mine too."

"Have you seen Douglas recently, Miss Merrick?"

"No, I haven't seen him. I've talked to him, though."

"When?"

"He telephoned me last night."

"Here?"

"Yes. After Claire had gone to bed."

"How did he know you were here?"

"I presume he called the house first and Mother gave him this number."

"Do you think that's likely, in view of the resentment she feels towards him?"

"He probably didn't give his name." She added with a touch of scorn, "I assure you *I* haven't been keeping in touch with him. As far as the Clarvoes are concerned, I've had it. They're a good family to stay away from."

"What was Douglas' reason for calling, Miss Merrick?"

"I don't know. It's the first time I've heard from him since the annulment. He sounded lonely and confused. I was a little of both myself, so we talked. Mostly about old times, years ago when Helen and I were at school together and I used to go home with her for holidays and weekends. Dougie, we called him then, and he was always tagging around after us, no matter how much we teased him. Even Helen was happy in those days. Funny how everything's turned out."

But she spoke with complete detachment, as if the Evelyn of those times had no connection with herself. Blackshear wondered when the split in her personality had begun. Perhaps it had been there from infancy and no one suspected. Or perhaps it had started during her teens, during the very times she'd been reminiscing about to Douglas, the "happy" days. It was possible that those were the "happy" days because she had already started on her flight from reality.

Of one thing he was almost certain, the split in her personality was complete. The woman he was talking to was unaware of the existence of her deformed twin. She remembered talking to Douglas on the telephone the previous night, and yet he knew that if he told her she had also talked to Mrs. Clarvoe, and in quite a different fashion, she would be incredulous and probably very angry. Nothing would be gained by antagonizing her. His job was to wait until the change occurred and the twin took over. Only the twin knew what had happened to Helen Clarvoe and where she was now. South Flower Street was miles long and had more brothels than restaurants.

Even if it had been safe to do so, there was no way of precipitating the change in Evelyn Merrick, because no one knew what caused it. It could be something external, a word, a smell, a sound, a chance phrase of music, or it could be something inside, a sudden chemical change in the body itself.

"It was funny," she said, "hearing from Douglas again. I expected to feel all sorts of resentment against him, but I didn't. Odd, isn't it, how people plan what they'll do and say in a certain situation and then when the situation actually occurs they don't do any of the things they've planned."

"What did you plan?"

"To make him feel like a worm. But I knew as soon as I heard his voice that I didn't have to say anything. He feels worse than any worm."

"Miss Merrick, how did you spend the day?"

"Looking for a job."

"Any particular kind of job, such as modelling, for instance?"

"*Modelling.* What on earth would give you that idea?"

"You're a very pretty girl."

"Nonsense. Thanks just the same, but it really is nonsense. I want a job with a future."

"You haven't been home, then, all day today?"

"No."

"Have you seen your mother?"

"No. I tried to get her at the flower shop this afternoon, but they told me she was taking the rest of the afternoon off."

"She went to see Mrs. Clarvoe."

"Verna? Why on earth would she do that?"

"Douglas died this morning."

Evelyn sat quietly, her eyes lowered, her hands folded on her lap. When she spoke finally her voice was clear and distinct: "The coffee must be ready by now. I'll get you a cup."

"Miss Merrick . . ."

"What do you expect me to say, that I'm sorry? I'm not. I'm not sorry he's dead. He's better off. I'm only sorry he wasn't happier while he was alive."

It was the kindest thing he'd heard anyone say about Douglas since his death.

She asked, "How did it happen?"

Blackshear explained the circumstances of Douglas' death, while she sat with her head half-averted, looking contemplative, almost serene, like a child listening to a story she'd heard a dozen times before.

When he had finished, she said with a sigh, "Poor Douglas. In some ways he was the best of the bunch, of the Clarvoes, I mean. He at least had some warmth in him. Directed towards the wrong people, perhaps, but at least it was there."

"Helen has it, too."

"Helen is cold to the very marrow of her bones."

A premonition of disaster struck Blackshear like a spasm of pain. He had a feeling that her remark was intended to be quite literal, that the woman was trying to tell him Helen was already dead.

"Miss Merrick, I will ask you again."

"Yes?"

"Have you seen Helen Clarvoe today?"

"No."

"Do you know where she is?"

"No."

"Do you know if she's alive?"

"No."

"Do you remember telephoning her at her hotel last Monday night around ten o'clock?"

"I can't remember something that never happened," she said gently. "I wish I could help you, Mr. Blackshear, but I'm afraid I don't know any of the answers."

It's useless, he thought, and turned towards the door. "Thank you for trying, anyway."

"You're welcome. When you find Helen, let me know."

"Why?"

"*Auld lang syne* or curiosity—you name it."

Anger rose in him like an overflow of bile, leaving a green and bitter taste on his tongue and a rawness in his throat. He couldn't trust himself to speak.

He opened the door and stepped outside. In spite of the lighted houses and the street lamps, the darkness seemed as impenetrable as a jungle.

15

SHE OPENED HER eyes and closed them again quickly because the light was so blinding, but in that instant she saw that she was in a small white room like a cubicle in a hospital and the enormous woman bending over her was dressed all in white like a nurse.

The woman said in a harsh, tired voice, "She's coming to. Give her some more of that whiskey."

"If she's drunk already, what you want to give her more of the same for, Bella?"

"Shut up and do as I say. Nothing brings a drunk around faster than the smell of another drink. Hand me the bottle, Mollie."

"Okay."

"Now hold her head up while I pour. Ha-ha-ha, sounds like a society tea, eh? Madame Bella poured."

Miss Clarvoe tried to protest. She did not want the whiskey; it burned like acid. She jerked her head to one side and began to scream, but a hand closed over her mouth.

"You don't want to do that, dear," the woman called Bella said quite softly. "Maybe you're seeing things, eh? Maybe little animals running around, eh? Just take a nip or two of this and they'll go away."

"No, no! I don't want . . ."

"What's the matter, dear? You tell Bella. Everybody tells Bella their troubles. Maybe you got a monkey on your back, eh, dear?"

Miss Clarvoe shook her head. She didn't know what the woman was talking about. There was no monkey on her back, no little animals running around.

"Tell Bella, dear."

"I can't tell, I don't know," Miss Clarvoe said, her voice muffled against the fleshy palm of the woman's hand. "Let me go."

"Certainly, dear, just so long as you don't scream. I can't have you disturbing my other customers. A man comes in after a hard day at the office, he wants a nice quiet massage, he don't want to hear a lady screaming—it upsets him."

Customers. Massage. It wasn't a hospital, then, and the woman in white wasn't a nurse.

"No more carryings-on, eh, dear? Promise Bella."

"Yes. I promise."

Miss Clarvoe opened her eyes. She was lying on a couch, and at the foot of the couch a very pretty blonde girl with acne was standing with a bottle of whiskey in her hand. The other woman, Bella, was enormously fat; her flesh quivered at the slightest movement and her chins hung in folds against her swarthy neck. Only her eyes looked human. They were dark, despairing eyes that had experienced too much and interpreted too little.

The mere exertion of talking made her pant, and when she removed her hand from Miss Clarvoe's mouth, she pressed it against her own heart as if to reassure herself that it was still beating.

"That's good material in her coat," the blonde girl said. "Imported from Scotland, it says, see right there on the label?"

"You can get back on the job now, Mollie."

"I don't have any more appointments for tonight."

"Then go home."

"What if she starts kicking up a fuss again?"

"I can handle her," the fat woman said. "Bella can handle her. Bella knows what the trouble is. Bella understands."

"So *that's* it," the blonde girl said with a contemptuous little smile. "Well, you can have it. *I* like the normal ones."

"Shut up, dear."

"I wonder what's so special about material imported from Scotland."

"Blow, dear, and close the door after you."

The blonde girl left and closed the door behind her.

Miss Clarvoe pressed her fingertips against her eyes. She couldn't understand what the two women had been talking about, none of it made sense to her. She felt nauseated and dizzy and her head ached just behind the left ear as if someone had struck her there.

"My head," she said. "My head hurts."

"Her head hurts yet. Listen to that. Naturally your head hurts, dear. You've been hitting the bottle."

"No. I never drink, never."

"You were reeking of the stuff when I found you out cold on my doorstep. I was saying good-bye to one of our regular customers who came in for his treatment, and when I opened the door there you were, lying against it. Stiff, dear. But stiff."

"That's impossible. I don't drink."

"Just rinse your mouth out now and then, eh?" The fat woman was laughing, every inch of her was laughing, mouth, chins, belly, breasts. When she had finished she wiped the moisture from her face and neck with a handkerchief. "That's my trouble, I'm too jolly. I laugh too much. It makes me sweat. Oh, how I sweat, dear, it's just not human the way poor Bella sweats. How about another nip of whiskey, dear?"

"No. No!" Miss Clarvoe tried to get up, lost her balance and rolled over onto the floor. "I must—I must get home—they're waiting for me."

The fat woman put her hands under Miss Clarvoe's armpits and helped her to her feet. "Who's waiting for you, dear?"

"I—I don't know."

"Well, if you don't know, there's no hurry, is there? Lie down for a bit. Bella will make you feel better."

"No, no." The fat woman's breath was hot against the back of her neck and smelled overpoweringly of aniseed. "I must . . . they're waiting." Someone was waiting for her, she knew that, but she couldn't remember who it was. The faces in her memory were blurred and indistinct, people were shadows, places were all alike. She leaned against the wall and said faintly, "May I—have some water?"

"Certainly, dear."

The woman brought her some water in a paper cup and watched her while she drank.

"Feeling better now, dear?"

"Yes."

"Your coat's dirty. Give it to me and I'll brush it off for you."

"No. No." She clutched the coat tightly around her body.

"Ah, you're one of the shy ones. Bella knows. Bella's been in this business for a long, long time. You don't have to be shy with Bella. Lots of ladies come in here. All they want's a little affection. Nothing wrong about that, is there? By the way, who recommended me, dear?"

"I don't understand."

"How did you get my name?"

"I didn't. I don't know your name."

The fat woman stood very still. Her eyes, tucked away under folds of flesh, were dead and purple like grapes. "How come you picked my place?"

"I didn't. I didn't pick any . . ."

"We mustn't tell fibs, dear. Bella hates fibs, they stir her to anger. Who gave you my name?"

"No one."

"You just came here by a lucky accident, eh? Is that right, dear?"

"I don't remember," Miss Clarvoe whispered. "I can't remember . . . Evelyn . . ."

"Is that who you are, dear? Evelyn?"

"No. No! I was—I was with Evelyn. She brought me here. She said . . ." Miss Clarvoe paused, holding her hands against her trembling mouth.

"What did she say, dear?"

"She said I belonged here."

The fat woman nodded and smiled and rubbed her chins. "She's a discerning girl, that Evelyn, oh my, yes."

"I don't understand what she meant."

"Don't you, dear. Well, lie down and rest a bit and Bella will show you."

"Show me what?"

"How to be happy, dear. How to be *so* happy. Men are pigs. They know nothing, they care nothing. Bella is different. Bella knows. Let me take your coat, dear. What sweet ankles you have. I used to have a well-turned ankle myself in the old days. Now I eat. I eat and eat because nobody loves me. Nobody loves Bella, she is fat as an elephant, yes, but she knows tricks. Give me your pretty little coat, dear."

Miss Clarvoe stood stiff with terror.

"I revolt you, eh, dear? No matter. They all say that at first, then later on they change their tunes. Bella makes them so happy. Bella will make you so happy you will want to come back and back and back."

"Stay away from me!"

"Don't be shy, dear. Bella knows her business, Bella will be gentle."

"You monstrous old slut," Miss Clarvoe said and lunged towards the door.

But the fat woman was there ahead of her. She stood with her back pressed against the door, her arms crossed on her enormous breasts.

"Bella hates to be called names, dear. It stirs her to anger."

"If you don't let me out of here, I'll scream; I'll scream until the police come."

Bella was quiet a moment, then she said bitterly, "I believe you would; you're a nasty piece if I ever saw one. Well, that's gratitude for you—I take you in, I look after you, you lap up my good whiskey, I say pretty things to you, none of them true, of course, your ankles are lousy, they're like pipestems . . ."

"Open that door."

Bella did not open the door, but she moved away from it, still talking, half to herself: "All the things I do for people and what do I get in return? Dirty names and looks. Bella is human, maybe she is as fat as an elephant, but she is human, she likes a little gratitude now and then. It's a wicked world, there's no gratitude in it. Get out of here, you nasty girl, get out. Bella is stirred to anger. Get out, get out."

But the nasty girl had already left, and she was talking to an empty room. She sat down heavily on the couch, one hand pressed against her heart. It was still beating, fluttering like a captive bird under smothering folds of flesh.

"People are no damned good," Bella said.

Helen Clarvoe couldn't run, her legs felt weak, as if the muscles had atrophied from long disuse, and the pain in her head had become worse. When she tried to think, her thoughts melted and fused and only one stood out clearly and distinctly from the others: I must get away. I must escape. I must run.

It was not important where she ran to. She had no plan, she didn't even know where she was until she reached the corner and saw the street signs: South Flower Street and Ashworth Avenue. She repeated the names to herself, hoping they would form a pattern in her mind, but neither of the names meant anything to her, and the neighnorhood was strange. She knew she had never seen it before just as she knew that she didn't drink. Yet she'd come here, had walked or ridden or been carried, and when she arrived she was drunk. *"Stiff,"* Bella had said, *"but stiff. Naturally your head hurts, dear, you've been hitting the bottle."*

"I never drink," Miss Clarvoe said. "I never touch liquor. Father said it coarsened a woman."

An old man waiting at the corner for the traffic light to change, looked at her over the top of his bifocals with interest and pleasure. He often talked to himself. It was nice to know other people did it, too.

Miss Clarvoe saw him look and she turned away and color flooded her cheeks, as if he had caught a glimpse of her, naked.

"Heh, heh, heh," the old man said and shuffled across the street, his shoulders shaking with mirth. Even the young ones talked to themselves these days. It was the age of the atom. Madmen have taken over. "Heh, heh, heh."

Miss Clarvoe touched her face. It was burning with humiliation. The old man had seen her talking to herself, perhaps he'd seen more than that. Perhaps he'd been walking by when she came out of Bella's place and he knew all about what kind of place it was. She must get away from the old man.

Miss Clarvoe turned and began running in the opposite direction, her coat billowing behind her, her thin legs moving stiffly like pipestems.

At the next corner she stopped, gasping for breath, and held on to a lamppost for support. The sign on the post read Figueroa Street. I am not lost, she thought. I know Figueroa Street, I will wait here on the corner until an empty taxicab comes along. But something in her mind, some sixth sense, warned her not to stand still, and she started out again. Not running. The running had attracted too much attention. She must be casual, ordinary. No one must find out that somewhere, along these streets, or other streets, she had lost the day. It was night. The day had gone, passed her by, passed without touching her.

She walked on, her head bent, as if she were searching the sidewalk and the gutters for her lost day. People passed, the cars roared by, the night was filled with noise and light and movement, but Miss Clarvoe did not raise her head. *I must pretend*, she thought. *I must pretend not to know I'm being followed.*

If she was clever enough, if she could control her panic, she might be able to find out who it was. Bella? The old man who'd caught her talking to herself? One of Bella's friends? None of them had anything to gain by following her, not even money. She had lost her purse, along with the day.

A bus was unloading at the next intersection and she quickened her pace and mingled with the crowd that was getting off the bus. Secure for a moment, she looked back, peering through the moving jungle of faces. Only one face stood out among the others, pale, composed, half smiling. Evelyn Merrick. She was standing in the shadowed doorway of a small TV repair shop, leaning idly against the plate glass window as if she had just paused for a rest during an evening stroll. But Miss Clarvoe knew it was not an evening stroll, it was a chase, and she was the beast in view.

She turned and began to run across the street, blind and deaf and numb with panic. She did not even feel the impact of the car that struck her.

When she returned to consciousness she was lying against the curb and people were standing over her, all talking at once.

"Saw her with my own eyes, out she dashed . . ."

"Red light . . ."

"Drunk, for sure. You can smell it a mile away."

"Honest to God, I didn't *see* her!"

"Let's get out of here. I don't want to be called as a witness."

"Come on, Joe, come on. I just can't stand the sight of blood."

Blood, Miss Clarvoe thought. I'm bleeding, then. It's all come true, what she said to me the first night. She saw it in her crystal ball, I was to be in an accident, bleeding, mutilated.

"What's a little blood, you watch prizefights all the time, don't you?"

"Must of been drunk . . ."

"With my own eyes . . ."

"Somebody call an ambulance."

"The lady in the green hat went to phone her husband; he's a doctor."

A young man wearing a cab driver's uniform took off his coat and tried to put it under Miss Clarvoe's head. She thrust it away and sat up painfully. "I'm all right. Leave me alone."

The words were muffled and indistinct, but the young man heard them. "You're supposed to lie there until the doctor comes."

"I don't need a doctor."

"I took a course in first aid and it says that in the book. Keep the patient warm and . . ."

"I'm not hurt." She dragged herself to her feet and began wiping the moisture off her face with a handkerchief, not knowing which was blood and which was sweat from all the running she'd done.

The crowd began to disperse—the show was over, no one was killed, too bad, better luck next time.

Only the young man in the cabbie's uniform lingered on, looking fretful. "It wasn't *my* fault. Everyone could see it wasn't my fault. You dashed right out in front of my cab, didn't give me a chance to stop, craziest thing I ever saw in my life."

Miss Clarvoe looked back at the doorway of the shop where she'd seen Evelyn Merrick just before the accident. The girl had left. Or else she had stepped farther back into the shadows to wait. That was the game she played best, waiting in shadows, walking in the night, watching for the unwary.

The cabbie was still talking, aggrieved and belligerent. "Everyone could see I did the best I could. I stopped, didn't I? I tried to minister first aid, didn't I?"

"Oh stop it, stop it! There's no time for argument. No *time,* I tell you."

He stepped back looking surprised. "I don't get . . ."

"Listen to me. What's your name?"

"Harry. Harry Reis."

"Listen Harry, I must get away from here. I'm being followed. She was—I saw her in that doorway over there a few minutes ago. She intends to kill me."

"You don't say." A faint derisive smile stretched his mouth. He didn't even glance back at the doorway she was pointing at. "Maybe you escaped from somewheres, huh?"

"Escaped?"

"Sure. Escaped. Climbed over the wires."

She shook her head in mystification. He seemed to be talking in riddles like the fat woman, Bella. Monkeys on the back, little animals running around, wires to climb over. They were all English words but Miss Clarvoe couldn't understand them. She thought, perhaps I am the foreigner, perhaps I have been out of touch too long; the language has changed, and the people. The world has been taken over by the Bellas, and the Evelyn Merricks, and little men like Harry with sly, insinuating smiles. I must get back to my own room and lock the door against the ugliness.

"I must . . ."

"Sure," Harry said. "Sure. Anything for a lady."

He led the way to his cab. Miss Clarvoe dropped the bloody handkerchief on the curb and followed him. She wasn't aware yet of any pain, only of a terrible stiffness that seemed to cover her entire body like a plaster cast.

She got into the back seat of the cab and pulled her coat close around her. She remembered the blonde girl in Bella's place asking what was so special about fabric imported from

Scotland. Miss Clarvoe didn't know, and it seemed important for her to figure it out. There were sheep, plenty of sheep, all over the world, but perhaps the Scottish sheep had finer wool. Wool. Sheep. Blackshear. She had forgotten about Mr. Blackshear. He was miles and years away, she couldn't even recall his face except that it looked a little like her father's.

The inside of the cab was dark and warm and the radio was turned on to a panel discussion on politics. All of the people on the panel had very definite ideas, firmly spoken, all of them knew exactly where the day had gone and what to expect from the night.

Harry got in and turned the radio off. "Where to?"

"The Monica Hotel."

"You live there?"

"Yes."

"You been living there long?"

"Yes."

"All the time steady?"

"Yes."

She could tell he didn't believe her. What did he believe? What were the wires she was supposed to have climbed over? She had never seen Harry before, never, she was sure of that. Yet he acted as though he knew secrets about her, ugly secrets.

"I will pay you," she said. "I have money in my hotel suite."

"Yes, ma'am."

"I'll send the boy down with it."

"Yes, ma'am."

She knew from his tone that he didn't expect any money, that he was humoring her as he would any drunk or liar or madman who happened to be his passenger. The customer is always right.

The headlights of the car following shone into the rearview mirror and Miss Clarvoe saw Harry's face for a minute quite clearly. It was young and pleasant and very, very honest. A nice, open face. No one would suspect what kind of mind lay behind it. The fat woman wore her malice and her miseries for all the world to see; Harry's were hidden underneath the youthful blandness of his face like worms at the core of an apple that looks sound from the outside.

Yet even Harry, even apple-cheeked, wormy-brained Harry knew where his day had gone. She had lost hers, dropped it somewhere like a handkerchief and picked it up again, soiled, from the dirty floor of a slut.

"Harry."

"Yes, ma'am." His tone was still sardonically polite.

"What day is this?"

"Thursday."

Thursday. Douglas died this morning. Mr. Blackshear came to the hotel to tell me about it. I promised to go home and keep Mother company. Mr. Blackshear offered to drive me, but I refused. I didn't want him to touch me again. I was afraid. I went and waited in front of the hotel for a cab. People kept passing, strangers, hundreds of strangers. I felt very nervous and upset. The people terrified me and I didn't want to go home and face Mother and hear her carry on about poor dead Douglas the way she did about Father. I knew what a dreadful show she would put on, she always does, but none of it's real.

Cabs kept passing, some of them empty, but I couldn't force myself to hail one. Then someone spoke my name and I turned and saw Evelyn Merrick. She was standing right beside me, smiling, very sure of herself. The strangers, the traffic, didn't bother her, she'd always liked crowds and people, the more the merrier. I held my head up high, pretending I was just as poised and confident as she was. But it didn't work. I could never fool Evelyn. She said, "Scared, aren't you?" and she took my arm. I didn't mind. I usually hate people to touch me, but somehow this was different. The contact made me feel more secure. "Come on, let's have a drink some place," she said.

Come on, let's have a drink, let's lose a day, let's drop a handkerchief.

"You say something, ma'am?"

"No."

"Like I told you, if you want to change your mind and go back . . ."

"Go back where?"

"Back where you came from."

"I don't know what you're insinuating," she said as calmly as possible. "I *am* going back where I came from. I live at the Monica Hotel. I have a permanent suite there and have had for almost a year. Is that clear to you?"

"Yes, ma'am." His tone added: Clear as mud. Harry had been around, he knew a thing or two, sometimes even three, and he was pretty certain that the woman had been playing around with narcotics, probably yellow-jackets. She was obviously a lady and ladies didn't go in so much for heroin. Nembutal was more genteel both to use and to procure. You didn't have to hang around a street corner or the back booth of a cafe waiting for your contact. You could get yellow-jackets just sitting in a nice, upholstered chair in some fancy doctor's office, telling how you were nervous and worn-out and couldn't sleep.

Sleep wasn't always what they got, though. Sometimes the stuff went into reverse, and they did crazy things like taking off all their clothes in the middle of Pershing Park or racing up Sunset Boulevard at eighty miles an hour and fighting with the police when they were arrested. Ladies could sometimes behave worse than women.

He glanced back at Miss Clarvoe. She was crouched in the right-hand corner of the cab, her arms pressed tautly across her chest, her lips moving slightly as if in prayer:

She took my arm, I remember that, she took my arm like an old friend and said, *Godiona gavotch.* It was our secret password in school when we were in trouble and needed help. *Godiona gavotch,* I repeated, and suddenly it was as if the years had never passed, and we were friends back in school, giggling after the lights were out and plotting against the French Mistress and sharing the treats from home. "Come and have a drink," she said. It was always like that—Evelyn was the one who initiated things, who formed the ideas and made the suggestions. I was the one who tagged along. I worshipped her. I wanted to be exactly like her, I would have followed her anywhere, like a sheep, the goat, the victim. I was marked, even then, and the marks have not faded with the years but have grown more distinct. Even Harry knows. He looks at me with contempt and his voice drips with it.

Apple-cheeked Harry, I see your worms.

"You want to go in the front or the back, ma'am?" Harry said.

"I am not in the habit of using a service entrance."

"I just thought, being you were messed up a little . . ."

"It doesn't matter." It did matter; she wanted nothing more than to go in the back entrance and sneak up to her room unnoticed, but it was impossible. Her keys had been in the purse she'd lost. "About the fare, I'll send a bellboy down with the money. How much is it?"

"Three dollars even." He stopped the cab at the marquee of the hotel, but he made no move to get out and open the door for her. He didn't expect a tip, he didn't even expect the fare, and for once it didn't matter much to him. She was a creepy dame; he wanted to see the end of her.

Miss Clarvoe opened the door for herself and stepped out onto the sidewalk and pulled her collar up high to hide the wound under her ear. The torn stockings, the rip in her coat, she couldn't hide, she could only move as rapidly as possible through the lobby, trying to outrun the stares of the curious.

Mr. Horner, the elderly desk clerk, was busy registering some new guests, but when he saw Miss Clarvoe he dropped everything and came over to her, his eyes bulging and his mouth working with excitement.

"Why, Miss Clarvoe. Why, Miss *Clarvoe*, for goodness sake . . ."

"I lost my keys. May I have a duplicate set, please?"

"Everybody's been looking for you, Miss Clarvoe. Just everybody. Why, they . . ."

"They need look no further."

"But what happened to you?"

She answered without hesitation. "It was such a nice day, I decided to take a little trip into the country." Had it been a nice day? She didn't know. She couldn't remember the weather of the day any more than she could its contents. "The country," she added, "is very beautiful this time of year. The lupine is in bloom, you know. Very lovely." The lies rolled glibly off her tongue. She couldn't stop them. Any words were better than none, any memory, however false, was better than a blank. "Unfortunately, I tripped over a boulder and tore my coat and my stockings." As she talked the scene came into sharper focus. Details appeared, the shape and color of the boulder she'd fallen over, the hills blue with lupine and dotted with the wild orange of poppies, and beyond the hills the grey-green dwarfs of mountains with their parched and stunted trees.

"You should," Mr. Horner said with reproach, "have let someone know. Everyone's been in a tizzy. The police were here, with a Mr. Blackshear."

"Police."

"I had to let them into your suite. They insisted. There was nothing I could do." He leaned across the desk and added in a confidential whisper, "They thought you might have been kidnapped by a maniac."

Color splashed across Miss Clarvoe's face and disappeared, leaving her skin ashen. Kidnapped by a maniac? No, it wasn't like that at all. I went with an old friend to have a drink. I was frightened and confused by all the strangers and the traffic, and she rescued me. She put her hand on my arm and I felt secure. By myself I was nothing, but with Evelyn there beside me I could see people looking at us with interest and curiosity, yes even admiration. "Come and have a drink," she said.

I could have stood there forever, being looked at, being admired, it is a wonderful feeling. But Evelyn likes excitement, she wanted to be on the move. She kept saying, Come on, come on, come on, as if she had some very intriguing plan in mind and wanted me to share it. I said, "I promised to go home and stay with Mother because Douglas is dead." She called each of them an ugly name, Mother and Douglas, and when I looked shocked she laughed at me for being a prude. I'd never wanted to be a prude, I've simply never known how to be anything else. "I've got a friend," Evelyn said. "He's a lot of fun, a real joker. Let's go over and have some laughs." Douglas was dead, my own brother, I shouldn't have felt like laughing, and yet I did. I asked her who the friend was who was such a joker and I remember what she answered. It's odd how the name has stuck in my mind when I've forgotten so many other things. Jack Terola. "He is an artist with the camera," Evelyn said. "He's going to take pictures of me that will be shown all over the country. He's going to make me immortal." I felt the knife of envy twisting in my heart. I wanted to be immortal, too.

"I had to co-operate with the police," Mr. Horner said. "I didn't have any choice. It was a question of handing over the keys to your suite or having them taken from me."

"I dislike the idea of anyone prying into my personal affairs."

"Everyone acted in your best interests, Miss Clarvoe."

"Indeed."

"After all, anything might have happened."

"What happened," she said coldly, "is that I went into the country with a friend of mine."

"Ah, yes. To see the lupine in bloom."

"That's correct."

Mr. Horner turned away, his lip curling slightly. It was November. The lupine wouldn't be in bloom for another three or four months.

He returned with the duplicate set of keys and laid them on the desk. "There are some messages for you, Miss Clarvoe. You are to call Mr. Blackshear immediately; he is at your mother's house."

"Thank you."

"Oh yes, and someone asked me to put this note in your box. A young lady."

The note was written in an ostentatious backhand on hotel stationery which had been folded twice:

I am waiting in the lobby. I must see you at once. Evelyn Merrick.

She wanted to run, but her legs ached with weariness, they would not carry her further. She'd already run too far, too fast, down too many strange and terrifying streets. She knew now that escape was impossible. Tomorrow, or the day after, or next week, behind some corner of time Evelyn Merrick would be waiting for her.

16

SHE TURNED AND saw Evelyn Merrick coming towards her across the lobby, picking her way fastidiously through the crowd. The day, which had changed Miss Clarvoe, had changed Evelyn too. She wasn't smiling and self-assured as she'd been when they met on the street. She was a grim-faced, cold-eyed stranger, dressed all in black as if in mourning.

"I see you got my note."

"Yes," Miss Clarvoe said. "I have it."

"We must have a talk."

"Yes." Yes, we must. I must find out how I lost the day, how the minutes passed overhead without touching me, like birds in a hurry. Wild geese minutes. I remember Father took us hunting once, Evelyn and me. Father was angry with me that day because the sun gave me a headache. He said I was a spoilsport and a crybaby. He said, *Why can't you be more like Evelyn?*

"Everyone's been worried about you," the stranger said. "Where have you been?"

"You know, you know very well. I was with you."

"What are you talking about?"

"We went into the country together—to see the lupine—we . . ."

The stranger's voice was harsh and ugly. "You've always told fantastic lies, Helen, but this is going too far. I haven't seen you for nearly a year."

"You mustn't try to deny it . . ."

"I'm not trying to deny it. I am denying it!"

"Please keep your voice down. People are staring. I can't have people staring. I have a reputation, a name, to protect."

"No one is paying the least attention to us."

"Yes, they are. You see, my stockings are torn, and my coat. From the country. You have forgotten how we went into the country, you and I, to see the lupine. I tripped over a boulder and fell." But her voice trailed upward into a question mark, and her eyes were uncertain and afraid. "You—you remember now?"

"There's nothing to remember."

"Nothing?"

"I haven't seen you for nearly a year, Helen."

"But this morning—this morning you met me outside the hotel. You asked me to have a drink with you, you said you were on your way over to see a man who would make you immortal and you wanted me to come along."

"It doesn't even make sense."

"Yes, yes, it does! I even remember the man's name. Terola. Jack Terola."

Evelyn's voice was quiet, insistent. "You went to see this man, Terola?"

"I don't know. I think we—we both went, you and I. After all, I wouldn't go to such a place alone, and besides Terola was your friend, not mine."

"I never heard the name before in my life. Until I read the evening papers."

"Papers?"

"Terola was murdered shortly before noon today," Evelyn said. "It's important for you to remember, Helen. Did you go there this morning?"

Miss Clarvoe said nothing, and her face was blank.

"Did you see Terola this morning, Helen?"

"I must—I must go upstairs."

"We have to talk."

"No. No. I must go upstairs and lock my door against all the ugliness." She turned, slowly, and began walking towards the lift, her shoulders hunched, her hands jammed into the pockets of her coat as if she wanted to avoid all physical contact with other people.

She waited until one of the lifts was empty, then she stepped inside and ordered the liftman to close the door immediately. The tired old liftman was no bigger than a child, as if the years he'd spent inside the tiny lift had stunted his growth. He was accustomed to Miss Clarvoe's idiosyncrasies, such as riding alone in lifts, and he'd been well enough tipped, in the past, to indulge them.

He shut the door and as the lift began to ascend he kept his eyes on the floor indicator. "A wintry day, Miss Clarvoe."

"I don't know. I lost mine."

"Beg pardon, ma'am?"

"I lost my day," she said slowly. "I've looked everywhere for it, but I can't find it."

"Are you—are you feeling all right, Miss Clarvoe?"

"Don't call me that."

"Ma'am."

"Call me Evelyn."

"Yes, ma'am."

"Well, say it. Go ahead. *Say Evelyn*."

"Evelyn," the old man said and began to tremble.

Back in her suite she locked the door and without even taking off her coat she went immediately to the telephone. As she dialed, she felt the excitement rising inside her like molten lava in a crater.

"Mrs. Clarvoe?"

"Is that—that's you, Evelyn?"

"Certainly it's me. I've done you another favor."

"Please. Have mercy."

"Don't snivel. I hate that. I hate snivellers."

"Evelyn . . ."

"I just wanted to tell you that I've found Helen for you. I have her all locked up in her hotel room, safe and sound."

"Is she all right?"

"Don't worry. I'm looking after her. I'm the only one who knows how to treat her. She's been a bad girl, she needs a little discipline. She tells lies, you know, awful lies, so she must be taught a lesson or two like the others."

"Let me talk to Helen."

"Oh no. She can't talk right now. It isn't her turn. We have to take turns, you know. It's very inconvenient, because Helen won't voluntarily give me my turn, so I just have to go ahead and take it. She was feeling weak from the accident, and her head hurt, so I simply took over. I feel fine. I'm never sick. I leave that to her. All the sordid things like being sick or getting old, I leave to her. I'm only twenty-one, that old crock is over thirty . . ."

Evelyn Merrick was waiting for Blackshear in the lobby when he arrived twenty minutes later.

"I got here as soon as I could," Blackshear said. "Where is Helen?"

"Locked in her room. I followed her up and tried to talk to her, but she paid no attention to my knocking. So I listened at the door. I could hear her inside."

"What was she doing?"

"You know what she was doing, Mr. Blackshear. I told you when I called you. She was telephoning, using my name, my voice, pretending to be me."

Blackshear was grim. "I wish that's all it was, a child's game, like pretending."

"What else is it?"

"She has a rare form of insanity, Miss Merrick, the disease I thought you had. A doctor would call it multiple personality. A priest might call it possession by a devil. Helen Clarvoe is possessed by a devil and she gives your name to do it."

"Why should she do that to me?"

"Are you willing to help me find out?"

"I don't know. What must I do?"

"We'll go up to her room and talk to her."

"She won't let us in."

"We can try," Blackshear said. "That's all I seem able to do for Helen, is try. Try, and fail, and try again."

They took the elevator up to the third floor and walked down the long, carpeted hall to Miss Clarvoe's suite. The door was closed and locked and no light showed around its edges, but Blackshear could hear a woman talking inside the room. It was not Helen's voice, tired, uninterested; it was loud and brash and shrill, like a schoolgirl's.

He rapped sharply on the door with his knuckles and called out, "Helen? Let me in."

"Go away, you old fool, and leave us alone."

"Are you in there, Helen?"

"Look at the mess you've got me in now. He's found me. That's what you wanted, isn't it? You've always been jealous of me, you've always tried to cut me out of your life. Now you've done it, calling in that man Blackshear and the police to hunt me down like a common criminal. I'm not a common criminal. All I did to Terola was touch him with the scissors to teach him a little lesson. How was I to know his flesh was soft as butter? An ordinary man wouldn't even have bled, my touch was so delicate. It wasn't my fault the poor fool died. But the police won't believe that. I'll have to hide here with you. Just you and me, how about that? God knows if I can stand it, you should be able to. You're dull company, old girl, you can't deny that. I may have to slip out now and then for a bit of fun."

Blackshear tried to call out again but the words died of despair in his throat: *Fight, Helen. Fight back. Stand up to her.* He began pounding on the door with his fists.

"Listen to that, will you? He's trying to break the door down to get to his sweetheart. Isn't that touching? Little does he know how many doors he'll have to break down; this one's only the first. There are a hundred more and that pitiful idiot out there thinks he can do it with his fists. Funny boy. Tell him to go away, Helen. Tell him not to bother us. Tell him if he doesn't go away he'll never see you alive again. Go on. Speak. *Speak*, you ugly crone!"

A pause, then Helen's voice, a tattered whisper, "Mr. Blackshear, Paul. Go away."

"Helen, hang on. I'm going to help you."

"Go away, go away."

"Hear that, lover boy? Go away, she says. Lover boy. God, that's funny. What a romance you had, eh, Helen. Did you *really* think anyone could fall in love with you, you old hag? Take a look in the crystal ball, you crow."

She began to laugh. The sound rose and fell, a siren screaming disaster, and then there was a sudden silence, as if the loud night were holding its breath.

Blackshear pressed his mouth against the crack of the door and said, "Helen, listen to me."

"Go away."

"Unlock your door. Evelyn Merrick is here with me."

"Liar."

"Unlock your door and you can see for yourself. You are not Evelyn. Evelyn is out here with me."

"Liar, liar, liar!"

"Please, Helen, let us in so we can help you . . . Say something to her, Miss Merrick."

"We are not trying to fool you," Evelyn said. "This is really Evelyn, Helen."

"Liars!" But the lock clicked and the chain slid back and slowly the door opened and Miss Clarvoe's tormented face peered out. She spoke to Blackshear, her pale mouth working painfully to form the words: "Helen is not here. She went away. She is old and sick and full of misery and wants to be left alone."

"Listen to me, Helen," Blackshear said. "You are not old and sick . . ."

"*I'm* not, no. *She* is. You're mixed up. I'm Evelyn. I'm fine. I'm twenty-one. I'm pretty, I'm popular. I have lots of fun. I never get sick or tired. I'm going to be immortal." She stopped suddenly, her eyes fixed on Evelyn Merrick, fascinated, repelled, "That girl—who is she?"

"You know who she is, Helen. She's Evelyn Merrick."

"She's an imposter. Get rid of her. Tell her to go away."

"All right," Blackshear said wearily. "All right." He turned to Evelyn. "You'd better go down to the lobby and call a doctor."

Miss Clarvoe watched Evelyn go down the hall and get into the lift. "Why should she call a doctor? Is she sick?"

"No."

"Why should she call a doctor, then, if she isn't sick?" She added peevishly, "I don't much like you. You're sly. You're a sly old man. You're too old for me. Not much use your hanging around. I'm only twenty-one. I have a hundred boyfriends . . ."

"Helen, please."

"Don't call me that, don't say that name. I'm not Helen."

"Yes, you are. You're Helen and I don't want you to be anybody else. I like you exactly as you are. Other people will, too, if you'll let them. They'll like you just as you are, just for yourself alone, Helen."

"No! I'm not Helen, I don't want to be Helen! I hate her!"

"Helen is a fine young woman," Blackshear said quietly. "She is intelligent and sensitive, yes, and pretty too."

"Pretty? That crock? That hag? That ugly crone?"

She started to close the door, but Blackshear pressed his weight against it. She released the door and stepped backwards into the room, one hand behind her back, like a child concealing a forbidden object. But Blackshear did not have to guess what she was concealing. He could see her image in the round mirror above the telephone stand.

"Put down the paper-knife, Helen. Put it back on the desk where it belongs. You're very strong, you might hurt someone accidentally . . . How did you meet Terola in the first place, Helen?"

"In a bar. He was having a drink and he looked over at me and fell in love with me at first sight. Men do. They can't help it. I have this magnetism. Do you feel it?"

"Yes. Yes, I feel it. Put down the knife, Helen."

"I'm not Helen! I am Evelyn. Say it. Say I'm Evelyn."

He stared at her, saying nothing, and suddenly she wheeled around and ran across the room to the mirror. But the face she saw was not her own. It was not a face at all, it was a dozen faces, going round and round—Evelyn and Douglas and Blackshear, Verna and Terola and her father, Miss Hudson and Harley Moore and the desk clerk and the little old man in the elevator—all the faces were revolving like a Ferris wheel, and as they revolved, they moved their mouths and screamed out words: *"What's the matter with you, kid, are you crazy?" "You've always told the most fantastic lies." "What a pity we didn't have a girl like Evelyn." "You can't make a silk purse out of a sow's ear." "Why can't you be more like Evelyn?"*

The voices faded into silence, the great wheel of faces stopped, and there was only one image left in the mirror. It was her own face, and the mouth that moved was her own mouth, and the words that came out were uttered by her own voice: "God help me."

Memory stabbed at her with agonizing thrusts. She remembered the bars, the phone booths, the running, the strange streets. She remembered Terola and the odd, incredulous way he looked just before he died and the acrid smell of the coffee boiling over on the stove. She remembered taking the bills from her own money clip and then thinking later that they'd been stolen. She remembered the cat in the alley, the rays from the night air, the taste of rain, the young man who'd laughed because she was waterproof . . .

"Give me the knife, Helen."

In the mirror she could see Blackshear approaching, slowly and cautiously, a hunter with a beast in view.

"It's all right, Helen. Don't get excited. Everything's going to be all right."

A pause, and then he began to talk again in a low persuasive voice, about doctors and hospitals and rest and care and the future. Always the future, as if it was definite and tangible, rosy and round like an apple.

She stared into the crystal ball of the mirror and she saw her future, the nights poisoned by memories, the days corroded by desire.

"It's only a matter of time, Helen. You'll be well again."

"Be quiet," she said. "You lie."

She looked down at the knife in her hand and it seemed to her that it alone could speak the truth, that it was her last, her final friend.

She pressed the knife into the soft hollow of her throat. She felt no pain, only a little surprise at how pretty the blood looked, like bright and endless ribbons that would never again be tied.

AN AIR THAT KILLS

To the Grushes, my favorite house haunters,
Paul
Bernis
Diane
Douglas
Dale

1

THE LAST TIME his wife saw Ron Galloway was on a Saturday evening in the middle of April.

"He seemed in good spirits," Esther Galloway said later. "Almost as if he was up to something, planning something. More than just a fishing trip to the lodge, I mean. He's never really enjoyed fishing, he has a morbid fear of water."

This was true enough, though Galloway wouldn't have admitted it. He tried desperately hard to be a sport. He fished, played golf and cricket in the summers, curled at the Granite Club in the winters, wore a crew cut, and drove his Cadillac convertible with the top down even in weather which forced him to turn the heater on full blast to keep from freezing to death. Now in his late thirties, he still appeared somewhat lacking in coordination in spite of all the exercise he took, and his round face showed residual traces of teenage acne and adolescent uncertainty.

He was packing a duffel bag when his wife, Esther, came into his bedroom. She was going out for dinner and she had on a new pink taffeta dress trimmed with seed pearls and topped by a white mink stole. Galloway noticed the dress and approved of it, but he made no remark about it. There was no point in spoiling women by paying them compliments.

"So here you are, Ron," his wife said, as if it were a surprising and interesting coincidence that a man should be found in his own bedroom.

Galloway did not respond.

"Ron?"

"Esther, angel, I'm right here, as you just pointed out, so if you have anything to say, go ahead."

"Where are you going?" Esther knew where he was going, but she was the kind of woman who liked to ask questions to which she already knew the answers. It gave her a sense of security.

"I told you last week. I'm going over to Weston to pick up Harry Bream and we're driving up to the lodge to do some fishing with a couple of the fellows."

"I don't like Harry Bream's wife."

"Harry Bream's wife is not coming along."

"I know that. I was merely making a remark. I think she's queer. She called me last week and asked if there was anybody dead I wanted to get in touch with. I couldn't think of anyone offhand except Uncle John and I'm not sure he'd want to be gotten in touch with. Don't you think that's queer, her call, I mean?"

"Harry's away a lot. Thelma has to do something to keep herself from getting bored."

"Why doesn't she have children?"

"I don't know why she doesn't have children," Galloway said impatiently. "I haven't asked her."

"You and Harry are such cronies, you could broach the subject to him casually some time."

"Perhaps I could, but I don't intend to."

"If Thelma had children she wouldn't have time to go around being psychic and making other people nervous. *I* haven't got time to be psychic."

"Thank God for small mercies."

Galloway fastened the straps of the duffel bag and set it near the door. The act was a definite invitation for Esther to say good-bye and be on her way, but she declined it. Instead, she moved across the room with an elegant swish of taffeta and stood in front of the mirror smoothing her dark hair. Over her shoulder she could see Galloway watching her with a prodigious frown of annoyance. He looked quite comical.

"I'm sick of my hair like this," she said. "I think I'll become a blonde. An interesting and psychic blonde like Thelma."

"You're psychic enough. And I don't like phony blondes."

"What about natural ones, like Thelma?"

"I like Thelma all right," he said obstinately. "She's my best friend's wife. I have to."

"Just all right?"

"For Pete's sake, Esther, she's a fattish little hausfrau with some of her marbles missing. Even your imagination can't build her up into a femme fatale."

"I guess not."

"When are you going to get over these crazy suspicions?"

"Dorothy . . ." She swallowed as she spoke the name, so that he wasn't sure what it was until she repeated it. "Dorothy had no suspicions."

"Why bring her up?"

"She didn't suspect a thing. And all the time behind her back you and I were . . ."

"Be quiet." His face was white with anger and distaste. "If your conscience is bothering you at this late date, that's too bad. But leave mine alone. And for God's sake let's not have a scene."

Esther had been going in for scenes lately, picking at the past like a bird at a stale loaf of bread, dislodging a crumb here, a crumb there. He hoped it was merely a passing phase and would soon be over. The past didn't often worry or interest Galloway. When he thought of his first wife, Dorothy, it was without pity or regret. Even his vindictiveness against her on account of the divorce had faded with the years. Divorces in Canada are not common or easy to obtain, and the Galloway scandal had been an ugly one, widely publicized throughout the country and the border states.

Esther let her hands drop to her sides and turned from the mirror. "I heard she's dying."

"She's been dying for years," Galloway said brusquely. "Who told you that, anyway?"

"Harry."

"Harry's a pill salesman. He likes to think everybody's dying."

"Ron."

"I don't want to be rude, but if I don't start moving, the fellows will be kept waiting at the lodge."

"The caretaker can let them in."

"Even so, as the host I should be there first."

"They'll be too boozed up to care."

"Are you deliberately trying to start another argument?"

"No. Really, I'm not. I guess I just wish I were going with you."

"You don't like fishing. All you do is sit around moaning about how sorry you feel for the poor little fish and what did they ever do to deserve a hook in the throat."

"All right, Ron, all right." She approached him rather shyly and put her hands on his shoulders and kissed him on the cheek. "Have a good time. Don't forget to say good-bye to the children. Next time perhaps we can all go."

"Perhaps."

But she looked a little sad when she went out the door, as if she had borrowed some of Thelma's psychic powers and sensed that there wouldn't be a next time or even a this time.

Galloway stood in the doorway for a moment listening to the rustle of her dress and the tapping of her heels muted by the stair carpet.

Suddenly, without knowing why, he called out in a loud urgent voice, "Esther! Esther!"

But the front door had already closed behind her and Galloway felt a little relieved that she hadn't heard him because he hadn't planned anything to say to her. The call had come from a part of his mind which was inaccessible to him and he didn't know what it meant or why it happened.

He leaned against the door frame, dizzy, breathing very hard, as if he had just awakened from a dream of suffocation, and while the dream was forgotten, the physical symptoms of panic remained.

I'm ill, he thought. She shouldn't have walked out on me like that. I'm ill. Perhaps I ought to stay home and call a doctor.

But as his breathing returned to normal and the dizziness abated, it occurred to him that a doctor wasn't really necessary as long as Harry was around. Harry worked for a drug company and his pockets were always bulging with pills, his briefcase full of pamphlets describing the newest medical discoveries which some of the doctors didn't even know about until Harry told them, or gave them the pamphlets to read. Harry was extremely liberal with free pills, diagnoses and advice. On occasion, he was more effective than a regular doctor since he was unhampered by training, medical ethics or caution, and some of his cures were miraculously quick. These were the ones his friends remembered.

"I will get some pills from Harry," Galloway said, and the very thought was soothing. Harry had a pill for everything, even sudden and inexplicable calls to one's departing wife: *It's your nerves, old boy. Now, my company has just come out with a dandy little item . . .*

Galloway flung his trench coat over his arm, picked up his duffel bag, and went down the hall to say good-bye to the two boys. They were ostensibly in bed; that is, the bedroom door was open and the night light was turned on. But they were not asleep. Their low, furious voices bounced across the room and back again.

"Mama said the dog could sleep on my bed tonight. Let go of him."

"Won't, won't, won't."

"I'll scream for Annie."

"I'll tell her you pinched me. I'll tell Annie and Mrs. Browning and old Rudolph and Mama and my Sunday School teacher . . ."

"Why not tell me?" Galloway said, and pressed the light switch.

The two boys stared at him, silenced by amazement. They saw little of Galloway, and when they noticed the duffel bag he was carrying, they weren't sure whether he was coming or going.

Gregory, who at seven was already an opportunist, made a quick decision. "Daddy's home," he shouted. "Goody, goody, Daddy's home! Did you bring me something, Daddy? What did you bring me?"

Galloway stepped back as if he had been shoved in the chest. "I—haven't been away."

"Well, then, you're going away."

"Yes."

"So if you're going away you've got to come back."

"Yes, I guess I do."

"So when you come back will you bring me something?"

Galloway's face was flushed and a nervous tic nagged at one corner of his mouth. That's all I mean to them, he thought.

Or to Esther. I'm the guy who brings them something.

"You could bring everybody something," said Marvin, who was five and a half. "Annie and Mrs. Browning and old Rudolph and my Sunday School teacher."

"I suppose I could. What do you think they'd like?"

"Dogs. Everybody would like dogs."

"Everybody? You're sure?"

"I asked them," Marvin lied emphatically. "I asked them what did they want brung in a suitcase, and they all said dogs." To prove his point he ran over to his brother's bed and flung both arms around the little dachshund. The dog was quite used to these outbursts of affection and went on placidly chewing a corner of the blanket. "Everybody could have a dog like Petey on their beds every single night, even old Rudolph."

"Rudolph says dogs dig holes in the flower beds."

"Petey never digs holes. *I* dig holes. I dig about a million holes a week."

Galloway smiled sadly. "That's a lot of work for a little man like you. You must be pretty strong."

"Feel my muscle."

"Feel mine too," Greg said. "I can dig a million holes too if I want."

Muscles were being duly tested when Annie, the maid who looked after the boys, appeared in the doorway. During the daytime when she wore her blue and white uniform, Annie was prim and self-contained and respectable. Tonight, dressed and groomed for an evening out, she was barely recognizable, with her mouth swollen by lipstick, and her eyebrows coyly arched in black, and her eyes cavernous behind a coating of mascara.

"Oh, it's you, Mr. Galloway. I thought the boys were alone arguing about that dog again."

"They won't have to argue about Petey much longer. I have orders to bring them another dog when I come back."

"Indeed."

"Surely you want me to bring you something too, Annie? Everyone else does."

She looked a little startled and disapproving. "I have my wages, thank you, sir."

"I'm certain you could think of something if you tried, Annie. Perhaps a necklace? Or a bottle of perfume to stun the senses of the local boys?"

"Bring Annie a dog," Marvin shouted. "Annie wants a dog!"

"I do *not* want a dog," the girl said sharply. "Nor anything else. Now you two settle down and go to sleep without any more nonsense. My boyfriend's waiting for me, but I'm not going to set one foot outside this house until you two are quiet." To Galloway she added in a whisper, "They get overexcited sometimes."

"You want me to leave, is that right?"

"I really think it would be better, sir. They were tucked in an hour ago."

He looked over Annie's head at the two boys. For a minute, before Annie came on the scene, he had felt quite close to them, he had thought what handsome and precocious children they were. Now, once again, they were strangers to him, a couple of little barbarians who wanted nothing from him but presents, who liked to see him go away because he would come back with something in his luggage.

The dizziness returned, and with it a sharp sour taste in his mouth. He said quickly, "Good night, boys," and stepped out into the hall and moved unsteadily toward the stairs. The duffel bag was like lead in his hand. He walked like an old man.

I must get some pills from Harry. Harry has all kinds of pills.

Esther's pink and cream De Soto was missing from the garage, but Galloway's Cadillac convertible was in its place with the top down, freshly washed and waxed, the way old Rudolph liked to keep it, as if it were an irreplaceable heirloom instead of something that would be traded in within a year.

It was cold, even for April. But Galloway left the top down and climbed, shivering, into the front seat.

Upstairs, the two boys continued their argument but its content had changed.

"What if he forgets to bring the dogs?"

"He can't forget."

"Or maybe he will never come back, like old Rudolph's wife."

"Oh shut up," Gregory said fiercely. "When you go away, you *got* to come back. There's no place else to go, you got to come back."

For Gregory it was that simple.

2

WHEN GALLOWAY REFERRED to his friends as a group he usually called them "the fellows." Two of the fellows, Bill Winslow and Joe Hepburn, drove up together from Toronto and arrived at the lodge, which was located on Georgian Bay a few miles beyond Wiarton, at about ten o'clock. A third, Ralph Turee, came alone a few minutes later.

They were admitted by the caretaker, and each of them launched immediately into his special task. Turee took the luggage upstairs, Hepburn started a fire in the huge stone fireplace, Winslow pried the lock off the liquor cabinet, and, as Esther had predicted, the fellows began the process of getting themselves boozed up.

These were Galloway's special friends, of approximately the same age, and with a mutual aim, having as good a time as possible when they were away from the pressures of business and family: Bill Winslow, an executive in his father's milling company; Joe Hepburn, manager of a firm which manufactured plastic toys and novelties; and Ralph Turee, who taught economics at the University of Toronto. Except for Turee, they were men of average intelligence and above average income. Turee never let them forget this. Chronically broke, he made fun of their money and borrowed it; possessing a superior education, he jeered at their ignorance and used it to his own advantage. But the group was, on the whole, a congenial one, especially after small differences had been dissolved in alcohol.

It was Turee who first remarked on the passage of time and the absence of Harry Bream and Galloway. "Peculiar thing Galloway hasn't come yet. He makes such a point of being punctual."

"I hate punctuality," Winslow stated. "It is the hobgoblin of small minds. Right, fellows?"

Hepburn said it was chastity that was the hobgoblin of small minds and Turee corrected them both, as usual, and said it was consistency, and eventually they got back to Galloway.

"Galloway called me last night," Turee said, "and told me he was going to pick Harry up in Weston and drive on up here and arrive about nine-thirty."

"There," Winslow said. "There you have it."

"Have what?"

"The crux of the situation. Harry. Harry's always late for everything."

It was a logical as well as an agreeable theory, and they were all having another drink to toast Harry, the crux of the situation, when, about eleven-thirty, Harry unintentionally ruined the whole thing by walking in the front door. He was wearing a mackintosh, a deerhunter's cap with the flaps up, and carrying his fishing gear.

"Sorry I'm late," he said cheerfully. "Something went wrong with the fuel pump the other side of Owen Sound."

They all stared at him in such a peculiar and disgruntled way that even Harry, who was not given to subtleties, sensed something was wrong.

"What's the matter with you guys anyway? Have I broken out in spots or something?"

"Where's Galloway?" Turee asked.

"I thought he was here."

"Wasn't he supposed to come with you?"

"That was the original plan, but I had an emergency call to make at a clinic down in Mimico, so I left word with Thelma to tell Galloway to go ahead without me. I know how he hates to be late. You don't suppose Thelma got her signals switched?"

It was generally agreed among the fellows that Thelma had been born with her signals switched, but none of them wanted to state this outright because it might hurt Harry's feelings. Harry adored his wife. Her little eccentricities seemed endlessly fascinating to him and he was always entertaining his friends with detailed reports of her opinions and experiences.

Because he'd been the sole support of his parents, Harry had not married until they were both dead and then he wasted no time. His marriage, at the age of thirty-five, to a woman who worked as a receptionist in a doctor's office, came as a shock to his friends, especially to Galloway who had become used to having Harry at his beck and call, and ready for anything. The carefree bachelor Harry had been suddenly replaced by the hopelessly married Harry, subject to rules and restrictions and at the mercy of whims and worries. Though Thelma and Esther did not get along well, the two men remained the best of friends, partly because Thelma seemed to like Galloway and encouraged Harry to see him, and partly because the two men had been friends ever since their prep school years together. As a senior, Harry had been president of the class. He still possessed the yearbook with his graduation picture in it, and the caption: *Henry Ellsworth Bream. A great future is predicted for our Harry, who holds a warm place in all our hearts.*

He still held a warm place in a good many hearts but the future remained elusive. He had missed a number of boats, by inches or minutes, by oddities of fate like a flat tire, a delay in traffic, a wrong turning, a misplaced key, a sudden blizzard, a mistake in a telephone number.

"Poor Harry," people said. "Always running into bad luck."

It was generally expected that when his parents died fate would step in and make up to Harry for all his misfortunes by handing him a real stroke of luck. By Harry's standards, fate had. The luck was Thelma.

"She probably didn't give him the message," Turee said. "Perhaps she suddenly decided to go to a movie or something and Galloway's still sitting there waiting for you to turn up."

Harry shook his head. "Thelma wouldn't do a thing like that."

"Not on purpose, of course."

"Not accidentally, either. Thelma's got a wonderful memory."

"Oh?"

"That girl's never forgotten a thing in her life."

"Well, all right, all right. It just seemed the logical explanation, that's all."

It was midnight by this time, and Bill Winslow, who couldn't hold his liquor but would die trying, had reached the point of saturation. The excess fluid was seeping out of his eyes in the form of tears.

"Poor old Galloway, sitting down there on his can, sitting on his poor old lonely can, while we're up here lapping up his liquor and having a swell time. It's not cricket. Fellows, I ask you, is that *cricket?*"

Turee scowled at him across the room. "For God's sake, stop blubbering, will you? I'm trying to think."

"Poor old Galloway. Not cricket. Here we are having a swell time and there he sits on his poor old . . ."

"Hepburn, see if you can haul him off to bed."

Hepburn put his hands under Winslow's armpits and pulled him to his feet. "Come on, Billy-boy. Let's go beddy-bye."

"I don't want to go to bed. I want to stay down here and have a swell time with you fellows."

"Look, Billy-boy, we're not having a swell time."

"Y'aren't?"

"No. So let's get moving. Where'd you leave your suitcase?"

"I don't know."

"I put it upstairs with mine, in the room next to Galloway's," Turee said.

"I don't want to go to bed. I'm sad."

"So I see."

Winslow tried to brush the moisture off his cheeks with his forearm. "I keep thinking about poor old Galloway and poor little Princess Margaret."

"How did Princess Margaret get into this?"

"Ought to marry somebody, have kids, be happy. Everybody should be happy."

"Certainly."

"*I'm* happy."

"Sure you are."

"I'm having a swell time with you fellows, aren't I?"

"Not for long, Billy-boy. Come on."

With the tears still spouting from his eyes, Winslow shuffled across the room and began to ascend the staircase on all fours like a trained dog going up a ladder. Halfway up he collapsed and Hepburn had to drag him the rest of the way.

Turee got up and put another log on the fire and kicked it impatiently with his foot. "Well, what do we do now?"

"I don't know," Harry said gloomily. "This isn't like Ron, to keep people waiting."

"He might have had an accident."

"He's a good driver. He's got a real bug on safety, seat belts and everything."

"Even good drivers occasionally have accidents. The point is, since there's no phone here, if something happened we'd have no way of finding out unless Esther sent a telegram to Wiarton and it was delivered out here."

"Esther would be too upset to think of doing that."

"All right, here's another theory: Galloway never left home. He suffered an attack of indigestion, perhaps, and decided not to come."

"Now that's more like it," Harry said with enthusiasm. "Last time I saw him he was complaining about his stomach. I gave him a couple of those new ulcer capsules my firm's putting out."

"Galloway hasn't got an ulcer."

"He may have. The capsules worked like a charm."

Turee turned away with an expression of distaste. He was the only one of the group who refused to have anything personal to do with either Harry's diagnoses or Harry's pills.

"All right, all right. Galloway's ulcer started kicking up and he went to the hospital. How does that sound?"

"Splendid," Harry said, beaming.

When Hepburn returned, a conference was held and it was decided that Turee, the brainiest, and Harry, the soberest, should drive back to Wiarton and call Galloway's house to test the ulcer theory.

The road wound along the cliffs above the bay and Turee had to concentrate on his driving while Harry, in case the ulcer theory might be incorrect, kept his eye peeled for signs of a Cadillac in distress. They met only two cars, neither one a Cadillac.

By the time they reached the town of Wiarton, nearly all the lights were out, but they finally located a pay phone in the lobby of a small tourist hotel which was just opening for the season. Since both the men were wearing fishing clothes, the manager of the hotel assumed they were customers and treated them very cordially until he learned they merely wanted to use the telephone. When, in addition to suffering a disappointment, he had to make change for five dollars, he became quite bitter about the whole thing and sat behind the desk glowering as Turee stepped into the phone booth.

It required ten minutes or more to put the call through to Galloway's house in Toronto, and then the connection was bad and the conversation was punctuated by what sounded like static.

"Esther?"

"Ron?"

"No, this is not Ron. Is that you, Esther?"

"Just who is this, please?"

"Ralph. Ralph Turee. Is that you, Esther?"

"Yes," Esther replied, rather coldly, since she'd been awakened from a sound sleep and even under the best of circumstances didn't care much for Turee, Turee's wife, or any of the little Turees. "Isn't it rather *late?*"

"I can't hear you. Would you speak up?"

"I'm practically screaming already."

"Listen, Esther—what in hell is that noise? Operator, operator, do something about that noise—Esther? Are you there? Well, listen a minute. Is Ron all right?"

"Of course he's all right."

"No attack of indigestion or anything?"

"Are you drunk, by any chance?" This was one of Esther's favorite questions and after long practice she read the line with spirited contempt, rolling the *r* in drunk and broadening the *a* in chance.

"I am not drunk," Turee shouted. "Why should I be?"

"I'm sure you have reasons. Now what's all this about Ron?"

"Well, it's like this. Harry's up here at the lodge with the rest of us."

"So?"

"Ron hasn't arrived. Harry drove up alone in his own car. He had a business appointment to keep in Mimico and he told Thelma to tell Ron not to wait for him but to come up to the lodge by himself and Harry would get here when he could. Well, Harry got here all right, but Ron hasn't. The fellows were beginning to get worried so we thought we'd better call you."

Esther suffered from a chronic case of jealousy, and the first image that flashed through her mind was not of Galloway lying dead somewhere in a car wreck, but of Galloway lying cosily beside Thelma in a bed. She said, "Maybe Ron was delayed."

"Where?"

"In Weston."

"How?"

"How? Ask Harry. He's married to the woman."

"Now that," Turee said irritably, "is the silliest remark in history. What's got into you, Esther?"

"Just an idea."

"Honest to God, I gave you credit for better sense. I can't say more than that right now because I'm shouting as it is and Harry's not ten feet away. Do you understand?"

"Naturally."

"Listen, Esther . . ."

At this point the operator's voice cut in and demanded another ninety cents. Turee deposited the money, cursing audibly. "Are you still there, Esther?"

"Naturally."

"I think you should call the police."

"Why? It might embarrass poor Ron. He's rather sensitive about being caught by the cops in bed with another man's wife."

"For Pete's sake, Esther, get off that kick, will you? This might be serious. Ron could be lying in some hospital or even a morgue."

"He carries all kinds of identification in his wallet. If there'd been an accident I would have been notified."

"Then you're not worried?"

"Worried? Yes, I'm *worried,* but it's not the kind of worry I want to share with the police department."

"I'm amazed at your attitude, Esther, genuinely amazed."

"You go right on being amazed, I can't stop you."

"But what about Ron?"

"Ron," she said dryly, "will be home in due course with a perfectly believable story which I may even believe, for a time. You needn't concern yourself about Ron. Wherever he is and whatever he's doing, I assure you he's not concerning himself about you, or me, or Harry, or anyone else."

"That could mean he's dead."

"The trouble with you and the fellows is that you all get maudlin when you've been drinking."

The statement contained such a large element of truth that Turee didn't attempt to refute it. "I must say that's not a very friendly remark."

"I'm not feeling too friendly at the moment. Now look. You and the fellows went up to the lodge for a weekend of fishing. Or whatever. If Ron shows up here I'll tell him you're worried and ask him to wire you. If he shows up there, you might do the same for me. Right?"

"Right," Turee agreed, though he didn't feel it was right at all. The whole thing was wrong, Galloway's absence, Esther's attitude, Winslow's wild, drunken sobbing. *What a weekend this is shaping up to be,* he thought. *I ought to turn right around and drive home.*

The air in the telephone booth had become hot and stale and when Turee opened the door and stepped out into the lobby he was sweating, red-eyed and ill-tempered.

Harry was standing beside the window looking intently out over the bay, as if there were many interesting things to be seen. But the bay was dark, nothing could be seen, and Turee knew that Harry had been listening—listening and perhaps hearing.

"Well, well," Turee said with an attempt at heartiness. "It seems as though we were getting all discombobulated for nothing."

"Ron's at home, then?"

"Not exactly. But I assure you Esther's not in the least worried about his well-being."

"That sounds as if she's worried about something else."

"Oh, you know Esther. She's hatched the idea that Ron went off on a bat. Who can tell, maybe she's right."

"Maybe." Harry turned back to the window, his jaw clenched so tight that his voice seemed to be coming from some other place, like a ventriloquist's. "I thought I heard you say something about me."

"You? Oh, certainly. I explained about the mix-up in Weston, how you had to keep your business appointment and . . ."

"I don't mean that."

"All right," Turee said quietly. "What else did you hear?"

"You told Esther you couldn't talk anymore about something because I was only ten feet away."

"That's right."

"What were you referring to?"

"Well, it's like this." Turee was an inexperienced liar, and the circumstances—the wearing off of the drinks he'd had, the lateness of the hour, and the presence of the hotel manager behind the desk, wide-eyed with curiosity—contributed to his awkwardness. "The fact is, Esther had a suspicion that you and Ron went off on a bat together."

"Esther should know me better than that. In the old days, well, perhaps, she might have had a point, but I'm a married man now."

"Yes."

"Esther *does* know me better than that."

"What Esther knows and what she feels are often miles apart."

"Are you telling me the truth?"

"About what?"

"Come off it, Ralph. We're friends."

"Well, as one friend to another, I suggest we go back to the lodge and get some sleep." Turee took a couple of tentative steps toward the door, but when he saw that Harry didn't intend to follow, he turned around and came back. "We can't stay here all night, old boy."

"Can't we?"

"Look, Esther's crazy suspicions shouldn't make the least difference to anyone. Now come on, let's go back to the lodge. There's nothing more we can do here."

"Yes, there is," Harry said. "I'm going to phone Thelma."

"Why?"

"You don't have to have a reason for phoning your own wife. Besides, I want to find out if Ron ever showed up at the house."

"But it's late, Thelma will be asleep. She may not even hear the phone."

"It's right beside our bed."

"Go ahead and call her then. Just don't say I didn't warn you."

"Warn me?"

"What I mean is, if I phoned my wife at this hour of the morning she'd think I was drunk, and the next time I was invited to come up here with the fellows she'd raise a hell of a smell."

"Thelma's not like that. She wants me to have a good time. She's a remarkably unselfish woman."

Turee didn't argue. It was one of Harry's most ingratiating qualities, to attribute to other people the virtues he himself possessed.

As Harry slid into the phone booth and closed the door, Turee watched anxiously, thinking, *God, suppose Esther's right for once and Ron's there with Thelma . . . No, that's impossible. Thelma's just as crazy about Harry as he is about her.*

He began to whistle, almost inaudibly, *I'm just wild about Harry.*

3

THELMA WAS NOT asleep, as Turee had predicted. She answered the phone on the second ring and her voice sounded alert, as if she'd been expecting the call. Or one like it.

"This is the Bream residence."

Harry laughed. "I know that, sweetheart."

"Oh, it's you, Harry."

"None other. I hope I didn't wake you up."

"No."

"Are you glad to hear from me?"

"Of course."

"Cross your heart and hope to die?"

"Cross my heart," she said flatly, "and hope to die. How you enjoy playing games, Harry. You're like a child. But isn't it too late for games? Oughtn't children to be in bed? I think so. Tomorrow," she added, "tomorrow you can play all the games you like."

In their three years of marriage she had never addressed him in such a wearily patronizing manner. Harry colored, as if his face had been slapped. "Thelma, what's the matter?"

"Nothing."

"That's not true. I know it's not true. What's happened, Thelma? Tell me. Tell Harry."

Her only response was a sigh. He could hear it quite plainly; it was long and deep and sad.

"Thelma. Listen to me. If you want me to come home, I will. I'll start out right this minute."

"No! I *don't* want you to come home!"

"What's the matter, Thelma? Are you feeling all right?"

Again she made no reply. Harry felt smothered by her silence. He pulled open the door of the phone booth a few inches and breathed in the new air deeply and rhythmically. With the door open Turee could overhear, but Harry didn't care. He was not timid or embarrassed about sharing his troubles with his friends since he had so frequently shared theirs.

"I'm ill," Thelma said finally. "I've been ill all evening."

"Get a doctor. Get a doctor right away."

"I don't need a doctor. I know what's the matter."

"What is it, sweetheart?"

"I can't tell you. This isn't—the time or place."

"Look, Thel, take it easy. Lie down and relax. I'm coming home right away."

"If you do, I won't be here."

"For God's sake . . ."

"I mean it, Harry. I'll run away. I've got to be alone for a while to think. Don't come home, Harry. Promise me."

"But I . . ."

"Promise me."

"All right, I promise. I won't come home, not tonight, anyway."

She seemed relieved by his promise and when she spoke again her tone was quite friendly. "Where are you calling from?"

"A hotel in Wiarton."

"Haven't you been to the lodge yet?"

"Yes, but Turee and I drove back to find a phone so we could call Ron's house."

"Why on earth should you call Ron's house at this hour?"

"To find out why he hasn't arrived here."

"He hasn't arrived," she repeated dully. "Is that what you said? Ron's not there?"

"Not yet."

"But he left here hours ago. He came before eight and I gave him your message and we had a drink together. And then . . ."

She stopped, and Harry had to urge her to continue. "And then what, Thelma?"

"I—I asked him—I begged him not to go up to the lodge."

"Why?"

"Because I had this feeling when he came in—it was so strong I nearly fainted—I had this *feeling*." She began to weep and the rest of her words were distorted by great choking sobs. "Oh, my God—warned—my fault—Ron's dead—Ron—Ron . . ."

"What are you saying, Thelma?"

"Ron . . ." She repeated the name half a dozen times while Harry listened, his heart on fire, his face like stone.

Turee came over to the phone booth and opened the door. "Is anything the matter?"

"Yes. But I don't know what."

"Perhaps I can help."

"I don't think so."

"Let me try, anyway. Go and sit down, Harry, you look terrible."

The two men exchanged places at the telephone and Turee spoke briskly into the mouthpiece: "Hello, Thelma. This is Ralph."

"Go away."

"Listen, Thelma, I don't know what the situation is, but calm down for a minute, will you?"

"I can't."

"Why don't you have a drink? I'll hang on for a minute while you go and pour yourself . . ."

"I don't want a drink."

"All right, all right. Just a suggestion."

"It wouldn't stay down anyway. I'm ill. I've been vomiting."

"Maybe you have a touch of flu."

"I haven't got the flu." She hesitated for a moment. "Is Harry standing anywhere near you?"

"No, he went outside."

"You're sure?"

"I can see him walking up and down on the veranda."

"I'm pregnant."

"'What? What did you say?"

"I'm going to have a baby."

"Well, for—well, I'll be double-damned. That's great, Thelma, that's wonderful!"

"Is it?"

"Have you told Harry?"

"Not yet."

"God, he'll be thrilled to pieces when he finds out."

"Maybe he will. At first."

"What do you mean, at first?"

"When he starts thinking about it he won't be so thrilled."

"I don't get the point."

"Harry and I haven't taken any chances along that line for over a year," she said slowly. "Harry didn't want me to have a baby, he was afraid complications might develop because I'm nearly thirty-five."

"No method is foolproof. You could have had an accident."

"It wasn't an accident. It was quite deliberate, on my part anyway. I wanted a baby. I'm getting old, pretty soon it would have been too late. I talked to Harry, I told him how I felt, many times. But he was terrified that something might happen to me. That's what he said, anyway. Maybe his real reasons were deeper, subtler, I don't know. Maybe he was jealous at the idea of my dividing my affections. But whatever Harry's reasons were, at least now you know mine. I want this child. I love him already."

"Him?"

"I have a feeling it's a boy. I call him Ron."

"For the love of God," Turee said. "Ron. Ron *Galloway?*"

"Yes."

"You're sure?"

"Now that's rather insulting, isn't it? It sounds as though I've been promiscuous."

"I only meant, in a thing like this you've got to be absolutely positive."

"I am."

"For the love of God," Turee repeated. "What a mess this is going to be. Think of Harry. And Esther."

"I can't afford to. I have my child to think about. Esther never loved Ron anyway. She married him for his money, he told me so. As for Harry, I feel sorry for him, of course. He's a good man, I hate to hurt him, but . . ."

"But you will?"

"I will. I must. I have my child to consider."

"That's just it, Thelma. Think a minute. For the child's sake, wouldn't it be better to keep this whole business a secret? Harry would make a wonderful father, and the child could be brought up without any fuss or scandal."

"That's impossible. I don't want to keep this whole business, as you call it, a secret."

"I strongly urge you to think about it."

"I've thought of nothing else for three weeks, ever since I found out I was pregnant. And one thing I'm sure of—I can't go on living with Harry. He doesn't even seem *real* to me anymore. How can I explain it? The only thing that's real to me is this baby inside me. Ron's baby. They are my life now, Ron and his baby."

The simple statement, spoken with such conviction, appalled Turee more than the actual circumstances behind it. For a moment he could hardly speak, and when he did, his voice was cold with disapproval. "I don't imagine Ron will feel quite so single-minded about it. After all, he's sired one child by his first wife and two by his second, so this is hardly a unique occasion for him."

"If you're trying to make me jealous or angry, don't bother. Ron's had other women, other children, yes, but this is special. The baby's special. I'm special."

There was no answer to this. Turee could only sit and stare silently and helplessly into the mouthpiece of the telephone, wishing with all his heart that he had stayed home and painted the garage, as his wife wanted him to.

"Ralph? Are you there?"

"Yes?"

"Ralph, I don't want you to get the idea that I'm—that I thought this all out ahead of time, that I planned it. I really didn't. It just happened, but once it happened, I realized how right it was for me."

"*Right.* Are you out of your mind, woman? What you're doing, what you've done, is completely and unjustifiably immoral."

"Don't preach at me. Words aren't going to change anything."

"Well, for God's sake, consider Harry. This will kill him."

"I don't think so. Oh, he'll be upset for a while, but eventually he'll meet some nice clinging-vine sort of woman who'll let him fuss over her and pour pills down her throat."

Turee was shocked. "You sound as if you actually hate him."

"No. Just the pills. He was making an invalid out of me. I'm really quite strong. The doctor says I should have a fine, healthy baby. It's what I've wanted all my life. I was an only child living with a maiden aunt, and terribly lonely. I used to dream of growing up and getting married and having a dozen children so I'd never be lonely again."

"You may," he said heavily, "be lonelier than ever. People around here take a dim view of . . ."

"Oh, people. I don't care about them. All I need is Ron and the baby."

"You're pretty sure of yourself, Thelma."

"Yes."

"Are you equally sure of Ron?"

"Yes. I told him about the baby tonight when he came over to pick up Harry. It seemed the right time to tell him."

Turee wasn't certain he agreed with her. "How did he take the news?"

She said defensively, "Naturally I didn't expect him to be deliriously happy about it right at first. He needs time to think, to adjust to the situation. Any man would."

"I'm glad you realize that," Turee said dryly.

"He loves me, that's the important factor."

"Is it?"

"Don't worry, everything will work out fine. I have a feeling."

Thelma's was a contradictory nature. This new feeling, that everything would work out fine, immediately eclipsed the old feeling that something had happened to Ron. Thelma could, in fact, superimpose one feeling on another feeling, like bricks, and it was always the latest, the top one, that was valid.

She added, "Oh, I know it's going to be messy in some ways, the divorce, for instance."

"Ron can't get a divorce from Esther. He has no grounds."

"I meant, Ron will pay her off and she can get the divorce."

"Suppose she refuses?"

"Oh nonsense. Esther loves money. Besides, why should she refuse?"

"Some women," Turee said with heavy irony, "aren't exactly thrilled at the prospect of breaking up their home and family."

"Don't sentimentalize Esther. I haven't done anything more to her than she did to Ron's first wife. Except that my motives are cleaner."

"How does Ron like the idea of going through the courts and the newspapers again as an adulterer?"

"Oh, for heaven's sake, can't you say something *cheerful?*"

"I can't think of anything cheerful," Turee said truthfully. "This isn't the type of situation that appeals to my sense of humor. Maybe Harry will be able to think of something cheerful. He's still outside on the veranda. Shall I call him?"

"No!"

"How are you going to tell him, Thelma?"

"I don't know. I've tried, I've led up to it, but—oh, it's all so difficult."

"You should have thought of that when you and Ron were hopping into bed together."

"What a terribly coarse remark!"

"The situation isn't exactly genteel either."

"Listen, Ralph. About telling Harry. I was wondering, you're such a good friend of his . . ."

"Kindly leave me out of it."

"I only thought, you can be so tactful when you choose . . ."

"On this occasion, I don't choose."

"Very well. But *I* won't tell him. I can't. I don't even want to see him again."

"For God's sake, woman, you owe him that much, an apology, an explanation."

"Why should I apologize? I'm not sorry. As for an explanation, how can I explain something I don't understand myself? I didn't know it was going to happen to Ron and me. If I had, maybe I would have asked Harry for a pill or something, a love-preventative pill." She laughed briefly and bitterly. "He's got every other kind."

"When did it all begin?"

"A couple of weeks before Christmas. I went into town to buy Harry's gift and I met Ron in Eaton's by accident. We had lunch together at the Park Plaza and afterwards we went out on the terrace in the snow and looked down at the city. It was so pretty. I'd never cared much for Toronto before, I was brought up in the West, Vancouver. Well, that's all, we just stood there. There was no flirtation, no hand-holding, we didn't even talk personally or look at each other much. But when I got home I didn't tell Harry. I had no reason not to. But I didn't. I even made up a lie for him, told him I had lunch with a nurse I used to work with at the Murray Clinic in Hamilton. The next day I took a bus into Toronto again because I'd forgotten to buy Harry's Christmas present. At least that was the excuse I gave myself. I went back to the same store, at the same time, and hung around the Yonge Street entrance for nearly an hour. I had this terribly strong feeling that Ron would show up. He didn't, but later he told me that he'd wanted to very much, that he'd thought of me all morning but he couldn't get away because Esther was giving a luncheon party at the club."

A couple of dimwits, Turee thought contemptuously, dramatizing themselves, out of boredom, into a situation that neither of them was equipped to handle. He said, "And Harry hasn't suspected a thing?"

"No."

"For your information, Esther has and does."

"I thought as much. She was very cold when I called her last week and invited her to go to a séance a friend of mine was giving. I was only trying to be affable."

"Why?"

"For Ron's sake. I don't want him cut off from Esther's children the way he was cut off from his first wife's. It's not fair."

"The courts seem to think so."

"The courts in this country, yes. Oh, this place is so stodgy and provincial. I wish we could live in the States, Ron and I and the baby."

The front door opened and Harry came back into the hotel lobby walking unsteadily and with his feet wide apart like a newly debarked sailor bracing himself against the pitch and roll of a ship that was no longer under him. Although the night air was still balmy, his lips were blue with cold and his eyes had a glassy stare as if unshed tears had been trapped there and frozen.

". . . some place where they don't have these long terrible winters," Thelma was saying. "Oh, how I hate them! I've reached the point where I can't even enjoy the spring anymore because I know how short it will be and how soon fall is coming when everything is sad again, everything dying."

"Let's go into that some other time," Turee said brusquely. "Now tell me, was Ron driving the Cadillac when he came to your house tonight?"

"I think so."

"Did it have the top down or up?"

"Down, I think. Yes, definitely down. I remember waving out the window to him and wondering if he might catch cold with all that draft on the back of his neck. He complained of feeling ill anyway."

"I can believe it."

"No, I mean he complained about it *before* I told him anything about the baby. Really, Ralph, you're in a nasty mood tonight."

"I wonder why."

"After all, it's not *your* funeral."

Harry walked slowly but directly toward the telephone booth and in spite of Turee's restraining hand he forced open the door. "Let me talk to her."

Turee said, "Thelma, here's Harry. He wants to talk to you."

"I don't want to talk to him. I have nothing to say."

"But . . ."

"Tell him the truth or give him a story, I don't care. I'm going to hang up now, Ralph. And if you call back I won't answer."

"Thelma, wait."

The click of the receiver was unmistakably final. "She hung up," Turee said.

"Why?"

"Didn't feel like conversation, I guess. Don't let it worry you, old boy. Women can get pretty flighty at . . ."

"I want to call her back."

"She said if you did, she wouldn't answer."

"I know Thelma," Harry said with a wan smile. "She can't resist the ringing of a telephone."

Once again the two men exchanged places and Harry put in a collect call to Mrs. Harry Bream in Weston.

The operator let the telephone ring a dozen times before she cut back to Harry. "I'm sorry, sir, there's no answer at that number. Shall I try again in twenty minutes?"

"No. No, thanks." Harry came out of the booth wiping his forehead with the sleeve of his fishing jacket. "Sonuvabitch, I don't get it. What's the matter? What did *I* do?"

"Nothing. Let's go back to the lodge and have a drink."

"What were you and Thelma talking about all that time?"

"Life," Turee said. Which was true enough.

"*Life,* at three o'clock in the morning, long distance?"

"Thelma wanted to talk. You know women, sometimes they have to get things off their chest by talking to somebody objective, not a member of their family. Thelma was in an emotional state."

"She can always count on me to understand."

"I hope so," Turee said softly. "I hope to God so."

"It's this uncertainty that gets me down. Why won't she talk to me? Why did she keep saying Ron's name over and over again?"

"She's—fond of Ron and worried about him. We all are, aren't we?"

"My God, yes. He's my best friend. I saved him from drowning once when we were in school together, did I ever tell you that?"

"Yes," Turee said, not because it was true but because he'd had enough irony for one day, he couldn't swallow any more; his throat felt tight and raw and scraped. "Come on, Harry, you look as if you need a drink."

"Maybe I should stay in town for the night, take a room here and get a couple of hours' sleep and then try to reach Thelma again."

"Leave the woman alone for a while. Give her a chance to collect herself."

"You may be right. I hope she remembers to take the orange pills I left for her. They're very good for relieving tension. I'm told they're the ones that cured the Pope of hiccups when he had that bad spell."

Turee felt, simultaneously, a certain sympathy for Thelma and a twinge of impatience with Harry. He would have liked to point out that Thelma's ailment was quite remote from hiccups and that it would require more than orange pills, or blue, or pink, to cure her. "There's nothing more we can do here," he said, "unless we inform the police that Ron is missing."

"He may not be missing anymore. By the time we drive back to the lodge, he'll very likely be there. Don't you agree?"

"It's possible." But not, Turee added to himself, very probable. If I were in Ron's shoes, the last thing in the world I'd want to do would be to come up here and face Harry. Ron may have taken a room at a hotel for the night. Or gone down to his cottage near Kingsville. Or maybe he's just driving around alone the way he does sometimes when he and Esther are on the verge of a quarrel. Ron can't stand scenes, trouble of any kind makes him sick. The time Bill Winslow and I had the big argument about politics Ron simply disappeared, and Esther found him later, retching behind the boxwood hedge.

Harry looked at his watch and the very sight of it made him yawn and brought water to his eyes. "My God, it's nearly four o'clock."

"I'm well aware of it."

"In another hour or two the fellows will be up and raring to go. We'd better start back, don't you agree?"

"I agreed some time ago."

"By Jove, you know something, Ralph? I feel better, I feel much, much better. I don't know what you said or did exactly, but you've given me a little perspective on things."

Turee forced a feeble smile. "Good."

"Yes sir, you've given me a new slant. Why should we worry over two perfectly mature adults like Ron and Thelma? After all, neither of them would ever do anything foolish."

"That's the spirit."

"Let's go back to the lodge and have a drink to celebrate."

"Celebrate what?"

"I don't know, I felt so bad before and now everything's fine again and I feel like celebrating."

He went ahead to open the door. He was smiling and his step was jaunty.

"By Jove, it's a glorious night," Harry said. "Smell that air, will you?"

Turee had little choice. He smelled the air. It carried the scent of wind and water, delusion and betrayal.

4

THE RIDE BACK to the lodge began quietly enough. After a brief spurt of conversation Harry climbed over into the back seat, folded himself up and went to sleep.

Turee drove slowly, his mind oppressed by the problem of telling Harry the truth in a way that would cause him a minimum of shock. Pain was inevitable—there was no way of sparing him that—but it might be possible to break his fall and lessen the concussion.

Until tonight Turee had always considered Thelma as something of a birdbrain. He now began to realize how cleverly Thelma had maneuvered him into the role of custodian of the secret. It was like finding himself custodian of a fissionable mass of uranium; if he didn't get rid of some of it, the whole thing might blow up in his face. The problem, then, was to unload it a little at a time, with due respect for its explosive powers.

"Tell him the truth or give him a story," Thelma had said, but it was clear that she intended him to tell Harry the truth, not because she felt he could do it in a more kindly and tactful way, but because she wanted to save herself the trouble. Thelma could no longer be bothered with Harry, she had no compunctions about hurting him, no apologies to offer him, no explanation to give him, no intention of ever seeing him again. This final fact seemed somehow more incredible to Turee than any of the others. For three years the Breams had been regarded as a model couple. They did not argue or correct each other in public, take verbal potshots at parties or confide their mates' failings to friends. Turee had always envied them a little, since he and his wife, Nancy, engaged in frequent and spirited arguments which usually culminated in a series of glib psychological terms: *Your Uncle Charles has that same paranoid streak—you're a cyclic depressive, that's all—it's no wonder the kids are going through a manic phase . . .* Instead of throwing ashtrays at each other, the Turees, in the modern manner, threw Oedipus complexes, father fixations and compulsive neuroses.

In the back seat Harry began to snore, rather gently and apologetically, as if he expected to be told to turn over and shut up. For some reason the sound exasperated Turee. It was like a sick puppy whimpering in its sleep.

"Harry," he said sharply.

"Umph," Harry said, as if he'd been prodded in the stomach by an elbow. "Aaaah. What? What?"

"Wake up."

"Must have dozed off. Sorry."

"Don't apologize all the time. It gets on my nerves."

"Nearly everything does," Harry said with a patient sigh. "I don't intend that as a criticism, old boy. Far from it. You're too high-strung, that's all. You ought to learn to relax. Say, you remember those orange pills I told you about, the ones that cured the Pope of hiccups?"

"They're quite difficult to forget."

"I happen to have a few in my pocket. You could take one now and let me drive for a while."

Turee had as little faith in Harry's driving as he had in Harry's ministrations. "Thank you, no. I prefer to remain tense."

Harry climbed back into the front seat and then, out of a habit that was becoming almost a compulsion, he began to talk of Thelma again, of her rare and various virtues. Harry didn't claim that all other women were clods, he merely let it be implied.

". . . so Thelma took the old man in the house and made him a cup of tea. Thel's like that, opens her heart to everyone . . ."

"Harry."

". . . even a total stranger. Then she got in touch with the old man's daughter-in-law . . ."

"Harry, I have something to tell you."

"All right, old boy, I'd practically finished anyway. Go ahead."

"Don't expect Ron to be at the lodge when we get there."

"Why not?"

"I don't think he's going to show up at all, either at the lodge or any other place he's likely to run into you."

"What have *I* got to do with it?"

"I believe Ron may be trying to avoid you."

"Avoid me? Why?"

"Because he's become quite fond of your wife."

"Why, he's always been fond of Thelma. They hit it off fine, right from the start."

"Now they're hitting it off finer." Turee took his eyes from the road for an instant to glance at Harry's face in the dim light from the dashboard. Harry was smiling. "Did you hear me, Harry? Ron's in love with your wife."

"That's Thelma's story, of course?"

"Yes."

"Don't let it worry you, there's nothing to it," Harry said firmly.

"You seem pretty confident."

"Listen, Ralph, I wouldn't tell this to anyone else in the world, but you're my friend, I can trust you with a secret."

Turee opened the car window. He had a sensation that he and Harry were stationary and the night was moving past them swiftly, turbulent with secrets. To the right the bay was visible in the reflection of a half moon. The waves nudged each other and winked slyly and whispered new secrets.

"The fact is," Harry said, "Thelma daydreams. Nothing serious, of course, but once in a while she gets the notion that so-and-so is in love with her. There's never anything to it. A week later she's forgotten the whole thing."

"I see."

"This time it's Ron. Once, it was you."

"Me. Why, for God's sake, I never even . . ."

"I know. Thelma imagines things. She can't help it. She's got a romantic streak in her nature. It gives her satisfaction to believe that someone is hopelessly in love with her, makes her feel glamorous, I guess." Harry sighed. "So she thinks Ron is in love with her, that's what she was upset about? That's what she told you?"

"She told me that among . . ."

"Poor Thelma. This daydreaming—well, it's like the séances she goes to. Thelma doesn't really believe in them and she hasn't anybody dead she'd like to communicate with. It's just she wants to be different, exciting, ah, you know, don't you, Ralph?"

"I suppose so."

"I've never talked about my wife like this before," Harry said solemnly. "I hope you won't think I'm being disloyal."

"Of course not."

"The séances, they're new, a neighbor of ours got her interested. But the daydreaming started when she was a girl and she's never managed to get over it. It makes up for some of the things that are missing from her life, romance and excitement. I try to provide them but I'm afraid I'm not the type who—put it this way: I sell pills. That's not very glamorous, I guess. Thelma makes up for it by daydreaming a little."

Or a lot, Turee added silently. "You don't think daydreaming can be dangerous?"

"Not to Thelma and me. How could it?"

"A prolonged dream can become mixed up with reality."

"Now, look here, Ralph, you have this tendency to be critical. I know you mean well, but it's not always wise. Thelma and I are perfectly happy as we are. If daydreams make up for certain inadequacies in her life . . ."

"You're contradicting yourself."

"All *right,*" Harry said, with the first sign of irritability he'd shown all evening. "That's my business. I can contradict myself to hell and gone if I feel like it."

"Certainly. Do that."

Harry lit a cigarette before he spoke again, in a softer tone. "You're smart, Ralph, you're deep, you know a lot of things me and the other fellows don't on account of your advanced education and so on. Only . . ."

"Only what?"

"Just don't start analyzing Thelma. I love her the way she is. Let her have her dreams."

"She's welcome to them, as far as I'm concerned."

"My marriage is the most wonderful thing that ever happened to me. I wouldn't do anything in the world to undermine the relationship between Thelma and me."

"You won't have to," Turee said, but the noise of the engine and the sound of the water below the cliffs submerged his words. He didn't try to dredge them up. Well, that's that, he thought. Harry wants to stay on cloud seven. Let him.

They covered the remaining miles, not in silence, since Harry had begun to whistle very cheerfully, but at least without conversation. Turee shut his ears to the whistling and busied himself sorting out the various images of Thelma that had flashed across his mind throughout the night.

First there was, of course, the Harry's-wife Thelma, a short, placid, pleasant-looking woman in her early thirties. An excellent cook and skillful housekeeper, she seemed to have few interests outside the small red-brick house she and Harry had bought in Weston. Turee had always found her a little on the dull side since she seldom made any observations or remarks of her own, but instead, chimed in her agreement with Harry, in a kind of wifely echolalia: *Harry's perfectly right—as Harry was saying only yesterday—Harry told me and I agree that* . . . She appeared, on the surface, to be a woman unwilling to make any decisions by herself, and incapable of originating any plans or ideas. Even her recent addiction to séances, and the ensuing psychic feelings, had been instigated by a neighbor.

But Turee's mind was getting ahead of itself, because the séances belonged more properly in the second picture of Thelma, Thelma the daydreamer, who fed her mediocrity with meaty chunks of dreams until it was fat beyond her own recognition. Under this system of mental dietetics Thelma became a woman equipped with great psychic powers, as well as a femme fatale with whom men fell hopelessly in love. It was girl stuff, this daydreaming, and Thelma was no girl. Perhaps she was no daydreamer either; the possibility occurred to Turee that Harry might have invented the whole thing to protect himself from the truth, that Ron Galloway actually was in love with Thelma.

This led to the third picture, blurred and more distorted yet somehow more real than either of the others, of Thelma, the woman who wanted a child, and with single-minded determination and not a trace of moral misgiving, had gone ahead and found the means to conceive one.

Harry had stopped whistling and was peering out of the window for the turnoff to the lodge.

"Why do you feel," Turee said suddenly, "that if I start to 'analyze' Thelma, as you call it, something will happen to your marriage?"

"I don't feel that."

"It was implied."

"Oh, Ralph," Harry said with sadness, "don't. Don't go on. Some things are better left alone. Analyze your students, if you like, or your family, anyone else but Thelma. Perhaps she isn't entirely happy, but I'm doing my best to change that. There are certain factors involved that I won't go into."

"She wants a child."

Harry looked surprised. "How did you know?"

"She told me."

"Just tonight? On the phone?"

"Yes."

"Oh, then that's what upset her. She must have gone to sleep and been awakened by another of her nightmares. She's had quite a few of them this spring. She dreams she's borne a baby, only something happens to it, it's deformed, or it gets sick and dies; once it was kidnapped by a Chinaman. She'd been to the laundry to pick up my shirts that day, that's how the Chinaman got into it, I guess . . . I haven't told Thelma yet, I want it to be a surprise, but I've visited two adoption agencies this week, making inquiries . . . The turnoff should be along here some place."

The turnoff was months ago, Turee thought. *You missed it, Harry.*

The lodge had been built by Galloway partly as a wedding present to Esther and partly as a place to hide out in until the scandal of his divorce from his first wife had blown over. It turned out not as a hideaway but as a showplace the natives around the bay, all the way from Penetanguishene to Tobermory, came to admire and criticize. The structure was, in fact, too elaborate for its setting and its function. The lower story had been built of native stone and the second story was in English half-timbered style, with a shake roof angled sharply to shed the heavy snow that fell during the long winters.

The caretaker's quarters over the garage, which was an exact miniature of the house proper, were inhabited from spring to fall by an elderly, morose ex-mechanic named MacGregor. Theoretically, MacGregor's job was to keep the house and ground tidy, the woodboxes filled and the plumbing in order. In actuality, he spent most of his time down in the boathouse fussing over Galloway's Estron, a diesel-powered launch.

MacGregor and only MacGregor operated the boat. He did not insist on this prerogative, he merely let it be understood that the Estron was high-spirited and temperamental, and, like any such woman, needed a strong and knowing hand if she were to avoid the disastrous impulses of her nature.

No one, not even his wife, knew why Galloway had bought the boat. Galloway hated and feared the water, the slightest swell made him seasick, and he had no talent for or interest in the Estron's mechanical aspects. When MacGregor was at the wheel, Galloway sat up front beside him, his fists clenched, his eyes moving uneasily in their sockets so that they seemed to be separately afloat, responding to every wave. When the trip was over and he was back on dry land, he always looked pale but exhilarated, as if he had proved himself by conquering an ancient enemy.

MacGregor's quarters were dark. When there was a weekend party going on he kept aloof, disdaining what he called the shenanigans, and appearing only when Galloway and his guests wanted to use the boat.

Turee parked his car between two jack pines and the two men began walking toward the lodge, single file and in step, like a pair of convicts chained together by invisible irons. Only one light was burning, in the main room downstairs, and the fire in the grate was barely alive.

Hepburn had gone to sleep in the red leather lounging chair, a book on his lap. He woke up at the sound of the front door opening, squinted across the room and said crossly, "About time somebody showed up. I feel as if I've been conducting a one-man wake."

Turee raised a sardonic eyebrow. "Maybe you have."

"No luck finding Ron?"

"He's not at home. We called Esther and she hasn't seen him or heard from him and doesn't seem to care one way or another. Then we talked to Thelma." He shot a glance at

Harry to see if he would react to the name, but Harry was standing in front of the dying fire, his back to the room. "Thelma says Ron came by to pick up Harry, they had a drink together and some talk and then Ron left, presumably to come up here."

It was merely the skeleton of the truth. Only an expert could add the flesh and blood and muscle and all the vital organs that would make it a whole, borrowing a little here, a little there, from Thelma, from Harry, from Ron, from Esther, from all the other people who had affected all these people. A truth is as complicated as a man. Constructing and articulating a skeleton is not enough. It must be made to live.

So now what, Turee thought. What do I do now?

Hepburn provided a temporary answer. "You fellows want a drink?"

Harry had turned from the fire and picked up a magazine from the drum table. The magazine was an old *Maclean's* left over from the last time the lodge had been occupied, October of the previous year. The sight of the date sent a spasm of pain across Harry's eyes. *Last year,* he thought. *Last year at this time I was happy. I owned the world. Only last year . . .*

On a sudden impulse he folded the magazine and threw it with vicious accuracy into the center of the fire. It began to smolder.

"Now what the hell did you do that for?" Hepburn said.

"I don't know."

"There was an article in it I wanted to read."

"Sorry." The magazine had caught fire. Harry watched it burn with a kind of bitter satisfaction. Last year was over. "It's late. I'm tired. I'd better be going to bed."

"I've just made you a drink."

"I don't want it."

"You need it, Harry-boy."

"No thanks. It's been a long day. Good night."

"Take it easy, Harry-boy."

"Oh yes. Sure."

He dragged himself upstairs, leaning heavily on the banister as if his legs had withered. A minute later Turee heard the dropping of shoes, the squeak of springs, a long sigh.

Hepburn handed Turee his drink. "What's the matter with him, anyway?"

"What he said. A long day."

"Baloney. I've never seen Harry tired in my life."

"Now you have."

"There must be a reason. Something's up with Thelma, maybe?"

"Maybe."

"Thelma's a funny girl, if you ask me."

"I don't have to ask you," Turee said, staring gloomily into the fire, trying to imagine what Thelma was doing right now. Planning? Weeping? Having second and third thoughts, or sleeping peacefully in the conviction that she'd been absolutely right the first time? It was impossible to tell.

"But I guess all women are."

"Not all. Nancy's different." Turee believed this, and would continue to believe it until the next time he and his wife had a misunderstanding.

"You're prejudiced." Hepburn finished his drink and laid his empty glass decisively on the stone mantel. "Well, anyway, thank God I'm not married. On which cheerful note I shall depart."

"Go ahead. I'll turn out the lights."

"Perhaps you'd better leave a couple of them on in case Ron . . ."

"Oh. All right."

"Goodnight, Ralph."

"Goodnight."

Hepburn hesitated, stroking his chin. He was already beginning to need a shave, his eyes were red from too little sleeping and too much drinking, and his flannel shirt was dirty and lacking a button.

Why, he looks like a bum, Turee thought. Maybe he is. Maybe they all are, and this is no place for me. I should be home with my family, not up here pretending to be like the rest of them.

"Go to bed and get some sleep," he said roughly, irritated by his own thoughts. "God, what a night this has been."

"It's not finished."

"Well, finish it."

"Okay, but don't go into one of your famous grouches. That's not going to help. We're all in this together."

5

THE FOLLOWING MORNING, a few minutes after eight o'clock, Turee was awakened by the heavy pounding of the lion's-head knocker on the front door and the simultaneous ringing of the old cowbell that served as a mess call. Making little noises of distress, he reached for his shoes and put them on. This was all the dressing he had to do because he had, like the others, slept in his clothes. It was part of the tradition of these weekends at the lodge, originated many years before by Harry Bream. ("Makes me feel sporty," Harry had said. "Roughing it and all that.")

Feeling somewhat less than sporty, Turee stepped out into the hall, where he met Winslow, wild-eyed and trembling, his back pressed against the wall.

"My God," Winslow croaked. "I'm dying. Dying."

"There's some bromo in the bathroom."

"My God. That bell. Tell it to stop. My ears . . ."

"Pull yourself together."

"I'm dying," Winslow said again and slid down the wall like a puppet whose strings had broken.

Turee stepped fastidiously around him and went on down the staircase. The encounter had done nothing to dispel the feeling he'd had the previous evening, that he didn't belong in this place, with these people. Though they were old friends, they seemed, under stress, to have become strangers, and their ways of living—or, in Winslow's case, dying—were alien to him. As he walked down the stairs the air from the room below rose up and struck his nostrils, and it seemed to him subtly poisonous, smelling of stale drinks and stale dreams.

He drew back the heavy wooden bolt on the front door and opened it, half expecting to see Ron.

During the early morning hours the wind had died down and the temperature had dropped. The ground was covered with hoarfrost glittering so whitely in the sun that, by contrast, Esther Galloway's skin looked very dark, as if she had quite suddenly and unseasonably acquired a tan.

She appeared to have dressed in a hurry and not for a trip. She was hatless, the shoes she wore were summer shoes without toes, and the Black Watch plaid coat she had clutched around her was one Turee remembered from a long way back. Esther always made such a point of elegance that it was a shock to see her looking quite ordinary, if not actually dowdy.

"Why, Esther."

"Hello, Ralph," she said crisply. "Surprise, surprise, eh?"

"Come in."

"I intend to."

He held the door open for her and she came inside, peeling off her gloves and agitating her head as if to shake the frost out of her hair.

"My ears ache. I drove with the windows open to help keep me awake. Silly, I guess." She laid her gloves on the mantel between two empty glasses left over from the night before. Then she picked up one of the glasses and sniffed with distaste. "Gin. When will Billy Winslow ever learn?"

"That's a difficult question."

"Did you have a nice party?"

"Not very."

"Ron—he's not here, of course?"

"No."

"No word at all?"

"None."

"Damn his eyes."

Some time during the early morning the fire had gone out, and the room was so cold that Esther's breath came out in little clouds of mist like smoke from a dragon's mouth.

Turee thought it suited her mood admirably.

"Damn his beady little eyes," she said. "All right, start making excuses for him, as usual, why don't you?"

Turee didn't answer because he was afraid of saying the wrong thing and there seemed no possible right thing.

"The way you fellows stick together, it's a scream really."

"Sit down, Esther, and I'll go and put on some coffee."

"Don't bother."

"It's no bo—"

"MacGregor's coming over in a minute to set the fires and make some breakfast." She turned and looked carefully around the room, one nostril curled very slightly. "The place needs an airing. It smells."

"I hadn't noticed." He had, though.

"I didn't expect him to be here, of course. I don't even know why I came except that I couldn't go back to sleep after you called last night, and I hate waiting, waiting and doing nothing. So I drove up here. I don't know why," she repeated. "It just seemed a good idea at the time. Now that I'm here I realize there's nothing I can do, is there? Except possibly help nurse a few hangovers. How's yours?"

"I don't have one," he said coldly.

"It couldn't have been a very good party, then."

"I said it wasn't."

"You could have another one today. Perhaps I'll even be invited to join in for once?"

"It's your house."

"All right, I'll invite myself. We'll all sit around and be jolly until His Nibs decides to reappear."

"You think it's that simple?"

She turned and addressed him very slowly and distinctly, as if she were talking to someone quite deaf or stupid. "Ron has complete identification papers in his wallet and his car registration fastened to the steering wheel. If there had been any accident I would have been notified. Isn't that correct?"

"I suppose it is."

"There's no supposing about it, surely. When an accident happens, it's reported immediately. That's the law."

It hadn't seemed to occur to her, and Turee didn't mention it, that laws could be broken.

Sounds of rattling and crashing from the kitchen indicated that MacGregor was at work making breakfast. This was not part of his regular duties, and Turee knew from past experience that MacGregor would make himself as objectionable as possible; the coffee would be like bitter mud, the bacon burned and the eggs unrecognizable except for bits of broken eggshell that would crunch between the teeth like ground glass.

"MacGregor's in a sour mood," Turee said lightly. "We'll probably all be poisoned."

"At this particular moment I wouldn't care."

"Esther, for Pete's sake. . ."

"Oh, I know—you think I'm a drag and a droop. You think I always go around with a long face, spoiling for a fight."

"I don't . . ."

"You're Ron's friend, naturally you're on his side. I have to admit, I guess, that Ron makes a pretty good friend. But he's a lousy husband."

"Spare me the details."

"I wasn't going into details," she said flatly. "I was just about to make a generalization."

"Go ahead."

"Oh, I know you loathe generalizations, Ralph. You prefer intimate statistics like how many tons of mackerel were shipped last month from Newfoundland."

Turee's smile was wan. "Let's have the generalization."

"All right. Some men just shouldn't get married, they have nothing to give to a woman, not even the time of day. Oh, they can bring her an expensive diamond watch so she can tell the time of day for herself, but that's not *sharing* anything."

She sat down on the leather hassock in front of the unlit fire as if the sudden release of emotions had exhausted her, like a blood-letting. "I wanted very much to come up here with Ron this weekend. Not that I'm particularly keen on fishing or even outdoor life, but I thought it would be fun to do the cooking and eat in front of the fireplace and take walks in the woods with Ron and the two boys. I asked him if I could come along and he didn't even take me seriously, the whole idea was so incredible to him."

She paused to take a long breath. "Why, the boys hardly know this place. They've only been here three times. Ron keeps making excuses—the boys might fall over the cliff, they might get bitten by a snake, they might drown, etcetera. But the real excuse he never mentions—the boys might interfere with him, they might want something from him that can't be bought with money, they might demand two or three ounces of Ron's very own self. They might even take a bite of his precious hide, not knowing, as I do, that it's quite unpalatable and indigestible."

"Esther . . ."

"That's all. I've finished."

"I don't mean to shut you up."

"You do, of course. But it's nice of you, anyway, to say you don't. I blab, don't I? But not to everybody. I wouldn't dream of saying any of these things to Billy Winslow or Joe Hepburn or even to Harry. They're a pretty stupid lot."

Turee was inclined to agree but he didn't care to encourage her in a new subject. He said, "You need some hot food and coffee, Esther. I'll go and see how MacGregor is getting along."

MacGregor was getting along exactly as Turee had anticipated. The bacon was already burned, the eggs were having convulsions in the skillet, and the odor of coffee was sharp as acid. MacGregor, wearing a chef's apron over his grease-stained overalls, was trying to sedate the eggs with liberal doses of salt and pepper.

"I'll take over," Turee said.

"What say, sir?"

"I'll carry on from here. You go and set the fire in the main room."

"Things got a mite burned," MacGregor said with satisfaction, as he removed the apron and handed it to Turee. "It's the will of the Lord."

"It's a funny thing that whenever the Lord picks something to be burned He chooses you as His instrument."

"Aye, sir, it's peculiar." He headed for the main room, whistling cheerfully through the gap between his two remaining front teeth. He had scored a victory, not just a personal victory, but one on behalf of all employees over all employers, and while Turee was not exactly an employer, still he was lined up on the same side. That was good enough. Let the bastard eat burned bacon. It was the will of the Lord.

After breakfast they sat in front of the pinewood fire MacGregor had built and drank the bitter coffee out of heavy stoneware mugs. Food and warmth had improved the situation. The pinched look around Esther's mouth and nostrils disappeared, and the uneasy little animals that Turee had felt moving around in his stomach were temporarily placated.

There was no sound at all from the upper rooms. Either Billy Winslow had gone back to sleep, or else his own prediction had been accurate and he had died. In either case, Turee didn't much care at the moment. The heat and color and movement of the flames held him in a kind of pleasant stupor. He listened to Esther talking the way one listens to background music, recognizing the songs but without paying any real attention. Esther's songs were about her two boys, Marv and Greg, and their latest pranks, and such was Turee's state of mind that he was able to listen without even wanting to cap her stories with stories about his own children.

". . . are you paying attention, Ralph?"

"Eh? Oh, certainly, certainly."

"Well, don't you think I'm right?"

"Absolutely." This was safe enough. Every woman wanted to be told she was absolutely right, especially if she had some doubt of it.

"Well, she got quite unpleasant about it. She said I shouldn't spank either of them, no matter what they did. She said I shouldn't even *threaten* to spank them, that it would destroy their confidence in me, and that I was simply indulging my own anger. Now I ask you, how can you bring up two normal, lively boys without a spanking now and then?"

"I wouldn't know. I have four girls."

"That's a different matter. Girls are more—well, you can *reason* with them."

Turee was extremely surprised to learn this. "You can, eh?"

"Besides, she's got her nerve telling me how to bring up my children when she doesn't even have any of her own." Esther paused long enough to take a sip of coffee. "It's funny about that."

"About what?"

"She's so crazy about children," Esther said, "why doesn't she have some of her own?"

"Who?"

"The *who* we've been talking about."

"I must have missed the name."

"Thelma. She's so crazy about children, it's funny she doesn't have any of her own."

Turee rose and went over to the fire and kicked one of the logs with his foot. The pleasant stupor had vanished; the background music had turned into a loud cacophonous modern symphony, and he was compelled to listen to it carefully, to make sense out of it, distinguish the parts and players—Harry moaning on the trombone, Esther nagging at the drums, Thelma crowing through the clarinet, Ron off-stage with a silver whistle waiting for his cue. And the conductor out to lunch.

"After all, she's still young and healthy," Esther said. "Harry makes a decent salary, and he's just as fond of children as she is, I think. Don't you agree?"

"I haven't given it much thought."

"Neither have I, really. But it's not the kind of thing that needs much. I mean, the way he horses around with our two boys, you can tell he loves children. I think a baby would do them both a world of good."

A baby, yes, Turee thought. But not this baby. He remembered what Harry had said while they were driving back to the lodge from Wiarton: *"I haven't told Thelma yet, I want it to be a surprise, but I've visited two adoption agencies this week, making inquiries."*

"Well, don't you agree, Ralph? That's what they need, a baby?"

"Yes. For heaven's sake, *yes*."

Esther looked at him in surprise. "What's gotten into you all of a sudden? Did I say something wrong?"

"No. I just consider it a subject that's none of my business."

"And none of mine either, is that what you're implying?"

Her face had hardened. "Very well, let's drop it. I don't like Thelma much anyway, if you want the truth."

"I've gathered that."

"Am I so obvious?"

"Obvious enough."

"Well, do you?"

"Do I what?"

"Like Thelma."

"I don't like anybody this morning," Turee said with an attempt at lightness. "Not even myself."

Esther smiled without humor. "We're in the same boat, then . . . Listen, do you hear a car?"

"No."

"I'm sure I heard a car." She hurried to the front door, pulling her plaid coat around her in anticipation of the cold air. "Maybe it's Ron. I'm *sure* it's Ron."

In spite of all the things she'd said about him she sounded excited and eager at the prospect of seeing him. Turee followed her outside. He could hear the car now quite plainly, and a moment later it came into sight, winding up the driveway between the spruce trees, leaving parallel black tracks in the frost.

It was a black and white car bearing the insignia of the Ontario Provincial Police on the front door. Esther turned, without a word, and went back into the lodge.

Turee waited while two uniformed policemen climbed ponderously out of the car and began walking toward him. *Well, this is it. Ron's been hurt. Or killed. They've come to tell us. This is it.*

The two policemen moved slowly, looking around at the property with the careful scrutiny of a pair of assessors. The older man was heavy-set and red-faced with a scar along the crease of his right cheek that gave him a false one-sided smile.

He spoke first. "Hello there. Is this where Mr. Ronald Galloway lives?"

"Yes," Turee said. The single word came out with difficulty. His contact with policemen had been limited to minor traffic tickets and he felt tongue-tied and uneasy, as if they had come to accuse him of a crime he had committed unawares.

"You're not Mr. Galloway, by any chance?"

"No. A guest."

"Mr. Galloway is here, then?"

"No. We—the other guests and myself—have been waiting for him since last night. I thought—that is, when I first saw you, I presumed you had some news of him."

"A missing report, if that's news. I'm Lieutenant Cavell and this is my colleague, Sergeant Newbridge. May I ask your name, sir?"

"Ralph Turee. I'm an associate professor at the University of Toronto." The words and the tone sounded snobbish and pretentious, as if he were deliberately attempting to lay a cloak of respectability over himself, like a child covering himself with a blanket and thinking he was well hidden. Yet the image irritated him. It seemed unfair to himself. He had committed no crime, he had nothing to hide, no reason to feel guilt.

Lieutenant Cavell's eyes narrowed, and the scar along his cheek deepened into a smile, as if he was quietly amused by such boyish antics as hiding under blankets. "Is that a fact, sir. Now suppose we go inside and talk a little about Mr. Galloway. Newbridge, you can look around out here."

"Yes sir," Newbridge said, but he appeared puzzled, as if he hadn't any idea what to look for or what to do if he found it.

Turee and Cavell went into the lodge. Esther had taken her place in front of the fire and was sitting with her legs crossed and her hands in her lap, looking poised and casual. Too casual. Turee suspected that she'd been hiding behind the door listening to the conversation.

She acknowledged the introduction to Cavell politely enough, but she didn't rise or offer her hand or even appear anxious to hear what he had to say.

It turned out to be very little. "I have only the barest facts. Less than an hour ago I received a radio message from the Toronto division that Mr. Galloway had been reported missing by his wife. I have the time and place he was last seen, the make, model of his car, and that's about it. I am not in charge of the case or anything like that. I was merely asked to check up at this end, see if he had arrived or anything had been heard from him."

"Nothing," Esther said brusquely. "Not a word."

"Well now it seems to me that if he's still on the road it will be an easy matter to spot him. Late model Cadillac convertibles aren't common in this neck of the woods, and if he had the top down in this weather, as I've been informed, he should stick out like a fire engine. If, on the other hand, he got tired and pulled into some motel for the night, we shouldn't have too much trouble there either. Motels aren't common in this area."

"Suppose he isn't in the area."

"Why should we suppose that, Mrs. Galloway? He intended to come up here, didn't he?"

"Intentions can change."

"Is he the unpredictable kind who might take a notion to go off on a trip somewhere?"

Esther shook her head. "No. At least, not in the past."

"Is he a heavy drinker?"

"He gets drunks sometimes, but it's a quiet thing with Ron. He simply goes to sleep."

"I hesitate to ask this, Mrs. Galloway, but it's my duty. Have you any reason to believe he was interested in another woman?"

Esther glanced briefly at Turee before she answered. "Absolutely none."

Her tone was so positive that it seemed to fluster Cavell. As if to cover his confusion with some activity, he removed from an inner pocket of his jacket a small brown notebook. "According to my information, Mr. Galloway was last seen by a Mrs. Bream who lives in Weston. Is she a friend of yours, Mrs. Galloway?"

"Her husband and mine have been friends since Upper Canada College. Ron went to Weston to pick up Harry, that's Mr. Bream, and bring him along to the lodge. Only Harry had an emergency call to make first, so he came on alone. He's upstairs now, still asleep. I can wake him up, if you like."

Turee made a grimace of protest, but if Esther noticed it she paid no attention.

"I don't think Harry can tell you any more than you already know," Turee said. "I suggest we let him sleep. He had a rough night."

Cavell raised his eyebrows. "Rough in what sense, Mr. Turee?"

I've got to learn to curb my tongue, Turee thought, *and not to volunteer any information. Eventually they'll find out everything, about Thelma and the baby and Ron, but it's not my business to bring it out.* He said cautiously, "We were up nearly all night attempting to track Ron down."

"We?"

"Harry Bream and I, and the other two guests, Bill Winslow and Joe Hepburn."

"And just what form did these attempts take?"

"Harry and I drove back to Wiarton and called Esther—Mrs. Galloway—on the chance that Ron hadn't left the house for some reason or other. She told us he had left so then we called Harry's wife. She said that Ron had turned up on schedule, stayed long enough for a drink and then set out again."

"Is that all?"

"Well, Thelma—Mrs. Bream—said Ron had complained of feeling ill. There's a possibility there, don't you think?"

"Such as?"

"Well, Ron takes his symptoms pretty seriously. He may have stopped off to see a doctor, he may even be in a hospital somewhere."

"He's as healthy as a horse," Esther said.

"Yes, but *he* doesn't think so."

"Besides, he's scared to death of hospitals. He had to be practically dragged to come and see me when the boys were born."

Cavell stared at her thoughtfully. "It seems to me you're not very willing to accept any theory, Mrs. Galloway."

"Willing, yes. Able, no. I know my husband quite thoroughly and none of the possibilities suggested so far has seemed plausible."

"Have you any theory of your own, Mrs. Galloway?"

"I might have."

"If you had," Cavell said dryly, "what would it be?"

"I think Ron may be trying to avoid me, for some reason."

It was so close to what Turee himself was thinking that he made a little sound of surprise, like a man who's just had his mind read.

Cavell said, "Why should your husband be trying to avoid you, Mrs. Galloway?"

"I don't—know." She flashed another sharp look at Turee as if she half suspected that he could supply the answer if he chose to.

Turee thought, *She's too damned bright for her own good. And too honest to hide it. No wonder she and Ron have some bad times.*

"You might," Esther added, to Cavell, "talk to Harry Bream."

"Why?"

"He and my husband are what you might call buddies." She put a sneer in the word. "If Ron has any secrets, Harry is his most likely confidant."

Turee made one more attempt to spare Harry the ordeal. "No more likely than I, surely, Esther?"

"Much more and you know it."

"All right then. I'll go and wake him up."

6

HARRY WAS STILL asleep, lying on his stomach and without a pillow, like a baby; and, as a baby will suck at things for comfort and security, so Harry had seized a corner of the blanket and had it pressed tightly against his mouth.

The night table beside the bed held an unlabeled bottle of red capsules and a nearly empty water glass.

"Harry? Hey. Harry."

He did not respond either to his name or the touch of Turee's hand on his shoulder. Turee leaned down and with great effort rolled him over on his back. Then he put his hand firmly under Harry's chin and moved his head from side to side several times until Harry's eyes opened.

"Don't do that," Harry said.

"Come on, wake up."

"It's cold."

"It's warmer downstairs. Get your shoes on. We have a visitor."

"Don't care." He closed his eyes again. "Don't care a damn."

"How many of those red capsules did you take?"

"Don't remember. Doesn't matter."

"It matters now." Turee put his hands under Harry's shoulders and forced him to a sitting position. Harry's head lolled back and forth as if his neck was broken.

"Why?" Harry said. "Why it matters?"

"There's a policeman downstairs, he wants to talk to you."

"Why?"

"About Ron. They're still trying to find Ron. Esther reported his absence to the police and then she drove on up here."

"Esther? Here?" He shook off Turee's hand and sat up by himself. His tone was more alert and his eyes had begun to focus properly. "Esther shouldn't have come here."

"Why not?"

"The place is a mess."

"So?"

"We'll have to clean it up a bit. Esther hates a mess."

Like the other fellows, Harry stood in considerable awe of Esther. It was not that she was unpleasant to them, but she had a subtle way of always being right that reduced them to a state of self-doubt and confusion. She could, without saying a word, walk through a room and indicate, merely by her posture and a faintly lifted eyebrow, that there were cobwebs on the rafters and dust under the rugs. And sure enough, if anyone took the trouble to look, the cobwebs would be there, and so would the dust.

Harry peered down at his wristwatch. "It's not even nine o'clock."

"I know."

"Esther—she must have stayed up all night."

"Practically."

"Why did she decide to come here?"

"To check up on Ron for herself."

"She doesn't trust us, I guess."

"Not very much."

"What does she think we're doing, covering up for him?"

"Maybe."

"Covering up what, I'd like to know. Does she think we bring *women* up here or something?"

"Could be."

"My God, that's a laugh."

"Not to her, it isn't."

"Esther's a funny girl. When I compare her with Thelma, for instance—why that's the last thing in the world Thelma would suspect. Thelma *likes* me to go away and have a good time. There isn't a selfish bone in her body."

Turee felt like gagging but he managed to say quite calmly, "Hurry up and get ready."

"All right." Harry swung his legs over the side of the bed and began putting on his shoes. "A policeman, eh?"

"Yes."

"What kind?"

"One of the Provincial Police on duty in this area. He got the report from Toronto by radio and was asked to check up."

"And you say Esther reported it?"

"Yes."

"Funny, when you talked to her last night she wasn't worried at all, wouldn't hear of bringing in the police."

Turee, too, had noticed the discrepancy but had ascribed it merely to the unpredictability of women.

Harry stood up, ran a comb through his hair, and buttoned the collar of his flannel shirt. "I ought to shave, Esther being here and all that."

"There isn't time."

"Thelma wouldn't like it if she . . ."

"Thelma's not here."

"Well, all right."

"And Harry, listen, this inspector, he seems pretty cagey. Watch yourself."

"How do you mean?" Harry asked.

"Don't talk too much."

"About what?"

"About anything you and I discussed last night."

"We discussed a lot of things last night."

"You know what I'm referring to."

"But I don't. So help me, I don't."

"About Thelma—Ron's having a crush on her, I mean. Don't mention it."

Harry blinked. "Why should I? It's not true. I told you that last night. Thelma likes to daydream, to pretend things. I told you that last . . ."

"I know you told me."

"Well, don't you believe it?"

"Certainly, certainly," Turee said, trying to keep the irritation out of his voice. "But the Inspector might not. He doesn't know Thelma the way we do. So keep quiet about it, eh?"

"You never give me any damn credit for any damn sense. You'd think I was a moron."

"Everybody's a moron about something."

"Meaning?"

"No meaning, no meaning at all," Turee said and walked out of the room with Harry following along behind, taking short angry little steps.

Downstairs, Esther and the Inspector had apparently reached the end of their conversation. Cavell, an unlit pipe in his hand, was studying the rows of books in the bookshelves, while Esther stood with her back to the fire, watching him with silent intensity. She was smoking a cigarette, rapidly and furiously, as if she had a great many things that she wanted to say and couldn't, and was using the cigarette as a cork to bottle them up.

Turee introduced Harry and Cavell, and then he turned and said pointedly to Esther, "You and I can wait in the game room. The Inspector might want to talk to Harry alone."

Esther gave him a sharp look, but she made no verbal objection as he put his hand on her elbow and guided her out into the hall.

The game room, which was across the hall from the kitchen, contained ample proof that the fellows were not as enthusiastic about fishing as they were about certain other sports: a well-used poker table with ivory chips, a pinball machine, an elaborately carved billiard table with a dozen cues racked up on the knotty pine wall.

Esther perched on the side of the billiard table, her right leg swinging aggressively as if it wanted to kick at something or someone.

She said, "All right, let's have it."

"Have what?"

"The reason you spirited me away from Harry and the Inspector."

Turee smiled. "My dear Esther, no one spirited you away. You're too big a girl to be spirited away, for one thing."

"Don't go off on verbal maneuvers. Why were you so anxious to get rid of me?"

"I wasn't anxious. I simply thought it would be polite if you and I let the Inspector talk to Harry in private."

"Politeness. That was one reason?"

"Certainly."

"Now what are some others?"

"Others?"

"You always have an ulterior motive, Ralph, sometimes several of them. You remind me of a set of boxes the boys used to play with when they were younger—when you open the largest one, you find a smaller one, and inside that, still a smaller one, and so on."

"I'm not sure I follow you."

"Every time you give me a motive for doing something, I know there's another reason inside it, and yet another inside that one. Inside every box there's a motive."

"It can't go on ad infinitum. What's in the smallest box?"

"Your fat little ego."

Turee's laugh had a brittle note. "You make me sound extremely complicated."

"Or devious."

"I'll make you a promise, Esther. If I ever open that last box, I'll invite you over. Will you come?"

"With bells on," Esther said primly. "I wouldn't miss it for the world."

"Of course, I don't guarantee there'll be much of a surprise inside. Just one fat little ego." Turee could see that she was enjoying the game; he was even beginning to enjoy it himself. "What do you suppose it'll look like?"

"A kewpie doll. One of those tiny celluloid kewpie dolls you can buy in the dime store."

"That's not very flattering."

"Oh it is, really. Compared to what I think mine would look like. Or Ron's."

"What about Ron's?"

"Ron would never get to the last box. Or if he did, he'd never invite me over to see it, or anyone else. It would be strictly a private showing."

"I wish you could think more kindly of Ron."

"I wish I could, too," Esther said slowly. "I happen to love him."

MacGregor had laid a fire in the fireplace and the room by this time was so warm that the windows had steamed up. Turee had a childish impulse to go over and write his name in the steam, or print a message or draw a picture—a heart with an arrow piercing it, and underneath, ESTHER LOVES RON.

"I'm not very sensible," Esther said, in a detached manner. "I appear to be sometimes—very sensible and efficient and practical. Actually it's all a front. I'm a fool, and the worst kind, too, the kind that knows it, that sees ahead of time all the wrong things to do and does them anyway. I fell in love with Ron the first time I met him. I knew he had a wife and child. I knew he was spoiled by too much money and a terribly foolish set of parents, I knew our backgrounds and our tastes were completely different. I went after him anyway, tooth and nail. It was easy. Ron was a perfect setup. He still is."

"How do you mean that?"

"If I could do it, any woman could. Or can."

"Now, Esther, don't go . . ."

"Ron is a patsy. The perfect patsy."

"Your circumstances aren't quite the same as Dorothy's."

"Oh, they're different, all right. But are they any better?"

It was, perhaps, the opportune time to tell her everything he knew about Thelma and Ron, but Turee had neither the courage nor the desire, nor even all the facts. It seemed to him a fateful piece of irony that Esther should now find herself in the same position into which she had forced another woman a long time ago. Somebody would have to tell her. Who, he wondered, had told Dorothy?

Turee had not seen Ron's first wife, Dorothy, for a number of years. Dorothy was a wispy blonde, the daughter of a furniture manufacturer, and as badly spoiled in her own way as Ron was in his. A confirmed hypochondriac before she was out of her teens, by the time she married, at twenty-one, she had become the prey of every quack in the city. Her infrequent outings with her husband, to concerts or plays or dinner parties, were always interrupted between acts, during intermission or before dessert, by sharp and mysterious pains that sent her home, usually alone. Her one pregnancy, spent largely in bed, had resulted, to everyone's surprise, especially Dorothy's, in a perfectly normal girl child. The girl was raised from the beginning by a governess, so that Dorothy was left free to concentrate on her multitude of symptoms. If Ron had been, as Esther claimed, the perfect setup, it was, without doubt, largely due to Dorothy.

The last news Turee had had of Dorothy was from Harry, who went to see her once or twice a year for old times' sake. Harry reported that she was living in her mother's town house on the north side, with two special nurses in attendance, a recluse before she was forty. She had confided to Harry, whom she had always liked, perhaps because of his interest in drugs and medicines, that she was suffering from an obscure malady of the bloodstream and would not last the year. She invited Harry to attend her funeral and Harry, ever one to oblige, had accepted the invitation.

Dorothy and Esther—they were poles apart, and Turee wondered how Ron could have married them both. Perhaps Dorothy's frailty had made him feel more masculine, but after a liberal dose of that, he married Esther as an antidote, someone he could lean on.

Esther said suddenly, "Would you like to play a game of billiards?"

"Not much."

"Nor I, really. I just thought it would help pass the time. I guess I shouldn't have come up here. There's nothing I can do, is there?"

"Now that the police are in charge we'd better let them handle everything. A bunch of amateurs milling around won't help."

"Ah, yes, the jolly old police."

"Come here a minute." Turee took his handkerchief and rubbed some of the steam off one of the windows. Outside, the younger policeman, Newbridge, was examining the tire tracks on the driveway. "Look out there."

Esther looked. "Well?"

"The police know what they're doing."

"Do they?" She turned from the window. "They can examine all the tire tracks to hell and back, but they're not going to find Ron that way."

"All right, be cynical," Turee said. "At least you had sense enough to call them in."

"That was sense?"

"Yes."

"Maybe you're right. But it wasn't mine."

"What do you mean?"

"I didn't call the police," Esther said. "I didn't call anyone."

7

THE INSTANT SHE put down the phone she knew she'd done something foolish. Not the call itself, that was necessary, but claiming to be Mrs. Galloway—that was the mistake. And yet, while she was talking, it had seemed so natural to pretend to be Ron's wife. "This is Mrs. Ronald Galloway"—the sound of it was exactly right.

After the phone call she went back upstairs to bed and to sleep, but in less than an hour she was awakened again by a bad dream. She could not remember the details of the dream, only that they had all been caught in a great flood, she and Ron and the baby and Harry, and they were being swept, screaming, out to sea. She awoke with the scream on her lips.

Her first thought was not of Ron or of Harry, but of the baby growing inside her. She pressed one hand gently to her stomach to calm the child in case it had been disturbed by the dream. Staring wide-eyed up at the ceiling she tried to imagine through her fingertips the child's contours, the tiny head, the curved neck, the curled-up little body. Thelma had worked in a doctor's office before she married Harry, and she knew quite well that the fetus at this early stage was quite hideous and bore almost no resemblance to a human baby. But when she pictured her own baby in her mind, it was beautiful, and perfectly formed and proportioned, like a tiny doll.

She kept her hand pressed to her stomach until she was satisfied that she'd felt a very faint movement, then she swung her feet over the side of the bed and stood up. Almost immediately a wave of nausea flooded over her. She opened her mouth and breathed deeply, watching herself in the bureau mirror and thinking how funny she looked and how glad she was that Harry wasn't there to see her, or to ask questions or give advice.

Throughout most of her life Thelma had suffered from a nagging self-consciousness about her appearance. She knew she was not pretty, and now that she was beginning to gain weight she looked almost dumpy. But Harry's unlimited devotion had given her both self-confidence and a sense of herself as a woman, so that the overall impression she presented was one of graciousness and femininity. Her friends spoke of her as "attractive," a term intended to obscure some of nature's mistakes. What justified the term in Thelma's case was the quality of her expression, which was warm and friendly and humorous. Children passing on the street smiled at her spontaneously, clerks in stores usually gave her special attention, and strangers she met at bus stops confided in her the most intimate details of their lives, mainly because Thelma looked at them as if she were really interested. Occasionally she was. But most of the time her expression was automatic and had nothing to do with how or what she was feeling. Turee called it "Thelma's wan smile," Harry called it her "sweet look," Ron had never noticed it.

When the nausea had passed, Thelma put on her Sunday housecoat and combed her long hair carefully and tied it back with a ribbon to match the housecoat. Her eyes were still swollen from last night's weeping, and the lids were transparent and tinged with purple like the skin of an onion. She bathed them in cold water and applied witchhazel pads before going out to the back veranda to pick up the milk and the Sunday paper.

It was a beautiful spring day, alive with promises. Her neighbor, a widow named Mrs. Malverson, was already out in the garden cultivating her daffodils which had just come into bloom.

"Hi there, Thelma."

"Good morning, Mrs. Malverson."

"This is a day, isn't it? Isn't this a day, though?"

"It's lovely, yes."

"You don't look so good, dear."

"I'm fine." A minute ago it had been true, but now the stab of the sharp sunlight hurt her eyes and its warmth made her feel feverish. She hugged the cold milk bottle to her breast.

"I bet you're tired this morning. I saw your lights on till all hours last night."

That snoop, Thelma thought, that nasty old snoop. But she couldn't have seen Ron here—she always goes to the movies on Saturday night. "I couldn't sleep."

"Couldn't sleep, my land, you should have asked your husband for some pills. The ones he gave me last month for my neuralgia, they were a real blessing."

"My husband went up north, fishing."

"Did he now. Well, he couldn't have picked nicer weather. I suppose you've noticed my early daffodils?"

"You showed them to me yesterday."

"Mulching, that's the secret. You and your husband should start a compost heap. How long's he going to be away?"

"I'm not sure."

Mrs. Malverson pushed back her straw gardening hat and wiped the perspiration off her forehead with her canvas glove. The gesture left a streak of dirt. "I'll tell you what. Let's go to church."

"No, thank you just the same. I don't feel . . ."

"You should come and get better acquainted at our little church. Today we're having a very special service. Our leader is going to read the flowers."

"Read the *flowers*?"

Mrs. Malverson threw back her head and laughed. "Spoken like a true unbeliever, curl of the lip and all. Well, I don't mind. I was an unbeliever once myself. I said those very words exactly the way you just said them. Reads the *flowers,* I said, just like that. Nevertheless, that's what our leader does. He reads the flowers that we bring, and in every flower there is a message from someone dear to us who is far away."

Thelma stood nervous and indecisive, still clutching the Sunday paper and the milk bottle, which was beginning to weigh a ton. Yet she could not seem to drag herself away. Mrs. Malverson's tongue and eye held her as securely as a lepidopterist's pin holds a moth.

"Thelma," Mrs. Malverson said softly, "you've changed. What's happened to you?"

"Nothing."

"I see such sorrow in you lately. Have you lost touch with someone dear to you?"

Thelma stared at her, pale and silent.

"Ah, that's it. You've lost touch with someone dear to you and now you want a message, don't you? Yes, I can see you badly want a message. Well, that's easy. Come to church with me and bring a flower to be read."

"No, I really . . ."

"Fresh, the flower must be fresh, and if you bring its root too, smelling of God's earth, so much the better. Often the messages are stronger when the root is attached. This person you want a message from, is it a woman?"

"No."

"A man, then. A man you have lost touch with. No, Thelma, I'm not prying. I only need to find out one other detail, for the color of the flower you bring will depend on it."

"Color?"

"The color's important. If he is alive, you will take a red flower, bright as blood. If he is what you call dead—we hate to use that term, it's so misleading—but if he is dead, you will take a white flower."

Thelma closed her eyes and began to sway. She could feel the milk bottle slipping out of her hands, she could hear the crash of glass and Mrs. Malverson's cry of dismay, but she was powerless to respond. *If he is what you call dead—we hate to use that term—dead . . .*

"My goodness, I hope I didn't say anything to upset you." Mrs. Malverson lifted her skirt, stepped over the tiny boxwood hedge that divided the two properties, crossed the driveway, and started up the steps of Thelma's back veranda. "Here, let me help you clean up that mess."

"No!"

"Well, it's the least I can do, seeing I . . ."

"Go away. Just go away."

"Well, my goodness, you fly off the handle at anything these days. A body might think you were pregnant."

"Shut up and leave me alone!"

"Well. Well," Mrs. Malverson said and retreated to her own yard, her straw hat bouncing angrily as she moved. This was the thanks you got for trying to bring a little joy into someone's life.

Ignoring the mess on the veranda, Thelma went back into the house and sat down at the kitchen table. A pair of curious houseflies chased each other in and out of the open window and Thelma watched them, thinking, Harry must put on the screens this week . . .

She had been doing this quite often lately, considering the future as if it were going to be a repetition of the present, thinking of little things that should be done around the house or yard, making tentative plans for the Decoration Day weekend. She knew better. She knew that Harry and she weren't going to live in this house any longer; whoever put the screens on for the summer, it would not be Harry. She knew, too, that there were other, greater changes waiting for her around the next corner of time. She could not avoid this corner, every tick of the clock brought her inexorably closer to it, no matter how tenaciously a part of her mind tried to stay on a secure day-to-day basis.

Harry will . . .

No, Harry will not, she thought. I must get used to the idea we won't be here. Some stranger will be putting on the screens, at the request of his wife, also a stranger. They will live in our house, these two strangers, and pretty soon it will be theirs entirely. Well, I mustn't get sentimental about it. I've never liked the place much. It's the same as thousands of other houses in Ontario, a square red-brick box. I want to live in a house without stairs, a climate without winter.

The telephone began to ring in the dining room. She was sure it was Harry calling but she was not sure enough to keep from answering it.

"Hello?"

"Thelma, is that you, honey?"

"Yes."

"Are you feeling all right again?"

"Yes."

"Listen, dear, I'm phoning from Wiarton. Ron hasn't shown up yet. I don't suppose you've had any news at that end?"

"No."

"Well, don't worry, everything will turn out right."

"Will it," Thelma said, and hung up.

A minute later the phone began ringing again. Thelma turned her back on it. As she walked toward the kitchen she counted each ring deliberately, like a defiant child counting the number of times she is called to supper: "Thelma. Thelma? Thelma! Thelma . . ."

Long after the final ring, the sharp shrill sound kept echoing in her ears, stirring up memories.

"Thelma? You hear me, Thelma?"

Oh yes, Aunt May, I hear you. Everyone in the city can hear you.

"You come in this house right away and finish up these dishes."

No, Aunt May.

"Hiding again, aren't you, pretending you don't hear me, well, you don't fool me. Thelma!"

I can fool you any time.

"Sneaky, that's what you are, a born sneak. If you don't march right in this house, I'm gonna write your ma and tell her I can't look after you. The Lord knows you're eating me out of house and home, and not a penny does she send for your keep. We'll all end up in the poorhouse, how would you like that, Miss Royalty too good to do dishes?"

If you end up in the poorhouse I'll come and visit you dressed in mink and diamonds.

"Thelma Schaefer, where are you hiding?"

Under the porch. You could reach out and touch me. Do. I'll bite.

"That no-good sister of mine, what else would you expect from her but a no-good child. You answer me, you hear?"

Aunt May had been dead for years, but every shrill sound reminded Thelma of her, an alarm clock, a telephone, a doorbell. Each was the voice of authority, the call to duty: Come in and do the dishes. Get up and go to work. Answer the phone and talk to Harry.

The child hiding under the porch was imprisoned forever within Thelma. Aunt May's voice still soured the sweetest melody, and the bile green of her nature had colored the universe.

Thelma began to make breakfast, moving around the kitchen with a kind of grim efficiency, as if she had in some way been challenged to prove her worth.

Aunt May was wrong, she thought. I won't end up in the poorhouse. There's Ron's money, a lot of money. My baby will have security and love. There'll be no Aunt May for him, no poverty, no fear. He'll have a house without stairs, a climate without winter, no running nose for him from fall to spring like the kids around here. He'll have the best care, the best clothes, the best schools . . .

She ate her breakfast as if in a dream, not enjoying it, not even tasting it, eating for the sake of the baby which needed nourishment. After she had finished, she took her coffee into the parlor at the front of the house.

The room was cool and dark, the shades still drawn from the previous night when she had waited there listening for the sound of Ron's car on the driveway. It was spring now, but the parlor still smelled of winter, of the long weeks of unopened windows and artificial heat, a close dusty smell which, even into autumn, never quite disappeared.

Thelma pulled up the shades and opened two of the windows. Summer sounds drifted in, the children from down the street fighting over a bicycle, the whirr of roller skates, the pounding of a hammer. The young married man who lived across the road was busy removing his storm windows while his wife watched him with great pride as if he were performing some unusual feat. The sun had drawn everyone out of doors like a magnet, but because the spring was new and people were still a little self-conscious about being outside, idle, and bare-armed and bareheaded, they had to find excuses to stay out. Cars were being washed, screens painted, babies walked, lawns rolled, gossip exchanged.

And Thelma, watching, thought, I wonder how much each of them knows about me. When it all comes out in the papers—and it will, I must face that fact—when they find out, will they be surprised, or will they claim they suspected it all along because they'd often seen Ron's car here?

The telephone in the dining room began to ring again. She was positive this time that it was Harry, and she would have let the call go unanswered, except for the fact that the front windows were now open and the people across street could hear the phone ringing quite plainly. They knew she was at home, they'd seen her at the window, and they would wonder why she didn't answer. It was the kind of neighborhood, the kind of country, where little things like that didn't go unnoticed.

She hurried into the dining room and picked up the receiver, annoyed by Harry's persistence. "Hello."

"Is this the Bream residence?"

"Yes."

The woman's voice was low and soft, and self-consciously cultured. "Is Mr. Bream at home?"

"No. I'm his wife, Thelma Bream."

"This is Joyce Reynold calling, Mrs. Bream. You may recall we met two or three years ago, and of course I've known Harry for a long time. He's been very kind to my poor daughter, Dorothy. Do you expect him home soon?"

"I'm afraid not. But if there's anything I can do . . ."

"Sweet of you, my dear, but I'm not sure, I'm simply not sure. A very perplexing thing has happened. It happened last night, actually, but it seemed too late to call Harry and besides I wasn't sure what I was expected to do. I'm still not. You didn't receive a rather peculiar call from Ron Galloway last night?"

"No." Thelma took a deep breath. "How do you mean, peculiar?"

"Confused. Rambling. Those are Dorothy's words. You see, the call wasn't to me but to Dorothy. I was tucking her in bed for the night when the telephone rang and it was Ron wanting to talk to Dorothy. We haven't heard from him in years, and I assumed it must be important so I allowed Dorothy to talk to him. She'd had a good day and was feeling stronger than usual, and I like to let her have a bit of excitement when I'm certain no harm will come of it. I was wrong, of course. I should have realized the man was drunk or out of his mind. Dorothy's been in a frightful state ever since."

"How does Harry come into it, Mrs. Reynold?"

"He mentioned Harry several times, something about making amends and regretting what he'd done to Harry. Now obviously that doesn't make sense, does it? Ron would never do anything to Harry, the two have been thick as thieves ever since they were children. And why, after all these years, should Ron suddenly call Dorothy and get maudlin about his treatment of her?"

"I don't—know."

"The poor child has suffered enough. I thought perhaps if Harry were there and could come and talk to her it might calm her down a bit. She's always been fond of Harry, and she seems to think, from Ron's conversation, that Ron wanted her to see Harry."

"Why?"

"He seemed to believe he'd done something terrible. Has he?"

"No." The word was sharp and final.

"Have you seen him recently?"

"Yes."

"Did he seem quite normal to you?"

"Yes. Quite normal."

"How very puzzling. Surely a normal man doesn't suddenly call up a former wife he hasn't seen in years and tell her he wants to apologize before he leaves."

"Leaves?"

"He said he was going away. And when Dorothy asked him where, he said he couldn't tell her, it was an undiscovered country. According to Dorothy, it sounded as if he was quoting a line of poetry."

Thelma leaned back and closed her eyes. *The undiscover'd country, from whose bourn no traveller returns.*

"Mrs. Bream? Are you still there?"

"Yes." A reluctant whisper. When Aunt May called, Thelma could hide and pretend she hadn't heard. But this time there was no place to hide. "Yes, Mrs. Reynold, I'm here."

"Did Ron say anything to you or Harry about taking a trip?"

"No."

"I'm perplexed, I truly am. How inconsiderate of Ron to annoy people like this, and I shall tell him so the first chance I get. As a matter of fact, I tried to call his house a little while ago but no one answered. Do you suppose he's already left?"

"I don't know."

"Undiscovered country," Mrs. Reynold said. "Undiscovered country, *indeed.*"

"I must—I must go now, Mrs. Reynold."

"Of course. I'm sorry to have taken up so much of your time. And I do hope I haven't upset you in any way."

"I'll—I'll give Harry your message when he comes home."

"Thank you, child. I'm sure Harry will know what to do."

"Good-bye."

When she'd put down the telephone, she wiped her right hand carefully with a handkerchief, as if she had touched something dirty and had been contaminated. Then she rose and groped her way to the stairs. The child in her womb felt as heavy as stone.

She reached her room, exhausted, and fell across the bed on her stomach with her arms outstretched. *High school. The smell of books and dust, and oiled wood floors. Memory work today, class. It's your turn, Thelma. We had the first part of the soliloquy last week. No need to repeat. Start with "For who would bear . . ." Quiet, class, while Thelma recites.*

> *"For who would bear the whips and scorns of time,*
> *Th' oppressor's wrong, the proud man's contumely,*
> *The pangs of despis'd love, the law's delay,*
> *The insolence of office, and the spurns*
> *That patient merit of th' unworthy takes,*
> *When he himself might his quietus make*
> *With a bare bodkin? Who would these fardels bear,*
> *To grunt and sweat under a weary life . . ."*

Go on, Thelma.

No, I can't. I don't remember!

Go on, Thelma.

> *". . . But that the dread of something after death*
> *The undiscover'd country, from whose bourn*
> *No traveller returns . . ."*

Such beautiful language, the teacher said. Lovely, lovely. But do put a little more feeling into it, Thelma.

8

IT WAS TEN o'clock Sunday morning, and a woman unknown to any of the principals in the case was getting ready to go to church. Her name was Celia Roy, she lived alone on the outskirts of the small town of Thornbury on Georgian Bay. She was a widow with a pension and two married daughters and no hope of much more in this life.

She was the kind of woman to whom nothing extraordinary had ever happened. True, she'd seen people die, babies born, mistakes committed, tragedies enacted, sacrifices made, but this was all run-of-the-mill stuff to Celia. What she dreamed of, in her declining years, was winning a new car on a radio quiz program, or an all-expense trip to Hollywood in a slogan contest, or a thousand dollars for submitting the best recipe. She would have settled for a really good night at the church bingo on Thursday, but even that hadn't happened.

She put on her hat in front of the sideboard mirror. She'd worn the hat for three years and could have put it on properly in pitch darkness, but she stood in front of the mirror out of habit, not really seeing either the hat or herself under it. Her hands were trembling with excitement and fear. It was the Sabbath, she was on her way to church, and she'd done something wrong, perhaps quite wrong. What was more, she had no intention of telling anyone about it. The dog was dead. She'd buried him herself in the dark of night, and no one knew a thing about it.

She heard her daughter Mabel's old Ford wheeze up in front of the house and cough to a stop. Each time Celia heard this noise she expected it to be the car's last—it sounded exactly like old Mr. Thurston's death rattle—but each time, under Mabel's expert pumping and pounding and shouting, the car would miraculously come to life in every joint and pulsate vigorously as if to deny all charges of age and infirmity.

Mabel bounded in the front door. She was a lively young woman with a hearty laugh and a quick temper and little or no patience with people who slunk, as she called it, through life.

"Hi. Ready, Mom?"

"Just about," Celia said. "I look a fright. It's this hat. It's getting out of shape."

"Who isn't," Mabel said cheerfully. "I told you to get a new one for Easter."

"And what to use for money?"

"Speaking of money, I don't have a cent for the collection plate. John didn't get his check, this is the third time in a row it's been late." She saw her mother's purse lying on the wicker jardiniere and picked it up. "Mind if I borrow a quarter?"

Celia had turned quite white. "Stop. Wait."

"What's the matter with you?"

"I—I don't like other people opening my purse."

"You never objected before."

"Well, I am now. Give it here."

"Honestly, honestly, you'd think I was trying to steal from you or something."

"I want none of your lip. Give me that purse."

"I just don't like your attitude, like I was a thief or something. What's wrong with you anyway? You're shaking like a leaf."

"You show some respect, girl. Now give me . . ."

"All right. Here's your old purse. Catch."

Celia's reflexes were no longer quick enough to respond to the unexpected, and the purse landed at her feet, the clasp open, the contents strewn on the hooked rug: a lace handkerchief, a pencil, a tarnished silver compact, a creased snapshot of Mabel's two children, a worn calfskin change purse, a prayer book, a post card, an alligator wallet.

"Gee, I'm sorry," Mabel said. "Honestly, I thought you'd catch it. Here, I'll pick everything up for you."

But Celia was already on her knees, scooping up her things and stuffing them back into her purse with fierce determination.

"*Mom.*"

"Fresh. That's what you are. Fresh."

"I didn't know you had a wallet, Mom."

"There's lots you don't know, including how to behave to your elders."

"Where did you get it?"

"Someone gave it to me. As a gift."

"It looks like genuine alligator."

"So?"

"Mom. It don't make sense. Who would give you a genuine alligator wallet?"

"A man, a very rich man." Celia rose, clutching her purse to her chest. "Now that's all I can tell you. The rest is my business, and my business alone."

"You don't know any very rich man."

"I do, too."

"Where did you meet him?"

"On the road, just outside."

"Mom."

"It's the truth, so help me. I met him on the road."

"And he just came up and tipped his hat and said, madam, I'm a very rich man, here is my genuine alligator wallet. Mom."

"Stop saying *Mom* like that."

"Well, it don't make sense."

"What's more," Celia said loftily, "you use bad grammar. That's what comes of marrying beneath you. Well, I warned you. I said, he's a common laborer, he'll drag you down with him and you with a high school education . . ."

"Don't change the subject, Mom. I want to hear more about the very rich man. He intrigues me."

"And don't get ironical-sounding either. It so happens I'm telling the truth and I don't expect my own child to be ironical-sounding to me."

"What are you going to do when other people notice the wallet? Tell them the same story you told me?"

"Nobody else is going to notice it."

"How come?"

"I'm going to get rid of it, that's how come."

"Get *rid* of it! Mom, are you losing your mind? Someone gives you a genuine alligator wallet and now you say you're going to get rid of it. It's worth, well, ten dollars at least. And now you say you're going . . ."

"Stop it. Stop pestering me."

"But it just don't make sense, Mom. A real genuine alligator wallet and you want to get rid of it, I never heard anything so crazy."

They stared at each other across the room, Celia pale and grim, and her daughter red-faced and bewildered.

"I'll keep the money," Celia said finally.

"What money?"

"There's money in it."

"How much?"

"Nearly a hundred *dollars*."

"A hundred dollars?"

"Not quite. Nearly." Celia clung to the word as if it somehow provided a saving grace.

"Mom. Where did you get it?"

"I told you. The man gave it to me."

"When?"

"Last night."

"Why?"

"For Laddie. To pay for Laddie."

"What's Laddie got to do with it?"

"Don't you shout at me! I haven't done anything wrong!"

"Something happened to Laddie?"

"Yes."

"He's dead?"

"Yes."

"And you don't even sound sorry," Mabel said coldly. "You don't even sound sorry. Your own dog."

"I *am* sorry! Only it wasn't my fault, he ran out in the road. He couldn't see very well anyway anymore, and the car was speeding."

"What car?"

"One of those sporty kinds without a roof."

"A convertible."

"I guess so. There was a man driving. He had on one of those fancy plaid caps people wear sometimes in the movies. He knew right away he'd hit Laddie; I guess he must have heard me scream too. He slowed up and yelled a word back at me, it sounded like 'sorry.' Then he threw something out of the car. At first I didn't know what it was."

"But you found out quick enough, eh?"

"I don't like your tone. It's not respectful."

"Stop bothering about tones and get back to facts. What happened then?"

"The car went on. Laddie was lying by the side of the road. I picked him up and I could tell right away he was dead. So I buried him myself, in the backyard."

"And kept the wallet."

"Why shouldn't I?"

Mabel shook her head. "It just don't sound right to me. It sounds sneaky, if you want the truth."

"The money's mine. It was given me fair and square, in just payment for my dog. Laddie was a very valuable dog."

"He was a half-blind, ten-year-old mongrel and you know it."

"Even so."

"Mom, last night when it happened, why didn't you call me?"

"Why didn't I? *This* is why, all this questioning."

"I'm only trying to get things straightened out so we can decide what to do."

"I've already decided. I'll get rid of the wallet so nosy people won't see it and ask nosy questions. And I'll keep the money because it's mine, given me fair and square."

"How do you know?"

Celia pursed her lips. "How do I know what?"

"The man driving the car, he might have thrown the money out on purpose to keep you quiet, so you wouldn't tell anyone you saw him."

"Why should he do that?"

"Maybe he was a criminal escaping from the scene of a crime."

Celia was shaken but refused to admit it. "Oh, nonsense."

"He hit Laddie and didn't stop to leave his name or to see if he could help. That's hit-and-run driving, right there. That's a crime in itself." Mabel's imagination was like her car. Once it started to move, it moved all over, in every joint and with a great deal of noise. "How do you know he wasn't a bank robber escaping with his loot?"

"The banks," Celia pointed out, "are closed on Saturdays."

"Or a murderer. How do you know he won't come back?"

"Why would he come back?"

"To make sure your lips are sealed."

"Oh, my goodness." Celia sat down abruptly in a wicker chair and began fanning herself with a handkerchief. "I'm not well. I feel—I feel faint."

"I'll fetch you a glass of water, wait there."

The water was administered, and with it, since nothing else was readily available, a chunk of Mabel's horehound. Mabel sang soprano in the choir and used horehound as a ladder to some of the higher notes.

"Are you feeling better, Mom?"

"No thanks to you, I'm not dead," Celia said bitterly. "Giving me a fright like that, at my age."

"I was only trying to make you see reason."

"Reason, is it, to throw away nearly a hundred dollars? If that's reason, I want to be crazy, thank you."

"All I'm asking you to do is to tell someone about what happened."

"Such as who?"

"The Reverend Wilton might know what to do."

"Over my dead body," Celia said. "He and I don't see eye to eye on too many things as it is."

"The constable, then, Mr. Leachman."

"Mr. Leachman has fits."

"Now what has that got . . ."

"His own sister told me. He has fits. He even," Celia added with an air of triumph, "foams at the mouth."

Mabel's face was so red it seemed ready to burst its skin like an overripe tomato. "Will you stop changing the subject?"

"I didn't change the subject. You brought up Mr. Leachman and I merely pointed out that he has fits. Bad ones."

"That's simple gossip."

"Gossip, is it? How is it that when you find out something interesting about a person you get information, *I* merely get gossip."

"Put your coat on, Mom. We'll be late for church."

"I don't feel like going to church."

"Maybe you don't feel like it but you need it. I think maybe I do too. And after church we'll go see Mr. Leachman. And I don't care if he's foaming like bubble bath, you're going to tell him what happened and show him the wallet and describe the man in the car."

"I didn't see him very well, only by the streetlight."

"The wallet had a name in it?"

"Yes. Galloway. Ronald Gerard Galloway."

"Sounds phony to me," Mabel said. "Come on, let's get going."

9

THE NEWS THAT Ron Galloway had been seen alive at Thornbury at approximately ten o'clock Saturday night was relayed to Esther late on Sunday afternoon.

She had just returned home from the lodge and was having early tea with the two boys in their playroom on the second floor. The boys were on their worst behavior. Sensing Esther's remoteness and preoccupation, they were using every trick in the book to draw her back into immediacy and refocus her attention on them. Food was thrown, epithets exchanged, tears shed. Through it all Esther tried to remain firm and kindly, but the cumulative strain of the past twenty-four hours proved too much for her and she herself had almost reached the point of tears when Annie came in to announce that Mr. Bream was waiting for her in the library.

"I told you I wasn't at home," Esther said sharply, in a transfer of anger. "To anyone."

"I couldn't help it, Mrs. Galloway. He said he had some very important news. And anyway, it's Mr. *Bream.*" She inflected the name to give it special importance, partly to excuse her disobedience of orders and partly because she liked Harry. He treated her with respect.

"All right. Take over these hellions. I can't do a thing with them."

Annie gave her a superior you-never-could glance which Esther pretended not to notice. Esther was well aware that Annie had more power over her than she had over Annie. The balance of power lay in the boys, and Annie handled them with the ease and poise of a skilled animal trainer who realizes the exact limitations of her beasts and expects no more from them than what they can give.

"They're really quite good boys," Annie said firmly.

"Yes, of course they are."

Harry was waiting for her in the library. Even before she entered the room she could hear him pacing up and down as if he were angry.

Esther said, "Annie tells me you have news."

"Of a kind."

"Is it about Ron?"

"Some of it is."

"Don't talk in riddles, Harry. This isn't the time or place."

"I can't help that. It is a riddle. Everything is." His hair and clothing were disheveled and his face feverish-red as if he'd just been battling a high wind. He was rather a short man but he usually held himself straight and tall so that people seldom thought of him as short. Yet during the afternoon he seemed to have shrunk by inches, his shoulders sagged, his neck was bent, and he looked small and wizened and old.

Perhaps I've changed just as much as Harry has, Esther thought, and she was grateful that there was no mirror in the room to tell her so.

"It's bad news, of course," she said sounding very detached.

"No. No, it's not. Not about Ron, anyway."

"Tell me."

"Some woman saw him last night in a little town called Thornbury, about ten o'clock. He ran over her dog."

"He what?"

"Ran over her dog and killed it. He slowed down, saw what he'd done and threw some money out of the car to pay for the dog. The woman described the car, and Ron, the cap he was wearing and so on. It was Ron, all right."

"How can you be sure?"

"There was all kinds of identification in his wallet. I guess he didn't have time to take the money from his wallet so he just threw out money, wallet and everything. It was one of those impulsive things Ron does without thinking."

"Without thinking? Oh no. He thought, all right. He thought, as usual, that money will pay for anything."

"Now look, Es, I might have done the same thing myself if I'd been in a terrible hurry."

"Why should he be in a terrible hurry?"

"I don't know. I just say maybe he was."

"And that's why he didn't stop the car, because he was in this terrible hurry?"

Harry hesitated. "He could have been scared, too."

"That's better. That sounds much more like Ron. He makes a mistake and runs away, throws money out of cars instead of stopping. Oh, it must have been Ron, all right. Even if there hadn't been any identification in the wallet, I'd know it was Ron. Will he ever grow up? Will he ever just once stand and face things?"

"Now Es, don't start . . ."

"Where's Thornbury?"

"Well, it's about halfway between Collingwood and Owen Sound. You pass through it on the way to the lodge. You must have seen it today."

"I didn't notice." She let out a long deep sigh, as if she'd been holding her breath, waiting for an attack. "And that's all the news?"

"Yes."

"It's worse than none."

"I don't see how you figure that."

She turned away so that when she spoke again she seemed to be addressing the window. "All this time, right up until now, I've been thinking that Ron went away deliberately to avoid me. Perhaps he drove to Detroit, I thought, and after wrestling with his conscience for a while, he will call me and tell me where he is and everything will be all right again. Or as close to all right as it ever has been. That's what I've been thinking, that he did something wrong and couldn't bear to face me and ran away."

"That's quite possible."

"No, it isn't. Not now. If he wanted to run away he wouldn't run to the one place in the world where I'd look for him first. If he was seen in Thornbury, that means he was on his way to the lodge, or had been there and was coming back. In which direction was he going when he went through Thornbury?"

"I never thought to ask. There actually wasn't time. The Inspector returned to the lodge right after you left for home and told me about the Thornbury business. I thought you'd want to know right away so I drove down here."

"You could have phoned."

"I wanted an excuse to leave anyway."

"Why?"

"I'd been trying to get in touch with Thelma. I got through to her once but she hung up on me. I tried again several times after that. The phone kept ringing all right, but no one answered. I know the reason, now."

His tone was so peculiar that she turned to stare at him. "What's the matter, Harry?"

"She's left me," Harry said, and began suddenly and silently to cry. He covered his face with his hands in an effort to hide his tears but they dribbled out between his fingers and down his wrists into his cuffs.

Esther had never seen a grown man cry before, and the shock of it temporarily immobilized her. She couldn't speak, and her only thought at first was that Harry needed a handkerchief, somebody should give poor Harry a handkerchief, he was getting his shirt wet.

When she finally found her voice it fitted her strangely, it was so tight and small. "Harry? I'll make you a drink, eh, Harry?"

"No. I'll be—all right. Give me—a minute."

She turned back to the window. She had looked out of this window a thousand times and she still had the same impression, that somewhere, beyond the circling driveway, the high hedges and the iron gates, life was going on without her and she hadn't been invited to the party. Sometimes, over the high hedge, she fancied she could hear the strains of distant music and between the iron rails could catch a glimpse of couples dancing.

"I went home," Harry said. "She wasn't there. Just a letter on the kitchen table saying—saying she'd left me."

"Did she give a reason?"

"Not anything I could understand. She wanted a chance to think things over, she said. I can't believe it. We were so *happy*." He stumbled over the word and picked himself up again. "Everybody knows how happy we were. I can't understand. What's she got to think over?"

"Perhaps quite a bit."

"But what?"

"It's an interesting coincidence, don't you think? Now they're both gone, Ron and Thelma."

"You're not implying they went off together?"

"Maybe you and I have been pretty stupid about the whole thing."

"They're not together," Harry said sharply. "I *know* where Thelma is. She said in her letter she was going to stay for a while with a cousin of hers over on Eglington Avenue. She asked me not to try and get in touch with her. I did, though. I called Marian, that's her cousin, and Marian said she was there all right but didn't want to talk to me just yet."

"Cousins," Esther said dryly, "have been known to lie."

"Not Marian. She and Thelma aren't that close, for one thing."

"I never heard Thelma mention a cousin in town."

"I just told you, they're not very close. Lunch together downtown twice a year, that sort of thing. Marian's never even been to visit us at the house."

"Then why should Thelma go to stay with her now?"

"She had no place else to go, I guess." He sounded as if he were going to start crying again, but he didn't. Instead, he swallowed hard several times before he resumed speaking. "She must have been desperate, to decide to go to Marian's. She doesn't even like her. She must have been desperate. Poor Thelma."

Esther turned abruptly from the window, her fists clenched tight against her sides. "Poor Thelma. I'm getting bloody sick of the poor Ron, poor Thelma routine. I'd like to hear a little more about poor Harry and poor Esther!"

"No, Es. Don't. Don't be harsh."

"It's time I was harsh."

"It's never time, if you love somebody. I don't know what Thelma's problem is. All I know is that she's in trouble and I want to help her."

"Suppose you can't."

"I've got to," Harry said with quiet firmness. "She's my wife. She needs me. I would do anything in the world to help her."

Esther knew it was true. She stood, pale and motionless, thinking that if Ron ever said that about her she would be the happiest woman in the country. She would feel that at last she'd been invited to the party and the music was no longer distant but in the same room, and the couple dancing to its strains was herself and Ron.

"I wish I had your faith, Harry," she said finally.

"I wasn't born with it. I built it up brick by brick, until now it's so high I can't see over it."

"You don't want to see over it anyway."

"Thelma has done nothing shameful," Harry said. "Whatever your suspicions are about her and Ron, they're wrong, believe me."

"I'd like to."

"Read her letter."

He took the letter out of his coat pocket and handed it to her, but she drew away. "No, I don't want to. It's private."

"Thelma wouldn't object."

"I don't want to," she repeated, but even while she was speaking her eyes were seeking out the words on the paper, written in green ink in a highly stylized backhand. The effect of style was ruined by some misspellings, several clumsy erasures, and one place where the ink was blurred as if by a teardrop.

> *Dear Harry:*
>
> *I have gone to stay with Marian for a time. It is so hard to explain to you, I feel so teribbly mixed up, and I thought if I went away by myself to think things over it would be better for all of us, including you. It is hard for me to figure out the right answers when I am so emotionaly upset like this. I can't talk to you just yet, so please don't call me or try to get in touch with me.* Please, *I mean it, Harry. If Mrs. Malverson or any of the neighbors wonder why I'm not there, just tell them I've gone to visit with a cousin, which is the truth anyway.*
>
> *I know you are wondering what's the matter with me, have I lost my mind or something. Well, I don't think so but right now I'm not sure of anything except that I must go away and figure things out without having to think of other people or feel sorry for anyone. The past is all very well but it's the future I've got to live in. I must find the right course and stick to it.*
>
> *Please try to be patient with me, Harry. I'll get in touch with you as soon as I feel that I can talk sensibaly and without breaking down. By the way, Marian knows* nothing, *so please don't try and pump her. I told her you and I had had a little spat.*
>
> *Thelma*
>
> *P.S. Mrs. Reynold called this morning and said Dorothy Galloway wants to see you as soon as possible about Ron.*

Esther almost dropped the letter in her amazement. "Mrs. *Reynold.* Why on earth should she call *you?*"

"I've no idea. I hardly know the woman. As for Dorothy, well, I go to see her now and then, but God knows we never talk about Ron. If his name were mentioned she'd stage a heart attack."

"Do you think it's possible she's heard something about Ron that we haven't?"

"How?"

"By mistake, perhaps. She's still Mrs. Galloway, a message could have been sent to her by mistake, instead of to me." The idea excited her, splashed color into her cheeks. "Isn't that reasonable?"

"I guess it is."

"You must go and find out, Harry."

Harry sagged against the desk, his head bowed. "Not now."

"You've got to."

"I can't face anyone right now."

"You're facing me."

"That's because we're both in the same spot."

"Not quite," she replied sharply. "You know where your wife is, you know she's alive and well. So we're not *quite* in the same spot, are we?"

He raised his head, slowly and with effort, as if it had turned to stone. Their eyes met, but he didn't speak.

"Harry. I need your help. You'll go and see Dorothy?"

"All right."

"Now?"

"Now," he said wearily.

10

HE REACHED OUT and switched on the radio in his car. The six o'clock news broadcast was just beginning. Trouble in Israel. A train wreck in California. Stock market still going up. A warehouse on fire near the waterfront. A plane crash outside Denver. No mention of Ron's disappearance. Probably because it's Sunday, Harry thought. This whole damn city goes dead on Sundays. Maybe Thelma's right and we ought to move to the States. I'll call her and tell her—no, she said to wait. I must be patient.

He turned north on Avenue Road and west on Grant, and about two miles from the intersection he came to what Dorothy's mother called her town house.

The neighborhood was beginning to crumble around it but the house itself remained intact, as impervious as a stone fortress with its three-storied turrets and barred windows. *A medieval castle,* Harry thought as he parked his car in the driveway. *And inside the castle awaits the princess in her tower of ivory. Not the sleeping beauty, however. Poor Dorothy has insomnia.*

He could laugh at the house, make fun of Dorothy, and even feel pity and contempt for her, but at the same time he was a little awed and uneasy and resentful in the presence of wealth, like a dwarf who has been denied some secret hormone that stimulated growth, suddenly finding himself among giants.

He pressed the door chime and waited, bracing himself as if for attack the instant the huge mahogany door opened. When the door finally opened he almost laughed out loud at the sight of a little old woman in a black uniform, no bigger or braver than Harry's dwarf-image of himself. She stared up at him, round-eyed, as if male visitors to the household were scarce, and objects of suspicion.

"Mrs. Galloway wanted to see me," he said. "I'm Harry Bream."

She didn't speak, and only the slightest nod of her head indicated that she had heard him. But she opened the door wider and Harry took it as an invitation to enter. Then she closed the door, gave a little curtsy in Harry's general direction and darted off down the hall and up the stairs with several backward glances as if she perhaps feared pursuit.

The hall was like a museum, with a domed ceiling and marble floors and massive pieces of statuary. Harry would have liked a cigarette but there were no ashtrays in sight and the walls seemed to be posted with invisible No Smoking signs. The only evidence of life in the room was a pair of battered roller skates abandoned at the bottom of the staircase. The skates struck a note of sad surprise in Harry: he was always forgetting that Dorothy had borne a child and that the child still lived here in this house. Harry hadn't seen her for years. She was kept, or chose to remain, out of sight.

He put his hands in his pockets and waited, and in a few minutes the little old woman came darting back down the steps, her white cap bobbing up and down on her head like a captive bird.

"Mrs. Galloway will see you in her room." She spoke very slowly and not too clearly, as if at some time in the past, through illness or injury, she had lost the ability to speak and had had to learn the use of words all over again.

Harry followed her upstairs. The pace she set was so brisk that Harry was breathing hard by the time he reached the first landing, and openly puffing when he came to the top.

Dorothy's suite was in the south turret and the door was open.

Dorothy was stretched out on a chaise longue in a tangle of satin pillows, wearing a white lace negligee like a bride still dressed and waiting for a bridegroom long overdue. She was almost forty now, but she resembled a frail and fretful child. Extreme emaciation and years of discontent had ruined her good looks without aging her. It was as if she had been kept inaccessible to the weather in the streets. Neither sun nor wind nor rain had ever penetrated her high window.

Her mother sat in a slipper chair at Dorothy's right, and between the two women was a long low table holding a Scrabble board with a half-finished game laid out on it.

"Harry, dear, how nice of you to come." Dorothy extended her hand and Harry took it and pressed it for a moment, disliking the feel of the long fleshless fingers that were like claws. He noticed what an unusually high color Dorothy had and the extreme brightness of her eyes and he thought at first that she was in the throes of a fever. But her hand felt cool and her voice was alert and Harry was forced to change his opinion. Dorothy was suffering not from fever but from fury. She was, in fact, as sore as a boil.

"Harry, you remember Mother, of course?"

"Certainly. Good evening, Mrs. Reynold."

"Good evening, Harry. So good of you to come."

"Not at all," Harry said politely. "I hope I'm not interrupting your game?"

"Game," Dorothy repeated with a twist of her mouth. "It's not much of a *game.* I'm miles behind as usual."

Mrs. Reynold flushed with embarrassment. "Now, Dorothy dear, that's not true and you know . . ."

"It is true. Besides, I *loathe* Scrabble. It gives me a headache."

"I can't help winning once in a while if I happen to get the right letters."

"It's not that I mind losing, not in the least. I've always been a good sport, I've made it a *point* to be a good sport, in spite of everything. Losing means nothing at all to me. It's just that you have *all* the luck."

"Now, dear, remember last night, you got the Q and the Z right at the beginning and made QUARTZ."

Dorothy couldn't decide between signalizing last night's triumph and losing the argument about luck, so she turned away deliberately and said to Harry, "You must forgive us. Mother takes her Scrabble very seriously."

"I've never played it," Harry said.

"Don't. It's a tiresome thing. It always gives me a headache, especially when other people have all the luck. Sit down, won't you? I'll ring for tea."

"Don't bother."

"It's time for my medicine anyway and I can't take it without tea. It's the foulest stuff."

"I'll get the tea," Mrs. Reynold said, rising. "I hate to bother Miss Parks when I can just as easily do it myself."

"It's her job to be bothered."

"Even so, dear. I'd rather do it myself. Sometimes she forgets to scald the pot."

Mrs. Reynold seemed both grateful for an excuse to leave and guilty about using it. As she passed Harry she gave him an anxious little look. It seemed to ask him to be kind to Dorothy, or at least tolerant.

When she had gone Dorothy said, "Mother's bored with all this hospital routine. I am, too, only I have to stand it. I wouldn't last a week without expert care."

"You're looking better, Dorothy."

Harry knew right away that this remark was a mistake. Dorothy frowned with displeasure and her fingers plucked at one of the satin pillows. "I don't see how I can be. I was *so* upset this morning Miss Parks had to call the doctor. I've got a new doctor, the last one was hopelessly out of date. Nothing but psychology, psychology. What good is psychology when your heart is beating like a triphammer, and the least excitement makes you feel faint?"

"What was the cause of the excitement?"

"Ron's call. I thought your wife might have told you."

"She didn't."

"I'm much calmer tonight, my pulse is just a shade under ninety—the doctor gave me an injection. Honestly, the way I've been prodded and poked with needles!"

"What about Ron?"

"He called here last night and told Mother he wanted to talk to me, and Mother, for some obscure reason, put him on to me. Mother means to do the right thing." Dorothy paused and let the implication go on without her, like a riderless horse: *but she never does, of course.* "I wasn't feeling very well anyway and it was after nine o'clock, past my bedtime, and I'd had a nagging pain in my left kidney all day."

"How long after nine o'clock?"

"A few minutes. I remember taking my pulse after the call. It was," she added with an air of satisfaction, "nearly a hundred and twenty."

"Why did the call upset you to such an extent?"

"It was so unexpected, for one thing. Ron hadn't called me, hadn't communicated with me in any way, for years. He had no reason to. At the time of the divorce I asked for nothing from him but Barbara, and of course I was given sole custody of her, in view of his behavior with that terrible woman—what was she, a stenographer or something? Common, anyway."

"She was a copywriter for an advertising agency."

Dorothy raised her brows. "That's common enough, surely? At any rate, I was totally unprepared for any call from Ron. I'd almost forgotten he existed. He never had a very strong personality, he's not the kind of person one remembers. My father, for instance, died when I was barely ten and yet I can recall him so much more distinctly than I can Ron."

"What was the call about?"

"I'd like to know, really. His words were distorted, confused."

"What was the matter with him?"

"Plain and simple intoxication, that's what I've since decided. He was roaring drunk, maudlin drunk. You know Ron—he never could hold his liquor like a gentleman."

It seemed to Harry that this was the dozenth time in the past twenty-four hours that someone had said to him, "You know Ron." Yes, he knew Ron, better than anyone did, and one of the things he knew very well was that when Ron was drinking, before he reached the point of confusion he always got sick and sobered up. If he had a weak head he also had a weak stomach, and the latter canceled out the former.

"He seemed terribly *contrite,*" Dorothy went on. "He apologized for the harm he'd done to me and said he was going to straighten everything out, pay all his debts, I think that was the way he put it. He asked about Barbara. I told him he had no right even to ask. I told him Barbara was being brought up to believe that her father was dead."

"That was pretty . . . cruel, wasn't it, Dorothy?"

She smiled. "Wasn't it, though? But I thought while he was paying his debts, I'd pay one of mine. I owed him a little cruelty. All those times when I was so ill I could scarcely move and he went off partying—that was the year I had my liver trouble. The doctors says I'm not over it to this day. Just last week I had to have a bromsulfalein—that's the dye test for liver functioning. *More* needles. I tell you I'm getting heartily sick of needles. I'm little better than a pincushion. And what good does it all do anyway. I haven't much longer. They all know it, they simply refuse to admit . . ."

"Dorothy."

Her name, spoken sharply, almost contemptuously, shocked her into a brief silence. She looked at him with her mouth half open, as if he had ordered her to be quiet. But she could not be quiet for long; an order was what she gave, not took, and a minute later she was off again.

"I know you think I'm feeling sorry for myself, that I oughtn't go on like this about my illness. But what else have I to talk about? What ever happens to me—shut up in this hideous house with an old woman and a pair of incompetent nurses who can't even take a temperature properly? It's always normal—that's what they tell me—it's *normal,* they say, when I know perfectly well that I'm running a fever, when my head feels as if it's burning up. And they're careful, oh, they're very careful, not to leave the thermometer around so I can take my own temperature. They hide it."

Harry was disturbed by what was to him this new development in Dorothy. In the past her egocentricity and her symptoms had been just as extreme, but now they were underlined by delusions of persecution. No longer did the princess dwell at ease in her ivory tower: she was imprisoned in a hideous house at the mercy of an old woman and bumbling nurses who lied and hid thermometers.

She continued to talk, her words coming faster and faster, and it seemed to Harry that she was incapable of stopping voluntarily and must be helped. He wondered how he could draw her attention away from herself without antagonizing her to the point where she would faint or go into hysterics or use any of the other tricks which by this time came as naturally to her as breathing.

He said, "Ron disappeared last night."

She stopped in the middle of a sentence, and her right hand, on the point of making a gesture, dropped quietly into her lap. "Why didn't you tell me before?"

"I tried."

"Disappeared, that could mean anything."

"In this case it means that he failed to keep an appointment, one that he was looking forward to, and that he hasn't communicated with anyone since."

"Not even his—that woman?"

"Her name is Esther," Harry said with a trace of irritability.

"You needn't bite my head off. I have quite enough trouble as it . . ."

"Esther has not heard from him."

The words seemed to please her. "Well, well. That's very interesting. Have you a cigarette, Harry?"

"I thought you didn't . . ."

"I can smoke if I want to. I want to."

He gave her a cigarette and lit it for her. The smoke curled up from her mouth in a quiet smile.

"Very interesting," she repeated. "Doesn't it suggest anything to you?"

"No."

"He told me on the telephone that he was going away on a long trip. Well, he did. Without taking her along."

"What do you mean?"

"He's walked out on her, exactly the way he did on me."

For the first time since he'd known her Dorothy looked contented. Her eyes were serene, her mouth had lost its bitter lines, and when she spoke again her voice was almost dreamy. "I wonder how she feels now. How funny life is sometimes, a mammoth hoax. I was the butt once, now it's her turn."

"Dorothy, it's not . . ."

"Who is the other woman, this time?"

"There *is* no other woman," Harry said brusquely.

"How can you be so sure?"

"I'm as sure of that as I am of anything. In this life nobody gets a written guarantee of anything, but you do get eyes and ears and the ability to form conclusions. I've formed mine."

"Tell me just one thing, Harry."

"I'll try."

"When Ron first became interested in this woman, this Esther, did he tell you? Did he confide in you?"

"No." It was a lie, but Harry knew the truth would have destroyed whatever relationship he had with her.

The truth was that Harry had been the first to hear about Esther. To this day he remembered Ron's initial reference to her: *"I met a girl at the Temples' last night. She's very attractive, and smart as a whip. I know I sound like a heel but I'd like to see her again. What do you think I should do?"* And Harry had said in reply all the things dictated by his conscience and common sense: Go easy, forget her, you've got a wife and child, and so on. Ron sincerely agreed with everything Harry said. Equally sincerely, he called Esther the next day, took her to lunch and fell in love.

"Well, you see?" Dorothy said with satisfaction. "If Ron didn't tell you about Esther, why should he have told you about this new one?"

"There is no new one."

"Wait and see."

"There isn't much else I can do."

"I know what *I'd* do. Want to hear?"

"All right."

"I'd get the police after him, and when they caught him, I'd make him pay and pay and pay."

I'll bet you would, Harry thought. He felt suddenly too weary to continue talking.

In contrast, Dorothy appeared more and more lively and cheerful, as if she drew some secret nourishment from the woes and afflictions of other people. This was a real banquet: Ron disappeared, Esther deserted, Harry grieving.

She eyed Harry greedily as if he were holding back some fancy tidbit she wanted for dessert. "Poor Esther. I suppose she's taking it *very* badly. Well, that's life. Ye shall reap what ye sow. You'll stay for tea, of course, Harry?"

"No, I really can't, thanks just the same."

"What a pity. I've so enjoyed talking to you. You're a veritable tonic for me, Harry. I feel better than I have for weeks and weeks. I *do* wish you'd stay a bit longer."

"Sorry, I have to get home."

"Home. Of course. I keep forgetting you're married now. I keep forgetting my manners too, I'm afraid. How is your wife?"

"Thelma's fine, thank you."

"Thelma. What a pretty name, it just suits her. Oh, by the way, I forgot to tell you one other thing Ron said on the telephone. I couldn't quite understand it myself. Perhaps you can."

"I'll try."

"He seemed to be under the impression that he had harmed you in some way. I'll see if I can give you his exact words. 'I've done something terrible to Harry and I'm sorry, I want him to know I'm sorry.' Do you know what he meant?"

"No."

"You must have some idea."

"None. None at all." Harry rose. His face felt stiff, like cardboard, as if it would crack if he tried to move it. "I don't know what he was talking about."

"How very odd, don't you think?"

"I—yes. Yes, it is."

"But you mustn't let me keep you with my chattering."

She extended her hand and Harry took it just as he had when he greeted her, but this time he wanted to squeeze it hard, as hard as possible, until he could hear the bones squeak.

"Is something wrong, Harry? You're so pale."

"Nothing is wrong."

"Well, give my best to Thelma. You're a lucky man, she's such an *attractive* young woman."

"Yes. Please say good-bye to your mother for me."

"Of course. It was sweet of you to come, Harry. We must get together more often."

They exchanged brief farewells and Harry went out into the hall, leaving the door of Dorothy's room open as he'd found it.

He should have closed it. All the way down the steps he fancied he heard noises coming from the tower, little chuckling sounds. Dorothy was laughing. The princess was burping after her banquet. Harry wished she would choke.

11

MARIAN ROBINSON, A spinster at thirty by choice, was now in her middle forties and the choice had long since been taken out of her hands. Marian's reaction to this fact was characteristic: she had begun to hate men, all men, with an almost religious intensity. She saved clippings, and collected stories, of men who had murdered, embezzled, kidnapped, beaten their wives, been unkind to cats, or committed any of fifty other acts which she found distasteful. She was, therefore, in the correct frame of mind when her cousin Thelma phoned and asked if she could share Marian's apartment for a time.

To Marian this could mean only one thing, that Thelma had finally discovered she was married to a brute, a lecher, or at the very least an alcoholic, and the poor girl needed sanctuary. Marian's apartment was small, closet space minimal and bed linen insufficient, but Marian was quite prepared to make sacrifices for a good cause, such as the dissolution of a marriage. When Thelma, upon arriving, made it clear that Harry was not a brute or even an alcoholic, Marian swallowed her disappointment along with two aspirin tablets and a cup of strong hot tea.

Thelma did not confide in Marian either the fact of her condition or the rather circuitous route by which she'd reached it. She told her merely that she and Harry had had a slight argument.

The two women had a light supper in the kitchen and Marian was washing the dishes and Thelma drying when the front doorbell rang.

"I'm not expecting anyone," Marian said. "Are you?"

Thelma shook her head listlessly.

"You don't suppose it's that husband of yours, do you? I told him quite distinctly on the phone that as far as he was concerned you were incommunicado." She wiped her hands on her apron. "Well, I'll just go and give him a piece of my . . ."

"No. No, Marian. I'll answer it. You sit down and have another cup of tea, it will do you good."

"I don't need any good done to me," Marian said crisply. "It's you I'm worried about, you look like a ghost."

"I can face—handle things. You just wait here and stop worrying."

Marian would never have admitted it aloud but she found it rather pleasant to be told what to do for a change. At the insurance office where she'd worked for twenty-three years she gave the orders. It wasn't always easy but it had to be done. She had some dozen girls under her. She knew none of them liked her, some of the younger ones made fun of her behind her back and called her Old Corsets, and others sat around hoping she'd fall down and break a leg. Marian knew the whole office would go to pot without her, so she was careful about falling and kept right on giving orders whether or not they made her popular. In the past Marian had never actually paid much attention to Thelma, but now she thought how different Thelma was from the girls in the office, not silly, and not timid by any means, just sort of sweet, in a womanly way.

Marian poured herself a third cup of tea and sat down at the kitchen table to enjoy it. She did not intend to eavesdrop, heaven forbid, but it was surprising the way sounds carried in a small apartment.

When Thelma opened the door Harry did not wait to be asked to enter. He thrust his way inside like an overzealous salesman, then closed the door and stood with his back against it in a kind of childish defiance, as if he were daring her to evict him.

He looked so silly that Thelma wanted to laugh, but she knew if she laughed she might also cry. The two, laughter and tears, seemed inextricably knotted inside her so that she couldn't move one without disturbing the other. She said quietly, "You shouldn't have come here."

"I had to."

"I asked you to wait. I can't—I don't feel *qualified* to discuss anything with you reasonably."

"Okay. Be unreasonable."

"Don't play games, Harry."

"I think it's you playing games," he said, with a little smile to soften the criticism. "Mysterious notes, hints, forebodings. I'm just an ordinary man. I don't understand mysterious notes, I've never had a foreboding in my life, and I guess I can't take hints very well either. What's it all about, Thelma?"

Instead of replying, she moved to the opposite side of the room as if she feared intimacy or anger and wanted to get as much distance between Harry and herself as possible. It seemed safer and easier to face him across Marian's mohair sofa and rose and brown Axminster rug.

Harry raised his voice to bridge the distance. "We're not a couple of kids anymore, Thelma. We're married. We've shared a great many things. Whatever's bothering you, we've got to share that too."

"We can't."

"Why not?"

"I have to share it with—with somebody else."

"Marian?"

"*Marian.*" She began to laugh, and almost instantly she could feel the sting of tears inside her eyelids.

He looked away, giving her time to compose herself. "All right, not Marian. Who, then?"

"I begged you not to come here, not to force me to talk before I was ready, before I *knew*."

"Knew what?"

"What's happened to Ron. I can't—I *can't* talk to you until I know where Ron is."

"Ron, he's part of your trouble?"

Her face disintegrated like paper crushed in a fist. "Oh God, I begged you, I asked you not to . . . Why did you come? Why can't you let me *alone?* Why didn't Ralph tell you?"

"Tell me what?" Harry said, but she just kept moaning, "My God, my God," and swaying back and forth with her hands covering her face.

He waited, watching her quietly, noticing for the first time the slight thickening of her abdomen, and thinking, *this is it. She doesn't have to tell me. I know.*

The things Ralph had said and Esther had suspected and Dorothy had subtly implied—they all added up to the little bulge at Thelma's waistline.

"There's a child," he said finally. "Ron's?"

"Yes."

"How—how far along are you?"

"Three and a half months."

"And Ron knows?"

"I told him. Last night."

He leaned heavily against the door frame, staring down at the roses of Marian's rug. They had pink, fretful faces like babies. "What does Ron intend to do about it?"

"The right thing, of course."

"After having done quite a number of wrong things, do you think it's going to be easy for him to do the right one?"

"There's no use getting sarcastic. It won't accomplish anything. I've thought the whole thing out. It's not going to be easy, but Ron and I, each of us will have to get a divorce and then we'll be married."

"By that time your child will be born a bastard."

The name staggered her like a blow and she might have fallen except that there wasn't room to fall. She was jammed between the wall and the mohair sofa.

"Thelma!"

He started across the room to help her but she waved him away. "No. I'm—all right."

"Let me . . ."

"No." She clung to the back of the sofa for a moment and then she straightened up, looking strangely dignified. "Don't use that word. Don't use that word about my son."

And Harry, watching her, thought, she's got it all planned, two divorces, a marriage, even the child's sex. "A lot of words are going to be used which you won't like, Thelma. You'd better start thinking of them now so you won't be surprised when they come up."

"I don't care what anyone says about *me*."

"Yes, you do. Try and face reality."

"I am. *This* is reality." She pressed her hand to her abdomen. "This child, this is my reality. I've wanted a baby ever since I can remember, and now I have one right here growing inside me."

"Reality isn't a single fact like that. It's a combination of thousands, millions . . ."

"You denied me a baby, Harry. You made excuses, you said I was too old to have a first child now, you were afraid something would happen to me and you'd lose me. Well, you have lost me."

He shook his head helplessly, unable to speak.

"It's your fault, Harry. That's why I'm not even apologizing to you, because I think it's your fault, not mine. I wanted this one thing more than anything in the world, and I could see the years slipping by and I was getting older, with nothing to show for it. I felt dead inside, dead and useless. Don't talk to me about reality, Harry. No matter what happens, I'm not sorry. I *won't* be sorry. I have my son to keep me alive."

It sounded almost like a speech she had prepared and practiced in front of a mirror, day after day, so that she would be ready for this moment.

"You had the whole thing planned," Harry said, "in advance?"

"That's not true."

"To put it coarsely, you hooked him."

She looked at him with a kind of contempt. "Believe whatever you want. It's too late to change anything."

"But why? Why Ron? Why my best friend with a wife and family of his own? For God's sake, couldn't you have stopped to think? Couldn't you at least have talked it over with me, told me how you felt?"

"I tried. You never listened. You only heard what you wanted to hear. To you everything was idyllic, you had a house and a wife to look after it, your meals were on time, your clothes laundered . . ."

"I was satisfied just having you," Harry said. "I didn't require anything or anyone else because I loved you. I still do. Oh God, Thelma, couldn't we forget this nightmare and go back?"

"I don't want to go back. Even if I could. I may be in trouble but at least I feel alive, I've got a future and a child to share it with. And Ron." Her voice shook a little over the name in noticeable contrast to the confident way she spoke of the child. "Ron, too, of course."

"Of course."

"Oh, I know what you're thinking about—that silly notion I had that he was dead. It's not true. Mrs. Malverson got me all upset with her talk about spiritual messages. What nonsense. I know he's not dead. I know where he is."

"Where?"

"Oh, not specifically. I just know he's hiding somewhere for a while because he's frightened. Of Esther, probably. Of course she'll be impossible about the whole thing but he'll simply have to face up to her. She'll make trouble, I expect that, she's the type."

"Name a type who wouldn't, under the circumstances."

"Esther's special, she's so determined. Well, I'm determined too. Let her make trouble. Ron and I won't be living here anyway. When everything is over we'll move to the States, California perhaps. I've never been there, but they say that children brought up in California are bigger and healthier than any other children in the world."

The change in her tone indicated that she was off on another dream, an express train whizzing across the border and through the states toward California. Nothing stood in the way of this train. If it did, it was demolished. Harry knew this from experience. He had stood on the tracks once too often.

". . . and because they play outdoors all the time even in winter. They eat outdoors, too. Everyone cooks over a barbecue pit or they go down to the beach and build a bonfire."

Harry stepped in front of the train with the fearlessness of one who had nothing to lose. "Stop. Stop it, Thelma."

"Why should I?"

"Don't start living a year from now when you have to get through tonight, tomorrow, next week."

"I'll get through. Don't worry about me, Harry. Get angry, call me names, anything, but don't *worry* about me."

"I can't afford to get angry. I might—hurt you."

From the kitchen came a sudden sharp crash like a plate breaking.

"Marian," Thelma said. "Dear heaven, I forgot about Marian."

As if she'd been waiting for her cue, Marian thrust herself through the swinging door, head down, like a charging ram.

She didn't look at Harry or give any indication of his presence. She shouted at Thelma, "You slut. You nasty little slut. Pack up your things and get out of here."

Thelma appeared pale but composed, as if her dream of California had blunted the sharp corners of the present. "Do you always eavesdrop on your guests, Marian?"

"Eavesdropping is one thing, cuckolding is another. And I want none of your insolence, do you hear me?"

"I hear you. You sound just like Aunt May."

"You leave her name out of it. We're a respectable family and you've disgraced us all. I want no part of you. You can go on the streets for all I care."

"I might do that. And if business gets too heavy I'll send some customers on to you. The experience might improve you."

"Why, you dirty—you cheap . . ."

"Shut up!" Harry ordered. "Shut up, both of you! Thelma, go and pack your stuff. You, Marian, sit down."

Thelma disappeared hastily into the bedroom, but Marian stood pat, her hands on her enormous hips. "I don't take orders from any *man.* I will not sit down."

"All right, you can stand on your head as far as I'm concerned. Just stop shrieking like a fishwife. You have neighbors, neighbors have ears."

"She insulted me. You heard her, she *insulted* me."

"You insulted her first."

"But she deserved it, she asked for it. After what she's done to you, how can you stand there and take her part?"

"She's my wife."

"Wife. A fine word, but that's all it is, a word. She's used you, deceived you, made a fool of you. And she intended to do the same thing to me. To think I was taken in by that sweet smile of hers and that soft 'Sit down and have a cup of tea, Marian, it will do you good.' As if she *cared.* Lies, lies. The soft-talkers, they're the worst. I've been taken in by them before. You'd think I'd have learned my lesson."

Her voice broke and spots of color blotched her face and her neck. In a moment of perception Harry realized that she was not so much angry as disappointed. She had been looking forward to having Thelma around for a while to alleviate her loneliness and lend her life a little excitement. Thelma's visit would have meant a transfusion of vitality; now the transfusion had been stopped almost before it began. Marian had closed the valve herself: she could not accept the blood of a slut, she would prefer to die.

"The girls at the office," Marian said, "maybe they're silly, yes, even malicious, but there's not one of them bad like her. Not one of them's ever gotten into that kind of trouble."

Harry found himself saying, without conviction, "Thelma's not bad. She made a mistake."

"When people make a mistake they're *sorry.* They're not proud of it like her. They don't go around bragging about a trip to California. I want to go to California too, I've dreamed of it for years, but you can bet I'll choose a more respectable way of getting there."

"I'm sure you will." The dry irony of his tone added, *I'm sure you'll have to.*

"This man she called Ron. Who is he?"

"I'm afraid," Harry said, "that it's none of your business."

"News like that gets around. I'll find out."

"I'm sure of that, too." Not only would Marian find out. Once Ron's disappearance hit the newsstands, the whole city, the whole country would find out, and Thelma would have to get used to stronger words than bastard and slut. Harry wondered, with weary detachment, if anyone dared print the word cuckold.

Thelma came out of the bedroom wearing the navy blue coat and hat she'd bought for Easter and carrying a rawhide suitcase which had been a wedding present from Ralph and

Nancy Turee. She ignored Marian, who was standing tense, braced for the next round, and said to Harry, "I'm ready. We can go now."

"And good riddance," Marian said.

"The same to you."

Harry interrupted quickly, "Come on, Thelma. I'll take you home."

"I'm not going home. You can drop me at a hotel."

"The house is yours. You need it more than I do. I won't bother you."

"I wish you'd stop being *noble.* I can't stand it!"

"I'm not being noble. It's just that I'd feel better if I knew you were looking after yourself properly. Me, I can stay anywhere, with Ralph, or Billy Winslow or Joe Hepburn. I'm used to bumming around. You're not. You have to take care of yourself, now more than ever."

She bit her lip in indecision, weighing her pride against her common sense and her concern for the baby.

"I won't bother you," he repeated. "I'll just take you home and pack up some of the things I'll need."

"All right." Her voice was tight and squeaky. "Thank you, Harry."

Harry took her suitcase and opened the door, and she walked out into the hall with quick, impatient steps. Harry hesitated, as if he wanted to say something pleasant to Marian before he left, but Marian had turned her back, and it was like the closing of a steel safe to which he didn't know the combination. No one did.

Outside a spring rain had begun to fall, lightly and steadily. Neither of them seemed to notice. They walked in silence for a time, unaware of any weather but their own, inside.

"Harry?"

"Yes."

"Where will you stay? In case anything happens and I have to get in touch with you . . ."

"I don't know. I haven't decided yet. With Ralph and Nancy, perhaps."

"But they have four children."

"Yes, I know," Harry said quietly. "I like children."

12

THE PRIVATE DAY school which the two Galloway boys attended had been closed for two weeks because of an epidemic of measles. One of the ways Esther had devised to keep them busy, and presumably out of mischief, was to give them certain duties and responsibilities previously assigned only to adults. The particular duty the boys enjoyed most, since it involved a rare freedom, was that of collecting the mail. They were allowed to walk all the way down to the end of the driveway, unescorted except by the little dachshund, Petey, and wait at the gate for the postman.

When the postman handed them the day's mail, they assumed it was a gift, and so they usually took him a gift in return, a cookie coaxed out of the housekeeper, Mrs. Browning, or a new drawing by Marvin or the prize from a box of cereal. On Monday they had a special gift for him, the first angleworm of the season, a scrawny specimen elongated by considerable handling and rather dried out after a time spent in Greg's shirt pocket.

The boys arrived early and the postman was late, so they had plenty of opportunity to indulge in the usual arguments and fights about who was to present the gift, who was to carry the mail into the house and who was to occupy the place of honor at the top of the iron gate. But on this particular morning neither of the boys seemed inclined to fight. Their energies were directed not against each other but against the mysterious tensions which now seemed to dominate the household. The boys had not been told, or allowed to overhear, anything about their father's absence. They had no means of understanding their mother's strange preoccupation, Mrs. Browning's snappishness, Annie's sudden lapses into silence, or the unusual permissiveness of old Rudolph, the gardener who lived over the garage. Rudolph, the most continuous male contact the boys had, loomed large in their lives. When the holes Petey, the dachshund, had dug in the rose bed on Sunday afternoon were filled quietly and without comment, both of the boys realized that something was the matter.

Their reaction was instinctive. Instead of remaining brothers, each jockeying for position in the household, they became friends, joined together against the world of adults. They climbed to the top of the iron gate and stuck out their tongues in the direction of the house and chanted derisive insults.

"I'm the king of the castle," Greg sang, and named individually the people who were dirty rascals: Annie, Mother, old Rudolph, Mrs. Browning. Marvin was all for including Daddy, but Greg reminded him sharply that Daddy had promised to bring them a new dog when he came home, and shouldn't be listed among the dirty rascals.

"What if he forgets?" Marv said. "He'll be a dirty rascal, then can we sing him in it too?"

"He won't forget. He'll bring something. He always does."

"A cat maybe, huh? I wouldn't say no to a cat."

"Petey would. Petey hates cats. Petey's a real cat-killer."

Petey, who had never seen a cat, responded to his new, unearned distinction with a happy yelp. This settled the matter as far as the boys were concerned. They couldn't possibly keep a cat, and if Ron brought one home by mistake they would simply hand it over to old Rudolph to trade in on a dog. Until the previous day they'd been willing to settle for any kind of dog, but now, sensing that a very large one would be more annoying to the adults, they decided on a Saint Bernard.

"We can teach it to bite Annie," Greg said. "When she makes us go to bed we'll say sic 'em, and then *boiiing*, Annie gets bit."

Marv laughed so hard at this delightful picture that he nearly fell off the gate. "*Boiiing*, Annie gets bit. *Boiiing, boiiing*, Mrs. Browning gets bit. *Boiiing, boiiing*, everybody gets bit."

" 'Cepting us."

" 'Cepting us."

They screamed with laughter and the gate shook and Petey broke into excited yelps. By the time the postman arrived, the boys' faces were red as tomatoes and Marv had started to hiccup as he always did after a laughing fit.

"Mr. Postman! Hi, Mr. Postman!"

"Hello boys." The postman was long and lean, with a weather-cracked smile. "How come you're not in school this morning?"

"Measles."

"You shouldn't be out here if you got measles."

"*We* don't got measles," Marv explained. "The other kids got them."

"Well, I declare. I was never that lucky when I was a boy. The whole town could be dying of plague but they never closed the school, no sir." He put down the heavy mail sack, propped it against the fence, and stretched his arms high in the air. "That's how I got an education. Force. I didn't want one."

"What's a plague?" Greg asked, climbing down from the gate.

"Like measles, only worse."

"You got something for us in your bag?"

"Sure thing."

"We got something for you, too."

"Well, how about that."

"You want to guess what it is?"

"I guess it's a cookie."

"No."

"An apple."

"No. You can't eat it. A human bean can't eat it, I mean."

"What does a human bean do with it?"

"Keep it as a pet."

"Oh. Well, I'm just about ready to give up. What is it?"

"Let *me* tell him!" Marv shouted. "Let *me!* It's an angleworm!"

The postman took off his cap and scratched his head. "An angleworm, eh? Let's see it."

The angleworm, now fairly moribund, was duly produced from Greg's pocket and placed carefully in the postman's hand.

"Well, now, isn't he cute? I must admit no one's ever thought of giving me an angleworm before."

"You'll take good care of him?" Greg said anxiously.

"You bet I will. I think I'll put him in my garden where he'll find other angleworms to play with. There's nothing worse than a lonesome angleworm, so I've been told."

"How do you know he'll meet the kind of angleworms he likes to play with?"

"They're not fussy." The postman opened his sack and distributed the mail as impartially as possible to the two boys. "Well, I've got to be on my way now."

"Someday," Greg said, "can we come with you and carry the sack?"

"Someday, sure. So long, fellows."

"So long."

They watched him until he turned the corner, then they set out for the house. Usually they hurried at this point. It made them feel important to hand over the mail to their mother or Mrs. Browning. But this morning their feet lagged and they kept glancing back at the gate as if they half expected the postman to reappear and offer to take them along on his rounds.

Their mother was waiting for them at the front door. "What a lot of mail. It must be heavy."

"I could carry the whole sack," Greg said, "if I wanted to. Someday I will, he said I could."

Marv put up an immediate protest. "He said both of us, me too."

"That will be very nice, I'm sure," Esther said and began glancing through the mail, putting the bills in one pile on the hall table and the circulars in another. There was only one letter.

For a long time Esther stood staring down at the handwriting on the envelope. Then she said in a cold, quiet voice, "You boys had better go to Annie."

They were afraid of this voice, but they couldn't admit it, to each other or to themselves.

"I hate Annie," Marv shouted. "I don't want . . ."

"Do as I say, Marvin."

"No! I won't! I hate Annie!"

"I hate her too," Greg said. "We're going to teach the new dog to bite her."

"Boiiing!"

"Boiiing, boiiing, Annie gets bit."

"Boiiing, boiiing, old Rudolph gets bit."

"Stop it," Esther said. "*Please.* Please be good boys."

"Boiiing, boiiing, everybody gets bit."

" 'Cepting us."

"Boiiing . . ."

"Oh God," Esther said and turned and ran across the hall into the library.

Her sudden flight and the loud shutting of the door stunned the boys for a minute. Then Marv said, tentatively, "Boiiing?"

"Oh, shut up. You're such a baby. Shut up."

Marv began to cry. "I want Mummy. I want my Mummy."

The letter postmarked Collingwood, was addressed to Esther in Ron's handwriting.

She knew in advance that it would contain bad news and she tried to prepare herself for it by imagining the worst, that he'd left her for another woman and wasn't coming back.

She was only half right.

> *Dear Esther:*
>
> *By this time you may know the truth, that Thelma is carrying my child. I won't try to excuse myself or explain.*
>
> *I can't. It happened, that's all I can say. I didn't know about the child until tonight. It was a terrible surprise, too terrible for me to face. My God, what I've done to you and Harry.*
>
> *I don't ask your forgiveness. I give you instead my promise that I will never hurt you or anyone ever again. I'm not fit to live. I'm sick in mind and body and soul. God help me.*
>
> *Ron*

She did not faint, or cry out, or weep. She stood like a stone; only her eyes moved, reading and rereading the words on the page.

She was not aware of the door opening and when she looked up and saw Annie her eyes wouldn't focus properly. Annie seemed misty and remote as if she were surrounded by ectoplasm.

"Mrs. Galloway?"

"Please don't—don't bother me right—right now."

"But I can't do a thing with the boys. They've both gone wild, screaming and laughing and carrying on. And Marvin just bit me." Annie exhibited her wounded wrist. "I'm not sure but what they're coming down with something. Do you think I should phone the doctor?"

"All right."

"You don't look so good yourself, Mrs. Galloway. Maybe you're coming down with the same thing. Can I do anything for you?"

"Yes," Esther said. "Call the police."

"The police?"

"I've had a letter. From my husband. I think he's killed himself."

Marvin came bouncing into the room, screaming, "Boiiing! Boiiing, boiiing!"

Esther turned with a sob and picked him up in her arms and held him tight. Too tight. There seemed to Marvin only one logical thing to do and Marvin did it. He bit her.

13

WHILE THE TWO Galloway boys were waiting for the mailman in Toronto, little Aggie Schantz was on her way to the small country school she attended near Meaford. In the winter when Aggie had to follow the road because snowdrifts made exploring foolhardy, if not impossible, she took the quick and direct route. But it was spring now, and the only snow left lay in crevices between rocks, in the hollows of tree trunks along the snow fences sagging under the weight of winter.

Aggie was a quiet child of eleven. She behaved decorously at school and obediently at home, and no one ever suspected what an adventurous spirit lurked behind her brown braids and black bonnet, or what itchy feet were buckled inside her canvas galoshes. Aggie came from a family of Mennonites whose outside contacts were limited and whose meager amount of traveling, to and from church or from one farmhouse to another, was done by horse and buggy. Aggie dreamed of a larger world. Sometimes when she was looking at a map in geography class, she grew quite dizzy thinking of all the hundreds, the thousands, of places she wanted to visit. They were all places of extremes—the highest mountain, the largest ocean, the biggest city, the oldest country, the hottest desert, the highest waterfall, the fastest rapids—Aggie intended to see each and every one of them.

While her dreams were wild, her plans for escape showed both common sense and resourcefulness. As a farm child she knew enough about horses to realize that they were a slow and unsatisfactory means of transportation. Horses had to be fed and watered and sheltered and rested and groomed. Trains and buses were equally impossible since she had no money. And so Aggie's eyes turned to the lake, to the fleets of fishing boats and the passing freighters that were so large one small stowaway wouldn't be noticed. She couldn't stay away from the lake, she scanned it constantly as if she were shipwrecked on an island, waiting, cold and hungry, for rescue.

As soon as the spring sun melted the snow from the cliffs above the lake, Aggie began taking an indirect route to school. Carrying her books and her lunch in a gray canvas bag, she climbed up to the top of the cliff and then down to the beach by a special steep path used only by agile children and venturesome dogs. The beach along here was very narrow, six feet at its widest, and strewn with boulders and rocks of all sizes. To keep from getting wet she was forced to leap from one boulder to another, but this proved tiring work and she sat down for a minute to rest, tucking her legs modestly under her long full cotton skirt. Her time sense told her she was going to be late for school, and her conscience warned her she'd better do something about it.

"There'll be hell to pay," Aggie said aloud, and the sound of the forbidden word was as intoxicating as a strange tropical drink. "Maybe I'll go there. It's the hottest place."

Half-shocked, half-delighted with her own wit and daring, she began to giggle self-consciously, turning her face sideways so that it was almost hidden by the folds of her black bonnet. And it was then, out of the corner of her right eye, that she spotted the red and black plaid cap wedged between two rocks.

She often found things on the beach, especially in the summertime, sometimes a piece from an old tire, a soaked and dilapidated shoe, a rusty tin can, or an empty bottle, but these were all worthless things, discarded by the owners and battered by the waves. The cap was dry, and no one would ever have discarded it because it was brand-new. It had a plastic visor at the front and a scarlet pompon on the crown, and to Aggie, who had never owned anything bright-colored in her life, it was a thing of beauty. She pushed back her bonnet, letting it hang from her neck by its strings, and put the plaid cap on her head. It came down grotesquely over her ears and eyes, but Aggie did not know that this wasn't correct. Nor did she, like most eleven-year-old girls, long for a mirror to see how she looked. Mirrors were banned in the house she lived in, and the only glimpses of herself she ever caught were chance and fleeting reflections in a sunny window or in the pond behind the barn on a still day. Therefore she didn't realize that she looked foolish; she knew only that the cap was beautiful, and so it must look beautiful on anyone, anywhere.

But because it was beautiful, it was, by the same token, forbidden. She looked around to check her privacy, and finding it complete, she took off the cap, compressed it as carefully as possible and tucked it inside her waist blouse. Under her bulky clothes it was barely noticeable, and it might have escaped detection entirely if Aggie herself had not been so extremely conscious of its presence, partly from pride in its possession and partly from discomfort over its location.

By the time she reached the small brick schoolhouse the final bell was ringing and the pupils were already lined up to go inside. Red-faced and panting, holding her arms across her chest, Aggie slipped into her place in line, and began marching into the smaller of the two classrooms.

Here Miss Barabou taught, or tried to teach, the four upper grades. They were a mixed group, not only in age and ability, but in background and religion. Miss Barabou herself was a Presbyterian of French Canadian ancestry, and among her pupils she counted Anglicans, Baptists, Mennonites, Christian Scientists, Methodists, and even two Doukhobor children from Alberta. Like many teachers, Miss Barabou chose her favorites principally on the basis of their obedience. The Doukhobor children were wild and unruly, often disrupting the class or flouting authority, and with them Miss Barabou was sharp and critical and sarcastic. On the other hand the Mennonite children were quite docile, they never questioned adult authority or criticized adult behavior or expected adult privileges. While Miss Barabou disparaged the Mennonite religion, she was often grateful for its results, and Aggie was her special pet. Aggie's position was not entirely enviable, however, for Miss Barabou expected a great deal from her special pets and easily became exasperated when she didn't get it.

After the class had bowed their heads and mumbled the Lord's Prayer in unison, they sat down at their double desks and began removing their books from their school bags. Miss Barabou took her place at the front of the class. She was large and majestic, and though she seldom punished her pupils, most of them stood in awe of her.

"Spring is here," Miss Barabou announced with satisfaction, as if she'd had a personal part in its arrival. "Did anyone see a robin on the way to school?"

Hands were raised and seven robins counted. An American eagle was offered by Boris, the Doukhobor boy, but was turned down on grounds of improbability.

"We do not have American eagles in this part of the country, Boris."

"But I saw one."

"Indeed. Describe it."

Boris described the eagle with such complete accuracy that Miss Barabou was visibly shaken.

But she was also determined. "We do not have American eagles in this section of the country. Ever. Now will someone please mark our seven robins on the bird chart? You, Agatha?"

Aggie sat motionless and mute.

"Agatha, I am addressing you. Do you know where we keep the bird chart?"

"Yes, ma'am."

"Will you kindly mark our seven robins?"

"I can't."

"Indeed, and why not?"

"I can't find my crayons."

"Well, stop squirming like that and take another look."

"I can't."

"Which do you mean, you can't stop squirming or you can't take another look?"

Aggie didn't answer. Her face was burning and her tongue felt fuzzy and dry.

"If you have an itch, Agatha, kindly go into the cloakroom and relieve it," Miss Barabou said in exasperation, thinking, *The awful way they dress their children, it's no wonder they itch. I'll bet she's got on six layers of clothing at least.* She added, more gently, "Agatha, is anything the matter?"

"No, ma'am."

It was at this point that Miss Barabou noticed Aggie's empty desk. "Where are your books, Agatha?"

"I—don't know."

"You lost your school bag, is that it?"

"I don't know."

The rest of the class had begun to titter and whisper behind their hands. Miss Barabou ordered them brusquely to start work on their book reports, and went down the aisle to Aggie's desk, her heavy step warning the class to behave. She was positive now that something was the matter with Aggie; the child's face was such an odd color and she was trembling. *Maybe she's coming down with something,* Miss Barabou thought. *That's all I need right now is an epidemic. Oh well, if it gets bad enough they may close the school and I'll have a holiday.*

"Do you feel ill, Agatha?" Miss Barabou asked, somewhat heartened at the idea of a holiday. "Stick out your tongue."

Aggie stuck out her tongue and Miss Barabou studied it with a professional air. "I can't see anything wrong. Does your head hurt?"

"I guess so."

"Let's see, you had measles and chicken pox last year. No mumps yet?"

"No, ma'am."

"Well, think of a lemon."

"A what?"

"Pretend you're eating a lemon. Or a pickle. Can you pretend that?"

"I guess so."

"All right now, does your throat feel queer on both sides just under your chin?"

"No, ma'am."

"Perhaps you're not pretending hard enough. Keep picturing that pickle, it's very, very sour and you're eating it. Now do you feel anything?"

"No, ma'am."

Sylvia Kramer raised her hand to announce that she had a real dill pickle in her lunch box and would gladly offer it for the sake of research. Miss Barabou replied that that wouldn't be necessary, and led Aggie into the cloakroom for further and more private diagnosis.

"Have any of your brothers or sisters been ill, Agatha?"

"Billy has the toothache."

"That's not catching. Why are you squirming and clutching your chest like that?"

Aggie shook her head.

"Do you have a pain there?"

"No, ma'am."

"Honestly, the way they dress you children, it's a crime. Are you still wearing your long underwear?"

"Yes, ma'am."

"I've a good notion to write a note to your parents. It's hard enough teaching without having to teach itchy children. For all I know, you have lice."

Tears welled in Aggie's eyes. She blinked them away, hard. "Agatha," Miss Barabou said quite gently, "now tell me truthfully, what is the matter?"

"I lost my school bag."

"Perhaps you forgot and left it at home."

"No. I lost it. On the beach."

"When were you on the beach?"

"This morning on my way to school."

"The beach isn't on your way to school. Besides, all you children have specific instructions not to go near the beach by yourselves. A lonely spot like that, you can't tell what will happen." Miss Barabou paused, significantly. "*Did* anything happen?"

Aggie merely looked up at her in helpless bewilderment, and Miss Barabou realized that the child didn't understand. She tried to explain patiently that little girls didn't go to lonely beaches by themselves because there were some bad men in the world who might do nasty things to them. "Did you see any men down there?"

"No."

"I hate to be suspicious, Agatha, or to nag. But I have the distinct impression that you're not telling me the whole truth."

Though Miss Barabou's voice was kindly, her eyes burned with such intensity that Aggie had the feeling they were looking right through her waist blouse at the red and black plaid cap.

"What occurred down at the beach, Agatha?"

"Nothing!"

"You know how important the truth is. What happens at home when you don't tell the truth?"

"I get the strap."

"As you very well know, I don't have a strap, and wouldn't use it if I had. Now you're not going to *cry*, are you?"

Aggie was, indeed. Tears spilled out of her eyes and she had to wipe them away with her sleeve. It was when Aggie raised her arm that Miss Barabou noticed the extra bulk under her clothes.

"What on earth have you got stuffed in the front of your blouse? So that's what you've been fidgeting about. You've got something hidden in there. What is it, Agatha?"

Aggie shook her head, helplessly.

"You won't be punished if you tell the truth. That's a promise. Now stop crying and tell me—no, better still, show me what it is."

"It's—nothing. I found it."

"Nobody finds a *nothing*," Miss Barabou said dryly. "It's impossible factually, as well as grammatically. What did you find?"

"A cap. An old cap somebody left on the beach that didn't want it anymore."

"Well, why didn't you say so before? All this fuss and fume about an old cap. Honestly, I sometimes wonder what kind of homelife some of you children have that makes you afraid to speak up. Now remove the cap, and we'll leave it here on the shelf in the cloakroom, and you can take it home with you after school."

Aggie turned her back, removed the plaid cap from under her waist blouse and handed it to Miss Barabou.

Miss Barabou appeared surprised. "'What an odd-looking thing. I've never seen one like it. Where did you find it, Agatha?"

"Between two rocks, just sitting there. I guess somebody just threw that old cap away."

"It isn't old. It's hardly been worn at all."

"It looks old to me."

But Miss Barabou seemed to have lost interest in Aggie. She was examining the inside of the cap, and when she spoke again it was more to herself than to Aggie. "There's a label. Abercrombie & Fitch, New York City. Funny. There aren't many Americans around at this time of year. The thing's new, no doubt about it. Expensive, too. Abercrombie & Fitch, I think they sell sporting goods. I wonder what kind of sport this would be worn for. Curling, perhaps, except that I've never seen a curling cap with a sun visor. Or golf. But the golf courses won't be open for ages. I'm not even sure if it's a man's cap or a woman's."

"Miss Barabou . . ."

"You may go back to your desk, Agatha."

"Is it my cap if I found it?"

"I can't promise you that," Miss Barabou said thoughtfully. "I better consult with Miss Wayley."

Miss Barabou escorted Aggie back into the classroom, pronounced her free of disease, assured the pupils they could associate with her without fear and warned them not to start getting symptoms out of the blue. Then, leaving the class in charge of one of the seniors, she made a beeline to Miss Wayley's room next door.

Social visiting between the two teachers during school hours was forbidden by the school inspector. But the inspector was miles away and not due for another month.

Miss Wayley, upon being apprised of the situation, put her entire class, including those who hadn't yet learned to write, to work on a composition entitled "How I Will Spend My Summer Vacation." Then she and Miss Barabou retired to the tiny room at the rear of the school where they ate their lunch and made coffee during recesses and conducted their private business in general. The room was cold and cramped and ugly, but it had two distinct advantages: a lock on the door which had so far resisted even the expert picking of Boris, and a telephone installed the past winter after a bad storm left the school marooned for nearly twenty-four hours.

Miss Wayley lit a cigarette, took three quick, furtive puffs, and butted it before any of the smoke could seep under the door and cause alarm or suspicion among the students. She saved the butt in an empty Band-Aid box inside the first aid kit.

"I think," Miss Barabou said, "we should phone somebody."

But Miss Wayley was busy trying on the cap in front of the yellowed, broken mirror hanging on the wall, "Don't I look sporty, though? Say, this is kind of cute. I wouldn't mind having one myself. Makes me feels years younger."

"Be serious."

"I am."

"It looks like a man's cap to me. Have you seen any strange men around town lately?"

"If I had," Miss Wayley said cheerfully, "I'd be on leave of absence tracking him down, believe you me."

"Be *serious.*"

"I can't. I feel sporty. Here, you try it on, Marie."

"I wouldn't dream of . . ."

"Go on. See how it looks. Just for fun."

Miss Barabou took a quick glance at the door to make sure it was locked, then she, too, tried on the plaid cap. For one instant, in the cracked mirror, she did indeed look sporty, but the instant was overwhelmed by years of common sense. "It's ridiculous. I wouldn't be caught dead wearing such a thing."

"Well, I would. I can just picture myself whizzing along in some snazzy convertible . . ."

"Why a convertible?"

"Because that's what the cap's for, riding in a convertible with the top down. I've seen them in the movies."

"That's how it happened, then."

"What did?"

"Someone was riding along the cliff road in a convertible and his cap blew off and landed on the beach where Agatha found it."

"It couldn't blow off, easily, anyway. That's what the elastic band at the back is for, to keep it tight-fitting so the wind won't blow it off."

"How odd," Miss Barabou said, and for the first time she appeared disturbed by the possibilities. "I know it sounds silly, but—well, you don't suppose there's been a *crime* committed?"

"No such luck."

"Please be serious."

"I am. I said no such luck and I mean it. Nothing ever happens around here."

"There's always a first time."

The noise from the two unattended classes was increasing by the minute—thuds, screams, laughter, whistling—but neither of the two teachers paid any attention. Din was a part of their lives and a few decibels one way or another didn't matter.

"I'd feel like a fool," Miss Barabou said, "if I called in the police and it turned out to be absolutely nothing."

"Call anyway." Miss Wayley selected one of the dozen or so cigarette butts she kept stored in the first aid kit, and lit it with a reckless air. "We might as well whip up a little excitement while the whipping's good. Here, help yourself to a butt."

"No thanks. It wouldn't be sanitary."

"Sorry I can't offer you a fresh one. Gee, it'd be wonderful to buy cigarettes cheap the way they do in the States."

"I'm not sure whom to call."

"The local constabulary. What a marvelous word, constabulary, isn't it?"

"The way you chatter, I can't *think.*"

"You don't have to think. Let the local constabulary do the thinking. You and I, we're teachers, we don't get paid for thinking, we get paid for teaching, and what a whale of a difference there is."

"Oh, *stop* it, Betty."

Miss Barabou picked up the phone.

Constable Lehman arrived at the school about nine-thirty, a small, droll-faced man in his fifties who took his work, but nothing else, quite seriously. He came in his own private car, an old Buick, a device intended to allay the curiosity of the students. Through no fault of his own the device backfired. A good half of Miss Barabou's class, and even several members of Miss Wayley's lower grades, recognized him immediately and such excitement spread through the school that a recess had to be declared.

The children, with the exception of Aggie Schantz, were herded into the yard like wild ponies, and a conference was held in Miss Barabou's room with the plaid cap on exhibition on her desk. Instead of being nervous, as Miss Barabou had expected, Aggie luxuriated in the special attention she was receiving. She told her story in full detail, and Lehman, who'd had experience with children of his own, did not interrupt her even when she included such nonessentials as what she had for breakfast and how many robins she saw en route to school.

"We count robins," Miss Barabou said by way of apology and explanation. "For the bird chart. Natural history, you know."

Lehman's nod indicated that he understood perfectly, and was, in fact, an old hand at counting robins himself.

"I see more than anybody," Aggie said, with becoming modesty, "mostly because I have a longer way to go to school. Boris saw an American eagle."

Lehman pursed his lips. "Did he, now? Well, they say more and more American people are coming up this way every year, why not eagles, too, eh? Can you show me this special path you take down to the beach, Aggie?"

"I can *show* you. You can't go down it, though."

"I can't, eh? Why not?"

"You're too old."

"You may have something there," Lehman said, and sighed for Aggie's benefit, and winked for Miss Barabou's.

Miss Barabou, who was not accustomed to being winked at, blushed in confusion and turned to Aggie. "Of course you'll show the Constable the path, Agatha. I'll excuse you from school for the rest of the morning. You go with Constable Lehman."

"I don't want to."

"Get your coat and galoshes on."

Aggie didn't move.

"Agatha, did you hear me?"

"I don't want to go without you."

"You know perfectly well I have to stay here and supervise my class."

"You could send them all home," Aggie said hopefully. "They wouldn't mind."

"No, I'm sure they wouldn't. Neither would I, until it came time to explain to thirty howling parents. Why on earth don't you want to go with the Constable?"

"The bad men."

"What bad men?"

"That do nasty things to little girls on beaches."

"Oh, for heaven's *sake.*" Miss Barabou's blush had spread to the tips of her ears and down her neck to the collar of her jersey dress. "I was only trying to—oh well, it doesn't matter. I give up. I'll go along, there's no point in arguing."

Miss Barabou sat in the back of the Buick alone, holding herself stiff and resistant to the feeling of adventure that was growing inside her with every turn of the road and every glance at the Constable's face half visible in the rear-view mirror. *He's really quite a nice man. Humorous, too. Betty said she heard he's a widower, all his children are grown and he lives by himself. He needs a haircut.*

She tried to discipline her thoughts by planning the next eighth grade British History assignment, but she could not seem to concentrate properly. The scarlet pompon on the plaid cap which lay on the seat beside her seemed to be taunting her: *Come on, live now. The Magna Carta is very old; King John is very dead. Be sporty.*

She looked sternly, ponderously, out of the window, though her head felt quite light and empty, as if giddy little bubbles were whirling around inside, released by some strange alchemy she did not understand.

"We're almost there." Aggie's voice pealed with excitement. "Right around the next corner."

"Roger," Lehman said.

"What's that mean?"

"It means right-ho. Roger, dodger, you old codger, I'm a major too."

"Oh, you make me laugh."

"I aim to please."

He stopped the car on the side of the road and all three of them got out, Aggie still giggling behind her hand, Miss Barabou very sober and dignified as if to make up for the levity of the others. Looking down at the water a hundred feet below, and the path by which she was expected to descend, she offered up a short silent prayer.

Lehman said to Aggie, who was impatient to start down the path, "Hold your horses a minute, lass. Now when you found the plaid cap, was it directly below here?"

"No sir. I walked along a piece first until I got tired and sat down and then I found it."

"About how far did you walk?"

"I don't know. I can show you down there."

"Show me up here first."

"I don't know if I can."

"Try. Start walking."

They began walking single file up the road with Aggie in the lead like a general with delusions of troops.

The road was not a main one, and though it was marked on maps as "improved," the improvements had long since disappeared in the throes of winter. The surface had buckled in places and some of the potholes were as large as Aggie's head.

Lehman appeared to be watching his footing very carefully, paying no attention to Miss Barabou struggling along in the rear. Aggie was skipping on ahead, not looking down at the road at all but avoiding every bump and hole as if she had made a complete mental map of the route and knew its every pitfall.

"I'm beginning to get tired," Aggie said, "so I guess it was right about here."

She looked up expectantly, as if awaiting Lehman's commendation, but he seemed too preoccupied to notice her. He was staring down at the mud along the side of the road, his eyes narrowed against the morning sun.

"Well?" Miss Barabou said when, out of sorts and breath, she finally caught up with the others.

"Look here, ma'am."

"I can't see anything out of the ordinary."

"No?"

"Some tire marks, that's all. It's a road, you'd expect to find tire marks."

"Not ones leading over the top of the cliff." Lehman turned to Aggie, who was bouncing all over the place. "Be a good lass and stay out of the way. In fact, how about you going back and waiting in the car?"

"But I haven't showed you anything yet."

"You've shown me quite a lot more than I expected."

"Tell me what."

"Well, stand still a minute. See these marks here? They were made by the tires of an automobile, a new one and a heavy one, my guess is a Lincoln or a Cadillac. Now where do they lead?"

"Nowhere. They just stop."

"Exactly. They just stop."

Lehman walked to the edge of the cliff and Miss Barabou followed him, wide-eyed and nervous. "What does it all mean?"

"It means there's a car down there, perhaps with people in it."

"*People.* But we've got to do something right away, help them . . ."

"I'm afraid it would be too late. The marks aren't fresh and the water's deep."

"Perhaps you're being too pessimistic. It could be that some people just stopped here for a look at the view and went on again. That's more likely than . . ."

"There's no sign that the car turned around."

Miss Barabou's hand moved to her throat. "I'll—I'd better take Aggie back to the car."

But she stood peering down at the water below, as if she hoped to distinguish the outlines of a car, the contours of people. The glare of sun on water dazzled her eyes and she stumbled back half-blinded.

Lehman caught her by the arm. "Watch it. That's a long fall."

"Yes."

"It's a city car, I'll bet you that."

"How can you tell?"

"Around these parts a person driving an expensive car would still be using snow tires at this time of year. The kind of winters we have up here, we need them. But in a city where the roads are kept clear, snow tires wouldn't be necessary." He paused. "I wonder."

"You wonder what?"

"What makes a person drive over a cliff."

Lehman drove Miss Barabou and Aggie back to school and left them there with instructions to say nothing to anyone. Then he called the Provincial Police and returned to the cliff. Three police cars were waiting for him when he arrived, as well as the resuscitation squad of the local fire station, all ready to go into action.

No action was necessary.

Two barges, sent down from Meaford with winches and dredging equipment, located the car in twenty feet of water just below the cliff where Lehman had found the tire tracks. The car was barely damaged, the windows and windshield were unbroken, and Ron Galloway was still inside, fastened snugly to the driver's seat by his safety belt.

14

RALPH TUREE RETURNED to his office from his eleven o'clock seminar feeling hungry and exhausted. He had got up too early for sufficient rest and too late for breakfast. Harry had spent the night at his house and the two men had talked until after three in the morning. Talked and talked and settled nothing beyond what was already settled—Galloway was missing, and Thelma was waiting for him to come back and claim her as his future wife.

He sat down at his desk and was unpacking the lunch Nancy had made for him when the door opened and Nancy herself appeared.

Turee looked up in surprise. It was not a rule that Nancy should stay away from his office during working hours, but her visits were so infrequent that she looked strange in the surroundings, like a new graduate student perhaps, or someone who'd lost her way in the corridors and merely stopped by for directions. She was a small pretty woman with a round cherubic face and rather short sturdy legs—"practical" legs, Turee called them, in contrast to what he considered her impractical mind. She was wearing her new violet-colored Easter suit, which meant that the occasion, whatever it might be, was important.

He rose and kissed her briefly on the forehead by way of greeting. "How did you get here?"

"Took a cab."

"A *cab.* My God, Nancy, I told you we're short of money this month after those Easter outfits you bought for the kids and . . ."

"Save your lecture. This is an emergency."

Her tone rather than her words stopped him. "Has one of the kids been . . ."

"Nothing like that. Esther called. She wants me to spend the rest of the day with her."

"Why?"

"Ron's been found."

"Dead?"

"Yes."

Something inside Turee that had been stretched tauter and tauter like a violin string broke suddenly with a twang. Along with a dozen other sensations he felt a sense of relief that the suspense was over. Ron was, in a way, now safe; safe from Esther's cold scorn, and Thelma's demands, and Harry's reproach, and the ridicule of the world. "How did it happen?"

"He drove off a cliff into the bay, somewhere not too far from the lodge. He had the convertible with the top down. Esther said the policeman who came to tell her said Ron mightn't have been found for days, or weeks even, if he hadn't had his safety belt fastened." Her lower lip projected childishly and began to tremble. "I don't know, there's something so f-f-funny about that, Ron was always p-playing it s-s-safe."

"Don't cry."

"I can't help it."

"All right then." He watched with detachment while she dabbed at her eyes, wondering for the hundredth time at what peculiar things roused a woman's emotions. The fact that Ron drove over a cliff to his death didn't seem to bother her as much as the safety belt being fastened. "Ron did it intentionally?"

"Yes. Esther had a letter from him this morning—he'd posted it Saturday night in some little town up north. She told me about it on the phone."

"And?"

"Well, this will come as a great shock to you, Ralph, but—well, Thelma's pregnant. By Ron. It's incredible, utterly incredible, he and Harry were such good friends. I can't *believe* it. Can you?"

He turned away deliberately, without answering.

"You don't even seem surprised, Ralph. You mean you *knew?* All along? And you didn't tell me?"

"We'll go into that another time."

"But you . . ."

"How is Esther taking it?"

"I don't know. She sounded calm enough. She seemed anxious for me to come and stay with her, though, so I will."

"Good girl."

"I couldn't very well refuse. Oh yes, and I've made arrangements with Mrs. Sullivan to go and meet Janie's school bus. The other kids are big enough to look after themselves for a while."

"They won't have to. My last class is a two o'clock. I'll be home before four."

"No, dear, you won't."

He looked exasperated. "What the hell does that mean, no-dear-you-won't?"

"I've been thinking it over. Somebody has to tell Thelma. It wouldn't be humane to let her hear on the radio or read it in the newspaper. Someone has to drive to Weston and tell her in person."

"Meaning me."

"You're the logical one. I thought of Harry, but it's so difficult locating him when he's on the job going from office to office. Besides, having Harry tell her wouldn't be very—well, delicate, would it? So that leaves you."

"Obviously."

"You don't mind very much, do you?"

"I mind like the very devil."

"Someone has to do it. I'd volunteer, but I don't trust myself. I'm angry with her, bitterly angry, I couldn't even pretend any sympathy."

"Can I?"

"No, but you can *feel* it," she said earnestly. "You're much kinder than I am about human frailties."

When he reached Weston it was five o'clock and his nerves were rubbed raw by traffic tensions and anticipation of his errand. At the very outskirts of the city he was still thinking up excuses to turn around and go back, or to call Bill Winslow or Joe Hepburn and pass the buck to one of them.

Though it was still bright and sunny, the blinds were already drawn on the windows of the square red-brick house where Thelma lived. Turee had to ring the doorbell half a dozen times before Thelma finally appeared.

Freshly scrubbed, without make-up, and with her long fair hair combed straight back, Alice-in-Wonderland style, she appeared younger and more vulnerable than Turee remembered her. Although he had talked to her on the telephone, he hadn't seen her since the last time the fellows had gathered at Harry's house a month ago, and on that occasion, as on other similar ones, she'd been unobtrusive and efficient, quietly refilling glasses and passing sandwiches, more like a good maid than the mistress of the house. Looking at her now, Turee tried to recall whether at any time during that night she'd paid special attention to Galloway, whether hands had touched briefly, or significant glances had passed back and forth, or knowing smiles been exchanged. The only incident Turee could think of happened late in the evening: Galloway had dropped and broken his glass and Thelma had cleaned up the mess. No one thought anything of it at the time, no one saw anything significant or symbolic in Thelma's kneeling docilely at Galloway's feet, picking up the pieces of glass and blotting the carpet with paper towels. Galloway had not offered to help. He'd seemed, in fact, stunned by the accident, as if he'd broken some valuable crystal by Steuben instead of an ordinary tumbler from the dime store.

"Hello, Ralph."

"Hello, Thelma. How are you?"

"Fine. I think, fine." She was carrying a man's blue and white striped shirt and a threaded needle. "Come in, won't you? I'm just sewing."

The three lamps in the living room were turned on but the room still looked gloomy, and the atmosphere was cool and damp as if the place had been shut up all day and used as a refuge by someone hiding from the sun or the neighbors.

Thelma sat on the chesterfield beside a pile of men's clothes, socks and shirts and undershorts. "Harry called at noon. Thanks for letting him spend the night with you."

"He's welcome to stay anytime. The kids are crazy about him."

"Oh."

"He likes them, too. He doesn't even mind them climbing all over him at six-thirty in the morning. That's a true test."

"Is it?"

"My own opinion is that Harry would make a very fine father. He's got all the . . ."

"You're wasting your time," she said, flatly and finally. "Harry is not the father of my child. I couldn't possibly go on living with him, pretending that he was. If that's what you're suggesting."

"I'm not merely suggesting, I'm strongly urging you to reconsider. Harry and I talked it over last night. He's willing, he's actually eager to assume responsibility for the child. He loves you, Thelma."

"I know that. But I don't love him. And if I had to continue living with him under such false pretenses I might grow to hate him. No child should be brought up in a house of hate as I was. No, Ralph, don't argue. The future is settled."

"Is it?"

"Yes. Oh, there'll be a lot of talk, a lot of scandal, but it will blow over. Then Ron and I can move somewhere else and start a life of our own." She spoke quickly, glibly, as if she had said these exact words to herself many times, perhaps because she believed them, perhaps because she was merely trying to believe them. "You don't mind if I go on sewing, do you? Harry's coming for his things after be finishes work and I want them to be in order. He won't have anyone to look after him for a while."

"For a while?"

"He'll get married again some day . . . I know he thinks his love for me is unique and undying and so on, but I understand Harry pretty well. Some nice woman will come along and give him the kind of life he wants."

"You've given him the kind of life he wants."

"He's easily satisfied. I'm not."

"You put up a good front."

"I have my pride. Oh, I guess you think that word sounds peculiar coming from me, but what I said is true. I couldn't very well go around telling people like you and Nancy that I was bored and lonely sitting around this house all day, knowing the future would be exactly the same. The only person I ever told was Ron. He told me things too—that Esther was smarter than he was and he was always embarrassed when they went out together and she dominated the conversation and everything. He said it made him feel as if he were her idiot son whom she dragged along out of duty."

It was, to Turee, a rather bizarre picture of the Galloways' relationship, and yet he realized instantly that it showed some true colors and some bold, clear lines.

"I told him he needn't fear anything like that from me, I'm not very smart. Or if I am, nobody's ever mentioned it."

Suddenly she put down her sewing and flashed him a glance so sharp and direct that he blinked trying to meet it. "What are you doing here, Ralph? You're usually home by this time. I know you and Nancy eat early because of the children. Did you just come to hear me chatter?"

"No."

"I knew as soon as I opened the door and saw you, I knew there must be a reason. An important one. Is it about Ron?"

"Yes."

"If it were good news you'd have told me right away. So it's bad news. How bad?"

"He's dead."

"You're not—there can't be any mistake?"

"No."

She bunched forward until her forehead rested on her knees and stayed there motionless, as if she'd lost the will to move. Street noises seeped in through the cracks of the windows and streaks of light past the edges of the drawn blinds. Turee wished he were outside with the noise and the light, instead of in this room where everything seemed to have died, not even a clock ticked or a fly buzzed.

Thelma spoke finally, her voice muffled by the folds of her skirt. "The car."

"What about the car?"

"He had an accident?"

"There is reason to believe," Turee said cautiously, "that the act was intentional."

"What reason?"

"He posted a letter to Esther before he died."

"To *Esther.*" Her head snapped up like a puppet's jerked by a string. "Not to me. Why not to *me?* Why not to me? I'm the one who loved him. I gave up everything for him, my home, my husband, my good name, and I'd have given up anything more I had. Why not to me? Why not . . . Oh God, I can't stand it. Ron, Ron, Ron. Oh God, come back, Ron, come back. Don't leave me alone. I'm scared. I'm scared."

"Thelma. Please."

"Ron, Ron, Ron darling. Oh, my God!"

She kept on moaning, her teeth pressed into her lower lip until the blood began to run, as if she were consciously inflicting mutilation on herself as punishment. Presently the metallic taste of the blood made her cough, and the moans turned into a fit of coughing. She held one of Harry's shirts against her mouth to stifle the sound. When she put it down again it was stained with blood and tears, and Turee thought what a sharp piece of irony it was that Harry, who had done nothing against anyone, should have to sop up the tears and wipe off the blood.

"Let me fix you a drink, Thelma."

"No!"

"Well, perhaps Harry has some pills lying around that will help calm you down a little."

"Pills!" She spat the word into the center of the room as if she were aiming at an invisible cuspidor. "Harry has a million pills lying around. Go take them all as far as I'm concerned."

"Damned if I wouldn't if I could find them," Turee said, rather pleased by her fit of temper. It meant that she wasn't too submerged in her grief to react to ordinary stimuli.

She held Harry's shirt to her mouth again, and if Turee hadn't known better he might have taken it for a gesture of affection. "What was in the letter he wrote to—to Esther?"

"I don't know."

"You haven't seen it?"

"No."

"Then she could be lying, deliberately lying, pretending there's such a letter to make me feel bad."

"That's not very reasonable, is it?"

"You don't know Esther."

"Only for ten years."

"Nobody knows what goes on inside somebody else."

"There's the circumstantial evidence of their actions and words. When you see a man obviously enjoying his dinner you can assume he feels hungry and thinks the food is good."

"Assuming and knowing—there's an appalling gap between them. And I fell into it." Fresh tears spilled down her cheeks and she jabbed at her eyes viciously as if they were traitors betraying her. "The night—Saturday night—when I told Ron about the baby I could see he was surprised, shocked even, but I thought he was pleased too, pleased because he loved me, and the baby was the bond of our love, and we would all be together in the future. That's what I *assumed.* What I know now is that he didn't want any future with me in it, he'd rather die. He'd rather *die.*"

"Don't blame yourself so much, Thelma."

"There's no one else to blame." Her lower lip was beginning to puff and her eyes had swollen and reddened. "How could he have done it, deserted me, left me to face everything alone?"

"Thelma . . ."

"I thought he was a man, not a nasty little coward. No, no, what in God's name am I saying—he wasn't a coward! He—I don't know. I don't know! Oh Ron. Oh *Ron!"* She seemed to be clinging wildly to a pendulum that swung between the extremes of love and hate, grief and fury. "I can't stand it. I can't go on living without him."

"You must."

"I can't, I can't do it."

"You have to think of your child."

She folded her arms across her abdomen as if she suddenly had a notion that the fetus was already aware and must be protected from the sight and sound of strangers who might be hostile. "What will happen to us, Ralph, to him and me?"

"I don't know."

"I had such high hopes, such wonderful plans."

This was Thelma stripped down to essentials, like a hot rod with its top removed, its fenders missing, its engine exposed and unmuffled and its twin pipes roaring, *I* and *me.* All of Thelma's high hopes had been built on deceit and her wonderful plans made entirely at the expense of other people.

Something struck the front window and landed on the porch with a plop. Thelma jumped, as if the little sound had been loud as a cannon, aimed at her.

"Probably the evening paper," Turee said. "I'll bring it in if you like."

"I don't like. I—will it be in, about Ron?"

"Perhaps."

"And me?"

"I'm not sure who knows about you, except for Harry and Esther and myself." A few minutes later he was forced to add, silently, *and the entire police department.*

The account of Ron's death was headlined on the front page of the paper, PROMINENT TORONTONIAN FOUND DEAD IN GEORGIAN BAY. Esther had apparently refused to provide a recent photograph of Ron, so some newspaperman had scrounged around in the file room and came up with a picture taken several years previously at a New Year's Eve party at the Granite Club. Ron was grinning self-consciously into the camera, serpentine tie entwining his neck and bits of confetti clinging to his hair and his dinner jacket. Both the picture and the caption, GALLOWAY IN A GAYER MOOD, were in incredibly bad taste. Turee had a futile hope that Esther wouldn't see it. That Thelma should see it was inevitable, but somehow this seemed more fitting to Turee, since all of Thelma's recent actions indicated her lack of the sense of propriety that was so strong in Esther.

Although Thelma hadn't wanted him to bring in the newspaper in the first place, she was now watching him with nervous impatience, twisting and untwisting her small plump hands. "Well, what does it *say?"*

"Read it for yourself."

"No. I can't. My eyes hurt."

"All right. First, there's a factual account of how and where he was found. I see no point in reading that aloud, it will only upset you."

"Go on from there, then."

" 'An autopsy has been ordered. Authorities are still investigating the possibility of accidental death, although the present evidence points to suicide. A letter received this morning by his wife, the former Esther Ann Billings, allegedly indicated Galloway's intention of killing himself. This letter is now in the hands of the police, who, because of its delicate and personal nature, refused to release its contents to the press.' "

"She gave the letter to the *police?*" Thelma's tone was incredulous, and Turee's would have matched it if he'd spoken. It seemed incongruous to him that Esther should have handed such a personal letter over to the police. The locker rooms of a police department could spring as many leaks as locker rooms anywhere else, and Esther was sophisticated enough to know this. Perhaps she'd had no choice and the police had demanded the letter as evidence of intent to commit suicide. Or perhaps Esther had meant, without thinking of the consequences to herself or her children, to involve Thelma, immediately and publicly.

Thelma said, "I'm in the letter, I suppose?"

"Yes."

"By name?"

"I think so."

"So it's only a matter of time until everybody in town knows. My God, how can I face it?"

"You have friends."

"Ron's friends, and Harry's. None of my own, not one."

"There's still a solution," Turee said. "If you'll accept it, if you'll be reasonable."

But she turned away, closing off the face of reason as if by a stone door. "I won't."

"You haven't even . . ."

"Hide behind Harry, that's your solution?"

"Harry's willing, I told you that. Don't underestimate him. He's a fine man, a generous man."

"Oh, I know. Good old Harry, always willing to give his last shirt to a friend—or lose it to him in a poker game. Harry's such a good loser, is that why everyone likes him so much? He loses so gently and gracefully. But he loses. He always misses the boat. Why?"

"Maybe he doesn't want to go any place."

"Well, I do. And I will. Anything will be better than going on living with Harry, in this house, in this town."

Her tone was final, and as if for emphasis she picked up her needle again. In and out of the holes of a button her hand moved, quick, precise, without a tremor. Either the pendulum had stopped swinging, or Thelma had let go of it.

Turee rose and crossed the room, awkwardly and painfully. His legs had gone numb and his feet felt as if they were being pierced by a thousand needles, all sharper than the one Thelma was wielding. She looked up and met his questioning gaze. "Stop worrying about me," she said bluntly. "I'll be all right as long as I keep busy, keep doing things. Tomorrow I'll start on the baby's layette. Everything will be sewn by hand . . . You're not leaving, Ralph?"

"It's getting rather late."

"I was hoping you'd stay until Harry comes for his clothes. He's probably seen the papers and he'll be very upset. He's terribly emotional about things—friends, home, mother, lost dogs."

"Aren't you?"

"Me? I haven't any friends, and I never had either a home or a mother or owned a dog. Does that answer your question?"

"Not very satisfactorily."

"How you love to analyze people, Ralph, but please don't try it on me."

Turee remembered Harry's saying similar words early Sunday morning while they were driving from Wiarton back to the lodge: *Just don't start analyzing Thelma. I love her the way she is. Let her have her dreams.*

Well, she had them, Turee thought dryly. What a blind fool Harry had been. Not like a husband, but like a too-permissive parent, overly ready to cover up a child's errors, and eager to accept the most comfortable explanations.

"I'll make you some tea, Ralph. Perhaps you'd like a sandwich, too?"

"No thanks to both. I'll wait for Harry, though."

"That's good of you." She picked up the pile of clothes from the chesterfield and rose, a little clumsily, as if she were not yet used to the new proportion of weight in her body. "If you'll excuse me, I'll finish Harry's packing."

"Where is he going to stay?"

"He told me he's taking a room at a hotel. I don't know which one. I didn't ask."

"Will he keep on with his job here?"

"I didn't ask that either." She paused in the doorway. "I keep telling you, but you still don't seem to understand. Harry and I are through. He is part of the past. We must both start right now forgetting each other. I've made my decision—it wouldn't be fair to Harry if I kept in touch with him, if I fostered any hope in him that we would get together again. I don't want to know where he's living or what he's doing. I wish him good luck, that's all. And happiness too."

"How magnanimous."

She missed the irony. "I bear no grudge against Harry. Why should I? He did his best."

After she'd left the room, Turee picked up a magazine, but it was impossible for him to read. He found himself listening to Thelma's step, on the stairs and along the hall, heavy and uncertain as if she were dragging something behind her. He could hear her moving around in the bedroom directly overhead, opening drawers, closing them, mumbling to herself now and then, muted sounds that disintegrated before they could reach Turee as words.

She's frightened silly, he thought. If Harry could force himself to take a really firm stand with her, she might be willing to give in, to lean on him. Thelma's repeated protestations of independence seemed to be covering up a real need to lean. Perhaps the reason she couldn't yet do it was her fear that Harry might not be able to bear her weight. It was now up to Harry to prove his strength.

The telephone began to ring in the next room and Thelma came downstairs to answer it, quite slowly, as if she knew in advance that the call couldn't be important, all the important things had already happened to her.

"Hello . . . Yes, this is Mrs. Bream . . . Is he hurt? . . . Oh, I see . . . No, I can't come myself, it's impossible. I'll see if I can get somebody else . . . Thank you for telling me. Good-bye."

Turee met her at the door of the living room. "Harry's been injured?"

"Not badly. He jammed the back of a streetcar on College Avenue and he has a few head cuts. He's in the emergency ward at Toronto General. They're going to keep him there overnight."

"Why, if it's nothing serious?"

"Why?" The corners of her mouth twisted in bitterness. "Because he's too drunk to go anywhere."

15

THE CURTAINED CUBICLE was so small that Turee barely had room to stand beside the bed. Harry lay on his back, his eyes closed, his entire head bandaged very tightly, so that the skin of his forehead had contracted into a petulant frown.

"Harry . . ."

"He's out," the nurse said. She was a type Turee recognized, stout, middle-aged, efficient, with a false front of maternality that wouldn't deceive a child but had fooled many an adult. She added, "He talks a blue streak, then passes out, and a minute later he's talking again."

"I thought he was only slightly hurt. All those bandages . . ."

"They don't mean anything. Head cuts bleed a lot so the doctor usually applies a pressure bandage for a day or two in case of hemorrhage. Actually he's only got eleven stitches. He'll suffer more from the hangover. And other things."

"Such as?"

"As soon as he's released from here they'll take him down and book him for drunk driving. He'll get a stiff fine. Too bad, him with no job and his wife pregnant. Maybe that's why he did it."

"Did what?"

"Drank so much. Some men get all emotional over their first baby. I guess it strains their sense of responsibility. Do you want to stay here with him for a while?"

"Yes."

"Good. I have things to do. If he gets rambunctious, just give me a buzz."

"All right."

"I'm Miss Hutchins."

Turee stood in silence at the foot of the bed, observing the differences that lack of consciousness emphasized. Harry's affability seemed to be unmasked as weakness, his urge to please as anxiety. And this is what Thelma sees, he thought, Harry with his guards down. This is what she based her decision on. She can't afford to lean on a straw.

"Harry."

Harry shook his head back and forth on the pillow as if he was trying to shake off the sound of his own name nagging him back into a world he wanted to forget.

"It's Ralph, Harry. You don't have to talk. I just want you to know I'm here."

"Thelma?"

"She's all right. She's at home. The next-door neighbor is staying with her, a Mrs. Mal—somebody."

"My head hurts. Wanna sit *up*."

"I'm not sure you . . ."

"Wanna sit up."

"All right." Turee cranked the bed up halfway. "That better?"

"Nothing's better. Nothing's better in the whole world." His slurred speech and glassy, unfocused eyes made it clear that either Harry was still drunk or under the influence of a sedative. "*Nothing*. See?"

"I see. Sure."

"You're a good head, Ralph. There's no better head than you, nowhere. See?"

"Sure, sure. Now take it easy."

Harry closed his eyes and lapsed into incoherence for a time. Only the odd word was distinguishable, but his angry, guttural tone and his bellicose expression indicated strongly that Harry was telling somebody off.

Turee moved up to the head of the bed and put his hand lightly and firmly on Harry's shoulder. "Harry, can you hear me?"

"Can't hear you. Go away."

"What's bothering you?"

"I bumped into a streetcar. Damn thing wouldn't move. I was in a hurry."

"Where were you going?"

"No place. No place to go."

"Before you hit the streetcar, Harry, what happened?"

"I had a little drink."

"I know that."

"One little drink. 'S what I told the policeman. 'S what I'm telling you."

"I thought you were at work. You don't usually drink between office calls."

"No office calls. No more office calls."

"What do you mean?"

" 'Take your goddam pills,' I said, 'I quit.' I said, 'The whole bloody bunch of you can go jump in the lake.' Lake." He repeated the word, wincing, as if it had pierced his consciousness like a needle. "Lake. I was in a bar. I heard them talking about a lake. Ron. That's what Ron did. Jumped in the lake. Isn't that funny, hah? Isn't that funny?" Tears were streaming down his face, and he had begun to hiccup. "Wanted to jump in the lake too. Couldn't find it. Couldn't find the bloody lake."

"You can find it some other time," Turee said dryly. "Right now you're supposed to take it easy."

"Streetcar in my way. Wouldn't move. 'Giddyap,' I said, 'giddyap,' and I stepped on the gas. Didn't mean to hit it, just wanted to push it along, get it started. I was in a hurry. I was—where was I going? Can't remember."

"It doesn't matter."

Harry wiped his face on a corner of the bedsheet, then held it against his mouth to stem the flow of hiccups. "My head hurts. I broke something. Did I—broke something?"

"No." He wishes he had, Turee thought. It would be easier on him if he could misdirect his misery at something physical. But all Harry's breaks are in places no doctor could reach to use a splint or apply a cast. "You've got a hangover," Turee added bluntly. "How much did you have to drink?"

"Just one little . . ."

"Come off it. I'm not a policeman. How much?"

"Don't, don't, don't. I can't remember."

"All right."

"I needed a drink. I quit my job."

"Why? You've always liked your job."

"No wife anymore, no home, might as well have no job, start from scratch."

"That's pretty childish logic. How do you expect to live?"

"I don't know. I don't care."

"Do you think the company will take you back? You've been with them for years."

"I'm not going back."

"You could apply for a transfer to another city."

"No wife, no home, no job."

"Also no friends, if you want to play it that way."

"Friends." Harry spit the word across the room as if it had a foul taste. Then he turned and buried his face in the pillow and started to curse. He kept it up for a long time.

"You're beginning," Turee said finally, "to repeat yourself."

"Shut your goddam . . ."

"All right, all right, all right."

"How the hell did you get here anyway? Who asked you to come?"

"Thelma. I was with her when the hospital phoned."

"Doing what? Or is that too personal?"

Turee, white with anger, explained in very elementary language what he was not doing with Thelma. "Now is that clear enough for you or shall I draw pictures?"

"Goddam you, shut up! Shut up, shut up!"

As if on cue, Miss Hutchins, the nurse, reappeared. She wore the professional smile which she picked up outside the door like a surgical gown and left there when she departed. "Just what is going on in here? Do you want to wake the whole hospital? How does your head feel?"

Without waiting for any answers, she began adjusting the tray holder on Harry's bed. "Here we are. Some nice Cream of Wheat. And a cup of chocolate with a marshmallow—one of the new dietitians is bugs on marshmallows, puts them in everything. And two little pills to help with the jitters."

Harry glanced briefly at the pills. "Chlorpromazine."

"Now how did you know that?"

"Never mind. I won't take them anyway. I want my clothes."

"What for?"

"I've got to get out of here. Where are my clothes?"

"Where I put them. So let's not have a hassle, Mr. Bream. In a hospital when the doctor says you stay, you stay. Might as well pretend you're a guest and be polite about it."

"I have to talk to my wife. It's urgent."

"Look, Mr. Bream, even if you managed to get out of here, you wouldn't be allowed to go home. You were driving while drunk and involved in an accident. You'll have to be taken down to the jail and booked. There's a policeman at the desk now waiting to question you about the accident. This isn't the Royal York Hotel but it's better than a cell in the local pokey."

"Bail. I could get bail. Ralph, how much money have you got?"

"Here?" Turee said. "About a dollar and thirty-five cents. In the bank, a little more."

"Well, there's Bill Winslow or Joe Hepburn. Or Esther. No, we couldn't bother Esther. But Bill would . . ."

"Bill won't," Miss Hutchins said bluntly. "Not tonight, anyway. Now if you behave yourself, you can stay here. You're warm, comfy, well looked after. But if you start throwing fits they'll haul you up to the psycho ward. Some of the beds there have cages around them. Now do you want to spend the night locked up like a monkey in a zoo, or are you going to be a good boy, eat your Cream of Wheat, take your pills and stop arguing?"

Harry peered at her resentfully from under his bandages. "You're very *rude.*"

"Am I now?" Miss Hutchins' smile for the first time was one of genuine amusement. "Well, I've been handling drunks for thirty years. I guess it's not the best way in the world to learn manners. Think you can feed yourself?"

"Of course I can feed myself."

"Try."

Harry tried. He picked up the spoon and dipped it in the dish of cereal, but his hand was shaking so badly he didn't attempt to raise the spoon to his mouth. He lay back and closed his eyes. "I'm not hungry."

"None of you are," Miss Hutchins said dryly. "But some protein helps with the shakes. The pills ought to help, too. Are you going to take them?"

"I—guess so."

Miss Hutchins gave him the pills in a tiny paper cup and Harry swallowed them like an expert, without any water.

"There now," Miss Hutchins said. "I'll take your tray away and we'll try eating again later after you've had a little rest."

"Chlorpromazine never affects me. I've had it dozens of times."

"Is that a fact?"

She removed the tray and cranked down the bed. Within a few minutes Harry was asleep again, snoring heavily through his open mouth.

Turee followed Miss Hutchins into the corridor. "Should I stay around?"

"Oh, there's no reason to. He'll be fine. It's nearly eight o'clock, he may sleep clear through the night."

"I hope so," Turee said, wishing he could do the same, sleep through the night right up until noon the next day. By noon some things would be settled. Harry would be free, and Esther would have weathered the first day of widowhood. Perhaps, too, the autopsy would be completed and any uncertainty about Ron's death dispelled. Turee wondered, and felt a little shocked at himself for wondering, if Ron had made a will, and if he, or any of the rest of Ron's friends, were mentioned in it. *I can't help it. I have a dollar thirty-five in my pocket.*

". . . a funny thing about Mr. Bream," Miss Hutchins was saying. "Before I took in his tray, I checked the result of the blood alcohol test they ran on him. It was only one-tenth of one percent. In a normal person that's not even intoxication level, yet Mr. Bream was almost dead drunk when they brought him in. I guess he's the kind who can't hold his liquor."

"I guess he is."

"Or else he's under some severe emotional strain which aggravated the effect of the alcohol. It's odd his wife didn't come to see him." Miss Hutchins' tone was casual, there wasn't the faintest emphasis on the word *wife.* But her eyes gave her away. They were honed sharp as a fortune teller's on the lookout for some slight reaction that would indicate she was on the right road to her client's secrets. "When I talked to her on the telephone she sounded quite cool and collected, just the kind of person you'd think would rise to an emergency."

Noon. Noon tomorrow, Turee said to himself as a child says Christmas. *By noon some things will be settled and Miss Hutchins will have faded into the past and good riddance.*

He had no reason to suspect that a long time later Miss Hutchins would reappear in his mind, her features distinct, her voice persistent, her outlines as precise as they were now while he was watching her bustle off down the corridor to the nurses' station.

Turee began walking in the opposite direction toward the exit door. The policeman Miss Hutchins had referred to was waiting at the registration desk, talking to a young man wearing a crew cut and a trench coat.

As Turee was about to pass, the young man turned and his face brightened with recognition. "Why, hello, Professor."

"Good evening."

"I guess you don't remember me. I'm Rod Blake. I was in a poli sci course of yours a couple of years ago."

"Blake. Of course." He recalled Blake now as a brash youngster whose good opinion of himself had been considerably higher than his grades. "What are you doing this year, Blake?"

"A little of this and that. I've got my sights set on a job. A good one. Why start at the bottom, I always say."

"Well, good luck."

Turee was impatient to leave, but the young man took a step to the left, blocking his way. It was an unobtrusive and expert motion, as if Blake were accustomed to people trying to get away from him and had practiced means of circumventing them.

"Nothing the matter with your family, I hope?" Blake said.

"They're all well, thank you."

"That's good. I thought your being here in this ward might indicate . . ."

"I was visiting a friend who had an accident."

"Nothing serious, I trust?"

Turee glanced at the policeman who appeared bored, either by the conversation, his job, or Blake. "Nothing serious, no. Well, good night, Blake."

"It was a real pleasure bumping into you like this, Professor."

They shook hands, firmly, like old friends or secret enemies, and Turee went out into the spring night.

The cold wind evaporated the moisture on his brow and spread a chill through his entire body. *I flunked him in the course. He hates my guts. I wonder what his angle is.*

16

IT WAS CHARACTERISTIC of Blake that when he wanted something badly he went after it with such tactless determination that he weakened his own chances. The job at the *Globe and Mail* was a case in point.

He had decided on journalism as his field because it apparently offered glamour and excitement and a chance for advancement. "Wait'll I'm editor," he'd told one of his girlfriends. And he had chosen the particular newspaper, the *Globe,* because it was old, established, solvent, and the news editor was a man named Ian Richards whom Blake respected as much as he could respect anyone.

Every day or two, for the past month, he'd been dropping in at Richards' office, trying to prove, by means of story ideas, plans for a new sports column, revamping the front-page format and so on, that the *Globe* had tired blood and needed a quick transfusion of Blake. He oversold himself. Richards' preliminary interest had turned into dislike, his amusement into acidity. Yet no matter how clearly Richards indicated these changes, Blake seemed to remain obdurately unaware of them.

Late Tuesday afternoon he appeared at Richards' office in an elated mood. Richards didn't pay much attention to the mood. He'd seen samples of it before, and it usually meant only that Blake had been thinking beautiful thoughts of himself again.

"I'd ask you to sit down," Richards said, "but I'm busy."

Blake grinned. "I can talk on my feet."

"You can talk on your head, I'm still busy."

"You'll be sorry if you don't listen. I'm on to something."

"Again?"

"This time it's big. You've been following the Galloway case?"

"I read my own newspaper, naturally. What about it? Suicides are a dime a dozen."

"And the stories behind them?"

"I'm sure they're all very interesting, but it's not the kind of thing we print."

"You might want to print this one. You, or some other newspaper. I'm giving you first chance. Nice of me, eh?"

"Dandy." Richards' mouth puckered as if he'd bitten into something sour. "Just dandy."

"Well, the whole thing started in kind of a chancy way. Last night I dropped in at the Emergency Ward at General. It's a good place to pick up things, there are always policemen around waiting to question accident victims and so on. Anyway, I was just standing there minding everybody else's business when I happened to see an old prof of mine from U. C., Ralph Turee. He handed me a bum deal in his course but I figured, let bygones be bygones. Besides, I had a hunch—it seemed like the last place in the world you'd meet a guy like Turee. I mean, he's just not the type you associate with accidents or emergencies or the like. He's cold, and cautious, probably never even had a parking ticket in his life—maybe a little like you, eh, Richards?"

"So you had a hunch. Go on."

"It seems Turee was in the ward, visiting a friend of his who had an accident. That much I got from him, the rest I got from the nurse in charge. I had no trouble at all. Nurses always go for me. I gave her the treatment and she opened up like a flower. The friend Turee was visiting was a guy named Harry Bream who'd been brought in drunk after hitting a streetcar. Bream did a lot of ranting and raving during which he dropped some names. Galloway was one, Ron Galloway. As soon as I heard that, bells started to ring."

"Same old bells, or new ones?"

Blake brushed away the sarcasm as he would a fly, with a sweep of his hand. "So I began checking. First the records at City Hall, then your file room downstairs. When Galloway was married, nine years ago, to his present wife, Harry Bream was his best man. And get this, he was also best man at Galloway's first marriage to the heiress Dorothy Reynold. The conclusion's obvious: Bream and Galloway have been very good friends for a very long time."

"So?"

"Well, Bream now has a wife himself. They were married about three years ago, no children, live out in Weston. Her name is Thelma. Mean anything to you?"

"Not a thing."

"You should get around, Richards. Like me. That suicide note Galloway left—well, let's put it this way: I've got a pretty good friend in the police department."

"He let you see the note?"

"No, but he told me what was in it."

Richards looked grim. "For how much?"

"Not a cent. He likes my pretty blue eyes."

"I suppose policemen find you as irresistible as nurses do?"

"You might," Blake said with a smile, "put it like that, yes."

"You're a fresh kid, Blake. Full of ideas, some of them good, full of stories, some of them true. But mostly full of you-know-what. I wouldn't give you a job here even if I could. You're trouble."

"Trouble or not, I have some very valuable information."

"My advice is, take it to the *News*."

"The *News* has no class. Besides, I hear it's going to fold. I don't want to start a trip on a sinking ship. I can't swim."

"You'd better learn."

"Okay, the hell with you, Richards. Let a silly personal prejudice cut you off from a scoop."

"We don't depend on scoops for our circulation."

"All right, but would you turn one down?"

Richards hesitated, drumming his pencil on the desk.

"Listen, Blake, if you've got a story, I might buy it. I won't buy you."

"How much?"

"That depends on the story. If it's good, if it's true. And if it's printable."

"I'd print it, if I were news editor."

"We don't always think alike. Let's hear the story."

"Not yet. I have to check out one more thing before everything's positive. Oh, it'll check, don't worry. My methods may not come under the Boy Scout rules, but they work." He perched on the edge of Richards' desk, clasping his hands together as if he were congratulating himself. "You know, that's the trouble with this paper, you need a live wire around with some high voltage."

"You might blow the fuses."

"Think it over. I've got guts, energy, youth, a nose for news . . ."

"What makes you hate yourself so much?"

"I've got to talk myself up. Who else will do it?"

"Haven't you got a mother?"

"Oh, come off it, Richards. How do you pick reporters around here, for their modest smiles and the way they sweet-talk you? Anybody can do that. Oh, you're a great man, Mr. Richards, sir, I don't really deserve to work for such an outstanding newspaper, sir, but I'll do anything, I'll scrub floors, I'll wash out the cuspidors . . ."

"Beat it, Blake. I told you I was busy."

"Okay, but I'll be back. Unless I get a better offer somewhere else."

"If you do, take it." He picked up a piece of copy from his desk and began reading.

Blake craned his neck to look at it. "The autopsy report on Galloway, eh? You know what I bet you'll do with it? Take your little red pencil and reduce it to something as dull as a stock quotation."

"That's my business."

When he had gone, Richards took off his spectacles and rubbed his eyes. They felt gritty, as though he'd been bucking a strong and dirty wind. He felt more distaste than interest in Blake's promises. If the police department had so many leaks that a kid like Blake could find out the contents of a supposedly secret suicide letter, this was a story in itself, perhaps a bigger story, in the long run, than any Blake could dream up.

He replaced his spectacles and turned back to the autopsy report. It was, as far as Richards was concerned, considerably duller than a stock quotation: death had been caused by drowning, water was found in the stomach and lungs, and foamy mucus in the trachea, and the blood chlorides on the left side of the heart were thirty percent lower than those of the right, a positive indication of drowning in fresh water.

The report revealed only one surprise, that Galloway had made a previous attempt at suicide in the earlier hours of the night, Saturday, that he had died. Considerable amounts of a barbiturate compound were found in the stomach and other vital organs. When questioned about this point, Dr. Robert Whitewood, the pathologist who performed the autopsy, stated that it was fairly common to discover traces of previous suicide attempts, which he compared roughly to the "hesitation marks" frequently found on victims of suicide who had used razors, knives, or other sharp instruments.

Nothing in the early part of the report affected Richards—water in the lungs, chloride content of the heart, mucus in the trachea, these meant only that Galloway was a dead man. But the phrase, hesitation marks, conjured up a live one.

"Hesitation marks." Richards repeated it aloud, thinking, Galloway was a man, like himself, going through all the motions of living, until one day he no longer felt any incentive to move. He had tried to kill himself, and failing, had tried again. Between the two attempts there was the time of hesitation. At what point had he written the letter to his wife?

And who, Richards wondered, was Thelma?

17

THELMA SELDOM READ the newspapers. She was not actually concerned about other people, and though she had her share of female curiosity Thelma's ran round and round on a limited track like a toy train stopping only at certain junctions, responsive only to the level of Thelma's immediate interest.

On the front lawn the morning paper lay unopened, already yellowing under the sharp spring sun. For several hours Turee had been trying to reach her by phone to warn her about the small but strategically placed paragraph on the second page of the *News*, headed MYSTERY WOMAN HINTED IN GALLOWAY DEATH. Thelma had heard the phone ringing and had refused to answer. She was practically certain that the caller was Turee and that he merely intended to repeat what he'd been telling her for the past two days, that, in the interests of good taste if nothing else, she was not to attend Galloway's funeral. Thelma had resisted this advice with voluble obstinacy. For one reason, quite unconscious, it presented her with something definite to rebel against, and so helped to take the edge off her grief. Turee's interference served as a counter-irritant, and the time she spent resenting and opposing it was time she would otherwise have spent in self-pity and regret and guilt.

The funeral was scheduled for three o'clock that afternoon at the Galloway home, and though it was not yet one, Thelma was already dressed for the occasion in an old black wool suit that didn't quite accommodate her new proportions. She had bathed her eyes to reduce the swelling and used powder on the lids to hide their blisterlike transparency. She wore no other make-up, and her light hair was pulled back from her face into a small tight knot. She looked more like a sorrowing widow than Esther could have looked after a month of practice. She was aware of this fact, too, and it gave her a grim sense of triumph.

But the thought of Ron brought tears to her eyes and she was on the point of breaking into sobs when the telephone began to ring again, and, almost simultaneously, the front-door bell.

"Damn you," she whispered. "Damn you, leave me alone!"

Then she turned deliberately away from the ringing phone and, wiping her eyes on her sleeve like a small girl, she went to answer the front door.

On the threshold stood a good-looking young man with a crew cut, a handful of pamphlets showing the advantage of owning a water-softener, and such a fast opening spiel that Thelma didn't even hear all of it.

" . . . not more than a few pennies a day, ma'am, and the luxury of rain water right out of your tap."

"It's no use wasting your time. I simply haven't the money right now."

"A softener will save you twice that amount in soap and detergent, water bills, wear and tear on clothing, and what's more, it will conserve your water heater. If I could just step inside a minute and show you the actual figures . . ."

"Well, I don't know."

The young man took quick advantage of her hesitancy. Feigning clumsiness, he dropped one of the folders he was carrying, and in bending down to pick it up he changed position expertly so that when he rose again he was inside the house. The maneuver was so smooth that Thelma couldn't help admiring it. At one period of her life she'd sold cosmetics from door to door and she knew some of the tricks, but this one was new to her.

Thelma closed the door behind him, somewhat amused at the idea of playing dumb and letting the young man think he was getting away with something. It did not occur to her that he actually was, that until an hour ago he'd known no more about water-softeners than a baby and the pamphlets he was presenting to her were distributed free at the Hydroelectric office.

"My name is Blake, ma'am. Rod Blake."

"I'm Mrs. Bream. Sit down if you like."

"Thanks. Now about this water-softener, of course it may seem like a large initial expense, but in the long run it will more than pay for itself, believe me. Now take this model. Begging your pardon, ma'am, but if we could have a little more light . . ."

Thelma pulled open the drapes, unaware that Blake wanted more light so that he could study her more carefully. Observing the bulge beneath the shabby black suit, the pallor of her skin, her tear-swollen eyes, he felt no pity at all, only a glow of exultation that his hunch had been right. This was the woman. He was more sure of it than ever when he noticed the framed tinted picture on top of the piano. A wedding picture, obviously, and the self-conscious, stiffly smiling bridegroom was the man he'd seen in the emergency ward at General Hospital on Monday night. The bride was Thelma, looking ten years younger than she did now, though Blake knew the Breams had been married for only three years.

"My house is so small," Thelma was saying. "There wouldn't be room for it."

"Ah, that's the story I hear all the time. It usually turns out that there's some corner nobody's thought of. Mind if I take a look for myself?"

Thelma didn't answer or turn from the window. She was staring out at the street, her small plump hands clenched rigidly together like desperate lovers.

"Ma'am? I asked if I could . . ."

"Be quiet."

Surprised, Blake followed her gaze. He could see nothing extraordinary, nothing even worth watching: a couple of children having a tricycle race, an elderly lady walking slowly between two canes, a young mother wheeling a pram, a man painting his porch, a trio of small, giggling girls lurching along in their mothers' high-heeled shoes.

"Mrs. Bream . . ."

"Is that your car parked in the middle of the block facing this way?"

"I don't have a car. I'm just getting started in the business."

"The car—I don't see very well these days—is it a Buick?"

"I think so."

"About five years old?"

"About that, I guess. I don't under—"

"Is there a man in it? My eyes—all this crying—I'll go blind if I don't stop . . . Is there a man in the car?"

"Yes."

"Oh, my God, he's watching me. Maybe he's been there for hours, all morning . . . My God, what will I do? Why can't he leave me alone?"

Blake shifted uncomfortably. What had started out, on his part, as a kind of lark was disintegrating before his eyes, like a sawdust doll spilling its insides. "I think maybe I'd better be on my way. If your kitchen's too small and all that . . ."

"You can't go now."

"But I . . ."

"He's getting out of the car, he's heading here. You can't leave me here alone with him."

"It's none of my business."

"God knows what he's thinking, seeing you come into the house. He may believe that you and I—oh, I don't know. But you can't leave now, without explaining to him that you're just a salesman. You must have some card or identification from the company you work for."

Blake had begun to sweat. "I'm new at the job. This is my first day. The company's just trying me out."

"You can tell him that."

"No, no. I mean, I don't work for any particular comp—"

"The pamphlets are from the Hydroelectric Company."

"Yes, but . . ."

"All right, you work for the Hydroelectric Company. You needn't be afraid," she added contemptuously. "Harry can be unpleasant but he'd never hurt anyone."

"Why drag me into it, for Pete's sake?"

"You dragged yourself. No one invited you."

Harry knocked on the door, and when Thelma didn't answer it immediately he let himself in with his own key . . .

They met in the hall.

"Hello, Harry," she said. "So you got out of the hospital. How are you?"

He peered at her through the dimness, blinking, like a man accustomed to wearing spectacles, who without them finds the world strangely altered. "You're dressed funny."

"Am I?"

"I don't remember that suit."

"I had it before we were married."

"Black . . . You're going to the funeral?"

"Yes. Are you?"

He shook his head. "Turee says it would be bad form if either of us went, under the circumstances."

"Turee says this, Turee says that . . . Well, Turee can run your life for you but he's not running mine. I'm going to the funeral. I have a *right* to go."

Harry smiled at her sadly. "We all have rights we don't, or can't, use. Technically, I have a right to come into my own house, kiss my own wife, make love to her if I want . . ."

"Is this another of Turee's ideas?"

"No. My own."

"Well, you can stop that kind of talk, speaking of bad form. If you and Turee pretend to have such fancy manners, why don't you practice them?" She turned away. "Besides, I—we have a visitor."

"I'm aware of that."

"He's nothing, nobody. A man selling water-softeners. Claims they save money. I wonder if they really do."

"I wonder." Harry still wore his smile but it seemed oddly changed. It was sly, wary, incongruous, a cat smile on a cocker spaniel. "You have a perfect right to have visitors, to buy water softeners . . . But then, as I said, I have rights too. It's when our rights conflict that there's bound to be trouble."

"I'm not afraid of your threats."

"You're trembling."

"Oh, I admit you make me nervous, only it's like walking in front of a small boy with a supply of snowballs—the idea of being hit by a snowball makes me nervous. But even if one should hit me it wouldn't be so bad. It's only snow. So go ahead. Throw one."

"It's spring. There's no snow. Small boys might switch to rocks."

"Oh, stop all this talk. Do what you came to do and get it over with!"

"I will. I thought I'd better explain myself first. I've appealed to you in various ways, Thelma, to save us both. I've begged for your mercy, and I've asked for your pity. But no matter what words were used it always amounted to me asking you. Now I'm *telling* you."

She looked at him, silent and sullen.

"My bags are out in the car, Thelma. I haven't unpacked since I left here on Monday afternoon."

"Why not?"

"Because I'm coming back," he said calmly. "I'm moving back into my house with my wife."

"Stop talking like a fool."

"I'm not a fool. Or a small boy. And I have something in my pocket more authoritative than a snowball or a rock."

"What?"

"A gun."

"You must be cra—Harry! Harry, listen to me . . ."

She put out her hand to stop him, but he brushed past her and went into the living room. She could see, quite distinctly, the contours of the gun in the lower left pocket of his suit coat.

Blake was standing in the far corner of the room, clutching his pamphlets as if they were a passport to the outside world. Drops of sweat wriggled down his temples and behind his ears, leaving moist, shiny trails like slugs.

"Hello there," Harry said brightly. "About this proposition of yours, I think my wife and I might be interested. Tell me, does soft water make shaving any easier?"

"I—I don't know."

"Come, you're old enough to shave, surely? How old are you?"

"Twenty-one."

"A mere boy. Do you throw snowballs?"

"I . . ."

"Never mind. You must excuse my wife and me for ringing you in on our private little difference of opinion. My wife hasn't been well lately. We're expecting a child in a few months, our first. Say, that's going to mean a lot of extra washing, isn't it? I think a water-softener might be a good investment. How about it, Thelma?"

"Harry," she said dully. "Don't. Stop."

"Go take a pill, Thelma. You're not well." He turned back to the young man who had managed one surreptitious step toward the door. "You look familiar to me. Have I seen you before?"

"No," Blake said, thinking, it's true. He couldn't have seen me, he had his eyes closed when I was talking to the nurse. She said he was out, out like a light . . .

"What's your name?"

"Rod Blake."

"Funny, I'd have sworn we met some place. A hospital—have you been in a hospital recently?"

"No."

"Well, no matter. Tell me more about your product."

"We have—several models."

"Go ahead, talk about them. Speak your piece."

"Well—well, as I was just saying to your wife, this is my first day on the job."

"So?"

"I don't know much about it yet." Though he was still pouring sweat, he had begun to shiver, as if a cold wind was blowing through the house up from the basement of the past. "I—I've thought of a good idea."

"Let's hear it."

"Perhaps I could leave these folders with you and you can study them for yourself, facts and figures and so on. Then when you decide . . ."

"I've already decided. We'll take one."

"Which—which model?"

"Any model."

"But . . ."

"Any model," Harry said graciously. "All we want is enough soft water for the baby's clothes. I'll probably be doing some of the washing myself, so my motives aren't entirely unselfish. Are you married?"

"N-no sir."

"Ah well, you've plenty of time. I was well over thirty when I got married—took me that long to find the right girl. I found her, though, I found her. And I don't intend to lose her."

"Well—ah, I'd better be going now."

"What's your hurry?"

"I—the fact is, I have to get hold of an expert to come and measure—measure things."

"I can see you're a real eager-beaver. Ever see a beaver dam, by the way?"

"No sir."

"Highly interesting. You should go out of your way to find one some time."

"Yes sir. I will."

"Industrious lot, beavers."

"They certainly are." Blake began moving toward the door, breathing heavily, as if he had just completed building a dam entirely by himself with no help from any beavers. "I'll—I'll put your order in right away and see about installation."

"Oh, there's no great rush about it." Harry smiled fondly at his wife. "We can't hurry Mother Nature anyway."

"Harry. Listen to me."

"Now, dear, don't be embarrassed or upset about a perfectly natural process."

"Be quiet." Thelma watched Blake approach her and she stood squarely in the middle of the doorway, so that he couldn't pass her on either side without pushing her away. "We don't want a water-softener. My husband is merely amusing himself at your expense and mine. He's probably been drinking."

"Not drinking," Harry said. "*Thinking.*"

"Drinking," she repeated to Blake, softly, as if she were confiding a secret. "And he has a gun."

"I know, I know, but what the hell am I supposed to do? I want to get out of here."

"You can't leave me alone with him."

"You said before you weren't afraid."

"I didn't know about the gun then."

"Sweet Jesus," Blake whispered, and he felt his knees buckle like a sick colt's. *Let me out of here in one piece and I'll go to church every Sunday for a year.*

"Thinking," Harry went on, as if he had not heard the exchange or else considered it too trivial to bother about. "Yes, my dear, that's what I've been doing, a lot of plain, common sense thinking. And I've decided that you're in no condition to make the decisions for the family, now that there are going to be three of us. You're too emotional to be allowed a freedom of choice. It's up to me to take a firm stand, and I will. I'm head of this house, it's time you realized that. *I* will decide the future. You hear that, Thelma?"

"Yes," Thelma said. "I hear."

"I'm glad you're coming to your senses. I don't want to hurt your feelings, but the fact is, you've always been a little unstable."

She looked grim. "Have I?"

"So it's up to me to take over, to make all the decisions. Now the first decision I wish to make is about the water-softener. I want a water-softener and I intend to get one. Is that clear?"

"Yes."

"You see how easy your role is going to be from now on? All you have to do is agree."

"Yes."

"Actually, it will save you trouble, it will be easier on you if I shoulder the burden of responsibilities. It puts too much of a strain on a woman, making decisions, being boss. It puts a strain on anyone." He passed the back of his hand across his forehead. "A great strain. I'm—I'm really quite tired. Haven't been sleeping much. Working all day, thinking all night, thinking . . ."

"You should lie down here, Harry, and get a good rest." She crossed the room and began arranging the pillows at one end of the davenport. "Lie down, Harry."

He didn't have to be told. He sank back among the pillows, limp with exhaustion. "Lie down with me."

"I can't right now. I have to go out."

"Not to the funeral? You're not . . ."

"Of course not. If you don't want me to, I won't. You're the boss, Harry."

"Where are you going, then?"

"To the store. Now that you're moving back into the house I have to stock up on groceries. What would you like for dinner?"

"I don't know," he said, closing his eyes. "I'm so tired."

"Fried chicken?"

"I don't know. Kiss me, Thelma."

Her lips touched his forehead briefly. It felt hot and dry, like something cured in the sun, or slow-baked in an oven. "You rest now, Harry. It's such a strain, all this thinking and being boss, it's given you a fever."

His eyes snapped open, painfully, as if he had been pierced by a splinter of irony from her voice. "You don't care. You don't care about anything."

"I do care, very much."

"No . . . You listen to me, Thelma. I'm the boss. I want fried chicken for dinner tonight. Hear that?"

"Yes."

"I make all the decisions from now on. Is that clear?"

"Of course."

With a sound of desolation he turned and buried his face in the pillows.

She stood looking down at him, tight-lipped, cold-eyed. "I'll need the car keys if I'm going to do the shopping. Are they in your pocket?"

He didn't respond. She waited for several minutes, still as a stone, until Harry began to snore. Then she bent over him, and, moving with delicate precision, she took the car keys from one pocket and the gun from the other, and put them both in her purse. Blake watched her from the doorway with the awed expression of a man witnessing the dismantling of an unexploded bomb.

When she turned and saw that Blake was still in the house she seemed surprised and displeased. "I thought you'd left."

"No."

"You're free to go any time." She went into the hall, closing the door behind her, and began putting on her hat, arranging the black veil over her face, tucking in wisps of hair. There was a mirror built into the hall rack but she didn't even glance toward it. "You're free to go," she repeated. "You were so anxious to leave a few minutes ago."

"Naturally. What did you expect me to do, tackle a crazy man?"

"He's not crazy. He's emotionally exhausted."

"Same difference, as far as I'm concerned. You'd better watch out for yourself, Mrs. Bream." He appeared reluctant to leave, as if he had misgivings about his behavior and wanted to confess and apologize but didn't know how to go about it. "What are you going to do about the gun?"

"I have no idea. What does anyone do about a gun?"

"Unload it, that's the first thing. Let me see it."

She opened her purse. She knew nothing about guns but it seemed odd to her that it wasn't heavier, more substantial.

"It's not real," Blake said, in a high, tinny voice.

"Pardon?"

"It's a toy, a cap pistol." The color of shame and fury spread across his face. "A cap pistol. And I was taken in. I was . . ." *I was a coward. I was scared by a toy gun and a little man years older than I am. Scaredy-cat, scaredy-cat.*

"I'm so relieved," Thelma said. "I should have guessed, of course. Harry just isn't the type to harm anyone even if he wanted to. People can't get away from their own type no matter how hard they try."

"Can't they?"

"Poor Harry. A toy gun. Well, I suppose we'll all look back on this some day and laugh. I mean, there was I, scared out of my wits, and you—I thought you were going to faint, you looked petrified."

"I wasn't frightened in the least," he said, and giving her a look of hatred, he turned and opened the door and ran down the porch steps, fleeing from his own identity, pursued by his own shadow.

Thelma started to call after him, to tell him not to bother about the water-softener, but at that moment the telephone began ringing again. This time she answered it promptly because she didn't want Harry to wake up.

"Hello?"

"Thelma, this is Ralph. I've been trying to reach you for hours."

"I was out." I don't even have to lie, she thought. I was out. Out of patience. "Is anything wrong?"

"Maybe. Harry came to my office this morning. He looked in terrible shape, as if he'd been on a binge for a week. I know that can't be true, though. He's afraid to drink since he had to pay that two hundred dollar fine after the accident."

"Why worry about him?"

"He was talking—well, pretty unrealistically. About you, and going home, and how he intended to get a firm hand on the reins, that sort of thing."

"So?"

"I thought you should be warned. He's a hell of a good guy, Thelma, it's up to us to keep him out of trouble."

"Not us," Thelma said dryly. "You."

"What does that mean?"

"He's here now. Sleeping. After making a delightful scene in front of a total stranger. It's the last straw. If he's going to be kept out of trouble you'll have to do it, you and Bill Winslow or Joe Hepburn. You're his friends. *I'm not.*"

"What are we supposed to do?"

"I'm going out now, to Ron's funeral—and you can start raving and ranting about bad form or anything else, but it won't do any good. I'm going. And when I get back, I want Harry out of here, out of this house. If he's still here when I come back, I'm going to phone the police and have him arrested for threatening me with a gun.

"A gun?"

"Oh, just a cap pistol, as it turned out. But the threat was real and I have a witness. Harry can be arrested."

"You wouldn't . . ."

"Wouldn't I? Listen, I'm fed up. I'm sick and tired and fed up. These scenes are tearing me apart. I have my health to consider, and my baby. I need peace and quiet, relaxation. How can I get any, with him barging around like a maniac? I would do anything to get rid of him. And I will, if you don't prevent it."

"I'll do my best."

"He won't be here when I come back?"

"No."

"Promise?"

"Yes."

"I suppose I should thank you in advance, only—well, whatever you do will be for Harry's sake, not mine. I ask no favors from anyone."

"I understand that. Go-it-alone Thelma, as usual."

"I'm not quite alone." She hung up.

In the living room Harry lay crushed among the pillows, dreaming of triumphs and defeats, the rhythm of his gentle snoring broken now and then by a catch of his breath, a pause, a sigh.

What long eyelashes he has, Thelma thought. Then she said softly, "Good-bye, Harry."

18

HARRY REMAINED AT home and slept through the funeral, partly from a desire to escape it, partly from genuine weariness. By the time Turee and Bill Winslow arrived at the house, he was awake and sitting up on the davenport, though still dazed.

"How did you fellows get here?"

"Thelma left the door unlocked," Turee said.

"No, I mean, what brought . . . ?"

"Action now, explanations later. Come on, Harry."

"Come on where?"

"To my house."

"I don't want to go to your house. I'm staying here. I'm waiting for Thelma."

"Thelma's not coming back until you leave."

"But she has to. She promised to make me fried chicken for dinner. I *commanded* her to."

"Oh, great, great," Winslow said. After the funeral, he'd had three quick, long martinis which had submerged his sorrow but left a lump of anger sticking in his throat like an olive pit. "You *commanded* her to. Fine. With a toy gun. Even better. What makes you pull such damnfool stunts?"

"I was only trying to prove . . ."

"What you were trying to prove and what you proved are a couple of light-years apart. You threaten a woman and she gets frightened. But after the fright goes away, what's left? Revenge."

"Not Thelma."

"Exactly Thelma. Get it through your thick skull that she wants you to get lost, or else. All these damnfool antics of yours, I don't blame her. Now let's hurry up and shove out of here. I need a drink."

"Well, gee whiz," Harry said plaintively. "What's everybody so sore about?"

"Who's sore?"

"You are."

"The hell I am."

"Quiet, both of you," Turee said. "Come on, Harry. Bill has his car, he'll drive us over to my house."

"Where's my car?"

"Thelma said she'd leave it at the house for you. Nancy's expecting us, let's get going."

"I don't want to go. I'm not a child. I can't be ordered around."

"You are and you can."

"I thought you were my friends!"

"If we weren't your friends, we'd both be home having a nice quiet dinner. Now let's go."

"All right, *all right.*"

Harry got up and went out the door, muttering to himself. He paused at the bottom of the veranda steps and glanced back at the door as if he had an irrational hope that Thelma was going to appear and ask him not to leave.

Mrs. Malverson was out on her front lawn watering a bed of daffodils. She spotted Harry and waved the hose playfully by way of greeting.

"Hello there, Mr. Bream."

"Hello, Mrs. Malverson."

"Beautiful weather for daffodils, isn't it?"

"I guess so." He hung back while the other two men approached the car parked at the curb. "Mrs. Malverson, I'm—well, I won't be around for a while. Business, you know how it is. I was wondering perhaps if you could drop in on Thelma now and then, cheer her up a bit. She hasn't been well lately."

"I know. I told her that myself only last Sunday. Child, I said, you look as if you've been up all night, and crying too. I'm sure it was Sunday. Yes, it was, because I remember now I asked her to go to church with me for the reading of the flowers. She dropped a bottle of milk, she was that nervous. And all this week she's been avoiding me. Me, her friend. Of course that's what you can expect from a woman at certain times."

"Certain times?"

"Oh, come now, Mr. Bream. Surely you've suspected that a little stranger is coming into your life?"

"Stranger? Yes. Yes, that's the right word." He turned so abruptly that he almost lost his balance, and walked toward the waiting car.

Mrs. Malverson stared after him, her mouth open in surprise. *Now what does that mean? Maybe I shouldn't have blurted it out like that, but my goodness, these are modern times. People don't hide things like a baby, they go around shouting it from the housetops as soon as they're sure. Unless . . .*

"Oh, that's ridiculous," she said aloud, with a violent tug on the hose. "Never have I seen a more devoted wife than Thelma Bream. Keeps the house spotless, airs the mattresses every second Thursday. And never a cross word between the two of them. She's always quoting Harry, Harry this, Harry that, as if he was some kind of god instead of an ordinary little man that sells pills, and some of them no darn good either. And every morning when he leaves for work out she traipses to the car to kiss him good-bye. A real womanly woman, if I ever saw one."

Unless . . .

"Absolutely ridiculous," Mrs. Malverson repeated weakly. "I ought to be downright ashamed of myself."

When they reached Turee's old three-story house on Woodlawn, Nancy came to the door to greet them. Though she looked red-eyed and worn, she spoke cheerfully: "Hello Harry—Ralph . . . Where's Billy? Isn't he coming in for a drink?"

"Not tonight," Turee said. "His wife has a cold and he wants to go home and catch it, so he'll have an excuse to cry."

"What a time to try to be funny."

"I'm quite serious."

"Well shush, anyway. Harry, where's your suitcase?"

"In my car. Wherever that is."

"Thelma left it for you in the driveway. Here are the keys. Now go get your suitcase."

"I can't stay here. I've been enough bother . . ."

"Nonsense. You're perfectly welcome to sleep on the sun porch. This is practically the only time of year it's usable. You won't freeze and you won't stifle. Now how's that for an offer?"

"Well . . ."

"Of course you'll stay. It'll be just like old times, before you were marrie—"

Nancy's tactlessness was sometimes as overwhelming as her hospitality, and Harry stood silent and embarrassed in the face of both, looking down at the carpet which was muddy with the tracks of children and worn in places right through to the padding.

Nancy touched his arm in gentle apology. "I'm always saying the wrong thing. Without meaning to. Come on, I've got dinner ready for you. Ralph will get your suitcase later."

The children had already been fed and sent upstairs with instructions to amuse themselves, no holds barred, and the two men were left alone at the round oak table in the big old-fashioned kitchen. They were both preoccupied and hungry and the meal was disturbed only by the sounds from upstairs, sometimes loud, sometimes muffled, running feet, squeals and giggles, stifled screams, an occasional howl.

There was a hectic quality in the children's playing, as if they knew something secret and strange and terrifying had happened and they were combating the knowledge with hysterical denial. "Uncle Ron is dead," Nancy had told them calmly. "Now if you have any questions I'll answer them as best I can." It was like asking a roomful of grade-schoolers if they had any questions about the mechanism of a hydrogen bomb. No questions were asked, out loud.

Death. A sacred word, yet an evil one, a beginning and a finality, heaven and hell, streets of gold and pits of fire, angels and demons, bliss and brimstone. *If you have any questions . . .*

The din from the second floor grew louder and more frantic. Nancy's voice plunged into it, sharp as a scalpel. "What are you four doing up there? Avis? Sandra? You hear me?"

Sudden and complete silence, as if all four, simultaneously, had been anesthetized.

"I want an answer. What are you doing?"

A girl's voice, brassy with defiance, "Nothing."

"It doesn't sound like nothing."

"It's *nothing.*"

"Well, please do it more quietly."

Whispers. A gasp. A frightened giggle. Then the muted chant of children:

"Galloway was laid to rest
In his Sunday pants and vest.
Galloway was laid to rest . . ."

The sounds floated down into the kitchen and Harry shivered and turned white. "I missed it."

"Missed what?"

"Ron's funeral."

"That doesn't matter. Barbaric custom, anyway."

"Thelma, she was there?"

"Yes."

"There wasn't any scene, any trouble? I mean, with Esther?"

"The ladies," Turee said with some irony, "are ladies, and don't make scenes at funerals."

"I was just wondering."

"You wonder too much."

"Yes."

"You've got to stop it."

"I know."

"Start thinking on the positive side. You're young, healthy, competent, you've got a future."

"I can't see it."

"Not with your eyes closed and pictures of Thelma pasted inside the lids. Start looking around. The sky hasn't fallen. The city is still here. The blood is still bouncing around in your veins. Here, have some of this port. An uncle of mine sent me a dozen bottles. He had to choose between his wine cellar and his ulcer."

Harry eyed the glass of port with suspicion, then shook his head gravely. "No thanks. I haven't had a drink since Monday."

"Why not?"

"I was afraid it might interfere with my thinking."

"Something should have." Turee sipped at his port and made a wry face. "No wonder the old boy developed ulcers. This stuff's god-awful. Try it."

Harry tried it. "It's not so bad."

Nancy came into the kitchen to ask Turee to go upstairs immediately and discipline the children.

Turee seemed unperturbed at the request, as if it was a very familiar one. "What do you want me to do?"

"I don't know. Something, anyway."

"Be more explicit."

"I can't. All I know is, if I'm expected to do all the disciplining in the family, the children will grow up thinking I'm an ogre. They'll have complexes."

"Ogress. And they'll have complexes anyway."

"Sandra's the instigator of this whole thing. I feel like spanking the daylights out of her."

"Go ahead and do it, then."

"You're no help at all!"

Turee rose, kissed her on the left cheek, and pushed her gently toward the doorway.

The wine, the warmth of the kitchen, the playing-out of the little domestic scene, all combined to cast a flush across Harry's face. He fidgeted with his empty glass, rolling the stem back and forth between his palms, and a glint of moisture shone in his eyes. "I can't stay here, Ralph. I wish I could. But seeing you and Nancy—and the kids—well, I guess I couldn't stand it. You understand."

Turee was grave. "Make your own decision. I was only trying to help."

"No one can help me. I've got to go it alone."

It was the same sentiment Turee had heard Thelma express, and he wondered how deeply either of them meant it and how far either of them would go alone. Together, leaning on each other, entwined in marriage, they'd been able to remain upright, as cornstalks in a field can withstand a high wind.

"What you suggested on Monday," Harry continued, "about leaving town, applying for a transfer, it's beginning to make sense to me now."

"Good."

"I'm sure they'll give me a transfer. I'm a good salesman and there's nothing in the record against me, except that business on Monday. Maybe if I go away for a while Thelma will actually miss me, eh?"

"Maybe."

"She might even change her mind. I could always send for her then, her and the baby, couldn't I? I mean, it's not impossible, is it?"

"Not at all."

"She's always wanted to leave this town anyway."

Not with you, Turee thought, refilling Harry's glass. "I realize that."

"Say, you know something, Ralph? For the first time in days I'm beginning to feel that things are making sense again. Don't you feel that, Ralph? Things will work out?"

"Certainly."

"I guess I was practically going off my rocker for a while there, staying up all night, thinking, trying to figure things out, not eating, not seeing anybody. I feel quite different now. Almost *hopeful*, you know?" He paused to sip at his wine and wipe the beads of moisture from his face with the back of his hand. "Now why did I say *almost?* I don't mean it. I mean very. Very hopeful. You were right, Ralph. I've got a future. I've really got a future, haven't I?"

"Of course." Turee saw Harry's bright new smile, and the bright new confident look in his eye, and anxiety began to gnaw at his mind with the teeth of rodents. Harry was on his way up again, the long erratic journey up, like a crazed bird, or a misguided missile darting wildly in and out of the orbits of meteorites. "Harry. Listen. Don't get too high."

"Now that's a funny remark. A few minutes ago you were trying to cheer me up and now that I'm cheered up, what are you trying to do? Puncture me? Well, you can't, old boy. I feel wonderful, see, I feel . . ."

"Harry, before you leave town, I think you should hire a lawyer."

Harry's jaw dropped in astonishment. "Lawyer? What for?"

"For Thelma."

"So she can divorce me? Is that what you mean?"

"No, no," Turee said impatiently. "She's going to need someone to protect her interests, that's all."

"Why? *I'm* going to protect her interests. I'll send her every cent I can spare."

"I know that. But suppose something happens to you—you become sick and can't work, you get hurt in an accident—what then? Thelma would be left alone with a child to support."

"I don't see how a lawyer would help that."

"You're not thinking straight, Harry. The child is Ron's—he's admitted paternity—therefore his estate should be made responsible financially for the child's upbringing."

"Thelma would never take a cent from Esther. She's too proud."

"Pride be damned. There should be nothing personal in this situation. Thelma may be proud, Esther may be reluctant, you may be all churned up, but the fact remains that the child has a legal right to support. That's where the lawyer comes in. He'll act in the child's best interests. His own, too. I understand in cases like this where a considerable amount of money is involved, they work on a percentage basis."

"What exactly do you mean, a considerable amount of money?"

"I didn't mean anything exact. All I'm saying is that Thelma should have a lawyer."

"But then there'd be a lawsuit. Everything would come out in the newspapers."

"If Esther's lawyers advise her to fight the case, there'd be a lawsuit, yes, but I don't think they will. And if they did, I don't think she'd accept their advice. At the moment Esther's pretty bitter about Thelma, but she's not really a vindictive woman. She'll simmer down between now and the time the child is born."

"What it boils down to, then, is begging Esther for money. Well, I won't do it. To hell with it. I can support Thelma and the child, and no *begging* necessary."

"Oh, be reasonable, Harry. Why deprive the kid of its legal right? I know how willing you are to support it, but it's going to grow up, to need things, housing, clothing, education. Ask me, I'm an expert. I've been broke for fourteen years and no doubt will continue that way for another fourteen. Kids are expensive. They don't always stay in the cradle, wearing diapers and living on milk. They need shoes, dolls, new suits, bicycles, baseball mitts, piano lessons, there are doctors' bills, dentists' bills . . ."

"All right," Harry said listlessly. "Don't go on. You're telling me I can't afford all those things."

"No. I'm telling you you don't *have* to. Thelma and the child are entitled to be kept in comfort and there's no sensible reason why they shouldn't be, except your pride and Thelma's, if pride is the right word."

"I don't need charity."

"Keep yourself out of it, Harry. Because you're not really in it. You'll have to face that squarely." Turee paused, pressing his fingertips against his temples as if to press his thoughts into the right phrases. "You're not really in it," he repeated. "I think you've been daydreaming this past week, Harry. I think you've half convinced yourself that nothing took place between Ron and Thelma, that the child is actually your own. Don't keep on like this, Harry, it's dangerous."

"But suppose . . ."

"There's no supposing about it. The child is Ron's. Now accept the fact and go on from there. If you keep setting up delusions to stumble over, you'll get nowhere. Why can't you face the truth?"

"I guess—I'll have to." The long erratic journey up had ended for Harry. The crazed bird had grown weary, the misguided missile had struck a meteorite and was falling through space. "I couldn't give her the child she wanted. I tried. God knows I tried. I've been going to a doctor for over a year without telling her. I covered up for myself by pretending that I didn't want her to have a child because of her health, her age."

"Why didn't you tell her the truth, Harry?"

"I wasn't sure, at first. Then when I was sure, I was afraid to tell her. After that, when I began taking treatments and pills—well, I kept hoping things would change. They changed all right," he added grimly. "In a way I never thought possible. My best friend, and my wife."

"It's happened before."

"Yes, but didn't they ever stop to think of Esther, of me?"

"There are times," Turee said, "when people don't stop to think of anything."

19

As far as the newspapers were concerned, the Galloway story died on the obit page, but rumors were flying wildly around town like kites without tails. One of them got entangled in Esther's telephone wire: an anonymous caller accused her of murder and demanded five thousand dollars as the price of his silence.

After this episode, Esther refused to take any calls or to see anyone except the lawyers concerned with the probate of Ron's will. It was a curiously simple will for a wealthy man to make. No trust funds or other safeguards had been set up for the children; except for a few minor bequests, everything was left outright to Esther, as if Ron had had greater faith in her good judgment and common sense than he had in his own. The lawyers came with papers for her to sign, and went away again, and came back with more papers. These visits were, for a time, Esther's only contact with the outside world.

She stayed indoors, wandering from room to room of the huge house, trying to find things to do, straightening pictures that weren't crooked, dusting ashtrays that hadn't been used, moving chairs that had been moved only a few hours before, reading aloud to the two boys in a new gentle faraway voice which had a strangely quieting effect on them. The extremes of unexpressed grief and rage, which characterized the early period of her mourning, began gradually to moderate with the passing of the days, leaving behind a kind of acceptance, and a broader perspective. She came to realize that she was not the only injured and bereaved person, that it was Thelma, perhaps, who would ultimately suffer more than anyone else. She had a growing urge to call Thelma, partly out of pity, partly out of curiosity, but she was a little timid about doing it directly, since she couldn't be sure how Thelma would interpret such a call.

As a compromise she tried to get in touch with Harry at his office. She was informed that Harry had left the country a week previously and his present location was unknown since the head office in Detroit handled all transfers to the United States.

The following afternoon she received a badly typed letter from him, postmarked Kansas City, Missouri.

Dear Esther:

I tried to say good-bye to you but I was told you were ill. I hope you are feeling better by this time and bearing up under the terrible strain. As you probably know by now, Thelma and I decided to separate, and I applied for a transfer and landed here, of all places. It's a lot like home, even the climate, though I guess it's warmer here because there's no lake.

I feel the way I did when I first left home for boarding school, like a mass of jelly inside from sheer homesickness. The nights are the worst. In the daytime I keep busy. I have to. This is a big city and I have to get to know it the way I know Toronto, if I'm to be any good to the company. They've given me a company car to drive, by the way, and everyone is very nice, so I've really nothing to complain of, jobwise. If I could only get over this sick, empty feeling inside.

I have just reread the first page of this letter, and for a guy who has nothing to complain of, I certainly complain! Forgive me, Esther. You have your own sorrows, I'm a dog to add to them.

I've sent Thelma three special-delivery letters but she hasn't answered. I know you two aren't likely to go out of your way to meet each other, but if you hear any news of her through Ralph or Billy Winslow or Joe Hepburn, please let me know.

I have so many things to say to you but somehow I can't say them. I want you to know one thing, though—I accept full responsibility for what happened. It was entirely my fault, I should have been more alert, more suspicious, more everything, I guess. I can't go into the details, they are too personal, but I repeat—it was all my fault and mine alone. *Ron would be alive today if it weren't for my weakness and vanity. Last night I dreamed I was a murderer, so I guess this is how I really feel inside.*

I will try to be more cheerful next time I write. Meanwhile, take care of yourself, Esther.

Love,
Harry

It was the second time within a week that the word murder had come up.

She reread the last part of the letter, thinking how simpleminded Harry was to believe that a catastrophe could be caused by any one person. A lot of people were involved, not just the leading characters, but the bit players, the prop man, the stagehands, waiting in the wings.

In the same mail a letter, with an imposing letterhead of six names and the address of a law firm, contained an incongruously informal message:

Dear Esther:

I'd like to drop in early Friday morning. No papers to sign, but a few matters to discuss.

Yours,
Charles

Charles Birmingham was a tall, austere man in his early sixties with a strong British accent which he had picked up at Oxford and managed to retain for forty years, intact. His too-formal manner of dressing gave the impression that he was always on his way to a wedding or a funeral, and his cold fishy eyes indicated that it didn't matter which.

Esther didn't like him, and he considered her a fool, so there was little room for a meeting of minds.

He came to the point of his visit without any preliminary niceties. "Mrs. Bream has retained an attorney."

"Yes, I just had a letter from Harry yesterday telling me he and Thelma have separated."

"I'm afraid you miss the point." *Women always do,* his tone implied. "This has no bearing on the separation. It concerns Mrs. Bream's unborn child. If Ron hadn't been so idiotic as to write that letter and you hadn't been so precipitate about handing it over to the police, we'd have an excellent chance of winning our case."

"Winning our case? You intend to fight?"

"To the best of my ability. As your attorney, it is my job to protect your financial interests."

"Have I any say in the matter?"

"Naturally, but it's customary for clients to take the advice of their attorney."

"Is it, indeed?" Esther's smile was chilly. "Well, I don't always do the customary thing."

"I'm sure you don't. However, in this case, I do hope your negativistic attitude toward me personally won't interfere with your better judgment."

"I don't like the idea of going into court, not one bit."

"If you're sued, you'll have to."

"Well, fix it so I won't be sued. Why can't the whole thing be handled in a friendly, civilized manner?"

Birmingham's lifted brows indicated his low opinion of this suggestion. "My dear Esther . . ."

"I don't want any scandal or fuss."

"There already is scandal."

"I know that." She remembered the soft, queer voice on the telephone, and her own terror, so paralyzing that she couldn't answer, couldn't even hang up. "It's got to be stopped. I'm afraid to go out, afraid to send the boys to school. I have this feeling that we're being watched."

"By whom?"

"I don't know."

"What do you propose we do about it?"

"Offer Thelma money to leave town. Once she's gone, the rumors will die down, people will forget, I can begin to live again."

"How much money?"

"Fifty thousand dollars. It would be worth that much to me to see the end of her."

"Suppose she refuses?"

"I don't see why she should. She has nothing to gain by staying here, except shame and humiliation and ridicule."

"Perhaps that's what she wants, self-punishment, self-debasement."

"Thelma's too sensible for that."

"My dear Esther, one of the things you learn early in my profession is that you can't tell from the outside who's sensible and who's not, and a great deal of the time you can't tell for certain what's sense and what's not. As far as I was able to gather, Mrs. Bream is not the usual femme fatale with a string of extramarital affairs behind her. She's an ordinary virtuous woman who has committed the kind of sin which ordinary virtuous women don't permit themselves to commit. If they do, they suffer. Mrs. Bream is suffering, suffering doubly because of the drastic consequences of her infidelity. In such a frame of mind she'd be unlikely, I think, to accept the kind of pay-off you suggest."

"Why?"

"It might seem to her a reward for having done something she loathes herself for."

"You read too much psychology."

Birmingham permitted himself a small tight smile. "Not at all. I practice it."

"I still think you're wrong about Thelma."

"Quite possibly. I talked to her only once, yesterday, in the presence of her attorney. She said very little, seemed uninterested, detached. Finally she complained of feeling ill, stomach cramps, dizziness, and so on. Purely psychosomatic, of course."

"Have you ever," Esther asked coldly, "been pregnant, Mr. Birmingham?"

"Fortunately, no. When I left, Mrs. Bream was trying to get in touch with the doctor, and her attorney was hopping around the office like a nervous stork. I deplore such excitements. Her attorney, by the way, hinted delicately at a small monthly stipend from the estate until the baby is born. This is impossible, naturally."

"Why?"

"Any payment—including the one you suggested—would be a virtual admission that your husband was responsible for the child. Then, later, when the child is born, we wouldn't have any grounds to fight the case. Mrs. Bream, or rather, her attorney, who will probably receive twenty-five percent of any settlement, would be in a position to make some pretty stiff demands." He added on a note of cheer, "Of course there's always the possibility that Mrs. Bream won't carry the child to term, or that it will be born dead, in which case our responsibility ends."

"What an inhuman remark to make." Esther had turned white with anger and her hands trembled as she lit a cigarette.

"It wasn't intended as such. You have an unfortunate tendency to over-emotionalize the issue. A natural womanly reaction, of course, but it increases the difficulty of my position."

"What is your position, to distort the facts?"

"My dear Esther . . ."

"You know the truth and so do I. Let's face it."

"Facing the truth," Birmingham said bluntly, "is going to cost you a heap of money."

"All right. I've got a heap of money, haven't I?"

"Considerable, yes. You also have two arms, but that's hardly a reason for discarding one of them."

"A very poor analogy. Look, Mr. Birmingham, let's get this straight. I hold no brief for Thelma. I don't like her and never have. But I feel a certain obligation toward her because I . . ." She hesitated, coloring slightly. "Because I understand her position. It could happen—has happened—to other—other women. I don't intend to fight any claims she makes on the estate. My conscience wouldn't allow it."

Birmingham had not been Galloway's lawyer at the time of his divorce, but he remembered the case and Esther's role in it and be began to realize that it was futile to argue with her. Whether or not she liked or approved of Thelma Bream, she had made a very strong identification with her: *There went I. Only I was luckier.*

"Very well," he said. "We'll let the matter ride for the present."

You will, I won't, she thought. But aloud she said cordially, "Of course. I'll see you to the door."

"That won't be necessary."

"It will be a pleasure."

She stood at the door watching his departure. He walked stiffly down the broad stone steps of the veranda and crossed the driveway to his car with ponderous dignity, like a penguin crossing an Antarctic waste, never missing the warm places of the world because he did not know they existed.

Though she had disliked Birmingham for years, she had never before openly opposed him. Now, like a child who has suddenly issued a declaration of independence, she felt a new power and vitality, as if some secret well of energy had been tapped. She ordered old

Rudolph to check her car and bring it around to the front of the house. Then she went upstairs to dress for town. For the first time in a month she passed the closed door of Ron's room without the increased heartbeat of fear and guilt.

"You're out of practice," Rudolph said. "You better let me drive you, Mrs. Galloway."

"No thanks. You can stay and help Annie with the boys. Tell them," she added, "tell them they'll be going back to school tomorrow."

Usually, when Esther drove downtown, she avoided the heaviest flow of traffic. Today she deliberately sought it out, feeling a pleasant, reassuring sense of anonymity. She was a woman in a car among hundreds of other women in cars. There was nothing special about her to attract attention. No one would bother watching her. No one but some crank on a telephone would believe she murdered her husband.

At the Bank of Commerce, on the corner of King and Yonge, she withdrew from her checking account two hundred dollars in twenty-dollar bills, sealed them in an envelope and addressed it to Thelma. It was not an act of kindness or of pity, but one of compulsion, and the emotions behind it were deeper and stronger than kindness or pity.

Whatever the reasons, it was, for Esther, the first step back into the flow of life. Others followed, as spring passed into summer. She met friends for lunch at the King Edward or the Royal York or the Plaza. She and Nancy took their combined brood of six to Sunnyside for a day of rides. She wrote to Harry, cheerful, impersonal letters which he answered in the same vein. She went to dinner at the Winslows' house and to several outdoor concerts with Joe Hepburn, who was tone-deaf but liked fresh air and crowds. The first week in July she drove the two boys and Annie up to the lodge near Wiarton, and promised them a return trip before school started again in September.

Aside from sending the money to Thelma once a month she had no contact with her, but she heard from Turee that Thelma was having a difficult time during her pregnancy. She had rented her house in Weston and taken a small apartment in town to be nearer her doctor in case of emergency. Esther wrote down Thelma's new address in her address book, and the following day, a stifling morning in early August, she drove slowly past the apartment house on Spadina, trying to find enough courage to stop and ring the bell. But the car kept right on going as if of its own volition, and Esther thought, *There was no parking space anyway. And it's so hot. And early—she might not even be up. Besides, I have nothing special to say to her, no comfort to offer her, no special formula, no guarantee.*

Throughout the summer she had been making similar excuses to herself, and while they oiled the surface of her mind, they did not seep down and touch the grit and gravel underneath. She was stoned by dreams of identification in which she became Thelma, harassed and trying to defend herself, accused and trying to justify herself, continually at the mercy of some cold-eyed stranger or some false friend. The accusing figures in the dreams varied—Birmingham, Turee, an unknown policeman who resembled her father, a schoolteacher she had once hated—but the accused was always the same, Thelma-Esther, like a double exposure, one image superimposed on the other.

She took the two boys back up to the lodge again for the final week in August, and on returning she began outfitting them for the school year ahead.

The meeting which she had both anticipated and dreaded for a long time took place in Eaton's College Street. She had just started up the escalator to the children's wear department when some woman stumbled getting off at the top. There was a little flurry of excitement by the time Esther reached the scene—the escalator attendant had propelled the woman to a chair, a floorwalker was waving his handkerchief in front of her face in the vague hope of whipping up more oxygen, and a clerk had been sent for some water.

The woman, heavy with child, seemed embarrassed at all the fuss, and when the clerk returned with a paper cup full of water she refused it. Instead, she rose with awkward dignity, made her way to the nearest counter and stood there a moment to steady herself.

Esther approached the counter and said, "Thelma?" and the woman turned, squinting, as if she'd been summoned from some dark world into sunlight.

"Are you all right, Thelma?"

"Yes. I'm fine." Her face was puffy, like rising dough, and her legs distorted by swelling. Her maternity dress, soiled around the collar, clung in wet patches between her shoulder blades and under her arms. Perspiration and oil had seeped through her make-up and stood out in droplets along her forehead.

"It's good to see you," Esther said. "I've thought of you so often."

"Have you?" Thelma smiled dryly. "Thanks."

"I—look, couldn't we go some place for a cup of tea? We can't talk here."

"I have nothing to say. Besides, my intake of fluids is very limited. Thanks all the same."

"I'll admit I felt bitter toward you at first, but not anymore. I wish we could be friends."

"Do you?" Thelma turned back to the counter which was filled with infants' toys, rattles and teethers and rubber dolls and stuffed animals. "I've gone this far alone. I think I can manage the rest of the way."

"How much longer do you have to wait?"

"Why all the sudden interest?"

"It's not sudden. Listen, we could go over to the Honey Dew for some toasted scones. Or some butter cakes at Child's."

"I'm on a diet."

"All right then, a leaf of lettuce and a dab of cottage cheese."

"Why are you being so persistent?"

"I want to talk to you," Esther said truthfully. "I've wanted to all summer, actually, but didn't have the nerve."

"Nerve?"

"Well, whatever you want to call it. I was—embarrassed, I guess."

"That's a word I'm beginning to understand quite well."

"Have things—has it been hard for you?"

Tears appeared in Thelma's eyes. She blinked them away, obstinately. "Why should you care?"

"I don't know why, exactly, but I do."

"It's been hell."

"I'm sorry."

"Don't, *don't* be sympathetic. It's the one thing I can't stand. Oh, for God's sake, let's get out of here, people are staring, I think I'm going to cry."

She didn't cry, though. By the time they reached the nearest Child's she seemed to have herself under good control. The coffee break crowd had left and the early lunchers hadn't arrived, so the place was nearly deserted. They chose a table in the corner farthest from the windows, and Esther ordered butter cakes and black tea, and Thelma a chicken salad which she looked at ravenously but barely touched, as if she knew too well the penalties of such a splurge.

"My blood pressure's up," she explained. "The doctor's afraid of eclampsia. I have to count every ounce of fluid, every grain of salt."

"Does Harry know?"

"Know what?"

"That you're not well."

"I *am* well," she said stubbornly. "I have to be careful, that's all. Harry." She repeated the name, frowning, as if she had trouble identifying him. "No, Harry doesn't know. I haven't written to him since June."

"He's been writing to you, though?"

"Oh yes. He sends me money twice a month, more than he can afford, actually—a money order from Kansas City and two hundred dollars from here—I guess he arranges the two hundred through the local office. I don't know why, it seems an odd way of doing things, but I'm grateful for the money. He must have been given a raise in pay."

Esther didn't even blink. "That's very likely. Wages are higher over there."

"His letters have changed recently. Oh, nothing definite you can put your finger on, he still misses me and so on, but I have the feeling—well, that it's only words, that he's doing quite nicely by himself. Or *not* by himself."

"What does that mean?"

"Maybe he's found somebody else," Thelma said in a low voice. "Oh, I don't blame him. I *wanted* it to happen."

"Are you sure it has?"

"No. But I have this intuition. And I know Harry. If some woman ogles him at an office picnic he's not going to run away, he'll stand there and be ogled and love every minute of it."

"I grant you there may be something in intuition, but carrying it as far as an office picnic and an ogling woman . . ."

"There actually was an office picnic. He mentioned it in his last letter. He said he'd had a very good time. Oh, not that I care. I want him to have a good time, to be happy. He deserves it. Only . . ."

"Only what?"

"I wish he wouldn't tell me about it. I'm so miserable. I'm so miserable." She dabbed at her eyes with a piece of Kleenex. "Office picnic. To *hell* with him."

"Now don't cry."

"I can't help it."

"Think of the future, the baby. How much longer do you have to wait?"

"Nearly three weeks."

"That's not very long."

"It seems—it feels like an eternity."

"Is there anything I can do to help?"

"No. No, thanks." She took another bite of the chicken salad, then pushed the dish away from her. "The next letter I get from him, I'm not going to read. I won't even open it."

"Aren't you being a little unreasonable?"

"Just as unreasonable as I can get, I know that. I'm a dog in the manger. I don't want Harry back, I could never live with him again. It's just—well, the thought of him carousing around with other women, going to all kinds of parties. . ."

"One office picnic."

"That's all he mentioned. There are probably dozens of occasions he didn't mention." She dabbed at her eyes again. "It's not that I begrudge him anything. I want him to be happy. I'll give him a divorce so he can marry her."

"By her, you mean the woman who ogled him at the picnic and pursued him relentlessly through a round of wild parties?"

"You needn't laugh at me," Thelma said sulkily. "I can read between the lines."

"Some people become so expert at reading between the lines they don't read the lines. You're letting your imagination run riot. You've taken an office picnic and blown it up into a series of orgies."

"No. Harry wouldn't enjoy orgies. He's not like that. He's just the kind of man who should be married."

"He already is."

"No, not anymore."

"Someday, perhaps, the two of you will get together again . . ."

"No. Never."

"How can you be positive?"

"Because I was never in love with him. I was over thirty when we met—I'd never had a real proposal before and I knew it was my last chance to—well, to have a full life, a baby—my God, how I wanted a baby." She looked down at her distended abdomen pressing against the table, and smiled, very faintly. "I didn't dream it would be so difficult."

20

THELMA'S BABY WAS born at the Women's College Hospital on a cold rainy morning during the last week of September. She'd gone to the hospital alone by taxi in the middle of the night without notifying any of her friends or neighbors.

Ralph Turee was the first person outside the hospital to hear of the birth. Thelma's doctor called him just before he left for a nine o'clock class, and told him that Thelma had been delivered of a fine, healthy eight-pound boy. Thelma's condition was "only fair" after two blood transfusions, and she was allowed no visitors for the present, but the baby could be seen through the glass walls of the nursery.

Feeling that something in the nature of a celebration was in order, Turee called a meeting of the remaining fellows for lunch at the Plaza. Over martinis and steak pie, Turee broached the subject of relaying the news to Harry.

"I think we should send him a telegram."

"Why?" Joe Hepburn asked. "To *congratulate* him?"

"Well, no. But he ought to be told Thelma and the baby are all right."

"I don't know, it strikes me a telegram would be in bad taste under the circumstances."

"Harry wouldn't know the difference and it wouldn't matter to him if he did. The only thing that concerns him is Thelma. The poor guy's probably sitting around biting his fingernails."

Bill Winslow spoke for the first time. The combination of the weather, the martinis, and a breakfast quarrel with his wife had put him in a sullen mood. "The hell he's sitting around biting his nails. Poor guy, my eye."

"What does that mean?"

"Never mind."

"I do mind," Turee said sharply. "Come on, what's the big secret? What do you know?"

"Plenty."

"Such as?"

"Such as Harry's not sitting around biting his nails over Thelma. He's not sitting around, period."

"You seem pretty positive."

"Why shouldn't I be? I had a letter from him yesterday. We haven't been corresponding much, I don't know why he picked me to confide in instead of one of you."

"Well, what did he say?"

"Read it yourself. I've got it here somewhere, been carrying it around. Kind of a shock."

The letter was passed across the table and Hepburn and Turee read it simultaneously. Its contents were simple enough: Harry had met a girl, a perfectly wonderful, marvelous girl named Anne Farmer. She was divorced, through no fault of her own; her husband had been a brute, a real cad and so on, but through it all Anne had remained faithful, sweet, kind, and so on. He intended to get a divorce and marry this paragon of virtue as soon as possible, and he hoped that the fellows would wish him luck. Not that he needed it, because Anne was so wonderful, so understanding, et cetera. All the best, Harry.

"Je—*sus*," Turee said and flung the letter down on the table.

Winslow picked it up and replaced it in his pocket. "Nice timing, eh?"

"I just can't believe it."

"Try a little harder."

"In all his letters to me, he's never mentioned another woman. I was led to believe he spent all his time working."

"Does that sound like Harry? Not to me."

"Hooked," Hepburn said gloomily. "Hooked again, and we're not there to protect him. Her husband was a brute. Naturally. All ex-husbands are brutes. All future husbands are angels. *Then* comes the switch."

"Shut up," Turee said. "I'm trying to think."

"The time for thinking is past."

"Listen. We'd better send that telegram to Harry after all. Suppose he suddenly decides to write Thelma a letter like this. The shock might kill her. The doctor said her condition was only fair. That's hospital jargon for anything-can-happen. We've got to warn Harry."

The telegram was drafted by all three men and Turee telephoned it in when he returned to his office: *Thelma delivered of healthy son. Her condition fairly serious. Imperative that you do nothing to upset her. Wait for letter. Ralph.*

Later the same afternoon Nancy took a dozen roses to the hospital for Thelma and stopped at the nursery to see the baby. A masked nurse wheeled the bassinet to the glass wall and pulled the coverlet part way down to reveal the baby's face. He was quiet, but not asleep, a beautiful child with a shock of black hair and brilliant blue eyes.

Nancy tapped against the glass, smiling and cooing. She was unaware that she herself was being observed until a voice spoke suddenly beside her, "Hello, Nancy."

Nancy turned with a little jump of surprise. "Why—why, Esther."

"I came, too. I had to see for myself." Her yellow raincoat and hat were still dripping with rain. "I guess I'm making a mess on the floor."

"You can't help it, in this weather."

"I—he's a lovely baby, isn't he?"

"Yes, very."

"He looks like his father. Don't you agree? He looks like Ron?"

Nancy agreed but said nothing.

"Well, I had to see for myself," Esther repeated, and with one more brief glance through the glass wall she turned and walked briskly down the corridor, her raincoat rustling around her legs like dead leaves.

It was two weeks before Thelma was released from the hospital. She left as she had entered, by taxi, but this time she wasn't alone. She held her son in her arms, with a pride and joy she had never known before, or believed possible.

She moved back into the house in Weston. Her neighbors all knew or suspected the truth by this time, but they were kindly people, especially Mrs. Malverson next door who threw herself immediately into the role of grandmother. She helped Thelma with the shopping, the washing, the cleaning, she clucked and cooed over the baby and took him for long walks in his pram, she measured out the ingredients of his formula with the severe precision of a pharmacist.

Mrs. Malverson believed herself to be Thelma's closest friend and confidante. She was, therefore, extremely surprised when she went over to Thelma's house one afternoon in late October and noticed a For Sale sign posted on the front lawn. She found Thelma upstairs sorting through the contents of an old trunk while the baby slept beside her in his bassinet.

"I saw the sign," Mrs. Malverson said flatly.

"Oh, is it up already? Good. I asked the realtor to hurry."

"You've been crying."

"Not much. Looking over old things always gives me the blues—I don't know why, I'm happier now than I ever have been."

"So you're going to move."

"Yes."

"When?"

"As soon as I can."

"Where?"

"Nevada."

"But that's in the States."

"Yes. I have an appointment at the American Consulate for Friday morning. I'm applying for a permanent visa."

"Well. *Well.*" Mrs. Malverson plopped down on the side of the bed. "I've got to catch my breath. This is all so *sudden.*"

"Not to me."

"Ronnie's too young to travel that far."

"No, the doctor said this is actually the best time, especially if we go by plane."

"But well, there's the lawsuit coming up and everything . . ."

"It won't be coming up. Esther has agreed to a settlement out of court. I didn't want to take it—she's been so nice about things since that day I met her in Eaton's—but my attorney said I'd be a fool to turn it down. It's quite a lot of money."

"And well it should be." Mrs. Malverson was on the point of asking how much, but she desisted, in the hope that Thelma would volunteer the information.

Thelma didn't. "Anyway, it's all settled now. I signed the papers."

"Nevada. I ask you, why Nevada? I hear it's a wicked spot. Gambling, even on the Sabbath, that's what I heard."

"It's a good place to get a divorce," Thelma said grimly. "Six weeks, and it's all over."

"A divorce?"

"Yes. My husband . . ." She stumbled awkwardly over the word, and her face flushed. "Mr. Bream called me long distance last night. He wants a divorce. He's in love with another woman.

"Well. *Well.*"

"Don't be so shocked. I wasn't. I've actually been expecting it for some time now. It's almost a relief to have it confirmed."

"You poor child. You poor . . ."

"*No.* I don't really care. I thought I might when I heard his voice again, but last night on the telephone he didn't even sound like himself, it was like talking to a stranger. Her name's Anne."

"Her?"

"The woman." She slammed down the lid of the trunk, but the gesture, like Pandora's, was a little too late. Too many things had already escaped. She said roughly, "All this old junk of Harry's, I might as well throw it away."

She left the first week of November. Turee offered to drive her out to the Malton Airport but she refused. She said all her good-byes briefly and by telephone, as if she preferred not to risk any display of emotion which might make her change her mind.

She sent air-mail letters to Mrs. Malverson, the Turees and Esther, assuring them of her safe arrival in Las Vegas. The trip had been pleasant and Ronnie a perfect angel all the way, but she didn't like Las Vegas. The countryside was too desolate and the town itself full of very odd people. When her residence requirements were up she intended to move on, perhaps to Southern California. There was no mention of homesickness, loneliness, regret. Or Harry.

At Christmas time she sent large, elaborate baskets of fruit to all her friends, belts of hammered silver and Indian turquoise to the Turee children, and hand-tooled leather holsters to Esther's two boys. On the back of a Christmas card to Joe Hepburn which didn't arrive until New Year's she wrote that she had her divorce papers and she and Ronnie were staying temporarily in a motel in Pacific Palisades until she decided on a permanent place.

She did not give the name of the motel, or the exact location of Pacific Palisades, which Hepburn had never heard of and couldn't find on the map.

It seemed as though the Breams, who had once lived in such close proximity, were now trying to get as far away from each other as possible. In Harry's next letter to Turee, in February, he said he had maneuvered a transfer to Florida. The Kansas City climate was proving too rigorous for Anne, who was inclined to be frail. Enclosed in the letter, almost as an afterthought, was the formal announcement of his wedding. Mr. and Mrs. Paul Davis Dugan announced the marriage of their daughter, Anne, to Mr. Harry Ellsworth Bream.

"Well, that's that," Turee said and passed the announcement and the letter across the breakfast table to his wife.

"Yes. Yes, I guess it is."

"You don't sound very happy about it. I thought you *liked* people to get married and live happily ever after and so on. What's eating you?"

"Oh, there's something so final about it, seeing it in print like this."

"Let's hope it's final."

"I can't help—well, Thelma and Harry always seemed so right for each other. I kept hoping things would work out between them."

"You're a great hoper."

Nancy reread the letter, making little snorting noises of disapproval. "Frail. Huh. She was born and raised in Kansas City, now suddenly she's too frail. Oh, I bet Harry has picked himself a lemon. A real *lemon*."

"Nancy, love . . ."

"What's more, I hear Florida is hotter than hell in the summer and people are always getting lost in swamps."

The new Mrs. Bream did not get lost in a swamp. She did, however, become dissatisfied with Florida rather quickly, and once again Harry found himself on the move, this time to a new job, obtained through one of Anne's relatives, with an oil company in Bolivia. Since he knew nothing about either oil or Bolivia, he expected to be extremely busy and would not have the chance to write as frequently as in the past.

By the time another Christmas rolled around, his letters had ceased entirely.

21

THELMA'S CHRISTMAS CARD that year consisted of an enlarged snapshot of her son standing in a shallow wading pool, staring sober and wide-eyed into the camera. He was now some fifteen months old, a handsome child, dark-haired like his father, stockily built like his mother.

The enclosed letter to the Turees was unlike any Thelma had written before. Even her handwriting had altered: it was larger, less controlled, and the lines slanted ebulliently upwards.

Dear Nan and Ralph:

Would you ever have recognized Ronnie? I bet not. He's getting to be so big I can scarcely carry him anymore (23 lbs!), but fortunately, I don't have to. He's very good at getting around by himself, too good, sometimes! It is so long since I've written to you that I hardly know just where to start. First things first, though, so here goes. I am going to be married this week, and if I were any happier I'd burst! His name is Charley, he's a widower with grown children, and he's quite the nicest person in the world. I met him last summer on the beach at Malibu. He was walking his dog and the dog bit me on the leg. Not very romantic! We'll be going to live in Charley's house in Santa Monica. (As a matter of fact, I'm writing this from there—Charley is out in the yard making a swing for Ronnie.) I hope you will find time to convey my good news to Esther and the Winslows and Joe and Mrs. Malverson and to give them my regards. I won't be writing again for a long time, nor hearing from any of you. I'll do my best to explain why, and I can only hope your feelings will not be hurt. Charley knows nothing about my past life. He thinks I am a widow—I told him that on the spur of the moment when we first met, and I've had to stick to my story. Please try to understand my position, and my reasons for not giving you Charley's last name or my new address. He's a wonderful man, and even if he found out the truth about me I think he'd forgive me, but I can't afford to take that chance. I love him too dearly.

I feel that I'm on the brink of a whole new life for myself and for Ronnie. (He needs a father now, you should see the cute way he trails behind Charley!) I can't do anything to endanger our happiness, even if it means no more communications from my dearest friends.

Please *try to understand, and give me your blessing.*

Love,
Thelma

Nancy was extremely happy over the news. "I think it's terribly romantic."

"Indeed," Turee said. "How do you know he's not marrying her for her money?"

"What money? All she has is the settlement out of Ron's estate."

"Do you happen to know how much it was?"

"No, and neither do you, smartie. Esther won't discuss it."

"Other people aren't so particular. One of the assistant professors in the French Department is related by marriage to Martindale, the attorney Thelma hired. It seems that right after Thelma left town, Martindale bought himself a new house and car with his percentage of the take. So the take must have been considerable."

"Even so, you have no reason at all to believe that this Charley is marrying Thelma for her money. She says right in the letter he has a house of his own, so he can't be exactly poverty-stricken. You're an incurable cynic, that's all."

"Really."

"I *still* consider the whole thing very *romantic.*"

"You needn't shout," Turee said. "Oh, there's one more point that occurs to me. If I were Charley, I think I'd be a little suspicious of my wife having no contacts whatever with her own past."

That spring Turee received an offer of a guest lectureship at the Santa Barbara campus of the University of California for the summer session. The pay was excellent, he couldn't afford to turn it down. Nor, on the other hand, could he afford to transport a wife and four children across the continent and rent adequate housing for them. They were all very eager to go with him and emotions were running at an all-time high when Esther unexpectedly provided a compromise solution to the problem. She decided to take the two boys to Europe for July and August and offered Nancy and the children the use of the lodge while she was gone.

Nancy accepted with gratitude, and the Turee household returned more or less to normal. Tempers calmed down, tears stopped, sulks disappeared, and preparations for the summer began.

Turee departed in early June, traveling by bus as far as Detroit and then by air coach to the West Coast. He intended to live as cheaply as possible during the summer so that he could return home not merely with some memories and experiences but with some hard cold cash. With this objective in mind, he rented a small furnished apartment at the rear of an old house set in the middle of a lemon grove near the campus.

Time passed quickly at first. There was work to be done, and sightseeing, and exploring the strange little Spanish city crushed between the mountains and the sea. The members of the faculty and their wives were friendly and hospitable. They invited Turee to dinner, to concerts, to barbecues; but there were still left some long evenings to spend by himself, especially over the weekends when his colleagues were busy with their own families. It was on one of these evenings, a Friday, that the thought occurred to him of going down to Santa Monica the next day and trying to find Thelma.

He knew that the idea must have been in the back of his mind before he even left Toronto because he had packed in his suitcase Thelma's last letter enclosed in the Christmas card with the snapshot of Ronnie on it. He remembered packing it, surreptitiously, without mentioning it to Nancy, and as he took it out now to reread, he realized that he had intended, from the first moment he'd been offered the appointment in California, to find Thelma. He wasn't certain why, whether he wanted to see her again out of curiosity, or for old times' sake, or merely to make sure she was all right.

He read the letter over twice, looking for facts. Then he got out his AAA tour books, a map of Southern California and a scratch pad to make notes.

Charley. Last name unknown. Occupation: not stated. A preyer on women, for all I know, Turee thought grimly. Age: a widower with grown children, which might place him between forty-five and fifty. Maybe older, but this wasn't likely, in view of Thelma's infatuation. Other facts: he owned a house in Santa Monica, and a dog which bit, and he sometimes visited the beach at Malibu.

Turee checked the map and the tour book. There were miles and miles of beach along Malibu, and the city of Santa Monica, to the south, was listed as having a population in excess of seventy-one thousand. The chances of finding a middle-aged man named Charley who owned a house and a biting dog seemed extremely remote.

The letter, then, was useless, as far as leads were concerned. This left the picture of the boy, Ronnie. It was sharp and clear, and the boy's unsmiling features quite distinct. It had obviously been snapped by someone more skillful with a camera than Thelma. Probably by Charley. Maybe Charley was a camera bug. That hardly narrowed the search down, though; camera bugs were as common in California as bleached blondes.

But as Turee studied the picture he felt a growing sense of excitement, as if an idea had already begun to germinate in the depths of his mind and was trying to push its way up through several layers of consciousness.

A very cute kid, he thought. Looks strong and healthy. Thelma probably watches him like a hawk, and has him checked by the doctor at least once a month. Not just any old doctor, either, but a specialist. A pediatrician.

Pediatricians. Of course. It's so simple, why didn't I think of it before? To hell with Charley, who needs him?

Once again he consulted the tour book—Santa Barbara, population about 50,000—then he picked up the local telephone directory. In the yellow pages, listed under Physicians and Surgeons, he found eight pediatricians. If Santa Monica had a similar ratio, he could expect to find about a dozen.

A dozen pediatricians and a picture of a little boy. Perhaps, with luck, that would be enough.

He checked the southbound bus schedule by telephone, wrote an enthusiastic note to Nancy outlining his plan, set his alarm for five, and went to bed.

That night in a dream he saw Thelma walking along a wide and desolate beach, her long fair hair streaming in the wind. Suddenly from behind a boulder a man appeared with a little dog. The man pointed toward the sea, and Thelma turned and walked slowly and methodically into the water until it covered her head. The man laughed, and the little dog began to bark, and the air was filled with the screaming of gulls and the black whirring wings of cormorants.

He woke up with one alarm ringing in his ears and another, shriller one in the back in his mind.

It was still dark, and the cool foggy air pushed heavily into the room, redolent of lemon blossoms. Turee got up and closed the windows. The smell was sickeningly sweet. Like flowers at a funeral. He thought of Thelma drowning in his dream, and the last letter she had written with its strange alteration of style and handwriting which Nancy had explained away by saying people's writing changed with their moods, that at last Thelma was happy.

Perhaps she had not written that letter at all. Perhaps, even then, she had been dead, and Charley himself had sent the letter to mollify Thelma's friends and at the same time discourage them from trying to find her.

And the boy, Ronnie? He, too, might be . . .

"No," Turee said aloud. "No. It's those damn lemon trees. The smell makes me sick. The kid's all right."

It was the damn lemon trees.

"The kid's perfectly all right," he repeated, as if someone in the room had denied it.

He reached Santa Monica shortly after nine o'clock, obtained a map of the city at the bus depot, and, with the aid of a telephone directory, made a list of the pediatricians in the area. Checking two of them by phone he learned that they would be in their offices only until noon, since it was Saturday.

That gave him two and a half hours. And a decision to make. He made it, with a silent apology to Nancy: he committed his first extravagance of the summer by hiring a car.

Neither his wife nor his friends considered Turee very methodical or efficient. Working against time, he turned out to be both. Instead of visiting the doctors in alphabetical order, he grouped them according to address. Five he was able to eliminate at once—they practiced in one building as a children's clinic. None of them remembered seeing the boy in the picture.

A sixth was on vacation in Montana. A seventh had gone to Los Angeles to see a patient at Children's Hospital.

It was half-past ten when Turee reached the eighth name on the list, a Dr. Hamilton who occupied an office in a diagnostic clinic. Turee was informed at the main desk that Dr. Hamilton was at St. John's Hospital but expected back any minute. Could his secretary do anything to help? Down the hall, three doors to the left.

Dr. Hamilton's secretary turned out to be a harried-looking blonde wearing spectacles and a snug white uniform. "I'm Miss Gillespie. Are you waiting for Doctor?"

"Yes."

"He should be in any minute. He has a patient scheduled for 10:45. Please sit down."

"Thank you."

He didn't sit down, however. He looked at his watch, picked up a magazine and discarded it, paced the length of the room twice, until finally Miss Gillespie said, "Is there anything I can do for you?"

"Well, perhaps. How long have you worked for the doctor?"

"Over three years."

"My name is Ralph Turee. I came from Toronto in the hope of finding an old friend of mine. I know she lives—or lived—in Santa Monica but I've lost her address. Since moving here she has remarried and I don't know her new husband's name."

"Are you sure you came to the right office? Dr. Hamilton is a *pediatrician.*"

"Yes, I'm coming to that. The woman I'm looking for has a little boy. The only hope I have of finding her is through this boy. She sent me a picture of him last Christmas. He'd be nearly two years old now. His name's Ronnie."

"We have dozens of Ronnies," Miss Gillespie said with distaste, as if every single Ronnie gave her a pain in the neck. "Perhaps if I could see the picture? Actually, I know Doctor's patients better than he does. I'm the one who entertains them and keeps them quiet until their turn comes. And if you think that's easy, just come around some afternoon about four when we're running behind schedule and emergencies keep popping in like flies and the kids are all howling and the phone's ringing—well, you get the idea."

"Vividly. I have four of my own."

Turee handed her the picture of Ronnie and she studied it intently for a moment. "Yes, he's one of our patients, I'm sure of it. Comes in quite frequently. He's allergic—chocolate, eggs, milk, and so on."

"Who brings him in?"

"His mother. She's one of these fussy mothers, doesn't care in the least about getting Doctor out of bed at one o'clock in the morning if the kid has the slightest symptom. Overprotective."

It sounded like Thelma. She was not dead. It had been the lemon trees, after all. He said, "What does she look like?"

"Oh, nothing much. I mean, it's hard to describe an ordinary-looking woman. Except her hair, it's really beautiful." Miss Gillespie glanced at the picture again and handed it back with a puzzled frown. "Did you say the boy's name was Ronnie?"

"Yes."

"I'm sure you're mistaken. Or I am. One of us is."

"Why?"

"That boy is little Harry Bream."

22

THE HOUSE LAY high in the hills and at the foot of a cliff, behind the city. The mailbox at the beginning of the curving concrete driveway was shaped like an old-fashioned stagecoach. It bore no name, only the street number 2479. The hinged doors were open, and the mail delivered but not yet picked up—a copy of *Life* magazine, nothing more.

A wind was blowing down the canyon. It shook the rows of eucalyptus trees, and the pods struck the roof of the car and rattled off with the sound of scurrying mice.

The house itself was simple and elegant, of stained redwood, with a wide expanse of patio which had recently been hosed down. Steam rose from the flagstones as if secret fires were smoldering underneath. Except for the rising steam there was no sign that the house was now occupied. Turee pressed the door chime, waited, pressed it again several times, but no one answered.

He crossed the patio and picked his way down a steep path through massed geraniums to the rear of the house. Here he found a second patio, more secluded, shaded by a plexiglass roof and decorated with camellias in redwood tubs.

He saw the child first, sitting quietly in a sandbox, completely absorbed in the operations of a dump truck. Then he saw the woman. She may have been inside the house and seen his car stop, or she may merely have heard the door chime and the unfamiliar footsteps on the path. At any rate, she seemed to be expecting him, waiting for him. She was sitting bolt upright, tense, in a canvas sling chair made for lounging. Her hands were pressed tightly against her knees as if they had been frozen there.

"Hello, Thelma."

Her only response to the greeting was a blink of her eyes.

"It's been a long time."

"Not long enough. Not nearly long enough." She watched warily as he approached. "How did you find me?"

"Through the picture of the boy."

"Yes. That was a mistake, wasn't it? Well, it can't be helped now." She leaned back in the chair and looked up at the sky, as if she were making some silent plea. "I was afraid that some day I'd be sitting here just like this and suddenly you'd turn up. Now that it's happening, it hardly seems real."

"It's real."

"Yes."

"How is Charley?"

There was no response.

"And Anne?"

This time, by way of answer, she gave a tired little shrug.

"There never was any Charley," Turee said. "Or any Anne. There never was—a lot of things."

"That doesn't sound very grammatical, but it's true, of course. There never was any Charley, or any Anne."

"Just you and Harry?"

"Just Harry and me."

"And Ron?"

"Ron." She spoke the name as if it were one she hadn't heard or thought about for a long time. "Yes. You'll be wanting to talk about Ron, of course?"

"Won't you?"

She smiled crookedly. "Not exactly. I—sit down, Ralph. I'd better put the baby to bed for his nap." Climbing awkwardly out of the sling chair, she crossed the patio to the sandbox where the boy was playing and held out her arms. "Come on, wee one. Put the truck down for now. It's time for our nap."

Wee one let out a rather perfunctory howl of protest.

"Now, Harry, don't make a fuss. We have company. Come say hello to the man."

Harry crawled out of the sandbox on all fours, grinned shyly at Turee, and ran ahead of his mother into the house, slamming the screen door behind him.

"I won't be long," Thelma said. "He's very good about naps. He's a—I wish . . ."

She pressed her hand to her throat as if to ease the pain of the unspoken words. Then she turned and walked swiftly into the house.

Turee wondered what she'd been going to say. *He's a wonderful boy—I wish you'd go away and leave us alone—I wish you had never come . . .*

Sounds filtered out of the kitchen, the opening and closing of a refrigerator door, the clink of glassware, the whirring of a mixer.

"Here's your orange juice, Harry."

"I want milk."

"Now, dear, you can't have milk, you know what the doctor said."

"I want milk."

"You know something, Harry? When I was a little girl we didn't have oranges the way you do now. Only at Christmas time did I see an orange, and then it looked too beautiful to eat, like pure gold. So I used to keep it in my room, dreaming of the day I'd eat it. But I never did eat it because it got all hard and shriveled and it was no good anymore."

It seemed that she was talking not to the child but to Turee, trying to explain, to excuse: the orange of pure gold which she had plucked was shriveled.

"There, you drank it all up like a good boy. Now come on, off to bed with you."

Images rose to the surface of Turee's mind like a series of colliding bubbles, each of them bursting until the final one remained fixed and clear. A figure in white. The nurse at the hospital after Harry's accident, with the phony smile and starched behind.

Miss Hutchins. He'd met her only once, over two years ago. He hadn't expected ever to see or think of her again, yet she had traveled nimbly over the years and miles to reappear on Thelma's sunlit patio and talk about Harry: ". . . dead drunk when they brought him in—his blood alcohol test showed only one-tenth of one percent—that's not nearly intoxication level in a normal person—he's the kind that can't hold his liquor."

But Harry had always been able to hold his liquor very well. Long after Winslow had slid under the table and Galloway was retching over the railing of somebody's back porch and Turee himself had reached a state of doldrums, Harry would still be bouncing around, the life of the party.

He hadn't been dead drunk, then. He'd been pretending. He'd been acting out one of a series of scenes, expertly timed, carefully planned, with himself in the role of tragic victim to distract attention from the real victim, Galloway. The whole thing had been staged, right from the first telephone call to Thelma from Wiarton, to the final letter about his new job with the oil company in Bolivia. And the gullible audience reacted as they were expected to. Act one, poor Harry, what a terrible break for such a nice guy. Act two, Harry starts on his brave search for a new life and finds it. Act three, Harry gradually fades away into the oil fields of Bolivia.

Bolivia, yet. My God, what fools we all were. We never questioned any of it for a minute. Thelma's renunciation of Harry, his attempt and failure to win her back, her courageous persistence in carrying on alone, her refusal to answer his letters, her reaction to his "marriage"—none of it had been real. All the time the Breams were supposedly drawing farther apart, they were binding themselves closer and closer to each other, not only by ties of love but by the stronger ones of guilt.

Thelma came out of the house. She had put on a sweater and was buttoning it at the neck, as if for her the day had suddenly turned chilly. "I called Harry at the office. He'll be right home."

"He has a job?"

"No. He's at the doctor's. He hasn't been well." She hesitated over the final word, then spoke very quickly to cover the hesitation. "You look fine, Ralph. How is Nancy? And the children? Are they with you?"

"No. They're all up at the lodge for the summer."

"The lodge, how far away that seems, and long ago. I wish—well, it doesn't matter now." She sat down in the green canvas glider and began to swing back and forth, as if, childlike, she found comfort in the motion of rocking. "You came all the way out here to find Harry and me?"

"Not Harry. You."

"You didn't expect to find Harry?"

"No," Turee said, coloring slightly. "I thought—we all thought he was in Bolivia."

"Naturally." She sounded grave, but a trace of sardonic humor flickered in her eyes for a moment. "That was Harry's idea, about the oil job in Bolivia. Harry's very—imaginative."

Once again she hesitated over the final word, as if other phrases had occurred to her first, more damaging and more precise ones which her personal censor refused to pass. She must have realized that her hesitancy had piqued Turee's curiosity, for she added by way of explanation, "It's very hard to describe someone you love deeply. Try it."

"This hardly seems the time or place."

"Perhaps not."

"Who dreamed up Charley?"

"Harry."

"He threw a boomerang. If it weren't for Charley I wouldn't be here. I was suspicious of him. I wanted to make sure you and the boy were all right."

"You came here because of Charley? How funny. How terribly *funny.*" She didn't laugh, though. She merely swung back and forth on the glider, her eyes fixed on Turee's face. "What are you going to do now?"

"I'm not sure. It's a very complex situation."

"Don't hurt Harry. Please don't hurt Harry."

"How can I help it?"

"Blame me. I'm the one responsible. I planned everything."

He didn't believe her but he kept his doubts to himself. "Why?"

"Why? There wasn't any one why. There were dozens, going back years. I'd always resented Ron, the way he had everything handed to him on a platter, the way he used to order Harry around. It rankled to see Harry toady to him." She paused. "Poor Harry, he's always had such bad luck."

Perhaps Harry's worst luck had been meeting Thelma, but apparently this notion didn't occur to her.

"Like your coming here and finding us like this," she said. "Sheer bad luck."

"Someone would have found you eventually."

"No. You were the only person interested enough to try. And you would never have found me if it hadn't been for the picture of little Harry. I wanted to show him off, I couldn't help it. That was my mistake. Pride. Vanity."

"Not pride or vanity. Your mistake was greed."

"I didn't want anything for myself, only for my husband and my child."

"And the child belongs . . ."

"To Harry," she said sharply. "He is *Harry's* child. Ron never came near me until I was certain I was pregnant. Then, of course, I arranged it. I had to. It was part of our plan, the hardest part of all for me, but the most vital. Ron had to believe sincerely that the baby was his. Otherwise Harry could never have persuaded him to write the final letter to Esther, which was so necessary to the suicide buildup."

"Persuaded?"

"No force was necessary. Ron had been drinking before he arrived, and he had more, some Scotch, with Harry and me. He was always easy to handle when he was drunk. Besides, when he found out about the baby, he was so overcome with guilt and shame he actually *wanted* to confess, to atone, in some way, for what he'd done to Harry and to Esther."

"Harry told him what to write?"

"Harry suggested. Ron was too upset to do his own thinking. He was very fond of Harry, you know. Everyone was. Everyone is, I mean." Color splashed her face. "What a silly mistake, using the past tense like that, as if he were dead or something."

"Or as if he had changed."

"He hasn't changed, not a bit."

But the denial was too quick and too vigorous, and Turee wondered what the years of pretense and deceit, of remorse and guilt, had done to Harry. "The phone call Ron made to Dorothy Galloway's house the night he died . . ."

"It wasn't Ron. Harry made the call. Like the letter, it was part of the suicide buildup. The idea of suicide had to be so strongly implanted ahead of time that no one would even think of murder. Because if anyone had thought of it, if anyone had started to make a real investigation, Harry and I were wide open. Neither of us could account for our time that Saturday night. Harry didn't make any emergency call at a clinic in Mimico, he was with me, waiting for Ron, waiting to go ahead with our plan. Nor did his car break down, the excuse he gave you and the others for being late arriving at the lodge. He wasn't even driving the car. I was. I was following him so that when the time came he could take over our car and go on ahead to the lodge. It was a tight schedule but we'd planned very carefully. Harry drove me into Meaford and I caught the 10:30 bus back to Weston. I arrived home barely ten minutes before Harry's phone call from Wiarton."

"That was planned too, of course?"

"Every word."

Turee looked bewildered, confused. "I can't—I can't quite believe it."

"I can't quite believe it myself, sometimes."

She turned her head suddenly as if she'd heard a sound she'd been waiting for and knew well. Half a minute later Harry appeared from around the side of the house.

He was a little paunchier, a little balder, than Turee remembered, but his step was still bouncy and his grin still boyish. It looked quite real, as if he was genuinely glad to see an old friend.

He crossed the patio, his hand extended. "Ralph, old boy. By God, you're a sight for sore eyes. You don't look a day older. Does he, Thelma? Sit down. How about a drink, fellow? What would you . . ."

"Let's not play games, Harry," Thelma cut in sharply. "Please."

"Come now, we've got to be polite, sweetheart. What's the matter with a little drink for auld lang syne?"

"I'm not sure Ralph would accept a drink from either of us."

"Nonsense. He's our friend."

No one spoke, but the words *So was Galloway* hung in the air like dust in a shaft of sunlight.

Finally Turee said, "Did Galloway?"

"Did he what?" A fretful little frown appeared between Harry's eyebrows. "I don't know what you're talking about."

"The night he died, did Galloway accept a drink from you?"

"Two, as a matter of fact."

"Loaded with barbiturates?"

"Loaded with nothing more than Scotch."

"How did you manage to drug him?"

"Drug him? Absurd. He came in, he said he was feeling sick and wanted something to settle his stomach. I gave it to him. Maybe I gave him too much. Quite accidentally."

"Harry . . ."

"Must we go into all this? It's done, it's over, it's been over for years. Besides, I've got a headache. Every time I go to the doctor I get a headache. I hate his guts. All these psychiatrists are quacks and fools."

"Why go to him, then?"

"Thelma insists. There's nothing the matter with me. The whole thing's absurd. I feel fine. I only go to please Thelma. Isn't that right, Thelma?"

Thelma was silent.

"Well, tell him, Thelma. Tell him there's nothing the matter with me, I only go to the doctor to please you, Thelma?"

She sat mute, not looking at him but staring upwards, as if she were lost and alone on an island, searching the sky for signs of rescue.

"Tell him the truth, Thelma. Go on. The truth."

"God help us," she said and turned and began walking toward the house.

"Thelma, come back here."

"No. Please."

"I command you to come back here. You must obey me. I'm the boss. We settled that years ago, didn't we? I'm the boss, aren't I?"

She hesitated a moment, biting the corner of her mouth.

Then she said quietly, "Yes. Sure you are, Harry."

"You mustn't walk out on me like that. It's disrespectful. I don't like it. I won't tolerate it. You hear?"

"Yes, Harry."

He held out his hands toward her, palms up, and Turee saw on each wrist a red scar in the shape of a cross. "You know what I've got to do if you don't treat me right, if you don't behave yourself. And this time I won't fail. I'll cut deep."

"No, Harry. Don't. Don't make me suffer anymore."

"You suffer? Thelma, Thelma, you've got it all wrong. I'm the one who must suffer. I must wash away your sins with my blood. Now sit down and be polite. Ralph came all the way down here to see us. We must be hospitable. He's our old friend. Eh, Ralph? How many years has it been, Ralph?"

"About a dozen," Turee said.

"Only a dozen? Ron and I were friends for twice that long. Ron's dead," he added, as if he were imparting a piece of news. "It's my turn next."

"Why do you think that?"

"Thelma and the doctor keep asking the same question. It's not something I think. It's something I know. Some people know things. Without rhyme or reason they just know. There's a special day ahead for me. I will recognize it when it comes. There will be signs, in the sky, the air, the trees, so I will know, *this is it, this is the day.*"

"What about your wife and your little boy?"

"My little boy? So you believed her, too. I don't blame you, it's quite a convincing story she tells. Only it's not true. The boy belongs to Galloway. Thelma lied to salve my ego. She's a very talented liar. For a long time I believed her when she said she was pregnant before Ron ever went near her. I believed her because I so very much wanted to. I managed to convince myself that all the tests I'd taken back in Toronto were wrong, that I wasn't sterile, I was a man like other men. Then one day, when I was giving the boy his bath, I noticed the way his left ear stuck out from his head a little more than the right ear, like Ron's. And the shape of his hands and feet—exactly like Ron's. And I knew then Thelma had lied to me. Oh, her reasons were noble, but she'd lied to me, deceived me, made a fool of me. She'd sinned. I had to do something, I kept thinking something must be done, Thelma must be saved. I tried to wash away her sins with my blood." He held out his scarred wrists. "She didn't understand. She thought it was a mere suicide attempt. She called the fool-doctor and they took me to a hospital. They couldn't keep me there, though. I'm too smart. I was polite, I behaved myself, I answered their questions. They let me go in a couple of weeks. The trick is to tell them enough but not too much. Let them think you're communicating but keep your secrets to yourself. Talk all you want about your childhood but not about your child. Especially if he's not really yours. Thelma."

She raised her eyes to him. They looked pale and pure as if they'd been washed a thousand times with tears. "Don't leave me alone, Harry. I love you."

"I know that," he said wearily. "I love you too. But the time has come when I must know the truth. I have been living with so many lies, I can hardly tell anymore what's real and what isn't. Like Charley. Your husband, Charley. I know he isn't real, we made him up together, you and I. Yet sometimes I can see him quite distinctly, sitting in my chair, driving my car, walking into your bedroom and closing the door. And if I listen hard enough I can hear the two of you whispering together, I can hear the creak of bedsprings, and I know you're making love in there, you and Charley, and I want to kill him for the same reason I killed Ron, because he dared to touch you."

"Don't go on, don't think about it."

"You never knew that before, did you, Thelma? I didn't want Ron's money. I wanted his life. I killed him out of rage and hate and jealousy. When he was in the back seat unconscious and I was driving his car, wearing his cap, carrying his wallet, I felt like a man. Funny, isn't it? He wasn't really much of a man. But he had something I didn't, something I wanted. And later when I was strapping him into the safety belt on top of the cliff, and you were waiting on the road in our own car, all I could think of was, you'll never touch her again, Galloway, you'll never touch another woman, cuckold another friend, beget another bastard . . ."

"Stop. Please stop."

"Not now. This is the time for truth. You're such a natural liar, Thelma. You lie the way other people breathe, without thinking about it."

"No!"

"But you must tell the truth now. There isn't much time. The boy—my boy—he's not really mine, is he, Thelma?"

"I lied for your sake. I wanted you to be happy. I . . ."

"The boy is Ron's?"

"Yes," she said in a ragged whisper. "Don't hate me for it. Please don't hate me."

"Thelma, Thelma, you are my love, how could I ever hate you? You've told me the truth. That's the first step."

"Step?"

"To atonement, to peace." He looked up at the sky, smiling and composed. "You see that single cloud up there, Thelma? That's one of the signs I've been waiting for."

"It's only a cloud, Harry. Don't imagine . . ."

"Only a cloud? Ah, no. This is the day."

"Stop."

"Don't you feel how different it is from other days? You, Ralph, don't you feel it, too?"

"It's an ordinary day," Turee said. "How about that drink you offered me a while ago?"

"Not now. You can pour it yourself after I've gone."

"You just got here, don't talk about leaving."

"I must. Look, Ralph. There. See it? A bird flying across the cloud. If I'd had any doubts at all, that would dispel them."

Turee tried to catch Thelma's eye for some hint on how to handle the situation. But her eyes were closed. She seemed to have fallen into a troubled sleep. Her hands twitched and tears glittered on her lashes.

"You can't leave Thelma."

"No," Harry said. "I won't leave Thelma. She's coming with me. She wants to." He reached down and touched her gently on the shoulder. "You want to, don't you, Thelma? We've been down some pretty dreary roads together. This last won't be any rougher."

Turee said, "Stop this foolishness and let me help you."

"It's too late to do anything for me. Help the boy, if you can. He's a good boy. He deserves to be brought up by a good man. You don't have to be afraid he'll grow up to be like me."

"I won't let you walk off like this . . ."

"You can't stop us. Besides, I don't think you really want to. They still hang people in Canada." He leaned down and kissed Thelma on the forehead. "Come on, dear."

Thelma rose silently, hanging on to his arm.

"For God's sake, don't go with him, Thelma," Turee shouted. "Stop and think."

"I've already thought," she said quietly.

They walked together hand in hand across the patio and up the steep path along the side of the house.

A minute later Turee heard the roar of a car engine. He thought of the cliffs of Santa Monica above the sea, like the cliffs of Wiarton above the lake, and he could see behind the next corner of time the last dreary road Harry had chosen.

They still hang people in Canada, Turee thought. *It's better this way. Better for the boy. He's got a life to live, I must see that he lives it right . . . My God, I wonder what Nancy will say. . . .*

THE LISTENING WALLS

to Vera Cooper, woman of letters

1

FROM HER RESTING place in the broom closet Consuela could hear the two American ladies in 404 arguing. The closet was as narrow as the road to heaven and smelled of furniture polish and chlorine, and of Consuela herself. But it was not physical discomfort that disturbed her siesta; it was the strain of trying to understand what the Americans were arguing about. Money? Love? What else was there, Consuela wondered, and wiped the sweat off her forehead and neck with one of the clean towels she was supposed to place in the bathrooms at exactly six o'clock.

It was now seven. She refolded the towel and put it back on the pile. The manager might be a little crazy on the subject of clean towels and exact times, but Consuela was not. A few germs never hurt anybody, especially if no one knew they were there, and what was an hour, one way or the other, in the face of eternity?

Every month the manager, Señor Escamillo, herded the members of the housekeeping staff into one of the banquet rooms, yapping at their heels like a nervous terrier.

"Now hear this. I have had complaints. Yes, *complaints.* So once again we are here, and once again I say to you the Americans are our most valuable customers. We must keep them so. We must speak always American; we must think American. Now. What do the Americans hate the most passionately? Germs. So we do not give them germs. We give them clean towels. Twice a day, clean towels absolutely without germs. Now, the water. They will ask questions about the water and you will say this water from the tap is the purest water in all of Mexico City. Now. Any questions?"

Consuela had a number of questions, such as why did the manager use bottled water in his office, but self-preservation kept her silent. She needed the job. Her boyfriend had a bent for picking the wrong horses at the Hipódromo, the wrong numbers in the lottery, the wrong jai alai player in the *quiniela.*

The argument between the two ladies was continuing. Were they arguing about love? Not very likely, Consuela decided. Pedro, the elevator operator and chief spy of the establishment, addressed each of the American ladies as señora, so presumably they had husbands somewhere and were in the city on vacation.

Money? Not likely, either. Both of the ladies looked prosperous. The taller one (Wilma, her friend called her) had a genuine full-length mink coat which she wore constantly, even going down to breakfast; and when she moved along the corridor she clanked like a trolley car she had on so many bracelets. She left nothing behind in her room except a locked suitcase. Consuela had, as a matter of routine, searched through the bureau drawers, and they were all as empty as a sinner's heart. The locked suitcase and the empty drawers were naturally a great disappointment to Consuela, who had refurbished her wardrobe considerably during the months she'd worked at the hotel. Taking the odd garment here and there was not actually stealing. It was more a matter of common sense, even of justice. If some people were very rich and others very poor, things had to be evened up a bit, and Consuela was doing her part.

"Everything locked," Consuela muttered among the brooms. "And all those bracelets. Clank, clank, clank."

She picked four bath towels off the top of the pile, swung them over her left shoulder and stepped out into the hall, a handsome young woman with a haughty tilt to her head. Her confident stride and the casual way she wore the towels made her look like an athlete headed for the showers after a good day on the court or in the field.

Outside 404 she paused a moment to listen, but all anyone could hear, even with ears of a fox, was the roar of traffic from the *avenida* below. Everyone in the city seemed to be going somewhere, and Consuela had an urge to run down the back stairs and go with them. Her feet, large and flat in their straw *espadrilles,* ached to be running. But instead they stood quietly outside 404 until the tall one, Wilma, opened the door.

She was dressed to go out to dinner in a red silk suit. Every curl, every ring, every bracelet was in place, but only half her make-up had been applied, so that one eye was dull and pale as a fish's and the other sparkled with a gold lid and a bright black fringe under a gaily improbable arch. When the paint job was completed she would be, Consuela had to admit, imposing, the kind of woman who would not have to catch the eye of a waiter because his eye would be already on her.

But she is not hembra, Consuela thought. *She has no more bosoms than a bull. Let her keep her underwear locked up. It wouldn't fit me anyway.* And Consuela, who was conspicuously *hembra,* if not downright fat, inflated her chest and rhumbaed her hips through the doorway.

"Oh, it's you," Wilma said. "Again." She turned her back with abrupt annoyance and addressed her companion. "It seems to me every time I take a breath in this place someone's pussyfooting around turning down beds or changing towels. We get about as much privacy as in a hospital ward."

Amy Kellogg, standing by the window, made a sound of embarrassed protest, a kind of combination of *ssshh* and *oh dear.* The sound was Amy's own, the resonance of her personality, and an expert could have detected in it the echoes of all the things she hadn't had the nerve to say in her lifetime, to her parents, her brother Gill, her husband Rupert, her old friend Wilma. She was not, as her brother Gill frequently pointed out, getting any younger. It was time for her to take a firm stand, be decisive and businesslike. *Don't let people walk all over you,* he often said, while his own boots went tramp, crunch, grind. *Make your own decisions,* he said, but every time she did make a decision it was taken away from her and cast aside or improved, as if it were a toy a child had made, crude and grotesque.

Wilma said, giving herself another golden eyelid, "I feel as if someone's spying on me."

"They're only trying to provide good service."

"The towels she put in this morning stank."

"I didn't notice."

"You smoke. Your sense of smell has deteriorated. Mine hasn't. They stank."

"I wish you wouldn't—do you think you ought to talk like this in front of the girl?"

"She doesn't understand."

"But the travel agency said everyone on the hotel staff spoke English."

"The travel agency is in San Francisco. We're here." Wilma made *here* sound like a synonym for *hell.* "If she can speak English why doesn't she say something?"

Wouldn't you like to know, Consuela thought, swishing cold water nonchalantly around the washbasin. She not speak English, ha! She, who had once lived in Los Angeles, until the immigration authorities had caught up with her father and sent the whole family back with a busload of wetbacks; she, who had a genuine American boyfriend and was the envy of the whole neighborhood because she would one day, with the cooperation of the right horses, numbers and jai alai players, return to Los Angeles and walk among the movie stars. Not speak English! *Ho ho to you, Wilma, with no more bosoms than a bull!*

"She's really very pretty," Amy said. "Don't you think so?"

"I hadn't noticed."

"She is. Terribly pretty," Amy repeated, watching Consuela's reflection in the bathroom mirror for some sign that the girl had understood, a blush, a brightening of the eye. But Consuela was an older hand at pretense than Amy was at exposing pretenses. She came out of the bathroom, smiling, bland, and turned down each of the twin beds and plumped up the pillows. For Consuela the pretense was like a game. It could be a dangerous one, if the Americans complained to the manager, who knew she could speak English perfectly. But she couldn't resist it any more than she could resist pilfering a pretty nylon slip, a gaudy belt, or a pair of lace panties.

Amy, who knew a little about games too, said, "What's your name? Do you speak English?"

Consuela grinned and shrugged and spread her hands. Then she turned so quickly that her *espadrilles* squeaked in protest, and a moment later she was speeding down the hall to her broom closet. The grin had dropped off her face, and her throat felt tight as a cork in a bottle. In the narrow darkness, without quite knowing why, she crossed herself.

"I don't trust that girl," Wilma said.

"We could move to another hotel."

"They're all the same. The whole country's the same. Corrupt."

"We've only been here two days. Don't you think . . ."

""I don't have to think. I can smell. Corruption always smells."

Wilma sounded positive, as she always did when she was wrong or unsure of herself. She finished her make-up job by applying a dot of lipstick to the inside corner of each eye while Amy watched, hoping that Wilma's "nerves" were not going to erupt again. The signs were all there, like the first wisps of smoke over a volcano; the trembling hands, the hard, fast breathing, the quick suspicions.

Wilma had had a bad year, a divorce (her second), the death of her parents in a plane wreck, a bout of pneumonia. She had planned the holiday in Mexico to get away from it all. Instead, she had taken it all with her. *Including,* Amy thought grimly, *me. Well, I needn't have come. Rupert said I was making a mistake and Gill called me an imbecile. But Wilma has no one left but me.*

Wilma turned away from the bureau mirror. "I look like a hag."

The wisps of smoke were becoming clouds.

"No, you don't," Amy said. "And I'm sorry I called you a poor sport. I mean . . ."

"This suit hangs on me like a tent."

"It's a beautiful suit."

"Of course it's a beautiful suit. It's a fine suit. It's the hag inside that's ruining it."

"Don't talk like that. You're only thirty-three."

"Only! I've lost so much weight. I'm like a stick." Wilma sat down abruptly on the edge of one of the beds. "I feel sick."

"Where? Is it your head again?"

"My stomach. Oh, God. It's like—like being poisoned."

"Poisoned? Now, Wilma, you mustn't *think* like that."

"I know. I *know.* But I feel so sick." She rolled over sideways across the bed, her hands clutching her stomach.

"I'm going to call a doctor."

"No, no—I don't trust—foreigners . . ."

"I can't sit here and watch you suffer."

"Oh God. I'm dying—I can't breathe . . ."

Her groans reached the broom closet, and Consuela pressed against the listening wall, as still and alert as a lizard on a sunny rock.

2

A DOCTOR ARRIVED before eight, a small, jaunty man with a red camellia in his buttonhole. He seemed to know what to expect; his examination was perfunctory, his questions brief. He gave Wilma a small red capsule and a teaspoon of a viscous peach-colored liquid, the remains of which he left on the bureau for future administration.

Afterward, he talked to Amy in the sitting room adjoining the bedroom. "Your friend, Mrs. Wyatt, is very high-strung."

"Yes, I know."

"She claims to have been poisoned."

"Oh, that's simply her nerves."

"I think not."

"No one would want to poison poor Wilma."

"No? Well, that's not for me to say." The doctor smiled. He had friendly eyes, the sheen and color of horehound. "But she has, in effect, been poisoned. Her malady is very common among visitors—*turista,* it is called, among other less reputable names."

"The water . . . ?"

"That, yes, but also the change of diet, injudicious eating, the altitude. The medicine I left for her is a new antibiotic which should take care of her digestive problems. The altitude is a different matter. Even to please the tourist trade, we cannot alter it. So here you are at approximately 7400 feet when you are accustomed to sea level. San Francisco, I believe you said?"

"Yes."

"It is particularly hard on your friend because she is suffering from high blood pressure. Such people are inclined to be overactive by nature, and at this altitude overactivity can be most unwise. Mrs. Wyatt must be more cautious. Impress that on her."

Amy did not point out that nobody had been able to impress anything on Wilma for years; but she sighed, and the doctor seemed to understand.

"Explain a little, anyway," he said. "My countrymen do not take their siestas out of sheer laziness, as the comic strips would have you believe. The siesta is a sensible health precaution under our circumstances of living. You must so advise your friend."

"Wilma doesn't like to lie down in the daytime. She says it's procrastination."

"And so it is. A little procrastination is exactly what she requires."

"Well, I'll do my best," Amy said, sounding as if her best would be only a slight improvement over her worst. In fact, it seemed to Amy that the two sometimes got mixed up, and her best turned out disastrous and her worst not so bad.

The doctor's eyes moved back and forth across her face as if they were reading lines. "There's another possibility," he said, "if you're not pressed for time."

"What is it?"

"You might go down to Cuernavaca for a few days and give your friend a chance to acclimatize more gradually."

"How do you spell that?"

He spelled it and she wrote it down on a little steel-backed pad with a magnetized pen attached. Rupert had given her the set because she couldn't keep track of pens and was always having to write notes with an eyebrow pencil or even a lipstick. The lipstick ones were necessarily abbreviated. R: G.G.w.M B'k s'n. A. Only Rupert could have deciphered this to mean that Amy had taken the Scottie, Mack, to Golden Gate Park for a run and would be back soon.

"Cuernavaca," the doctor said, "is only about an hour's drive, but it's some three thousand feet closer to sea level. Pretty town, lovely climate."

"I'll tell Mrs. Wyatt about it when she wakes up."

"Which probably won't be until tomorrow morning."

"She hasn't had any dinner."

"I don't think she'll miss it," the doctor said with a dry little smile. "You, on the other hand, look as if you need something to eat."

It seemed heartless to admit to hunger with Wilma ill, so Amy shook her head. "Oh, I'm not really hungry."

"The dining room remains open until midnight. Avoid raw fruit and vegetables. A steak would be good, no condiments. A Scotch and soda, but no fancy cocktails."

"I can't very well leave Wilma."

"Why not?"

"Suppose she wakes up and needs help."

"She won't wake up." The doctor picked up his medical bag, stepped briskly to the door, and opened it. "Good night, Mrs. Kellogg."

"I—we haven't paid you."

"My charges will be added to your hotel bill."

"Oh. Well, thank you very much, Dr. . . .?"

"Lopez." He presented his card with a neat little bow and closed the door behind him loudly and firmly as if to prove his point that Wilma wouldn't wake up.

The card read, Dr. Ernest Lopez, Paseo Reforma, 510, Tel. 11-24-14.

He left behind him a faint smell of disinfectant. While he'd been in the room the smell had been rather reassuring to Amy: germs were being killed, viruses were falling by the wayside, bad little bugs were breathing their last. But without the doctor's presence, the smell became disturbing, as if it had been put there to cover up older, subtler smells of decay, like spices on rotten meat.

Amy crossed the room and opened the grilled door of the balcony. The sound from the *avenida* was deafening, as if everyone in the city, fresh and rested after a siesta, had suddenly erupted with excitement and noise. It had rained, briefly but heavily, during the late afternoon. The streets were still glistening and the air was thin and crisp and pure. It seemed to Amy like very healthful air, until she remembered Wilma's high blood pressure. Then she closed the door again quickly, as if she half believed that the room was pressurized and she could shut out the altitude with a pane of glass and some iron grilling.

"Poor Wilma," she said aloud, but the sound didn't emerge the way she intended it to. It came out, tight and small, from between clenched teeth.

She heard her own voice betraying her friendship, and she walked away from it with guilty haste, toward the bedroom.

Wilma was asleep, still wearing her red silk suit, and her bracelets, and her golden eyelids. She looked dead enough to bury.

Amy switched off the lamp and went back to the living room. It was eight o'clock. Across the *avenida* a church bell began to toll, striving to be heard above the clang of trolley cars and the horns of taxis. Back home it was only six o'clock, Amy thought. Rupert would still be working in the garden, with Mack nearby stalking butterflies and Jerusalem crickets, and letting them go, of course, if he caught any, because Scotties were very civilized dogs. Or, if the fog had moved in from the bay, the two of them would be inside, Rupert reading the Sunday papers in the den, with Mack perched on the back of his chair looking gloomily over Rupert's shoulder as if he took a very dim view of what was going on in the world.

The big man and the little dog seemed so vivid, so close, that when the knock came on the door she jumped in shock at the intrusion on her private world.

She opened the door, expecting only the girl with the towels again. But it was an elderly Mexican man carrying an object loosely wrapped in newspaper.

"Here is the box the señora ordered this afternoon."

"I didn't order any box."

"The other señora. She wished it initialed. I bring it in person, not trusting my no-good son-in-law." He removed the newspaper carefully as if he were unveiling a statue. "It is a beautiful box. Everyone agrees?"

"It's lovely," Amy said.

"The purest silver. None purer. Feel how heavy."

He handed her the hammered silver box. She almost dropped it, its weight was so unexpected in spite of his warning.

He grinned with delight. "You see? The purest of silver. The señora said it looks like the sea. I have never see the sea. I make a box that looks like the sea and I have never see the sea. How is it possible?"

"Mrs. Wyatt—the señora is asleep right now. I'll give it to her when she wakes up." Amy hesitated. "The box is paid for?"

"The box, yes. My services, no. I am an old man. I run like lightning through the streets, not trusting my no-good son-in-law. I run all the way here so the señora would have her beautiful box tonight. She said, 'Señor, this box is of such beauty I cannot bear to be without it for one night.'"

It was practically the last thing on earth Wilma would have said but Amy was in no mood to argue.

"For the señoras," he added righteously, "I run anywhere. Even though I am an old man I run."

"Would four pes—"

"A very old man. With much family trouble and a bad kidney."

In spite of his age and infirmity and running through the streets he seemed ready to talk at considerable length. She gave him six pesos, knowing it was too much, just to get rid of him.

She put the box on the coffee table, wondering why Wilma, who always made such a fuss about being charged for extraweight baggage on planes, should have bought so heavy an object, and for whom it was intended. Probably for herself, Amy thought. Wilma rarely squandered money on other people unless she was in an elated mood, and God knew there was no evidence of that on this trip.

She opened the box. The initials were on the inside of the lid, engraved so elaborately that she had difficulty deciphering them. R.J.K.

"R.J.K." She repeated the letters aloud as if to clarify them and to conjure up an image to match them. But the only R.J.K. she could think of was Rupert, and it didn't seem likely that Wilma would buy so expensive a gift for Rupert. Most of the time Amy's husband and her best friend were barely civil to each other.

3

IT WAS SUNDAY afternoon when Wilma awoke from her long sleep. She felt weak and hungry, but her mind was extraordinarily clear, as if a storm had passed through her during the night leaving the inner air fresh and clean.

As she showered and dressed, it seemed to her for the first time in many years that life was very simple and logical. She wished there were somebody around to whom she could communicate this sudden revelation. But Amy had gone, leaving a note that she would be back at four, and the young waiter who brought her breakfast tray only grinned nervously when she tried to tell him how simple life was.

"When you're tired, you sleep."

"Si, señora."

"When you're hungry, you eat. Simple, logical, basic."

"Si, señora, but I'm not hungry."

"Oh, what the hell," Wilma said. "Go away."

The waiter had almost ruined her revelation, but not quite. She opened the balcony doors and addressed the warm, sunny afternoon: "I shall be absolutely basic all day. No fuss, no frills, no getting upset. I must concentrate only on the essentials."

The first essential was, obviously, food. She was hungry, she would eat.

She removed the cover from the ham and eggs. They were black with pepper, and the tomato juice tasted strongly of limes. Why in God's name did they have to put lime juice on everything? It was difficult enough to be basic, without fools and incompetents thwarting you at every corner.

I am hungry, I will eat turned into *I am hungry, I must eat* and finally *I'll eat if it kills me.* By that time she was no longer hungry. The revelation joined its many predecessors in oblivion and life once more became, as it always had been for Wilma, complex and bewildering.

Later in the afternoon Amy returned with an armload of packages. She found Wilma in the sitting room reading a copy of the *Mexico City News* and drinking a Scotch and soda.

Wilma peered over the top of her spectacles. "Buy anything interesting?"

"Just a few little things for Gill's children. The stores were jammed. It seems funny, everyone shopping on Sunday." She put her packages on the coffee table beside the silver box. "How are you feeling?"

"All right. I must have passed out like a light after the doctor gave me that junk."

"Yes."

"What did you do all evening?"

"Nothing."

Wilma looked faintly exasperated. "You can't have done nothing. Nobody does nothing."

"I do. I did."

"What about dinner?"

"I didn't have any."

"Why not?"

"I was—upset." Amy sat down stiffly on the edge of a green leather chair. "The box came."

"So I see."

"It looks very expensive."

"It was," Wilma said. "The least they could have done was wrap it. My purchases are my own private business."

"Not this one."

"Obviously not." Wilma tossed the newspaper on the floor and took off her spectacles. She couldn't read without the spectacles, since she was far-sighted, but she could see across the room better without them. Amy's face looked pale and numb. "I gather you noticed the initials?"

"Yes."

"And concluded, of course, that Rupert and I are madly in love; that we have, in fact, been carrying on an affair for years and years behind your . . ."

"Shut up," Amy said. "I hear the girl in the bedroom."

Consuela had let herself in with her passkey and was now making up the beds. Her shoulders slumped and her feet dragged from weariness because she'd had a fight with her boyfriend that had lasted well into the night. The cause of the fight was, to Consuela, absolutely ridiculous. All she did was pilfer a black nylon slip from 411, but her boyfriend became very angry and told her she would lose her job and accused her of trying to steal the smell off a goat if she got the chance. Besides all that, the slip had been too small for her and she'd torn the seams attempting to force it over her hips.

Life was unfair. Life was cruel as a bull's horn. Consuela groaned as she changed the sheets, and made small suffering sounds as she slopped a little water around the washbasin. *Why would I steal the smell off a goat?*

"You're jealous," Wilma said softly. "Is that it?"

"Of course not. It just doesn't seem proper to me. And if Gill finds out he'll make a big fuss about it."

"Don't tell him, then."

"I never tell him things. But he always finds out in some way."

"Why do you still care what your brother thinks, at your age and weight?"

"He can cause a lot of trouble," Amy said. "He's always been suspicious of Rupert anyway. I don't know why."

"I could tell you why, but you wouldn't like it. You probably wouldn't even listen."

"Then why bother telling me?"

"I'm not going to." Wilma finished her drink. "So you don't care whether I give Rupert the box, just so long as Gill doesn't find out about it. That's very funny."

"Not to me, it isn't. And I don't see why you had to buy such an expensive gift in the first place."

"Because I wanted to. You wouldn't understand. You haven't done anything because you *wanted* to in your whole life. I have. I do. I saw this box in the window of a little shop and it reminded me of something Rupert said once, that the sea looked like hammered silver. I never really understood what he meant until I saw the box. So I bought it. I simply went in and bought it, without thinking of money, or you, or Gill, or all your weird, complicated . . ."

"Not so loud. The girl . . ."

"The hell with the girl. The hell with the box, too. Take the damn thing and throw it over the balcony!"

"We can't very well do that," Amy said quietly. "There are too many people on the street. Someone might get hurt."

"But that's what you'd like to do, isn't it?"

"I don't know."

"Oh, admit it. Admit something for a change. You want to get rid of the box."

"Yes, but . . ."

"Do it then. Chuck the thing over the railing. That'll be the end of it. And good, good riddance."

In the bedroom Consuela let out a little bleat of protest. To throw a silver box out into the street like garbage would be a terrible sin. Suppose someone very rich saw it falling through the air and caught it and became even richer—Consuela groaned at the thought of such injustice and cursed herself for her stupidity in pretending to the two ladies that she couldn't speak English. Now she could not present herself to them and state her case: I am a very poor and very humble peasant. Sometimes I am even tempted to steal . . .

No, that would not have been good, giving them ideas about her stealing. Perhaps it was just as well that she had pretended not to know English. This way she could simply confront the ladies, looking very poor and humble and honest, and they might offer to give her the box.

Consuela glanced in the mirror above the bureau. How did one go about looking honest? It was not easy.

She picked up the carpet sweeper and headed for the sitting room, already making plans for the silver box. She would sell it and buy lottery tickets for tomorrow's drawing. Then, on Tuesday morning when her winning number was published in the papers, she would tell her boyfriend to go kiss a goat, thumb her nose at the hotel manager, and leave immediately for Hollywood where she would have her hair bleached and walk among the movie stars.

She spoke in Spanish, sounding very poor and humble. "If the good ladies will excuse me, I have come to clean the room."

"Tell her to go away and come back later," Wilma said.

Amy shook her head. "I don't know how."

"I thought you took Spanish in high school."

"That was over fifteen years ago and only for a semester."

"Well, find the book of common phrases for tourists."

"We—I left it on the plane."

"Oh, for God's sake. Well, get rid of her some way."

Consuela had discovered the silver box on the coffee table and was making excited noises over its beauty, its craftsmanship, and the number of lottery tickets it was worth.

"She must be talking about the box," Amy said.

"Let her talk."

"If you're just going to throw it away anyway, you could give it to her instead."

"I could," Wilma said, "but I won't. And who said I intended throwing it away?"

"You did. You practically promised."

"Nothing of the sort. I said if *you* wanted to throw it away you were to go ahead and do it. But you didn't have enough nerve, so you lost your chance. The box is mine. I bought it for Rupert and I'm giving it to Rupert."

Consuela, cheated out of her blonde hair and her movie stars, squawked in protest and held her hand against her heart as if it were breaking.

Wilma glared at her. "Go away. We're busy. Come back later."

"Oh, you are a wicked one," Consuela moaned in Spanish. "A selfish one, a bad one. Oh, may you spend eternity in hell."

"I can't understand a word you're saying."

"Oh, I wish you could, you black witch with the evil eye. Children grow pale and sicken when you look at them. Dogs put their tails between their legs and slink away . . ."

"I've had enough of this," Wilma said, addressing Amy. "I'm going to the bar."

"Alone?"

"You're perfectly welcome to come along."

"It's so early, barely five o'clock."

"Then stay here. If you can dig up some of that high school Spanish of yours, I'm sure you and the girl can have a ball."

"Wilma, don't drink too much when you're in this mood. It will only depress you."

"I'm already depressed," Wilma said. "*You* depress me."

At seven o'clock Amy set out to look for her.

The hotel operated two bars, an elaborate one on the roof with a lively orchestra, and a smaller one between the lobby and the dining room for people who preferred martinis without music. Amy tipped the elevator boy two pesos and asked him what direction Wilma had taken.

"Your friend in the fur coat?"

"Yes."

"First she went up to the roof garden. A little time later she came down again. She said the marimbas made it too noisy to talk."

"Talk?" Amy said. "To whom?"

"The American."

"What American?"

"He hangs around the bar. He is what you call homesick, for New York. He likes to talk to other Americans. He is harmless," the boy added with a shrug. "A nobody."

They were at a table in a corner of the crowded bar, Wilma and the harmless American, a dark-skinned, blond-haired young man in a garish green and brown striped sport coat. Wilma was doing the talking and the young man was listening and smiling, a trained professional smile without warmth or interest. He looked harmless enough, Amy thought. And he probably was—except to Wilma. Two marriages and two divorces had taught Wilma nothing about men; she was both too suspicious and too gullible, too aggressive and too vulnerable.

Amy crossed the room uncertainly, wanting to turn back, but wanting even more to be reassured that Wilma was all right, not drunk, not nervous. *This is the wrong place for her. Tomorrow we'll go to Cuernavaca as the doctor suggested. It will be more restful, there will be no homesick Americans.*

"Why there you are," Wilma said, very loudly and gaily. "Come on, sit down. I'd like you to meet a fellow San Franciscan. Joe O'Donnell, Amy Kellogg."

Amy acknowledged the introduction with a slight nod and sat down. "So you're from San Francisco, Mr. O'Donnell?"

"That's right. But call me Joe. Everybody does."

"I somehow got the impression you were from New York."

O'Donnell laughed and said easily, "Woman's intuition?"

"Partly."

"Partly the sport jacket, maybe. I had it tailored in New York. Brooks Brothers."

Brooks Brothers, my foot, Amy thought. "Indeed? How interesting."

"Let's have a drink," Wilma said. "You sound too sober, Amy dear. Sober and mad. You're always getting mad; you just don't show it like the rest of us."

"Oh, stop it, Wilma. I'm not mad."

"Yes, you are." Wilma turned to O'Donnell and put her hand on his sleeve. "You want to know what she's mad about? Do you?"

"I can take it or leave it," O'Donnell said lightly.

"Sure you want to know."

"You're drunk."

"A little. A very very very little. Make up your mind. Do you want me to tell you what she's mad about?"

"All right, spill it and get it over with."

"She thinks—Amy is always thinking, it's a very bad habit—she thinks I have designs on her husband because I bought him a silver box."

O'Donnell grinned. "And have you?"

"Of course not," Wilma said vigorously. "Rupert's like a brother to me. Besides, I *like* to buy things for people. Sometimes, when I'm feeling good, that is. Other times I get depressed and stingy and I wouldn't give the time of day to a blind man."

"Right now you're feeling good, eh?"

"Very good. Let me buy you a drink. Or perhaps you'd like a silver box?"

"We could start with the drink."

"Okay. Waiter! Waiter! Three tequilas with lime."

"Wilma," Amy said. "Listen. Why don't we go and have dinner?"

"Later, later. I'm not hungry right now."

"I am."

"*You* go and have dinner, then."

"No. I'll wait for you."

"All right, wait. Just don't sit there looking mad. Try to be cheerful."

"I'm trying," Amy said grimly, "harder than you think."

O'Donnell's smile was becoming a little strained. The evening wasn't turning out as he'd planned—a few free drinks, some talk, perhaps a small loan. One woman he could usually handle nicely. Two women, especially two women who didn't like each other, might become a burden. He wished there were some quick, quiet way of ditching them both without any hurt feelings. Hurt feelings could result in complaints to the manager, and he didn't want the welcome mat pulled out from under him. The bar was his headquarters. He never got into any trouble. The Americans who came in were always glad to set up drinks for a fellow Friscan or New Yorker or Chicagoan or Angeleno or Milwaukeean or Denverite. Some of the cities he claimed as home he had visited. The others he'd read about or heard about. He'd never been to San Francisco but he'd seen many pictures of the Golden Gate Bridge, Fisherman's Wharf and the cable cars. That was enough real information. The rest he could fake, including an address if he was asked for one. He always used the same address, Garden Street, because every city had a Garden Street.

"Eleven-twenty-five Garden Street," he told Amy. "You probably never heard of it. It's over on the east side of town. Or it was. They may have torn the whole district down by now and put up hotels or department stores. Are the cable cars still running?"

"Some of them," Amy said.

"It makes me homesick just thinking about them."

"Does it?" She wondered what place he was really homesick for; a farm in Minnesota, perhaps, or a little desert town in Arizona. She knew she would never find out. She couldn't ask and he wouldn't tell. "Is there anything to stop you from going home, Mr. O'Donnell?"

"Just a small matter of money. I've had some bad luck at the track."

"Oh."

His smile widened until it seemed almost genuine. "Yes. I'm a naughty boy, Mrs. Kellogg. I gamble. I have to."

"Oh?"

"There's no other way of making money. I can't apply for any job without working papers and so far I haven't been able to get any working papers. Say, this is beginning to sound like Be-Sorry-For-Joe O'Donnell night. Let's can it. Let's talk about you. What have you two ladies been doing for amusement in Mexico City?"

"Amusement?" Wilma lifted her brows. "I hardly know the meaning of the word anymore."

"We'll have to change that. How long will you be here?"

"We leave tomorrow," Amy said. "For Cuernavaca."

"That's too bad. I was hoping to show you. . ."

"Cuerna—who?" Wilma said loudly to Amy.

"Cuernavaca."

"And we leave tomorrow?"

"Yes."

"Are you out of your mind? We just got here. Why in God's name should we take off for a place I never even heard of, Cuern—whatever it is?"

"Cuernavaca," said Amy patiently.

"Stop repeating it. It sounds like a disease of the spine."

"It's supposed to be very beautiful and. . ."

"I don't care if it's the original Garden of Eden," Wilma said. "I'm not going. What put such a crazy idea in your head anyway?"

"The doctor suggested it, for the sake of your health."

"My health is fine, thank you. You look after your own."

The drinks came and O'Donnell sat without embarrassment while Wilma paid for them. A year ago, or two years, he might have been a little embarrassed. Now he was merely tired. The two ladies were, as he'd feared, becoming a burden. He wished they would go to Cuernavaca right away, tonight.

He said firmly, "No visitor to Mexico should miss Cuernavaca. Cortés' palace is there, and the cathedral, just about the oldest cathedral in the republic. And birds, thousands of singing birds. If you like birds."

"I hate birds," Wilma said.

He went on to describe the climate, the tropical foliage, the beautiful plazas, until he realized that neither of the two women was paying the slightest attention to him. They had begun to argue again, about a man called Gill, and what Gill would think if he walked in right now, or if he ever found out.

O'Donnell got up and left.

Consuela quit work at eight o'clock and went down to the service entrance where her boyfriend was supposed to meet her. He wasn't there, and one of the kitchen help told her he'd gone to the jai alai games.

Consuela cursed his pig eyes and his black heart and returned to her broom closet, determined on revenge. It wasn't much of a revenge but it was all she could think of, to stay in the closet all night and let him worry about her and wonder why she didn't come home and where she was.

She made herself as comfortable as possible on a bed of towels. There was no ventilation in the closet but Consuela didn't mind this. The night air was bad anyway. It caused consumption, and if you had consumption you couldn't get into the United States. The immigration authorities wouldn't give you any papers.

She dozed off and dreamed that she was on a bus going to Hollywood. Suddenly the bus stopped and a bearded man who looked a little like Jesus opened the door and said, "Consuela Juanita Magdalena Dolores Gonzales, you have consumption. You must get off the bus immediately." Consuela flung herself at his feet, weeping and pleading. He turned away from her sternly, and she began to scream.

When she first woke up she could hear herself screaming, but a moment later, sitting up, fully awake now, she realized it was not herself she'd heard screaming. It was one of the ladies in 404.

In spite of the lateness of the hour there were a dozen eyewitnesses who'd been passing on the *avenida* below the balcony of 404, each of them eager to give his version of what had happened.

The American lady paused at the railing and looked down before she jumped.

She did not look down. She knelt and prayed.

She didn't hesitate a moment, just ran across the balcony and dived over.

She screamed as she fell.

She didn't make a sound.

She carried in her arms a silver box.

Her arms were empty, flung wide to the heavens in supplication.

She turned over and over in the air.

She fell straight down and head first, like an arrow.

The eyewitnesses all agreed on one point: when she struck the pavement she died instantly.

In the hotel manager's office Dr. Lopez gave a brief statement to the police. "I treated Mrs. Wyatt last night for a case of *turista.* An unhappy woman. Very nervous, very high-strung."

"Very drunk," said the bartender.

"Very rich," Consuela said with a nervous giggle. "What a pity to die when one is rich."

The doctor held up his hand for silence. "Kindly allow me to finish. My rounds begin in less than five hours and even a doctor requires some sleep. As I said before, you'll get the complete story from Mrs. Kellogg when she recovers. How soon that will be depends on the hospital authorities. She's suffered a bad shock. Moreover, when she fainted she struck her head on the bedpost, so she may have some degree of concussion as well. That's all I can tell you."

"I, too, am very nervous and high-strung," said Mercado, the older of the two policemen. "Still, I do not leap off balconies."

Dr. Lopez smiled without amusement. "You might one day, one balcony. Good morning, gentlemen."

"Good morning, Doctor. Now you, Consuela Gonzales. You claim you were in the broom closet and heard a woman screaming. Which woman?"

"The small, brown-haired one."

"Señora Kellogg?"

"Yes."

"Was she just making a noise or was she screaming words?"

"Words. Like 'stop' and 'help.' Maybe others."

"Just as a matter of curiosity, what were you doing in the broom closet at that hour?"

"Sleeping. I was very tired after work. I work hard, very very hard." She threw a glance at Escamillo, the manager of the hotel. "Señor Escamillo doesn't realize how hard I work."

"That I don't," Escamillo said with a snort.

"No matter, no matter, no matter," Mercado said. "Go on, señorita. You woke up and heard screaming. You rushed into 404. And?"

"The small one, Señora Kellogg, was lying on the carpet beside the bed. Her head was bleeding and she was unconscious. I couldn't see the other one anywhere. I never thought to look over the balcony. How could I think of such a thing? To take one's own life, it is a mortal sin." Consuela crossed herself, fearfully. "The room smelled of drinking and there was half a bottle of whiskey on the bureau. I tried to give the señora some to wake her up but it just spilled all over."

"So you drank the rest yourself," said Escamillo, the manager.

"The merest drop. To keep my strength up."

"Drop. Ha! You reek of it," said Señor Escamillo.

"I will not be insulted by any pig of a man!"

"So you dare to call me a pig of a man, you *ladronzuela!*"

"Prove it. Prove I am a *ladronzuela!*"

Mercado yawned and reminded them that it was late; that he and his colleague, Santana, were very tired; that he, Mercado, had a wife and eight children and many troubles; and would everybody, please, be friendly and cooperative? "Now, Señorita Gonzales, when you failed to rouse the señora, what did you do?"

"I telephoned down to the room clerk and he sent for the doctor. Dr. Lopez. He has an agreement with the hotel."

"He has a contract," Escamillo said. "Signed."

Consuela shrugged. "Does it matter what you call it? When a doctor is necessary, it is always Dr. Lopez they send for. So he came. Immediately. Or very soon anyway. That is all I know."

"You stayed with the señora until the doctor arrived?"

"Yes. She did not wake up."

"Now, señorita, what do you know of a silver box?"

Consuela looked blank. "Silver box?"

"This one. See, it has blood on it and is badly dented where it struck the pavement. Have you ever seen this box before?"

"Never. I know nothing about it."

"Very well. Thank you, señorita."

Consuela rose gracefully and crossed the room, pausing for a moment in front of Escamillo's desk. "I do not take insults. I quit."

"You don't quit. You're fired."

"I quit before I was fired. So ha!"

"I shall count every single towel," Escamillo said. "Personally."

"Cochino."

Consuela snapped her fingers and went out, slamming the door firmly and finally behind her.

"You see?" Escamillo cried, beating the air with his fists. "How can I run a hotel with help like that? They are all the same. And now this terrible scandal. I am ruined, ruined, ruined. Policemen in my office! Reporters in my lobby! And the Embassy—Mother of Jesus, must the Embassy be brought into this, too?"

"We must, of course, inform the Embassy in such cases," Mercado said.

"These crazy Americans, if they want to jump do they not have places to jump in their own country? Why must they come here and ruin an innocent man!"

Everyone agreed that it was most unfair, most sad, but God's will, after all. No one could argue with God's will, which was responsible for national and domestic disasters like earthquakes, unseasonable rains, temperamental plumbing, difficulties with the telephone exchange, as well as cases of sudden death.

It was comforting having someone to blame, and Escamillo was beginning to feel better when another point suddenly occurred to him. "What of the suite, 404? It is empty and yet it is not empty. I must charge for it or lose money. But I cannot charge if there is no one in it. And I cannot put anyone in it while the señoras' belongings are still there. What must I do?"

"You must learn not to think so much of money," Mercado said firmly and picked up the silver box and nodded to his colleague, Santana. "Come along. We will examine 404 once more and then lock it until the little señora recovers."

The balcony doors had been left open but the suite still reeked of whiskey, from the carpet where it had spilled and from the bottle itself which Consuela had left uncorked on the bureau.

"It would be a shame," Mercado said, reaching for the bottle, "to let this product stand here and evaporate."

"But it is evidence."

"Evidence of what?"

"That the señora was drunk."

"We already know from the bartender that she was drunk. We must not accumulate too much evidence. It would only confuse matters. The case is, after all, quite simple. The señora was drinking much *tequila* and became depressed. *Tequila* is not for amateurs."

"Why did she become depressed?"

"Unrequited love," Mercado said without hesitation. "Americans make much of these things. It is in all their cinemas. Have a nip."

"Thank you, friend."

"One thing we can be sure of. It was not an accident. I thought at first, the señora, after drinking heavily, may have rushed out to the balcony to get some air, perhaps also to relieve her stomach. But this is not possible."

"How is this not possible?"

"She would never, in such an emergency, stop to pick up the silver box." Mercado sighed. "No. She killed herself, poor lady. It is a sad thing to think of her wandering around in hell, is it not?"

Dawn was breaking through a gray drizzle.

"It rains," Santana said.

"Good. It will wash off the sidewalk and drive the people home."

"There are no more people. It is all over."

"Amen," Mercado said. "Still I wonder, along with Señor Escamillo, why did she jump from this particular spot with all the American places to choose from."

"The Empire State Building."

"Of course. And the Grand Canyon."

"The Brooklyn Bridge."

"Niagara Falls."

"And others."

"Many others." Mercado closed the balcony doors and locked them. "Well, one must not argue with the will of God."

"Amen."

4

RUPERT KELLOGG'S OFFICE was on the second floor of a new concrete building that stood just on the edge of Montgomery Street's ancient prestige. Here he ran a small accounting business with the aid of his secretary, Pat Burton, a spinster addicted to changing the color of her hair, and an apprentice, a young man named Borowitz who was working his way through San Francisco State College.

Rupert was forty, a tall, bland-faced, soft-talking man who'd been in the accounting business for nearly twenty years. He was moderately efficient, and moderately successful, in his work, but he didn't enjoy it. He would have preferred to do something more interesting and amusing, to own a pet shop, for instance. He had a profound love for animals and an intuitive understanding of them. The hours he spent at Fleishhacker Zoo seemed to him to be full of the fundamental meanings of life, but he never told this to anyone, not even his wife Amy; and the only time he'd suggested the possibility of opening a pet shop there'd been such a rumpus among his in-laws that he'd given up the idea. At least he'd given up mentioning it. It was still in the back of his mind, hidden away like a deformed child from the disapproving gaze of his brother-in-law.

On Monday morning he arrived late at the office, a habit that was growing on him, especially since Amy had left. Miss Burton, pumpkin-haired for the beginning of the autumn season, was on the telephone looking distraught. This she did easily and with so little provocation that Rupert paid no attention. He found Miss Burton's anxiety states more tolerable if he stayed beyond their boundaries as much as possible.

"Hold on, operator. He's just this minute coming in the door." Miss Burton pressed the telephone dramatically to her chest. "Thank God you've come! A Mr. Johnson in Mexico City wants to talk to you."

"I don't know any Mr. Johnson in Mexico City."

"He's from the American Embassy. It must be terribly important. You don't suppose something awful has . . ."

"Isn't this the wrong time to suppose, Miss Burton? I'll take the call in my office." He closed the door behind him and picked up the phone. "Rupert Kellogg speaking."

"One moment, please, Mr. Kellogg. All right, go ahead. Here's your party, Mr. Johnson."

"Mr. Kellogg? This is the American Embassy in Mexico City, Johnson speaking. I have bad news to report so I might as well give it to you now and straight."

"My wife . . ."

"Your wife's going to be all right. It's her companion, Mrs. Wyatt. She's dead. To be quite blunt about it, she went on a drinking spree and killed herself."

Rupert was silent.

"Mr. Kellogg, are you still there? Operator, I've been cut off. Operator! *Telefonista!* For the love of the Lord, couldn't I make just one phone call without interruption? *Telefonista!*"

"You haven't been cut off," Rupert said. "I was—this is a—shock. I—I have known Mrs. Wyatt for many years. How did it happen?"

Johnson told him what details he knew, in a sharp, disapproving voice, as if he considered Wilma's death a breach of international etiquette.

"And my wife?"

"She's suffering from shock, naturally. They've taken her to the American-British-Corday hospital. Do you want that address?"

"Yes."

"It's Mariano Escobedo, 628. The telephone number is 11-49-00."

"Will she be able to talk to me if I call?"

"Oh no. She's under sedation. She has a head injury incurred when she fainted, nothing serious as far as I know."

"How long will she be in the hospital?"

"It's impossible to tell," Johnson said. "Do you have any friends here who could look after her?"

"No. I'd better come down myself."

"That's a good idea. Shall I call the Windsor Hotel where she was staying and ask them to hold the suite for you?"

"Please," Rupert said. "I'd also appreciate it if you left a message at the hospital for her: I'll be down there tonight."

"What if you can't make it tonight?"

"I'll make it. There's a flight leaving in two hours. My wife took it last week."

"Do you have a tourist card? They won't let you on the plane without one."

"I'll get one."

"Very well. I'll leave the message for her. One more thing, Mr. Kellogg. The police were unable to find any next of kin to Mrs. Wyatt. Has she any relatives?"

"A sister in San Diego."

"Name?"

"Ruth Sullivan."

"Address?"

"I don't know where she's living, but her husband is a lieutenant commander attached to the Eleventh Naval District. It shouldn't be hard to find out his home address. Earl Sullivan."

"Thanks, Mr. Kellogg. And if there's anything the Embassy can do for you while you're down here, let me know. The number is 39-95-00."

"Thank you. Good-bye."

"Good-bye."

Miss Burton appeared in the doorway, slump-shouldered and spaniel-eyed, as befitted the gravity of the situation. "I couldn't help overhearing, people talk so loud over long distance."

"Do they?"

"That's a terrible thing about Mrs. Wyatt, dying in a foreign country like that. All I can say is, God rest her soul." It seemed enough. Miss Burton straightened her shoulders, put on her spectacles and said briskly, "I'll call Western Air Lines right away."

"Yes."

"Are you feeling all right, Mr. Kellogg?"

"I—certainly. Certainly."

"I've got some aspirin."

"Take them yourself."

Miss Burton knew better than to argue. She merely dropped two aspirins on his desk and went out to the reception room to phone the air lines. Rupert stared at the aspirins for a long time. Then he got up and went over to the water cooler and swallowed them both at once.

Miss Burton sailed in on a note of elation. "Success. You leave on flight 611. But goodness, the arguing I had to do. Some snip of a clerk kept saying that the people leaving on 611 were already checking in at the airport. And I said, listen, this is an emergency. I spelled it right out for him, e-m-e-r-g-e-n-c-y . . . Oh, I see you took the pills. Good. How are you fixed for money?"

"I'll need some."

"Okay, Borowitz can run over to the bank. Now, here's your schedule. Depart International at 11:50. Lunch on plane. Stopover in L.A. for about an hour. Leave L.A. at 2:30. Dinner on plane. Arrive Mexico City at 10:10, Central Standard Time."

Miss Burton might go to pieces over smaller crises, but when the larger ones came along she expanded to meet them. She arranged for money, tourist card, toothbrush, clean socks and pajamas, care of the Scottie, Mack, and message to Amy's brother, Gill Brandon. When she finally got Rupert on the plane and he waved good-bye to her from the window, she was moist-eyed but relieved, like a mother sending her son off to school for the first time.

She drove Rupert's car back to the city and parked it in the garage of his house on 41st Avenue. Then she let Mack out to run while she washed and dried the dishes Rupert had left in the sink. In all the years she'd worked for him, this was only the second time she'd been inside his house, and it gave her a curious feeling, like watching somebody sleeping.

After she finished the dishes she wandered through each of the rooms, not snooping really but merely taking mental notes like any good secretary interested in her boss: *Mahogany and lace in the dining room, that's too formal for him, must be her doing . . . I'll bet he sits in the yellow chair, there are hair oil marks on the back and a good lamp beside it. He loves to read, he'd need a good lamp . . . A grand piano* and *an organ, fancy that. She must be musical, he can't whistle a note . . . I'll never get used to those colored johns . . . The maid's room, I bet. Every bit as nicely furnished as the others, which goes to show how generous he is. Or maybe it's her. Borowitz says she comes from a very moneyed family . . . The hall table looks like genuine rosewood, the kind you polish with your bare hands if you're crazy that way and have lots of time. A postcard. I wonder who from. Well, postcards aren't private. If you've got something private to say, say it in a letter.*

Miss Burton picked up the postcard. It bore a colored photograph of the Old Faithful geyser on one side and a penciled message on the other.

> *Dear Mr. and Mrs. Kellogg:*
> *I am having a real good time on my holliday. I saw Old Faithful already six times. It is a site. It gets cold here at nite, blankets needed. There is a swimming pool that smells bad owing to minrals in the water. The smell don't come off on you fortunately. No more room on the card. Hello to Mack.*
>
> *Yours truly,*
> *Gerda Lundquist.*

Yellowstone yet, Miss Burton thought. And I can't even afford Sequoia. Not that I want to. People are always saying how small you feel under the big trees, which isn't my idea of fun at five foot one-half inch.

Having finished her unofficial tour of the house and mail, Miss Burton let the Scottie in at the back door and fed him several dog biscuits. Then she walked over to Fulton Street to catch a bus back to town.

She had no premonition of disaster. The day was sunny and her horoscope that morning had been exceptionally favorable. So had Rupert's, which she always looked up even before her own: *This is a wonderful day for you Leos and Librans.*

Wonderful day, Miss Burton thought, and skipped along the sidewalk, quite forgetting that Mrs. Kellogg was in a hospital and Mrs. Wyatt was dead.

The plane was on schedule. Rupert called the A.B.C. Hospital from the airport and made arrangements to see his wife in spite of the lateness of the hour.

He arrived at the hospital shortly before midnight and was met at the main desk by a dark young man who identified himself as Dr. Escobar.

"She's alseep," Escobar said. "But I think, under the circumstances, it would do her good to see you. She has called for you several times."

"How is she?"

"That's difficult to say. She's been crying a great deal, whenever she wakes up, in fact."

"Is she in pain?"

"Her head may hurt a bit, but I think the crying is explained more by emotional reasons than physical ones. It is not merely the death of her friend that has disturbed her, though that certainly is bad enough in itself. There were additional circumstances, the fact that the two women were alone in a strange city without friends, that they'd been drinking a good deal . . ."

"Drinking? Amy has never taken more than a cocktail before dinner."

Escobar looked a little embarrassed. "There is considerable evidence that both your wife and Mrs. Wyatt had been drinking *tequila* with an American barfly named O'Donnell. The women had a loud argument."

"They were very good friends," Rupert said stiffly. "Ever since childhood."

"Very good friends sometimes argue together, sometimes drink together. What I am trying to tell you is that Mrs. Kellogg feels extremely guilty, guilty about the drinking, guilty about the argument, guilty, most of all, because she was unable to prevent her friend's suicide."

"Did she try?"

"Anyone would try, naturally."

"Has she told you what . . ."

"She's told me very little. She has very little to tell. *Tequila* is a formidable concoction if one is not used to it." Escobar turned to the elevators. "Come along, we'll see her now. We've moved her from Emergency to a private room on the third floor."

She was asleep with the night light on. Her left eye was black and swollen, and there was a bandage over her temple. Crumpled pieces of Kleenex littered the floor beside her bed.

"Amy." Rupert bent over his sleeping wife and touched her shoulder. "Amy, dear, it's me."

She was hardly awake before she began to cry, holding her fists against her eyes.

"Amy, don't. Stop that, please. Everything's going to be all right."

"No—no . . ."

"Yes, it is. I'm here to take care of you."

"Wilma's dead." Her voice began to rise. "Wilma's dead!"

Escobar stepped swiftly over to the side of the bed and grasped her hand. "Now, Mrs. Kellogg, no more hysterics. The other patients on the floor are sleeping."

"Wilma's dead."

"I know," Rupert said. "But you must think of yourself now."

"Take me home, take me out of this terrible place."

"I will, dearest. Just as soon as they let me."

"Come now, Mrs. Kellogg," Escobar said smoothly. "This isn't such a terrible place. We'd like to keep you here for a few days of observation."

"No, I won't stay!"

"For a day or two . . ."

"No! Let me go! Rupert, get me out of here. Take me home!"

"I will," Rupert said.

"All the way home? To my own home and Mack and everything?"

"All the way, I promise."

It was a promise which, at the moment, he intended to keep.

5

GILL BRANDON CAME downstairs wearing his composite morning expression: anticipation over what the day would bring and suspicion that something was bound to spoil it.

He was a short, stocky, vigorous man with a forceful manner of speaking that made even his most innocuous remark seem compelling, and his most far-fetched theory sound like a self-evident truth. To heighten this effect he also used his hands when he talked, not in any dramatically loose European style, but severely, geometrically, to indicate an exact angle of thought, a precise degree of emotion. He liked to think of himself as mathematical and meticulous. He was neither.

Gill kissed his wife, who was already at the table with the morning paper in front of her opened to the lovelorn column. "Any phone calls?"

"No."

"It's damned peculiar."

"What is?" Helene said, knowing perfectly well what was, since Gill had talked of nothing else for a week. Thank God it was Monday and he had to go into the city to work. If the stock market was fluttery, so much the better. It would take his mind off other things. "Here's a terribly funny letter from some woman in Atherton. I wonder if it's anyone we know. It could be Betty Spears. Listen. 'Dear Abby: My problem is my husband is so stingy that he even snitches my green stamps.' I know for a fact Johnny Spears saves green stamps . . ."

"Will you *listen* to me?"

"Of course, dear. I didn't know you were saying anything."

"Rupert's been down there for a week now and I haven't heard a word since that first phone call from his secretary. Not a word about how Amy is and what's going on, when they'll be back, nothing."

"He may be busy."

Gill scowled at her across the table. "Busy doing what, may I ask?"

"How should I know?"

"Then stop making up nonsensical excuses for him. Nobody's too busy to pick up a phone. He's damned inconsiderate. And what Amy ever saw in him I'll never know."

"He's very good-looking. And very nice."

"Good-looking. Nice. Great Scott, is that what women marry men for?"

"You're hungry, dear. I'll ring for breakfast."

Helene pressed the buzzer under the table, feeling a mild surge of power. She had been born and raised in an Oakland slum, and never, in all her twenty years of marriage, had she become accustomed to the miracle of ringing for anything she wanted. Breakfast, martinis, chocolate creams, tea, magazines, cigarettes—you pressed a button, and bingo, whatever you wanted, there it was. Sometimes Helene just sat and thought of things to want so she would have the pleasure of pulling the tasseled bell cord or pressing the buzzer underneath the table.

Occasionally she visited Oakland but more frequently her parents came down the Peninsula to see her, Mrs. Maloney wearing her teeth and Sunday clothes, Mr. Maloney sober as a judge and dry as a herring. After the initial greetings of genuine pleasure, both parents stiffened into silence, too stunned by the luxurious surroundings to do much of anything except sit and stare. Back home they were affectionately voluble about their daughter Helene, who had gone to Mills College on a scholarship and lived in a fine house in Atherton with her wealthy husband and three beautiful children.

Face to face with her, they became mute and embarrassed, and their visits were a nightmare, especially to Gill, who tried harder than Helene did to make the Maloneys feel at home. His tactics were peculiar: he sought to minimize his wealth by calling attention to some of his economies, by talking forcefully of having his thirteen-year-old son take a paper route and his seventeen-year-old daughter work her way through college. The result of this stratagem was more confusion on the part of the Maloneys and complete frustration for Gill, who meant, as usual, only to do the right thing. No one had ever been able to figure out why such good intentions as Gill's often had such disturbing consequences.

"Amy's association with the Wyatt woman," Gill said, "has meant nothing but trouble. She was obviously unbalanced. Anyone but Amy would have seen that and avoided her."

Helene mentally crossed herself. "Now Gill. *De mortuis* . . . Besides, they were friends. You don't go back on a friend because she's having, well, a few emotional problems. Wilma could be a very charming and entertaining person when she wanted to. That's the way I prefer to remember her."

"You have a very simple and convenient memory."

"And I intend to keep it that way. Eat your breakfast."

"I'm not hungry," Gill said irritably. "Personally, I'm inclined to blame Rupert for this whole business. He should have vetoed the trip as soon as the subject was broached. Two women wandering alone around a foreign, uncivilized country—why, it's preposterous."

It sounded rather pleasant to Helene whose traveling was confined to shopping trips to the city and summers at Tahoe. She munched on a piece of crisp bacon, listening to Gill the way one listens to waves breaking on a beach, knowing the noise will always be the same, only varying in volume now and then with the tides and the weather.

So often the noise was about Amy, and Helene listened out of habit, without interest. In her opinion, Amy was a dull little creature, invested with wit by her brother and beauty by her husband, and having, in fact, neither. Helene, too, had often wondered about the relationship between Amy and Wilma, but she wondered from quite a different point of view from Gill's: why should such an intense and energetic person as Wilma have wasted so much time on a mouse like Amy?

Gill turned up his volume. "I still think the American Embassy should have called me about this unfortunate affair."

"Why?"

"Amy's my kid sister."

"She is also a grown woman with a husband. If she needs looking after, let Rupert do it."

"Rupert is incapable of handling certain situations."

"What's to handle?" Helene said blandly.

"There are probably decisions to be made, actions to be taken. Rupert's too soft. Now if I were down there I'd be firm with those foreigners."

"If you were down there, dear, you'd *be* the foreigner."

"I suppose you think that's terribly clever?"

"It's just the truth."

"You seem," he said with a dry little smile, "to be hitting on a great many truths these days."

"Oh, I am. Some large, some small."

"Tell me a few of them."

"Another time. You'd better hurry if you're going to take El Camino instead of Bayshore." She smiled at her husband across the table. In spite of his manner of talking she knew him for a gentle man, more like Amy than he would ever realize. "You'll drive carefully, won't you, Gilly?"

"I wish you wouldn't call me that. It sounds absurd."

"You don't object when Amy calls you . . ."

"It was my nickname when we were children. She uses it unconsciously. And I do object. Remind me to speak to her about it when she comes home."

Helene's expression didn't change, but she felt a sudden sick feeling in her stomach and the coffee she was drinking seemed to have turned sour. *I don't want her to come home. She is two thousand miles away. I like it this way.*

David, the thirteen-year-old, bounced into the room, wearing the uniform of the military day school he attended. "Morning, all."

"What on earth," Helene asked, "is the matter with your face?"

"Poison oak," he said cheerfully. "Roger and Bill got it, too, when we were out on maneuvers. Boy, the sergeant was mad. He said the Russians could have landed while the whole bloody bunch of us were chasing around after poison oak."

"I'll call for you after school and take you to the doctor."

"I don't want to go to any bloody doctor."

"Stop saying that word. It's not very nice."

"The sergeant uses it all the time. He's an Englishman. They always say bloody. Oh, I forgot to tell you, Uncle Rupert's home. He phoned last night when you were out."

"You might," his father said, "have told me before."

"How could I, when you were out?"

"Is Amy all right?"

"I don't know. He didn't say anything about her."

"Well, what *did* he say?"

"Just that he was going to be home all day today and would like to see you about something important."

"I'll call right . . ."

"He said not to call. It's a very private matter. He wants to talk to you in person."

Gill was already on his feet.

The two men shook hands and Gill said immediately, "Amy's all right?"

"Yes."

"Where is she? Still in bed?"

"She's—we can't talk out here. You'd better come in."

The house was dark and quiet and musty, as if the people who lived there had been away for a long time. No sun filtered through the drawn blinds, no sound crept past the closed windows. Only in the den, at the end of the long, narrow hall, had the drapes been pulled open, and the morning sun hung dusty in the air. On the tiled coffee table was a half-empty highball glass smudged with lipstick, and beside it, an unstamped envelope with the name "Gilly" written across the front in Amy's boarding-school script.

Gill stared at it. The letter was wrong; the silent man at the window, the too-quiet house, the half-empty glass, all seemed ominous. He cleared his throat. "The letter—it's from Amy, of course."

"Yes."

"Why? Why a letter, I mean."

"She preferred to do it that way," Rupert said, without turning.

"Do what?"

"Explain why she went away."

"Went away? Where?"

"I don't know where. She refused to tell me."

"But this is preposterous, it's impossible."

Rupert turned to face him. "All right, have it your way. It's preposterous and impossible. It happened, though. Some things *can* happen without your knowledge or permission."

They glared at each other across the sunny room. When Amy was around to smooth things over, the two men had been civil to each other and observed the amenities. Now, without her presence, the unspoken gibes and unvoiced criticisms that had accumulated through the years seemed to hang between them, ready to be plucked out of the air and used as strings to either bow.

"She took her clothes," Rupert said, "and her dog, and left."

"The dog, too?"

"It was hers. She had a right to."

"Taking the dog, that means . . ."

"I know what it means."

They both knew. If Amy had intended to come back, she wouldn't have taken the dog with her.

"You'd better read your letter," Rupert said.

Gill picked it up and held it in his hands for a moment, very carefully, as if it were a bomb that might detonate at any sudden movement. "Do you know—what's in it?"

"It's sealed and addressed to you. How should I know?" He did know, though. He remembered every word in the letter. He'd gone over it a dozen times looking for flaws. He'd found some, but only after it was too late.

Gill read slowly, mouthing the words like a beginning reader.

> *Dear Gilly:*
>
> *I have told Rupert to give you this letter, rather than mailing it, because I know you will want to ask him questions. Some he'll be able to answer, some he won't. Some even* I *can't answer, so how can I make you understand the reasons why I am going away for a while? The main thing is, I am. It is a very big decision for me. I can't phone you to say good-bye because I know you'd argue with me and I'm afraid my decision might not be strong enough to stand up under an argument from you.*
>
> *It is a week now since Wilma died, a week of regret and grief, but also one of reexamination of myself. I didn't come out very well. I am thirty-three, and it seems that I've been living like a child, always leaning on other people. I didn't enjoy it, I just could never get around to not leaning. I never will, if I simply stay here and sink back into the same old rut. I must get the feeling of being alone and being myself. I know that if I had been a mature, responsible person, used to making decisions and acting on them, I would have been able to prevent Wilma's death. If I had not been drinking myself, I could have stopped Wilma from drinking to the point of depression . . .*

"She'd been drinking," Gill said in surprise. "How much?"

"A lot."

"That doesn't sound like the Amy I know."

"Perhaps there's another one. She was not only drinking, she was drinking in the company of an American barfly named O'Donnell."

"I don't believe it."

"That's your privilege."

> *. . . All this may seem nonsensical to you, Gilly. But I can be practical, too. I have given Rupert the necessary authority to handle my financial affairs, so you needn't worry on that score. And please, Gilly, whatever you do, don't blame Rupert for my going away. He's been a wonderful husband to me. Be kind to him, cheer him up, he's going to miss me. You will, too, I know, but you have Helene and the children. (Give them my love and tell them I've gone east to recuperate or some such thing. Don't tell them I've gone off my rocker which is probably what you're thinking. I haven't gone off, I'm just getting on.)*
>
> *Best love, and don't worry about me!*
> *Amy.*

Gill returned the letter to its envelope, slowly and methodically, as if it were a bill he was thinking twice about paying. "Has she been doing much talking along these lines the past week?"

"Quite a bit."

"Then she had planned on leaving even before she came home?"

"She came home to pick up Mack."

"You should have warned me ahead of time, sent me a wire or something. I might have prevented this."

"How?"

"By telling her not to go."

"That's the pattern she's trying to break out of," Rupert said, "being told what to do."

"Have you any idea where she went?"

"No. I'm not even sure she had a definite place in mind."

"Well, how did she leave?"

"She called a cab, but I persuaded her to cancel it and let me drive her to the station."

"What time?"

"About eight."

"Is there any possibility she was coming down to Atherton to see me?"

"None," Rupert said. "She wrote you the letter, for one thing. For another, she had Mack with her. There are no baggage cars on the commuters' trains to accommodate animals."

"There are on the Lark. It leaves for Los Angeles around nine o'clock. By God, that's it, that's where she is, Los Angeles."

"There are trains *leaving* as well as arriving at Los Angeles."

"Even so, she shouldn't be too difficult to trace, a young woman traveling by train with a bad-tempered Scottie."

"Mack's not bad-temp—Oh, for heaven's sake, get it through your head, Gill. Amy doesn't *want* to be traced."

"She's a woman. Half the time women don't know what they want. They have to be told, guided. I've always thought you should have kept a firmer hand on the reins."

"Funny, I thought you were holding them."

Gill colored. "What do you mean by a remark like that?"

"Just what I said. The reins were never in my hands. Nor have I ever considered my wife in the same category as a horse."

"Horses and women have a lot in common. Put them in an open field and they run to hell and gone."

"Where did you learn so much about women, Gill?"

"I don't want to quarrel with you," Gill said firmly. "The situation is too serious. What are you going to do about it?"

"Nothing. What do you suggest I do?"

"Call the police. Tell them to locate her and bring her back."

"On what grounds? Amy's of age, considerably overage, in fact."

"We'll be able to think of some reason."

"Oh, for . . . All right. Suppose we do and suppose they find her. What then?"

"They'll bring her home and we'll have an opportunity to talk some sense into her head."

"By 'we' I presume you mean 'you'?"

"Well, I've always been able to handle her, make her see reason."

"Perhaps she *is* seeing reason," Rupert said. "Her own. Not yours."

Gill struck the arm of the davenport with his fist. Particles of dust scurried up and away in alarm. "You're being pretty damn cool and collected for a man whose wife has disappeared."

" 'Disappeared' isn't quite the word."

"It is to me."

A sudden draft rippled the moted shafts of sunlight, and a woman's voice called out from the back door, "Mack. Here, Mack. Come on, boy. Time for your run."

At the first word Gill had risen expectantly, but as the woman continued to call the dog he sat down again heavily as if he'd been pushed in the chest by Rupert's fist. Rupert had not moved.

"Here, Mack. Come on, now. If you're on that bed again I'm going to tell on you! Mack? Boy?"

Miss Burton appeared in the doorway, her cheeks pink with cold, her hair bleached to the color and texture of straw. "Why, Mr. Kellogg. My goodness. Why I had no idea you were home. Barging in like this, what must you think of me?"

"It's all right, Miss Burton," Rupert said. "I should have given you advance notice. You know Mr. Brandon, of course?"

"Why yes. Good morning, Mr. Brandon."

Gill rose and nodded briefly. He'd seen Miss Burton at least a dozen times but he would never have recognized her meeting her casually on the street. She seemed to assume different faces and personalities with each new hair color. Only her voice remained the same, brisk brunette, no matter how blonde her inanities.

Miss Burton fondled Rupert with her eyes. "This is such a nice surprise finding you home. I just came by to give Mack his breakfast and take him for a run, and lo and behold, here you are instead. My goodness. How is Mrs. Kellogg?"

"She's fine, thank you," Rupert said.

"Where's Mack? Now that I'm here I might as well . . ."

"You run along to the office, Miss Burton. I'll—take care of Mack."

"All rightie, whatever you say."

"I'll be down this afternoon sometime."

"Good. Things are getting a mite behind. Borowitz has a new girlfriend and can't concentrate. She's absolutely nothing to look at, just young."

"Yes. Well. You'd better run along now, Miss Burton."

"I'll do that. Good-bye, Mr. Brandon. It was real nice seeing you again. And you'll be along later then, Mr. Kellogg?"

"Yes."

"My, I'm glad you're back. Borowitz is making a real fool of himself."

After she'd gone Gill said heavily, "What are you going to do about Amy?"

"Wait."

"Just sit on your rear and wait?"

"That's right."

"You're a fool."

"That's your opinion."

"You're damned right it is," Gill said and stamped furiously out of the room and down the hall to the front door.

I handled him wrong, Rupert thought. *He may do something crazy, like go to the police.*

6

ON FRIDAY OF the same week, when Rupert returned from lunch, he found Helene Brandon waiting for him in his office. She was wearing a sable-trimmed suit and matching hat, and she carried the commuters' essential, an enormous handbag. She had obviously been passing the time going through the handbag. Half its contents were on Rupert's desk: paperback books, a magazine, two pairs of spectacles, cigarettes, pills, a candy bar, a collapsible umbrella, plastic rain boots and a pair of low-heeled black shoes.

The feminine clutter reminded Rupert of Amy and he tried to avoid looking at it by keeping his eyes fixed on Helene's face. A pretty face, round and plump and without secrets.

She began thrusting everything back into her handbag. "Gill would have a cat fit if he knew I was here, so it goes without saying that I'm not, eh?"

Rupert smiled. "For a lady who isn't even here you're looking very pretty."

"We Peninsulans have to dress to the teeth when we come to the city just to prove we haven't gone to seed in the suburbs."

"That hardly seems likely in Atherton."

"Oh, you think not? Listen, I haven't had on a pair of high heels for weeks. My feet are killing me."

"Change your shoes."

"No, I'd rather suffer. I'll enjoy the trip more in retrospect if I suffer now."

"That's logic, I presume?"

"No. It's just true." She snapped the handbag shut and said with no change of tone, "I know about Amy. Gill told me."

"I'm glad he did. I wanted you to know."

"You haven't heard from her?"

"I didn't expect to. She told me she wouldn't be writing for a time."

"She could at least let you know where she is."

"She could, yes," Rupert said. "But she hasn't. And I'm not in a position where I can tell her what to do."

"Maybe that's what she wanted."

"What is?"

"To be where people can't tell her what to do. I wouldn't mind it myself for a few weeks." Helene contemplated this idea with half-closed eyes. Then she dropped it, with a sigh, and said abruptly, "Listen. Gill's spoiling for trouble. I thought I'd better warn you."

"What kind of trouble?"

"I'm not sure . . . You'd better close the door. If Miss Burton's ears perk up any further she'll take off in the first high wind."

"I have no secrets from Miss Burton."

"Well, *I* have," Helene said dryly. "And you might be going to."

Rupert closed the door. "What does that mean?"

"Gill has ideas."

"About what?"

"You and Miss Burton."

Rupert let out an explosive sound like an angry laugh. "Oh, for Christ's sake!"

"I think it's funny too, but I'm not laughing. Gill's dead serious. He's managed to convince himself that you don't want Amy back because you have—other interests."

"What possible basis could he have for such a screwy idea?"

"Miss Burton has a key to your house."

"Naturally. I gave it to her so she could feed Mack twice a day while I was away."

"Gill said you usually put him in a kennel."

"The last time we left him in a kennel he picked up mange."

"You see? There's a logical explanation for everything but Gill just won't believe it. He's practically irrational on the subject of family. I don't know why, and I prefer not to think about it since there's nothing I can do about it."

"I often think about it," Rupert said.

"So do I, really. It's useless, though. We might just as well say 'Gill is a nice guy but he's nuts on the subject of Amy,' and let it go at that."

"Consider it gone."

Helene took a deep breath to signify that that subject was closed and another about to be opened. "Then there's the lipstick."

"What lipstick?"

"On the highball glass in the den. Gill says it was exactly the same shade as Miss Burton was wearing."

"And thirty million other American women. It was a new color introduced last spring, something or other sherbet."

"Tangerine sherbet?"

"Right. I gave it to Amy for Easter in one of those fancy doodad cases. Now is that all?"

"Not quite."

Rupert struck his palms together in helpless fury. "What else, for God's sake?"

"I wish you wouldn't keep swearing. It upsets me. And if *I* get upset heaven knows what will happen. I seem to be the only calm one in the whole caboodle. Now what was I going to say?"

"I'd be a fool to guess," Rupert said grimly and sat down behind his desk to wait while Helene sorted through her mind, as she had sorted through her handbag, coming across all sorts of odds and ends she thought she'd lost.

"I should have taken notes, but I couldn't very well because Gill thought he was talking to me in confidence. I mean, he had no idea I'd come here and tell you. He'd have a cat fit if it . . ."

"You said that."

"Did I? Well, it only goes to show. Oh, I remember now. The cigarette butts in the den."

"There were no cigarette butts in the den."

"That's just it. None in the ashtrays, none in the fireplace. Amy's a very heavy smoker—it's one of the few things she's ever defied Gill about. And since she was particularly nervous that night, Gill said you'd expect to find all the ashtrays overflowing."

"With fifty years of training, Gill might make a detective."

"Well, he *does* notice things," Helene said defensively, "even if they turn out to be wrong."

"Even if, yes. In this case he didn't notice far enough. Amy spent no more than five minutes in the den. He should have taken the trouble to examine the rest of the house. Tell him that next time he's to bring his microscope."

"You're mad, aren't you?"

"You're damn right I'm mad. What's he trying to prove?"

"Nothing definite. He just thinks you're not telling the truth."

"The truth about what?"

"Everything. I warned you, he's simply not rational."

"That's a quaint way of putting it. The man's a maniac."

"Only where Amy is concerned."

"Isn't that enough?" Rupert pounded the desk with his fist in a half-conscious imitation of Gill. "Ever since Amy and I have been married he's been trying to break us up. He's been sitting around hoping I'd beat her or chase other women or turn into a lush or a drug addict, anything. Anything at all, just so Amy would leave me and climb back into the family nest like a goddamn baby bird. Well, he's half succeeded. She's left me, but she didn't head back for the nest."

"She hasn't left you, Rupert. Not really. I—I read the letter." She flushed slightly and twisted one of the rings on her plump fingers. "Gill asked me to read it."

"Why?"

"He wanted my opinion about whether it made sense—female sense, as he called it—and about whether I thought the handwriting was, well, authentic."

"And was it?"

"Of course. I told Gill the handwriting was unmistakably Amy's. Only . . ."

She paused, working at the ring again as if it had shrunk in size and was hurting her. It was the diamond Gill had given her twenty years ago. Amy had still been in the nest then, baby bird Amy, featherless, formless, her mouth constantly open not because of hunger, bird-style, but because of a bad case of adenoids. The adenoids had been removed, feathers grew, wings developed; but there'd been no place to fly until Rupert came along. Helene remembered Amy's wedding day more clearly, and more happily, than her own. *Bye bye, blackbird.*

"Only what?" Rupert said.

"He didn't trust my judgment. Yesterday he took the letter to a handwriting expert, a private detective named Dodd."

Rupert leaned forward, mute with shock. From Borowitz's office next door came the spasmodic coughing of the adding machine. Business as usual, Rupert thought, Borowitz feeding figures into the machine and coming up with answers. And a few blocks away, in another office, Gill was coming up with answers too, only there was something the matter with his machine, a loose screw. "What," he said finally, "does he think has happened to Amy?"

"He's not thinking, he's *feeling*, don't you see that? None of his ideas makes sense. That's why I came here, to warn you. Also because I'm worried, I'm worried sick. It's not good for Gill's health to have these ideas."

"It's not good for mine either, obviously. Tell me some of these ideas of his."

"You won't get mad again?"

"I can't afford to. The situation's too serious."

"All right then. He said last night he's not sure Amy ever came home at all."

"Then where is she?"

"Still in Mexico."

"Doing what?"

"Doing nothing. He thinks—no, I don't mean thinks, I mean feels. He *feels* she's dead."

Rupert didn't even look surprised. The surprises were over, he knew now Gill was capable of anything. "A psychiatrist would have a ball with that one. Has he managed to feel how she died?"

"No."

"Or when?"

"During the week that you were down there."

"So I went to Mexico City," Rupert said, sounding very detached, "and killed my wife. Did I have any particular reason?"

"Money. And Miss Burton."

"I wanted to inherit Amy's money and marry Miss Burton, is that it?"

"Yes." She had managed to work the ring off her finger. She sat now with it in her lap, not looking at it, only partly conscious that it was there. "Oh, he doesn't really believe all this, Rupert. He's hurt because Amy didn't confide in him, and angry at you for letting her go away."

"There's more to it than that. You oversimplify. Why do you suppose Gill feels that Amy is dead?"

It was a question she'd been avoiding in her own mind for several days, and it disturbed her to hear it spoken aloud. "I don't know."

"Because he wants her dead."

"That's not true. He loves her. He loves her best."

"He also hates her best. She is—or he believes she is—the source of his emotional troubles. If Amy's dead, his problems are over. He's free. Oh, sure, he'll suffer at the conscious level, he'll feel grief and pity and all that, but down at rock bottom he's free." He paused. "Only he isn't. She's not dead."

"I never thought for a minute that she was." But Helene looked relieved to hear it, guiltily relieved. It was as if she, too, scraping along rock bottom, grubbing for satisfactions, had come across a dead Amy, a drowned, bedraggled baby bird with its mouth still open. "Listen, Rupert. You seem to understand that Gill isn't—himself. You'll be tolerant, won't you?"

"That depends."

"On what?"

"How far he goes."

"I'm sure the worst is over. When something upsetting like this comes along Gill thrashes around for a while but he eventually sees reason." She had convinced herself, if not Rupert. She picked up the ring from her lap and put it back on her finger, only partly aware that she'd taken it off in the first place. "I must go now. I'm late for a dental appointment. You'll let us know right away if you hear from Amy?"

"Certainly. I'll even bring the letter over so Gill can have the handwriting analyzed."

"Don't be bitter."

"I'm not. I'm quite serious about it. What have I got to lose?"

"You're being an awfully good sport over all this," Helene said warmly. "I think Amy's made a terrible mistake, walking out on you."

"She didn't walk. I drove her. And if she made a mistake, that's her business. For her to do anything on her own is a good thing, even if it's wrong. Perhaps eventually Gill will understand that."

"He will, give him time."

"She's never done anything on her own before. The trip to Mexico City was intended to be a declaration of independence. But it was merely a change in dependence: Wilma planned every inch of the way."

Helene mentally crossed herself at the mention of Wilma, whom she hadn't really liked very well but who at least had never appeared in her dreams as a dead bird. "Listen, Rupert. You may think this is silly, but have you thought about advertising for Amy in some of the big newspapers throughout the country? I mean, let her know we're worried and want to know where she is. You see ads like that all the time: Bill, contact Mary; Charley, write to Mother; Amy, come home. Things like that."

"Amy, come home," he repeated. "Gill's idea, I suppose?"

"Well, yes. But I agree with it. It might do some good. Amy isn't the type who'd want people to worry about her unnecessarily."

"Perhaps she is. How do we know? She's never had much of a chance to prove what type she is."

"You could try advertising anyway. It can't do any harm. There wouldn't even be any publicity if you made the ad vague enough and didn't mention last names. We certainly don't want publicity."

"You mean Gill doesn't."

"I mean *none* of us does," she said sharply. "This whole business—it would look very queer in the newspapers."

"It won't take long to reach the papers if Gill goes around sounding off that Amy is dead and I'm about to establish a love nest with Miss Burton."

"So far he's sounded off only to me."

"And to the private detective, Dodd."

"I don't think he told Dodd much, just enough to make it plausible that he wanted the handwriting in Amy's letter compared to other samples of her writing." She got up and leaned across the desk. "I'm on your side, Rupert, you know that."

"Thanks."

"But you have to make some concessions to Gill for your own protection. If he thought you were really *trying* to find Amy and get her back, it would help put him straight. So try."

"Advertise, you mean?"

"Yes."

"All right, that's easy enough."

"The library should have the names of all the leading newspapers in the country." She hesitated. "It might be quite expensive. Naturally, Gill and I will pay for . . ."

"Naturally?"

"Well, it was our idea. It's only fair that . . ."

"I think," Rupert said, "that I can afford to advertise for my own wife."

Amy, come home. He could already see the letters in print, but he knew Amy never would.

7

ELMER DODD WAS a brash, bushy-haired little man, who'd been, at various times and with varying success, a carpenter in New Jersey, seaman on a Panamanian freighter, military policeman in Korea, bodyguard to a Chinese exporter in Singapore, and Bible salesman in Los Angeles. When, at forty, he met a woman who persuaded him to settle down, he found himself experienced in many things and expert in none, so he decided to become a private detective. He moved his bride to San Francisco. Here he hung around the Hall of Justice to get the feel of things, attended trials, where he took notes, and haunted the morgues of the *Chronicle* and the *Examiner*, where he read up on famous criminal cases of the past.

All this might eventually have helped, but it was sheer coincidence that set him up in business. He was having a snack one day in a spaghetti joint in North Beach when the proprietor shot his wife and mother-in-law and the mother-in-law's boyfriend. Dodd was the sole surviving witness.

During the years that followed, Dodd's name became familiar to every newspaper reader in the Bay area. It popped up in divorce cases, felony trials, gossip columns and, more regularly, in the personal section of the want ads where he offered his services as an expert in various fields, including handwriting analysis. He owned a couple of books on the subject, which, in his own opinion, made him as much of an expert as anyone else since handwriting analysis was not an exact science. He knew enough, at any rate, for run-of-the-mill cases like this Amy business.

Amy sounded like a bit of a nut (Dodd also owned a book on abnormal psychology), but nut or not, she had certainly written all four of the letters Gill Brandon had brought in for comparison. Dodd had known this immediately, even before Brandon had left his office. But it would have been impractical to admit it. Experts took time, they checked and re-checked, and were suitably reimbursed for their trouble. Dodd took a week, during which he checked and rechecked Gill Brandon's financial standing and decided on a fee. It was just enough to make Brandon squawk in protest, but not so much as to cause him to refuse payment.

Dodd was satisfied.

So, in spite of the fee, was Gill. "I don't mind telling you, Dodd, that this is a great load off my mind. Naturally, I was almost positive she wrote the letter. There was only a small element of doubt."

What a liar, Dodd thought. "Which is now dispelled, of course?"

"Of course. As a matter of fact, we heard from her again yesterday. By 'we' I mean she wrote to her husband and he forwarded her letter to me."

"Why?"

"Why? Well, I—he realizes I'm very concerned about my sister. He wanted me to know she is all right."

"And is she?"

"Certainly. She's in New York. I should have guessed she might go there—we have relatives in Queens and Westchester."

"Did you bring the letter with you?"

"Yes."

"I'd like to see it. There'll be no extra charge, of course," Dodd added, after a quick study of Gill's expression. "I'm just curious."

Gill passed the letter across the desk, reluctantly, as if he were afraid that Dodd might suddenly alter his opinion and claim all the letters were forgeries.

Dodd knew at first sight that the handwriting was identical with that in the other letters, but he went through a few motions for Gill's benefit. Using a magnifying glass and a ruler, he measured and compared spaces between lines and words, margins, paragraph indentations. It was, however, the text of the letter that interested him: it seemed so much sharper and more positive than any of the others. The handwriting was the same, certainly. But was the woman?

> *Dear Rupert:*
>
> *Whatever made you do such an absurd thing? I couldn't believe my eyes when I saw the ad in the* Herald Tribune. *Gill will be furious if he finds out. You know how livid he gets at the mere mention of publicity.*
>
> *Of course I'll come home. But not right away. As you can see by the postmark, I'm in New York. It's a good place to be when you want to figure things out by yourself. Everyone lets you alone. For the time being, this is just what I need.*
>
> *Don't worry about me. I miss you, but in a way I'm quite happy and I know this is what you would want for me.*
>
> Please *take that advertisement out of the paper. (Or is it papers? I hope to heaven not!) Also, please phone Gill and Helene and tell them everything's fine. I'll write to them eventually. This business of writing is very difficult for me—it seems to bring before me so clearly and sharply some of the very things I'm trying to forget—not forget, but get away from. The old Amy was a baby and a bore, but the new one isn't quite sure of herself yet!*
>
> *Mack is fine. There are quite a few dogs in New York, mostly poodles, but we meet the odd Scottie now and then, so Mack is not lonesome.*
>
> *Before I forget, the Christmas card list is in the top left drawer of the desk in the den. Order the cards early and have both our names printed on them, naturally.*
>
> *Take care of yourself, dear.*
>
> *Love,*
> *Amy.*

"Christmas card list," Dodd said without expression. "This is September."

"I taught Amy—that is, we were both brought up to attend to such matters well in advance."

"Isn't this overdoing it a bit?"

Gill knew it was, but he asked, "What do you mean?"

"It sounds to me as if she doesn't intend to be home for Christmas and is trying to tell you in a nice way."

"I can't believe that."

"Well, you don't have to," Dodd said cheerfully. "Maybe it's not true. Have you talked it over with your brother-in-law?"

"No."

"I suggest you do. He's probably better acquainted with his wife than you are."

"I doubt that. Besides, Rupert and I are not exactly on the best of terms."

"Family friction, eh? Maybe that's the real reason Amy decided to leave town."

"There was no family friction until she left. Some has developed since, of course."

"Why 'of course'?" When Gill didn't answer, Dodd went on, "Cases like this are a lot commoner than you might imagine, Mr. Brandon. Most of them don't get as far as the police files or the newspapers; they're kept within the family. A lady gets bored or disgusted or both, and off she goes on a bit of a wingding. When the wingding is over, she comes home. The neighbors think she's been on a holiday, so nobody's any the wiser. Except maybe her. Wingdings can be rough on a lady."

Dodd was an expert on wingdings, without owning any books on the subject.

"My sister," Gill said, "is not the kind of woman who would be interested in wingdings." He coughed over the unfamiliar word as if it had stuck in his throat like a fishbone. When he had finished coughing he wiped his mouth and stared at Dodd, suddenly hating the bushy-haired little man with his metallic eyes and his tarnished, keyhole views of the back bedrooms of life.

He rose without speaking, not trusting his voice, and reached for the letters on Dodd's desk.

"No offense intended," Dodd said, observing Gill's trembling hands and the bulging veins in his temples with detachment. "And none given, I trust?"

"Good day."

"Good day, Mr. Brandon."

That night at dinner Dodd's wife asked, "How was business today?"

"Fine."

"Blonde and beautiful?"

"That's strictly in books, sweetheart."

"Glad to hear it."

"Mr. Brandon is neither blond nor beautiful," Dodd said, "but he's interesting."

"How so?"

"He has a problem. He thinks his sister was murdered by her husband."

"And what do you think?"

"Nobody's paid me to think," Dodd said. "Yet."

8

ON SUNDAY, THE twenty-eighth of September, three days after Gill's visit to Dodd, the Kellogg's maid, Gerda Lundquist returned from her month's vacation in Yellowstone National Park.

She called Rupert from the bus depot in the hope that, since it was Sunday and he wouldn't be working, he might offer to come and pick her up. No one answered the telephone so she grudgingly took a taxi. The vacation had been hard on her pocketbook, and on her nerves too, especially toward the end when the snows began and people swarmed out of the park, leaving it to the bears and the chipmunks and the antelopes for the winter. Gerda was looking forward to a nice paycheck and some warm, cozy evenings in front of the television set the Kelloggs had given her the previous Christmas. Television was so restful she often went to sleep watching it, and Mrs. Kellogg would come to her door and rap softly and ask, "Gerda? Did you forget to turn off the television, Gerda?" Mrs. Kellogg never commanded, never gave a direct order. She asked politely, "Would you mind . . ." or "What do you think of . . ." as if she respected Gerda's superior age and wider experience in life.

She let herself into the house with her latchkey and went immediately out to the kitchen where she filled the teakettle with water to heat for some postum and a boiled egg. The kitchen was very clean, the dishes washed, the sink shining, signs that Mrs. Kellogg must be home from Mexico. Mr. Kellogg was more willing than able around the kitchen.

As the kettle began to hum, so did Gerda, an old song from her childhood in Minnesota, the words of which had long since been forgotten. She did not hear Rupert come in, she was only aware of a sudden change in the room, and she turned and saw him standing in the doorway to the hall. His hair was disheveled, and his face and ears were pink with wind as if he'd been running in the park with Mack.

He stared at her in silence for a few seconds. He seemed to be trying to figure out who she was and what she was doing in his house. Then he said, "Good evening, Gerda," in a flat voice with no welcome in it.

"Good evening, Mr. Kellogg."

"How was the vacation?"

"Oh, it was grand. But I don't mind telling you it's good to be back home."

"I'm glad to have you back."

But he didn't sound glad or look glad, and Gerda wondered what she had done to displease him. *How could I have done anything? I was in Yellowstone. Ach, it's just one of his moods. Not many people know about his moods.* "How's Mrs. Kellogg?" she said carefully. "And Mack?"

"Mrs. Kellogg is away on another holiday. She took Mack with her."

"But . . ." The kettle began to whistle as if in warning. Gerda compressed her lips and busied herself at the stove, trying not to look at the wooden peg beside the back door where Mack's red and black plaid leash was hanging. She could feel Mr. Kellogg's eyes pointing at her back like a double-barreled gun.

"But what, Gerda? Go on."

"I wasn't about to say anything. Would you care for an egg, Mr. Kellogg?"

"No thanks. I've had supper."

"Eating in restaurants for so long like I did makes you hungry for something real homey like a soft-boiled egg."

The egg cracked in the boiling water. Gerda added a pinch of salt to the water so the egg white wouldn't all drool out of the shell. Her hand was shaking and some of the salt spilled on the stove, turning the blue flame of gas momentarily to orange. *That's Mack's leash hanging by the door. He's a well-behaved dog, the best, but no one would ever take him out without his leash because of the traffic. Especially not Mrs. Kellogg. She's nervous about cars. She's never even learned to drive.* She said aloud, "Have you been eating in restaurants or at home while Mrs. Kellogg is away?"

"Half and half."

"I must say you've kept the kitchen real nice and neat."

"Miss Burton dropped by this morning on her way home from church and helped clean up."

"Oh," Gerda said. Miss Burton, that creature with the dyed hair. On her way home from church, was she, and what were the churches coming to these days, pray tell?

She took the egg out of the saucepan and put it in an egg cup. Then she buttered a piece of bread and sat down at the table to eat. Mr. Kellogg was still standing in the doorway watching her with that funny expression in his eyes. It made her so nervous she could hardly swallow.

"By the way," Rupert said, "you'll be interested to know that Mack left in high style. My wife brought him a new leash from Mexico, one of those fancy, hand-tooled leather jobs."

"Well, isn't that nice."

"Mack thought so."

"I bet he looked too cute for words."

"Yes." Rupert stepped back with a grimace as if he'd had a sudden twinge of pain. "When you've finished eating, I'd like to have a talk with you, Gerda. I'll be in the den."

The talk turned out to be quite simple. She was fired. No reflection cast on her abilities, of course. A matter of simple economics. Mrs. Kellogg would be away in the East indefinitely, and it just wasn't feasible to keep Gerda on. He made a lot of nice remarks about her efficiency and cooperation and so on, but it all amounted to one thing: she was fired. A month's wages in lieu of notice and the best of references, which Miss Burton would type up and have waiting for her at the office. Good-bye and good luck.

Gerda said, "You mean you want me to leave right away?"

"Yes."

"Right now *tonight?*"

"It might be simpler that way," Rupert said, "since you haven't unpacked yet. I'll drive you wherever you want to go."

"I got no place to go."

"There are hotels. And the Y.W.C.A."

Gerda thought of the warm, cozy evenings in front of her television set, now suddenly to be replaced by cold, deadly ones in the lobby of the Y.W.C.A. with a lot of other women as dull as herself. Resentment stabbed her eyes until they bled tears.

"Now, Gerda," Rupert said uneasily. "You mustn't cry. This isn't actually a personal matter."

"It's personal to me!"

"I'm sorry. I wish—well, we all wish things could be different."

"This is a terrible homecoming."

"There have been worse," Rupert said, remembering his own.

"What about the TV set?"

"That belongs to you. I'll have a man come to disconnect it and deliver it to you when you get settled."

"If I get settled."

"I'm sure you'll have no difficulty finding another job, one you'll enjoy more. Things would be pretty dull for you around here without Mrs. Kellogg and Mack. I suggest you try an employment agency."

Gerda sniffed. She didn't like employment agencies and the snippy way they asked questions and pretended that jobs were scarce just to make themselves look good when they got you one. "I think I'll call the Brandons."

"Who?"

"The Brandons, Mrs. Kellogg's brother and his wife. They got that big place to keep up in Atherton and many's the time I've heard her complain how she couldn't get decent help."

He didn't say anything. He just kept staring at her as if he thought she'd lost her mind.

Flushing, Gerda said, "Maybe you think I wouldn't fit into such a fancy place, me and my country ways, is that what you're thinking? Well, let me tell you I heard Mrs. Brandon with my own ears call me a jewel. That was no more than three months ago, and if I was a jewel three months ago I guess I'm a jewel right here and now."

"Of course. Of course you are," Rupert said, and he kept his voice very quiet because he felt like screaming. "I happen to know, however, that Mrs. Brandon has a complete staff at the moment."

"That's not saying she will have tomorrow or next week, things being like they are in this world."

"You might not like living on the Peninsula."

"The climate's nice. All this fog in the city is hard on my bronchial tubes. That's my weakest spot."

"The Brandons have three children. They're very noisy."

"A little noise won't hurt me none." She turned to leave. "Well, I better go find some cartons so I can pack the rest of my stuff."

"Gerda. Wait."

She looked back, surprised at the urgency in his voice. "Yes sir?"

"I'll call Mrs. Brandon, if you like, and ask her if she has an opening and what salary she's prepared to pay and so on."

"I don't want to put you to any trouble."

"It's no trouble at all."

"Well, that's real kind of you, Mr. Kellogg. I'm much obliged, I'm sure."

"I might as well call now, while you're still here, and get the matter settled." He gave her a dry little smile. "You may even enjoy working at the Brandons. Everyone to his taste."

While she was in her room packing the rest of her things she could hear him talking on the main phone in the kitchen. His voice was very loud and distinct, and she wondered if Helene Brandon was possibly getting a little deaf.

"Helene? This is Rupert . . . Fine. And you? . . . Glad to hear it . . . Oh, she's having a great time, seeing every play in New York. Helene, the reason I called is Gerda. She returned from her vacation tonight, and I had to tell her that I couldn't afford to keep her on. She's first-rate at her job, as you know . . . A jewel. Yes, she remembered that you called her that when you were talking to Amy some time ago . . . I can't help it if Amy will be mad. It's a matter of simple economics . . . I can eat most of my meals in restaurants and hire a cleaning woman once a week. To get back to the subject of Gerda . . ."

Gerda, the jewel, fought a brief brisk battle with Gerda, the woman. The woman emerged victorious and tiptoed down the hall to the extension telephone in the master bedroom. She had no need to lift the receiver to hear Rupert; his voice veritably boomed from the kitchen. Mrs. Brandon must certainly be getting deaf. Or perhaps she always had been and covered it up by lip reading.

Gerda's hand, slowed by guilt, reached for the telephone. *I really shouldn't. I'm a jewel . . .*

"I thought it would be nice if we kept Gerda in the family, as it were . . . I realize you don't need anyone right now, Helene . . . Frankly, I think you'd be missing an excellent opportunity if you didn't snap her up. Her qualifications are most unusual, you know that for yourself. I think she'd be good with the children, too . . . Of course, if you haven't a place for her, you haven't . . ."

Meticulous as a surgeon, Gerda lifted the receiver. The dial tone buzzed in her ear. For a second she thought that Mrs. Brandon had, in sudden pique or boredom, hung up. Then she heard Rupert's voice again from the kitchen: "Naturally she'll be disappointed. So am I. But we can't ask you to do the impossible, Helene . . . Yes, I'll tell her to try you again in a few months. Goodbye, Helene."

9

"THIS GERDA LUNDQUIST," Dodd said, rubbing his chin, "she's reliable?"

Until the past twenty-four hours Gill Brandon had barely been aware of Gerda's existence; he was not competent to answer the question. But because he wanted to believe her, he nodded vigorously. "Absolutely reliable. I'd trust her with my life."

Dodd smiled the dry little smile that indicated disbelief in practically everybody. "There are a lot of people I'd trust with my life that I wouldn't trust to give an accurate account of something they saw or experienced."

"Miss Lundquist is not an imaginative type. Nor would she have any reason for trying to put my brother-in-law in a bad light."

"Revenge for being fired?"

"She already has a better job," Gill said stiffly.

"With you?"

"With us."

"Why?"

"Why? We needed an extra servant, that's why."

That's not why, Dodd thought. *Now that he's got the first shred of evidence against his brother-in-law he intends to keep it in a safe place. I'm glad I'm not in Kellogg's shoes. This Brandon means business.*

Gill said, "You understand, Gerda knows nothing about Amy's disappearance. She thinks that Amy is simply on a vacation in New York."

"And you think she isn't?"

"I know she isn't. I told you previously we have relatives in Queens and Westchester. I called both places last night after Gerda had come to us with her story. No one has seen or heard from Amy."

"That proves nothing."

"It would if you knew Amy. She's always been very conscientious about keeping in touch with members of the family. If she were anywhere near New York she would have called Cousin Harris or Aunt Kate. Whether she wanted to or not, she would have contacted them out of duty."

"How long is it since you've seen your sister?"

"She left for Mexico City on the third of September, a Wednesday. I said good-bye to her the previous day."

"Was she acting normally?"

"Of course."

"In good spirits?"

"Excellent. Very excited at the prospect of the trip, like a kid who's never been any place on her own before."

"Was Mrs. Wyatt with her at the time?"

"Yes. They'd been doing some last-minute shopping and called me from the St. Francis to come and have lunch with them."

"What kind of woman was Mrs. Wyatt?" Dodd asked.

"Eccentric. Oh, some people found her very amusing, and I think Amy was rather fascinated by her, in the sense that she never knew what Wilma would do next." He added grimly, "She does now."

"Yes, I guess she does. What day was it that Mrs. Wyatt killed herself?"

"A little over three weeks ago, on a Sunday night, the seventh of September. I was informed the following day when Miss Burton, Rupert's secretary, called me at my office. Rupert went down to Mexico City that same day, the seventh."

Dodd wrote the dates in a notebook, more because he wanted something to do than because he thought he'd ever be referring to them again. Still a firm believer in wingdings, he was convinced that Amy would pop up one of these days with an unlikely everything-suddenly-went-black story.

"I heard nothing from him," Gill continued, "until a week later. I was out that night, but he left a message with my son that I was to come to the house to discuss something important. When I got there he told me Amy had left and gave me her farewell letter, the one I first brought to you. You may recall its contents."

"Yes."

"She wrote that she'd been drinking the night of Wilma's death."

"And?"

"Rupert added something to that. He told me she'd been in the company of an American barroom hanger-on named O'Donnell. I think he was lying. My sister is cultured, well-bred. No well-bred woman would walk into a bar and pick up . . ."

"Wait a minute, Mr. Brandon," Dodd said. "Let's get something clear. If I'm to find your sister it's more important to me to know her faults than her virtues. She may be kind and gentle and sweet and so on. That doesn't tell me a thing. But if I know she has a weakness for barflies named O'Donnell, then I start looking up all the barflies named O'Donnell in my files."

"Your humor isn't very funny."

"It wasn't intended to be. I was making a point."

"You may consider it made," Gill said coldly. "It doesn't alter the facts, however. My sister has no weaknesses of the kind you mean. Besides, Rupert has been proven a liar."

"You're referring to Gerda Lundquist's account of his pretended telephone conversation with your wife?"

"Among other things, yes."

"Why do you think he falsified that call?"

"It's obvious. He wanted to prevent Gerda from making any attempt to get a job at our house."

"Why?"

"He was afraid she would give us damaging information about him."

"By 'us' do you mean you and your wife?"

"I mean myself only. Mrs. Brandon is inclined to believe the best of everyone. She's a very trusting soul."

"So is Rupert," Dodd said, "or he would never have attempted the phone trick, knowing there was an extension in the bedroom."

"Trusting? Perhaps. Perhaps only stupid."

"Amateur, anyway."

"Amateur." Gill nodded vigorous agreement. "That's what he is. And that's why he'll be caught."

Dodd folded his hands and closed his eyes, like a minister about to pray for some lost souls which he strongly suspected would remain lost. "Tell me, Mr. Brandon, has Gerda Lundquist given you any damaging information about your brother-in-law? For instance, did he have a bad temper? Did he quarrel frequently with his wife? Was he a lush or a chaser?"

"No, not to my knowledge."

"What's the worst Gerda had to say about him?"

"He was—moody."

"And that's all?"

"She also said that last spring he was frequently late coming home. He claimed he was working overtime."

"At what period in the spring?"

"March, I believe she said."

"March," Dodd pointed out, "is income-tax time, and your brother-in-law is an accountant. He was lucky to get home at all."

Gill flushed. "Just whose side are you on, anyway?"

"I never take sides until both teams are out in the field and I know what game they're going to play."

"This is no game, Mr. Dodd. My sister is missing. Find her."

"I'm trying," Dodd said. "Did you bring the pictures?"

"Yes."

The pictures were in a manila envelope: two formal photographs and about a dozen large colored snapshots. In most of the snapshots Amy was smiling, but both the photographs showed her grave and self-conscious, as if she hadn't wanted to be in front of a camera at all, knowing in advance the results wouldn't satisfy anyone. *Repressed*, Dodd thought. *Anxious to please. Too anxious.*

One of the snapshots showed her sitting on a lawn with a small black dog on a leash beside her. Against the green grass the red and black plaid of the dog's leash and collar stood out distinctly.

"That's Mack?" Dodd said.

"Yes. He's a pedigreed Scottish terrier. I gave him to Amy for her birthday five years ago. She's devoted to him, too much so, in fact. He's only a dog, after all, not a child, but she takes him everywhere she goes, downtown shopping and so on. She even wanted to take him with her to Mexico City but she was afraid of a possible quarantine at the border."

"She kept him on a leash?"

"Always. And always on this particular leash. You may not notice anything special about it, unless you're an expert on tartans, but this tartan is not very commonly seen. It represents the Maclachlan clan. Mack was registered with the American Kennel Club under his official name, Maclachlan's Merryheart, and Amy got the fanciful idea of having a collar, leash and sweater made up for him in the proper tartan. The set cost a hundred dollars, almost as much as the dog itself."

Gill paused to light a cigarette. The pictures of Amy, spread over Dodd's desk, smiled up at him mockingly: *All this fuss over me and my little dog. We're in New York, Gilly. We're doing all the shows. Mack's wearing the new hand-tooled leather leash I bought him in Mexico City . . .*

"Wherever Amy is," Gill said, "she didn't take Mack with her. His leash is still hanging in the kitchen."

"Rupert had an explanation for that. He told Gerda . . ."

"I know what he told Gerda, but it isn't true."

"I agree that it doesn't seem likely," Dodd said cautiously. "It's possible, though."

"If you knew Amy you wouldn't think so. She's childishly proud of Mack's tartan."

"Then where is the dog?"

"I'd give a great deal to know the answer to that."

You may have to, Dodd thought. Finding people was tough enough. Finding a Scottie that looked like a thousand other Scotties seemed impossible. There wasn't even any guarantee that the dog was still alive. He said, "Why should Kellogg have told you in the first place that Amy took the dog with her?"

"To convince me that Amy came home and went away again of her own accord."

"Is there any evidence that she did come home?"

"Rupert's word."

"No one else saw her?"

"No one, to my knowledge."

Dodd consulted his notes. "Let's see, she came back from Mexico City, allegedly, on Sunday, September the fourteenth, and left again that same night without calling anyone to say good-bye and without being seen by anyone we know of except Rupert. Right?"

"Yes."

"Have you any idea why?"

"Why she didn't call me and wasn't seen? Certainly I have an idea. She never came home. Perhaps she never even left Mexico City."

"Let's be frank, Mr. Brandon. Do you believe your sister is dead?"

Gill looked down at the smiling pictures on Dodd's desk. *Me, dead? Don't be absurd, Gilly. I'm in New York. I'm having a ball.* He said, through tight lips, "Yes. I believe he killed her."

"And his motive?"

"Money."

Dodd sighed, very faintly. If it wasn't money, it was love. Perhaps they both boiled down to the same thing, security.

"He has her power of attorney," Gill said. "He doesn't even have to wait for proof of death so he can inherit her money."

"Did your sister make a will?"

"Yes. Rupert inherits half her estate."

"Who gets the other half?"

"I do."

Dodd said nothing but his black, bushy eyebrows moved up and down his forehead. *Very interesting, Mr. Brandon. I know—and you don't know I know—that you've been living beyond your income for some time now, taking bites out of your capital to feed some pretty undernourished investments.* "It would, then, if your sister is dead, be to your advantage to prove it as quickly as possible."

"What do you mean?"

"As long as Mrs. Kellogg is simply missing, the power of attorney she gave her husband is in force. He has full control over her property, and how much will be left for you or anyone else to inherit depends entirely on his discretion. Let's assume your sister is dead. From your point of view—that is, keeping her property intact and at full value—it would be an advantage to get proof of death immediately. From his point of view, the longer the delay, the better it will be for him."

"I don't like to—to think of these things."

You've already thought of them, old boy; don't kid me. "Come now, Mr. Brandon, it's just a little game we're playing. Your sister, by the way, must have trusted Rupert completely or she would never have given him a power of attorney."

"Perhaps. But he might have applied some form of pressure to get it."

"You said he has a small but successful business of his own?"

"Yes."

"And he lives modestly?"

"There's no guarantee he intends to continue living modestly," Gill said. "That calm exterior of his might be hiding some pretty fancy and wild ideas."

"Do you believe his dismissal of Gerda Lundquist was, as he claimed, a matter of economic necessity?"

"Not unless he's been having some unusual expenses."

"Such as gambling debts?"

"Such as another woman."

"That's pure speculation on your part, is it, Mr. Brandon? Or impure, as the case may be."

"You may call it speculation. I call it simple arithmetic. Two and two add up to Miss Burton, his secretary." Gill ground out his cigarette in an overflowing ashtray advertising Luigi's Pizza House on Mason Street. "I have two secretaries, but I assure you that neither of them has a key to my back door, neither of them looks after my dog, neither of them drops in after church to clean up my house."

"It will be easy enough to check up on Miss Burton."

"Do it subtly. If she suspects anything she'll tell Rupert immediately and he'll find out I hired you. He mustn't know a thing about any of this. Surprise must be the basis of our tactics."

"*My* tactics, if you don't mind, Mr. Brandon."

"All right, yours. So long as he's caught. And punished."

Dodd leaned back in his swivel chair, interlacing his fingers. It seemed clear to him now that Brandon wanted Rupert punished more than he wanted his sister found. He shivered slightly. It was three o'clock on a sunny afternoon. It felt like midnight in the dead of winter.

He got up and shut the window, and almost immediately opened it again. He didn't like the sensation of being in a closed room with Gill Brandon. "Tell me, have you talked to your brother-in-law since the morning he gave you the letter?"

"No."

"You haven't communicated any of your suspicions to him?"

"No."

"It might clear the air if you did."

"I'm not giving him any advantage by tipping my hand."

"Are you sure you have a hand?"

"I'm sure. Nobody lies the way he's lied unless he has something to hide."

"All right," Dodd said. "Let's leave Rupert out of this for a minute. Where, to your knowledge, was your sister last seen?"

"At the hospital where she was taken after Wilma's death sent her into shock. The American-British-Corday, I believe it's called."

"And what was the name of the hotel she and her friend were staying at?"

"It was their intention to stay at the Windsor. Whether they did or not, I'm not sure. Mrs. Wyatt was very changeable, and if some little thing didn't suit her she would have gone someplace else. Wherever they stayed, you can bet that it was Mrs. Wyatt's decision. My sister has never learned to stick up for her rights."

Dodd wrote: Windsor Hotel? Sept. 3. A.B.C. Hospital, Sept. 7. Then he gathered up the pictures of Amy, put them back in the manila folder and marked it A. KELLOGG. "I'm going to send a couple of these down to a friend of mine in Mexico City."

"Why?"

"He might be willing, for a fee, to do some investigating. That's where the trouble seems to have started. Let's get an objective report, since you're reluctant to believe anything your brother-in-law says."

"Who is this friend?"

"A retired cop from L.A. called Fowler. He's good. And expensive."

"How expensive?"

"I can't give you an exact figure."

Gill took an unmarked envelope out of his pocket and put it on Dodd's desk. "There's five hundred in cash. Is that sufficient for the time being?"

"That depends."

"On what?"

"On how much bribe money my friend's going to need."

"Bribe money? Whom does he have to bribe?"

"In Mexico," Dodd said dryly, "practically everyone."

10

THURSDAY WAS PAT Burton's dancing night at the Kent Academy. She didn't bother going home after work. She took her dancing equipment to the office with her—a pair of transparent plastic shoes with three-inch heels and a bottle of strongly scented cologne because the Academy always had a rancid smell like an unventilated school gymnasium. The cologne was, therefore, an asset if not a necessity; the Cinderella shoes were not. They impeded Miss Burton's progress. After eleven months of lessons (Learn to Dance the First Night) she was still having considerable trouble with the mamba, and her tango included numerous extracurricular totters which were the despair of the instructor. "Miss Burton, save your wiggles for the cha-cha-cha. Keep your *balance.*" "I can do it perfectly well at home in my bare feet." "Since when do we teach the tango so people can do it at home in their bare feet?"

It didn't matter very much anyway because no one invited Miss Burton out mambaing or tangoing. Her infrequent dates preferred less sophisticated or less strenuous entertainment. She continued going to the weekly class, however. It represented to her, as well as to the majority of the others, a social rather than an instructive evening.

The class was already in progress when Miss Burton arrived. One of her frequent partners, an elderly retired lawyer, a widower named Jacobson, waved to her out of a fast rhumba and Miss Burton waved back, thinking, *one of these days he's going to drop dead right on the floor. I just hope it's not me he's dancing with when it happens.*

The instructor screamed over the music at no one in particular, "Don't sway your hips! Forget about your hips! If your feet are doing the right thing your hips will do the right thing. Do I make myself *heard*?"

He made himself heard but hips refused to be forgotten.

Miss Burton tapped her foot and surveyed the room from the doorway. Not many spectators tonight. A woman with a little girl. A pair of teenagers, a boy and a girl, with matching shirts and matching expressions of boredom. A middle-aged woman wearing a pound of pearls. And, standing right next to Miss Burton herself, a man with bushy gray hair that seemed to emphasize the youthful alertness of his face. He looked as though he had wandered into the place by mistake, but now that he was there he was determined to get the most out of it.

He said, with a slight frown, "I don't understand the business about not swaying your hips. That's a rhumba they're doing, isn't it?"

"Yes."

"I thought in a rhumba you were supposed to sway your hips."

Miss Burton smiled. "You're new here, aren't you?"

"Yes. My first time."

"Are you going to be in the class?"

"I guess so," the man said, sounding rather pained. "I guess I have to."

"Why? There's no law about it."

"Well, you see I won a scholarship. I can't very well waste it."

"What kind of scholarship?"

"There was this advertisement in the paper showing pictures of people doing various kinds of dances. If you identified the dances correctly you were given a scholarship, thirty dollars' worth of free lessons. I won. I can't understand it exactly," he added. "I mean, there are a lot of people know more about dancing than I do, thousands of them. But I won."

Miss Burton didn't want to hurt his feelings but she didn't want him to be taken in, either. He was so naïve and earnest, a little bit like Mr. Kellogg. "I'm sure you could win lots of *real* contests if you put your mind to it."

"This one wasn't real?"

"No. Everybody won. It was just a come-on so the Kent Academy could get the names of people who are interested in dancing."

"But I'm not interested in dancing. I'm just interested in contests."

Miss Burton whooped with laughter. "Oh dear. That's a good joke on the Academy. What other kind of contests do you go in for?"

"Any kind. Also tests. I buy all the magazines and do the tests, like, for instance, 'Would You Make a Good Engineer?', or 'What Is Your Social I.Q.?', or 'Can You Qualify as a Quiz Contestant?' Things like that. I do pretty well in them." He added with a sigh: "I guess they're rigged too, like this here contest."

"Oh, I don't believe that," Miss Burton said loyally. "Maybe you really would make a good engineer."

"I hope so. I do some engineering occasionally."

"What kind of engineering?"

"It's classified."

"You mean, like secret missiles and things?"

"That's close enough," he replied. "What do you do?"

"Me? Oh, I'm just a secretary. I work for Rupert Kellogg. He's an accountant."

"I've heard of him." *Too often*, he thought. *Much too often.*

"He's the best accountant in town. The best boss too."

"You don't say."

"Other bosses I've had used to get their mean days. Mr. Kellogg never has a mean day."

"I bet children and dogs take to him right off the bat."

"Maybe you mean that as a joke, but it's absolutely true. Mr. Kellogg's crazy about animals. You know what he told me once? He told me he didn't really like being an accountant, he wanted to open a pet store."

"Why doesn't he?"

"His wife comes from a ritzy family. They wouldn't approve, I guess."

Old Mr. Jacobson, the retired lawyer, rhumbaed past, wriggling like a nervous snake, and gave Miss Burton a grin and a wink. His face was as moist and red as a sliced beet.

"He seems to be having a fine time," the man said.

"That's Mr. Jacobson. He knows all the dances perfectly, only he can't keep time."

"He's certainly caught the spirit of the thing anyway."

"I'll say. One of these days he's going to drop dead right on this very floor. It kind of spoils my evening thinking about it."

The music ended, and the instructor announced in a tired shriek that the next number would be a change of pace, the slicker waltz, and would the men kindly remember that a good strong lead was necessary in this one, especially at the turns?

Mr. Jacobson sped in Miss Burton's direction. Miss Burton turned red and whispered an anguished "Oh dear." But she didn't have enough nerve, or presence of mind, to head for the powder room. So she stood her ground and uttered a short, quiet prayer: *Don't let this be the night.*

Mr. Jacobson was as merry as Old King Cole. "Come on, Miss B. Let's have at it!"

"Oh, don't you think you'd better rest a bit?"

"Nonsense. I have the whole week to rest. Thursday's my night to shake a leg."

"Yes. Well."

Miss Burton surrendered reluctantly to Mr. Jacobson's bony arms and good strong lead. This might be, could very well be, Mr. Jacobson's last dance. The least she could do was to make it as pleasant as possible for him by trying to follow him properly, and at the same time watch his face for any telltale signs of the end approaching. She wasn't sure what the signs would be, and the strain of looking up at him gave her a crick in the neck.

"You're not concentrating tonight, Miss B."

"Oh yes, I am," Miss Burton said grimly.

"Loosen up a little. Relax. Enjoy yourself. This is supposed to be fun."

"Yes."

"What's the matter, something on your mind?"

"Just—the usual."

"Get it off. Tell someone. Tell me."

"Oh, dear me, no," Miss Burton said hastily. "Haven't we been having lovely weather this fall? Of course, we can't expect you—it to last."

Mr. Jacobson didn't catch the error because the instructor had raised his voice again. "This is ballroom dancing. This is not real life. In real life women don't like to be pushed around. In ballroom dancing they expect to be, they want to be, they have to be! So lead, gentlemen! You're not zombies! Lead!"

"You have a real good lead," Miss Burton said.

"And you have a mighty fine follow," Mr. Jacobson replied gallantly.

"No, I haven't, not really. I do all the dances much better at home in my bare feet. I get shook up when people watch me."

"Such as the man at the door?"

"Oh dear, is he watching me? My goodness."

"Watching people is his business, or part of it."

"What do you mean?"

"He's a private detective named Dodd. I used to see him hanging around the Hall of Justice. He had a lot of nicknames in those days, the least objectionable of which was Fingers, because he had a finger in every pie."

"It must be a case of mistaken identity," Miss Burton said in a high, tight voice. "He told me he was an engineer. He's doing secret work."

Mr. Jacobson chuckled. "On whom?"

"He's—he's here because he won a scholarship."

"Don't you believe it. That's Dodd. And he's here because he wants information from someone."

"Who?"

"Well, whom was he talking to?"

"Me," Miss Burton said, and both her heart and her feet missed a beat.

Dodd caught the startled look she threw him and knew that Jacobson had told her who he was. He thought, *I should have recognized Jacobson sooner, but he's lost fifty pounds. Well, there's no harm done. Let Miss Burton get fussed up. She might tell me more of the truth by lying.*

"But I don't have any information," Miss Burton insisted.

Mr. Jacobson winked. "Ah, don't you now."

"I really don't. Maybe Mr. Dodd is here after somebody else. That Mr. Lessups who enrolled last week, he looks like a crook."

"Don't we all. Now, Miss B., you're tightening up again. Relax."

"How can I, with a policeman staring at me like that?"

"He's not a policeman. He's a private detective."

"It's the same thing for my money."

"Then your money's wrong. Mr. Dodd has no authority whatever. You don't have to say a word to him. Tell him to go roll his hoop."

"I can't."

"And why not?"

"I—I'd kind of like to find out what he's doing here."

"In brief, your curiosity is greater than your fear. Ah, women. Well, the best of luck, my dear. And if you can't be good, be careful."

Dodd was waiting for her at the doorway. When she tried to pass him he put out his hand to stop her. "I gather Mr. Jacobson has introduced me? That's all right. I intended to do it myself eventually. Would you like to go someplace for a cup of coffee?"

"I definitely would not."

"That's honest anyway. Are you honest about everything, Miss Burton?"

"I don't go around telling people I'm an engineer."

"I told you I did some engineering. I do."

"Well, you're not going to do any engineering on me," Miss Burton said coldly. "You have no authority to question me about anything."

"That's what Jacobson told you?"

"Yes and he's a lawyer and he should know."

"Of course," Dodd agreed. "What interests me is, why are you so afraid of questions? I've learned quite a lot about you, Miss Burton, and it seems to me you have nothing to hide or be ashamed of."

"What do you mean you learned quite a lot about me? How? Why?"

"Hold on a minute. You're asking me questions. You haven't any authority to do that, have you?"

"I . . ."

"You see, this thing works both ways. I have no authority, you have no authority. Nobody asks questions, nobody gets any answers. Not an ideal way to run things, is it? Now let's sit down and have a reasonable talk. How about it?"

"Maybe I'd better ask Mr. Jacobson first."

"You haven't been accused of any crime. You don't need a lawyer."

Miss Burton sat down. "Okay, what do you want?"

"I'm looking for a missing person. I thought you might be able to help."

"How can I help? I don't even know any missing person."

"Yes, you do," Dodd said.

11

IT WAS COLD and late, and ghosts of fog were prowling the streets of the city, but Miss Burton didn't notice the time or the weather. She hurried along the sidewalk, propelled by fright, guided by instinct. Her handbag, containing the dancing shoes and the bottle of cologne, hung heavy from her shoulder and knocked against one hip as she moved.

From his parked car Dodd saw her turn the corner toward Market Street. He made no attempt to follow her since he was sure of her intention. He had planted the intention himself, deliberately, and watched it grow in her transparent eyes the way a botanist watches a seed grow between two layers of glass.

With a final flip of her yellow coat Miss Burton disappeared around the corner of Woolworth's and Dodd was left pondering some second and third thoughts about the advisability of dragging her into the case. She was a nice girl. He didn't like to use her, but business was business. If Rupert Kellogg was innocent of any wrongdoing, he deserved to be warned about Brandon's suspicions and operations. If he was guilty, a warning might jolt him into action. So far he'd done nothing but sit tight and tell stories, some thin, some tall. Brandon himself was certainly not admitting the whole truth. No living woman could be as flawless as Amy.

Dodd turned on the ignition of the little Volkswagen. He was tired and depressed. For the first time since entering the case he had the feeling that Brandon might be right about his sister. Wherever and whenever Amy was found, she wouldn't be found alive.

The house was dark. Miss Burton had never seen it at night, wrapped in fog, and she was not sure it was the right place until she went up on the veranda and saw the bronze nameplate on the door, Rupert H. Kellogg. A few hours ago the sight of the name would have given her a pleasant little thrill. Now it seemed strange, without any relation to the man who owned it. She pressed the door chime and waited, shivering with cold and fear and self- doubt. *What am I doing here? What will I say to him? How can I act calm as if nothing had happened, as if Dodd had never told me those terrible things?*

Take care of yourself, Dodd had said. *A woman has disappeared, don't make it two.*

She turned her head quickly and peered through the fog at the street, hoping for a moment that Dodd had followed her. But there were no cars parked along the curb, and no one was walking along the street or waiting under a lamppost. She was alone. She could enter this house and never be seen again and no one would be able to say, "Yes, I noticed her, a small woman in a yellow coat, shortly after eleven o'clock—she went in and never came out . . ."

The hall light splashed through the window and she reared back as if someone had thrown it at her like acid. Panting, she leaned against a pillar and watched the door slowly open.

"Why, Miss Burton," Rupert said. "What are you doing here?"

"I—I don't—know."

"Is anything the matter?"

" Ev—everything."

"You haven't been drinking, have you?"

"No. I never drink. I'm a M-M-Methodist."

"Well, that's very interesting," he said wearily, "but I hope you didn't come all the way out here at this time of night to tell me you're a Methodist."

She pressed against the pillar, her teeth chattering like castanets. She wanted to run away but she was both afraid for him and afraid of him, and the double fear immobilized her.

"Miss Burton?"

"I—I was just passing by and I thought I'd—drop in and say hello. I didn't realize how—late it was. I'm sorry to have bothered you. I'd—better be going."

"You'd better not be going," he said sharply. "You'd better be coming in and telling me about it."

"About—what?"

"Whatever it is that's making you act like this." He opened the door wider, and waited. "Come on."

"I can't. It wouldn't be proper."

"All right, I'll call you a cab."

"No! I mean, I don't want a cab."

"You can't stand here all night, can you?"

She shook her head and her limp, blonde curls fell over her eyes so that she looked like a little old lady peering out at him through a lace curtain. He wondered what was going on behind the lace curtain.

He said, "You're cold."

"I know."

"You'd better come inside and get warm."

"Yes. All right."

He closed the door behind her and led her down the hall to the den. An unscreened fire was burning in the grate, its flames reflected in the silver box on the coffee table. He saw her glance at the box, but briefly and without interest. There was no danger here. She couldn't possibly know anything about the box.

"Sit down, Miss Burton."

"Thank you."

"Now, what's troubling you?"

"I—well, I went to dancing class tonight at the Kent Academy. I always do on Thursdays. Not that I'm a good dancer or anything, it's just a way of passing time and meeting people. Usually the people are okay, nothing special but okay. Nothing sneaky about them, I mean. If you meet someone there and he says he's an engineer, that's what he is, an engineer. So you're not suspicious, I mean."

She hadn't intended to tell him about the dancing classes for fear he would laugh at her, but the words just came tumbling out of her mouth like blown bubbles. He didn't laugh at her, though. He seemed very grave and interested.

"Go on, Miss Burton."

"Well, tonight I met this man. He's a terrible man. He said things, suggested things."

"I'm sure you know how to deal with improper suggestions, Miss Burton."

She flushed and looked down at her hands. "They weren't suggestions like the kind you mean. They were about you. And Mrs. Kellogg."

"Who was the man?"

"His name's Dodd. He's a private detective. Oh, he didn't let on he was a private detective. He tried to palm himself off as a new student, but I have this friend at the Academy, he's a lawyer . . ."

"What did this man Dodd say about Mrs. Kellogg?"

"That she was missing. Under mysterious circumstances."

"She is not missing. She is in New York."

"I told him that. But he just smiled—he has the nastiest smile, like a camel's—and said New York was a big place with a lot of people in it but he didn't think one of them was Mrs. Kellogg." Before the warmth of the fire Miss Burton's suspicions of Rupert were evaporating like fog under the heat of the sun. "If I were you I'd sue him for slander. It's a free country but people can't go around saying anything in their heads when it does harm to other people."

"Well, don't get excited."

"I'm not excited. I'm good and mad. I said to him, 'Listen, you keyhole cop. Mr. Kellogg's the finest man in this city, and if Mrs. Kellogg is missing it's not his fault, it's hers, and why don't you put the blame on the right person?' And he said, as a matter of fact, he'd been thinking along those same lines himself."

She waited, expecting his approval and his gratitude for her support. What she had no reason to expect was his quiet, malevolent whisper: "You imbecile."

Her face crumpled under the surprise attack. "What—what did I do?"

"What didn't you do!"

"But I was only sticking up for you, I was only trying . . ."

"You tried. All right. Let's leave it like that."

"I don't understand," she wailed. "What did I say wrong?"

"Probably everything." He went over to the window, lengthening the time and space between them so that he might have a chance to regain control of himself, and, consequently, of her. He had no doubt of her loyalty. But what was loyalty? Would it break under pressure, bend under heat? How much of the truth would it take?

He could see her reflection in the window, her eyes wide with bewilderment and pain: *What did I do?* She looked young and simple. He knew she was neither.

"I'm sorry, Miss Burton," he said, addressing her reflection because it was easier to lie to a reflection. "I had no right to speak roughly to you."

"You did so have a right," she said faintly. "If I did something wrong, even if I didn't mean to, you've got a perfect right to check me up. Only I still don't understand just what I . . ."

"You will, someday. For the moment we'd better both forget it."

"But how can I stop doing something if I don't know what I did?"

He closed his eyes for a moment. He was too weary to talk, to think, to plan, but he realized that he couldn't allow her to leave without some explanation or instruction. It would be all right if she remained as she was now, contrite, meek, low in energy. But what of the difference in her after a night's rest, a time to think, a good breakfast?

He could visualize her bouncing into the office in the morning (with some of the loyalty rubbed off like fuzz off a peach) and greeting Borowitz with the news: "Guess what, Borowitz? Last night I met a real private detective and he was asking me all kinds of questions about the boss's wife disappearing." And Borowitz, who was by nature and habit a gossip, would relay it to his girlfriend, and the girlfriend to her family, and within days it would cover the city, spread by mouth like a morbid virus. The initial carrier must be stopped. It no longer mattered how.

"Miss Burton, I have great faith in your discretion, as well as your loyalty and good will. I depend on them." He despised the false tone, the false words. They wouldn't even have fooled the little dog Mack, but Miss Burton was breathing them in like oxygen. "I am going to take you into my confidence, knowing you'll respect it."

"Oh, I will. My goodness, I certainly will."

"My wife *is* missing, in the sense that I'm not sure where she is. I've told people she is in New York because I had a letter from her postmarked New York and because I have to tell them something."

"Why doesn't she let you know where she is?"

"It was part of our agreement before she left. For lack of a better term, call it a trial separation. We were to let each other strictly alone for a period of time. Unfortunately, my brother-in-law, Mr. Brandon, doesn't believe in letting anyone alone. He hired a private detective to look for Amy. Well, I hope he finds her, not for her sake or mine, but for Mr. Brandon's. He's making a terrible fool of himself. His wife knows it and has tried to stop him. Failing that, she came and told me all about it."

"Was that the day she came to the office all dressed up?"

Rupert nodded. "Somewhere along the line Mr. Brandon picked up the idea that I wanted to get rid of my wife because I'm interested in another woman." He turned to face her. She was leaning forward in the chair, tense and excited, like a child listening to a fairy tale. "Do you know who the woman is, Miss Burton?"

"Why no. Why, my goodness . . ."

"You."

Her mouth fell open so that he could see the silver fillings in her bottom row of teeth. *Silver,* he thought. *Silver box. I must get rid of the silver box. First, I must get rid of her.*

He said, patiently, sympathetically, "I'm sorry this comes as a shock to you, Miss Burton. It did to me, too."

She had dropped back into the chair, pale and limp. "That—that awful man. To say, even to *think,* such a terrible thing—trying to ruin my good name . . ."

"Not yours. Mine."

"And all these years I've been a good Methodist, never even thinking about carnal things!" But even as she spoke the words, she knew they were not true. Rupert popped up too often in her mind, in her dreams, as father, as son, as lover. Perhaps he knew. Perhaps he could read it in her eyes. She covered her face with her hands and repeated in a high muffled voice, "Always a g-g-good Methodist."

"Of course. Of course you are."

"I—just because I touch up my hair. Nothing in the Bible says you can't change the color of your hair. I went to the minister and asked him. I always ask the minister for advice when I'm worried."

He looked down at her stonily, without compassion, seeing her not as a woman but as a threat, an unexploded bomb whose firing pin had to be removed with the most meticulous care. "Are you worried now, Miss Burton?"

"Worried to death."

"Does that mean you intend to talk this over with your minister?"

"I don't know. He's a very wise . . ."

"This is a delicate situation, Miss Burton. Undoubtedly your minister is a man of wisdom and good will, but are you sure you want still another person to hear the rumor?"

"What do you mean, *still another*?"

"Mrs. Brandon knows. And the detective, Dodd. Gerda Lundquist too, probably, since she's now working for the Brandons."

"They can't know anything," Miss Burton said shrilly. "There's nothing to know. It's just a vicious rumor. I'll deny it."

"Can you?"

"Yes, I can. There isn't a word of truth in it!"

"Not one word?"

She shook her head back and forth in silent pain.

"Miss Burton, suppose I told you there is some truth in it, that it's not just a rumor?"

"No. No! Don't tell me anything!"

"All right."

He watched the tears slither out between her fingers and roll down her skinny wrists. *She won't explode now,* he thought. *She'll just make a lot of noise and fizzle out.*

She was a crying woman, not a bomb anymore. He took a long deep breath and crossed the room toward her.

"Miss Burton—Pat."

"Don't come near me! Don't tell me anything!"

"I said I wouldn't. But you'd better stop crying now. Your eyes swell up when you cry."

"How—how do you know?"

"I remember when you came to work after your mother's funeral. Your eyelids were like blisters, and they stayed that way all day. You looked very funny."

Slowly she took her hands away from her face. He was smiling down at her, so gently and affectionately that her heart gave a sudden thrust against her chest wall like the kick of a fetus.

He said, "You don't want Borowitz suspecting you've had an emotional upset. If he sees that you've been crying he'll ask questions. You have no answers."

"I have—no answers."

"You're tired. Sit there quietly for a minute while I call a cab for you. Will you?"

"Yes."

"And no more tears?"

"No."

He called the cab from the phone in the kitchen, remembering the last time he'd called one, on a Sunday evening almost three weeks previously. He'd put in the order for a cab, and then three minutes later, according to plan, he'd canceled it. The cab company would have a record of the address and the cancellation. He didn't know how long the company would keep such a record. Long enough, he hoped, for Dodd to find out about it; so far he was finding all the wrong things, like a retriever bringing back the decoys instead of the dead ducks. No, it was the other way around . . .

When he returned, Miss Burton had stopped crying but she still looked moist and disheveled.

"You'd better straighten up a bit," he said. "You know where the bathrooms are."

She blushed at the word, which seemed suddenly intimate and full of meaning.

"We don't want the cab driver getting curious about your appearance," he added. "You'll be picked up, by the way, at the northwest corner of Cabrillo in ten minutes. I thought it would be more discreet than having him come here. Incidentally, discreet is a good word for you to remember."

"I never ever had to be discreet before," she said painfully. "I never ever had anything to hide before."

"Have you now?"

"I—I don't—know."

"If you don't know, you'd better act on the assumption that you have."

"I feel so confused."

"Try not to let it show."

"How can I help it? How can I go to the office tomorrow morning like nothing has happened?"

"You've got to," he said. "You have no choice."

"I can quit. Maybe under the circumstances, it would be better if I quit."

"Do you realize what will happen if you do? Mr. Brandon will immediately assume that I'm setting you up in a love nest, with my wife's money."

She shrank inside the yellow coat as if it were a hiding shell, a protection from the terrible intimacy of such words as *love nest*.

"I'm trying to help you, Miss Burton. But you have to help yourself too. And me. We're in this together."

"No," she whispered. "We're not. We're not in anything together. I haven't done anything, said anything. I'm innocent. I'm *innocent!*"

"I know you are."

"But I've got to prove it. How can I prove it?"

"By keeping control of yourself. Don't discuss me or my personal affairs with anyone. Don't answer questions, don't volunteer information."

"Those are all *don'ts*. What can I *do?*"

"The best thing would be to hurry up and get out of here. Now go and wash your face and comb your hair." The words were brusque but he spoke them in a kindly, almost paternal tone, and she reacted like an obedient child.

In the bathroom off the kitchen she washed her face and dried it on the only towel hanging on the rack. She knew it must be Rupert's towel and when she pressed it against her forehead and her hot cheeks she wanted to cry again, just stand there for a long time and cry.

He was waiting for her in the kitchen, wearing his topcoat and a fedora. His skin looked gray under the fluorescent lights. "I'll walk you to the corner."

"No. You must be tired. You should go to bed."

"I don't want you walking along a city street alone at midnight."

"Is it midnight?"

"Later than that."

Outside, the fog was dripping from the eaves like rain. They walked side by side, as far apart as they could get on the narrow sidewalk, self-consciously avoiding personal contact. But the contact was there, invisibly bridging the space between them. Miss Burton could feel it as she had felt it in the bathroom, pressing Rupert's towel against her face. She was exquisitely aware of every movement he made, every breath he took, the stride of his long legs, the swing of his arms, the sighs that seemed to be words which mustn't be said. *What words*, she thought, *and do I want to hear them?*

She spoke to hide her thoughts. "It's so—quiet."

"Yes."

"Funny, I feel so noisy inside."

"Noisy in what way?"

"Gongs. Gongs are clanking."

He smiled slightly. "I've never heard gongs. Thunder, though. Lots of that."

"I guess everybody has their own personal noise inside."

"I guess they do," he said. "Your cab's waiting."

"I see it."

"Here's five dollars to cover your fare."

She felt that by accepting the money she was accepting more than her taxi fare, but she didn't argue, didn't even hesitate. He put the five-dollar bill in her outstretched hand. It was the only physical contact they'd had all evening.

He returned to the house and, for the dozenth time that day, he reread the letter that had accompanied the silver box.

Dear Rupert:

I wish to thank you and Amy for the beautiful wreath, and you for the note of condolence. The funeral was very quiet, and though Wilma would have called it oversentimental, we found it satisfying. Perhaps, as Wilma always claimed, funerals are barbaric affairs, but they are a custom and a convention, and in times of stress we lean on custom and convention.

I hope that Amy has recovered from the shock by this time. It was unfortunate that she had to be a witness, or that anyone had to be. But Wilma may have planned it that way—she could never do anything in private, there always had to be an audience, whether it was an applauding one or a hissing one. Her other attempt at suicide, after her first divorce, was undertaken in the bathroom of a friend's house while a large party was going on. None of us there felt we could have prevented what happened, so Amy must not feel that she could have prevented it . . .

Rupert remembered the occasion well. Amy had been at Lake Tahoe with the Brandons at the time, so he had gone alone to the hospital to see Wilma. Without makeup, and wearing a regulation gown, she looked pale and haggard.

"Wilma?"

"Fancy meeting you here. Sit down and make yourself comfortable. If anyone can be comfortable in this stinking hole."

"What in God's name made you do it, Wilma?"

"Such a question."

"I'm asking it."

"Okay, I was bored. All those silly people chattering and laughing. I saw the pills in the medicine cabinet and took them. Have you ever had your stomach pumped out? It's quite an experience."

"I think you'd better go and see a psychiatrist."

"I've been seeing one for the past two weeks. He's very cute. He has the curliest eyelashes. I sit and look at his eyelashes for fifty minutes three times a week. It's fascinating. I may get a crush on him. On the other hand I may get bored. There's not a hell of a lot *to* eyelashes."

"You've got to take this seriously."

"I'm tired, pal. Get out, will you?"

In less than two months Wilma became bored with the psychiatrist's eyelashes and quit seeing him.

Rupert returned to the letter.

> *. . . I could talk about Wilma for hours at a time—and often have—but I never seem to reach any clearer understanding of her. What a pity that all her drive and energy wasn't channeled into constructive outlets. It would have been far better if she'd had to go out and support herself instead of living on alimony checks. We have not been able, by the way, to find out where Wilma's husband, Robert Wyatt, is to tell him about Wilma's death. He won't be very interested anyway, except that it will save him money.*
>
> *You're probably wondering about the silver box. It was among Wilma's things that were sent on to me from Mexico City. It must have been damaged in transit, but it is still a handsome piece of work. Earl and I assumed, from the monogram inside the lid, that she intended it as a gift for you. She always spoke of you with deep affection, and I know how patient you and Amy have been with what Earl called Wilma's "shenanigans." Please keep the box in memory of her.*
>
> *Give our best regards to Amy and thank you again for the beautiful wreath. Yellow roses were always Wilma's favorite. How thoughtful of you to remember.*
>
> *Sincerely,*
> *Ruth Sullivan.*

Yellow roses.

"I hope," Wilma had said once, "that when I die someone will send me yellow roses. How about it, Rupert?"

"All right. If I'm still around."

"Is that a promise?"

"Certainly."

"Promises to dead people are easy to break. When I think of all the promises I made to my parents—if I've kept any of them it's sheer accident. So forget the whole thing, will you?"

"I don't think," Amy had said primly, "that people ought to talk about their own funerals . . ."

He tossed the letter and its envelope into the fire. Then he picked up the silver box hesitantly, as if he didn't want to touch it. It looked like a coffin. But not Wilma's coffin. The initials on the lid were his own.

He went out to the garage, holding the box under his topcoat.

Half an hour later, as he approached the middle of Golden Gate Bridge, he threw the little silver coffin over the guard rail. It sank first into the fog, then into the sea.

12

THE RUNWAYS OF International Airport were steaming under the heat of a surprise sun, and planes that had been grounded overnight were taking off in all directions as fast as space could be cleared for them. Inside the glass walls the loudspeaker, like an invisible tyrant, gave out constant orders to its subjects: "Pan American, flight 509 for Hawaii, now boarding at Gate Seven . . . Mr. Paul Mitchell, report to United Air Lines, Mr. Paul Mitchell . . . Trans World Airlines flight 703 to Chicago and New York has been delayed half an hour . . . Do not attempt to board planes before your flight number has been announced . . . Gate Seven is now open for Pan American flight 509 to Hawaii . . . Mrs. James Swartz, repeat, Mrs. James Swartz, your ticket has not been validated for Dallas, Texas. Report immediately to the United Air Lines desk . . . Gate Ten is now open for flight 314 to Seattle . . .

Behind the Western Air Lines counter, a young pink-faced man in horn-rimmed spectacles was doing some paperwork behind a nameplate that identified him as Charles E. Smith.

When Dodd approached, the young man said, without looking up, "Can I do anything for you?"

"I'd like a ticket to the moon."

"What in . . . Oh, it's you. Dodd. Somebody been murdered?"

"Yeah," Dodd said pleasantly. "Your whole family, including cousin Mabel, has been wiped out by a mad bomber."

"I confess."

"Good boy."

"So what else is new?"

"I'm in the market for some information, Smitty."

"I'm listening."

"On Sunday night, September the fourteenth, a man and wife supposedly landed here after a flight from Mexico City. What I want to know is, did they both get off the plane, did one of them, did either of them?"

"That sounds simple enough," Smitty said. "But it isn't."

"You keep records, don't you?"

"Sure, we keep records. We have the names of every person who's boarded any of our planes for the last two years."

Dodd looked impatient. "Well?"

"I said *boarded.* We're not in business for our health. We collect the fares and get the passengers on board. Where they get off is not our concern."

"You mean if I bought a ticket to New York and got off at Chicago instead, no one would notice the difference?"

"It wouldn't be part of our records," Smitty said. "But someone might notice the difference."

"Such as?"

"A member of the crew. One of the stewardesses, for instance, might recall you particularly because you tried to get fresh or drank three martinis before dinner instead of one. Or the radio operator, the co-pilot, the pilot—they all take trips to the head and sometimes they stop and chat with the passengers."

"Do you keep records of the crew on each flight?"
"The dispatch clerk does."
"How about looking up September the fourteenth. Better check the thirteenth, too."
Smith took off his spectacles and rubbed his eyes. "What kind of business are you on, Dodd?"
"It's never clean."
"I know that, but what's involved?"
"Love, hate, money, take your choice."
"I'll take money," Smitty said blandly.
"Are you implying that you'd accept a bribe? This is a shock to me, son, a truly terrible sh—"
"Wait in the coffee shop. I get off duty in fifteen minutes."
The coffee shop was crowded to the doors. It was easy enough to spot the people who were waiting for their planes. They ate with anxious haste, one eye on the clock, one ear on the loudspeaker. The women fussed with their hats and handbags, the men rechecked their tickets. They looked tense and irritable. Dodd wondered where all the happy travelers were that he saw in the vacation ads.
He jostled for a place at the counter and ordered coffee and a Danish pastry. While he ate he eavesdropped on the conversation of the two middle-aged women beside him who were embarking on a trip to Dallas.
"I've got this feeling I forgot something. I just *know* . . ."
"The gas. Did you remember to turn off the gas?"
"I'm sure I did. I *think* I did. Oh, dear!"
"You brought the dramamine, I hope."
"Here it is. Not that it will do any good. I feel sick already."
"Imagine the nerve of them making me weigh my purse along with my luggage just because it's a little oversize."
"Even if I didn't turn off the gas the house wouldn't blow up, would it?"
"Take the dramamine. It will quiet your nerves."
When they left, Dodd silently wished them *bon voyage* and put his topcoat over one of the vacant stools to save it for Smitty.
He was on his second cup of coffee when Smitty came in. "Done?"
"Done," Smitty said. "Saturday, September thirteen. Pilot Robert Forbes, lives in San Carlos but now in flight. Co-pilot James Billings, Sausalito, now off duty. Radio operator Joe Mazzino, Daly City, now on sick leave. Three stewardesses. Two of them, Ann Mackay and Maria Fernandez, are now in flight. The third, Betty deWitt, turned out to be married and was fired last week. Her husband's Bert Reiner, a jet pilot attached to Moffett Field and they live in Mountain View down the peninsula. Mrs. Reiner's your girl, if you can get to her."
"How come?"
"She was the only one of the crew on both flights, the thirteenth and fourteenth, taking the place of another girl who was ill. The trouble is, Betty might not want to cooperate. She was sore as hell when they found out she was married and gave her the sack."
"I'll try my luck anyway. Thanks, Smitty. You're a model of efficiency."
"Don't applaud," Smitty said. "Just pay."
Dodd gave him ten dollars.
"Jesus, you're a cheapskate, Dodd."
"It took you fifteen minutes to get the information. That's forty bucks an hour. Where else could you make forty bucks an hour? See you later, Smitty."
He took the Bayshore Freeway back to town. When he reached his office his secretary, Lorraine, was on the phone and he knew from the sour expression on her face that she didn't like the assignment he'd given her.

"I see . . . Yes, Mr. Kellogg must have given me the name of the wrong kennels. Sorry to have bothered you."

She hung up, crossed out another number on the scratch pad, and immediately began dialing again.

Dodd reached over and broke the connection. "Aren't we speaking to each other this morning?"

"I have to save my voice for all these lies I'm telling."

"Any luck so far?"

"No. And I can feel an attack of laryngitis coming on."

"Until it arrives, keep phoning." Dodd knew better than to sympathize with Lorraine's ailments, which were numerous and varied enough to fill a medical textbook. "Any mail?"

"The letter came you were waiting for from Mr. Fowler in Mexico City. Special delivery. I left it on your desk."

Lorraine took a cough drop, parked it expertly inside her left cheek and began dialing again. "I am calling about Mr. Kellogg's Scottie . . ."

Dodd opened his letter. It was typewritten in the uneven hunt-and-peck style Fowler had used when he was a sergeant on the Los Angeles police force, and bore no date, return address or salutation.

Good to hear your voice again, you old sinner. But what's all the hurry and excitement about anyway? Everything at this end seems on the up and up.

Mrs. Kellogg was released from the A.B.C. Hospital on September twelve. I talked to the interne working on the ward she'd been in. He was reluctant, twenty-five bucks worth reluctant, but he admitted that the authorities weren't anxious to have Mrs. Kellogg leave so soon and gave their permission only when Kellogg offered to hire a nurse to accompany his wife on the trip home. According to the intern, there was considerable disagreement among the doctors about the severity of Mrs. Kellogg's concussion. Concussions can't be measured exactly even by an electroencephalogram test, which Mrs. Kellogg refused to submit to when she learned it involved needles inserted in the scalp. Personally, I can't see where Mrs. Kellogg's fear of needles fits into anything, but you wanted me to give you every single detail, so hang on. The intern's diploma is still wet, so naturally he knew all about concussions. He read it to me out of a book: the severity of a concussion can be judged by the degree of retrograde and anterograde amnesia involved. Ain't it the truth?

On the day of Mrs. Kellogg's release she and her husband returned to the Windsor Hotel. From there he put in a call to a Mr. Johnson at the American Embassy. Telephoning in this country is an art, not a science, and the switchboard operators have the temperament of opera stars. The wrong words, the wrong tone, and the telefonista *gets her wires crossed. Apparently, Kellogg used the wrong tone. There was a lot of trouble about the call, which is how I happened to find out about it from the* telefonista *herself. I went over to the Embassy and talked to Johnson. It turned out that he was the man who'd broken the news of the affair to Kellogg and offered his services when Kellogg came down here.*

Kellogg's request was simple enough. He wanted the name of a reputable lawyer who specialized in civil matters. Johnson sent him to Ramon Jiminez. Jiminez is a substantial citizen, active in politics, as well as a smart lawyer. He refused to give me any information. But when I told him I already had the information and merely wanted a confirmation or denial, he admitted that he had executed a power of attorney giving Kellogg control of his wife's affairs, financial and otherwise. Everything was legal and aboveboard. At the mere mention of the word coercion, he blew his stack (in a nice, quiet way, of course) and asked me to leave his office. My own feeling is that there can't have been any coercion involved or Jiminez wouldn't have touched the thing with a ten-foot pole. Why should he risk his reputation for the peanuts Kellogg could afford to pay? (I'm assuming that your statement about Kellogg's finances is accurate.)

Now, about the other matters you wanted me to check. No official hearing, like our American coroner's inquest, was held concerning Mrs. Wyatt's death, but some dozen eyewitnesses gave depositions to the police. The ground witnesses, i.e., those passing on the avenida, *must be discounted, their stories were so contradictory. A combination of excitement, darkness, superstition and religious awe doesn't make for accurate observation. Mrs. Kellogg's account of the tragedy agreed substantially with that of the chambermaid, Consuela Gonzales, who for reasons known only to herself was spending the night in a nearby broom closet and heard Mrs. Kellogg screaming. She rushed into the room. Mrs. Wyatt had already flung herself over the balcony and Mrs. Kellogg was lying on the floor in a dead faint. I tried to contact Miss Gonzales at the hotel but she was fired for stealing from the guests and being insolent to the manager. The bartender, while not a witness to the death of Mrs. Wyatt, testified that she was very drunk and in a belligerent mood. If you're looking for sour notes, you have one right there: belligerent drunks pick fights with other people, not themselves. But this is pretty slim—belligerence can turn to depression at the drop of another martini, or, as in this case,* tequila. *In any case, the police here—and they're not as carefree and inefficient as you've probably been led to believe—are thoroughly satisfied that Mrs. Wyatt's death was a suicide. They released her body and her effects to her sister in San Diego, Mrs. Earl Sullivan.*

As I said at the beginning of this report, everything at this end seems *on the up and up. There is a puzzling factor involved which may have something to do with the case, and then again it may not. I give it to you for what it's worth.*

It concerns Joe O'Donnell, the man you asked me to investigate. He dropped out of sight a week ago. He's been hanging around the Windsor bar every night for over a year. When he didn't show up three or four nights in a row Emilio, the head bartender, paid a visit to his apartment. O'Donnell wasn't there and hadn't been seen by any of the neighbors for some time. His landlady claimed he skipped out because he owed back rent. This may be true but it doesn't explain his absence from the bar, which he used to call his "office." Emilio was vague on what kind of business O'Donnell conducted from his "office," but he insisted it was legitimate, that O'Donnell had never been in trouble with the police or the management of the hotel. My guess is that he went in for any petty con game that came along, whether it was accepting loans from wealthy women he picked up, like Mrs. Wyatt; organizing poker parties for American businessmen, taking bets on the horses, stuff like that. Nothing illegal, nothing bigtime. O'Donnell has—or had—a lot of charm, apparently. Everyone has a good word to say for him: generous, kind, amusing, intelligent, good-looking. How come this superman is cadging drinks and playing gigolo at a bar every night? It doesn't add up.

I questioned Emilio further. It seemed odd to me that a bartender should go checking up on a customer simply because he failed to appear for a few nights.

Emilio was evasive—Mexicans are, usually, but they lie to please rather than to deceive, and once you understand this, it's easy to cope with. It turned out that a letter had been delivered to the hotel in care of Emilio, addressed to Joe O'Donnell. It had been sent airmail from San Francisco, and on the envelope the sender had written "urgente y importante."

When Emilio handed the letter over to O'Donnell, O'Donnell made some remark about being an Easterner and not even knowing anyone in San Francisco except people he'd met casually in the Windsor bar. Like Mrs. Kellogg and Mrs. Wyatt, I presume. Anyway, he sat down and read the letter over a bottle of beer. Emilio asked him, half kidding, what was so "urgente y importante," *and O'Donnell told him to mind his own goddamn business. He got up and left the bar immediately and that's the last anyone's seen of him.*

Naturally, Emilio's curiosity was aroused. Ever since Mrs. Wyatt's death, he's had suicide on his mind. For reasons not entirely religious, suicide has a more profound effect on the average Mexican than any other kind of violence. Emilio went to O'Donnell's apartment in the vague fear that O'Donnell had killed himself because of some very bad news he'd received in the letter.

Well, there you have it. I know O'Donnell's address and will check on him further. Also I've arranged with Emilio to contact me when and if O'Donnell shows up at the bar. He might. Then again he might be in Africa by this time. He would have no trouble getting out of the country since he's an American citizen and not in any trouble with the authorities.

To get back to Mr. and Mrs. Kellogg. They checked out of the Windsor early on the morning of September thirteenth and took a cab to the airport. There was no sign of the nurse Kellogg had told the hospital authorities he intended to hire to accompany his wife on the trip. Maybe he changed his mind, maybe he arranged to meet the nurse at the airport. When they left the hotel, Mrs. Kellogg was wearing a bandage over her left temple and she had a black eye. According to the doorman, she acted as though she'd been drugged, but I'd be inclined to take this with a grain of salt. It may be a case of that national characteristic of lying to please—i.e., he assumed from my questions that I suspected something was wrong and he was merely trying to "help."

I await further instructions.

Best,
Fowler.

Dodd read the report through a second time, then he buzzed for Lorraine.

"Send a wire to Fowler."

"Straight or night letter?"

"Night letter."

"Okay, you have fifty words." She copied Fowler's address from the envelope containing the report. "Shoot."

"Check all means of exit for O'Donnell. Search apartment for letters, bank statements, photographs, evidence of love interests. Get names of all friends he might contact. Keep up the good work. Sincerely. Dodd."

"That's not fifty words," Lorraine said.

"So?"

"Maybe you should add something, like 'give my best to your wife.'"

"I could," Dodd said, "but it might not be in the best of taste. He's a widower."

"Oh. But if you're paying for fifty words, and it's almost two dollars . . ."

"Kindly send it as is, with no further editing. After that I'd like you to call Moffett Field and get the address and phone number of a pilot named Bert Reiner. I don't know his rank. He lives in Mountain View with his wife."

Lorraine rose. "Well, that's a change from kennels and dog hospitals anyway."

"You'll get back to them."

"If I only knew *why* you wanted to find this Scottie, it would make my work less boring. I mean, I'm your secretary, I should *know* these things."

"Maybe you should, at that. Remind me to tell you, for Christmas."

The exchange had given Lorraine a headache. She took an aspirin to relieve the pain, half a tranquilizer to quiet her nerves, and a vitamin pill on general principles. Then she reached for the telephone again.

13

THE TOWN OF Mountain View cowered under the benevolent despotism of the jet age. Its older residents held public meetings and wrote letters of protest to the newspapers, complaining of sonic booms and broken windows, flaming crashes and altered skies. In return, the Air Force personnel and some of the more war-conscious citizens wrote letters which said in effect, "Where would you be without jet protection in case of attack?"

The Reiners lived in the lower half of a new redwood duplex near El Camino Real. Betty Reiner answered the door. She was a tall, slim, pretty brunette with green eyes and an automatic smile that looked less genial than a frown. She wore tight black Capri pants, a silk shirt, and a double strand of pearls that reached below her hips. Dodd wondered whether this was her ordinary housekeeping costume or if she had dressed for the occasion.

"I don't know what this is all about," she told Dodd as she led him into an immaculate black and white living room. "I was just going to have some coffee. Would you like some?"

"Thanks, I would."

"Sugar and cream?"

"A little of both."

She poured the coffee out of a white ceramic pot with a black lacquered handle. The only touches of color in the room were Mrs. Reiner's green eyes and the orange polish on her fingernails. "I wish I had a nickel for every cup of coffee I've doled out on the job. As soon as the passengers realized it was free they couldn't get enough of the stuff." She handed him his coffee. "So Smitty sent you here, eh?"

"Yes. He thought you might have some information I need."

"What gave him that idea?"

"He told me you had practically a photographic memory."

Mrs. Reiner was too shrewd to be taken in by such obvious flattery. "It's not that good. Some things I remember, some I don't. What do you have in mind?"

"A certain flight from Mexico City to San Francisco."

"Which one? I've made that trip fifty times."

"Saturday, September thirteen."

"That was about a week before I was fired. I suppose Smitty told you? They fired me when they found out I was married. It's a crazy rule. If marriage interferes with efficiency, why doesn't the Air Force discharge my husband and all the other married pilots. You'd think being a stewardess was some fancy, high-toned job when all you do really is play waitress and maid, without tips."

"Saturday, September thirteen," Dodd repeated patiently. "The pilot and co-pilot were Robert Forbes and James Billings, and the two stewardesses working with you were Ann Mackay and Maria Fernandez. Do you recall now?"

"Of course. That was the weekend a friend of mine got sick and I offered to return to Mexico City that night and take her place on the same flight the next day. It was against the rules, but as I said, they've got some crazy rules."

Dodd opened the manila folder marked A. KELLOGG and took out the pictures of Amy. "This woman, I have reason to believe, boarded your plane with her husband and possibly a third party."

Mrs. Reiner studied the pictures with interest but no immediate recognition. "She looks like a hundred other people I've seen. Was there anything special about her?"

"Two things. She wore a bandage over her left temple and she had a black eye."

"The woman with the black eye—of course I remember! Maria and I were kidding around about it, wondering how she got it, whether her husband beat her up or something. He didn't seem like the type. A good-looking man, very quiet and considerate."

"Considerate of whom?"

"Well, of her, mainly. But of us girls too. A lot of passengers get pretty demanding in the course of a long flight. He didn't ask for anything special. Neither did she. She slept most of the time."

"Quite a few stewardesses are also registered nurses. Are you, Mrs. Reiner?"

"No."

"Had any nursing experience at all?"

"Just the elementary stuff included in our training course, how to cope with air sickness, how to administer oxygen to asthmatics and cardiac patients, things like that."

"Then you wouldn't know if Mrs. Kellogg's sleep was a natural one or not."

"What do you mean 'natural'?"

"Is there any possibility that she was drugged?"

Mrs. Reiner fidgeted with her rope of pearls. "Her husband gave her some Dramamine."

"How do you know it was Dramamine?"

"Well, it was a little white pill that looked just like it."

"A lot of narcotics and barbiturates are in the form of little white pills."

"I guess I just assumed it was Dramamine because so many passengers use it these days. Don't forget, Dramamine makes some people very sleepy. Maybe the effect's only psychological, but it happens." She tied the pearls in a knot, untied them, reached for her coffee. "I can't believe—I don't want to believe—that one of my passengers was being doped against her will, right under my nose."

"Did she make any fuss about taking the pill, or pills?"

"I only saw her take one. There may have been others. She didn't make a fuss, no, but I thought she looked a little scared. Not about taking the pill, just scared in general. A lot of my passengers do look scared, though, especially when the weather's bad."

"Were Mr. and Mrs. Kellogg traveling alone or was there a third party with them?"

"They were alone."

"Are you sure? Mr. Kellogg was supposed to have hired a nurse to accompany his wife on the trip."

"They were alone," Mrs. Reiner repeated firmly. "They paid no attention to anyone else, as far as I know. Lots of times when we're passing over something interesting, the passengers will get out of their seats and fraternize. Mr. and Mrs. Kellogg didn't."

"This was a first-class flight?"

"Yes."

"Double row of seats on each side of the aisle?"

"Yes. Mrs. Kellogg was in the window seat."

"Who was sitting across the aisle from Mr. Kellogg?"

Mrs. Reiner wrinkled her forehead, then smoothed out the wrinkles with the tips of her fingers. "I can't swear to it but I think it was a couple of Mexican women, looked like mother and daughter."

"Which one had the aisle seat?"

"I don't remember. You don't seem to understand, Mr. Dodd. When you've made that same flight dozens of times as I did, it's hard to differentiate them. Why, I would never even have recognized Mrs. Kellogg's picture if you hadn't clued me in about the black eye. It takes something special like that to make one trip stand out in my memory."

"Now that this particular flight is standing out, you're remembering more and more about it?"

"Yes. There was a little girl up front who kept getting sick. And an elderly man, a cardiac patient. I had to give him oxygen."

Dodd said, "I understand the airline keeps a list of the passengers on board each flight."

"There are several such lists. I had my own."

"What other information was on this passenger list?"

"Where each of them was going."

"Where were the Kelloggs going?"

"They had return tickets to San Francisco. We only made one other stop, Los Angeles." She reached for the coffeepot again, but her hand suddenly stopped in midair. "Now that's funny. I could have sworn that the Kelloggs were booked through to San Francisco, and yet . . . Wait a minute. Let me reconstruct. The plane landed at L.A. and everybody got off, as usual, for the stopover, except the cardiac patient. I stayed behind with him. He was scared, poor guy, so I gave him all the attention I could. We were in flight again before I had a chance to resume my regular duties, making the new passengers comfortable, handing out pillows and so on. I went to the rear of the plane . . . I remember now," she went on, her voice rising a little with excitement. "As I passed by, I saw that there were two women in the seats where the Kelloggs had been sitting. I was just about to tell the women that those seats were taken when I noticed that Mrs. Kellogg's coat and carryall bag and Mr. Kellogg's hat and briefcase were missing from the baggage rack."

"They got off at L.A., then?"

"Yes. I might have been mistaken, though, about their tickets being through to San Francisco."

"You weren't."

"It seems peculiar, doesn't it? But then, I'm sure there's some logical explanation."

"I'm sure there's an explanation," Dodd said. "I'm just not sure how logical it is. In case you remember anything else, no matter how trivial it may be, call me at one of these numbers, any time."

"All right."

"And thank you very much, Mrs. Reiner, for the information."

"I hope you can use it."

"I can use it."

After he'd gone she sat down and poured herself the rest of the pot of coffee. Now that the flight had been singled out clearly in her mind, she couldn't stop thinking about it. By the time the plane landed at San Francisco, the old man with the heart condition was in bad shape and had to be taken off the field in an ambulance. The little girl who'd been airsick recovered in time to chew several wads of gum and get some of it stuck in her hair. It was removed with patience and an ice cube. The honeymoon couple departed with their transistor radio tuned into the final inning of a baseball game. The smart alec with the flask and the bum jokes almost fell off the landing platform. The two Mexican women who'd been sitting across the aisle from the Kelloggs and looked like mother and daughter, couldn't have been; they left the plane separately and without speaking. The younger one had her purse clutched in both hands as if it contained her whole future.

"It was just an ordinary routine flight," she said aloud, as if Dodd had been there to deny it. "Nothing sinister about it. Mrs. Kellogg's black eye was the result of an accident, not a beating up. The pill her husband gave her was Dramamine. She looked scared because she didn't like traveling by plane. They got off at Los Angeles because—well, there could have been any number of reasons: Mrs. Kellogg's condition, or Mr. Kellogg's suddenly remembering a business deal, or both of them deciding to visit a relative they hadn't seen for a long time."

A group of jets roared overhead in take-off. The house shook, the windows rattled, the sky changed.

14

HELENE BRANDON PLANNED the trip to the city as a surprise for Gill. Shortly before noon she appeared at his office looking chic and cheerful in her sable-trimmed suit and best pearls.

Gill's private secretary, Mrs. Keely, greeted her with restraint: *A wife's place is in her own office, not her husband's.* "Good morning, Mrs. Brandon. Mr. Brandon is not expecting you?"

"No, he's not. This is a surprise."

"Oh. He's very busy this morning. He left orders that he was not to be disturbed until lunchtime."

"It's lunchtime now."

She opened the door of his office, softly, in case he was dictating or talking on the telephone. But he was doing neither. He was bent over his desk, his head buried in his hands, while the ticker-tape machine beside him coughed politely for attention. She stood, quiet and motionless, watching him, thinking with surprise how vulnerable he looked and wishing she had never seen him like this. She would rather have had him arguing with her, shouting at her, criticizing her, anything but sitting there defenseless.

"Gill?"

He raised his head slowly. His eyes were red, as though he'd been rubbing them, trying to erase from them images he didn't want to see. "Hello, Helene."

"Your secretary told me you were busy. Are you?"

"Yes."

"Doing what?"

"Thinking."

"Not about . . . Oh Gill, stop it, stop worrying over things you can't do anything about."

"I have more reason to worry now than at any time since she disappeared."

"Why? Has something happened?" She crossed the room and put her hands on his shoulders. They seemed frail and stooped under the padded cashmere coat. "Gilly, dear. Tell me."

"Amy never came home that night, Sunday. Rupert came home alone. Every word he's spoken is a rotten lie."

"I can't believe . . . How do you *know*?"

"Dodd found out."

"Can you trust him?"

"Further than I can Rupert."

His shoulders twitched impatiently under her embrace. She stepped back, and her hands dropped to her sides. Thoughts began swimming to the surface of her mind, ugly and sharp-toothed, like barracuda coming out of the ambush of kelp and crevice. *I don't care if she never came home, never comes home, never is seen again.*

"They left Mexico City together on Saturday," Gill said, "bound for San Francisco. Their luggage was checked through. It arrived, but they didn't. They got off at Los Angeles. Their luggage wasn't claimed until Sunday evening."

"What does that prove?"

"It proves what I've suspected all along, that Rupert's whole story is a pack of lies. Amy didn't come home Sunday night, she didn't pick up her dog, he didn't drive her to any station, the highball glass with the lipstick stains wasn't hers . . ."

"How can you be sure of all that? Maybe they got off at Los Angeles together and took a plane up here the next day, still together."

"Why would they stop over in Los Angeles without any luggage? A man traveling alone might. No woman would." He stopped to rub his eyes again. "There is some evidence that Rupert doped her to make her more—manageable."

"Doped her? Why, that's crazy, that's utterly crazy!"

"I think," he said quietly, "you'd prefer to believe that I'm crazy rather than that Rupert is corrupt. Is that right, Helene?"

She leaned, suddenly and heavily, against the desk. "I—I've never said you were crazy, just some of your ideas."

"You're convinced, aren't you, that I have some sort of fixation on Amy which puts me in a position where I can't evaluate facts. Go on, admit it, Helene. You've been thinking it for a long time, tossing hints, making implications. You might as well say it outright."

Her mouth moved carefully, like a cornered animal feeling its way out of a trap. "I don't believe either that you're crazy or that Rupert is corrupt."

"You're straddling the fence, eh?"

"I'm trying to be detached and reasonable."

"You're detached, all right. I think you've been detached for a long time, from Amy, from me too."

She could feel words boiling in her throat like lye, but she swallowed them all and said calmly, "I couldn't be detached from you, Gill, you know that. But that doesn't mean I must agree with you on everything, all the time. You don't like Rupert and never have. I do."

"Why? Because he married Amy and took her off our hands?"

It was close to the truth. "I thought he would make a good husband for her. And he has, until . . ."

"Until. Yes. That's a very large word."

"Oh, Gill, stop it. Don't put me in the position of having to defend Rupert against you."

"You're defending him against the facts, not me. The *facts.* Do you hear me?"

"I'm sure everyone in the building can hear you."

"Let them!"

They glared at each other across the desk. But deeper than Helene's anger was a feeling of relief. *He's shouting, that's good. At least he doesn't look so vulnerable anymore. He's fighting, not just sitting with his neck bent and exposed as if to a guillotine.*

"While we're airing grievances," he said, more softly, "I must ask you not to wear your pearls when you take the train up to the city."

"Why not?"

"There've been too many jewel robberies lately."

"The pearls are insured."

"Not for what they're worth. And I can't afford to replace them. You might as well find out now, money's tight. Call it bad luck on my part, or poor judgment, or both. But the fact is, we have to cut down, perhaps even sell the house."

"Sell our house?"

"It might come to that."

"Why didn't you tell me before? There are a hundred ways I could have been saving money."

"You can start now."

"I don't mind." But it was more than not minding; she felt quite excited at the idea of a change, a challenge. Perhaps they could find a ramshackle old house, and Gill and the kids could all help fixing it up, painting, putting on a new roof, making over curtains, repairing doors and steps. The whole family working together for a common purpose . . .

"I've been poor before. I don't mind."

"I do," Gill said. "I mind very much."

She could still see the old house clearly in her mind, but no one was working on it. The roof leaked, the steps sagged, the windows were cracked and curtainless, the paint was peeling, and Gill was sitting on the front porch, his head in his hands, his neck exposed to any blow, any attack. "God damn you," she said. "Stand up and fight."

"Fight? Fight what? You?"

"Not me. You shouldn't be fighting me. We should be on the same side, pulling together. And we would be if . . ."

"If what? Let me hear your if's, Helene."

"If it weren't for Amy."

He looked pained but not surprised. "You may regret saying that."

"Maybe I already do," she said soberly. "But not because I don't believe it."

The intercom signaled for attention, and the voice of Gill's secretary insinuated itself into the room, as penetrating and genteel as the whisper of a lady librarian. "Mr. Dodd is on the telephone again, Mr. Brandon. Will you take the call?"

"Go ahead. . . . Dodd? Yes. Yes, I understand. When? How much? Good God, didn't anyone try to stop him? I know it's legal, but under the circumstances . . . No, I can't get away from the office until later this afternoon. Hold on a minute." Gill put his hand over the telephone and spoke sharply to his wife, "I must ask you to wait outside."

"Why?"

"This is a personal matter."

"Meaning it's about Amy?"

"Meaning it's none of your business."

"I couldn't care less," she said airily, but her cheeks burned red and when she walked to the door her legs felt weak and rubbery.

She stopped at the secretary's desk in the outer office. "Tell Mr. Brandon I couldn't wait. I have another—appointment."

Appointment wasn't quite the word, she thought, as she rode the elevator downstairs. Errand was closer. Errand of mercy. Or perhaps errand of mischief. It would depend on your viewpoint.

On the street she hailed a cab and gave the driver the address of Rupert's office.

"That's walking distance," he said.

"I know. I'm in a hurry."

"Okay. You from the Peninsula?"

"Yes."

He screwed up his face in soundless laughter. "I can always tell. After twenty-six years in this business you get intuition. I'm from the Peninsula myself. Redwood City. Every morning I take the train up here and I drive my cab all day and then I take the train back. Always been crazy about trains. The wife says I ought to of been an engineer. That way I wouldn't always be running into a bunch of knucklehead cops always telling me where to park and what to do and making with the one-way streets. You waste a lot of gas on these one-way streets."

You waste a lot of gas, period, Helene thought irritably. Any other time the cabbie would have amused her, she would have asked questions, drawn him out, and later made a funny story of the incident to tell Gill and the kids. Today he seemed merely a talkative, annoying old man with a grievance.

He parked at a red curb. She paid him and got out of the cab as quickly as possible.

When she reached Rupert's office, she found Miss Burton in the act of combing her hair.

"Why, Mrs. Brandon," Miss Burton said, returning the comb to her purse with nervous haste. "We weren't expecting you."

Editorial "we" or Rupert-and-I "we," Helene wondered. She had never paid particular attention to Miss Burton in the past, and she wouldn't have now if it weren't for Gill's suspicions. There was nothing special about her: eyes blue and rather solemn, short turned-up nose, plump, pink cheeks, temporary blonde hair, short, sturdy legs intended for long and loyal service. The composite picture she presented was one of directness and simplicity; not even Gill, with his emotional astigmatism, could have denied that.

Helene said casually, "Is Mr. Kellogg around?"

"He just left."

"I'll wait, if I may. Or perhaps I'll do some shopping and come back later."

"He won't be in the office anymore today," Miss Burton said. "He's not feeling well. I think he's coming down with the flu. He hasn't been taking good care of himself since Mrs. Kel—since he's been living alone."

"Oh."

"I mean, well, no proper meals for one thing. Good hot meals are very important."

"Do you cook, Miss Burton?"

"Cook?" She flushed from the base of her throat to the tips of her ears. "Why? Why do you ask that?"

"I'm just interested."

"I like to cook when there's someone to cook for. Only there isn't. I think that answers your question, and the other questions behind it."

"Other questions?"

"I think you know what I mean."

"But I don't. I have no idea."

"Your husband has." Miss Burton's voice trembled, and a pulse began to beat, hard and unrhythmically, in her left temple. "Lots of ideas."

"Has he been talking to you?"

"To me? No. Not *to* me. Behind my back. Hiring a greasy little detective to follow me, pump me—well, he was pumping at a dry well. He didn't find out a thing, the same as you're not going to because there's nothing to find out, because I never . . ."

"Wait a minute. Do you think I came here at my husband's request?"

"It's a funny coincidence, last night the detective, now you."

Helene's brief laugh was more like a cough of indignation. "Why, if Gill knew I was here, he'd—well, no matter. Let's put it this way. I don't agree with my husband on everything. If you're angry with him for something he's done, all right, that's your privilege. But don't let your anger spill over on me. I came here as a friend of Rupert's. You're his friend, too . . . Aren't you?"

"Yes."

"Well, then, hadn't we better work together, cooperate?"

Miss Burton shook her head, more in sorrow than in denial. "I don't know. I don't know who I can trust anymore."

"That puts two of us in the same boat. The question is, where's the boat going? And who's at the helm?"

"I don't know anything about boats." Miss Burton's voice was cold and cautious. "Not a thing."

"Neither do I, really. I went sailing once on the Bay with my husband. Years ago, just the two of us. Gill was the skipper and I was supposed to be the crew. God, it was awful. I was scared to begin with, because I can't swim very well, and then a strong wind came up and Gill began shouting orders at me. Only I couldn't understand them, they sounded like a foreign language or a child's gibberish—ready about, hard alee, jibe ho. Gill explained them all to me afterwards, but at the time I felt such terrible confusion, as if some immediate and urgent action was expected of me but I couldn't understand what. That's the way I feel now, right this minute. There's a strong wind, there's danger, I should be doing something. But I don't know what. The orders sound like gibberish, I can't even tell where they're coming from. And I can't get off the boat. Can you?"

"I haven't tried."

"And you won't try?"

"No. It's too late."

"Then we'd better get our signals straight," Helene said bluntly. "Don't you agree?"

"I guess so."

"Where's Rupert?"

"I told you, he wasn't feeling well, he went home."

"Straight home?"

"He may have stopped for lunch. He always eats at the same place at noon, Lassiter's, on Market Street, near Kearny."

Lassiter's was a moderately priced bar and grill that catered to the men of the financial district. They were a martini crowd, consisting of third vice-presidents, sales managers, West Coast representatives, all of them known as executives, a word which meant nothing except that it entitled them to a two-hour lunch.

She spotted Rupert immediately, sitting at the counter with a bottle of beer and a hamburger in front of him, both untouched. An open paperback book was propped against the beer bottle, and he was staring at it but not reading it. He looked tense and expectant, as if he was waiting for someone he didn't like or something he didn't want to face.

When she touched him lightly on the shoulder he jumped and the book fell on its side and the beer bottle teetered.

She said, "Aren't you going to eat your lunch?"

"No."

"I hate to see anything wasted."

"Help yourself."

He got up and she took his place at the counter and reached for the hamburger without embarrassment or self-consciousness.

He stood behind her while she ate. "What are you doing here, Helene?"

"Miss Burton told me you usually had lunch at this place so I came over and here you are."

"And now what?"

She spoke quickly and quietly so the man on the next stool wouldn't overhear. "Gill just had a phone call. From Dodd. I'm sure it was about you and some money. I could only hear Gill's part of the conversation and not much of that. He asked me to wait outside so I couldn't hear any more, but I think he's going to meet Dodd late this afternoon. They may be planning some kind of showdown."

"About the money?"

"I guess so."

"They have no grounds."

The man on the next stool paid his check and left, and Rupert sat down in his place.

"Listen," Helene said. "I've got to know more about this. I've put myself in a bad position trying to defend you. I want to be reassured that I'm doing the right thing."

"You are."

"What money was Dodd talking about?"

"I cashed a check on Amy's account, using her power of attorney."

"Why?"

"Why do people cash checks? Because they need money."

"No, I meant why all the fuss on Dodd's part, and Gill's? Gill said it was legal but that someone should have stopped you, under the circumstances."

"No one could have stopped me. No one even has the right to question me about it. As a matter of fact, whatever employee of the bank informed Dodd about the check was guilty of improper conduct. Dodd holds no official position, and private records shouldn't be open to him."

"What's he like?"

"I don't know. I've never met him."

"Miss Burton has," she said, with deliberation. "Last night."

He tried to look indifferent. She could see his face in the mirror behind the counter, trying on various expressions none of which seemed to fit. He said finally, "So she couldn't keep her mouth shut."

"She didn't intend to tell me anything, don't be hard on her. She thought I'd come to the office as a spy for the great Brandon-Dodd combine. That's a laugh, isn't it?" She pushed away the empty plate with an expression of distaste as if she'd suddenly decided that she hadn't been hungry after all and now regretted eating the hamburger. "Miss Burton's in love with you, I suppose you know that."

"No, I don't!" he said sharply. "You're imagining . . ."

"It's time you found out, then. It's written all over her, Rupert. I feel rather bad about it."

"Why should you?"

"Oh, empathy, I guess. It's happened to me too, being in love with someone who hardly noticed me. That was years ago, of course," she added quickly. "Before I met Gill."

"Of course."

"Are you in a hurry?"

"Why?"

"You keep looking at that clock on the wall."

"Well, I have to get back to the office pretty soon."

"I thought you weren't going back to the office this afternoon."

"What gave you that idea?"

"Miss Burton."

"Miss Burton," he said easily, "almost managed to convince me I wasn't feeling well and should go home. The fact is, I'm fine and I intend to spend the afternoon working." He swung round on the stool as if he intended to get up and leave. Instead, after a second's hesitation, he completed the full circle and faced the counter again. "Let's have some coffee, eh?"

The maneuver would have been obvious even if she hadn't already been suspicious of him. By tilting her head slightly, Helene could see in the mirror the reflection of the entrance door. A young woman had just come in and was surveying the room with an air of anxiety. She was well built and pretty, dressed in a skin tight woolen suit, a feathered hat, half a dozen strings of colored glass beads, and patent leather pumps with heels so high that she stood at a forward angle as if she were bucking a high wind. When she put up her hand to adjust the feathered hat over her blonde curls, a platinum wedding band gleamed under the lights.

"She's rather pretty," Helene said.

"Who is?"

"The young woman by the door. She appears to be looking for someone."

"I hadn't noticed."

"Well, notice now."

"Why should I?"

"Oh, you might be interested. She is. She's coming your way."

"She can't be. I've never seen her before in my life."

Rupert turned and gave the girl a long, cold, deliberate stare. She stopped abruptly, then headed for the cigarette machine, moving with little wobbly steps on the high, narrow heels.

Helene noticed that her feet were proportionately larger than the rest of her, very wide and flat, as if she'd spent a considerable period of her life walking barefoot. When she had fished the cigarettes out of the trough, the girl put them in her black patent leather handbag and walked toward the exit. One of the men sitting at a table gave a low whistle as she passed, but she paid no attention, as if she hadn't heard the sound or didn't know what it meant or for whom it was intended.

"I think she's a farm girl," Helene said. "That getup looks like something she's copied from a movie magazine. I suppose you might call her a blonde with a good tan or a brunette with a good bleach job, depending on your viewpoint."

"I have no viewpoint. I don't know the woman."

"She's probably one of the secretaries in your office building and has a mad, mad crush on you."

"You're being ridiculous. I'm not the type of man women get crushes on."

"Oh, but you are. You make a perfectly splendid father image, firm but kindly, strong but gentle, that sort of thing. It's fatal—for a girl that age. How old would you say she is? Twenty-two? Twenty-five?"

"I haven't thought about it and don't intend to."

"Years and years younger than Miss Burton, anyway, wouldn't you say?"

"Stop playing games."

Helene smiled. "I like games. If I didn't, I wouldn't be here. It's kind of amusing, isn't it, Gill and Dodd sniffing around like a pair of nervous bloodhounds and me trying to put them off the scent? Your scent."

"Why are you trying?"

"I told you, I like games."

"I like games too, when the grand prize isn't my own skin. This is the second time you've warned me about Gill's activities. What's your real reason, Helene?"

"It's too complicated to explain."

"Don't explain, then," he said.

"I won't."

"I want to thank you, anyway, for all the trouble you've gone to."

"You're welcome. At least I think you're welcome. I don't know. I—I'm beginning to feel like a traitor. I'd like to be reassured that I'm not, that I've done the right thing in coming here."

"You've done the right thing," he said gravely. "Thank you again, Helene. Someday, perhaps soon, Amy will be here to thank you too."

"Amy? Soon?"

"I hope so."

"She's coming back?"

"Of course she's coming back. What made you think she wasn't?"

"Nothing—special."

"Maybe by Thanksgiving, or at least by Christmas, we'll all be together again. Everything will be the same as it always was."

"The same," she repeated dully. "Of course. Precisely the same."

Precisely. Inevitably. Irrevocably.

She rose, one hand pressed against her mouth to stifle a sound she could never let anyone else hear.

Later, when she was asked, she couldn't remember exactly how she spent the next couple of hours. She recalled walking along many streets, staring into the windows of shops and the faces of strangers. For a long, or a little, time she sat on a bench in Union Square watching sad-eyed old men feed bread crumbs and popcorn to the pigeons. The pigeons were plump and sleek and did not resemble Amy at all, but Helene drew back in protest when one of them came too close to her foot. She was repelled by its dependence, its insistent docility, which it seemed to be forcing on her. *Amy. Amy again. By Thanksgiving. Or Christmas. No hope of never.*

It started to rain lightly and the old men abandoned their benches and ambled off to shelter. Helene put on her gloves and rose, ready to leave, when she saw the girl from Lassiter's grill entering the Square from Powell Street. She had no idea whether the girl would recognize her or whether it would be important if she did, but simply as a precaution she picked up a discarded newspaper from the grass and held it in front of her as a spying shield.

She thought at first that the girl was alone and that the man walking parallel to her was just about to pass her and be on his own way. He didn't pass. He kept right on walking beside her but at a distance, as if the two of them were in the midst or the aftermath of a quarrel. They approached the bench where Helene sat hidden behind the limp newspaper, with the pigeons cooing and coaxing at her feet.

The man had the same startling color contrast as the girl, very light hair and deeply tanned skin. They might have been brother and sister. The man was the older of the two, perhaps in his early thirties. There were clearly defined laugh lines around his eyes and mouth, but he wasn't laughing. He looked pale under his tan, and feeble under the loud plaid sport coat. Helene had never seen him before but she remembered others like him. Years ago during the depression in Oakland, her way to school led her past a poolroom where jobless young men used to hang out for lack of anything better to do. On their faces, in their posture, they all shared a common expression, not bitter or angry, but listless, as if they hadn't expected much anyway. The man in the plaid coat wore the same expression.

The farm girl and the poolroom buff. They looked out of place in the Square and with each other. She couldn't imagine what connection either of them could have with Rupert. I must have been mistaken, she thought. Rupert was telling me the truth when he said he didn't know the girl, had never seen her before. He's probably been telling the truth about everything. Suspicion is contagious. I caught it from Gill.

It was nearly four o'clock when she returned to Gill's office and found him with his topcoat on and his briefcase under his arm, ready to depart.

"You're soaking wet," he said. "Where have you been?"

"Oh, walking. Looking at things."

"If you hurry, you can catch the 4:37 train home."

"Aren't you coming too?"

"Later. I have to see Dodd."

"Why?"

"It's time we had a showdown with Rupert."

"But why now, today?"

"The dog's been found."

She looked at him stupidly. "Dog? What . . ."

"Amy's dog," he said.

15

"THE SIDALIA KENNELS," Dodd said. "It's a combination small-animal hospital and boarding kennel on Skyline Boulevard just outside the city limits. He brought the dog in Sunday night, the fourteenth of September. The vet himself wasn't there but a college kid, a Cal Aggie student who helps out during the summer, was on duty at the time. The dog had a spot of eczema on his back and Kellogg's instructions were to keep him there until further notice. He paid a month's board in advance. The dog was wearing a plaid harness but no leash. He's in good shape, according to the vet; the eczema's gone and he's ready to leave whenever Kellogg wants to pick him up . . . Did you call Kellogg's office, by the way?"

Gill nodded. "Miss Burton said he left at noon to go home."

"We'll catch him there then. You understand, don't you, that there's nothing much we can do except ask him questions and hope for answers. It's not illegal to park a dog at a kennel. And it's not illegal to use a power of attorney, even fifteen thousand dollars' worth."

"What would he want with all that money?"

"Let's go and find out. We'll take my car if you don't mind."

With the slackening of the rain, a wind had risen, and the little Volkswagen wavered with the gusts as if it were going to roll like tumbleweed across the road. But there was no place for it to roll. All the way out Fulton Street the five o'clock traffic moved bumper to bumper. Gill sat with his fists clenched against his thighs, and every time Dodd applied the brakes, Gill's foot stamped on the floorboard.

"It's a little car," Dodd said after a time. "It only needs one driver."

"Sorry."

"There's no need to get all tensed up about this, Brandon. When we confront him with what we know of the truth, he may break down and tell us the rest of it. Then again, he may have a nice pat explanation for everything."

"Including the money?"

"The money part's easy. He needed it to send to Amy—her expenses in New York are running higher than she expected."

"She isn't in New York."

"So if I were Kellogg, I'd say, prove it."

"I will, even if I have to wring the truth out of him with my bare hands."

Dodd was silent a moment, apparently engrossed in guiding the car through the traffic which had thinned out somewhat west of Presidio Boulevard. "Come on now, Brandon. You're not really figuring on that bare-hand bit."

"I am."

"Why are you carrying a gun, then?"

"I—don't know. I bought it this afternoon. I've never owned a gun before. It suddenly occurred to me that I ought to have one, that I needed one."

"And now you feel better?"

"No."

"Nor do I," Dodd said grimly. "Get rid of it."

"That won't be necessary."

"I think it will. You're not the type who should be messing around with loaded guns."

"I guess I knew that," Gill said. "It's not loaded. I didn't buy any cartridges."

Dodd made a little sound that seemed to indicate amusement or relief or some of both. "I can't figure you, Brandon."

"If I wanted to be figured, as you put it, I would have gone to a psychiatrist, not a detective. Turn right at the next corner. The house is in the middle of the third block."

"You'd better leave the gun in the car."

"Why? It's not loaded."

"Kellogg might get the idea that it is, and counter with one of his own that *is* loaded. That would leave us out on a pretty thin limb."

"Have it your way." Gill handed over the gun and Dodd locked it inside the glove compartment.

"There's one more thing, Brandon. Let me do the talking. At first, anyway. You can horn in later if you like, but right at the beginning let's not get this thing slobbered up with emotions."

Gill got out of the car, stiffly. "I don't like your choice of language."

Dodd's reply was lost in the wind. He pulled up the collar of his coat and followed Gill up the walk to the porch.

It was a middle-income neighborhood where great attention was paid to outward appearances. Lawns no bigger than an elephant's ear were groomed to perfection, hedges barely had time to grow before they were clipped. The roses and camellias were fed almost as well and regularly as the occupants of the houses, and were probably given more care and inspection for signs of disease. It was a street of conformity; where identical houses were painted at the same time every spring, a place of rules where gardens, parenthood and the future were planned with equal care, and even if everything went wrong the master plan remained in effect—keep up appearances, clip the hedges, mow the lawn, so that no one will suspect that there's a third mortgage and that Mother's headaches are caused by martinis, not migraine.

Dodd asked, "Who picked the house?"

"Amy did." Gill pressed the door chime. "That is to say, she took my advice. The property was part of an estate sale which I found out about before it was announced on the open market."

"She could have afforded something more elaborate, though?"

"She could, yes. But not Rupert. Amy has always insisted on living within Rupert's income."

"Why?"

Gill looked annoyed, and Dodd wasn't sure whether it was the question that bothered him or the fact that no one was responding to the door chime.

"My sister," Gill said, "believes in the good old-fashioned type of marriage where the husband provides the financial support. It is not a case of stingi—of thriftiness."

The quick switch of words interested Dodd. *So he really thinks she's stingy. That probably means he's tried to borrow money from her and she refused. I wonder how hard up he actually is and to what degree his desperate need for Amy is more financial than brotherly.*

Inside the house a telephone began to ring. It rang eight times, ten times, then stopped for a few seconds and began again, as if the caller suspected that the first dialing had been incorrect.

"He's not here," Dodd said. "There's no use wasting our time."

"Wait just a few more minutes. He might be in the shower."

"Or in Santa Cruz."

"Why Santa Cruz?"

"No reason." Dodd shrugged. "I just picked the name out of a hat as a place to go when you don't want to stay where you are."

"You must have had a reason for picking that name rather than any other."

"It may not be valid."

"Let's hear it anyway."

It was getting dark. The lights in the houses on both sides of the street began coming on almost simultaneously. For a few moments, before drapes were drawn and blinds shut, the street had a festive air, a look of Christmas.

"It's just a hunch," Dodd said. "Suppose Kellogg decided to skip town, what would be the first thing he'd do?"

"Get some cash together."

"He already did that this morning. What do you think his next move might be?"

"I don't know."

"I don't know either; I'm just guessing. But judging from what I've heard about some of his characteristics, I have a notion he'd pick up his dog. The Sidalia Kennel is on Skyline Boulevard, and Skyline Boulevard leads to Santa Cruz. If he left the office at noon, as Miss Burton claims, he could easily be in Santa Cruz by this time. From there he'd probably head for L.A."

"Santa Cruz isn't on the direct route to L.A."

"He may be trying to avoid direct routes."

"We can't assume that he's left town," Gill said. "Why should he? He doesn't know we've found out about the dog and the cash."

"Someone may have tipped him off."

"That's impossible. No one else knows about it."

"No one?"

"Just my secretary. And my wife, Helene. You can rule them out, of course."

"Of course," Dodd said, but the ironic tone nullified the words. "Where is your wife now?"

"On her way home, on the train." Gill consulted his watch. "No, she'd be home by this time if she caught the 4:37. Why? Helene has nothing to do with this."

"I didn't say she had."

Inside the house the telephone began to ring again. Dodd turned toward the veranda steps. "Wait here a minute. I want to take a look around."

"I'll come with you."

"You'd better stay here. In case Kellogg or anyone else shows up you can sound a warning to me."

"Warning? What are you going to do?"

"On the police books—and I hope it doesn't get that far—it's called breaking and entering."

"You can't do that. It's illegal. I won't be a party to it. I've got too much to lose. My reputation . . ."

Dodd had already disappeared around the corner of the veranda where a steep driveway led into a double garage that was attached to the rear of the house. The overhead aluminum door was unlocked and rattling in the wind. Dodd pulled it open. Rupert's car, a two-year-old Buick, was parked inside, with the key in the ignition.

Dodd stood for a moment, with his hand on the hood of the car. The engine was cold. He took out his flashlight and aimed its beam at the door that led into the house. The lock was, as he'd hoped and expected, a flimsy one. The attached-garage setup often proved a boon to burglars: people who were careful about protecting their front door frequently put an inefficient lock on a door that opened into a garage. In a matter of minutes he had pried the lock loose with his pocketknife and the door was swinging inward.

He turned off the flashlight and stood in the near-darkness, listening for some sound that would indicate the house was occupied. But the wind was too noisy, and on top of the wind the telephone resumed its shrill demands for attention.

Dodd followed its sound across the room and picked up the receiver, hoping that the idea he had was wrong. "Hello?"

"Rupert? Is that you?"

It wasn't wrong. "Yes. I just got home . . . Helene?"

"I've been trying to reach you for an hour. Listen. Gill went to meet that detective. He's planning some kind of showdown with you because the dog's been found."

"Where?"

"I don't know where. All I know is you've been lying to me about the dog. Haven't you? . . . Well, *haven't* you?"

"Yes."

"And that girl in Lassiter's at noon, the one you said you'd never seen before, you knew her, didn't you? You'd arranged to meet her there, hadn't you?"

"Listen . . ."

"I won't listen anymore. You've lied about everything. You've put me in an awful spot. I trusted you, I tried to help you. What if Gill finds out? He's crazy on the subject of Amy. He may do something terrible. I'm scared. I'm scared to death."

"Gill won't find out," Dodd said. "Take it easy."

"Everything's such a mess. I don't know what to do."

"Do nothing. I've got to go now, Helene. There's someone at the door."

"Gill?"

"Yes, I'm pretty sure it's Gill."

"Be careful of him," she said in a hurried whisper. "He's changed. I can't tell anymore what he's thinking, what he's going to do."

"I'll be careful. You be discreet. Good-bye, Helene."

She began to cry. He hung up softly, wondering if she was the kind of woman who cried easily or if she was as scared of her husband as she claimed to be.

Dodd's eyes had become adjusted to the gloom. He could see the outlines of the furniture in the kitchen, the chrome-trimmed breakfast set, the yellow work counters, the matching stove and refrigerator. His gaze lingered on the refrigerator. The top part was intact, but at the bottom its outlines broke off suddenly as if the whole base of it had been blown out by dynamite. *No, that's crazy,* he thought. *There's no hole in the refrigerator, it's a shadow. Something has been put in front of it.*

His fingers moved carefully along the wall to the light switch and clicked it on. A man was lying face down on the floor in a widening pool of blood that reached almost to Dodd's feet. Beyond the man's outstretched left hand, which bore a gold wedding band, was a kitchen knife with a dark-stained, ten-inch blade. Someone had tried, without success, to clean up the mess. Two or three bloody bath towels were lying in the sink along with an overturned box of detergent.

Dodd thought first and irrationally of the little dog waiting at the kennel to be picked up by his master. It would be a long wait, a long, long wait.

He turned and fumbled his way down the dark hall to the front door. When he opened the door he saw Gill take a couple of steps backward as if he intended to run away.

"You'd better come inside for a minute," Dodd said.

"I don't like this, I don't like it at all. Is he—is he here?"

"He's here."

"How's he taking it, your breaking in like this?"

"He hasn't made any complaints."

"Oh. Well. In that case." Gill stepped inside, moving his body rigidly as if he expected an attack. "I can't see. Turn on the lights."

"Later. Where have you been all day, Brandon?"

"At my office. Why?"

"You didn't pay a call on your brother-in-law earlier in the afternoon?"

"Of course not."

"When you left the office to go out and buy that gun, was there anyone with you?"

"No."

"How long were you away?"

"What difference does it make?"

"Arranging for me to come here with you like this would make a good cover-up in the event that you were here earlier, by yourself."

"I don't know what the hell you're getting at. Why can't we turn on a light? Where's Rupert? What's going on?"

"Nothing's going on," Dodd said. "It's all over. Rupert's lying in the kitchen, dead."

"Dead? He—he killed himself?"

"Possibly but not probably. Someone tried to clean up the mess afterwards."

"Mess? How . . . ?"

"A knife."

"Oh, God. Oh, my God. What am I going to do now?"

"You're going to come right back to the kitchen with me and phone the police."

"I won't. I can't. My family, my reputation. We've got to get out of here. Quick. Now. Before anyone comes. My God, fingerprints. Have I touched anything? The doorknob. I'll wipe off the doorknob . . ."

"Don't panic, Brandon." Dodd put his hand firmly on Gill's arm. "Take it easy."

"Let me go! I've got to get out of . . ."

"This is the wrong time to throw a fit, believe me. Now exercise some control, will you? I don't like this any better than you do. I could lose my license on this little gambit."

"It was your idea, it was all your idea."

"Okay, blame me if you like. Just don't flip your lid."

"What about Amy? Poor Amy, God help her."

"Amy isn't here. We are. If God's going to help anyone, I want priority. Now come on. We have work to do."

"I—I can't. I've never seen a—dead man before. I'm afraid I might be sick."

"Keep your head up and breathe through your mouth," Dodd said. "And kindly remember, as you view the remains, that you hated his guts anyway."

"You're a callous, insensitive brute."

"Sure. But right now you're stuck with me, so let's talk friendly."

As he spoke he gave Gill a little push and Gill started down the hall, holding a handkerchief to his mouth. When he reached the doorway of the kitchen he paused and let out a sound of surprise. The handkerchief fluttered to the floor, unnoticed.

"That's not," he said in a whisper, "that's not Rupert."

"Are you sure?"

"Rupert's bigger and his hair's much darker."

"Who is he, then?"

"I don't know. I can't see his face from here."

"Go over and take a look at it, then. Be careful not to touch him."

Gill walked cautiously around the pool of blood and leaned over the dead man. "I've never seen him before."

"Think hard, think of Rupert's friends, Amy's friends . . ."

"I don't know all of their friends, but I'm pretty sure this man wouldn't be one of them."

"What makes you say that?"

"That haircut, those clothes. He looks like a hoodlum or one of those beat boys that hang out around Grant Avenue."

"There's quite a difference between a hood and a bohemian."

"I'm simply saying that I don't believe Amy or Rupert would consort with a man like this."

"Then what's he doing in their kitchen?"

Gill's face was gray and shiny like wet putty. "For God's sake, how should I know? It's all crazy, preposterous."

"Well, you'd better call the police."

"Why me? Why can't you do it?"

"Because I won't be here when they arrive."

"You can't walk out and leave me holding the baby."

"I can. I have to."

"If you go, I go. I warn you, you're not getting out of here without me."

"Oh, for Christ's sake," Dodd said. "Take it easy and listen a minute, will you? We know now that Kellogg had a damn good reason to skip town. But his car's still in the garage. I want to find out how he left and if anyone was with him. I still think my hunch about the dog may be right, so I'm going to drive out to the kennel and check. If I stay here and wait for the police I'll lose several hours."

"But what will I tell them?"

"The truth. Why we came here together, how I got into the house, the exact truth. They'll probably send out either Ravick or Lipske of the Homicide squad. They're both friends of mine. They're not going to like my not sticking around, but tell them I'll contact them later and give them any information I have."

"Will I have to talk about—Amy?"

"You'll have to talk about everything. This is a murder case now."

Gill picked up his handkerchief from the floor and pressed it against his forehead. "I'd better call my lawyer."

"Yes, I think you'd better."

16

ALONG THE OCEAN front waves angered by the wind were flinging themselves against the shore. Spray rose twenty feet in the air and swept across the highway like rain, leaving the surface sleek and treacherous. Dodd kept the speedometer at thirty, but the thundering of the sea and the great gusts of wind that shook and rattled the car gave him a sensation of speed and danger. The road, which he'd traveled a hundred times, seemed unfamiliar in the noisy darkness; it took turns he couldn't remember, past places he'd never seen. Just south of the zoo, the road curved inland to meet Skyline Boulevard.

The Sidalia Kennel was built on a bare, brown knoll about half a mile beyond the city limits. It looked new and clean, a brightly lit, two-story Colonial structure with an expanse of galvanized iron fencing on each side, and a small neon sign at the entrance to the driveway: PET HOSPITAL. A second sign below elaborated on the first: TREATMENT AND BOARDING. SMALL ANIMALS ONLY.

As Dodd got out of the car an Airedale began pacing up and down its runway in restless curiosity. A jet shrieked across the sky and the Airedale raised his head to howl a complaint.

"It's no use, old boy," Dodd said. "That's progress."

The howling had roused the other dogs. Before Dodd even reached the front door every runway had come alive with noise and movement: wagging tails, bared teeth, sounds of welcome and sounds of warning.

As Dodd reached out to press the buzzer the door opened to reveal a short, stout, white-haired man who looked a little like a beardless Santa Claus. He wore a smile and a white coat, both of them fresh and tidy.

"I'm Dr. Sidalia. Come in, come in. Where's the patient? Not an automobile accident, I hope? Those I dread. So sad, so unnecessary." He shouted over Dodd's shoulder. "All of you fellows out there, be quiet, do you hear me? They're good chaps," he explained to Dodd, "just a bit excitable. Now what can I do for you?"

"My name's Dodd. I'm a private detective."

"Now that's interesting, isn't it? Wait till I summon my wife. She's a great mystery fan. She's always wanted to meet a real private detective."

"I'd rather you di—"

"Oh, it's no trouble at all. We have our living quarters on the second floor. It's noisy but more convenient. You wouldn't believe the number of night emergencies I must cope with, more than any obstetrician, I'm sure. When we lived in the city I no sooner arrived home for dinner than out I would have to rush again to treat some little chap in trouble."

"The chap I came here about," Dodd said dryly, "is a Scottie."

"A fine breed. Loyal, courageous, indepen—"

"His name's Mack. He belongs to Rupert Kellogg. I talked to one of your employees about the dog earlier in the day. He said Mack was ready to be taken home."

"He *was* taken home," the doctor said with a pleased smile. "Oh, it was a joyful reunion, for both man and beast. Scotties are true Scots. They don't spend freely, they don't squander their affections on just anyone, no indeed. Fine chaps, Scotties."

"Kellogg picked the dog up himself?"

"Of course."

"When?"

"I should say between three and four o'clock. I was treating a Yorkie at the time. The poor lass has distemper, I don't think she will live. Still, we keep trying, and hoping, and, if you want the truth, praying a bit too. My wife takes care of that end of it. She's a godly woman."

"Was Kellogg alone?"

"He came in here alone. His wife waited for him out in the car."

"His wife's supposed to be in New York."

"Really? Now that's odd, isn't it? I met Mrs. Kellogg a couple of years ago when I gave Mack a rabies shot. A pretty little woman, quiet but friendly."

"And you say that the woman in the car was Mrs. Kellogg?"

"Now that you've cast some doubt on it, I can't be sure. I assumed it was Mrs. Kellogg because she was with Mr. Kellogg. Why, I even waved to her . . . Wait a minute. Come to think of it, she didn't wave back. There's another thing I noticed too . . . Mack didn't seem too anxious to get into the car. Usually, when I've had a dog here for a while, he's very eager to jump into the family car and go home."

"I have good reason to believe that Kellogg wasn't driving the family car and wasn't traveling with his own wife."

"Dear me," Dr. Sidalia said, looking uncomfortable. "He certainly doesn't give the impression of being that kind of man at all. He's very fond of animals."

"So was Dr. Crippen."

"The English murderer?"

Dodd nodded. "In fact, it was Crippen's attachment to a dog that led to his capture."

"I didn't know that. I wonder what happened to the dog after Crippen was hanged?"

"I have no idea."

"Well, I hope a good home was found for him, poor chap. It can be quite a blow to a dog, losing his master." Sidalia spoke as if the Crippen case was recent, the dog still alive, although he must have known that everyone connected with Crippen had long since died. "Why did you bring up the subject of Crippen in connection with Mr. Kellogg?"

"Kellogg's in the same kind of trouble."

"You don't mean he—murdered somebody?"

"It looks that way."

"Dear me. This is quite a shock. I must sit down."

Sidalia lowered himself into a plastic-covered chair and began fanning his face with his hand.

"The police will be here to question you," Dodd said. "Probably in an hour or two. They'll want to know about the woman and about the car."

"I never notice cars. People and animals, yes. But cars, I pay no attention to them. All I can remember is that it was dirty. I notice dirt, I'm a very meticulous man."

"Was the car new?"

"Neither new nor old. Average-looking."

"Color?"

"Greenish."

"Coupé Convertible? Sedan?"

"I can't recall."

"You said that the dog didn't seem anxious to enter the car. That means you stood and watched. How did the dog get into the car?"

"Kellogg opened the door, naturally."

"Which door?"

"The rear."

"That would make the car a four-door sedan, wouldn't it?"

"Why yes," Sidalia said, looking pleasantly surprised. "Yes, I believe it would."

"How did the woman react to the dog? Did she make a fuss over him? Did she reach back and pet him?"

"No. I don't think she did anything."

"Assuming that the woman was Mrs. Kellogg, would you call that normal behavior under the circumstances?"

"Dear me, no! When one of my little patients is released, there's always a good deal of excitement on the part of the family. It's one of the joys of my life, to witness these reunions."

"How was the woman dressed?"

"I only saw her head. She wore a bright red scarf tied under her chin."

"What color was her hair?"

"I can't recall that any of it was showing. She was very tanned, I know that. I remember wondering how Mrs. Kellogg could have managed a tan like that with all the fog we've had this summer. Of course, we're fairly sure now that the woman wasn't Mrs. Kellogg, so perhaps she was not tanned at all but had a naturally dark skin. These days it's hard to tell the difference, the way women bake themselves like potatoes."

Dodd thought, *a tanned or dark-skinned woman, a greenish sedan, a black dog; that's not much to go on.* "When Kellogg left, in what direction did he turn?"

"I have no idea. I went back inside as soon as he started the car. As I told you, I had a patient on the table at the time, the little Yorkie with distemper. A cruel disease, distemper, inflicted on the poor beasts usually by the carelessness of their masters. Would you care for a pamphlet on the subject of distemper immunization?"

"I don't own a dog."

"Cats also can become victims."

"I don't own a cat, either."

"Dear me, you must be a lonely man," Sidalia said with sympathy.

"I get along."

"As a matter of interest, I have two little chaps in here right now who are looking for a good home, a beautiful pair of pedigreed cocker spaniels, brothers."

"I'm afraid I . . ."

"You have a kind face, Mr. Dodd. I noticed, as soon as I opened the door, that you have a very kind face. I'll wager you have a way with animals."

"I live in an apartment," Dodd lied. "My landlord won't allow dogs."

"He must be an unfeeling man. I'd move out of there immediately if I were you."

"I'll think about it."

"Mark my words, a man prejudiced against animals is a man not to be trusted."

Dodd opened the door. "Thanks for the advice. And the information."

"Must you go so soon? My wife will be very disappointed at missing the chance to meet a real private detective. I'll buzz her, it won't take a minute."

"Some other time."

"Duty calls, I presume. Well, I hope I've been of some assistance. Not that I would like to get Mr. Kellogg in any trouble, he's a fine, dog-loving man."

"Whatever trouble he's in, he got there himself."

"Such is the way of the world," Sidalia said with more pity than censure. "Good-bye for now, then. And don't forget, when you move to a new place, there's no better company in the world than a pair of cocker spaniels."

"I won't forget."

Dodd realized as he got into his car that if he'd spent ten more minutes with Sidalia the back seat would now contain two cocker spaniels, and a lot of trouble. *And a lot of fun. I wonder what Doris would say if I . . . No, that's crazy. One dog, maybe. But two, she'd think I'd lost my marbles. Still, not everybody is offered a pair of beautiful pedigreed cocker spaniels. By God, I bet they're cute . . .*

The doctor was standing on the lighted porch, waving good-bye. Dodd pressed down hard on the accelerator and the little car jumped across the driveway as if all of Sidalia's chaps were biting at its heels.

He took Portola Drive back to the city. He wasn't in any hurry. An hour ago he'd been overoptimistic about finding out what car Kellogg was driving, the make, the year, even the license plates; he had imagined himself following Kellogg, reaching him before the police did, breaking the case before they even knew there was a case.

"Dodd, boy dreamer," he said aloud. "Me and my kind face."

He was aware that the police would be waiting for him at Kellogg's house and taking a dim view of his absence, but a few more minutes wouldn't make much difference. The telephone call he intended to make had to be made in private, without Brandon or any policemen listening in.

He parked the car in front of the building where his office was located, and took the elevator up to the third floor. Lorraine, his secretary, had left a message for him in her typewriter, as she usually did when something important came up during his absence: "Spec. Del. letter from Fowler on your desk." To make sure he didn't miss the letter she had propped it between two ashtrays, as if she mistrusted either his eyesight or his ability to find anything.

Dear Dodd:
Had just returned from posting my previous letter to you when Emilio called me from the Windsor bar to tell me that something milagroso *had happened to him. I don't agree that it's miraculous, but it's interesting. Someone sent him two ten-dollar bills in an envelope postmarked San Francisco. He thought at first the money came from some lady tourist who'd taken a fancy to him. Then he remembered that O'Donnell had borrowed two hundred fifty pesos from him several months ago, roughly twenty bucks. I draw several conclusions from this:*

1. O'Donnell is in S.F.
2. He has some means of support.
3. His conscience is bothering him, and he's scared. (In my experience "conscience money" usually has little to do with the debt or theft involved. It's a pay-off for other things, triggered by fear.)
4. Whatever is on his mind, it's serious enough to make him send the money anonymously, but not so serious as to make him cover his tracks completely.

These are my conclusions. Draw your own. And happy hunting!

Fowler.

Happy hunting. Dodd repeated the words grimly, remembering the dead man on the kitchen floor. There were many mistakes in Fowler's letter: all the tenses were wrong. The hunt was over.

He picked up the phone and called a number in Atherton.

A woman answered on the second ring. "This is the Brandon residence."

"I'd like to speak to Mrs. Brandon, please."

"Mrs. Brandon has retired for the night."

"It's very important."

"She's got a headache. I have orders not to dis—"

"Is that Miss Lundquist?"

"Why yes."

Dodd oiled up his voice. "I'm a friend of Mr. Brandon's. He's often spoken of you, Miss Lundquist."

"He has? Well, my goodness."

"My name is Dodd. I must talk to Mrs. Brandon. Tell her that, will you?"

"I guess, being as it's so important, she won't mind. Hold on."

Dodd held on, cradling the phone between his shoulder and his ear while he lit a cigarette. He could hear nothing from the other end, no whispers or sounds of movement. He thought the line was dead. Minutes passed, and he was on the point of hanging up when Helene Brandon spoke suddenly and sharply in his ear: "Hello, who is this?"

"Elmer Dodd."

"We're not acquainted."

"We are, in a sense, Mrs. Brandon. We had a telephone conversation a couple of hours ago."

"Is this your idea of a joke? I've never talked to you on the telephone or any other way."

"I was at Kellogg's house when you called. Kellogg wasn't."

After a brief pause, she said in a low, muffled voice, "Is my husband with you?"

"No."

"Does he know—about my call?"

"I haven't told him. But he's going to find out. So is everybody else in Northern California when this hits the newspapers."

"The newspapers? Why should the newspapers be interested in a private conversation between me and my brother-in-law, or what I thought was my brother-in-law? And why should you want to tell them?"

"I don't want to," Dodd said. "I have to. I've got a license to hang on to. I can't withhold evidence."

"Evidence? Of what?"

"Brandon hasn't been in touch with you?"

"No. He's not home yet. I'm beginning to worry. He's never this late, I don't know where he can be."

"He's still at Kellogg's house."

"You shouldn't have left him alone with Rupert," she said shrilly. "God knows what will happen."

"Kellogg isn't there. He's skipped town, with the police on his tail."

"Police? Why? Have they found—Amy?"

"Not Amy. A man, a stranger. He was murdered in Kellogg's house with a kitchen knife, sometime this afternoon."

"Oh, my God! Rupert—Rupert . . ."

"I think Kellogg meant to get rid of the body. He started to clean up the mess but there was too much of it. He decided to leave town instead. So he picked up his dog, and his girlfriend, and left."

"What girlfriend?"

"The one he lied to you about. You saw her in Lassiter's at noon." Dodd paused. "What happened, Mrs. Brandon? Did you walk in unexpectedly and louse up the rendezvous?"

She didn't answer immediately. He thought she might be crying, but when she spoke again her voice was clear and crisp, with no evidence of tears. "She came in while I was talking to Rupert at the lunch counter. She was heading straight for him until he turned and stared at her. I'm not a mind reader, but I know there was a message in that look of his. Anyway, she bought a package of cigarettes and left. When I asked Rupert about her, he said he'd never seen her before. I had a feeling then, that he was lying. I still have. But it's only a feeling, there's no evidence to back it up."

"There might be. What did the girl look like? And how much of a girl was she, and how much of a woman?"

"Early twenties. Blonde, quite pretty, a bit overweight. She looked ill at ease and uncomfortable, as if her clothes were too new and too tight. I thought at the time she was a girl from the country, used to doing a lot of outside work. The tan she had wasn't the kind we get around these parts. It was more like the kind you see on the migrant workers who pick fruit and cotton on the ranches in the Valley."

"A lot of the migrants are Mexican," Dodd said.

"A lot are white too. They both end up with the same color skin."

"You said her hair was blonde?"

"Bleached."

"By the sun or the bottle?"

"Even in the Valley the sun doesn't get that strong."

"Have you any reason to believe the girl came from the Valley?"

"Her feet. They were very wide and flat, as if she was used to going barefoot."

He didn't argue the point, but he knew that very few of the Valley pickers went barefoot if they could afford shoes. Under the noon sun the ground grew hot as a kiln.

"I saw her again later," Helene said. "She walked through Union Square with a man about ten years older than she was. I thought he might be her brother. He had the same coloring, and they had the same general air about them, as if they were ill at ease in the city and didn't belong there. I'm pretty sure they were arguing about something, though I didn't overhear any actual words."

"The man was wearing a plaid sport jacket?"

"Why—why yes. How did you know?"

"I saw him."

"Were you in the Square too?"

"No. I saw him later." *The rest of a lifetime later.*

"Who is—was he?"

"An acquaintance of your sister-in-law, I think."

"You make that word 'acquaintance' sound dirty."

"Do I? Well, let's face it, Mrs. Brandon—when I dress for a job like this I don't put on clean, white gloves."

"You mean Amy and this man were . . ."

"Acquainted."

"It still sounds dirty."

"Maybe you're just hearing it dirty," Dodd said. "Amy and O'Donnell met in the bar of a Mexico City hotel. Amy's gone, O'Donnell's dead. Now you know as much about it as I do. For further information consult your local newspaper."

"The papers. Oh God. This will be in all the papers. Gill will . . ."

Dodd didn't want to be told what Gill would. He'd seen and heard enough of the man. He said brusquely, "Mrs. Brandon, when you met Kellogg at Lassiter's at noon, did he mention his wife?"

"Yes. He said Amy would be coming back soon. By Thanksgiving or Christmas."

"That's not very soon."

"Isn't it? I guess that depends on your viewpoint." She paused, as if she was trying to decide whether to tell him how she really felt about Amy. Then she said, "Do you think she's coming back?"

"I'm beginning to wonder," Dodd said, "if she ever went away."

A kitchen knife wasn't generally the kind of weapon used in a planned or premeditated murder. It was a weapon of emergency, seized upon suddenly in a moment of fury or fear. Fists were a man's customary instruments of quick attack and defense. A woman's were whatever happened to occur to her or to be handy. The knife may have been lying on the kitchen counter, ready to be picked up.

There were only five women involved in the case. One of them, Wilma Wyatt, was dead. The others were living, or presumed living: Miss Burton, Helene Brandon, the young woman with the bleached hair, and Amy herself. Of these four, only the young woman and Amy were definitely known to be acquainted with O'Donnell. But it was possible that Miss Burton had met him through Kellogg, and that even Helene Brandon, for all her protestations of innocence and ignorance, had known the dead man. Known him, and had reason to fear him. In that case, Helene's blundering phone call to Kellogg's house might not have been a blunder at all, but part of a plan with a triple purpose: to try and establish her own innocence, and to find out if the body had been discovered and identified, and to make sure that the girl with the bleached hair was brought into the case. Bringing in the girl would direct attention away from herself and her own still-obscure part in the affair.

But what possible connection, he wondered, could Helene Brandon have had with O'Donnell? And if there had been any connection, would she have freely admitted seeing O'Donnell in the Square?

No, he thought, *it doesn't make sense. The woman at the bottom of this is not Helene, it's Amy. It all comes back to Amy—where did she go and why did she leave?*

A wild idea rose to the surface of his consciousness like some improbable sea monster. Suppose Amy hadn't left at all, suppose she'd been living in that house all the time, under cover, for reasons no one yet knew. Incredible as the theory seemed, it would account for a number of things: the dismissal of the maid, Gerda Lundquist; the removal of the little dog, Mack, who might have given Amy's presence away; the letters, which had certainly been written by Amy, but not necessarily from a distance, perhaps right in her own bedroom.

Doors began opening in his mind, revealing rooms that were peopled with shadows and voiced with echoes. None of the shadows could be positively identified, and the echoes were like the nonsense syllables produced by a tape recording running backward. But in one corner of one room, a faceless woman sat at a desk, writing.

The telephone conversation with Helene Brandon continued.

"Mr. Dodd? Are you still . . .?"

"I'm here."

"Listen to me. Please listen. There's nothing to be gained by dragging me into this."

"You have important evidence."

"But I gave it to you. *You* have it now. That's what counts, isn't it—the evidence itself, not who tells it to the police. Can't you keep me out of it? I'll pay."

"If I keep you out of it, I'll be the one who ends up paying."

"There must be ways."

"Name one."

She was silent a moment. He could hear her heavy, irregular breathing, as if thinking was to her a violent physical exercise.

"You," she said finally, "you could have been the one who saw Rupert and the girl at Lassiter's, at lunch time."

"Maybe I could, except I ate my lunch out of a paper bag in my office."

"Alone?"

"A couple of flies joined me for dessert."

"Please, for heaven's sake, be serious. You don't know what this means to me and my family. My three children are all in school. They're old enough to suffer from this, suffer terribly."

"You can't prevent their suffering. Their uncle is wanted for murder."

"At least he's not a blood relative. I am. I'm their mother. If I'm dragged into this, God help them."

"Okay, okay," Dodd said flatly. "So I saw Rupert and the girl at Lassiter's. What was I doing there?"

"Having lunch."

"My secretary knows damned well I took my lunch to work."

"All right then, you were trailing Rupert—or is it tailing?"

"Either."

"When the girl came into the picture you decided to tail her instead, so you did. She went to Union Square where she met . . ."

"How did she get to Union Square?"

"Took the Powell Street cable car."

"Do you know that or are you making it up?"

"Making it up. But it sounds plausible, isn't that what we're aiming at? Besides, she entered the Square from Powell Street."

"What time?"

"I don't know, I sort of lost track of time. I was—thinking about Amy coming home. And other things." She coughed, as if to warn herself not to step on dangerous ground. "I remember it started to rain, and the old men who were feeding the pigeons got up and left."

"It started to rain about three o'clock." He wouldn't have noticed the time or the rain particularly, except that his secretary had come into his office to tell him in her own peculiar way, that she was going down to the drugstore to buy a bottle of cold pills. *"Some people believe that rain cleanses and washes the air. But I happen to know for a fact that what it does is bring down all the viruses and bacteria from outer space, also Strontium 90. I suppose you don't care about Strontium 90, but when your bones begin to decay inside you . . ."*

"Three o'clock," Helene said. "Yes, it must have been about that."

"Where did she meet her friend in the plaid sport jacket?"

"I have no idea. It was simply a coincidence that I saw her again. I wasn't following her or looking for her or anything. She just appeared."

"Okay, that's how I'll have to play it, as a coincidence. The police don't like coincidences, though."

"Coincidences like that happen here all the time. In L.A. you can go downtown every day for a month and never meet a soul you've ever seen before. But here, the downtown's so small I invariably meet someone I know when I go shopping or out to lunch. It's sort of like a village in that respect."

"The natives would get restless if they heard you say that."

"It's true, though. It's one of the things I love about the city."

"All right," Dodd said. "So it was a small coincidence. I wasn't tailing the girl, she just appeared."

"Mr. Dodd, you're going to help me? You're really going to help me?"

"Not you. The kids." He wanted to, but didn't, tell her why. When he was a junior in high school, his father had been arrested on a drunk charge. It wasn't much, but it made the newspapers. He'd left school and never gone back. "Your job now, Mrs. Brandon, is to be discreet. If the police question you, answer them. But don't volunteer any information."

"What if they find Rupert and he tells them the truth, that I was the one who saw him at Lassister's with the girl?"

"Rupert," Dodd said, "will have a lot of other talking to do before he gets around to that."

17

When Miss Burton turned the corner it seemed to her that someone on the street was staging a huge outdoor pageant with all the neighbors serving as members of the cast and crew. It was impossible to tell what kind of pageant it could be, the characters and costumes were so varied and numerous: small boys on bicycles; women in housedresses, bathrobes, pajamas; men carrying cameras, babies, briefcases; groups of girls twittering and chirping like birds, and grim-lipped old ladies watching in silence from the back of the stage, as if the scene they were witnessing was old, remembered stuff to them.

Both sides of the street were lined with cars, some with engines still running and the headlights on and people peering out from the open windows. Miss Burton stopped and leaned against a lamppost, feeling suddenly dizzy and breathless. *What are they trying to see?* she thought. *What do they expect to see? What are they waiting for?*

The wind clawed her hair and pinched her lips blue and tore at her yellow coat, but she was unaware of any physical suffering. People pressed past her, shouting to each other above the wind. A large white dog paused to stare at her as if she was usurping his own private lamppost.

A woman wearing a battered muskrat coat over striped pajamas called the dog away. "He won't hurt you, he's gentle as a lamb."

"I'm not—afraid," Miss Burton said.

"You looked like you were."

"No."

"You can't see much from here, but if you go any closer you might get involved. Believe me, it doesn't pay to get involved."

"What happened?"

"Murder is what happened. In the Kelloggs' house. I've always known there was something funny about those people. Oh, they seemed nice enough, on the surface . . . Where are you going? Hey, wait a minute, you dropped your scarf!"

But Miss Burton was already on her way, running through the crowd, weaving in and out like a little quarterback pursued by giants.

Dodd was parking his car around the corner when he spotted her, recognizing her first by her yellow coat. She didn't see him, she would have passed by without knowing he was there if he hadn't called out to her: "Miss Burton!"

She turned to look at him, briefly and blindly, then she resumed her running. He started after her, without any plan or intention, like a dog chasing a moving object simply because it was moving. He hadn't gone fifty yards when he began to puff and a sharp pain stabbed his side. He would never have caught up with her if she hadn't stumbled over a crack in the sidewalk and fallen to her knees.

He helped her up. "Are you hurt?"

"No."

"It's a funny time to be practicing up for the four-minute mile."

"Go away. Just go away."

"What are you doing here?"

"Nothing. *Nothing.* Please leave me alone. Please."

"A lot of people are suddenly saying please to me," Dodd said dryly. "I guess it takes trouble to make people talk polite."

"I'm not in trouble."

"Any friend of Kellogg's is in trouble. Have you heard from him?"

"No."

"He didn't call to say good-bye?"

"No."

"And you wouldn't tell me if he had, would you?"

"No."

"You can get away with saying no to me, but the police aren't going to like it. They're probably at your apartment right now, waiting for you. And from now on that's the way it will be. You'll be watched, followed, every place you go. If they can get to your mail before you do, they will. Your apartment will be bugged and your phone tapped."

"I have no information."

"You're loaded with information, Miss Burton. And they'll get it all. They'll take you apart like a watch, your insides will be laid out on a table. No watch ever works the same once it's been taken apart like that, unless it's done by an expert. The police aren't expert, they can be pretty damned clumsy."

As if to emphasize his point, a police car with its siren open turned the corner on two wheels. A few drivers pulled over to the curb, the rest proceeded as if they'd heard and seen nothing.

"Why," she said painfully, "why are you being so cruel?"

"Maybe, someday, you'll realize it's kindness, not cruelty, to warn you what to expect when the police start asking questions."

"I can't give out information I don't have."

"And you won't give out what you do have?"

"I told you . . ."

"Miss Burton, what are you doing in this neighborhood?"

At first she shook her head as if she didn't intend to answer. Then she said, slowly and carefully, "Mr. Kellogg left the office at noon. He wasn't feeling well. I decided to drop by his house and see if there was anything I could do to help."

"That's what you intend to tell the police?"

"Yes."

"They'll think you're a most solicitous and devoted secretary."

"I am."

"In fact, they might think you're more than a secretary."

"I can't help the dirt in other people's minds. Including yours."

"My mind doesn't have any dirt in it, where you're concerned."

"No?"

"No," he said firmly. "I believe you're exactly what you claim to be, a devoted secretary, with very little talent or taste for lying. Miss Burton, why were you running away when I stopped you?"

"I heard that there'd been a—a murder."

"Who told you?"

"A woman, a stranger. She said a murder had been committed in the Kellogg house."

"That's all?"

"That's all. I didn't wait to hear any more. I didn't want to get involved so I left."

"Without asking any questions?"

"Yes."

"Weren't you even curious about who was murdered?"

She turned away, silent and obstinate.

"Miss Burton, your employer was living alone, or presumably alone, in that house. Wouldn't it have been natural for you to assume that he was the one who was killed? Wouldn't it also have been natural for you to stay long enough to find out?"

Her lips moved but she didn't speak. He wondered if she was praying. He hoped so; she was going to need all the help she could get.

"Miss Burton, did you have a good reason to believe that the victim was not Rupert Kellogg?"

"No!"

"I suggest that he called you to tell you he was leaving town because something had happened. Perhaps you didn't believe him and that's why you came out here tonight, to check up on him. Or perhaps he didn't tell you exactly what had happened and you wanted to find out for yourself. Which was it?"

She put her hands over her ears. "I don't have to listen to you! I don't have to talk to you! Go away! Go away or I'll scream!"

"You are screaming," he said.

"I can scream louder."

"I'll bet you can. But you don't want to see the police any sooner than you have to, so let's play it calm, eh? You can't drown out the truth by screaming."

"What you think isn't necessarily the truth."

"Then why all the reacting? Simmer down. Do some thinking. Your story doesn't hold up. The police won't believe it any more than I do."

"I can't help . . ."

"You can help. Tell the truth. Do you know where Kellogg is?"

"No."

"You haven't seen him since he left the office at noon?"

"No."

"Or been in touch with him?"

"No."

"Miss Burton, a woman has disappeared and a man has been killed. Under those circumstances, withholding information is a very serious matter."

"I have no information, for you or anyone else."

"Well, I have some for you." He paused, letting her wait, giving her time to wonder, to worry. "When Kellogg left town he wasn't alone. He took his girlfriend with him."

She didn't move and no expression crossed her face, but a column of color rose up from her neck to her cheekbones and the tips of her ears. "That's a very old and very cheap trick, Mr. Dodd."

"For your sake, I wish it were a trick. But it happens to be a fact. They were seen together at noon, and again later when he picked up the dog at the kennel."

"I don't believe it. If he had a—a woman with him it must have been his wife."

"Not a chance. The girl was a pretty blonde, years younger than his wife."

"Younger." She mouthed the word as if it had an acrid taste but must be swallowed.

"Twenty-two, twenty-three."

"What's her—name?"

"If I knew, I'd tell you."

She was silent, huddling inside her yellow coat for protection, not from the wind outside but from the storm inside. She said at last, "I guess you've told me enough for tonight."

"I had to. I can't watch a woman like you jeopardize herself for a worthless man without trying to stop you."

"How do you know what kind of woman I am?"

"I do know. I knew last night when I talked to you at the dancing academy." It seemed, to Dodd, a very long time ago.

She glanced at him bitterly. "I suppose you followed me last night when I went home after class."

"You didn't go home, Miss Burton."

"So you were following me."

"No."

"Then how can you be sure where I went?"

"Kellogg told me."

"That's a lie. He doesn't know you, he's never spoken to you in his life."

"Let's say his actions spoke for him. This morning he used his power of attorney to take fifteen thousand dollars out of his wife's bank account. I deduced that someone had warned him I was on his trail. You."

He guessed from her shocked expression that it was the first time she'd heard about the money and the power of attorney. He pressed his advantage: "Did Kellogg forget to mention the fifteen thousand to you? He has a convenient memory."

"It was—the money was—is—none of my business."

"Even if he used it to skip town with a blonde? I suppose he also forgot to mention the blonde."

"You're a bad man," she said in a whisper. "A hateful man."

"If, by that, you mean you hate me, I'll have to accept it. If you mean I'm full of hate, I must correct you. I'm not full of hate. I wish you well, I'd like to help you."

"Why?"

"Because I think you're a nice girl, who's doing some wrong things with the right intentions."

"I've done nothing wrong."

"Let's say ill-advised, then." He jammed his fists into the pockets of his topcoat as if to prevent them from taking a poke at someone. "You went to Kellogg's house last night to warn him. I know that, so don't bother denying it. Now listen. This is important. You went to the front door and Kellogg let you in?"

"Yes."

"There's a long hall with several rooms off it. Did you walk down that hall?"

"Yes."

"Were the doors to those rooms open or closed?"

"Open."

"Where did you and Kellogg talk?"

"In the den, at the back of the house."

"Did you go into any of the other rooms?"

"Just what are you getting at?" she said shrilly. "Are you implying that he and I . . ."

"Please answer."

"I went to the bathroom. Make something of that. I went to the *bathroom,* and combed my *hair* and washed my *face* because I'd been *crying!* Now make something of it!"

He looked pained, as if the thought of her crying depressed him. "I'm not going to ask you why you were crying, Miss Burton. I don't even want to know. Just tell me one thing. Did you get the impression, while you were there, that someone else might be living in the house besides Kellogg?"

"I suppose you mean the blonde?"

"You suppose wrong. I mean Amy."

"Amy." One corner of her mouth jerked upward in a sudden little half-smile. "That's a funny idea, that's really funny." She drew in her breath and held it like a swimmer about to go underwater. "No, Amy wasn't in the house, Mr. Dodd. Not alive, anyway, not listening, not able to listen."

"How can you be sure?"

"He would never have said the things he did if anyone else had been there. Especially Amy."

So the bastard made love to her, some degree of love. Dodd found himself wondering, too hard, what degree of love. "Thank you, Miss Burton. I realize how difficult it was for you to tell . . ."

"Don't thank me. Just please leave me alone."

"Are you going home?"

"Yes."

"I'll drive you. My car's just down the street."

"No. No thanks. There's a bus due in five minutes."

So she even knows the bus schedule, Dodd thought. *That means she's made a lot of trips to these parts, too many.* "Well, at least let me walk you to the corner."

"I'd rather you didn't."

"All right. Go by yourself. Good night."

Neither of them moved.

He said brusquely, "Hurry up or you'll miss your bus."

"I wish I knew what side, whose side, you were on in this business."

"I was hired to find Amy. Kellogg's various extracurricular activities, like murder, theft, adultery, don't interest me except to the extent that they might lead me to Amy. Dead or alive. So you might say I'm on nobody's side. I could be on yours, but you don't want to play it that way."

"No."

"That suits me. I work better as a free agent anyway." He turned to leave. "Good night."

"Wait. Just a minute. Mr. Dodd, you can't—you can't really believe Rupert did all those things."

"I can. I'm only sorry you can't."

"I have—*faith* in him."

"Yeah. Well. That's that, isn't it?"

He wondered how long her faith would last after she'd had a talk with the police.

They were waiting for him at Kellogg's house, a sergeant whom he didn't recognize, and Inspector Ravick whom he did. Only a few hours before, the place had been, except for the dead man in the kitchen, very orderly and well-kept. Now it was a shambles; the furniture had been disarranged, cigarette butts and used flash bulbs were scattered on the floors, rugs were caked with mud, and everything in the kitchen, walls and woodwork, stove, refrigerator, sink, taps, chairs, bore the black smudges of fingerprint powder.

"I see you've been making yourself at home, Inspector," Dodd said. "Is this your version of gracious living?"

A scowl crossed Ravick's broad, pock-marked face. "Okay, Weisenheim, where the hell have you been?"

"The name's Dodd. Only my best friends call me Weisenheim."

"I asked you a question."

"Well, I'm thinking of an answer."

"Make it good. Start talking."

Dodd started talking. He had a lot to say.

18

FOR FIFTY MILES the road had been winding tortuously along the cliffs above the sea. In places the cliffs were so high that the sea was invisible and unheard. In other places they were low enough for Rupert to see the foam of the breakers in the light of the quarter-moon.

The little dog had begun to whimper in the back seat. Rupert spoke to him soothingly and quietly. He said nothing to his companion. They had not spoken since Carmel, and they were now passing through the Big Sur, where the redwoods stood in massive silence, disowning the wild wind and the reckless sea.

She was not asleep, although her eyes were closed and her head rested against the door. He thought, not for the first time, *what if the door should fly open on a curve, what if she fell out? That would be the end of it all. I could drive on by myself* . . . But he knew it wouldn't be the end, the end wasn't even in sight. He reached across her suddenly and locked the door she was leaning against.

She shrank back as if he'd aimed a blow at her head. "Why did you do that?"

"So you won't fall out." *So I won't be tempted to push you out.*

"Is it much farther?"

"We're not even halfway."

She muttered some words that he didn't understand; they might have been a prayer or a curse. Then, "I feel sick."

"Take a pill."

"All these curves, they make my stomach feel bad. There must be another road, one that is straight and smooth."

"The better roads have more cars on them. You'd feel a hell of a lot sicker if you heard a siren behind you."

"The police are not watching for this car. They don't know Joe had a car. Maybe they even don't know who he is. I took his wallet out of his pocket. That will make it harder for them." But she didn't sound very sure of it, and after a time she added, "What will we do when we get there?"

"Leave that to me."

"You promised to look after me."

"I'll look after you."

"I don't like the way you say that. Why can't we make plans, right now, right here? There is nothing else to do."

"Watch the scenery."

"We could start deciding what . . ."

"The deciding's done. The plans are made. You're going back."

"Back? Not—all the way back?"

"You'll take up exactly where you left off. Tell everyone you've been away on a little vacation and now you want to resume your ordinary manner of living. Act natural and don't talk too much. And remember, this isn't advice I'm giving you, it's an order."

"I am not forced to obey. I have money. I can disappear, I can get lost in the city."

"Nothing would please me more, but it won't work."

"You mean you will not let it work," she said bitterly. "You will tell."

"I'll tell. Everything I know. That's a promise."

"You don't care what happens to me, do you?"

"Not a hoot in hell. If you went up in smoke I'd just open the windows and air the car out."

"You are—you are a very changed man."

"Murder changes people."

Even above the noise of the engine he could hear the sharp intake of her breath. He turned to look at her, wishing it were for the last time. She was tugging at the red silk scarf she wore on her head as if it constricted her, prevented her from getting enough air.

He said, "Leave it on."

"Why?"

"Your hair's rather noticeable. To say the least. Keep it hidden until you can get to a beauty parlor and have it changed."

"I don't want it changed. I like it this way. I have always wanted to be . . ."

"Keep the scarf on."

She retied the scarf under her chin, muttering to herself and shaking her head. He thought, *she's frightened enough to take orders. That's one good sign, the only good one, she's frightened.*

For half an hour they had not met or passed another car, or seen a dwelling or any sign of human occupancy. It was as if the last people to have passed that way were the builders of the road, and that had been, Rupert judged from its condition, a long time ago. Parts of it had melted in the rain as if the concrete had been mixed with sugar. *Sugar road,* he thought grimly. *If I have a future, if I live to come this way again, that will always be its name.*

At the next bend a faint glow was visible between the massive trees, like a light at the end of a long, dark tunnel. He knew she had seen it too. She began again to complain of her stomach and her head.

"I feel sick. I want a glass of water."

"We haven't any."

"There's a light up ahead. Perhaps it is a store. You could buy some aspirin for my head and get some water."

"It would be dangerous to stop."

"I tell you, I can't go on. I feel so sick, I feel like dying."

"Go right ahead."

"Oh, you are a monster, a fiend . . ." The rest of the epithets were lost in a series of deep, dry retches.

He said, "Stop play acting."

She kept on retching, her body bent double, her hands against her mouth.

The glow between the trees became a neon sign identifying a group of log cabins and a dilapidated coffee shop at the Twin Trees Lodge, *reas. rates, vacancy*.

Rupert pulled off the road and braked the car. Most of the cabins were dark but lights were on in the coffee shop and a man was sitting behind the counter reading a paperback book. Either he hadn't heard the car or he was at an interesting part of the book, because he didn't look up.

In the back seat the little dog began to yelp with excitement at the forest smells and the sound of a creek running behind the cabins. Rupert told the dog to be quiet and the woman to get out of the car. Neither of them obeyed.

"You wanted to stop," he said. "All right, we stopped. Now hurry up and buy a cup of coffee or whatever you want, and we'll be on our way."

He reached across her and opened the door and she half fell out of the car, at the same time making a sudden grab for her purse. The quick, cool gesture was a tip-off that her retching hadn't been genuine. It was part of an act, though he still didn't understand its purpose. For nearly a month now she had been acting a role, speaking lines not her own, in a voice and idiom not her own. She seemed almost to have forgotten who and what she was. On only one occasion had she stepped out of the role back into herself and that was when she stood in the kitchen talking to O'Donnell. *"I'm going away"* O'Donnell had said. *"No hard feelings, eh? Don't worry, I won't talk, I don't want trouble. Just give me the money to get home again . . ."*

Money. The key word. He watched her as she crossed the parking lot to the coffee shop clutching her purse to her breast like a little golden monster of a baby.

He waited until she sat down at the counter before he got out of the car and closed the door as quietly as possible behind him. South of the coffee shop were the restrooms and a public telephone booth. He headed for the booth, taking the long way around to stay out of the light of the neon sign. He knew that if he had been the one who had insisted on stopping she would have been suspicious and not let him out of her sight or hearing. As it was, she had forced the issue and so she was suspicious of nothing. She sat drinking her coffee and munching a doughnut, with the purse on the counter in front of her, where she could see it and touch it at all times.

He entered the telephone booth, put a coin in the slot and dialed long distance. It was getting late and the rush hours were over. The call went through immediately.

"Hello."

"Mr. Dodd?"

"Speaking."

"You don't know me personally, Mr. Dodd, but I have a proposition you might be interested in."

"Clean?"

"Clean enough. I know you're looking for Amy Kellogg."

"So?"

"I can tell you where she is. In return for certain services."

The man behind the counter had reheated the coffee on a little butane burner. "A bit of a warm-up, ma'am?"

She looked blank. "I beg your pardon?"

"That's my way of saying, how would you like another cup of coffee without paying for it?"

"Thank you."

He poured more coffee for her and some for himself. "Going far?"

"We are just traveling around seeing the country."

"Gypsying, eh? I like gypsying myself."

The word stung her ears. It meant wandering, homeless, poverty-stricken people who would steal anything. She said sharply, one hand on her purse, "We are not gypsies. Do I look like a gypsy?"

"Heck, no, I didn't mean that. I meant, like for instance you pick up and leave and you don't know where you're going."

"I know where I'm going."

"Sure. All right. Just making conversation anyway. Business is slow, not many folks around to talk to."

She realized she had made a mistake being sharp to him, he would remember her more vividly. She tried to make amends by smiling at him pleasantly. "What is the next city?"

"Highway 1 ain't long on cities. It's for scenery, finest scenery in the world. Lemme see, San Luis Obispo I guess you'd say is the next real city. When you get there you're on 101, that's the main highway."

"Is it far?"

"A good piece. If it was me, now, I'd cut across to Paso Robles from Cambria, you get to 101 faster that way."

"Is there a bus that goes by here?"

"Not often."

"But there *is* one?"

"Sure. I've been trying to arrange with the company to use my place as a lunch stop, only they say it ain't big enough and the service ain't quick enough. There's just me and the wife to handle everything."

"How many doughnuts do you have left?"

"Six, seven."

"I'll take them all."

"Sure. That'll be fifty-two cents all together with the coffee."

She opened her purse under the counter so that he couldn't see how much money she had. She wasn't sure herself, but it looked like a great deal, enough to make her free of Rupert. *If I could get away from him, if I could hide in the woods . . . I'm not afraid of the dark, only of the dark with him in it . . .*

Him. It was a curse, an epithet, a dirty word.

He was sitting behind the wheel of the car when she came out of the coffee shop. She had changed to flat-heeled shoes for comfort during the trip, and she moved with leisurely grace, not the way she moved in the city, wobbling and lurching along like a little girl wearing her mother's high heels for the first time.

Instead of coming toward the car she turned right. He thought she was going to the restroom and he settled down to wait. The clock on the dashboard clicked away the minutes as if they were merry ones. Five. Seven. Ten. At eleven, he cranked down the window of the car and called her name, as loudly as he could without attracting the attention of the man behind the counter. There was no answer.

The little dog began whimpering again, as if he realized, before Rupert did, what was happening and how to deal with it. Rupert opened the car door and the dog leaped across the back of the seat and out into the night. He circled the parking lot, nose to the ground, lifting his head at intervals to yelp in Rupert's direction. Then he turned suddenly and streaked off toward the rear of the cabins where the creek splashed down the hill to the sea.

Both the dog and the object of his chase were covered by darkness. Rupert didn't call out to either of them. He simply began following the sound of the dog's now frantic barking, walking silently among the vast trees, the noise of his footsteps muffled by layers of dense, damp redwood needles. He didn't hurry, he needed time for his eyes to adjust to the dark, and he knew the dog wouldn't stop chasing her as long as she kept running. If he had had a free choice, he would have whistled the dog to heel, put him in the car, and driven on, leaving her to wander in the woods by herself until she dropped of exhaustion. But he had no choice. She was his hope as well as his despair.

She had reached the creek and was about to cross when he caught up with her. The dog was running up and down in front of her, just out of reach of the kicks she was aiming at his head. His tail was wagging and his barking sounded more mischievous than angry, as if he thought this was a new game she was playing, throwing her foot at him instead of a tennis ball.

As Rupert approached, she began to scream strange curses at him: he was a pig, his mother was a sow, his father had horns, the little dog belonged to the devil.

He grabbed her by the wrists. "Shut up."

"No! Leave me alone!"

A light went on in one of the cabins and the silhouette of a man's head appeared at the open window. The head was cocked, listening.

Rupert said, "Someone's watching."

"I don't care!"

"You will."

"No!"

She struggled in his grasp. He could barely hold her; in her fury she was as strong as a man.

"If you don't behave," he said quietly, "I'll have to kill you. The water's deep enough. I'll hold your head under. You can scream all you like, then. It will just help things along."

He knew she was afraid of the water, she hated the very sight of the sea, and even the sound of water running in the shower made her nervous.

She had gone limp in his arms, as if she had already drowned of fright.

"You're going to kill me anyway," she said in a ragged whisper.

"Don't be absurd."

"I can see it in your eyes."

"Stop this nonsense."

"I can feel it in your touch. You're going to kill me, aren't you?"

Yes, I am. The words were in his mouth ready to be spoken. *Yes, I'm going to kill you. But not with my bare hands, and not now. The day after tomorrow, perhaps, or the day after that. There are things to be settled before you die.*

The beam of a flashlight flickered among the trees and a man's voice called out, "Hello out there! Hey! Ahoy!"

Rupert tightened his grip on her wrist. "You're to say nothing. I'll do the talking, understand?"

"Yes."

"And don't get any ideas about asking for help. *I'm* your help, I hope you have sense enough to realize that."

The man from the coffee shop appeared, his white apron luffing in the wind. The beam of his flashlight caught Rupert in the face like a slap.

"Say, what's going on here?"

"Sorry for the disturbance," Rupert said. "My dog jumped out of the car, and my wife and I were trying to catch him."

"Oh, is that all?" He seemed vaguely disappointed. "For a minute there I thought someone was being murdered."

Rupert laughed. It sounded genuine. "I imagine murders take place more quietly and quickly." He didn't have to imagine; O'Donnell had died almost instantly, and without a word or cry of pain. "Sorry to inconvenience you."

"Oh, that's all right. We don't get much excitement around here. I like a bit of it now and then. Keeps a person young."

"I never thought of it in that way." Rupert picked up the dog with one hand, keeping the other on his companion's wrist. There was less resistance from her than from the dog, who hated to be carried. "Well, I guess we'll be on our way. Come along, my dear. I think we've caused enough commotion for one night."

The man led the way back to the parking lot, shining his flashlight on the ground. "The wind's shifting."

"I hadn't noticed," Rupert said.

"Not many people do. But with me, it's my business to check the wind. From the way it feels now, the fog'll be rolling in pretty soon. Fog, that's our problem in these parts. When the fog comes in I might as well shut up shop and go to bed. You heading for L.A.?"

"Yes."

"If I was you, I'd cut inland as soon as I could. You can't fight fog. The best you can do is run away from it."

"Thanks for the advice. I'll bear it in mind." Rupert thought, *there are lots of things beside fog that you can't fight, that you have to run away from.* "Good night. Perhaps we'll be seeing you again."

"I'll be here. Got all my money tied up in the place, can't afford to go away." He laughed sourly, as if he'd played a bad joke on himself. "Well, good night, folks."

When he had gone, Rupert said, "Get in the car."

"I don't want . . ."

"And hurry up. You've already delayed us half an hour with your histrionics. Do you realize how far news can travel in half an hour?"

"The police will be looking for you, not me."

"Whichever one of us they're looking for, if they find us they'll find us both together. Understand that? Together. Till death do us part."

19

SEÑOR ESCAMILLO YANKED open the door of the broom closet and found Consuela with one ear pressed against her listening wall.

"Aha!" he cried, pointing a fat little forefinger at her. "So, Consuela Gonzales is up to her old tricks again."

"No, señor. I swear on my mother's body . . ."

"You could swear on your father's horns and I do not believe you. If I were not so desperate for experienced help I would never have begged you to come back." He thought briefly of the real reason he'd asked her to come back; perhaps he'd been a fool to lend his services to such a wild, American scheme. He consulted his big, gold pocket watch, which didn't keep good time but served as a useful prop to hold his staff in line. "It is now seven o'clock. Why are you not placing fresh towels in the rooms and turning down the beds?"

"I have already attended to most of the rooms."

"And why not all of them, pray? Are the towels so heavy, such a burden, that you must stop to rest every five minutes?"

"No, señor."

"I wait for the explanation," Escamillo said, with cold dignity.

Consuela looked down at her feet, wide and flat in their straw *espadrilles. Clothes,* she thought, *it's clothes that make the difference. Here I am dressed like a peasant, so he treats me like a peasant. If I had on my high heels and my black dress and my necklaces, he would be polite and call me senorita, he wouldn't dare to say my father had horns.*

"I wait, Consuela Gonzales."

"I have attended to all the rooms except 404. I was prepared to do that one too, but when I stopped at the door I heard noises from inside."

"Noises? How so?"

"People were arguing. I thought it would be wiser if I didn't disturb them, if I waited until they went out for the evening."

"People were arguing in 404?"

"Yes. Americans. Two American ladies."

"You swear it on your mother's body?"

"I do, señor."

"Oh, what a liar you are, Consuela Gonzales." Escamillo put his hand over his heart to show how much the situation pained him. "Or else you have lost your judgment."

"I heard them, I tell you."

"You tell me, yes. Now *I* tell *you.* The suite 404 is empty. It has been empty for nearly a week."

"That can't be. I heard, with my own ears. . ."

"Then you need new ears. Four hundred four is empty. I am the manager of this establishment. Who would know better than I which rooms are occupied and which are not?"

"Perhaps, while you were away from the desk for a few minutes, someone checked in, two American ladies."

"Impossible."

"I know what I hear." Consuela's cheeks were the color of red wine as if the blood in her veins had fermented with fury.

"This is bad," Escamillo said, "to hear things other people do not."

"You haven't tried. If you would place your ear here, at the wall . . ."

"Very well. The ear is here. And now?"

"Listen."

"I am listening."

"They are moving around," Consuela said. "One of them is wearing many bracelets, you can hear them clanking. There. Now they are talking. Do you hear voices?"

"Certainly I hear voices." Escamillo stepped briskly out of the broom closet, brushing lint off the sleeves and lapels of his suit. "I hear your voice and my voice. From an empty room I hear nothing, praise Jesus."

"The room is not empty, I tell you."

"And I tell you once again, stop this nonsense, Consuela Gonzales. I think you have not been saying your beads often enough lately and God is angry with you, making noises that you alone can hear."

"I have done nothing to make Him angry with me."

"We are all sinners." But Escamillo's tone implied strongly that Consuela Gonzales was the worst of the lot and she was to expect only a minimum of mercy, if any. "You had better go down to the bar and ask Emilio for one of those new American pills that ease the mind."

"There is nothing the matter with my mind."

"Is there not? Well, I am too busy to argue."

She leaned against the door of the broom closet and watched Escamillo disappear into the elevator. Globules of sweat and oil stood out on her forehead and upper lip. She brushed them off with a corner of her apron, thinking, *he is trying to frighten me, embarrass me, make me out a fool. I will not be made out a fool. It is easy to prove the room is occupied. I have a key. I will unlock the door, very quietly, and open it, very suddenly, and there they will be, arguing, moving around. Two ladies. Americans.*

Her ring of keys, suspended from a rope belt around her waist, struck her thigh and tinkled like coins as she moved toward 404. She hesitated at the door, hearing nothing now but the traffic from the *avenida* below and the quick rhythmical drumming of her own heart.

Only a month ago, two American ladies had occupied this very room. They too had argued. One of them wore many bracelets and a red silk suit, and painted her eyelids gold. And the other . . .

But I must not think of those two. One is dead, the other is far away. I am alive and here.

From her key ring she chose the key labeled *apartamientos* and inserted it quietly into the lock. A quick turn of the key to the left and of the doorknob to the right and the door would open to reveal the occupants of the room and Escamillo would be proved the cowardly liar that he was.

The key would not turn. She tried one hand and then the other, and finally both together. She was a strong woman, used to heavy work, but the key wouldn't budge.

She rapped sharply on the door and called out, "This is the chambermaid. I must change the towels. Please let me in. I have lost my key. Please open the door? Please?"

She caught her lower lip with her teeth to stop its trembling. *The room is empty,* she thought. *Escamillo is right, God is punishing me. I hear voices no one else can hear, I talk to people who are not there, I listen at walls that say nothing.*

She hesitated only long enough to cross herself. Then she turned and ran down the corridor to the service stairway. In flight, she tried to pray. Her mouth moved but no words came out, and she knew it was because she had not said her beads for a long time; she could not even remember where she had put them.

Four flights down, and she was in the little room behind the bar where Emilio and his assistants came to sneak cigarettes and finish off the dregs of bottles and count the day's tips.

She had made so much noise crashing down the steps that Emilio himself hurried back to see what the fuss was about.

"Oh, it's you." Emilio was bold and elegant in a new red bolero trimmed with silver buttons and orange braid. "I thought it was another earthquake. What do you want?"

She sat down on an empty beer case and held her head in her hands.

"How's Joe?" Emilio said.

The American was waiting in Escamillo's office, pacing up and down as if he couldn't find a door to escape through. He looked worried, as worried as Escamillo felt. Escamillo, from the beginning, had had grave doubts about the situation, but Mr. Dodd was very persuasive. He'd made the plan sound both reasonable and practicable.

Escamillo was afraid it was neither, although so far he hadn't indicated his misgivings. He said simply, "Everything is in readiness. They are arguing very well together, very real."

"And Consuela is listening?"

"Certainly. Listening, it is a long habit with her."

"Did you have the lock changed?"

"Just as I was instructed, so everything has been performed. She can gain access to the room only when the ladies are ready to receive her. Also, the silver box—I gave it to Emilio as you told me to do. However, I do not understand about the silver box. Why was it necessary to purchase an exact duplicate? I begin to wonder." Escamillo's face, normally as bland as a marshmallow, was contorted in anticipation of disaster. "I begin to have doubts."

"That makes two of us."

"Señor?"

"We all have doubts," Dodd said flatly. "Let's just hope hers are bigger."

"She is not a fool, you know. A cheat, a liar, a thief, all those, but not a fool."

"She's superstitious and she's scared."

"*She* is scared, ha! And who is not? I feel my liver turning cold and white like snow."

"There's nothing to be scared of. Your part in this is finished."

"I must remind you that this is *my* hotel, *my* reputation is at stake, *I* am responsible for . . ." The telephone on Escamillo's desk began to ring. He darted across the room and picked it up.

His small pudgy hands were quivering. "Yes? That is good, very good." He put the phone down and said to Dodd, "It has worked so far. She is with Emilio. He is very clever, you can trust him."

"I have to."

"Señor Kellogg will be here soon?"

"He's waiting in the lobby now."

"Suppose there is violence? Violence distresses me." Escamillo pressed his hand against his stomach. "You have not taken me entirely into your confidence, señor. A little voice keeps telling me that there is something questionable about all this, perhaps even something illegal."

A little voice kept telling Dodd the same thing but he couldn't afford to listen.

"How is Joe?" Emilio repeated.

"Joe?" She raised her head and stared at him blankly. For a moment the blankness was genuine—Joe was long ago and far away and dead. "Joe who?"

"You know Joe who."

"Oh, him. I haven't seen him. He was no good. He ran off with another woman."

"An American?"

"Why do you say that?"

"He sent me 250 pesos that he owed me. It was marked on the envelope, San Francisco."

"Ah, so? Well, I hope she is very rich so he will be very happy."

There'd been two rich ladies, Consuela thought. *They were ready to be plucked like chickens, but all Joe got out of it was a second-hand car and a few clothes to be buried in, because he lost his nerve, he began feeling sorry for people. His mind had turned soft as his belly.*

No, no, I must not think of that, of the blood . . .

"What happens with you?" Emilio said. "You look bad, like a ghost."

"I have a—a headache."

"Perhaps you would like a bottle of beer?"

"Yes. Thank you. Thank you very much."

"Do not thank me so hard," Emilio said dryly. "I expect you to pay."

"I will pay. I have money."

She thought, *I have money I can't spend, clothes I can't wear; I have bottles of perfume, yet I must go around smelling like a goat. You would steal the smell off a goat,* Joe had said.

It seemed funny to her now. She began to laugh softly, cupping her mouth in her hands so that no one would hear her and want to know why she was laughing. It would be too hard to explain; she wasn't quite sure of the reason herself.

Emilio returned carrying a bottle of cheap beer. He gave her the beer, then held out his hand for the money. She put a peso in it, grudgingly, as if it were her last.

"This," he said, "is not enough."

"It is all I have."

"I hear different. I hear you had a winning ticket last week."

"No."

"This is what I hear, that you took all your money and hid it away. If this is so. . ."

"And it is not."

"But suppose it is. Then you are in luck, because I have a fine bargain for you."

"I have seen too many of your fine bargains."

"Not like this." From one of the higher shelves behind the door Emilio took an object wrapped in a copy of *Grafico.* He removed the newspaper and held out, for her to see, a box of hammered silver. "A beauty, is it not?"

She pressed the cold bottle against her burning forehead like a poultice.

"As you can see," Emilio said, "it has a damage, a dent. That is why I am offering it at the absurd price of two hundred pesos. Go on, take it, feel its weight. It's genuine silver, as heavy as a mourner's heart, and what could be heavier than that, eh, Consuela?"

"Where," she said, "where did you get it?"

"Ah, that is my little secret."

"You must tell me. I must know."

"Very well. I found it."

"Where?"

"A lady left it behind in the bar, on one of the seats."

"What lady?"

"If I knew the lady I would return the box," he said severely. "I am an honest man, I would never keep what belongs to another, never. But," he added with a shrug, "since I do not know the lady's name, and since she looked very rich, with many gold bracelets, yes, even gold on her eyelids . . ."

The telephone rang in 404. Both the women jumped, as if they'd heard a shot. Then the one in the red silk suit crossed the room and picked up the telephone. "Yes?"

"She'll be back up soon," Dodd said. "Leave the door partly open so she can get in. Is Mrs. Kellogg all right?"

"Yes."

"And you?"

"I'm nervous. I feel so grotesque in this getup, with all this paint on. I don't know if I can go through with it."

"You have to, Pat."

"But I'm not an actress. How can I fool her?"

"Because she's ready to be fooled. The others have done their part—Escamillo, Emilio. Now it's your turn. Kellogg will be there shortly. So will I. I'll be in the other room, so don't worry."

"All right," Miss Burton said. "All right." She put down the telephone and looked across the room at the woman sitting on the edge of one of the twin beds. "She's coming up soon. We must be ready."

"Oh God," Amy whispered. "I'm not sure. Even now, I'm not *sure*."

"Everyone else is. All of us. We're sure."

"How can you be, if I'm not?"

"Because we know you and your character. We know you couldn't possibly . . ."

"But I tell you, sometimes I remember, I remember quite clearly. I picked up the silver box, I was going to throw it over the balcony as Wilma had challenged me to do. She tried to grab the box from me, and we struggled, and then I hit . . ."

"You can't remember what didn't happen," Miss Burton said sturdily.

". . . and a beautiful silk suit," Emilio said, "the color of blood. My most favorite color. Your most favorite too, Consuela?"

She didn't hear the question. She was staring at the silver box as if it contained all the imps of hell. "The woman who left it, you said you'd never seen her before?"

"Wrong. I told you I did not know her name. Of course I have seen her before. She and her friend, one night in the bar they had a long talk with Joe, very gay, very merry, lots of *tequila.*"

"No. I don't believe you. It's not possible."

"Ask Joe," Emilio said, "next time you see him."

"I won't be—seeing him."

"Ah, you might be surprised. One of these days you might open a door, expecting nothing, and there he'll be . . ."

"No, that is imposs—"

"There he'll be, the same as ever, as good as new." Emilio was grinning nervously. "And he'll say, 'Here I am, Consuela, I have come back to you and your warm bed and I will never leave you again. Always I will be at your side, you will never get rid of me.'"

"Quiet," she screamed. "Pig. Liar." She was holding the bottle of beer by the neck as if she intended to use it to silence him. The beer gurgled out on the wooden floor and through the cracks, leaving a trail of bubbles. "He will never come back."

Emilio's grin had disappeared and a white line of fear circled his dry mouth. "Very well. He will never come back. I do not argue with a lady with so many muscles and a bad temper."

"The box—the woman—it's all a trick."

"How do you mean this, a trick? I do not play tricks."

"Señor Kellogg gave you that box. And there is no such woman as you claim."

Emilio looked genuinely puzzled. "I know no Señor Kellogg. As for the woman, well, I saw what I saw. My eyes are not liars. She and her little brown-haired friend came in about 5:30. I served them myself. I said, 'Good afternoon, señoras, it is a great pleasure to see you once more. Have you been away?' And the señora in the blood- colored suit said, 'Yes, I have been away on a long, long journey. I never thought I would get back, but here I am, here I am again.'"

"My beads," she said, and the beer bottle dropped from her hand and rolled, unbroken, across the wooden floor. "I must find my beads. The closet—perhaps I left them in the closet. I must go and find them. My beads . . . Hail Mary, full of Grace . . ."

Rupert and Dodd waited in the bedroom.

"A devil on the one hand," Rupert said, "and a delusion on the other. And I was trapped between them. I could do nothing but stall for time, keep Amy hidden away until she was able to think clearly again, to distinguish between what had happened and what Consuela claimed had happened. I had to keep her hidden not only from the police but from her family or anyone else she might try to 'confess' to. I couldn't afford the risk of somebody believing her confession. There were times I almost believed it myself, it was so sincere and so plausible. But I knew my wife, I knew her to be incapable of violence against another human being.

"Consuela's lies started the delusion, but it was aggravated by Amy's own feeling of worthlessness. All her life she had suffered from a nameless guilt. Now Consuela had given it a name, murder. And Amy accepted it, because it is sometimes easier to accept one specific thing, no matter how bad, than to go on living with a lot of obscure and indefinite fears. But there were other reasons too for her acceptance. She was beginning to feel hostility toward Wilma and to resent Wilma's domination. These feelings were later translated into guilt. Also, remember that Amy was drunk, and consequently had no clear recollection of the facts to counteract Consuela's false version of them."

"You claim it's false," Dodd interrupted. "But are you sure?"

"If I weren't sure, would I have confided in you and put myself at your mercy? Would I have brought you and Amy down here, dragged Miss Burton into this, broken any number of laws? Believe me, Mr. Dodd, I'm sure. It's Amy who isn't. That's why we're here now. We can't let her spend the rest of her life thinking that she killed her best friend. She didn't. I know that, I knew it from the first."

"Then why didn't you give Consuela a quick, firm brushoff?"

"I couldn't. By the time I reached Amy at the hospital, the damage had already been done. Amy was convinced she was guilty and Consuela stuck to her story. If it had been a simple matter of dealing with the girl alone, there would have been no problem. But there was Amy too. And on my side, I had no evidence at all, only my knowledge of my wife's character. Bear in mind, also, that we were in a foreign country. I was completely ignorant of police procedure, of what the authorities might do to Amy if they believed her confession."

When Rupert paused for breath, Dodd could hear the two women in the adjoining room talking, Amy softly, nervously, Miss Burton with brisk assurance, as if by putting on Wilma's clothes and make-up she had assumed some of Wilma's mannerisms. The stage was set but the leading character had yet to appear. *The silver box should do it,* he thought. *She's got to come back up to check Emilio's story about the two Americans.*

"I had no choice," Rupert continued, "but to yield to Consuela's demands and to stall for time. I talked it over with Amy and she agreed to do what I suggested, stay out of sight for a while. We got off the plane at L.A. and I checked her into a rest home under a different name, without even her own clothes to identify her."

"That's why you let the luggage go through to San Francisco?"

"The luggage and Consuela," he added grimly. "She was sitting across the aisle from us. I was able to get official papers for her by pretending I was hiring her as a nurse-companion for my wife."

"Didn't Mrs. Kellogg object to the idea of entering a rest home?"

"No, she was quite docile about it. She trusted me and knew I was trying to help her. I felt reasonably certain that in a rest home, no matter what story she told, no one would believe her. As it turned out, she kept her secret to herself. And she obeyed my orders, gave me her power of attorney before we left Mexico City, wrote the letters I dictated in order to forestall any suspicions on the part of her brother Gill. I arranged with a business associate to have one of the letters postmarked New York but Gill wasn't taken in. I didn't realize how strong his suspicions would be or the extent of his dislike for me.

"As soon as I did realize, thanks to Helene, I began to get rattled and make mistakes. Big mistakes, like leaving Mack's leash in the kitchen and giving Gerda Lundquist a chance to catch me in that fake telephone call. It seemed that with each mistake I made, the next one became easier. I could no longer think clearly, I was so worried about my wife. I had relied heavily on the theory that the passage of time would bring Amy to her senses. I was too optimistic. Time alone couldn't do the trick; something more positive was needed. But I could do nothing positive, not even go down to Los Angeles to see her, to reason with her. I was trapped in San Francisco, with you and Gill Brandon on my tail. It was, ironically, Consuela herself who forced me to do something positive."

They'd met, by prearrangement, in the back row of loges of a movie theater on Market Street. Rupert arrived first and waited for her. When she finally arrived, she had doused herself so extravagantly with perfume that before he saw or heard her approach he could smell her as she walked up the carpeted steps.

It was not the time or place for amenities, even if she'd known or cared about them. She said bluntly, "I need more money."

"I haven't any."

"Get some."

"How much were you thinking of?"

"Oh, a lot. There are two of us now."

"Two?"

"Joe and I, we got married yesterday. I have always wanted to get married."

"For God's sake," Rupert said. "Why did you have to drag O'Donnell into this?"

"I dragged no one. I simply wrote him a letter because I was lonesome. You do not understand how it is, being without friends, seeing only people who hate you and wish you dead. So I wrote Joe a letter, telling him how well I was doing, and about my pretty clothes and jewelry and my new hair, more blonde than his even. I think it made him jealous. Anyway he borrowed some money and came up here by bus. Seeing him again, I thought, well, now that he's here we might as well get married and regain the blessing of the Church. So now there are two of us."

"To be supported by me."

"Not you. Your wife. You have done nothing to be ashamed of. Why should you pay? It is Mrs. Kellogg who must pay."

"This is blackmail."

"I do not concern myself with words, only money."

"You've told O'Donnell everything, I suppose?"

"We are man and wife," she said virtuously. "A wife must confide in her husband completely."

"You're a damned fool."

He felt her stiffen in the seat beside him. "Not such a fool as you might think."

"Do you realize the penalty for blackmail?"

"I realize that you cannot go to the police and complain against me. If you do, they will have to question Mrs. Kellogg and she will admit her guilt."

"That's where you're wrong," he said quickly. "My wife no longer believes your story about Mrs. Wyatt's death. She remembers the truth."

"What a bad liar you are. I can always tell a bad liar, I being such a good one."

"Yes, I know that well."

"Only I do not lie about vital matters, like Mrs. Wyatt's death."

"Don't you?"

"Must I keep telling you? I was in the broom closet, sleeping, and I woke up when I heard someone screaming in 404. I rushed in. The two women were struggling over the silver box—they'd been arguing about it when I was in the room before. As I approached, Mrs. Kellogg got hold of the box and struck Mrs. Wyatt on the head. The balcony doors were open. Under the force of the blow, Mrs. Wyatt stumbled backwards out on to the balcony and fell over the railing. My mind is very quick. I thought immediately, what a terrible thing if the police accuse Mrs. Kellogg of murder. So I picked up the box and threw it over the railing. Mrs. Kellogg had fainted from shock. I poured some whiskey down her throat from the bottle on the bureau, and when she came to a little, I said to her, 'Don't worry. I am your friend. I will help you.'"

Friend. Help. Rupert stared in silence at the oversized movie screen where a man was stalking a woman, intent on killing her. He had a brief, childish wish that he were the man and Consuela the woman. If Consuela died, naturally, or by accident, or by design. . .

No, he thought. It would solve nothing. I must try to save Amy, not to punish Consuela. With Consuela dead I would have no chance of proving to Amy that she is suffering from a delusion. I must keep the devil alive because without her I cannot kill the delusion.

"The sea and the fog," Consuela was saying. "They do not agree with my health. I want to go back home where it is high and dry. But of course I will require money."

"How much?"

"Fifteen thousand dollars."

"You must be crazy."

"Oh, I know it sounds like a great deal, but once you have paid, you will be rid of me. Is it not worth that much to be rid of me." She added softly, "Joe is not stupid. He has investigated. He has found out about the piece of paper you have that lets you cash checks on your wife's account."

"A check that large is bound to attract attention."

"You have already attracted much attention. A little more won't matter. You will get the money?"

"I guess I have to."

"Very well. Tomorrow, at noon, I'll come to the restaurant where you eat lunch, Lassiter's. I'll sit down beside you, as if by accident, and when you give me the money, that will be the end of the whole thing."

"Why meet at such a public place as a restaurant?"

"Simply because it is a public place. With so many people around, you won't change your mind and try to do something foolish. I am not afraid of you, but then I can't trust you either; you love that little wife of yours too desperately. How does it happen, such a love as this?"

"That's something," he said grimly, "you'll never find out."

They missed contact at Lassiter's because of Helene's surprise appearance. Rupert went home, and later in the afternoon . . .

". . .About 3:30," Rupert continued, to Dodd, "they drove up to the house in a second-hand car O'Donnell had bought with some of the money I'd already paid Consuela. They came around to the back door and I let them into the kitchen. They'd obviously been quarreling. Consuela was in a temper and O'Donnell seemed very nervous and frightened. I think he'd begun to realize that he had a tiger by the tail and the only thing he could do was to let go, run like hell, and hope for the best. O'Donnell's mistake was in announcing his intention of letting go. It gave the tiger a chance to prepare to spring.

"As soon as I handed the money over to Consuela, O'Donnell told her he wanted out, that he didn't intend to go with her back to Mexico City or any other place. I got the impression that they often had violent quarrels and that this one was no different. I went into the den. I could hear her screaming about marriage vows and the blessing of the Church. Then he said something to her in Spanish, and everything suddenly became very quiet. When I went back into the kitchen O'Donnell was lying in front of the refrigerator, dead, and Consuela was standing with the knife in her hand, looking surprised.

"The whole thing was so quick, so incredible, that it seemed to be taking place in a dream. I was too stunned to think clearly or to make plans. I could only act, automatically, by instinct. I tried to clean up the mess with bath towels, but it was no use, there was too much of it. Consuela kept crying and moaning, partly in regret over what she'd done, but more, I think, in dismay over what was going to happen to her now. It was at this point that I realized I had accepted too passive a role in the whole business. If I was to help Amy, I had to do something more positive. I couldn't just sit back and wait for time to restore her to her senses. And so it was, as I said, Consuela herself who forced me to action by her killing of O'Donnell.

"Armchair critics, and people who've never been in my position, may censure me for not immediately calling the police. But you know, Dodd, that I couldn't afford to; that if I had, my wife might very well be in jail right now. Consuela would have told the authorities her story of Wilma's death, and Amy, ten chances to one, would have confirmed it. So in order to protect my wife, I had also to protect Consuela. For a time, anyway.

"We started out, using O'Donnell's car for obvious reasons. When I stopped at the kennel to get Mack, I had some wild notion of ditching Consuela, picking up Amy at the rest home, and just taking off with her and Mack and disappearing. But I knew this wouldn't work out, that in some way I must get Amy and Consuela to confront each other. I figured that Amy was a little more sure of herself by this time, and Consuela a great deal less. From such a meeting I hoped the truth would emerge. That's why I called you from the Big Sur, and asked your help in arranging it. I'm aware that I've put you in a very difficult position, but believe me, it's for a good cause. My wife's whole future is at stake."

So is mine, Dodd thought, and started making a mental list of the number of laws he'd broken in the interests of Amy's future. He stopped at seven; the project was too depressing.

In the adjoining room the telephone began to ring and Dodd went to answer it. The two women watched in silence as he picked up the phone. "Yes?"

"I sent Pedro up with the silver box," Escamillo said. "Did you receive it?"

"Yes."

"Emilio is now in my office. He tells me she is on her way upstairs."

"Thanks." Dodd replaced the phone and turned to Amy, who was sitting on the edge of the bed looking pale and bewildered, as if she'd somehow wandered into the whole affair by mistake. "Are you ready, Mrs. Kellogg?"

"I guess I am."

"How do you feel?"

"All right. I guess all right." Her hands plucked listlessly at one of the chenille roses of the bedspread. "I wish Rupert were here."

"He's right in the next room."

"I wish he were here."

Exasperation showed in his face and posture. "Mrs. Kellogg, I needn't remind you that a lot of people have gone through a great deal for your sake, especially your husband."

"I know. I know that."

"You've got to cooperate."

"I will."

"Of course she will," Miss Burton said in a hearty voice, but her bracelets clanged nervously and one of her golden eyelids twitched in dissent.

When Dodd had left, Amy sat on the bed repeating his words to herself: *A lot of people have gone through a great deal for my sake. Especially Rupert. I've got to cooperate. Because a lot of people have gone through a great deal for my sake I've got to cooperate—got to. . .*

As soon as Consuela opened the door of her broom closet she could hear the voices again. They were indistinct, until she pressed her ear to the listening wall, and then she heard, quite clearly, the sound of her own name, Consuela. And again, Consuela, as if they were calling her, summoning her.

No, she thought, *no, that is impossible. Escamillo said the suite was empty, and I went to the door myself, and knocked, and no one answered. The voices are heard by me alone. Perhaps I have a fever. That must be it, of course. In a fever the mind often plays tricks; one imagines, one sees and hears things that are not so.*

She raised one hand and touched her forehead. It felt moist and cool, like a newly peeled peach. No trace of a fever. *Still, it must be there,* she thought. *So far it is all on the inside and hasn't yet come to the surface. I must go home and take precautions against the evil eye that someone has cast upon me.*

But when she stepped out into the corridor she saw that the door of 404 was partly open. She knew it could not have been blown open by the wind—half an hour ago it had been so securely fastened that her passkey wouldn't budge in the lock.

She crept along the wall to the half-open door and peered inside. There were two women in the room. One of them, the small brown-haired one sitting on the bed, was alive. The other, standing in front of the open balcony door, had died almost a month ago. Consuela had seen her die from this very doorway, had heard her final scream. Now she had stepped from her coffin, groomed and jeweled as if she'd been to a party, wearing the same red silk suit and the same fur coat, untouched by any worms or mildew or decay. A month of death hadn't changed her at all; even her expression, when she saw Consuela, was the same, annoyed and impatient.

"Oh, it's you," she said. "Again. Every time I take a breath around this place someone comes creeping in to change the towels or turn down the beds. I feel as if I'm being spied on."

"They just try to give us good service," her companion said.

"Good service? The towels all stink."

"I hadn't noticed."

"You smoke too much. Your sense of smell isn't as sharp as mine. They stink."

"I don't think you should talk like this in front of the girl."

"You can tell from her face she doesn't understand a word I'm saying."

"But the travel agency said everyone on the hotel staff spoke English."

"All right, why don't you try her out?"

"I will," Amy said. "What's your name, girl? Do you speak English? Tell us your name."

Consuela stood, mute as a stone, her right hand clutching the little gold cross she wore around her neck, her eyes fixed on the hammered silver box lying on the coffee table. *It has all happened before,* she thought, *and it will all happen again. It is not that the American lady died and has come back from her grave. It is that we are all dead, all three of us, dead and in hell. This is what hell is, everything goes on repeating and repeating, forever and ever, and nobody can change it. The whole thing has happened before, and it will happen again. Pretty soon they will start to quarrel about the silver box, they will struggle over it. And I will stand here and watch her die, and listen to her last scream . . .*

"No! No! Please! No!" She fell forward on her knees, pressing the little gold cross against her dry lips, mumbling in Spanish the words of her childhood: "Holy Mary, Mother of God, pray for us sinners, now and at the hour of our death."

She went on praying, only partly aware of other people rushing into the room, of men's voices shouting at her, asking her questions, calling her names.

"Liar."

"You must tell us the truth."

"What happened to Mrs. Wyatt?"

"You killed her yourself, didn't you?"

"You came into this room and found Mrs. Kellogg unconscious, and Mrs. Wyatt too drunk to defend herself. And you saw your big chance."

"You must tell us the truth."

She began again, for the fifth time, "Hail Mary, full of Grace. Blessed art thou amongst women . . ." But the words were automatic and had no connection with her thoughts: *I am in hell. This is another corner of it, when you tell the truth and no one believes you because you have lied in the past. So you must lie to be believed.*

"Consuela, do you hear me? You must give us the truth."

She raised her head. She looked stunned, as if someone had struck a blow in a vital place, but her voice was quite clear. "I hear you."

"What happened when you came into this room?"

"She was standing on the balcony with the silver box in her hands. She leaned over the railing and disappeared. I heard her scream."

"And Mrs. Kellogg had nothing to do with it?"

"Nothing." She kissed the little cross. "Nothing."

20

"Amy, dear." It was almost midnight. The others had gone, and Rupert was alone with his wife. "You mustn't cry anymore. It's all over. Tomorrow we'll go home, we'll both try to forget this past month."

She stirred in his arms like a fretful child kept up long past her bedtime. "I can never forget."

"Not entirely, perhaps. But it will become dimmer for you, more bearable."

"You're very kind to me."

"Nonsense."

"I wish I could repay you."

"You already have," he said gently. "By remembering the truth. By getting back your confidence and your belief in yourself."

"Your confidence in me was never shaken?"

"Never."

"That's because you love me."

"Partly. It's also because I know you, I know you better than you know yourself."

"Do you?" She stirred again and sighed. "You've been through so much for my sake, haven't you, Rupert?"

"Oh, not so much."

"What if I'm not worth it?"

"There you go again. Stop talking like that. It hurts me."

"Why?"

"Because I love you."

"I love you too, Rupert." She lay against her husband's heart, listening to its familiar beat, and to the noises of the alien city. *A lot of people have been through a great deal for my sake, especially Rupert. I've got to cooperate . . .*

They were at the airport when the plane landed, Gill looking flushed and a little sheepish, and Helene wearing a big, cheerful smile as real as the plastic carnation she had pinned to her lapel.

"Darlings!" Helene shrieked, and put her arms around them both. "How wonderful to see you! Did you have a nice flight? You're both looking simply tremendous. I've got a million questions to ask, but I promise to be good and not ask a one until we get in the car. Gill, dear, why don't you go and claim their luggage?"

"I'll go with you, Gilly," Amy said. "We have so much to talk about."

"Yes. Yes, we have." Gill took her arm and began guiding her through the crowd toward the baggage department. "You're looking well."

"Oh, I feel fine."

"I guess I have a lot of apologies to make to Rupert."

"That won't be necessary. He understands. He's a very understanding man. In some ways."

Gill glanced down at her, a little puzzled by her tone. "In some ways?"

"Well, I mean, he doesn't understand everything. The way you do."

"But I don't. I've never claimed. . ."

"I mean, about me. He doesn't understand about me, the way you do. You see, he loves me, it's given him a blind spot. With you it's different. I've never been able to keep anything from you. Somehow or other, you've always found out."

"Not always."

"Rupert's a marvelous man, Gilly. When I think of all he's been through for my sake, all he's suffered . . ." She hesitated, her hand on his arm, as light as a bird. "You mustn't ever tell him, Gilly. It would make him feel so bad."

He felt the bird on his arm growing, becoming heavier. "I don't know what you mean, Amy."

"It will be one of our secrets, the biggest one. You must never tell anyone else at all, especially Rupert."

"Tell him what?"

"That I killed Wilma."

ABOUT THE AUTHOR

Margaret Millar (1915–1994) was born in Ontario, Canada and was educated at Kitchener-Waterloo Collegiate Institute and the University of Toronto, majoring in classics. In 1938 she married Kenneth Millar (who wrote under the name Ross Macdonald). She published her first novel, *The Invisible Worm*, in 1941 and she worked as a screenwriter for Warner Brothers. She was active in the conservation movement in California in the 1960s and was named a Woman of the Year by *the Los Angeles Times* in 1965, and in 1982 she became a Grand Master of the Mystery Writers of America.

COLLECTED MILLAR

The Complete Writings of Margaret Millar in Seven-Volumes

Collect all seven to complete the illustration on the spine!

THE FIRST DETECTIVES

ISBN: 978-1-68199-031-6

$17.99

The Paul Prye Mysteries

The Invisible Worm (1941)

The Weak-Eyed Bat (1942)

The Devil Loves Me (1942)

Inspector Sands Mysteries

Wall of Eyes (1943)

The Iron Gates [*Taste of Fears*] (1945)

DAWN OF DOMESTIC SUSPENSE

978-1-68199-030-9

$17.99

Fire Will Freeze (1944)

Experiment in Springtime (1947)

The Cannibal Heart (1949)

Do Evil in Return (1950)

Rose's Last Summer (1952)

THE MASTER AT HER ZENITH

978-1-68199-027-9

$17.99

Vanish in an Instant (1952)
Wives and Lovers (1954)
Beast in View (1955)
An Air That Kills (1957)
The Listening Walls (1959)

LEGENDARY NOVELS OF SUSPENSE

978-1-68199-028-6

$17.99

A Stranger in My Grave (1960)
How Like an Angel (1962)
The Fiend (1964)
Beyond This Point Are Monsters (1970)

THE TOM ARAGON NOVELS

978-1-68199-029-3

$17.99

Ask for Me Tomorrow (1976)
The Murder of Miranda (1979)
Mermaid (1982)

FIRST THINGS, LAST THINGS

978-1-68199-032-3

$17.99

Banshee (1983)
Spider Webs (1986)
Collected Short Fiction (2016)
It's All in the Family (1948) (semi-autobiographical children's novel book)

MEMOIR

978-1-68199-033-0

$16.99

The Birds and the Beasts Were There (1968)

THE COMPLETE WRITINGS OF
MARGARET MILLAR
AVAILABLE AS EBOOKS FOR THE FIRST TIME

PAUL PRYE NOVELS

The Invisible Worm
ISBN: 978-1-68199-000-2

The Weak-Eyed Bat
ISBN: 978-1-68199-001-9

The Devil Loves Me
ISBN: 978-1-68199-002-6

INSPECTOR SANDS NOVELS

Wall of Eyes
ISBN: 978-1-68199-003-3

The Iron Gates
ISBN: 978-1-68199-004-0

TOM ARAGON NOVELS

Ask for Me Tomorrow
ISBN: 978-1-68199-005-7

The Murder of Miranda
ISBN: 978-1-68199-006-4

Mermaid
ISBN: 978-1-68199-007-1

NOVELS OF SUSPENSE

Fire Will Freeze
ISBN: 978-1-68199-008-8

Do Evil in Return
ISBN: 978-1-68199-009-5

Rose's Last Summer
ISBN: 978-1-68199-010-1

Vanish in an Instant
ISBN: 978-1-68199-011-8

Beast in View
ISBN: 978-1-68199-012-5

NOVELS OF SUSPENSE

continued

The Cannibal Heart
ISBN: 978-1-68199-024-8

An Air That Kills
ISBN: 978-1-68199-013-2

The Listening Walls
ISBN: 978-1-68199-014-9

A Stranger in My Grave
ISBN: 978-1-68199-015-6

How Like an Angel
ISBN: 978-1-68199-016-3

The Fiend
ISBN: 978-1-68199-017-0

Beyond This Point Are Monsters
ISBN: 978-1-68199-018-7

Banshee
ISBN: 978-1-68199-019-4

Spider Webs
ISBN: 978-1-68199-020-0

OTHER NOVELS

Experiment in Springtime
ISBN: 978-1-68199-022-4

Wives and Lovers
ISBN: 978-1-68199-025-5

STORIES

The Collected Short Stories
ISBN: 978-1-68199-021-7

CHILDREN'S BOOKS

It's All in the Family
ISBN: 978-1-68199-023-1

NONFICTION

The Birds and the Beasts Were There
ISBN: 978-1-68199-026-2